EVERYMAN,
I WILL GO WITH THEE,
AND BE THY GUIDE,
IN THY MOST NEED
TO GO BY THY SIDE

HENRIK PONTOPPIDAN

LUCKY PER

TRANSLATED FROM THE DANISH
BY NAOMI LEBOWITZ

WITH AN INTRODUCTION
BY GARTH RISK HALLBERG

EVERYMAN'S LIBRARY
Alfred A. Knopf New York London Toronto

390

THIS IS A BORZOI BOOK
PUBLISHED BY ALFRED A. KNOPF

First included in Everyman's Library, 2019

www.randomhouse/everymans
www.everymanslibrary.co.uk

ISBN 978-1-101-90809-9 (US)
978-1-84159-390-6 (UK)

Library of Congress Cataloging-in-Publication Data

Names: Pontoppidan, Henrik, 1857–1943, author. | Lebowitz, Naomi,
translator. | Hallberg, Garth Risk, author of introduction.
Title: Lucky Per / by Henrik Pontoppidan; translated by Naomi Lebowitz;
introduction by Garth Risk Hallberg.
Other titles: Lykke-Per. English
Description: New York: Everyman's Library, 2019. | Includes bibliographical
references.
Identifiers: LCCN 2018053817 | ISBN 9781101908099 (hardcover: alk. paper)
Subjects: | BISAC: FICTION / Classics. | FICTION / Coming of Age. |
FICTION / Literary. | GSAFD: Bildungsromans.
Classification: LCC PT8175.P6 L913 2019 | DDC 839.813/72—dc23
LC record available at https://lccn.loc.gov/2018053817

A CIP catalogue reference for this book is available from the British
Library

Book design by Barbara de Wilde and Carol Devine Carson

Typeset in the UK by Input Data Services Ltd, Isle Abbotts, Somerset
Printed and bound in Germany by GGP Media GmbH, Pössneck

LUCKY PER

INTRODUCTION

I

In the summer of 1937, Ernst Bloch, the redoubtable German-Jewish literary critic, utopian humanist, and exile from Nazi persecution, was browsing the paper in his new home of Czechoslovakia when an item brought him up short. The novelist Henrik Pontoppidan had died at the age of eighty in his native Denmark. Bloch moved swiftly to set down his thoughts and sent the resulting, impassioned eulogy to another newspaper, the German-language *Prager Weltbühne*, for publication. "A great writer has been pronounced dead," he lamented:

> This is one of those dark instances in which the world cheats itself of the few great things that are in it. Most people, it would seem, do not recognize the name of Pontoppidan, despite the Nobel Prize that crowns it. Even fewer have read *Hans im Glück*, that dense, deep, unique work.

The title was from the German edition of Pontoppidan's magnum opus, *Lucky Per* (*Lykke-Per* in Danish). Published in two volumes in Copenhagen in 1905, the book had also appeared in Swedish, Finnish, Polish, Romanian, and Dutch; won praise from such luminaries as Thomas Mann; and propelled its author to a 1917 Nobel Prize for Literature. Twenty years on, Europe may have had bloodier matters on its collective mind, but Bloch, ever hopeful, found himself dreaming of a more pacific world where *Lucky Per* would "be counted among the essential works of world literature"—a "near future," he wrote, in which Pontoppidan might "finally begin to live."

The embarrassment of this prediction was not so much that it was wrong as that it was premature. Bloch soon received a note from Pontoppidan, who pointed out tactfully that he was not in fact dead, but at home in a coastal suburb, celebrating his ninth decade. And what's more, still writing; the third volume of his memoirs would appear the following year, a fourth in 1940. (Only in 1943, after an abridgment of the whole had been published as *On the Way to Myself*, did the novelist, now eighty-six, finally breathe his last.)

The historical record in English doesn't indicate quite where the adjective "erroneous" belongs here—whether Czech journalists had accidentally misreported Pontoppidan's death or whether, as seems likely, they were simply saluting a Nobel laureate on his eightieth birthday, and Bloch, still adjusting to a new language, had misread. But perhaps the ambiguity is fortuitous, one of those places where life gusts up to reveal its stitching. In Denmark today, *Lucky Per* is a literary touchstone, and the basis for the most lavish film production in the country's history. Elsewhere, the name of Pontopiddan is virtually unknown. And because his legacy has amounted, in essence, to a tale of two audiences—one at home, one abroad—it seems only fitting that the first false report of this great writer's death should arise from things lost in translation.

II

Even in 1937, Pontoppidan's readership in his mother tongue was larger and more durable than Bloch, stranded elsewhere in a fragmenting Europe, could have understood. A pastor's son and engineering-school dropout, Pontoppidan had made his name and a modest living with his very first story collection, *Clipped Wings*, published in 1881, when he was twenty-four. Two more collections and assorted journalistic piecework followed over the next decade, along with a handful of promising books in the half-invented genre he called "*smaa Romaner*"— novellas, give or take a few thousand words. This early writing focused on life in the peasant towns of Jutland, the easternmost lobe of the Danish archipelago. It was Pontoppidan's home territory—his pen-name in the Copenhagen *Morgenbladet* was "Rusticus," the man of the country—and he aimed to "delyricize" it in the manner of a Nordic Flaubert, flensing away the sentimentality of his Romantic elders. The titles alone suggest a posture of wintry pragmatism: *From the Huts*, *The Polar Bear*, "The End of Life," "The Bone Man"; "Fate was not kind," a story called "A Death Blow" insists, perhaps superfluously. Yet these tales betray a tender streak, too, a kind of gallows humor, along with a deep-running feeling for the place. Even the bleakest of them abound with a quality of passionate seeing: the sun "melting the tar out of the timber walls," the wagon rolling out of the forest "as if out of another century."

It was a fourth collection, *Clouds*, that, in 1890, announced Pontoppidan's full range. To the early works' Flaubertian ironies, *Clouds* added Balzacian hunger, reaching from the provinces to a capital in the throes of modernization. Pontoppidan was now in his thirties, a husband and father, and perhaps this, too, had enlarged him. In any case, *Clouds* was his "most significant and most widely read work" to date, according to a critical biography by P. M. Mitchell.

In short order, Pontoppidan was trading letters with Georg Brandes, the leading promulgator of a "Modern Breakthrough" in Danish culture; living in Copenhagen year-round; and contributing to Brandes's brother's newspaper as "Urbanus"—the man of the city. Most importantly, he was beginning work on an ambitious cycle called *The Promised Land*, which would bid farewell to peasant life. Across three *smaa Romaner*, it traced the story of Emanuel Hansted, an idealistic young curate who moves from the city to the provinces and is ultimately destroyed by them: "Here lies Don Quixote's ghost," runs the epitaph in the novel, "who was born to be a good chaplain, but thought himself a prophet and a saint." The work was a popular success; English versions of its first two installments were printed in London in 1896. But even as the trilogy was being gathered into a single volume, Pontoppidan was embarking upon a still more ambitious project—indeed, one that claimed ambition as its central mystery.

He would name his new hero Peter Andreas Sidenius, and the book after a nickname, "Per." And if Emanuel Hansted's refined background and tragic end had been the projections of a young man on the make, Pontoppidan would grant Per something of his own "Aladdin's luck," along with great swaths of his personal history.

The most significant of these sharings was a family background: Per Sidenius would be the black sheep of an "old and extensive ministerial line" of pietist clerics. (Cue Pontoppidan's trenchant autobiography: "My father was a parson. That is basically my entire saga.") Estranged as a child from his Jutland home—marked out, he feels, by fortune—Per heads off at sixteen for the big city. He is following the map drawn by his realist forebears, but also, interestingly, reversing the trajectory of *The Promised Land*.

In Copenhagen, Per pursues his fortune along a series of charmed paths. Really, they are the same path. He enters the Polytechnic Institute and just as quickly departs it. He flirts with artistic circles but outgrows (he thinks) their "fleas and filthy bedrooms." He falls in and out of love at least five times. And through all these stormy impulsions, he clings to the ambition he has conceived for himself: to usher "little, poor" Denmark into the twentieth century by means of "his great work."

That the word "work" here indicates a feat of civil engineering, rather than of art, is one of several key ways in which *Lucky Per* tacks away from the traditions it otherwise reckons by: *bildungsroman*, yes, but also folk tale, religious confession, *künstlerroman* . . . Per's engineering schemes (as the critic Fredric Jameson has noted) link personal and national destiny in a way that even the boldest of the *künstler*'s creations cannot. When Per dreams of changing the world, he is thinking not only of moral sentiments but of shipping routes, capital flows, and the liberation of a rural proletariat through the power of the sea. Nonetheless, his projects encode, as eloquently as any poem or painting, a psychological self-portrait. Or does it not speak to his suppressed desires that his proposed masterpiece, a "tentacled canal system," will bring estranged Jutland towns like the one he's just fled into communion with all the ports of the great world? Such industrial-strength hubris bulks up the irony, too: Per seems a little crazy to dream so big, yet we nontechnicians feel uneasy dismissing him. And by the midpoint of the novel, via his rude charisma and his engagement to a banker's daughter who might civilize him, Per stands on the cusp of realizing his dream.

But fortune in *Lucky Per* is as mysterious as in life. For it is precisely at this moment that Per's rise stalls out. His outer attainments—funds, love, renown—seem only to underscore an inner emptiness. "Who am I? I can't say," he murmurs at one point, early on, and that remains his strength and his curse, the abyss from which no success can save him. Still, Per is nothing if not stubborn; his motto is the Nietzschean "I will." And so the book's second half completes the fairy-tale arc of journey and return. We watch him strip away his ambitions one by one, breaking the connections he's made, mending the ones he's broken, drawing ever closer to a new, perhaps unreachable goal.

Lucky Per appeared in seven installments, from 1898 to 1904. Pontoppidan, an obsessive reviser, kept editing well into the 'teens. Nonetheless, the book was already understood to place its author, in Mann's phrase, "within the highest class of European writers." Writing in Heidelberg, the Marxist György Lukács gave *Lucky Per* a prominent place in his influential *Theory of the Novel*, alongside *Don Quixote* and *A Sentimental Education*. Meanwhile, in Stockholm, Fredrik Vetterlund, a conservative who found Pontoppidan's generation insufficiently high-minded, commended *Lucky Per* and *The Promised Land* to the attention of the Swedish Academy: "These belong, by virtue of their richness, their portrayal of the soul, their narrative art, and their overall effect, to the most eminent works [of] Nordic novel-writing."

One imagines Pontoppidan as too skeptical a temperament to have cared much about accolades. He was now halfway through the last of his three great novel cycles, *The Kingdom of the Dead*, and his outlook on "the soul" had darkened considerably. A proximate cause was Europe's catastrophic plunge into war. Yet in one respect, fortune stayed with him. It was felt in the Academy—never exactly insensible to the literary charms of Scandinavia—that the Nobel was now best bestowed on writers from the small, neutral countries of the north. Pontoppidan, increasingly austere, would have to share the prize with his more moralistic countryman, Karl Gjellerup. But the award was widely understood not as a split decision for two half-qualified writers so much as a ticket brokered between extremes: "Gjellerup's idealism and Pontoppidan's talent," in the brisk assessment of the Norwegian daily *Verdens Gang*.

Gjellerup was almost instantly forgotten. Pontoppidan, on the other hand, would have an outsized influence on twentieth-century Danish literature. In 1906, when Martin Andersen Nexø published his own magnum opus, *Pelle the Conqueror*, the dedication was to Pontoppidan: "the master." And up through the 1950s, Danish novelists would apprentice themselves to his innovations. A writer so well known in his own time, and resolutely of no party, was perhaps destined to fall comparatively out of vogue amid the radical upheavals of the '60s and '70s. But his reputation soon recovered. When, at the turn of the millennium, Denmark's paper of record, *Politiken*, surveyed readers on "the greatest Danish novel of the twentieth century," *Lucky Per* came in second, edged out only by Johannes V. Jensen's historical epic *The Fall of the King*. And 2018's sumptuous three-hour film adaptation by the Oscar-winning director Bille August would seem poised to cement *Lucky Per* as Denmark's version of the Great Scandinavian Novel, full stop.

III

Still, overseas, *Lucky Per* and its author remain as unrecognized as Bloch seemed to fear eighty years ago. Only a few dozen pages of Pontoppidan's fiction have been translated into English since Volume II of *The Promised Land* appeared in 1896. And by 2007, these too were emphatically out of print, so that even as Denmark's Culture Ministry was inducting *Lucky Per* into the country's official canon, Bill Bryson could lump it in with the work of other Nobelists "whose fame would barely make it to the end of their own century." *The New Yorker*'s Adam Gopnik waxed similarly invidious a few years later: "Who wouldn't rather be in the company of Proust, Auden, and Nabokov, than of ... Henrik Pontoppidan?" Of course, neither of these writers made claims to have read him, so perhaps this is simply a way of begging the bigger question: why has so little of Pontoppidan's work reached the English-speaking world?

There is always the possibility that certain untranslatable

facts of culture have held Pontoppidan back—but this theory seems belied by both common sense and the work itself. To be sure, Denmark is a little nation ("Lilliputian," *Lucky Per* calls it) but that never stopped Kierkegaard or Isak Dinesen from finding readers. And, to be sure, there are elements of Pontoppidan's great social tapestry—ecclesiastical mores, "fascine constructions"—that history has rendered moot ... but *more* moot than the Chancery Court of *Bleak House*? More moot than *Middlemarch*'s Parliamentary Reform Act of 1832? It seems to me, rather, that one of *Lucky Per*'s major feats of engineering is to charge the putatively local concerns of 1870s Denmark with storm and strife that resonate today.

There is, more plausibly, the obstacle posed to translation by Pontoppidan's literary language. His reputation in Denmark is as an exemplar of classical prose. Aesthetically restless, Pontoppidan would gradually subsume the clipped lucidity of his youth into a larger panoply of modes that, in *Lucky Per*, amounts almost to an encyclopedia: satire and pathos, speechifying and repartee, lyrical evocations of Copenhagen's grit, moils of introspection that stretch logic as if attempting to engineer modernism itself, and—perhaps his favorite effect—a periodic clearing into transparence. The net result is high style, and high tension. "Pontoppidan keeps his [prose] as a pastor's wife does the floor of her living room," wrote the critic and friend Vilhelm Andersen. And he's right: given everything that's packed inside, the room is impressively well kept. But what really drew me in, when Naomi Lebowitz sent me her translation in 2010—the first I'd ever heard of this forgotten masterpiece—was the fire that so often seems on the verge of shooting from the walls.

In fact, returning to *Lucky Per* now, on the eve of its republication, I've begun to suspect that what has held it back from wider renown is the very thing that guarantees its posterity: what Bloch calls its "contradiction," Jameson its "cosmic neutrality," and Pontoppidan himself its "double vision." That is, the book elevates the tensions of its style, the wildness and the control, the passion and the doubt, to the level of a compositional principle, which in turn becomes a philosophical outlook on the most bracing paradoxes of life itself.

This is easiest to see in Per's family relationships. Pontoppidan's model for storytelling was, he wrote to Andersen, "the unattainable pattern: There once was a man named John," and *Lucky Per*'s opening gives us "a pastor named Johannes Sidenius" living among "the green hills of East Jutland." Within a few sentences, the mists of folklore clear, and we see this pastor as he appears to his town's gossipy citizens: the aloofness, the self-regard, the ascetic unconcern for the figure he cuts, the faintly ridiculous "dark blue glasses." By the end of the chapter, when the pastor's rebellious son Per leaves home on a boat "slowly steam[ing] out through the endless bends of the fjords," we'll be ready to throw our sympathies in with our hero.

Yet a funny thing happens on the way to the city: we glimpse an interior world that threatens to hold us back in the town. First a neighbor threatens, in a private meeting with the pastor, to report Per to the town council for stealing apples. As if translating appearances for one too myopic to read them, he emphasizes the cost to the pastor's position: such a report "will not make your appointment to this parish look good." But the echo that comes back suggests the pastor's true concern, not an indignant "my appointment!" but a broken "My son . . ."

In a later incident, when he confronts Per directly, we are securely grounded in the son's perspective, and participate in Per's "contempt" for the old man. For a moment, the feeling seems mutual. The father snaps, "It's gone that far with you, has it?" But then the perspective flits in an odd direction: he has said this, we are told, "without revealing that his worst anxiety"—Per committing some more fleshly sin—"has already, in reality, been allayed." There is the usual authorial bemusement here at an old man's prudery, but also a rare emotional force to his fear for his son's soul. And rarer still is the negative capability that would leave such a clash unresolved—the way our subjective sense of the father, deepening, doesn't overwrite our initial objections so much as sit alongside them in anxious correction.

This curious quality of suspension and reversal haunts the rest of *Lucky Per* no less than its folkloric echoes. Once in

Copenhagen, under the influence of new acquaintances, Per attempts to shed his bohemian indifference about attire:

He had already ascertained that, to certain eyes, a white shirtfront and an immaculately fitted coat could have more significance for a young man's future than a prolonged, dedicated, ascetic diligence. Nothing vital was lost so long as appearance was maintained.

Pontoppidan is a great poet of mood, in the sense that his characters are always in one, and that the moods are astutely observed, cross-hatched, even counterintuitive. Where a typical realist might show us a character doing one thing and feeling another, Pontoppidan gives us Per doing one thing, feeling another, and then, in some hidden vault of the self, feeling a third thing he doesn't even feel he feels. On the surface, he is rather proud of himself as he strides through the streets. But the word "ascetic" is enough for us to feel the pastor's memory ghosting along beside him, trailing the crowd of mocking neighbors we understand must have made Per ashamed. For us, at least, appearance has not been maintained.

And this Oedipal ambivalence is only one of the book's double visions. In the course of its long unfolding, dozens more characters bloom into parallactic dimension: from Chief Boatswain Olufsen, who prides himself on his "little miscellaneous garden," to his wife, who steals out to water it with her "nightclothes still under her apron"; from Trine, the good fairy of the Olufsen household, to Fru Engelhardt, who starts as Anna Karenina and ends as Mae West; and—still a startling conjunction—from the anti-Semitic painter Fritjof Jansen to Lea Salomon, a level-headed Jewish matriarch who loves her husband but, wonderfully, will not let him kiss her right hand.

IV

No discussion of this novel can be complete without addressing the depiction of Jewish life that takes up much of its middle act. That geometric fact alone would be noteworthy, issuing as it does from a pastor's son, but Pontoppidan's treatment of his Jewish characters is even more remarkable for its variety, its complexity, and its frankness. In this regard, his only real competitor among lapsed-Protestant writers is George Eliot, and with all due respect, *Lucky Per*'s Salomon family, among whom Per finds a fiancée and a fortune, leave her Daniel Deronda in the dust.

One strength of the portrayal is its lived reality. The Salomons palpably share the world in which their author moved, rather than being imagined *ex nihilo*, or researched into being. Indeed, we might say that the cosmopolitan Copenhagen of *Lucky Per* belongs more to them than to the title character. As the first long chapter dedicated to the Salomons makes clear, their links to the ghettos and shtetls are generationally attenuated; they are, rather, representative of the class of cultured, moneyed, and assimilated Jews who in the 1870s, along with their Gentile analogues, were leading sleepy Denmark into the future.

Yet with his mastery of implication, Pontoppidan makes clear that this belonging, in all senses, is unstable. Philip Salomon, the nature-loving "King of the Exchange," grows a little nervous when he steps out into the country, away from the protections of city life; his feeling of security has slipped. Meanwhile, the "jolly" Romantic Fritjof collapses into a hateful singularity of vision, a sort of fascist nostalgia for the lost privileges of race. And for all Per's unease at Fritjof's jeremiads, his complex and shifting feelings toward the Salomons seem driven by his own sense of a vanished birthright. It's not their money he's after, though that might help with his canal plan. It's what he perceives—incorrectly—as their comfort in their own skins.

One of the great strengths of *Lucky Per* is the way it gives play to all shades of anti-Semitism, often without the moral scare quotes we feel in Eliot. Against the charms of impetuous Nanny Salomon, or of her brother Ivan, an ingratiating bachelor whose "deepest self" is "altruistic, childlike, empathic," Pontoppidan sets the prejudice not only of Fritjof and his circle, but of Per himself. He sees Nanny, at first, as an "Oriental beauty" and dismisses Ivan as "a foolish little Jew." If he comes to feel pleasure, even admiration, in the company of the Salomons, it is less a mark of distinction in his character than a function of habitual exposure to other people, which in Pontoppidan can wear down a bias but never quite wear it out.

It might be tempting, early on, to mistake the character's point of view for the author's. When we enter the Salomon household, we enter, too, the tropes of phrenology. The father, Philip Salomon, must, among other qualities, have "uncommonly thick red lips." The court jester, Uncle Heinrich Delft, enjoyable for reasons that have little to do with any stereotype, must nonetheless have an "ape-like head." His sister Lea's beauty, and the suggestion that he himself is "a testimony to the irregularity with which characteristics peculiar to the Jewish race emerge," open up an interesting double reading: perhaps his ugliness is the aberration? Yet some "peculiar characteristics" certainly attach to the initial portrait of Jakobe, the brilliant oldest Salomon daughter, with her "large hooked nose ... wide mouth ... and ... short, recessed chin." The impression made on Per is "disagreeable," and it seems impossible to say in this moment that a novel that would see her so clinically doesn't share the sentiment.

But then something amazing happens. The instant Per leaves the room, Jakobe complains, "But the staring eyes! I found him rather repulsive." And for all her intellectual gifts, her distaste, driven home by another echo, is no less physical than Per's. "He made an unpleasant impression on me, like a horse with glass eyes." Later, Jakobe will decide that perhaps *she* has assessed too harshly *his* "peculiar attributes of character." And in the space of a phrase, we see stereotype become stereoscopic—every perspective has its opposite, everything is fathomlessly deep. And superficial: tom-ay-to, tom-ah-to. What is left but for the two of them to fall in love?

This surprising development is the largest single instance of double vision in the novel, as it grants us privileged and extended access to Jakobe's mind. Indeed, she becomes almost a co-protagonist; it is no stretch to call her, as Lebowitz has elsewhere, "one of literature's greatest and most interesting heroines." Jakobe is as intelligent as anyone out of James, as bold as anyone out of Austen, as perverse as anyone out of

Dostoevsky. Moreover, she is Per's *döppelgänger,* driven by her own ambitions and urges.

And she opens, in one of Pontoppidan's signature clearings, a view to the real wages of anti-Semitism. It is a flashback to a Berlin train station, where, waiting to depart for the south, she sees, "some way off on the platform, a group of pitiable, ragged people, surrounded by a circle of curious, gaping onlookers held back by police." And then

on the large, half-darkened waiting room floor, hundreds of the same kind of fantastic, ragged forms she had seen on the platform ... men, women, children, gray-bearded old men, suckling infants lying on their mothers' breasts. Some were almost naked; many had bloody bandages around their foreheads or hands; all were sallow, emaciated, dirty, as if they had been wandering for days in the sun and dust.

It dawns on Jakobe that these must be the Russian Jews she has heard about, refugees from a pogrom:

She had read in the newspapers, every day through the whole summer, about these crowds of refugees who were half wild with terror over the scandalous crimes perpetrated against them, abetted by the indifference of the authorities. ... She had tried to console herself by assuming the picture to be exaggerated, since such inhumanity, committed by a powerful and industrious populace, would be impossible in this century of freedom and enlightenment.

But this novel, with its relentless probing for what lies beyond our blind spots, will leave standing no final protection from the human truth—not class, not learning, not ideology—and in these moments when a character grows strong enough to drop her blinders and simply see, as the novelist sees, *Lucky Per* becomes not just great, but prophetic.

V

And still at its center stands Per Sidenius, likeable-unlikeable, mercurial and unchanging, Nietzschean and Darwinian and Freudian and perhaps even Marxian, all and none of the above.

He is the novel's largest paradox, its toughest selling point in a black-and-white world ... and, I've come to feel, its richest reward. For where Jakobe is the great positive presence in the novel, formed of earthly qualities and attributes, Per, her equal and opposite, is a kind of negative space, an emanation of spirit. In his parabolic fall away from Jakobe in the book's long third act, he passes through marriage, parenthood, homes, but no position is stable. The only things that seem to leave a mark are his lifelong sense of exile and his restless forward drive. It is Per's intimation, as he nears one of the great, strange conclusions in the history of the novel, that the burden is not his alone to bear:

We seek a meaning to life, an aim for our struggles and suffering. But one day, we are stopped by a voice from the depths of our being, a ghostly voice that asks, "Who are you?" From then on, we hear no other question. ... Is what we call the soul merely a passing mood? ... Or do we have as many souls in us as there are cards in a game of Cuckoo. Every time you shuffle the deck a new face appears: a jester, a soldier, a night owl.

The restless reshufflings of *Lucky Per* appear, in this light, an attempt to bring into focus an existential predicament we still, a century later, resist seeing clearly. Jakobe's vision in the train station may throw us into the realm of tomorrow morning's headlines, but Per is the most audaciously modern thing here: he is, like us, on the way to himself.

Whether he ever gets there is in some sense the engine of suspense driving us forward. But a clue lies in the title, a final obstacle of translation, a final doubling of vision. The Danish word "lykke," like the German "glück," means in a single stroke both "happiness" and "luck." No English word can quite convey the meaning, though Lebowitz lets it rustle through a range of nearby idioms—"by chance," "hazard," "fortunately." In the novel's stunning last chapter, our "lykke" Per is aging and alone on the Jutland heath, but in full (he feels) possession of himself. We are free to believe him or not, to see him as happy but not lucky, or lucky but not happy, or both things, or neither, but in any case the curious light that seemed to shine behind previous clearings in the text now pours through—"a conclusion of resignation," Bloch wrote in his misbegotten eulogy, "yet illuminated, like the final paintings of Rembrandt."

Per Sidenius in these pages is the apotheosis of Pontoppidan's prismatic vision, the transparency that is the sum of all colors. And naturally, he is the final reversal in a novel full of them. He may have failed at his "great work," but the author standing behind him manages to "keep the wound open," as real artists must do. If only for a few moments, he clears a channel that seems to connect what we would more comfortably view as incommensurable seas: proximity and distance, joy and sadness, the fairy tale and the avant-garde, the nineteenth century and the twenty-first. Whatever the vicissitudes of literary fortune, it is our luck he belongs to us now.

Garth Risk Hallberg

NOTES

vii. "In the summer": This anecdote appears in a footnote to Jon Helt Haarder's chapter in *Danish Literature as World Literature*, ed. Dan Ringgaard and Mads Rosendahl Thomsen, Bloomsbury, 2017, p. 169. Additional material can be found at www.henrikpontoppidan.dk.

vii. "A great writer": Bloch's piece is reprinted in *Literary Essays*, trans. Andrew Joron and Helga Wild, Stanford University Press, 1998, pp. 67–71.

vii. "also appeared": P. M. Mitchell, *Henrik Pontoppidan*, Twayne Publishers, 1979, p. 138.

viii. "*On the Way to Myself*": Title translations, publication dates, and much of the biographical data derive from Flemming Behrendt's entry on Pontoppidan (translated by Russell Dees) in *Danish Writers from the Reformation to Decadence 1550–1900*, Thomson Gale, 2004, pp. 383–95.

viii. "most lavish": "Esben Smed Begins Filming Lucky Per in Copenhagen," nordicdrama.com, August 9, 2017.

viii. "de-lyricize": Sven H. Rossel, *A History of Scandinavian Literature 1870–1980*, trans. Anne C. Ulmer, University of Minnesota Press, 1982, p. 44.

viii, ix. "Fate was not kind"; "as if out of another century": Mitchell treats the early work at length, with extensive quotations, pp. 26–54.

ix. "melting the tar": From a 1927 translation of "A Fisher Nest." (See Select Bibliography on p. xxiii of this volume.)

ix. "trading letters": e.g. those reprinted in Brandes's *Selected Letters*, trans. W. Glyn Jones, Norvik Press, 1990.

ix. "living in Copenhagen": Behrendt, p. 510.

ix. "Here lies Don Quixote's ghost": Quoted in Mitchell, p. 72.

ix. "English versions": See Select Bibliography, p. xxiii.

x. "pietist clerics": The ancestral surname, "Broby" (literally "bridgetown"), was Latinized in the 1600s, and subsequently borne by scores of priests around Denmark. J. G. Robertson, "Henrik Pontoppidan," *Contemporary Review*, 117 January–June 1920, p. 79.

x. "My father was a parson": Quoted in Claus Jensen's chapter on Pontoppidan and Gjellerup in *Neighbouring Nobel: The History of Thirteen Danish Nobel Prizes*, ed. Henry Nielsen and Keld Nielsen, Aarhus University Press, 2001, p. 163.

x. "Fredric Jameson has noted": "Cosmic Neutrality," *London Review of Books*, 20 October 2011, pp. 17–18.

x. "within the highest class of European writers": A facsimile of Mann's encomium to Pontoppidan appears at www.henrikpontoppidan.dk.

xi. "György Lukács": See *A Theory of the Novel*, trans. Anna Bostock, MIT Press, 1971.

xi. "Meanwhile, in Stockholm": The discussion here of the 1917 Nobel Prize follows Jensen's.

xii. "Danish novelists": See Rossel's entries on Jacob Paludan, Hans Kirk, and Frank Jaeger. Glyn Jones also points out that Pontoppidan's early focus on the poor lit the way for more proletarian realists ("Henrik Pontoppidan (1857–1943)," *Modern Language Review*, 52, no. 3, July 1957, pp. 376–7).

xii. "comparatively out of vogue": Behrendt, p. 514.

xii. "surveyed readers": Harder, p. 168.

xii. "out of print": The most recent edition to appear was James Massengale's terrific rendition of *The Polar Bear*, published in the University of Wisconsin-Madison's Introduction to Scandinavia pamphlet series in 2002.

xii. "official canon": q.v. nordicdrama.com.

xii. "Bill Bryson could lump": In *Shakespeare: The World as Stage*, Atlas Books/HarperCollins, 2007.

xii. "Adam Gopnik waxed": In "Writing and Winning," *The New Yorker*, October 18, 2010.

xiii. "exemplar of classical prose": Mitchell, p. 67.

xiii. "Pontoppidan keeps his [prose]": Quoted in Harder, p. 184.

xiii. "double vision": Jensen, p. 170.

xiv. "the unattainable pattern": Jensen, p. 177.

xvii: "one of literature's": See Lebowitz's "Magic Socialism and the Ghost of *Pelle Erobreren*," *Scandinavian Studies*, 46, no. 3, Fall 2004, pp. 341–68.

xx. "keep the wound open": A familiar quotation in Denmark, this is the final line of the painter Jørgen Halleger's speech in the *smaa Roman* called *Nattevagt* ("Night Watch"), published in 1894, per Behrendt, p. 511. Halleger makes a cameo in chapter 2 of *Lucky Per*.

SELECT BIBLIOGRAPHY

Pontoppidan's published work in Danish runs to some forty volumes, placing him among Scandinavia's most prolific writers, but his reputation rests on three long novels: *Det Forjættede Land* (1892–5), *Lykke-Per* (1898–1904), and *De Dødes Rige* (1912–16). Many of his writings were revised for successive republications, a few of the shorter pieces radically; no collected critical edition of his works has been published. The present translation is based on the revision of *Lykke-Per* completed in 1918. A full list of Pontoppidan's other works to have seen print in English follows:

- *The Apothecary's Daughters*, trans. Gordius Nielsen, Trübner, London, 1890.
- "Autobiographical Statement," trans. Russel Dees, *Danish Writers from the Reformation to Decadence: 1550–1900*, Thomson Gale, Detroit, 2004, p. 518.
- *Burgomaster Hoeck and His Wife*, trans. Martin A. David, Geelmuyden.Kiese/Scandinavian Airlines, Lysaker, 1999.
- "Eagle's Flight," trans. Lida Siboni Hanson, *American-Scandinavian Review*, 17, 1929, pp. 556–7.
- "A Fisher Nest," trans. Julianne Sarauw, *American-Scandinavian Review*, 15, 1927, pp. 476–86.
- *Emanuel, or Children of the Soil*, trans. Alice Lucas, Dent, London, 1896.
- "Gallows Hill at Ilum," trans. David Stoner, *Anthology of Danish Literature*, ed. Frederik J. Billeskov Jansen and P. M. Mitchell, Southern Illinois University Press, Carbondale, 1972, pp. 333–59.
- *The Polar Bear: A Portrait*, trans. James Massengale, Wisconsin Introduction to Scandinavia II, no. 12, Department of Scandinavian Studies, University of Wisconsin-Madison, Madison, 2002.
- *The Promised Land*. trans. Alice Lucas, Dent, London, 1896.
- "The Royal Guest" [short story], trans. Lida Siboni Hanson, *Denmark's Best Stories: An Introduction to Danish Fiction*, ed. Hanna Astrup Larsen, American-Scandinavian Foundation/Norton, New York, 1928, pp. 217–36.
- "The Royal Guest" [novella], trans. P. M. Mitchell and Kenneth H. Ober, *The Royal Guest and Other Classical Danish Narrative*, University of Chicago Press, Chicago, 1977, pp. 133–93.

The most comprehensive biographical source in English remains Mitchell's monograph of 1979, but the shorter portraits offered more recently by Claus Jensen and Flemming Behrendt are indispensable resources for readers wishing to learn more—the latter, in part, for its complete bibliography of the work in Danish.

Given the dearth of available translations, English-language scholarship on Pontoppidan has been surprisingly rich; critics have encountered the work in German, in French, and in Danish and, in the case of Naomi Lebowitz, have undertaken to bring Pontoppidan into English themselves. Her essay "The World's Pontoppidan and His *Lykke-Per*" (*Scandinavian Studies*, 2006), places Pontoppidan alongside major figures of Danish and European intellectual life and unpacks the novel's fairy-tale parallels—and appears here in revised form as a Translator's Afterword. Fredric Jameson's 2011 *London Review of Books* essay further situates *Lucky Per* in nineteenth-century history and literature, while Jon Helt Haarder offers a useful overview of *Lykke-Per* in "Towards a New World: Henrik Pontoppidan and Johannes V. Jensen," from *Danish Literature as World Literature*. An early and in some ways still unsurpassed appreciation of Pontoppidan by J. G. Robertson appeared in the *Contemporary Review* in 1920, and was republished in his *Essays and Addresses on Literature* of 1935.

More specialized insights into *Lykke-Per* appear in Ernst Ekman's study, "Henrik Pontoppidan as a Critic of Modern Danish Society," (*Scandinavian Studies*, 1957); Peter Tudvad's "Henrik Pontoppidan: Inspiration and Hesitation" (a chapter in *Kierkegaard's Influence on Literature, Criticism, and Art*, Ashgate Publishing, 2013); Liliane Weissberg's "Utopian Visions: Bloch, Lukács, Pontoppidan," (*German Quarterly*, 1994), and in a series of essays by W. Glyn Jones published in *Scandinavian Studies* and *Modern Language Review* in the 1950s and '60s.

Comprehensive studies in Danish by Vilhelm Andersen, Knut Ahnlund, and Georg Brandes remain untranslated, but an English-language summary was appended to Ahnlund's 1956 dissertation. Along with select other material in English, it is available at www.henrikpontoppidan.dk; further texts, including facsimiles of the mid-1890s translations of *The Promised Land* and *The Apothecary's Daughters*, can be found at the Danish Royal Library's website: kb.dk.

CHRONOLOGY

DATE	AUTHOR'S LIFE	LITERARY CONTEXT
1857	Birth of Henrik Pontoppidan in Fredericia, Denmark (24 July), to the Lutheran clergyman Dines Pontoppidan and his wife Birgitte Marie Christine (*née* Oxenbøll).	Børnstjerne Bjørnson: *Synnøva Solbakken.* Gustave Flaubert: *Madame Bovary.* Ludwig Feuerbach: *Theogonie.*
1858		Hans Christian Andersen: *New Fairy Tales and Stories* (to 1872).
1859		Charles Darwin: *On the Origin of Species.* John Stuart Mill: *On Liberty.* George Eliot: *Adam Bede.*
1860		Bjørnson: *A Happy Boy.* Ivan Turgenev: *First Love.*
1861		Meïr Goldschmidt: *Homeless.* Mill: *Utilitarianism.* Goncourt Brothers: *Sœur Philomène.*
1862		Henrik Ibsen: *Love's Comedy.* Turgenev: *Fathers and Children.*
1863	Moves to Randers, Denmark, where his father is transferred.	Andersen: *In Spain.* Ibsen: *The Pretenders.*
1864	Witnesses the invasion of Denmark by Austrian and Prussian forces.	Fyodor Dostoevsky: *Notes from Underground.* Goncourt Brothers: *Germinie Lacerteux.*
1865		Leo Tolstoy: *War and Peace* (to 1869).
1866		Feuerbach: *God, Freedom, and Immortality.* Dostoevsky: *Crime and Punishment.*

HISTORICAL EVENTS

Fall of Christian Albrecht Bluhme's Conservative administration in Denmark, and formation of a National Liberal government by Carl Christian Hall. Copenhagen Convention: the historic Sound Toll abolished and Danish Straits made international waterways.

First message sent by transatlantic cable.

Franco-Austrian War.

Garibaldi proclaims Victor Emmanuel King of Italy. Abraham Lincoln elected US president.
Emancipation of the serfs in Russia. Beginning of the American Civil War.

Otto von Bismarck becomes Prussian prime minister and foreign minister (September).
Death of King Frederick VII, and accession of Christian IX. "November Constitution" instituted, annexing the province of Schleswig to Denmark proper. Marriage of Princess Alexandra of Denmark to Albert Edward, Prince of Wales. Accession of Prince William of Denmark to the Greek throne as George I. Beginning of the unsuccessful January Insurrection in Poland against Russia (to 1864).
Outbreak of the Second Schleswig War between Denmark and an alliance of Prussia and Austria (February). Danish army defeated at the Battle of Dybbøl (18 April) and Jutland occupied. Treaty of Vienna cedes majority of Schleswig and Holstein to Prussia and Austria (October). Fall of the National Liberal government in Denmark, and appointment of a Conservative administration. First International (International Working Men's Association) (to 1876).
The Convention of Gastein, granting Prussia the administration of Schleswig and Austria that of Holstein. End of the American Civil War. Assassination of Abraham Lincoln.
The Seven Weeks' War between Austria and Prussia, ending with Prussian victory at the Battle of Königgrätz (3 July). The Treaty of Prague cedes Schleswig and Holstein to Prussia (23 August). New conservative Danish constitution instituted.

DATE	AUTHOR'S LIFE	LITERARY CONTEXT
1867		Goldschmidt: *The Raven.* Ibsen: *Peer Gynt.* Émile Zola: *Thérèse Raquin.* Goncourt Brothers: *Manette Salomon.*
1868		Dostoevsky: *The Idiot.*
1869		Ibsen: *The League of Youth.* Goncourt Brothers: *Madame Gervaisais.*
1870		Bjørnson: *Poems and Songs* and *Arnljot Gelline.*
1871		Darwin: *The Descent of Man.* Eliot: *Middlemarch* (to 1872). Zola: The *Rougon-Macquart* cycle (to 1893).
1872		Georg Brandes: *Main Currents in Nineteenth-Century Literature* (6 vols, to 1890). Jens Peter Jacobsen: *Mogens.* August Strindberg: *Master Olof.* David Friedrich Strauss: *The Old Faith and the New.*
1873	Commences studies in engineering at the Copenhagen Polytechnic Institute.	Ibsen: *Emperor and Galilean.*
1874		Eliot: *Daniel Deronda* (to 1876).
1875		Death of Andersen. Holger Drachmann: *Muted Melodies.* Bjørnson: *The Bankrupt* and *The Editor.* Tolstoy: *Anna Karenina* (to 1877).
1876	Disappointment at failure to be selected for an expedition to Greenland. Undertakes a formative trip to the Swiss Alps.	Sophus Schandorph: *From the Province.* Jacobsen: *Marie Grubbe: A Lady of the Seventeenth Century.*
1877		Brandes: *Danish Poets.* Drachmann: *Songs by the Sea, Venezia,* and *From Over the Border.* Goldschmidt: *Memories and Accomplishments of Life.* Ibsen: *The Pillars of Society.* Turgenev: *Virgin Soil.*

CHRONOLOGY

Swedish scientist Alfred Nobel invents dynamite. *Ausgleich* establishes the Austro-Hungarian Dual Monarchy.

Suez Canal opened.

Forenede Venstre (United Left) party established in Denmark. Outbreak of the Franco-Prussian War (to 1871). Italy annexes the Papal States (20 September).
King Wilhelm I of Prussia proclaimed German Kaiser in the Hall of Mirrors of the Palace of Versailles (18 January). Paris Commune.

Forenede Venstre obtains majority in the Danish *Folketing*, demanding reforms such as the restoration of the more liberal constitution of June 1849.

New Icelandic constitution granting domestic legislative power instituted. Jacob Brønnum Scavenius Estrup becomes prime minister of Denmark, leading a conservative government of the *Højre* (Right).

Queen Victoria proclaimed Empress of India. Alexander Bell patents the telephone.

Thomas Edison invents the phonograph.

DATE	AUTHOR'S LIFE	LITERARY CONTEXT
1878		Karl Gjellerup: *An Idealist, A Description of Epigonus.* Schandorph: *Without a Centre.* Drachmann: *The Princess and Half the Kingdom.*
1879	Discontinues his engineering studies to become a writer, and begins teaching at a folk high school in Frerslev, North Zealand, founded by his brother Morten. Death of his father.	Drachmann: *Weeds and Roses.* Ibsen: *A Doll's House.* Strindberg: *The Red Room.* Bjørnson: *The New System.* Dostoevsky: *The Brothers Karamazov.*
1880	Completes his military service in the corps of engineers of the Royal Danish Army.	Herman Bang: *Hopeless Generations.* Jacobsen: *Niels Lyhne.* Guy de Maupassant: *Boule de suif.*
1881	Publishes his first story, *Et Endeligt* [*The End of a Life*], and *Stækkede Vinger* [*Clipped Wings*], short stories. Marries Mette Marie Hansen, a country girl from North Zealand, where the couple make their home.	Harald Høffding: *Outlines of Psychology.* Gjellerup: *Heredity and Morals.* Drachmann: *Old and New Gods.* Ibsen: *Ghosts.* Strindberg: *Lucky Peter's Travels.* Maupassant: *La Maison Tellier.* Henry James: *The Portrait of a Lady.*
1882	Birth of his first child, Karen Pontoppidan.	Gjellerup: *The Teutons' Apprentice* and *Spirits and Times.* Ibsen: *An Enemy of the People.*
1883	Publishes his first novel, *Sandinge Menighed* [*Sandinge Parish*], and *Landsbybilleder* [*Village Sketches*], short stories, including "En Fiskerrede" ("A Fisher Nest").	Bang: *Faedra.* Brandes: *Men of the Modern Breakthrough.* Bjørnson: *Beyond Our Power.* Jonas Lie: *The Family at Gilje.* Friedrich Nietzsche: *Thus Spake Zarathustra* (to 1885). Maupassant: *Une Vie.*
1884	Birth of his second child, Johanne Elisabeth Pontoppidan. First meeting with critic Georg Brandes.	Gjellerup: *Brynhild.* Ibsen: *The Wild Duck.* Strindberg: *Getting Married.* Bjørnson: *The Heritage of the Kurts.* Maupassant: *Miss Harriet.*

CHRONOLOGY

Prussia and Austria rescind the stipulation of the Treaty of Prague (1866) that North Schleswig be ceded back to Denmark if demanded in a plebiscite.

Louis Pasteur's discovery of a vaccine for chicken cholera revolutionizes work in infectious diseases.

Assassination of Tsar Alexander II of Russia. Jewish pogroms in Russia (to 1914); *c.* 2.5 million Jews leave Russia and Eastern Europe, many emigrating to the USA.

Co-operative dairies established in Denmark. Formation of the Triple Alliance between Germany, Austria–Hungary, and Italy. First Aliyah (to 1903) – Jewish migration to Palestine.

Eruption of Krakatoa.

Berlin Conference (to 1885).

DATE	AUTHOR'S LIFE	LITERARY CONTEXT
1885	Publishes *Ung Elskov* [*Young Love*], novella. Death of his first child, Karen Pontoppidan.	Bang: *Quiet Existences.* Drachmann: *Once upon a Time.* Amalie Skram: *Constance Ring.* Maupassant: *Bel-Ami.* Howells: *The Rise of Silas Lapham.*
1886	Publishes *Mimoser* (*The Apothecary's Daughters*), novella. Birth of his third child, Hans Broby Pontoppidan.	Jacobsen: *Poems and Sketches.* Ibsen: *Rosmersholm.* Nietzsche: *Beyond Good and Evil.* Tolstoy: *The Death of Ivan Ilyich.* Benito Pérez Galdós: *Fortunata and Jacinta* (to 1887). James: *The Bostonians.*
1887	Publishes *Fra Hytterne* [*From the Huts*], short stories, and *Isbjørnen* (*The Polar Bear: A Portrait*), novella. Contributes to Copenhagen daily, *Politiken* (to 1889).	Bang: *Stucco.* Gjellerup: *Thamyris.* Strindberg: *The Father.* Skram: *People of Hellemyr* (to 1898). Høffding: *Ethics.* Nietzsche: *On the Genealogy of Morals.* Maupassant: *Le Horla.*
1888	Death of his mother.	Ibsen: *The Lady from the Sea.* Strindberg: *Miss Julie* and *Creditors.* Maupassant: *Pierre et Jean.*
1889	Separates from his wife.	Gjellerup: *Minna.* Bang: *Tine.* Brandes: *On Aristocratic Radicalism.* Schandorph: *Recollections.* Bjørnson: *In God's Way.* Nietzsche: *Twilight of the Idols.*
1890	Publishes *Skyer* [*Clouds*], short stories, including "Ilum Galgebakke" ("Gallows Hill at Ilum"); *Krøniker* [*Chronicles*], parables, and *Reisebilder aus Dänemark*, a travel guide to Denmark in German.	Drachmann: *Pledged.* Ibsen: *Hedda Gabler.* Knut Hamsun: *Hunger.* Maupassant: *L'Inutile Beauté.*
1891	Publishes *Det forjættede Land* (*The Promised Land*) (in 3 volumes, to 1895).	Gjellerup: *Herman Vandel.* Lie: *Fairy Tales* (to 1892).

CHRONOLOGY

Prince Valdemar of Denmark declines the offer of the throne of Bulgaria.

Construction of the Eiffel Tower begins in Paris. Queen Victoria's Golden Jubilee.

Accession of Wilhelm II as German Kaiser.

Second International (to 1916).

Resignation of Bismarck.

Old age pension law introduced in Denmark. Expulsion of Jews from Moscow.

DATE	AUTHOR'S LIFE	LITERARY CONTEXT
1892	Divorces Mette Marie Hansen, and marries Antoinette Caroline Elise Kofoed, the daughter of a civil servant.	Ibsen: *The Master Builder.* Skram: *Betrayed.* Hamsun: *Mysteries.* Theodor Fontane: *Frau Jenny Treibel.*
1893	Publishes *Minder* [*Memories*], novella.	Gjellerup: *Wuthhorn.*
1894	Publishes *Nattevagt* [*Night Watch*], *Den gamle Adam* [*The Old Adam*], novellas, and "Ørneflugt" ("Eagle's Flight"). Birth of his fourth child, and first by his second wife, Else Cathrina Pontoppidan. First of many summer visits to Rørvig.	Høffding: *History of Modern Philosophy* (to 1895). Gjellerup: *Pastor Mors.* Ibsen: *Little Eyolf.* Bjørnson: *Beyond Human Might.* Hamsun: *Pan.*
1895		Skram: *Professor Hieronimus* and *At St. Jørgen's.* Hans E. Kinck: *Bat Wings.* Fontane: *Effi Briest.* Thomas Hardy: *Jude the Obscure.*
1896	Publishes *Højsang* [*Song of Songs*], novella. Birth of his fifth child, and second by his second wife, Steffen Broby Pontoppidan.	Bang: *Ida Brandt.* Gjellerup: *The Mill.* Ibsen: *John Gabriel Borkman.* Anton Chekhov: *My Life.*
1897		Kinck: *From Sea to Mountain.*
1898	Publishes *Lykke-Per* (*Lucky Per*) (in 8 volumes, to 1904).	Johannes V. Jensen: *Himmerland Stories* (to 1910). Strindberg: *To Damascus* (to 1904). Bjørnson: *Paul Lange and Tora Parsberg.* Hamsun: *Victoria.*
1900	Publishes *Lille Rødhætte: Et Portræt* [*Little Red Riding Hood: A Portrait*], novella.	Schandorph: *Helga.* Jensen: *The Fall of the King* (to 1901). Strindberg: *The Dance of Death.* Joseph Conrad: *Lord Jim.*
1901		Høffding: *Philosophy of Religion.* Gjellerup: *The Soothsayer.* Thomas Mann: *Buddenbrooks.* Chekhov: *Three Sisters.*
1903		James: *The Ambassadors.*
1904		Chekhov: *The Cherry Orchard.* James: *The Golden Bowl.* Conrad: *Nostromo.*

CHRONOLOGY

Subsidized voluntary sickness insurance introduced in Denmark.

Resignation of Estrup as Danish prime minister. Accession of Nicholas II as Tsar of Russia. Beginning of the Dreyfus Affair in France.

Kiel Canal opens. Guglielmo Marconi invents wireless telegraphy. Sigmund Freud's *Studies in Hysteria* inaugurates psychoanalysis.

First modern Olympic Games held in Athens. Theodor Herzl publishes *The Jewish State.*

First Zionist congress at Basel.
Legislation for workers' compensation introduced in Denmark. The Danish physicist Valdemar Poulsen makes the first magnetic recording. Publication of Zola's letter, *J'Accuse...!,* in support of Alfred Dreyfus. First German Navy Bill begins German naval expansion.

Electoral victory of the *Venstrereformparti* (Left Reform Party). Institution of the "Change of System," including parliamentary supremacy, free-trade legislation, reforms of taxation, education, and religion. Death of Queen Victoria and accession of King Edward VII and Alexandra of Denmark as Queen Consort. First Nobel prizes awarded.
Entente cordiale between Britain and France. Wright brothers' first successful powered flight.
Iceland obtains home rule from Denmark. Russo-Japanese War (to 1905).

DATE	AUTHOR'S LIFE	LITERARY CONTEXT
1905	Publishes *Borgmester Hoeck og Hustru* (*Burgomaster Hoeck and His Wife*), novella.	Jensen: *The Wheel.* Edith Wharton: *The House of Mirth.*
1906		Martin Andersen Nexø: *Pelle the Conqueror* (to 1910). Gjellerup: *The Pilgrim Kamanita.* Jensen: *Poems 1906.* John Galsworthy: *The Forsyte Saga* (to 1921).
1907	Publishes *Hans Kvast og Melusine* [*Hans Kvast and Melusine*], novella.	Jensen: *Myths* (9 vols, to 1945). Strindberg: *The Ghost Sonata.*
1908	Publishes *Den kongelige Gæst* (*The Royal Guest*), novella.	Jensen: *The Long Journey* (6 vols, to 1922). Kinck: *The Drover.* Nietzsche: *Ecce Homo* (posthumous).
1910	Takes up permanent residence in Copenhagen.	Høffding: *Human thought: its forms and its problems.* Arnold Bennett: *Clayhanger* novels (to 1918).
1911		Theodore Dreiser: *Jenny Gerhardt.*
1912	Publishes *De Dødes Rige* [*The Realm of the Dead*] (in 5 volumes, to 1916).	Mann: *Death in Venice.*
1913		Marcel Proust: *À la recherche du temps perdu* (to 1927). Alain-Fournier: *Le Grand Meaulnes.* D. H. Lawrence: *Sons and Lovers.*
1914		Conrad: *Chance.* James Joyce: *A Portrait of the Artist as a Young Man* (to 1915).
1915		
1917	Wins the Nobel Prize for Literature "for his authentic descriptions of present-day life in Denmark," shared with fellow Danish writer Karl Gjellerup.	Nexø: *Ditte, Daughter of Man.* Gjellerup: *The Golden Bough.* Hamsun: *Growth of the Soil.*

CHRONOLOGY

The *Radikale Venstre* (Radical Left) party splits from Jens Christian Christensen's *Venstrereformparti* (Left Reform Party). Norway gains independence from Sweden. Prince Carl of Denmark appointed King of Norway, as Haakon VII. First Russian Revolution.
Death of King Christian IX of Denmark, and accession of Frederick VIII. Alfred Dreyfus exonerated. First Dreadnought launched.

Subsidized voluntary unemployment insurance introduced in Denmark. Formation of the Triple Entente between Britain, France, and Russia.

Bombing of the ship *Amalthea* in Malmö harbour by Swedish socialists.

Death of Edward VII and accession of George V.

Agadir crisis.

Death of King Frederick VIII of Denmark, and accession of Christian X.

Government formed from the *Radikale Venstre* (Radical Left) party, supported by the *Socialdemokratiet* (Social Democratic) party.

Assassination of Archduke Franz Ferdinand of Austria (28 June). Outbreak of the First World War. Denmark adopts a policy of neutrality, though is forced by Germany to lay mines in the Great Belt.
Revision of the Danish constitution, removing property qualifications from the franchise for electing the *Landsting*, introducing universal male and female suffrage for elections to both Houses, and establishing proportional representation (June). Trial by jury and land reform introduced.
Resumption of unrestricted submarine warfare by Germany poses a threat to Danish overseas trade. Sale of the Danish West Indies to the USA. Russian Revolution. USA declares war on Germany. Balfour Declaration of British support for a Jewish home in Palestine.

DATE	AUTHOR'S LIFE	LITERARY CONTEXT
1918	Publishes *Et Kærlighedseventyr* [*A Love Story*], novella.	Kinck: *The Avalanche Broke* (to 1919).
1919		
1920		Wharton: *The Age of Innocence*. Fitzgerald: *This Side of Paradise*.
1922		Nexø: *From the Soil* (3 vols, to 1926). Joyce: *Ulysses*.
1923		Italo Svevo: *Zeno's Conscience*.
1924		Halldór Laxness: *Under the Holy Mountain*. Mann: *The Magic Mountain*. Ford Madox Ford: *Parade's End* (to 1928).
1925		Brandes: *Jesus, a Myth*. Jacob Paludan: *Birds Around the Light*. Virginia Woolf: *Mrs. Dalloway*.
1926	Death of his third child, Hans Broby Pontoppidan, in the USA.	Franz Kafka: *The Castle*. Ernest Hemingway: *The Sun Also Rises*.
1927	Publishes his last novel, *Mands Himmerig* [*Man's Heaven*].	Paludan: *The Ripening Fields*. Laxness: *The Great Weaver from Kashmir*. Woolf: *To the Lighthouse*.
1928	Death of his second wife, Antoinette Caroline Elise Kofoed and their daughter Else Cathrina Pontoppidan. Moves to Ordrup, a suburb of Copenhagen.	Hans Kirk: *The Fishermen*.
1929		Nexø: *In God's Land*. Laxness: *The Book of the People*. Hemingway: *A Farewell to Arms*.
1931		Laxness: *Salka Valka* (to 1932). Woolf: *The Waves*.
1932		Nexø: *Jørgenstern* (to 1933). Joseph Roth: *The Radetzky March*. Herman Broch: *The Sleepwalkers*.

CHRONOLOGY

The Armistice ends the First World War (11 November). The Act of Union renders Iceland an independent kingdom under the Danish crown. Civil war in Russia (to 1921).
Treaty of Versailles. Weimar Republic in Germany (to 1933).
Plebiscites in North Schleswig determine that its northern portion be returned to Denmark. Denmark joins the newly formed League of Nations.
Fall of the *Radikale Venstre* (Radical Left) administration, and appointment of a Left government with Conservative support.
Failure of *Landmandsbanken*, Denmark's most important private bank. USSR founded. Mussolini forms Fascist government in Italy.

Failure of Hitler's Beer Hall Putsch in Munich. German hyperinflation. Appointment of a minority Social Democrat administration, led by Thorvald Stauning, supported by the Radicals. Death of Lenin.

Death of Alexandra of Denmark at Sandringham.

Financial crisis in Germany.

Stalin's first Five-Year Plan in the USSR.

Stauning's second ministry leading a coalition of Radicals, Social Democrats, and Liberals, proposing reform to the criminal code and the curtailment of defence spending. Wall Street Crash; beginning of worldwide Depression.
Increased taxation imposed to finance support for farmers and the unemployed through a "compromise agreement" with opposition parties. Denmark leaves the gold standard.
Ottawa Agreements institute British imperial preference, damaging Denmark's economy.

DATE	AUTHOR'S LIFE	LITERARY CONTEXT
1933	Publishes his memoirs (in 4 volumes, to 1940).	Mann: *Joseph and his Brothers* (to 1943).
1934		Laxness: *Independent People* (to 1935).
1935		
1936		Kirk: *Day Labourers.* William Faulkner: *Absalom, Absalom!*
1937		Laxness: *The Light of the World* (to 1940).
1938		Jean-Paul Sartre: *La Nausée.*
1939	Death of his former wife, Mette Marie Hansen.	Kirk: *The New Times.* John Steinbeck: *The Grapes of Wrath.*
1940		Hemingway: *For Whom the Bell Tolls.*
1941		Bertolt Brecht: *Mother Courage and Her Children.*
1942		Albert Camus: *The Outsider.*
1943	Publishes *Undervejs til mig selv* [*On the Way to Myself*], a condensed compilation of his memoirs. Dies at Ordrup, Denmark (21 August) and is buried at Rørvig.	Jensen: *Poems, 1904–41.* Laxness: *The Bell of Iceland* (to 1946).

CHRONOLOGY

The Kanslergade Agreement devalues the *Krone* and enacts social reforms.
Adolf Hitler becomes German Chancellor.
Hitler becomes Führer. Stalin's purge of Communist Party begins.

Nuremberg Race Laws institutionalize discrimination against Jews in Germany.
German troops enter Rhineland. Spanish Civil War (to 1939).

Kristallnacht – Jews attacked in Germany (November 9–10).
Failure of Stauning's efforts to establish a unicameral legislature. Treaty of Non-Aggression signed by Denmark and Nazi Germany (31 May).
Molotov–Ribbentrop Pact (August). Outbreak of the Second World War, and Danish declaration of neutrality (September). Outbreak of the Winter War between Finland and the USSR (to 1940).
Invasion and occupation of Denmark by Nazi Germany (9 April); Denmark becomes a German protectorate. German invasion of Norway. Fall of France, Belgium, the Netherlands, and Luxembourg; Battle of Britain.
Operation Barbarossa, the invasion of the USSR by Nazi Germany.
Denmark signs the Anti-Comintern Pact (November). Attack on Pearl Harbor, and American declaration of war on Japan and Nazi Germany.
Wannsee Conference co-ordinates Hitler's 'Final Solution' for the annihilation of European Jews. Death of Stauning; Vilhelm Buhl becomes prime minister (May) but is replaced by Erik Scavenius when the Germans insist on a change of government (November). King Christian X refuses anti-Jewish legislation called for by Germany (September).
German defeat at Stalingrad. Strikes and resistance to the German occupation in Denmark, which Christian X is forced to condemn (May). Danish government ends policy of accommodation. Germans impose martial law (29 August). Christian X makes speech attacking the German occupation and is incarcerated until the end of the war. Mass escape of Jews from Denmark to neutral Sweden.

xli

LUCKY PER

CONTENTS

BOOK 1

LUCKY PER, HIS YOUTH

CHAPTER 1

IN THE YEARS before and after our last war, a pastor named Johannes Sidenius lived in one of the small market towns of East Jutland that lie hidden among green hills at the base of a thickly wooded fjord. He was a pious and stern man. In his outer appearance, as in his whole way of life, he differed sharply from the other inhabitants of the town, who, for many years, viewed him as a troublesome alien whose peculiarities left them, by turns, cool or resentful. No one could help staring at him as he passed with his proud and austere bearing, striding through the crooked streets in his gray homespun tailcoat, peering through large, dark blue spectacles, and gripping the handle of a big cotton umbrella with which he forcefully stabbed the pavement at every step. Those who sat behind window mirrors on the lookout for him made faces or smiled at his reflection. The town's important merchants, its old country traders and horse breeders, never greeted him even when he was wearing his robe. Although they themselves wore wooden shoes and dirty linen coats and sucked on pipes in public, they considered it a disgrace and a scandal for their town to have such a beggar pastor who went dressed like a parish clerk, who obviously had trouble supporting himself and his brood of children. The community had been accustomed to an entirely different kind of clergy—to men in fine black suits and white cambric collars, men whose names had cast luster on the town and the church, and who later became archdeacons or bishops but still did not flaunt their piety, who did not feel that they were too good to interest themselves in the town's worldly affairs or to take part in its social entertainments.

In those days, the big red parsonage was a hospitable place where, when business with the pastor was finished, a petitioner was invited into the sitting room with the pastor's wife and the young daughters to have a cup of coffee or, when the visitor was distinguished, a little glass of wine or a home-baked cake and a lively chat about the day's local news. Now no one set foot in the house without a pressing concern, and no one came farther than Pastor Sidenius's sepulchral study, where the blinds were at half-mast so the pastor's eyes would not suffer the reflection from the walls on the other side of the narrow street.

Here the pastor almost always received guests while standing, did not ask them to sit down, finished with them quickly, apparently took little interest in them, and was even less forthcoming with those who thought they had a right to special consideration. Even the town's officials and their families had stopped paying calls to the house after Pastor Sidenius, instead of offering them refreshments, had taken to examining them on their faith as if they were confirmands standing before the altar.

He aroused especially strong exasperation at funerals of prominent citizens to which the public paraded with horns and guild flags entwined with flowers, the civil servants in plumed hats and uniforms embroidered in gold. After a light lunch and a little port wine at the house of the bereaved, they deemed themselves ready for devotion and edification. Instead of the customary ample eulogy, Pastor Sidenius invariably limited himself to the recitation of a prayer—what one would expect at the funerals of unbaptized children and the poor. Not a word about the deceased's upright character and tireless industry, not one allusion to his worthy service to the town's welfare, to his selfless interest in street projects and the municipal waterworks. The name of the deceased was scarcely uttered at the grave, and then always accompanied by phrases like "this wretched heap of dust" or "this food for worms." The greater and more distinguished the assembly where the pastor was speaking, the more flags and banners that fluttered around the grave in the wind, the shorter the prayer became, the more wretched the remains for which the town had gathered, so that the mourners dispersed filled with indignation that was more than once aired audibly in the graveyard.

The only inhabitants of the town who had connections with the parsonage were a pair of misshapen old maids from the home for unmarried ladies of rank, together with a pale Christ figure of a long-bearded journeyman tailor and a few so-called religiously "saved" paupers who, in Pastor Sidenius's home, found a refuge from their worldly surroundings. There could be no question of a social circle, because Fru Sidenius was sickly and for some years had taken to her bed, and Pastor Sidenius was entirely indisposed toward society.

His hangers-on sought him out only for religious concerns, but they were sure to go to church every Sunday, where they regularly assembled in a fixed place directly beneath the pulpit, annoying the other churchgoers by resoundingly singing even the longest hymns without consulting the hymnal.

Pastor Sidenius belonged to an old and extensive ministerial line that could trace its ancestry back to the Reformation. For three hundred years, the spiritual calling was like a sacred legacy from father to son—and, yes, to daughters, too, insofar as they often married the father's assistant or their brothers' fellow student. The self-confident authority for which the Sidenius preaching had long been known stemmed from this tradition. There were few parishes in the whole country where, over the course of the centuries, someone from the Sidenius family had not submitted his mind and heart to the rule of the church.

Naturally, not all of these servants had been equally zealous. There had been some fairly worldly minded among them—men in whom a long-repressed life force erupted into a certain recklessness. In the previous century, there was such a pastor in Vendsyssel—"Mad Sidenius"—who tried to live the unrestricted life of a hunter in the great forests of Jutland's hill country. He often sat in the taverns drinking brandy with the peasants, until one Easter Sunday in his drunkenness he struck down the parish clerk in the church and caused his blood to spatter onto the altar cloth.

Still, the overwhelming majority of this family had been pious champions of the church, many of them widely read as well, even learned theological seekers, who in their rustic seclusion had, beneath the gray monotony of the years, sought recompense for all their hardships in a quiet, introspective life of the mind, an absorption in their own inner world, where they at last found the true values of existence, its richest happiness, its real goal.

It was this scorn of all ephemeral things, passed from generation to generation in the family, that had been Johannes Sidenius's weapon in his life's struggle and kept his back unbowed and his mind upright despite the oppression of poverty and a multitude of adversities. For this struggle, he had a firm support in his wife, with whom he lived in a most heartfelt and happy marriage, though they were not at all alike. She, too, was possessed of a deeply religious disposition, but, in contrast to her husband, was of a melancholy, passionate nature that imbued her with restlessness and dark anxiety. Unsteady in her faith from her childhood home, she had, under her husband's influence, become a zealot in whom the daily struggle to survive and her many childbirths had generated morbidly exaggerated conceptions of life's hardships and a Christian's responsibility. The years since her last delivery—years in which she lay paralyzed in her darkened sickroom and, finally, during the recent unhappy war, endured the enforced billeting of enemy soldiers, levies, and bloody humiliations—hardly increased her confidence in life.

Though her husband often earnestly reproached her, she could never really find relief from her anxieties. She knew they reflected a sinful lack of confidence in the grace of Providence, and she kept instructing her children that outer contentment with everything was a duty before God and men. But she could become as agitated as over a crime when she heard of the townspeople's way of life, of their parties with many courses and three or four kinds of wine, about the women's silk dresses and the jewelry of the young girls—yes, she even had difficulty forgiving her own husband when now and then he came home from his walk with a modest gift and, with a kind of silent courtesy, laid it before her on the bedcover: a pair of roses in a cone, a bit of fine fruit or a little pot of ginger jam for her night coughs. She was both happy and moved by his attention, but she could never keep from saying, even while she gently kissed his hands, "You should not have done that, you good man."

A brood of children, eleven in all, pretty but pale and, from time to time, sickly, grew up in that house—five bright-eyed boys and six bright-eyed girls, all easily recognizable among the town's young people by, among other things, their unusual collars, which gave the boys a little girlish look and the half-grown girls a little boyish one. The boys wore their brown hair long and curly, reaching almost to the shoulders, while the girls, on the other hand, wore their hair combed smooth over their scalps and, at the temples, wound around the ears in tight, small braids.

Relations between parents and children, the overall tone of the house, were pervasively patriarchal. At the humble, meager mealtimes that invariably began with a prayer, the father sat at the end of the long, narrow table while his five sons, arranged by age, sat on one side and the six daughters, correspondingly aligned, on the other. The oldest daughter, the domestic Signe, took her absent mother's place at the other end of the table. No child ever dared to speak unless asked to, but the father spoke often to the children about their schooling, their lessons and comrades, and enjoyed putting himself into the story. In a pedagogic way, he described circumstances and incidents of his own childhood; he told about his schooldays, about his life in the mud-built parsonage of his father and his grandfather, and so on. Sometimes, when he was in a special mood, he would tell humorous anecdotes from his student days in Copenhagen, about his life in the regent's charity dormitory and student tricks played on night watchmen and the police. But if he had, in this way, induced the children to laughter, he never failed in the end to give his story a cautionary point, admonishing them to turn their thoughts to the earnestness of their lives and their responsibilities.

The large family and its successes, beginning in school, gradually became Pastor Sidenius's chief pride and, at the same time, evidence of God's blessings on his house, which he received with humble gratitude. They were developing into bright, studious, and very conscientious offspring—genuine Sideniuses—who, one after another, grew into their father's image and took after him in every aspect, even to the same self-conscious carriage and the measured military gait. Only one of the children, a middle boy named Peter Andreas, caused his parents concern. He was not only willful in school, so that they received constant complaints, but already, at an early age, a deliberate insubordination surfaced in him in the face of the rules and customs of the house. Before he was ten, he rebelled against his parents, and the older he became, the more his provocative, overbearing defiance showed itself able to counter every imposition of discipline, restraint, or divine injunction.

Pastor Sidenius sat often at a loss at his wife's bedside and dwelled upon this son, who stirred in them both a frightening memory of that degenerate Vendsyssel pastor whose name was stamped in blood on the family's genealogy; and the brothers and sisters were involuntarily affected by the reaction of the parents. They increasingly looked upon Peter Andreas with unfriendly eyes and banished him from their games. He had, as well, come into the world at an unlucky hour, just as his father was transferred from an isolated, poor moorland folk parish to a provincial town where he was saddled with extensive official duties. Peter

Andreas was, therefore, the first of the children to be handed over for his upbringing entirely to his mother, but she had more than enough to do during Peter Andreas's early years, taking care of the youngest of his brothers and sisters. In the end, paralyzed by ill health, she would gather them around her bed, but Peter Andreas was already too big for her to monitor his behavior.

So it happened that, from birth, Peter Andreas was a stranger in his own house. He first sought refuge in the maids' room and in the shed of an old woodcutter, whose sober reflections on all passing events influenced the boy's sense of the world from an early age. Later he found a second home in the big commercial houses of the neighborhood and their lumberyards, where he assimilated a worldly view on life and its pleasures from servants and trade apprentices. At the same time, this outdoor life developed his body and raised a brick-red color in his chubby cheeks.

He soon became dreaded for his strength among the crowd of youngsters of the streets and lumberyards, and he set himself up, finally, as the leader of a little troop of small mischief-makers who ravaged the neighborhoods. Without anyone in his house first suspecting, he grew up as a little wild boy. It was when he was older—especially when he was nine and entered the town's grammar school—that the boy's dangerous tendencies became evident. His parents and teachers tried hard to make good what they had missed, but it was too late.

One day, in late autumn, a member of the town's petit bourgeoisie was in Pastor Sidenius's study to arrange for a child's christening on Sunday. He accomplished his errand with as little delay as possible and already had his hand on the door latch when, after a short reflection, he turned again into the room and said assertively, "Incidentally, I could, at the same time, request you, Pastor, to be so kind as to keep your son out of my garden. He and some other boys find it very difficult to leave my apples in peace—and I am not happy about it, plain and simple."

Pastor Sidenius, who sat bent over his desk with his large, dark blue glasses pushed up on his forehead, about to inscribe the god-parents' name in the church record, raised his head slowly at this remark, pushed his glasses back into place, and said sharply, "What are you saying? Are you accusing my son of—"

"Yes, I am," continued the other with his hand on his hip, very satisfied to be able for once to lord it over the self-confident pastor. "Your son, Peter Andreas by name, is now a kind of chief of a group of small rogues who clamber over our fences. And justice is justice—even with a pastor's son. I will be compelled to turn to the police, and then you can well expect the town hall to hand down a public punishment for the boys, and that will not make your appointment to this parish look good."

Pastor Sidenius laid down his pen with a trembling hand and stood up. "My son . . . ," he repeated, and his whole body shook.

While this was transpiring in the pastor's study, the little sinner sat in school and hid his bad conscience from the eyes of the teacher and his comrades behind a tall stack of books. He had, on the way to school, encountered the angry citizen, who yelled at him from across the street, "Prepare yourself, my boy! I am just now going to have a little talk with your father!" Peter Andreas was not accustomed to taking his father's anger particularly to heart, but this time, he had an unusual sense of having done something unworthy, and grew increasingly uneasy as the hour drew near for him to return home.

He slunk with red ears through the parsonage door and past the entrance window where his father customarily watched out for him to call him in when he had done some mischief. But the window remained locked. Nor could he see any sign of his father in the courtyard or on the way to the kitchen door. Relieved, he began to breathe more easily. "The old man merely wanted to threaten me," he thought, and strolled into the kitchen, where he usually got news about dinner. Seized by a sudden overconfidence, he ventured into the bedroom to greet his mother. Here he was stopped immediately at the door by a dark look from the bed. With a hard, strange voice, his mother said, "Go to your room. I don't want to see you." The boy stood there for a while; he could see that his mother had been crying. "Don't you hear me? Stay in your room until your father calls you!" Dejectedly, he stole away.

Sometime afterward, the household's old one-eyed servant girl summoned him to dinner. His brothers and sisters already sat at their places around the table and waited. As soon as he appeared, they stopped talking, and from their silence and tight faces, he understood that they knew what was going on. He plopped into his seat and stuck his hands in his pockets in an attempt to appear cocky and confident, but no one looked at him. He did catch a glance from the big, soft, pensive eyes, under the joined dark brows, of his sister Signe at the end of the table.

Although he heard steps from the adjoining room, Peter Andreas started when his father opened the door. The pastor withheld his customary greeting. Silently he sat down at the table, bowed his head, and folded his hands, but instead of grace he began to speak of Peter Andreas.

"There is something," he said, with his eyes shut behind his dark glasses, "that weighs on my heart, a serious affair, about which I wish to talk a bit to my dear children before beginning the meal." Then he confirmed what most of them had already heard from their mother, about their brother's offense. "What has happened shall be neither hushed up nor excused. As it is God's will that everything that has been hatched in the dark shall one day become manifest, now is this deed come to light to receive His judgment. Peter Andreas has not respected God's law and command. As he has hardened his heart against his parents' admonitions, he has defied God's word that says, 'You must not steal.'

"Yes, my son, you shall not be spared having your sin *named*. But you shall also understand that it is out of love for you that your father and mother and all your big and small brothers and sisters speak to your conscience through my mouth. We cannot lose hope that we can succeed in finding a way to your heart so that you will not end up like that sinful brother over whom God pronounced that frightful curse: 'You will be a wandering fugitive in all the earth.'" Around the table the small red-and-blue-checked handkerchiefs of the children were set into motion. All the sisters cried, and the older brothers were deeply affected and could barely hide it.

The father finally stopped with this aspiration: "Now I have spoken. And if Peter Andreas will keep my words in his heart and honestly seek the pardon of man and God for his offense, this affair will not further be raised among us, but will be buried and forgotten. So let us, then, children, come together in prayer to God who is in heaven, that He will take your misguided brother in His hand, that He will both humble his rebellious spirit and lead him out from sin's thralldom, forth from perdition's path. Grant us, O Lord, who is in eternity, that not one of us shall be found wanting when your children, on the day of Resurrection, gather round your glorious throne. Amen."

Only Peter Andreas was affected in an entirely opposite way to what his father intended. He never allowed himself to be at all impressed by his father; rather, he had been a willing pupil of his older friends, outdoor servants, and trade apprentices, who had little respect for the pastor.

In spite of this, the boy was not yet entirely without feeling about these holy words and the threatening Bible commands his parents always sought to imbed in his conscience. When he, on Sundays, observed his father kneeling before the altar in his white robe or saw him standing under the richly carved pulpit sounding board, he sometimes felt seized by an ephemeral sense of awe.

On this occasion, the biblical words had no effect on him. At first he was apprehensive about the unusual form of his reprimand, but his fear did not last long. In his uncomplicated child's perception there was an altogether foolish disproportion between the solemn warning of God and the paltry pair of apples he had pilfered over a fence. The longer his father spoke, and the more audibly his brothers and sisters expressed their feelings, the more calmly and indifferently he viewed the whole scene.

At that moment a breakthrough occurred in the eleven-year-old boy's mind. He eyed the others, finally, with a full sense of superiority—yes, even over the twins, who had stared at their affected brothers and sisters uncomprehendingly, and now began to blubber so pitifully he had trouble suppressing a smile.

Nevertheless, under the general pressure, his cheerfulness was strained. The lessons on humility had hit him too hard in his most sensitive spot, his sense of honor. His cheeks had gradually lost their color. Deep in his heart after his father's speech, a frightful agitation stirred, a dark, muffled repressed thirst for revenge that gathered like a shimmering mist over his eyes.

The memory of that dinner hour was to have a fateful consequence for the boy. An unappeasable hatred of his family awakened in his hitherto carefree soul, a defiant and bellicose feeling of abandonment that would become the heart and driving force of his future life. From his earliest years, he had felt himself deserted, virtually homeless, under his parents' roof.

Now he began to ask himself whether he really belonged there, or whether he was an orphan his parents had taken in. The more he mulled this over, the likelier it seemed. Everything, even the increased reserve in his brothers and sisters as they avoided him, strengthened his suspicion. Hadn't he heard a hundred times that he was not like the others? And had his father ever given him a sign of affection, or even a friendly word? Then there was his appearance. When he viewed himself in the mirror, he seemed darker than his siblings, with redder cheeks and white, strong teeth. He also recalled how a neighbor's servant, apparently as a joke, had once called him a tramp and a gypsy.

This thought—that he was not his parents' child at all—remained his *idée fixe*; it obsessed him the entire time of his growing up. Not only did it supply the rationale for his exceptional position in the family, but it satisfied his boyish conceit. He had always felt it a kind of humiliation to be the son of an old, half-blind, and toothless man who was mocked by the whole town. In addition, he felt deep shame over the poverty of the family situation. He was not very old before he chose to go hungry all day at school rather than eat his lard sandwich in front of his comrades. Once, when his mother had made him a winter coat out of his father's old cassock, he refused to wear it because the shiny cloth revealed all too obviously its origin. And when his mother tried to force him to wear it, in a fit of defiance, on the verge of tears, he tore it to pieces, and flung it to the floor.

He abandoned himself to the dream of being a child left behind by one or another vagabond gypsy band, one of those wandering nocturnal families of which the old one-eyed servant girl had so often spoken, that had its haunt out there on the barren heath where his parents had once lived. He imagined his real father as a powerful chieftain with black locks hanging down his back, a cape flung over his shoulders, a wooden staff in his brown, strong hand, a supreme lord, a king over the dark heath's endless realm, the home of freedom and wild storms.

Peter Andreas was at that age of waking dreams when fancy's wings take flight. With all the doors of possibility flung open for him, he made his imagination an infinite field of play. No potential seemed impossible any longer. His dream would end in the airiest realms of Fairyland.

He regularly finished his flight by envisioning himself, at long last, as a king's son who, like the hero of a story just read in school, was abducted by an itinerate band, sold, and then held in captivity in the parsonage. He existed so completely in this story that sometimes it seemed that he could remember scenes and incidents from a childhood lived in happy surroundings—for example, a large hall with marble columns and many black-and-white-checkered floors over which his little feet glided . . . a blue lake surrounded by high hills . . . a monkey in a golden cage . . . a tall man in a red cape who seated Peter Andreas on his horse and rode with him into the large, dark woods.

Both his parents and his schoolteachers gradually became aware of the boy's brooding withdrawal, which sometimes could seem monomaniacal. At home, he wandered silently through the rooms, apparently indifferent to everyone and everything. Out of the house, he went his own unpredictable way. His father could not get a word out of him, and even toward his mother—who, before, had earned a little of his confidence and with whom, when he really needed it, he always found the most understanding and indulgence—even toward her he became, year by year, more remote. When, now and again, at the end of the day, he knew she was alone, he would sit by her bed and offer to massage her legs, afflicted with varicose veins. But he answered nothing other than "yes" or "no" when she sought to know why he was brooding. Nevertheless, she and her husband periodically tried to reassure themselves about him. His inaccessibility could, after all, simply be a sign that he had begun to be introspective. But one day, something happened that extinguished this last hope.

On a late-winter evening the family sat together in the parlor and waited for the song of the watchman in the street signaling time for bed. The housewifely Signe sat on the horsehair sofa behind the big mahogany table, zealously working at her knitting, while at the same time reading out loud to her father from the newspaper *Fædrelandet*, which lay spread out under the low-burning oil lamp. Her father sat in his usual evening spot, an old-fashioned high and stiff-backed armchair, upholstered with a flowery cover of the cheapest kind. He was tired and sunken, with bowed head. His arms were crossed on his chest. A large green visor hid more than half of his pallid, gray, wrinkled, beardless face. Almost asleep, he heard—and, really, didn't hear—the monotonous reading of a four-column article on foreign news. Pastor Sidenius was a morning man. Even in the middle of winter, he got up when the church bells rang six. In addition, he had no great interest in the worldly journals and papers. He used them chiefly as a kind of soporific to lull him to sleep in his after-dinner naps.

Two of the younger girls, in their large, checked cotton

smocks, sat beside Signe. Both, though red-eyed from sleepiness, diligently bent over their crochet. They looked like exact copies of their older sister, had the same slightly precocious expression, the same small tight braids in front of their ears, the same large bright eyes protruding a bit under strong, prominent brows. The door of the bedroom was open, and, in the half darkness, one of the smaller children sat by the side of the mother and massaged her aching legs.

Peter Andreas was also in the parlor. He stood by himself near one of the windows and sneaked secret peeks at the clock on the desk. He was now a fourteen-year-old boy, solidly built, his sleeves and pant legs too short for his strong limbs. His two older brothers were now young men studying at the university in Copenhagen. As currently the house's oldest son, Peter Andreas had inherited the little gabled room under the roof, where he stayed, for the most part, when he was home. As soon as Signe stopped her reading, he used the occasion to say goodnight and escape, but his father stopped him at the door with a question: why was he leaving them? He gave the excuse that he still had a school exercise to write.

When Peter Andreas had gone, his father, still a little blurry from sleepiness, inquired, "Is there nothing worth reading in the newspaper?"

"How late is it then, children?" his mother's weak voice asked from the bedroom.

"It's ten after nine," answered the little girls in unison as they looked at the clock.

There was still some time. They all knew the watchman would soon come. Only the voices of the people passing by in the street could be heard, since a layer of new-fallen snow made their steps soundless.

"Shall I read on?" asked Signe, turning to her father.

"Well, let it go," he said, got up, took off his eyeshade, and began to walk back and forth to shake off his drowsiness before the evening prayer.

A few minutes later, the deep hum of the old night watchman's song was heard. It sounded like a drunken man chatting loudly to himself. The two little girls began immediately to pack up their sewing things as Signe started to tidy up for the night. The two servant girls were summoned from the kitchen, and Signe sat down at the piano.

The mother's voice again emerged from the bedroom: "Shall we sing 'Praise God, He Is Near?' this evening?"

"You hear that?" said the father, who stood behind the big armchair and rested his folded hands on its back.

Signe had a full and very beautiful soprano voice, which, in contrast to the characteristic moderation that marked all her other modes of expression, she projected with a natural power. As she sat there, with her thick hands, reddened from work, on the old instrument's yellow keys, her eyes uplifted, it was not difficult to see what kind of faith, and hope, and love had given this young woman, not yet twenty years old, the strength to sac-rifice her youth to the service of her home and small siblings. It was no romantic ecstasy that lit up her little, round face. She did not sing in an otherworldly transport to the heavens that would open up and carry off the soul in a blessed vision. Like the genuine Sidenius that she was, she had no predisposition for Catholic mysticism.

The certain confidence mirrored in her glance and face that gave the voice such an unusual inner strength sprang from a corresponding sober and dogmatically grounded conviction that she belonged to the little troop of believers who walked on the narrow path of virtue and would find their reward in heaven, where, at last, glory would ransom all earthly pain and privation.

In the middle of the hymn's second verse, her father suddenly raised his head. "Quiet!" he exclaimed, and stopped the singing.

At the same time, her mother called out from the bed, "There is someone ringing the gate bell!"

Now the others heard the heavy clang of the night bell from the opposite end of the house, and it stirred, in the midst of the evening's stillness, an instinctive sense of alarm.

The father went through an adjacent room into his study next to the front door and opened a window.

"Who is it ringing in the night?" he cried out.

Inside the parlor a man's voice could be heard from the street. While the two little girls nervously looked at each other and then at Signe, who still sat at the piano, their father, from within, asked in a rather harsh tone, "Your sick child . . . What is your name, and where do you live? . . . Krankstuegyden? Oh, yes. How old is the child? . . . One year? Strange that the citizens of this town have no need of their pastor until danger threatens. Most of the time, you have no need to feel God's presence. How is it that you have neglected to baptize the child for so long? Yes, naturally I shall come. You should go home and arrange what is necessary, put everything in order before I come. And," he called after the man, who had already moved off, "you might see to it that there is a light on the steps."

When the pastor came back to the parlor, he asked for Peter Andreas.

"I'll call him," said Signe, who knew that her father, because of his weak eyesight, did not like to go out at night and on slippery streets without a companion.

"Signe, you can stay here and help me with my robe. Boel can fetch him," said the pastor, glancing at the old servant and going into the bedroom to get dressed.

In the meantime, the mother's night lamp was lit, and, in her usual depressed tone, she said, "Johannes, dress warmly. It's very cold tonight. I could sense it by the sound of the church clock. Signe, get Father's lined waistcoat. It's hanging in the closet."

Old Boel came back with the news that Peter Andreas was not in his room and she could not find him anywhere in the house.

The pastor reluctantly got up from his chair on which he had just settled himself in order to close up his collar at the back of his neck with a pin. He turned pale. Since he could see by the servant's disturbed expression that she knew more than she was telling, he moved close to her and asked emphatically, "What's going on? Out with it . . . You're hiding something!" Trembling with anxiety at the pastor's anger, she confessed that many times lately she, who had her room, like Peter Andreas, just under the roof, had heard the boy steal out into the night. Since she now found his room empty, she had investigated more closely and found the window in the entrance hall half open and fresh footprints in the snow outside.

The mother tried, then, to get out of her bed, but she fell back on her pillow with a bitter cry and held a hand before her eyes as if afflicted with vertigo. The pastor went to her and clasped her other hand.

"Calm down, Mother," he said, though his own voice trembled.

"God help us!" she groaned.

"Amen," said the pastor loudly, without letting go of her hand.

In the meantime, Peter Andreas could be found at the big hills around the northern part of town, where a merry troop of young people was vigorously sledding in the bright moonlight. They had chosen the Kongelige Amtschausse for their track, a broad, level, downward slope that led from the top of the hill in a single great swoop almost into the town. If you had sufficient speed and were not afraid of the watchman, you could hurtle down the steep Nørregade almost to the marketplace in front of the town hall.

During this long descent, the freest and widest view over the whole country opened up before your eyes—first, of the snow-covered town with the red lamps in the street and white moonlight on the roofs; next, of the frozen fjord, and the icy meadows; and, finally, of the far country with its villages, woods, and snowy fields. Over it all was a high cottony heaven where moon and stars seemed to play hide and seek with the clouds, as if this whole old planet were infected with the youngsters' joyfulness.

Hurray! The iron runners whizzed down the icy track through shrill whistles and joyful shouts, the sleds steered by long ice axes that trailed after them like a rudder, skipped over small stones, rode over each obstacle as easily as a boat over a wave. Here and there, along the way, small clusters of adolescent servant girls stood with thick kerchiefs around their heads and their hands tucked into their aprons as in a muff.

When it happened that one of the little athletes tipped over and remained sitting on the track like a rider thrown from a horse, while the empty sled flew down the hill at double speed, merciless laughter erupted from these groups of girls, mixed with a scornful hooting of the boys who happened to whiz by just then. The worst mocked were the grammar-school boys, the uninitiated, who were a decided minority. Peter Andreas's highest sense of disgrace came from the humiliation of belonging to this class.

He himself steered with conceited assurance his new, smart, long sled, painted red and named "Bloodeagle," which he had irresponsibly taken on credit from one of the town's wheelwrights and which, in the daytime, he hid in one of the lumberyards. It flew through the air lightly and soundlessly on its English racing runners while he continuously roared, "Out of the way!" His round cheeks glowed; his eyes were triumphant with competitive zeal. Now and then, in the middle of his rush, he raised himself upon his runners and swung his ice ax over his head, like a warrior his lance, shouting, "Heigh-ho!" His exuberant lust for life—all the giddy, ambitious, young joy he had to hide or suppress at home or school—broke out now, so spontaneously and rashly that he seemed a little ridiculous even to his best friends.

Suddenly a high, warning shout sounded from the bottom of the hill. In a flash, all the sledders steered off the track and tumbled into the deep ditches on both sides of the path. Those who were far up on the track hurriedly hid behind bushes and snowdrifts, while only the girls stood where they were, content to stick their heads together and giggle.

Down by the entrance to the town the watchman was going on his rounds. With his long greatcoat, his metal badge shining on his breast like a star, he stood there in the moonlight at the end of the dark street. In consideration of the horses of the farmers coming into town for purchases, sledding on the main road was strictly forbidden. Because of that, the boys had posted lookouts there and at the bottom of the hill to guard against a surprise attack.

Now the fearsome watchman stood there and surveyed the suddenly empty street. Here and there a "cluck cluck" or a "meow," followed by snickering and giggles, could be heard from the ditches. The watchman raised his threatening cudgel, and turned back into town, shaking his head. Shortly after, the watchman's signal again sounded, and a couple of minutes later the sporting on the hill was again in full swing.

Meanwhile, an older apprentice had lured one of the girls onto his sled, which immediately inflamed the ambition in Peter Andreas's breast. In the middle of the run, he braked in front of a group of girls, who were always on the verge of laughter, and invited the tallest of them to join him. After a little hesitation, she yielded and sat in front of him astride the sled. Boldly he wrapped his arms around his conquest, and off went Bloodeagle.

"Watch out!" he shouted at the top of his lungs to proclaim his triumph to the whole world.

"Did you see Peter Andreas?" "Yeah, that was Per!" he heard, in passing, from a pair of comrades who were going back up the hill with their sleds. His heart swelled with pride. He had caught their tone of reluctant admiration.

The black-eyed, dark-haired pauper girl turned around on the wild ride to look at him appreciatively and laughed with her large, red, half-open mouth that made his cheeks burn. Old dreams surfaced again in his chest: dreams of gypsy life and happiness on the wide heath, dreams of a carefree, wandering life, with a tent or a mud hut as a home, a life open to the stars and fleeting clouds.

The sled stopped just before the town. The girl wanted to stand up and turn to her new friend, but Peter Andreas forced her to stay seated—he didn't want to risk losing her—and began to pull the sled up the hill. Step by step he struggled with the heavy load. He imagined himself a warrior, a Viking going home from a triumphant campaign in a strange land, conveying his booty with him, a beautiful woman, a stolen princess, who would be willing to be with him in his beamed house deep in the woods. Spurred by his fantasy, he set his feet against the icy slope, straining with every muscle so hard that perspiration broke out on his forehead. When they had reached the top of the hill and he had again mounted the back of the sled to race down, the girl turned to him and asked, "Is it true what they say, that you are a son of the pastor?"

The question brought him so abruptly back to reality that he grew pale. He forced a "no" through his teeth—with an intensity he felt down to his toes. Meanwhile the sled flew down the slope as the runners seemed to sing.

He had never known so strongly as in that moment that he did not belong to his house, to that half-dark, stuffy room where his father and siblings now sat and sang hymns and muttered apprehensive prayers in the middle of a magical winter's night—in a sort of underworld blindness to the light and full of a dread of life and its glory. He felt himself a thousand miles from that scene, under a wholly different heaven, at one with the sun and stars and the sailing clouds. Listen! His ear caught once more a familiar sound from down under . . . the striking of the church clock. Like a message from the underworld it reached him through the silvery light of the frosty air—eleven heavy, dark, slow beats. How he hated that sound. Wherever he was and at all hours of the day it rudely broke into his happy dreams . . . calling and warning him. It was not possible to escape very long before it summoned him back. Like an invisible spirit it pursued him down all his prohibited paths. When, in the spring, he had stolen out to the meadows with his giant kite, "Heljo," or, in the summer, taken out a boat to the fjord to catch perch, each quarter hour that ghostly voice stole into his ear with its summoning sound. "Hello!" he shrieked to drown out the voice, and squeezed the tall girl, as if in provocative defiance, still harder. She turned again, smiling at him with a glance that sent a sweet shiver down his back. "You're beautiful," he whispered in her ear. "What's your name?"

"Oline."

"And where do you live?"

"On Smedestræde in the Riisagers' house. Where do *you* live?"

"I?"

"If you're not the pastor's son, who are you, then?"

"Who am I? I can't say. But why don't we meet tomorrow night on Voldstræde, when it gets dark?"

"I'd like that."

Without regarding the danger, Peter Andreas had run over the town boundary and was still going at full speed down Nørregade. He had not gone far before a large form sprang up from the street corner and with a thundering "Stop!" caught the sled with the crooked end of his cudgel, upsetting it and flinging both children into the snow. The girl, with a wild scream, fled the scene, while the powerful hand of Ole the watchman grabbed Peter Andreas's neck. "Come here, boy! I'll teach you devilish kids not to mess around with the authorities. To the town hall with you! No backtalk! Whose cursed kid are you, anyway?"

Peter Andreas understood immediately that it would take real ingenuity to get out of this jam. Quickly, breathlessly, he said, "It was good that I met you, watchman. There's a huge scuffle up there among the boys. Iversen's big apprentice has pulled a knife. You better hurry . . . he's really furious."

"What are you saying?"

"He stabbed the mayor's son. I hope he's not dead. He is lying in a big pool of blood."

"The son of the mayor!" groaned the watchman, and released Peter Andreas.

"I'll run to tell his family and fetch Dr. Carlsen," said Peter Andreas, and quickly grabbed the rope of his sled. Before the watchman could collect himself, he was gone.

It was almost midnight when he climbed the neighbor's fence and crawled in by the entrance hall window he had left half opened. He had taken his boots off outside in the snow and with careful steps was sneaking up the loft stairs. At that instant, the door of the study opened and his father stood before him with a lamp in his uplifted hand. For some seconds, father and son stood facing each other without saying a word. Only a rattling noise could be heard from the lamp globe in Pastor Sidenius's trembling hand.

"Like a thief you go in and out of your father's house," said the pastor, finally. "Where are you coming from?" he added in a half whisper, as if he barely had the courage to hear the answer.

Peter Andreas admitted, without beating around the bush or excusing himself, where he had been—in that second he felt such contempt for his father that he couldn't even lie to him. He confessed his purchase of Bloodeagle and his debt to the wheelwright.

"It's gone that far with you, has it?" said his father, without revealing that his worst anxiety had already, in reality, been allayed. He knew there were a few secret places of indecency in town, and he had been afraid that his son had been lured to such a spot by bad examples. "Go to bed," he added. "You are a sinful child! We'll talk more about it in the morning."

When Peter Andreas, early the next day, was called down for morning prayers in the living room, he was prepared for a repetition of the solemn scene of stigmatizing he had endured on the occasion of his apple theft. Signe sat at the piano under a single lighted lamp while the rest of the large room lay in darkness. It was so cold a frosty cloud came out of the hymn-singing mouths.

The first and second hymns were sung and the creed recited without any reference made to yesterday evening's incident. Nothing about it was said to him even later in the day. Pastor Sidenius had been sitting the whole morning at his wife's bed, and they had come to the recognition that it was fruitless to try any longer to influence the boy's mind by persuasion. They could only trust that, with God's mercy, time and life's discipline would straighten him out. They agreed to provide pointed nails for the top of the neighbor's fence. Besides this, the father would personally assure himself every evening that the youngster was in his bed.

Peter Andreas was indifferent. Whatever his parents did with him—whether it was good or bad—no longer made an impression on him. The time had passed when, to shorten his torment, he would plot adventures—an outright revolt or a secret flight, sallying forth into the world, seeking, by chance, the kingdom of his dreams. He was now both old and wise enough to realize he could most surely and quickly gain his longed-for independence if he patiently finished school, and, furthermore, it wasn't long before he found other ways to frustrate his father's vigilance. When everything was quiet in the house, he would, with a rope, lower himself out of the gable window onto the half-roof of the entrance hall and slide from there onto the gutter and into the street. Consequently, on many a moonlit night he still lolled out by the fjord with his beloved fishing line and, on the way home, gave the watchman his catch for keeping his mouth shut.

He had found a way as well to renew relations with the dark-eyed Oline from the Riisagers' house. A couple of times he made a night assignation with her in one of the big lumberyards. But that was soon over. The free and easy coarseness in the girl's expression and manners filled him with shame. When she, once, essentially, made an assault on his virtue, he shied away and stopped seeing her.

Continually stirred by the coal ships and the small Swedish lumber boats, he had a special predilection for the poor life of the harbor. He came to know the manager of a little provisions shop, and he often spent his free periods there to listen to sea stories, of adventures in foreign lands, of powerful steamships that could accommodate up to two thousand people, and of the activities of the big ports with their large shipyards and docks.

But the life of the seamen did not tempt him. He aimed higher. He wanted to be an engineer. That profession seemed to him to command the most possibility for the real fulfillment of his dream of a proud and free-roaming life, rich in adventures and exciting incidents. Also, the choice of a practical profession would give him the means to break away cleanly from his family and the glorified centuries-old traditions. His was a calculated challenge, especially in relation to his father, who would often disparage the general joyous anticipation of a great technological future. Once, when the public interest was roused among the citizens by a proposal to get the town's navigation moving through a deepening of the fjord's channel, his father viewed the project with special contempt: "These people with their per-petual concern about everything but the one thing necessary!" From that day, Peter Andreas wanted to be an engineer.

He got a push in that direction from his school. While most

of his teachers deemed him, at an early stage, someone who would never accomplish anything worthwhile, he had gradually found for himself a friend and protector in his mathematics teacher. An old military man, he spoke very highly of Peter Andreas's capabilities to the pastor when he had the chance a couple of times, and he resisted the pastor's impetuous plan to take his son out of school and make him learn a craft. The old soldier seemed to be impelled by an empathic understanding of the boy and to find satisfaction in reducing the strict priestly monitor to silence with his praise.

Then, too, the town's attitude toward Pastor Sidenius and his house was beginning to change. Times and practices had eventually moved the citizens to reconciliation. Many of the old merchants and horse breeders who had, almost up to the present day, determined the public opinion of the town, had died over the years. More important, neither in their businesses nor in the disposition of their wealth did they use their appropriated authority reasonably and fairly for the town's welfare. They had been businessmen of the old school, who, in their country pride, refused to realize that the times were leaving them behind as they disregarded changes effected by new developments in communication. Many of the town's best families that had lived lavishly on inherited fortunes sank almost into poverty after the war. As their status diminished, their need for religion's consolations grew. Pastor Sidenius's earnest words about earthly vanity and the true riches of poverty and deprivation began to find a way into the hearts of the people—most of all of those who had been his worst enemies in the past. The group of worshipers who gathered on Sunday to hear his preaching steadily increased, and citizens no longer refused to greet the pastor when he passed them—at least not when he was in his robe.

It was while these developments were taking place that freedom's hour finally sounded for Peter Andreas. Pressed by the old mathematics teacher's persistent advocacy, his father eventually consented to send him to the capital to study at the Polytechnic Institute. He was sixteen years old.

One pretty autumn evening, when the weekly passenger boat slowly steamed out through the endless bends of the fjords on the way to Copenhagen, Peter Andreas stood at the sternpost with a bag slung over his shoulder and looked back at the town that grew gradually darker against the pink evening sky. His departure from home had cost him no tears. Even his goodbyes to his mother were made without great emotion. Yet, as he stood there in his new, tailored suit with a hundred-daler banknote sewn into the lining of his vest and saw the town's swarm of roofs and the church's heavy brick tower disappear in the twilight, a sense of uneasiness seized him and there stirred in his breast a vague feeling of gratitude. He felt that he hadn't managed the farewells to his family well, and almost wished he could turn back to say goodbye again. As the distant sound of the church's evening bell—home's last greeting and warning—was carried out to him over the meadows, he experienced feelings of reconciliation.

This susceptible mood sustained itself during the first days in the capital. It got even stronger as he became prey to the typical feelings of loneliness that oppress the provincial pilgrim in the big city with nothing but strange and indifferent faces. He knew no one in Copenhagen. None of his schoolmates had come here—wanting, instead, to finish their schooling. He felt completely depressed in his loneliness; often he went down to the quay by the Exchange to see whether a skipper of an apple cargo from home might come, with whom he could chat about his town and common acquaintances. Only his disaffection for his father stayed constant; it was always to his mother that he wrote when he felt like it.

Of his older brothers, one, Thomas, had already, a year ago, completed his studies and was appointed to a country post as curate. The other, Eberhard, lived, to be sure, in the city, but was out of town just now; and even when he returned, they would never see each other. Eberhard was cautious, anxious, and self-contained—fearful of coming into contact with something that could hurt his reputation. He therefore felt very annoyed by this degenerate brother who came like a wild stray to make his way without having completed his schooling.

During the first two months, Peter Andreas lived in a wretched back room of an attic in the inner city with a view of a crowd of red roofs. Later, he moved into the lodgings of an old couple in Nyboder.

The day before Christmas Eve, he traveled home overland, after having announced his coming arrival in a very short letter. On the interminable daylong journey through Zealand and Funen, and at the sight of so many happy Christmas travelers who filled the compartments he was reminded with what excitement the homecoming of his older brothers was always anticipated, how lamps were lit in the rooms, and how the evening meal was postponed until after the train's arrival to make the reception all the more festive. And he thought of his old friends, who possibly already knew he was coming and might be at the station to greet him.

The compartment gradually emptied on the journey through Jutland, and finally he was left alone. It had grown dark, the ceiling lamps were lit, and heavy rain was hitting the windowpanes. When he heard the train running over a bridge, his heart began to race. He knew the sound, which would last five minutes. It was the Skærbaek Bridge. He rushed to the window and wiped off the pane ... yes, there was the brook ... and the meadows and the Skærbaek hills. And now the tracks turned and the town's lights could be seen dimly through the rain.

His sister Signe was on the platform to meet him. A slight sensation of discomfort shot through him when he saw her. She stood there, her shoulders a little stooped, in a short, frightfully old-fashioned coat. She wore black gloves, and, below a tucked-up skirt hem, her long, thin ankles could be seen above her large feet in galoshes. It embarrassed him that she had to be viewed like that, exposing her unfortunate appearance to general criticism. In addition, he had fully expected to see his younger twin brothers, and that raised the suspicion that only Signe met him because she was the one sibling with whom he had the least to do.

On the way home, through the streets, he soon divined that his parents were not really happy about his visit; they thought it unwise, Signe said, that he already was taking a vacation. Such a trip cost money—he should, first, at any rate, have asked for his father's permission.

Even before they reached the parsonage, Peter Andreas's feelings had become cool. And when he came into the parlor and saw his father sitting there in his usual place, on the old, faded chair, with his green eyeshade, he regretted not having stayed in Copenhagen. It was obvious that his father, patting his cheeks, welcomed him with reluctance. The door into the dining room was closed. Peter Andreas could hear the floor being scrubbed, and when his eyes lighted on a few sandwiches on a tray on the table, he understood that the others had already eaten. His mother was, as always, in her bed. Her welcome lacked neither

sincerity nor warmth; she kissed him on both cheeks, but his
heart remained chilled.

Peter Andreas was too young to understand that he had committed nothing worse than sharing the common plight of a
younger child in a large family in which the oldest had harvested
the first fruits of the parents' affection. Even if this love was not
diminished toward the younger children, it certainly was quali-
fied. For the parents, it missed the glamour of the new that
kindled every step of the future. At bedtime, when Peter Andreas
was alone up in his old attic room, he began to laugh. He made
fun of himself, mocked his own sentimentality that had made him
long for this so-called home, and he swore with all his heart that
he would never again be taken in by such a mood.

When Christmas came, with all its holy ceremonies he felt no
part of, with the constant churchgoing and so much hymn singing, he counted the hours until he could get away and again be
his own man in Copenhagen. His meeting with his friends was
disappointing as well. Influenced by their parents' view of him,
some of them pretended to hardly know him. His father and siblings had only reluctantly spoken about him, which led the town
to understand that he was someone who had gone astray. Many
of his classmates displayed, in addition, a vanity that came with
having graduated to higher studies. He had rapidly sought them
all out, but none of them asked him to come again.

Immediately after New Year's Day, he returned to
Copenhagen.

CHAPTER 2

IT WAS SAID that, in his day, the old, pensioned Chief Boatswain
Olufsen of Hjertensfrydgade was one of Nyboder's best-known
and most respected citizens. Every morning, when St. Paul's
clock tower rang eleven, his tall, thin, and a bit wobbly form
could be seen walking out of the rickety door of a two-story
building where he lived in the top apartment. For a moment, he
would stand on the sidewalk and, just like the seaman he was,
look up to the clouds and let his eyes run over the roof ridges as
over the rigging of a ship. He was dressed in a somewhat faded
but very neatly brushed overcoat, a wide Dannebrog ribbon in
his buttonhole. A gray top hat sat on his white hair, and he

steadied himself on the umbrella held in his left hand, on which he wore an old shriveled leather glove.

With his right arm behind his back, he shuffled along slowly and carefully down the uneven flagstones. At the same time, in the window mirror at the front of the apartment, his wife came into view, following him with her eyes until he was safely over the deep gutter at the corner of Elsdyrsgade. She was in her flowered night jacket with newspaper curlers in front of each ear, enjoying the vision of his well-cared-for form with proud self-satisfaction, as if he were exclusively her own creation.

At that moment, the boatswain passed Nyboder's guardhouse with the high gallows on which the alarm bell hung, and he switched his umbrella to his right hand in order to greet with the gloved hand any of the guards who should give him a military salute—something he prized and always carefully observed. Then he turned into Kamelgaden and walked toward Amalienborg Slotsplads, where he arrived every day on the exact hour of the changing of the guard. After he had listened to the music for a while, he went back across Store Kongensgade and by Borgergade farther into the city.

Here, where he was outside his former domain, where no one knew him as Boatswain Olufsen who had received his Dannebrog ribbon from the king's own hand, where he was, in short, just a common stroller that people could elbow with impunity—here something in his back and legs seemed to slow him down involuntarily, while he anxiously tottered forward on his aching feet through the rushing passersby. He never went farther than Købmagergade. What lay on the other side of that street was, for him, not the right Copenhagen, but a kind of suburb so far removed he couldn't understand how anyone could want to live there. In his eyes, Adelog-Borgergade, the town's main artery, together with the quarter around Grønne-Svaerte-Regnegade, the tollhouse, and Holmen, made up his world. When on his return walk he reached the last brush maker in Antonistræde or after visiting Frøken Jordan's subscription library in Silkegade to exchange a book for his wife, he turned around and went home.

Generally, there were a couple of hours before he returned to Hjertensfrydgade, because of his custom of stopping at each street corner to observe the stream of passing people and traffic. Above all, despite his eighty years and bleary eyes, he enjoyed looking at the servant girls, especially those with bare arms. If it happened that one of them, by chance, brushed close by him, he would whisper some little love-words and hurry away, giggling and ducking his head.

And he couldn't resist standing for a moment in front of the shop windows to look at the displays and memorize the prices of everything from underclothes in the knitted-goods shop to the diamonds in the jewelry store. Not that he had any intention of buying these things (he was, at any rate, strictly prohibited; his wife, knowing full well his weakness for young, pretty women, never trusted him to go out with money); but with his empty pockets, he was satisfied to go into the shops and have various goods laid out before him, ask prices of the most expensive items, and then trot off saying, "I'll let you know."

By afternoon the boatswain was home in his parlor—the "salon," as they called it in Nyboder slang—a low-ceilinged, cabin-like room with a row of small windows that looked out on the street. He sat here at one of the windows with a skullcap on his head and looked, hour after hour, at the crowds of half-domesticated crows coming in from the parks, either onto the roof ridges of the houses across the way, or croaking and fighting around the pavement's trash cans, which, at that time, still sat in front of every door on the quiet and empty streets. Now and then a film fell over his old, fading eyes. His head sank slowly onto his breast, and his lips puffed out.

"Now you are again cooking peas, little father," said his wife, referring to a peculiar hum that came from the boatswain when sleep overpowered him. She had her accustomed afternoon place on a low chair by the stove, where she sat and knitted, reading at the same time a tattered novel that lay before her on her knees, turning the pages with her elbow so as not to interrupt her knitting. A cage with a canary that hopped on its perch hung in the window, and a young blond girl, their foster daughter Trine, often sat sewing in the back room with the door open.

Madam Olufsen was almost as tall as her husband and had the figure of a cavalry rider, with a hint of a gray mustache. She was hardly attractive when she went around in the morning in her night jacket and paper curlers, but in the afternoon, after she had tied her stays, put on her black merino dress, and hidden her half-bald head under a ribboned cap—in front of which the now carefully arranged temple curls displayed themselves almost flirtatiously against the not altogether faded cheeks—the talk in Nyboder of her former glory could well be believed.

All in all, she and the boatswain had been a handsome couple. They had also been a happy couple. If the boatswain was not always strictly true to his vow to keep all the sworn Commandments, by compensation his wife was faithful enough for both of them, although, in younger years, she had not lacked temptations. If rumors could be believed, a prince who always stalked the young women of Nyboder when their husbands went on long journeys introduced himself one night on the corner of Marinade, and propositioned her. She deeply curtsied, lowered her eyes, and quietly followed him into one of the dark, isolated avenues behind the embankment. Here in this secluded spot, out of the goodness of her heart, she swiftly laid the little wizened highness over her knees and gave him a spanking, which was not the first chastisement an offended Nyboder wife had allotted him, but certainly the most powerful.

The reputation this old couple enjoyed with their fellow citizens was long-standing, and their house was still a popular gathering place for various of the quarter's elite. The kind of social events held here could not be found in many Nyboder houses. Outside of the usual church holidays—the so-called days of prayer and repentance, observed everywhere in Christendom with rich food and warm punch—a long line of family events and annually recurring special days of a private nature were celebrated. There was a birthday for Peter the canary's adoption by the family, and a commemorative day for the boatswain's big toe, cut off many years ago because of caries. Best of all was Madam Olufsen's cup day in the spring, when the air warmed up, which began with a large chocolate lunch for the barber who organized the event.

The gathering for these occasions consisted of the same seven or eight old friends of the house who for more than forty years had celebrated important family occasions together: pensioner Chief Carpenter Bendtz from Tulipangade, pensioner Quartermaster Mørup from Delfingade, Chief Gunner Jensen, and Riveter Fuss from Krokodillen, all with wives. Nor had the course of the celebration undergone any significant change in the last generation. When the guests were gathered in the back room, the boatswain would open the door into the salon, where the table was set, and invite his friends to eat, with the same amusing reminder that now was the time to "shovel something into their faces." When everyone was seated and the hostess had put the steaming goose or ham on the table, Riveter Fuss regularly, at that very moment, feigned surprise, tilted his chair back, and said, "Now, Madam Olufsen, you have laid an enormous egg!" Whereupon Madam called him an old fool and bade the guests to feel at home.

At this point, as it often happened, the door opened for a curly-haired young man, whose arrival was greeted with a general shout of joy. He was everyone's favorite. All the old people stood up courteously and extended their hands; little Trine blushed and busied herself with bringing a chair in from the next room, setting a new place at the table, and fetching a warm plate from the kitchen. The new guest, a twenty-one-year-old student at the Polytechnic Institute, was the Olufsens' tenant, Sidenius, who for a couple years had lived downstairs in a pair of small back rooms that belonged with the boatswain's apartment.

Gradually, as the decanters and brandy bowl were emptied, the mood became very high spirited. Only Trine remained quiet and still as she saw to attending the guests. She filled the glasses, passed the bread around, changed the plates, trimmed the candles, fetched saltcellars, retrieved lost handkerchiefs, and brought water for the ladies when they began to get sick or to hiccup—all so noiselessly that her presence was hardly noticed. It was as if an invisible spirit were serving the company. She was so little and undeveloped in spite of her nineteen years that she was easy to overlook. The old folk considered her still a child, a diminutive child; and, in truth, she was a little slow-witted as well. She was a poor, plain orphan the boatswain had adopted and whose origin was unknown. She was no beauty, and even for the young Sidenius, she was nothing more than the indiscernible instrument that brushed boots and washed linens.

As the punch bowl and the sugar-sprinkled apple cake appeared on the table, the company entertained itself with various songs of fellowship and patriotism. Madam Fuss made herself particularly noticeable—more for the power than the beauty of her highly admired treble voice.

While the singing continued, Trine went into the kitchen, after having made sure that the guests were well provided for. She lit a candle from the open hearth and carried it down the house's small and steep steps—a kind of ship's ladder—to put Herr Sidenius's lodgings in order for the night. They were two small, dark, and humid rooms, poorly furnished with a little oilcloth sofa and a folding table where books, drafting tools, and large rolls of pencil-marked papers lay helter-skelter.

Trine set the candle on the table, opened a window, and stood for a moment dreaming, with her hand on the window frame. She looked out on a romantic full moon shining over the tiny fenced garden and gardening shed. Suddenly she shuddered, as though frightened by her own thoughts, and patiently set about putting the untidy rooms in order. She collected clothing thrown over chairs and hung it up behind the corner curtain of the bed-room. She rearranged the books on the table and placed all the many small drafting tools in their designated cases.

Although the young gentleman had never troubled to give her instructions concerning these things, to tell her carefully where he expected, even demanded, them to be, the instinct that love creates in the simple taught her his habits, how to guess at his wishes, how to find her way steadfastly through the labyrinth of whims and disordered fancies that enter into such a young man's peculiar and decided will. He had once and for all let her know—and he had, on that occasion, made a frightful grimace as he lifted his finger—that she should consider her service to him as her life's work and special destiny, for which God would call her to account on Judgment Day.

It was, therefore, with a dedicated feeling of a high and sacred calling that she entered his small rooms and busied herself with his belongings. A special sense of devotion lingered in the little bedroom while she fussed with his bed, and arranged his slippers conveniently in place, the toes turned inward, and laid his matches by the lamp nearest his bed. When she finally took his pillow between her hands to fluff out the feathers she squeezed it for a moment to her heart, and with a worshipful expression closed her eyes.

In the meantime, the old folks in the salon were becoming more and more giddy. Riveter Fuss had fetched his guitar, and in spite of the ladies' objections began to sing the disreputable broadside ballad, "The Overfed Lady at Gammelstrand." The men shouted with joy as the young Sidenius laughed and, from eighty-four-year-old Chief Carpenter Bendtz, a muffled chuckle sounded as if it came from inside a bottle. But the women rose offended, and marched off to the back room, where coffee, candies, and blackcurrant liqueur were being served.

Not until it was almost morning did the company break up. The married couples toddled homeward, reconciled and in such a happy state of mind that they were beguiled into affectionate hugging and kissing in the street.

It was here, through these old people who emptied the cup of joy to the dregs, that Peter Andreas had found his first sanctuary—a provisional refuge on the way to that country of happiness his dreams had promised him. Here he had met the most beneficent understanding of just that part of his nature that, at home in the parsonage, had been oppressed or branded as the work of death or the devil. He had been especially thankful for this home during his lonely first year in Copenhagen, and for the whole cheerful and idyllic neighborhood that was a little hidden province in the midst of the capital. Later, after he had gradually widened his circle of acquaintances, his relation to the two old people and their little society acquired a more fleeting character, but he never broke with them, and the old couple remained fond of him and interested in his welfare, almost as if he were one of their own family. More than once he would be going to bed on an empty stomach and Madam Olufsen, considerately, would invite him to "try out" the new cheese or "give his opinion" of a freshly baked ham. (It had not taken them long to discover his poverty, despite the fact that he did everything to hide it.)

However, the Olufsens did not succeed in getting a real insight into him. Chatty and lively as he would be at times, he never spoke, or only jokingly, of himself or his goals. When they asked him directly, he liked to say, "I'm studying to become a government minister," and would be stubbornly silent about his home and family relationships, even though Madam Olufsen never grew tired of asking him. He had decided to consider all the past as something dead and forgotten; each bitter and humiliating remembrance must never be allowed to haunt his existence. He sought to make his mind a clean tablet for the glowing gold script of luck and triumph. There was no picture on the table or walls to remind him of the home he had left, or reveal it to others—at least, not until he could justify a demand there for vindication. If he were suddenly to die, no one would find in his most secret hiding place so much as a letter saved or any other sign that would reveal who he was and where he came from. He even changed his name. He no longer signed himself "Peter Andreas," but simply "Per," and he was sorry that he could not adopt another last name.

His connections with his childhood home had gradually shrunk to short letters in which he sent receipts quarterly for any money he received from his father to help him out—an entirely insufficient amount to cover such large expenses as lectures, books, and drafting and measuring instruments, which his studies demanded. From the time he was eighteen, he taught arithmetic in a boys' school and, to get by, copied out blueprint designs for a master craftsman.

At times he was depressed. He felt degraded by his poverty and, above all, by his job teaching in a boys' school, which he never mentioned. What is more, he became disillusioned with his studies and the future possibilities they could generate.

When, four or five years before, he was about to enter the Polytechnic Institute, he had an almost holy expectation. He had imagined it as a kind of temple, a solemn intellectual workshop where the future happiness and well-being of free men were forged by the thunder and lightning of the mind. He found, instead, a hateful, ugly building in the shade of an old bishop's see. Inside, there were many dark, melancholy rooms permeated with the smell of tobacco and sandwiches, where a group of young men stood bent over small tables covered with papers, while others sat with long pipes and read notebooks or surreptitiously played cards. He had expected his future teachers to be devoted preachers of natural science's sacred gospel; he met instead old, dry schoolmasters in the lecture halls, not much different from the teachers he had just left at home. One of them, a perfect mummy—whose voice, in the lecture, would give out at any moment and had to be renewed by a swig from a medicine bottle—taught what he remembered from Hans Christian Ørsted's day. Another, Professor Sandrup, his teacher of engineering proper, wore a white necktie and most resembled an old theological scholar or clergyman. He enjoyed a certain reputation for theoretical knowledge, but was a pedant who, out of pedagogical conscientiousness, had prepared long, scholarly accounts of the uses even of the simplest instruments, like axes and wheelbarrows. On the exams, he demanded a literal rendering.

Already for some time, Per had realized that a proficient engineer was, in any case, no longer a proud fairy-tale hero striding through the world, as he had once deceived himself into believing, but a common bureaucrat, a meticulous recording machine, a living tabulator, chained to a drafting table. Furthermore, most of his fellow students—especially those who were considered the most promising by both teachers and classmates—dreamt of a steady, secure position as an administrator, even if a subordinate one, that would allow them, as fathers with multiple responsibilities, to order their little house and garden. After forty years of faithful service, they could retire with a small pension, a token of distinction, or a "councilor of justice" title.

Per was tempted by no such prospect. He felt he had not been created for common or cheap happiness. He felt master-blood in his veins and demanded a seat of honor at life's table among the earth's free and chosen.

He had selected the means that would allow him to gain the desired proud independence. While he managed to go to lectures and seminars fairly regularly, attending to the humiliating trivial work that would secure him a future income, he had secretly busied himself with making a draft of a large water construction project—a fjord realignment that he had planned in his first student years in Copenhagen. Its origin lay even further back in time, all the way to his boyhood, when he had heard so much talk about reviving navigation through the fjord by deepening and realigning the channel and rebuilding the harbor—an undertaking, finally abandoned, of which his father had spoken disparagingly because of the considerable disturbance that arose in the town. Even then, Per had dreamt of completing that great plan, of directing the fresh flow of ocean and the golden outpouring of international trade into the town's poor harbor of apple barges. The dream—to become the savior of the city that had witnessed his humiliation—had never completely left him. After his last unhappy Christmas visit, it overpowered him. In his loneliness this *idée fixe* gave him no peace. With a kind of religious conviction, he saw the realization of this dream as his life's destiny and present goal.

For three years—since he had learned how to adapt a canal profile to the proportions of a professional map—he had been working on this. Night after night he had stolen time from his sleep to chart bed plans and current velocities, sketch fascine constructions, banked slopes, pier heads, and ringed spars. And through the years, he had developed his plan, adding something new, making it more and more massive. Influenced by some well-known German professional publications, he conceived the idea of extending the deepened channel to the other side of the town like a canal or a system of canals on the Dutch model. What he vaguely projected as a final, impressive goal was a network of broad arteries that would connect all the large rivers, lakes, and fjords of middle Jutland with each other and put the cultivated heaths and the flourishing new towns into contact with the sea on both sides.

But a depression intruded each time his thoughts flew to such a height. The shaggy monster of impotence settled itself on his worktable and laughed scornfully at his dreams of greatness: "You're crazy," it admonished. "Until you become old and gray, you cannot be allowed to carry through anything like that in this country, where it looks like presumption for a young man to have ambitions other than to seat himself hunched over in an office chair, and where an engineer who wants to preserve the highest esteem and confidence of his fellow citizens may hope for a post like a royally appointed highway bureaucrat. Have you already forgotten what your respected teacher, the revered Professor Sandrup, with his paternal earnestness, impressed on your mind when you began, in an examination, to trot out new views (not assigned) gleaned from reading modern German authors: 'Try, young man, to fight against the premature desire to show off your independence'—not true? Instructive words! Wise and weighty words."

After a while, he seldom allowed such bitter thoughts to chafe his spirits; he was too young and his mind too unsettled. In general, a brisk walk, a glance at a pretty girl, a small dinner party at the old couple's apartment, or an evening passed with some friends in a café was sufficient to dissipate the gathering storm clouds. Women were an especially helpful diversion when a bad mood threatened. He was now twenty-one years old, and attraction to the opposite sex was ready to dominate his imagination and give it a new horizon.

One evening he went with an acquaintance to an Old World Swiss café that was a favorite gathering place of the city's dispersed artistic and literary demimonde. While his comrade enthusiastically pointed out some of the day's most talked-about artists and authors among the company, Per, with little interest in such things, fixed his attention on a young woman standing behind the counter—a tall and slender figure with splendid strawberry-blond hair.

"That's 'Red Lisbeth,'" his companion explained. "The model for Iversen's *Venus* and Petersen's *Susanne*. Not bad, is she? What a complexion!"

From that day on, Per became a frequent patron of the café, especially at those times when it was not so crowded. He was very attracted to the young woman, and when it became evident that the feeling was mutual, he soon had an intimate relationship.

Per was, at this time, quite vain about his appearance. He had a strong and sturdy body, a high forehead, dark, curly hair, and large blue eyes under joined brows. Above his full mouth could be seen the beginnings of a mustache. Thanks to Madam Olufsen's motherly care, he had kept his bright young complexion, his cheeks their country color. When he circulated among people, he would smile without being aware of it, and that constant empty smile easily deceived those who did not know him; they simply looked upon him as a child in sweet harmony with all of existence. On the whole, he did not succeed in shedding his provincial air. Still, when he was in his best clothes he cut an imposing figure, carried himself well, and moved rather gracefully. Despite his continual destitution, he never neglected his clothes. At any rate, when he was seen in the street, he was always neat and trim. He had already ascertained that, to certain eyes, a white shirtfront and an immaculately fitted coat could have more significance for a young man's future than a prolonged, dedicated, ascetic diligence. Nothing vital was lost so long as appearance was maintained. At home, on the other hand, he was careless with himself and felt a certain comfort and satisfaction in wearing out his old clothes.

The café where he now had become an habitué and where he wasted more time and money than he could afford was called the Pot. It was frequented by a bohemian clique known as "the Independents," consisting of younger, and singular older, beautiful souls, genuine talents who nevertheless had, in some way, become stalled, either never really maturing or growing old before their time. The very controversial seascape painter Fritjof Jensen sat there in the evening, with his broad-shouldered Viking body and wavy black hair and beard, in a short sailor jacket. He was a genial, imaginative painter, an engaging, jolly brother with a foaming tankard, but as soft and unreliable as a boy in puberty. Each morning, the sick poet Enevoldsen, a lonely melancholic, polished his lorgnette or tenderly rubbed his hands or lost himself in the enjoyment of a cigar; he had sat that way, year after year, but, supported by all kinds of little jobs, had chiseled his verse of glowing color—small masterpieces that initiated a whole new tone in Danish poetry. Jørgen Hallager, the young, naturalist figure painter with a bulldog face, sat there—the inciter and anarchist who wanted to overturn society, reform art, abolish academies, and hang all professors, but who supported himself legitimately as a retoucher for a photographer. And there was the old mockingbird, the journalist and dramatist of comedies Reeballe, a bowlegged, wig-wearing dwarf with one shining eye and one dim, whose long yellowing goat's beard hung over his always dirty shirtfront—the inevitable target of all the caricaturists in the city's humorous papers. He willfully circulated among the tables, often in a fairly drunken condition, with a chewed cigar stump in the corner of his mouth and with one or both hands tucked behind him in his waistband, darting here and there among people he didn't even know and mixing his nonsense into their conversations. He too wanted to reform the world, but in the classic spirit. His ideal was Socrates, with his standpoint of clear, sober knowledge. In moments when his mind was fully befogged, he liked to strike his breast and call himself "the last Greek."

Despite the fact that Per was so much younger than these men and had not himself made any attempt to cultivate them, he enjoyed the honor of being involved in their circle—partly, as Fritjof Jensen once professed, for the sake of his "painterly red cheeks," but really because of his relation to Lisbeth, who was their favored pet. Some of them owed half their fame to her beautiful, silken hair and soft skin. As recompense, they paid her the special attention of always recognizing that moment's preferred admirer, including even those who in no way belonged to the artistic society.

Per continued, nonetheless, to feel a stranger in this group; and it was not merely because of his modesty that he seldom took part in the conversation. He had as meager a sense of painting as of poetry, but his imagination found sufficient nourishment in his studies. It remained so totally absorbed in his great future work that no passion was left for art.

However, he was not an indifferent spectator. He was silently amused by these curious men who could fly into a rage over a color combination and talk themselves into a state of ecstasy on the subject of four rhymed lines, as if mankind's welfare hung on their right conception. He enjoyed this kind of scene as he would a stage comedy, and he would laugh to himself when he noticed how much Lisbeth also was seized by the madness and, proud that her figure was so important to art, would gladly have her life understood as an inspired offering to beauty's glorification.

One of the men frequenting the Pot, who seemed particularly interested in Per, did not belong in the circle and, in general, did not even seem to be welcome there. This was a certain Ivan Salomon, a young Jew, the son of one of the richest men in the city—a little, adroit fellow, a brown-eyed squirrel, always smiling, very obliging, and very happy to be moving among so many famous artists. It was that man's most ambitious dream to discover a genius someday and champion him. He was always on the hunt for a hidden or unappreciated talent whose patron he could be. Every little particular aspect of appearance that he spotted—a pair of deep-set eyes, a firm forehead, or even just uncut hair—he took immediately as a sign of special gifts, and many funny stories were told about the disappointments he had suffered in this regard.

He had now pinned his hopes on Per, who was rather annoyed by his attentions. He even resisted his flattery. He felt uncomfortable when Herr Salomon—with distinct allusions to Per's quick success with Lisbeth—ingratiatingly claimed that he was marked out to be an Aladdin, a charmed boy on whose Caesar brow God's finger had written, "I come, I see, I conquer!" At the same time, such words really thrilled Per, made him quiver in his innermost, hidden being. It only pained and humiliated him that he should first hear this prophecy from the mouth of a foolish little Jew.

One evening Per came into the Pot around midnight and found himself in the middle of a riotous bacchanal. It was the great Fritjof Jensen—just "Fritjof," as he was called by everyone—who was letting go on the occasion of selling *Hurricane in the North Sea*, one of his four two-foot canvases, to a butter merchant. Some small tables had been lined up in the middle of a room that was divided from the other part of the restaurant by a corridor. Here, a score of guests sat around two wreathed bowls of champagne punch.

Fritjof, enveloped in a cloud of tobacco smoke, sat at the head of the tables, enthroned like an Olympian. His great private cup, called "the Deep," stood in front of him, and his blurry eyes and voice signaled his drunkenness. For more than twenty-four hours he had been feverishly running about, spending night and day in oyster and wine bars with prostitutes, and in the woods, dragging along any friend or friend's friend he encountered on the way.

Among a series of speakers, a pale young man with Mephisto-phelean features suddenly sprang up on his chair and loudly toasted an absent friend, a certain Dr. Nathan, of whom Per had often heard, always enthusiastically, at the Pot. He was a literary critic and beloved philosopher counted in certain young aca-demic circles as their spiritual leader, who, dissatisfied with his native land, had settled in Berlin. Per knew little else of the man, except that it was impossible not to come across his name in every serious or comic newspaper at hand—"Dr. Satan," as he was invariably called. That the man was Jewish had prevented Per from desiring more intimate knowledge of him. He simply didn't like that foreign race, nor did he have any leaning toward literary men. The doctor had even given lectures at the university, that theologically defiled womb for the whole of academic philistin-ism—in Per's eyes, the country's characteristic curse.

The pale, young speaker, who stood on his chair and gesticu-lated wildly, was a poet named Povl Berger. Cheered on by his drinking partners, he called Dr. Nathan his "hero," then his "God." After he emptied his glass, he crushed it in his hand to honor him, and blood ran over his fingers. Per sat openmouthed. He felt he was in a madhouse.

In the course of the night, new guests joined the company, and two small tables were brought in to accommodate them. For practical reasons, the tables were not placed in the row, but on the sides, so that the whole company formed a cross.

A bellow, a thunderclap, erupted. It was Fritjof shouting, "We will not sit here under this cursed sign of Galilee! Piety nauseates me! Let us form a horseshoe. We will bargain with the devil, honor his very footwear. Move out, friends!"

When everyone had indulged him and all had again taken their seats after the uproar, he lifted his full cup and proclaimed,

"I greet you, Lucifer. Holy rebel! You guardian spirit of freedom and happiness! The god of all younger devils! Grant me many fat butter merchants and I will build you an altar of oyster shells and empty champagne bottles . . . Hey, proprietor! . . . Gripomenus! More wine here! Hey, is anyone listening?"

The proprietor, a little Swiss man in a short jacket, popped in through the restaurant door, which had been closed and unlit for some time. Shrugging and gesticulating, he begged pardon, but he couldn't serve any more this night; it was past two, and the street's friendly watchman had already once knocked on the pane to warn him.

"The time! The time!" shouted Fritjof. "We are gods, Gripomenus! Time is for tailors and shoemakers!"

"Yes," answered the little proprietor, with his head tilted to one side and his hands folded on his chest. "And for restaurant owners—unfortunately." When he noticed that his joke had been well received, he added, with a smile, that he would be glad to accommodate the gentlemen again the next day; they could come early if they wished. "We open at seven."

But Fritjof flung himself back in his chair and reached deep into his right trouser pocket. "We shall have wine!" he bellowed, as he scattered a handful of clinking coins all over. "Here is the butter! Will you have more? Drink, friends. Let the mess be! We are not philistines."

But this grandiosity was too Olympian for his companions. They suddenly became sober and busied themselves picking up the coins that had rolled onto the floor, while Fritjof still went on shouting: "Wine—we shall have wine and women! Wine, I say!"

Gradually, the drinking bout broke up. The proprietor respectfully took every guest aside, and amicably asked each one to leave the premises "because of the police." He led them out through the back door. Only Fritjof was unyielding and kept shouting.

At last, only Per was left with him, but since he, too, wanted to leave, Fritjof grabbed his arms and tearfully threatened, begged, implored him to stay.

Per let himself, finally, be persuaded. He felt he couldn't be responsible for leaving the painter in such an inflamed state of mind. With Fritjof's promise to stay peaceful, "Gripomenus," shaking his head, brought in coffee and cognac and shuffled away.

Fritjof planted his elbows on the tabletop and propped his bearded head between his hands. He suddenly became silent and stared down through half-closed eyes.

Per sat at the other side of the table and lit a new cigar. A single half-lowered gaslight burned directly over their heads. The rest of the large room was barely visible through the gray veil of whirling dust and tobacco smoke. The clutter of empty tables and chairs was all around them just as the guests had left them: a mess of cigarette ashes, champagne corks, and broken glass littered the tables. But it was quiet now—so strikingly still after the wild noise that each sound could evoke a faint echo from all the corners of the room.

Since Fritjof sat without a word, Per thought that he had fallen asleep at last. He clinked his glass against Fritjof's: "Skål." Instead of answering, Fritjof began to talk mournfully of death. He looked shakily at Per with his purblind eyes and asked him if he ever felt uncomfortable when he thought *here* about what might be *there*—on the other side of the grave.

Per, who did not have such impulses and was far too concerned with his present life to project possibilities of a future life, thought, at first, that Fritjof was joking. But when he started to laugh, Fritjof seized his arm and said half anxiously, half commandingly, "Quiet, young man! Let us not forswear anything! It's very easy to be careless about it in your green years. But wait until you have your first gray hair and feel a queer sort of tingle when you think that your well-cared-for body one day shall be served as a celebratory meal for some hundreds of hungry worms. Just a little superfluous fat around the heart—done! A pillow of shavings under the head, eight screws in the coffin lid—and voilà, the table is set! Let us not forswear anything, I say. Perhaps there is still more beyond the stars than our modern Hebrew prophets dream of. In that case, what then? Won't there come a day of reckoning for us all? We imagine ourselves to be so smart. Yes, indeed! But happier? Skål!"

Per's eyes opened wide. He stared at that bearded wild bear, that high priest of happiness and the cultivation of beauty in life, who suddenly displayed himself as the soulmate of Per's father and mother, a spirit from the underworld who wandered in the realm of shadows, whose thoughts circled around the grave and the beyond—in dread of the powers of light he had, just a moment ago, so exuberantly conjured up.

This was not the only time Per got such a surprising insight into the inner feelings of the "Independents" and made out a dark side, an irrepressible remnant of a haunted self that, in an unguarded moment, would play unpleasant games with their day self. He would watch the "last Greek," Reeballe, when he was uncharacteristically sober, struggle fairly seriously to sustain his conscience, and Lisbeth regularly fetching her confirmation hymn book from the chest of drawers whenever she felt her hip pain or was frightened she was pregnant.

Gradually it dawned on him what it was, in general, that crippled the power of human beings and made the world a big hospital for invalids. Some sought consolation in drink, others drowned out the "inner voice" with childish boasting and wild games, a third kind, anesthetized, shut themselves up as in a snail's shell during a storm, while a fourth lost themselves in idle dreams of a future anarchistic brotherhood among men—so everyone, in general, belonged to one of these groups and struggled with ghosts, while life, ruddy-cheeked and smiling, invited them to the celebration around them. He recognized it all from his childhood!

Suddenly, the dizzying sensation swept over him that he would be someone exceptional, special, a man who already as a child, through a happy chance, had broken his chains while the age's freest spirits were still in thrall. Ivan Salomon's words—that Per had Aladdin's luck and God's legend on his brow—bore a fresh and extensive significance. He had only to wish, to desire without scruples, and all life's glories would be his!

So, conquer then; he was a king's son! He already wore the ruler's crown on his head. And there had already been one who had seen its glimmer and read the inscription: "I come, I see, I conquer."

CHAPTER 3

ONE DAY, AFTER long consideration, Per collected some rolls of drafting paper and computation copybooks and sought out Professor Sandrup in his private quarters to ask him to look at his canal and fjord realignment project and render his opinion. The professor ran his eyes over the plan, silently set his glasses on his long nose, and uttered small grunts of dissatisfaction. With the discomfiting capacity that old teachers develop, in the course of years, to be able instantly to finger a work's weak points, he quickly indicated a mistake in Per's calculation of the current's velocities.

Per could deny neither the existence of the mistake nor its consequence for the whole plan. He blushed a flaming red and made no attempt to defend himself. The professor again took off his glasses as he acknowledged Per's interest and industry evident in his work, but earnestly advised him not to spend more time on this kind of useless experiment—to apply himself, rather, to the practical and regular study of prescribed examination subjects.

When Per got home he again spread his papers out in front of him and studied them thoroughly. It didn't help. The mistake could not be disregarded. It had slipped in at the very beginning of his computations and the adjustment would have a consequence, as the professor had correctly seen, that the projected middle water level at the river's lowest point would be depressed below sea level. In other words, the whole plan rested on a false premise and could not be achieved.

Once again his face flushed with shame. His whole proud kingdom had collapsed in ruins. For over an hour he sat hunched inertly over the table with his head in his hands.

Suddenly he stood up, threw the sketches, calculations, and estimates pell-mell into a drawer, lit a cigar, and strode out into the city, where he spent the afternoon in a billiard room. He walked around, loudmouthed and in shirtsleeves, playing with anyone who asked him. He was, moreover, unusually sure in his strokes and won game after game. No one who saw him could imagine that he had, the same day, suffered such an ignominious disappointment.

Late in the afternoon, an acquaintance came in who offered a ticket for sale at half price to an artist and student carnival that evening. Per bought it instantly.

The next evening, he stood in snowy weather with his coat collar up and waited on one of the dark, quiet corners of Frue Plads. There wasn't a person in sight. No footprint could be seen in the white snow that carpeted the ground around the church. The statues of Moses and David in front of the entrance looked like a pair of Holberg lawyers with big, white wigs and black cloaks.

Per waited for a lady, a young woman he had met at the carnival and danced with half the night. He didn't entertain high hopes that she would come. This was his first love adventure with a genuine lady, and she had given him no promise. She had virtually rebuffed his bold request with a self-conscious jest.

The bell in the tower had long since sounded nine, and he was thinking of going home, when someone cleared his throat behind him. It was a messenger, who asked his name and then gave him a letter. Per moved under the nearest streetlight, and while his nostrils flared to take in the stationery's scent of violets, he read, "Obviously, I have not come. But I'll try to get you an invitation to a party at the manufacturer Fensmark's next Sunday. I think there is a shortage of gentleman dancing partners." The letter bore no signature, but there was a postscript: "I am really angry with you. I hope you are a little ashamed of yourself."

Per shoved the letter into a pocket and smiled with satisfaction. He thought of Lisbeth. He could now, finally, get rid of her. He had long felt a distaste for such virtual prostitutes with their crudeness and fickleness, fleas and filthy bedrooms. A richer and better love life would now begin for him. His fantasy rolled out a thrilling future of amorous adventures, dangerous assignations, secret cab rides, hidden hand squeezings under the table, stolen kisses behind a fan, horrendous confessions.

From Skoubogade he turned onto Vimmelskaftet, where he abruptly interrupted his beautiful fantasies with a coarse oath. A little man in a sable coat under a big umbrella came directly toward him on the sidewalk. Despite the fact that the umbrella hid the whole of his upper body, Per had recognized him immediately by the quick pace of his steps. It was Ivan Salomon.

To avoid him Per quickly stepped over the gutter to cross the street, but it was too late. A loud greeting—"Herr Sidenius! Isn't that Herr Sidenius?"—pinned him in place.

"If you are on your way to the Pot," said Salomon, "I would dissuade you. I have just come from there. This evening it's hard to endure the boredom. Only Enevoldsen is there; our good poet sits absent-mindedly and polishes his lorgnette. He was obviously having great difficulties over where to put a comma. Shall we go somewhere else? Will you give me the pleasure of dining with me this evening? You're free, aren't you?"

Per yielded; he couldn't think of any objection that Salomon wouldn't be able immediately to overcome. Besides, he didn't have any great desire to go home to be with himself in a rotten mood because of what lay in the bureau drawer. He wouldn't be able to sleep. Since the man wanted his company, why not this one time?

Shortly thereafter, they sat on a wine-red velvet sofa in a newly built elegant restaurant of a hotel favored by traveling country gentry and commissioned officers. An expensive Brussels carpet covered the floor, and large mirrors graced the walls. Service was quietly plied by waiters in formal jackets, and the patrons, several of whom were women, carried on soft-voiced conversations.

Per felt, at first, a bit ill at ease. Not only was he unused to moving in such distinguished circles, but he was especially embarrassed about being there with Salomon. The latter, with his raucous and uninhibited manner, attracted an ill-willed attention.

A patron sitting alone, whom Per had not yet noticed, looked up crossly from his newspaper. He was roughly forty years old, a tall, slack, skeletal figure, nearly bald, with an emaciated face, a long, blond mustache, and a gold pince-nez. He had scrutinized Ivan Salomon with a critical glance, but as soon as he caught sight of Per, a blush suffused his pale cheeks and he hid behind his newspaper so that nothing of his body was visible except a pair of long, crossed legs.

"What would you like to eat? Some oysters?" asked Salomon, as he pulled off his rich brown gloves and stuck them between the two lowest buttons of his waistcoat. "Do you have really fresh shellfish this evening?" he asked the waiter, who responded with a slight, nonchalant bow.

Per couldn't make himself admit that he didn't particularly care for this elegant dish, but, on the other hand, didn't want to miss the opportunity for a solid dinner. He was hungry from the long wait in the cold air. He yearned for meat, cheese, and eggs, many eggs. "Oysters are good," he said, "but I confess I am hungry as a wolf."

"Bravo, excellent!" Salomon rejoiced, and clapped his hands, inciting all of the highly vexed patrons, even the ladies, to turn toward them, and the single gentleman's lorgnette to peek out for a moment over the edge of the newspaper.

Salomon continued questioning the waiter: "Let me hear what else you have this evening."

The waiter rattled off a list of dishes.

"Let us have all of it—everything!" Salomon shouted with unbridled gaiety as his arms swept over the table. "Lay it on! A fine supper! And quickly, little friend! We are as hungry as wolves."

Per, who had seen that even the waiter's expression was condescending, knew no other way out of his embarrassment than to adopt Salomon's tone. He took a toothpick from the holder on the table, leaned back in the sofa corner, and cast a challenging glance around the room.

The shellfish was served on a bed of ice with a chilled bottle of champagne. Wild fowl, asparagus, omelets, cheese, celery, and fruit followed. Per ate heartily. He mused that since he might come here only once, he should really take advantage of it. It was the first time in his life he had been favored with such a royal offering.

While Salomon only pecked at the first dishes, his incessant conversation was lavish. He commenced his favorite theme, the Renaissance. "Mankind's Golden Age," he said. "Poets, artists, inventors—all the magnificent talents—were living like princes, honored by kings, loved by queens; geniuses in our day starve in a garret room and hardly count in good society. Consequently, their work so often misses the mark of greatness, the kind of power that irresistibly sweeps you away. I spoke before of Enevoldsen. God knows I hold his talent in high regard. I consider his *Creation* a lyrical masterpiece. But after that—is it not so? Filigree work, charming figments of imagination, pretty statuettes instead of monuments. For three days he has been pondering one adjective. He is missing great experiences, that's the thing. Ah, if one were rich, rich, rich!"

He leaned against the sofa back with hands clasped behind his neck and sat with a leg tucked under him, displaying a bit of a red silk stocking.

"I thought you *were* rich," remarked Per dryly, just to say something.

"Ah, rich! ... No, one should be able to strew millions around, scoop gold with both hands! Geniuses should be established like small princes around the country, surrounded by courts, hunts, masked balls, mistresses! Think of Rubens! Think of Goethe, of Voltaire!"

He stretched across the table to fill Per's glass. Then he tried to make his guest talk about himself and his future plans. An acquaintance he had in common with Per, also a student at the Polytechnic, had informed Salomon that the young man, outside of his regular studies, was working on some kind of invention. It bothered Salomon not to have been able to make Per reveal this in order to offer him support.

But Per was now less than ever inclined to this kind of confidence. He pretended not to understand anything. When he finished his meal, he lit a cigar and leaned back, no longer paying attention to the other's effusions. His thoughts, on fire from the wine, gravitated to Fru Engelhardt, the woman from the carnival. Meanwhile, his eyes traced swirling clouds of cigarette smoke transforming into a high, floating flower, a billowy alcove curtain from behind which Fru Engelhardt's ripe body was barely visible in all its sheer loveliness. He realized, for the first time, how much in love he was. Admittedly, if he were honest, he would confess that his feelings for her, until that moment, had not differed greatly from those he entertained generally for pretty, full-bodied women. The only thing that gave him pause was the matter of her age. Hardly young, yet certainly not over thirty, but even if she were, her dark brown eyes, as large as a pair of ripe chestnuts, her bold carriage in her enchanting Columbine costume, her heaving shoulders, the trembling nostrils of her little snub nose—all betrayed a youthful ardor, a proclivity to passion, that canceled out the age question.

His eyes fell on the gentleman with the gold lorgnette, who, at last, had laid aside his paper and now was summoning the waiter for the bill. When their eyes met, they both raised themselves up a little to make a ceremonial greeting.

"Good Lord, that's Neergaard!" Salomon exclaimed. "Do you know him?"

"Not really . . . I bumped into him by chance yesterday at the carnival."

"What? Were you there? . . . I didn't see you."

"It was terribly overcrowded. You were there too?"

"Yes, I was there; I was Hamlet! Didn't you see me?"

Per well recalled having seen a little black-costumed knight in the crowd with a lady dressed as a snow queen, who had kindled a sense of scandal in the other ladies, partly because of her daring décolleté, and partly because of the diamonds decorating her white veil like glittering rainbows of frost crystals.

"You were with a lady?" asked Per.

"My sister—yes."

"Ah . . ."

Meanwhile, the gentleman with the gold lorgnette had stood up and was, at that moment, about to don his coat with the waiter's help. Per observed with some envy his very correct and elegant clothes, the cool sophistication with which he let the waiter bring him both his hat and his cane, and then the way, with merely a movement of the hand, he requested a light for his cigarette.

The previous night, when Per had danced for the first time with Fru Engelhardt, Neergaard had popped up beside them and introduced himself. After that, he had steadily watched them from a distance, suggesting to Per that he must be a rival.

As Herr Neergaard passed their table to leave the restaurant, Salomon waved amicably and exclaimed, "Good evening, Neergaard . . . Good evening! How are you?"

Herr Neergaard lifted his eyebrows as if greatly surprised. Then he smiled indulgently and, not even taking the cigarette from his mouth, responded with a detached nod. In contrast, he greeted Per with almost exaggerated courtesy that obliged Per, once again, to get up to bow.

When he had gone, Per asked, "What kind of a fellow is he, really?"

Salomon shrugged. "Don't know what I can say . . . I don't really know him well. Merely met him now and again at social occasions. He was once an eminent person. He is a law graduate, bears a distinguished name, and has excellent connections . . . In other words, he had chances to make a brilliant career in our small circle. There was also once talk about appointing him to the diplomatic service . . . to the legation in London, I think. That interested even the Prince of Wales. I don't know what it was that blocked the way. In any case, he wouldn't take an appointment. He certainly is a peculiar man. Now he holds an extremely modest post in one of the ministries."

The day after Per received the invitation to the ball Fru Engelhardt had promised to get for him, he busied himself to improve his wardrobe so that his appearance in Copenhagen social circles would not appear shameful in the eyes of the other gentlemen. It was obvious that he needed to borrow some money.

He was introduced by one of his café acquaintances to an old one-time farmer who made his bit of capital grow by lending it out to young men at an interest rate of sixty percent, secured by the borrowers' life insurance policies, books, furniture, and christening and vaccination certificates. He required, as well, a ceremony of verbal guaranties, with a hand on the Bible, in the presence of witnesses.

Madam Olufsen was wide-eyed at the introduction of each new item that, almost daily, was brought into the house from the town's big stores. She and her husband often discussed what could be going on. Per said nothing. In fact, when he was at home, which had become seldom, he was very reclusive. The only one who could have shed some light on the situation was the silent Trine. Love's thousand-eyed instinct had quickly instructed the simple girl—so far as her understanding of this sort of thing could reach—as to what was developing here. And more frequently than ever, she would take refuge in the privy when sorrow overwhelmed her and she could be alone with her tears.

She devoted herself with even greater care to his small rooms, zealously attending to and fussing over everything that belonged to him, especially the new things she took to be his wedding wardrobe, as if it were a matter of her own happiness. She sewed labels on the fine linen, handkerchiefs, and silk stockings, and laid clean paper in the unlocked bottom drawers of Per's bureau, where they all would be placed. When the evening of the ball came, it was she who knotted his white necktie, buttoned his gloves, told him his new tailcoat fit him well and that his barbered hair looked good. And at eight thirty, when the ordered cab had not yet come, it was she who railed against the tardy fool of a driver and who, in the sleet and darkness, without a hat or shawl, ran up and down Adelgade, trying to get another cab.

By the time Per stepped into the ballroom, the dance had already begun. A dozen pairs waltzed elegantly over the floor, while an equal number stood or sat along the walls. Among these he quickly discovered Fru Engelhardt sitting in a fire-red silk dress and fanning herself with a large down-bordered fan. A gentleman with a shiny bald head, rocking his top hat on his knee, sat at her side. It was Neergaard.

The sight of that man put a damper on Per's mood, especially at the jealous thought that *his* presence also was owing to Fru Engelhardt's favor. Per did not dance in the first quarter hour, but stayed in the neighboring room where some older men were playing cards. Only toward the end of the first waltz did he bow stiffly before his young friend without looking at her escort. She seemed reluctant to recognize him. Finally, she stood up, gathered up her train with a half-motherly smile, and pressed her full body against his arm.

"What an ungrateful man you are," she said in her Copenhagen dialect after they had danced a few times around the room, without Per having uttered a word. "You haven't once thanked me for the invitation I got you. It wasn't so easy, I want you to know."

"I am deeply obliged, Fru Engelhardt."

"How formal! Is something bothering you?"

"Yes, a little."

"And what's that, if you can trust a lady?"

"Why is Neergaard here? I can't stand him. You'll do me a kindness if you don't dance with him."

"I must say, that request is a bit presumptuous." She laughed and pressed again against his arm. Per laughed as well. Her secret sign of trust, the scent of her hair, and the half-bare bosom resting on his chest inflamed him. They danced four rounds, and by the time he led her back to her place, Neergaard had disappeared. Per saw him a little later standing at the other end of the room, paying court to a young girl with long yellow braids down her back.

Meanwhile, the ball dragged on slowly through the first dances without anyone much enjoying the party except for the servants, who were permitted from time to time to look into the room. Only when the gentlemen in the side rooms discovered that refreshments had been brought out did things get more lively. This assemblage was somewhat mixed and the tone fairly unrestrained, as is generally the case in cultivated families without grown sons, whose ball partners are procured from acquaintances or acquaintances' friends with no voucher other than an address out of a directory. Since the guests felt in no way obliged to the house, they carried on freely, yawning and criticizing and making demands as if in a public place.

The host, a little white-haired man who didn't even know the names of his guests, moved about anxiously through the rooms and felt more alien than anyone. With a forced social smile, he conscientiously performed the duty laid on him by his wife and daughter, "to put the dancers to work." Whenever he found a gentleman idling before the paintings on the drawing room walls, or stopping a little too long for refreshments, he positioned himself at his side and initiated a conversation that began innocently enough with some observation about art, or theater, or skating, but invariably ended with the guest, under his supervision, turning back to the dance room, where he presented himself to one or another of the house's old friends whose dance card had some blanks.

Fru Engelhardt had promised Per the cotillion, but when refreshments were finished and the dance began, he sought her in vain in both the hall and the adjacent rooms. At last he found her in a little, dim, six-cornered tower room on the other side of the living room. She sat all alone on a sofa in a corner that could be seen only after entering.

She greeted him with a gentle, tired air of sadness and said that he had the right to be angry with her, but she had no more desire to dance, and understood that he would think it required him to leave the dance, too, to keep her company. She could not accept such a complete sacrifice on his part. He must not feel obliged to stay.

Even with his social inexperience, Per was not so naive as to miss her meaning. He shoved a chair over by her side, and for a time the two sat silently, while the music and noise—quite muted, since it had to pass through two or three large rooms—reached them from the dance. Suddenly Per took her hand resting on the sofa arm, and since she let him hold it, he declared, in plain words, his love and his desire for an assignation. She did not seem unwilling, and he bent over her white arm and planted one, two, three kisses up to her elbow. He had really thought she would prevent him; she did say she would be seriously angry if he did it again—but the glance of her moist eyes and her swelling bosom contradicted her words.

Footsteps were heard outside the room, and Per had just enough time to push himself back in the chair when Neergaard's tall form appeared at the door. He bowed politely, excusing himself, but remained standing there hesitantly with his hands behind his back.

"Come in," said Fru Engelhardt.

"Do you want company?" asked Neergaard in a provocative way that displeased Per.

"Not really. But if you have something amusing to tell us, we'll be glad to hear it."

"Ah yes . . . You and Herr Engineer Sidenius sit here so drearily alone . . . so completely abandoned by the world."

"Yes," she sighed, fanning herself gently and leaning back in the corner of the sofa. "It's so depressing how tired I am . . . completely done in by the dance and so many people. But you? Why aren't you dancing? You seemed so thoroughly engaged tonight."

"No, dear lady," he said, finally deciding to enter the room. "Now I think I, also, am in a gloomy mood and will practice saying a clean farewell to the world—you permit?" He pulled up a chair so that Per and he sat face-to-face without even having greeted each other.

Fru Engelhardt's tongue became very busy. She commented on several of the ladies' dresses, criticized the social conglomeration, and then, by contrast, strongly praised the food. Per looked at Neergaard and didn't say anything. Nor did Neergaard. He had bent forward so that his face was obscured. His elbows rested on his knees, and his long hands, slightly shaking, played with the gloves on his lap.

"How boring you have become, Neergaard," she blurted. "You who once were so entertaining. What really is wrong with you? It's probably something to do with a woman."

"Perhaps."

"Yes—there's the little Frøken Holm. Naturally! . . . She might be just your style. I'll say it to you, Herr Sidenius: Herr Neergaard has always been courteous enough to tell me that he goes for the blond and blue-eyed. And all the better bargain if she comes from the country." She turned once again to Neergaard. "The pure scent of clover, summer sun, and sweet milk . . . a genuine dairymaid—that's what I always wished for you . . . When shall the wedding be?"

Herr Neergaard, who had lifted his head, leaned back against his chair, with his hands folded on his top hat resting on his stomach and said with a sigh of resignation, "When you've reached my age, it's most sensible to look on yourself as already dead. Then you have only to take care that you have a dignified funeral."

Fru Engelhardt laughed. "You are really too bleak for this world. What should we poor women say? Look at the old cavalry captain Frich in there; he is sixty-two and leads a dance like a young lieutenant. I'm convinced he is still a lady-killer . . . Ah, no, at your age, men still have a lot of happiness in store."

Neergaard bowed to her. "I thank you, dear lady, for your consoling graveside speech. I well realize that today, men as well as women know the art of conserving the really striking freshness of youth into maturity in the way we have learned to conserve peas, asparagus, and other summer vegetables. But an old preserved cavalry captain is still, to me, an abomination. No, we should resign ourselves to our age, give to youth what is youth's—and save ourselves many tribulations. At my age, a man can have tribulations enough. Rheumatism, indigestion, gallstones, and then the operating table—these are the real assets on the wrong side of forty."

"Oh, but memories," Fru Engelhardt said softly. "The good memories, Neergaard, have you forgotten them?"

"Memories—hmm! Aren't those a kind of preserved commodity, a poor winter comfort against their loss from the vanished summer? No, let's not talk of memories! Just one more nuisance—so that, as we gradually age, they make us feel all life's incidents as a steadily weaker and wearier repetition."

"Ah, you're altogether impossible tonight. But I excuse you. You're sick, Neergaard . . . You live an altogether irregular life. You should really talk to a doctor. I'm certain he will prescribe a cure in Carlsbad."

"Perhaps . . . Or, instead, those tried-and-true iron pills in a fully loaded revolver. As a painkiller, they can't be beat."

"Ah, I won't talk to you anymore. You can't be serious for a moment."

During this exchange, Per had shifted his eyes from one to the other. Their intimate tone had once again made him a little troubled about this relationship, but he calmed himself by recalling Fru Engelhardt's remark on carnival night, that she and Neergaard knew each other from childhood. Also, save for the witty recommendation of a stay at the distant Carlsbad, he interpreted her consistent demeanor toward Neergaard as annoyance at his importunities.

The dance was virtually over; in the room's dusty mist only three or four couples, giddy with love, whirled on while the music repeated its band beats in faster and faster tempo. But it started to be lively in the rooms where tired and breathless pairs settled themselves around the always well-stocked refreshment tables.

Carriages began to ride off. Fru Engelhardt went around the room to make her farewells on the arm of her husband. He was a tall, stout, good-natured wholesaler who had spent the evening playing cards. When they were going past Per, to his dismay, the wife stopped and introduced him. The husband took his hand and uttered some polite words, but Per was so embarrassed he could not look him in the eye.

Why did she do that? he wondered, a bit disconcerted, when at the same moment he heard her say very loudly to her husband in the middle of a crowd at the door, obviously with the intention that Per should hear her, "Is it not Tuesday you go to London, dear?" The wholesaler confirmed this. Per turned red and smiled; then he turned pale and smiled again with a long, radiant look, his eyes following the white shoulders above the red silk dress. Yes, now his life would begin.

Toward three o'clock, Neergaard and Per were walking home in the moonlit night. It wasn't Per who had sought this company, but when Neergaard, on leaving, had asked him where he lived and whether he could join him since he was going the same way, he couldn't say no. He considered the offer as the final acknowledgment of his victory in the battle for Fru Engelhardt—a peace offering. In addition, he found it hard to resist the worldly man's show of politeness to him, in spite of the difference in their ages.

Neergaard spoke of the social gathering and of the whole evening's diversion. But Per was too busy with his own feelings and with the evening's events to take in more than the words alone. Despite the sharp frost and their slow pace—Neergaard's legs were a bit uncertain—Per walked with his coat unbuttoned. The sense of his victory warmed him. Smiling, he puffed thick tobacco smoke out into the bright air.

They turned from the canal at the Holmen Bridge and went farther up, on the left side, to Kongens Nytorv. They passed the national bank, whose heavy square mass rose up toward the starry heavens like a mighty sarcophagus. A sentry in a red cape guarded the entrance.

A while later, Neergaard stopped in front of one of the old small and unimpressive houses that were still permitted to stand next to the broad thoroughfare.

"So, here's where I live. Won't you, Herr Engineer, give me the pleasure of coming in for a glass of good wine? It's still not late."

Per thought it over, and said yes. He felt the need to let himself go and had, to be sure, no interest in returning home. From the day he had locked his papers in his bureau drawer, he moved around his room as if he had buried a body under the floor.

A few minutes later he found himself comfortably seated in a corner of the couch behind a large table on which a tall pedestaled lamp with a green shade burned. While Neergaard rummaged around in the next room to get the drinks ready, Per inspected the pretty and elegant bachelor's quarters, which made him dejected about his own poor, cramped rooms. How could he receive a lady like Fru Engelhardt there? Here, the whole floor was carpeted. Inlaid mahogany furniture. Vases and gilded branched candlesticks. All kinds of old inherited pieces in view. And there on the wall over the desk appeared, in the half-light, a host of large and small portraits: paintings in gold frames, daguerreotypes, silhouettes, small ivory medallions, lithographs, drawings, modern photographs . . . a shadowy row of the departed Neergaard clan. After a closer examination, he saw it was all, to be sure, a bit neglected. The carpet was nearly worn out, and the upholstery was faded. On the large, beautiful bookcase full of rows of bound books, he noticed a pair of cracks in the glass panes.

Neergaard appeared with a long-necked bottle and two green glasses. He seated himself in an armchair across from Per and poured out drinks with great care. "It makes me happy to have made your acquaintance," he said, as he lifted his glass. "Permit me to drink to your well-being, Herr . . . Herr Lucky Per!"

Per regarded him, somewhat surprised and annoyed by the unvarnished allusion to the evening's events. But since the intention was to pay homage to the victor, he wouldn't show himself to be offended. He took up his glass and downed his wine. "That particular, witty nickname is not *my* invention," volunteered Neergaard, and started to polish his lorgnette. "I'm only quoting one of your friends. I mean little Salomon, whom I saw you with the other day. He's your great admirer. The name, in my sense, is not really flattering. There's an old adage about luck—that it is the guardian of fools. And a venerable Latin author wrote this about luck—that it is the father of care."

Per thought, Yes, console yourself. Now you're even!

"So that this doesn't sound like a hateful paradox," continued the other, "I will say that the unlucky seem to me to be the luckiest. They have the satisfying situation of being able to grumble about fate, slander God, demand recompense from providence, and so on, while he who, as they say, sits on luck's lap can only accuse himself for unlucky occurrences."

"But why should he have bad luck?" remarked Per, smiling and gazing at the smoke from his cigar.

"Why?" said Neergaard, the whole time sounding a note of sympathy missed by Per. "I don't think you really understand me, Herr Engineer! I mean—despite my dislike for paradox—that especially the lucky are the most unlucky, and this can well be a man's lot particularly in our day. In nine-hundred and ninety-nine of every thousand cases, we lack the capacity to make good use of luck so that it becomes more gain than loss. And in our age, we have not learned to trust the marvelous—that's it. We feel, at the table of luck, like a peasant at a king's banquet. When it comes to it, we all prefer our old home's porridge and our mother's pancakes to the splendor of the land of milk and honey.

"You know, probably, the story of the young swineherd who wins the princess and half the kingdom. It's after the ending that interest precisely begins, I think, at least for grown-ups. *We* would see the peasant boy in velvet and brocade walk around pale and thin from sheer luck. We would see him lie in the princess's silk bed and blubber from longing for the milkmaid Maren's arms, thick as thighs. Because there's no doubt he will do that. He will not have a happy day before he wears again his wooden clogs and exchanges his crown and scepter for his father's dung fork."

He fixed his lorgnette on his nose and leaned back in his chair, his long hands folded under his bowed head. His tired eyes settled on Per, and with a momentary searching and compassionate, almost worried, expression, he continued: "With all our Danish wealth of fantasy, there remains in all of us a persistent predilection for the tried and tested. However passionately we storm forth in our youth to contend with the marvelous and adventurous world, when wonderland really opens its doors for us and the king's daughter beckons us from on high, we are tempted to peek back at the old chimney corner."

"You're really right, I suppose," said Per, as he gazed with a smile at the smoke cloud from his cigar. "In general it works like that. But there are exceptions."

"Not one in a thousand. Maybe even ten thousand. You yourself will experience what an uncomfortable magical power there is in all that is homely and habitual, even if we sometimes hate it. Just look, for example, how we drag around with a growing burden of family legacies that piles up as high as a Chinese wall we haven't the will to leave. We live in a sepulchral chapel of family remembrances and, finally, have no feelings other than piety."

"Well, it can't be like that for everyone," said Per. "I, for example, would find it difficult to be tempted, for what I drag about with me from my past could easily fit in a vest pocket."

"I congratulate you! But can we help it? The magical power of the homestead is not merely in material things. The mindless admonitions of our fathers, perhaps long dead, or the simple prejudices of our mothers, influence our personal stories even into our old age. And we have, in addition, our dear brothers and sisters, our concerned uncles and aunts."

"For my part, in this respect, I'm lucky to recognize nothing of all that."

"Well, I'd really like to congratulate you again. But you have had a home, probably one of those Danish pastors' houses renowned for their coziness. I infer that, you know, by your name." Per disregarded these last words and commented that he did not know now, nor ever had, what was called close relations.

"Really? You are—"

"Yes," said Per, deliberately interrupting him. "I am only myself."

Neergaard leaned forward with his hands on the arms of the chair and stared at Per as if newly awakened. "So little Salomon was not entirely mistaken. In fact, something of the fairy tale clings to you. No family relations! No concerned brothers and sisters, no well-meaning aunts and uncles! Free as a bird under heaven." Per confirmed this by failing to respond. Neergaard sank back into his chair, and, for a moment, there was a deep silence.

"You seem really to be an unusually blessed man, Herr Sidenius. If I weren't so old and doddering, I could be tempted to envy you. Free and unburdened in all your relations! And with an appetite for life like a blackbird in a cherry tree. Well, so be it. Still, where does this lead? We assume in the long course of life

the chains we are not born with. We are and remain slaves. We
feel at home only in irons. Don't you think so?"

"Frankly speaking, I don't follow what you are thinking," said
Per, and looked up at the clock by the bookcase, which said
4:15. He was tiring of the conversation's monotony—and he felt
a little put off by the frivolous tone of speech. A few moments
passed before Neergaard answered, still looking at Per with
intense interest.

"What I'm thinking . . . Ah, we pick up friends and habits in
the course of time, hog-tie ourselves with all sorts of obligations.
Not to speak of the glue that sticks us to women, called love,
desire, sexual attraction, or what you will. Even as free a bird as
you must concede that women have tentacles that, in spite of
their gentleness, can fetter a man like iron shackles."

"Ah, not so that it bothers us," laughed Per. "And least of all
when they squeeze hard."

"Yes, you are still so young. But suppose the opportunity was
handed to you that some woman or other who attracted you ero-
tically, even if you looked down on her, a tart, perhaps a nurse-
maid whom you in your youthful innocence kissed—in other
words, a creature to whom, because of habit or the force of an old
memory, you felt bound—suppose you discovered that woman
cold-bloodedly betrayed you behind your back. How would
such a free bird as you handle that situation?"

Where is he going with this? wondered Per. Aloud, he said,
"What would I do? Naturally I would get another woman."

"Very good, but if now that one also proves unsatisfac-
tory—would you then run the risk again—straightaway?"

"I'd take, in that case, a third, fourth, fifth—good Lord, there
are women enough in the world, Herr Neergaard."

"Yes, that's true, true . . ." He continued to repeat the word
while at the same time closing his eyes, as if he had found the
solution to the riddle of the universe.

Per gave signs of wanting to leave. He felt the conversation
was getting a little too personal. Also, it was late. A pair of
bakery wagons had already driven through the streets and
signaled the arrival of morning. But Neergaard was seized by
a sudden and strange surge of high spirits. He filled Per's
glass again and begged him to forget the time. "I consider myself really lucky to have made your acquaintance, Herr Sidenius.
You are an unusually fresh and delightful man. Don't take this

wrong, but it would give me pleasure to make you a proposal."

What now? thought Per.

The whole thing, Neergaard continued, might seem to Per, at first, a little bizarre, but after listening to him, Per wouldn't, surely, take things more critically than they deserve. It seemed there was one of Neergaard's friends, a near relative, who lay dying. He was very sick—had not long to live—sick in both body and soul. But that was beside the point. In short, the man, who was not married, could not decide what to do with his estate. It really consisted of nothing more than some pieces of furniture, a couple of bad paintings, a few books, approximately like what you see here. He didn't want to leave it to his family. He didn't want to keep them intact where they risked becoming objects of veneration. He demanded expressly that they should be sold lock, stock, and barrel, at auction—dispersed to the winds. That was the poor man's *idée fixe*. Since his own family, being well off, was likely to resist his wishes, because most of what he owned was inherited, he began to talk of leaving the profits to someone else who could use a little money or gain a moment's happiness. "And so," said Neergaard, "it occurred to me: Could I have permission to propose you to him? I'm convinced that, if he knew you, he would have arrived at the same thought. You're just what he often wanted to be. Free and unrestrained and unencumbered— no, I beg you—if you have nothing against this proposition, don't say anything. We'll say nothing more about it. All said, the whole is not such a significant matter . . . at best, two thousand kroner, when debts and other obligations are paid up."

He is surely drunk, thought Per, and deemed it not worth objecting. He passed the whole thing off as a joke. "Yes—that wouldn't be bad," he said. "I can always use money. But now it's time to go home, and I thank you for the evening."

"No, why are you going? Stay a bit longer! But it's stuffy in here. Let's open up!" He rose nervously and opened a window. The cold air rushed into the room and caused a long smoking tongue of fire to dart up in the lamp. "Sit down! We have been here talking and become so melancholy and the bottle is not empty. And the wine is good!"

But Per could no longer be tempted. He felt somewhat uncomfortable with Neergaard's agitation. He noticed now, as well, how pale his face had become, how clammy his hand, how he trembled at Per's farewell.

There are so many strange people in the world! he thought as he started down the street with a measured gait and a freshly lit cigar in his mouth, and began walking home through the city, where life was beginning to stir. He recalled his night scene with the great Fritjof in the Pot and reflected, "When you're tête-à-tête with them, you begin to see ghosts—graves open up and you preach your own funeral!"

Here and there a street sweeper moved in the morning haze. Small cellar shops and a single tobacco booth had opened. Although the streetlamps were still no longer lit, lights were shining from all the bakery shops and a scent of fresh-baked bread streamed out of the large window vents. Per stopped for a moment in front of one of these shops to watch a scene between a smart young girl standing on a stepladder, busying herself with putting large cake plates on a shelf, and a half-naked journeyman who sat on the counter almost under her and dangled his legs. Per couldn't hear what they were saying, but the fellow's broad grin and the feigned indignation of the girl, who, with the help of her feet, tried to keep his hands away from her, made all words superfluous.

Per smiled, while he played the same game in his thoughts with Fru Engelhardt. Yes, the night was over, life began anew, and the instincts of love had already firmly captured hearts. The factory whistles sounded now. He listened attentively to them. First he heard a few from Nørrebro, then one from Christianshavn, and finally from all over—a hundred-voiced cockcrow, matins for a new day that, for now, exorcized all the ghosts of darkness and superstition, not to be summoned again from under the earth.

CHAPTER 4

ONE DARK, MISTY evening a week later, a thin, gray-cloaked man got off a streetcar at the corner of Grønningen, went past the barracks, and walked over to the long three-cornered market just before Nyboder. He held one hand behind his back, and with the other, the handle of his umbrella, which, at each step, he forcibly stabbed at the sidewalk. He walked quickly and deliberately in the Nyboder quarter and sought to read the street signs at the corners by the weak lamplight.

When he had gone down a long stretch without having found the name he was looking for, and since there was, in that empty place, no one in sight he could ask, he turned at random at the corners and quickly became completely lost in the many small Nyboder streets, which all looked alike. There were fewer street-lights, as well, than in the marketplace. The windows of the sunken ground floors were shuttered and only a weak light fil-tered out through the small round or heart-shaped peepholes. But behind the shutters it was quite alive with a whirl of voices, the shouts of children, and, here and there, harmonica music. Outside, on the street, every word spoken could be clearly heard. Here or there a door would open and a woman in a bathrobe would, for a moment, come outside, or a couple of cats would run around in a love duet.

The gray-cloaked gentleman finally came across a few people who directed him to Hjertensfrydgade, which he set out to find. He read the numbers on the doors with the help of a match until he reached the house where Per lived. He felt for a rope bell, but when he couldn't find it, he jiggled the old-fashioned latch. Finally, he figured out how the door opened, and he entered the house's little front hall, which was so dark that he couldn't see his hand in front of his face. He cleared his throat loudly a couple of times to attract the attention of one or another of the inhabitants. The door of a ground-floor apartment, where a ship's carpenter's family lived, opened, and a woman peeked out, holding a child. Above her smoothly combed hair, the lamplight shone out toward the stranger and made visible a young, long pale face with red-bordered eyes and thin side whiskers.

"Doesn't Herr Sidenius live here?" the stranger asked without even a greeting.

"Yes, he lives in the back of the house, but he isn't home."

"Perhaps I'm speaking to his landlady?"

"No—he lives up above with the Olufsens—I'll call Madam Olufsen."

At that moment, the steep stairs creaked under a heavy tread and Madam Olufsen, who had stood listening behind her door, showed herself on the landing with a tin lamp in her hand.

"Would you like to speak to Herr Sidenius?" she asked.

"Yes, but he's not at home," answered the stranger in a tone that seemed to blame *her* for his fruitless trip. "Do you think it's worth waiting for him?"

"No, I don't think so. He went out just a short time ago."

"What time of day do you think I have the best chance to catch him?"

"Well, he's not often at home, lately. But you'd probably have the best chance in the early evening."

"Thanks. Goodbye."

"Who shall I say called?" asked Madam Olufsen.

But the stranger was already out the door. The sound of his deliberate steps and the jabbing of the umbrella point faded in the street.

"I'm sure that was a pastor; what does he want with the engineer?" said the ship carpenter's little wife, totally perplexed, to Madam Olufsen.

But Madam Olufsen was at that time not very inclined to talk about her lodger. She uttered a curt "Goodnight," and went back into her rooms.

The chief boatswain sat there, with his large silver glasses on his nose, reading *The Runaway Black Slave, or Shipwreck on the Coast of Malabar,* a novel in four volumes brought home every winter from Frøken Jordan's library and each time pored over with the same sense of awe and excitement.

"Was that someone who wanted to talk to Sidenius?" he asked without looking up from his book.

"Yes," answered Madam Olufsen, as she drew her shawl tight around her shoulders with a shiver and laid a shovel full of peat on the fire in the oven before sitting down in the armchair with her knitting. Neither she nor her husband was very talkative today. They couldn't keep from thinking that their lodger had changed lately, and not for the better. He had, to be sure, indulged himself before, but those bouts of dissipation were never played out for many days. Now he had seldom been home for nearly three weeks, and when they saw him he was silent, inaccessible, and annoyed with everything. He had even mentioned the possibility of moving. One day he had let slip that he had known the government minister who had been in all the papers lately for poisoning himself. If it were true, it could not be the best society that he had sought out.

And they had another cause for complaint. They were not receiving his rent, and, moreover, they kept running up against importunate collectors who arrived with his unpaid bills from shoemakers and tailors.

"Who was that downstairs who wanted to speak to Sidenius?" asked the chief boatswain after a while.

"I don't know him. But it does occur to me that I have seen him once before—a long time ago. I think Sidenius said that he was from the other world. But he didn't look very American."

Per was, at that moment, waiting for Fru Engelhardt on the same dark corner of Frue Plads where he had watched for her before. This time, he had a better-grounded expectation that she would come. To be sure, he had not seen her since the evening of the ball. She had sharply forbidden him to waylay her on the street or to seek any other means to come into contact with her, but today her husband was scheduled to travel to London, and she had, the day before, sent an unsigned note with the words "Tomorrow evening." He paced back and forth to make sure he was still in the right meeting place at the right hour.

He had that morning received another letter that concerned him almost more than this so impatiently awaited rendezvous. To his great sense of shock, Neergaard's lawyer announced that Neergaard, in a note left behind expressing his last wish, bequeathed to Per a sum amounting to the proceeds of an open auction of the deceased's furniture. The will, the letter added, was essentially invalid since it was not drawn up in a statutory form, but since the deceased's two sisters, the only legitimate heirs, were well off by marriage, there would be no basis to think they, both living out of the country at this time, would have to acknowledge the arrangements. The lawyer, in his capacity as estate executor, asked Per, therefore, to come by his office to discuss the matter at his convenience.

Per, feeling an inner embarrassment, could not decide what he should do about this situation. With all his fatalistic trust in his pact with luck, and though he desperately needed the money tossed into his lap, he could not consider a suicide's caprice as a heaven-sent gift. On the other hand, it seemed to him it would scarcely be responsible for him to reject such a significant sum that could relieve him of so many difficulties. There was nothing left of the loan he had procured, and the largest part of his wardrobe was not yet paid for.

But now a closed carriage rolled up out of a side street. A

bright-gloved hand appeared at the window opening. Immediately, Per jumped forward, held the carriage, tore open the door,
called out to the driver the name of a first-class restaurant in
Kongens Nytorv, and climbed in.

During the ride, he was beset by a rather sharp disappointment. He had expected to find Fru Engelhardt nervous and
restless—to see her blush and tremble under her fur coat from
anxiety and shame. He had prepared himself for some words that
could overcome her shyness; there was no need for an artful
seduction. Scarcely had he taken his seat and thanked her for
coming than she threw herself on his lap like a tart and pressed
against him so hard he almost lost his breath.

When they went up the well-lit steps to the restaurant, she hid
her face; but when a little table was brought in and set up by the
waiter in a separate small room, she threw her hat and coat off
without considering the presence of strangers. While Per acted a
little awkwardly in what was for him an unusual situation, she
seemed to feel entirely at home here, straightened her hair in
front of a mirror, drew off her gloves, and seated her full body in
the middle of a sofa behind the set table.

Per took his place in silence across from her. He gathered that
this was not the first time she found herself in such a place. He
was fairly certain he detected a restrained, knowing smile on the
waiter's bewhiskered face when he stepped in.

"Why are you looking at me?" she asked when they were
alone. She tilted her head coyly to one side and smiled a little too
youthfully. "Good God, you are virtually inspecting me. Is there
something wrong with my appearance?" She looked down at her
bosom, which bulged out over a square low-cut bodice. She was
dressed in black, tightly laced up, full-breasted, but slim around
the waist like a young girl.

"So talk, then, young man! You are a frightful bear. What's
wrong with you? You look like you just got bawled out!" She
busied herself with procuring projectiles, plucking off some red
berry blooms from the table's centerpiece. Pale from anticipation, Per gazed at her plump, white, soft fingers, their pearly
nails and the little row of dimples that opened and closed over
the rosy knuckles with every movement of the hands, like
little kissable mouths. He caught a berry that she flung at him
in the air, and seized her hand, drawing it over the table to
place it on his mouth—when, at just that moment, the doors

opened and the waiter and his helper appeared with the food.

Champagne was poured and the dishes uncovered. When they were again alone, Per smiled and raised his glass in a toast. Other glasses followed and quickly dissipated his bad mood. What the devil, he said to himself. What did her past matter? The main thing was that now she belonged to him, was his conquest. At dessert he began to talk about Neergaard's suicide. It was his opinion that the man had been depressed, and he indiscreetly told her about the nocturnal meeting in his room, about Neergaard's overwrought state of mind when he, then, decided on his will's provisions while Per was clueless. He jabbered also about a rumor that there had been a woman involved. One of his acquaintances, who claimed to receive information from Neergaard's landlord, had talked about a dark-haired woman who, for many years, had visited him, and probably was the same who, the evening of the funeral, had managed to enter the mortuary and strew floods of roses on his casket.

While Per was talking, Fru Engelhardt sat in thoughtful silence with her elbows on the table and let the tip of her little finger slide around the border of the glass. Her face had a half-absent look. It seemed as if she were just politely listening to a lengthy tale. But when Per started to dig into Neergaard's past and tell what he had heard about his abandoned diplomatic career, she manifested some impatience. She took a grape from the fruit bowl, dipped it in her wine, and began to suck on it; then she came out apologetically with a question about something entirely different that suddenly occurred to her and asked him to call the waiter to bring in the coffee. Since Per did not seem inclined to drop the subject, she got up resolutely, and said, "Thanks for the dinner," as she went over to the open piano.

"What shall I play?" she asked, after having tested the instrument with a few quick runs up and down the keys. "Do you know this?" The sound of flat notes surged from the piano's depth. "'Waldtraum,'" she declared in the middle of the performance.

Per had again become silent and introspective. It struck him as odd that she had no more interest in an unhappy man, who had been a part of her circle, her humble admirer, her dance partner, and who had, just the other night, killed himself. An uncomfortable suspicion, indeterminate and dark, fluttered into his consciousness: Could Neergaard have been something more to her? Was her indifference feigned? But he had time only to grasp at the thought in flight. Uneasy with his silence, Fru Engelhardt suddenly broke off her playing and got up; from behind she wrapped her arms around his neck and forced his head back so their eyes met. No, that's impossible, thought Per, when he saw her smiling face. She gently leaned over and gave him benumbing kisses on his forehead, his hair, both his eyes, until her lips, with sudden wildness, sought his mouth, and were glued to it so tightly it seemed as if they would never let go. She whispered something in his ear, and he got up. Without waiting for coffee, she threw on her coat while Per paid the bill, and they hurried down to the summoned carriage.

Tightly entwined, lips against lips, they drove to a hotel, where they signed the book as Herr and Fru Svensen from Aarhus.

But time after time in the course of the night, while Per lay awake in the half-lit hotel room, the suspicion again stole over him like a nightmare. He reviewed that night in Neergaard's room, remembered the words that were spoken and how he had not, then, realized their significance. With uncomfortable clarity he gradually saw through everything: the woman who lay there and slept by his side also belonged with the goods Neergaard had given him as a legacy. Yes, she had even been that man's fate, and by her lack of gratitude had driven him to death.

And he was guilty, too. His overexcited senses conjured up the shade of the dead man moving around the room. His bald head emerged everywhere in the half-light and his eyes looked with jocular melancholy at her beside him. There at Per's side lay the murderess who had stolen in to decorate Neergaard's casket with roses. Who could understand that? She was sleeping as peacefully as a baby in a cradle with her slow, regular breathing. While her husband was being tossed about on the sea, and before the body of a lover had started to decay in the casket, she was comfortably locked in another's arms. Yes, he himself was a guilty partner! Disgust and horror seized him. He could not remain lying there. He had to get up, go out.

At that moment Fru Engelhardt turned herself heavily in the bed, stretched her arms over her head, and said, half asleep, "Are you up?" He did not answer her. The mere sound of her voice made him shudder. She tried to open her eyes but did not have the strength. With a weak attempt at smiling, she fell asleep again.

Per hurriedly readied himself to leave. He wanted to disappear soundlessly without saying goodbye. He would leave a note at the desk with only one clear word: Neergaard.

But when he had put on his hat and coat and stood at the foot of the bed ready to sneak out, he fixed his glance once more on the half-naked form that lay there in an unattractive position on its back with both hands under the neck and one knee raised. The thin straps that should have held up her slip had fallen down and her face was pale with fatigue.

Per's heart beat loudly. His knees trembled. He could not tear his eyes away from that scene. Despite all his disgust and horror, he felt himself again powerfully pulled in by long white tentacles, by that swelling breast, the half-open lips flushed from kisses. He was almost afraid for himself.

He, who had not until now felt the contradictions and inner divisions in man's nature, and who had considered any given woman an innocuous play-toy, began to shudder from the dark power that drove the game with destiny and will like a storm the dust of the road. For the first time he felt engaged in battle with demons he had not wanted to believe in and had condescendingly smiled at. From deep inside him, his father's magisterial voice sounded half-forgotten words that turned him pale: "the power of darkness," and "Satan's snare."

Fru Engelhardt, awakened by his prolonged gaze, opened her big, brown eyes. Confused from her sleep, she brushed away a wisp of hair from her forehead and sat up.

"What? Are you dressed?" He didn't answer. "Is it morning already?"

He was still silent.

"Well, what's the matter? Are you sick?"

"No—not yet."

"Not yet? What do you mean? Why are you staring at me like that? What's the matter?"

"I mean, I must guard against becoming sick, deathly ill . . . like Neergaard."

A bolt of lightning flashed across her face, but then she smiled. Though she had become pale, she said in a fully controlled tone, "What kind of talk is that? What have you to do with your friend's sickness? Come to your senses!"

"I'm glad to see you refuse to utter his name now. But, at the same time, that gives you away, and I'll tell you, frankly, why I came to realize while you were asleep that you were Neergaard's lover and it was your betrayal and faithlessness that made him kill himself. Do you understand me now?" She had lowered her head and was biting her quivering lips. "Go!" she said in a low but commanding voice and while she flung a corner of the sheet over her breasts. "Go, I said, you country bumpkin."

Per leaned forward to hurl in her face the word "Bitch," but collected himself. His feeling of shared guilt kept him from speaking, and he turned around and left.

At the hotel desk he woke the night clerk and asked for his bill. While he counted out his money, he thought now there was no way he could accept Neergaard's gift. He walked home quickly through the dark and empty city.

It was that very late time of night when the streets are deserted and the houses send back echoes of the wanderer's steps. The café's last-night owls have staggered home and the police have left their posts to chat with each other. Only thieves and disreputable alley laggards are on the move. A gentleman with a rolled-up coat collar and a hat over his eyes hurried out of a hidden corner and passed Per under a streetlight. It used to amuse him to look at these kinds of sinners slinking home with impudent or guilty expressions, but this time he turned away to avoid the man's eyes. How might *he* himself look? He was not in the mood to see his own degradation reflected.

When he reached home in Hjertensfrydgade, it was with relief that he entered the two small rooms he had lately found so objectionable; now he felt an unusual sense of peace and safety. He hurriedly threw off his clothes, and when he settled into bed it was with a sensation that reminded him of how, as a boy in his childhood home, he had drawn his quilt up around his ears and, in the dark, listened to the old one-eyed servant woman tell ghost stories.

After some hours of sleep, troubled by disturbing dreams, he woke to the sound of a starling's whistle in the garden. He could tell by the tone that it was a sunny day. Still he continued to lie in bed and did not want to get up. He was tired. And why should he get up? He would miss nothing by staying in bed.

His only half-awake thoughts had, for just a moment, stolen

over to the top bureau drawer, and he turned to the wall to sleep longer. He didn't succeed. Vulnerable thoughts about that drawer and its unlucky sketches made him unhappy, kept him awake. For an hour or so he lay there with his hands behind his neck and stared at the low and rotting wooden ceiling with its blistered coat of paint. At the same time, in his sober morning mood, he went over the night's experience and was a little ashamed of his behavior. He thought he had exhibited some immaturity. In any case, a woman of Fru Engelhardt's quality deserved some respect.

After he got up and had his morning coffee, he was certain that he had done something really stupid. He had taken things too seriously, had, at any rate, been too overwrought. Had he perhaps had a little too much to drink?

Nonetheless, he continued to feel that great comfort at being home he had not felt in a long time. He lit his pipe and rocked in his dilapidated rocking chair while his eyes lingered on the ground-floor windows of a small house in the next street, visible over the fence. In one of the windows he saw a couple of red-cheeked children and a housewife who was mending socks, and outside, by a sunny wall, a hanging green cage with a linnet. He didn't know what there was of particular interest that fascinated him. It was the same little picture of trusting and peaceful every-day happiness that he had seen here for so many years. But there was something different about this morning; it was almost as if he were viewing the scene for the first time.

He was startled by a knock at the door. It was Madam Olufsen, who came in to tell him of the gentleman who had been there last evening and asked about him.

"What kind of man was he?"

"Well, I don't know that, but he didn't look very comfortable. In addition, I think he was here once before."

Probably a creditor, thought Per, and the question of Neer-gaard's inheritance pressed on him and made him anxious. Could he now defend his decision not to take the money that he needed so much? Madam Olufsen was standing in the open doorway, which was almost filled up by her tall, stout figure. "And I'd like to know, Herr Sidenius, how things sit with you. You spoke of moving."

Per smiled a little self-consciously. "I wasn't really serious. I'm staying here, Madam Olufsen. That is, if you'll have me."

"Well, yes, naturally."

"You seem to be somewhat annoyed. Well, I understand that completely. I have been a little thoughtless lately. Let's speak no more about it. But, good God, what's going on? You're all dressed up in the early morning! Are you going to communion?"

"No, but—don't you know? Skipper Mortensen came to town the day before yesterday. And this afternoon we're going to visit him."

"I'll come along. Let's meet on board. I'm really longing to see the old bird again."

"Aren't you mistaken, Sidenius? You don't seem to find such things amusing anymore."

"Nonsense, Madam Olufsen! Don't play the turkey-cock! As I said, we'll meet on board. That's that!"

However heavy her heart, Madam Olufsen had to smile. She could never resist him when he was in a good mood.

"Yes," she said, "you know you are always welcome with Mortensen. He's never happier than when he sees you. I think he's enamored of you."

Skipper Mortensen was an old friend of the house. He lived in Flensborg but came to Copenhagen two times a year with his ship to sell cheese, butter, and smoked provisions to some of the city's large delicatessens and to some personal acquaintances. When the chief boatswain had seen in his daily and thorough reading of the ship and harbor list in *Telegrafen* that the sloop *Karen Sofie* had passed through customs and was moored at the Exchange, he couldn't wait for the day and moment when a visit could be determined, and he sent Trine into the city to let young Didriksen know. A carriage driver, one of the family's friends, Didriksen lived in Store Brøndstræde, and had, for a number of years, on just such occasions, promptly put himself and his carriage at the disposal of the old couple. Punctually at three o'clock the carriage stopped in front of the house, ready to mount and so finely polished it seemed ordered for a merchant's wedding at the Vor Frue Church. After a while, the aging couple appeared, on view for the dozen or so children from the neighborhood who had gathered, and for the many grown-ups who watched the triumphant expedition from their doors and windows. Madam Olufsen was wearing a Vienna shawl and a large, bright blue bunch of grapes on her hat; the chief boatswain was dressed to the nines in his funeral suit with his twenty-five-years service medal, and his Silver Cross glimmering out from under his unbuttoned coat.

During the ride through the city, he attracted quite a bit of attention because of this badge of honor. As he sat there, white-haired and ceremonial, both hands firmly resting on the handle of his umbrella, he evoked an image of an old admiral from the beginning of the century, and it would have been no surprise if he had commanded a ready respect had not the young Didriksen—proud of his association—turned around every minute to speak to him loudly and familiarly.

First they went through the entire old city, looked at the large, new buildings that shot up everywhere, at the remains of ramparts just beginning to be razed, and the new covered omnibuses that came in from Frederiksberg and that, in the bustle of Østergade, resembled elephants with riders on their backs. From Kongens Nytorv they turned toward the canal, stopping for a moment outside the Holmen Church, where the couple had been married fifty-two years ago, and finally arrived at the Exchange on the quays.

Per was already there. He greeted them from the railing of the *Karen Sofie*, where, a bit tired out, he had seated himself to enjoy the spring sun, while the skipper—an elderly man with a full beard—came down to receive his guests. In the hull of the ship the cargo room was open—the belly, so to speak, of the *Karen Sofie*—where a ladder extended down from the deck; it was a kind of organized shop in which half-darkened hams, sausages, smoked legs of lamb, and big millstones of cheese shimmered mysteriously like a fairy-tale treasure in Aladdin's cave. With the assistance of Per and the skipper, Madam Olufsen was lowered down the ladder; the chief boatswain—who, on the sea, had to show himself pert as an old navy hand—followed, refusing any help. Meanwhile, he already stumbled on the first rung, and would doubtlessly have broken his neck if the skipper hadn't caught him in his arms. In spite of that, the chief boatswain made fun of the young Didriksen, who, the last to descend, carefully felt out each rung before putting his feet down. "That's the way a louse crawls over a comb," he shouted, a gibe heard in the Danish navy from the days of Christian IV.

After a half hour of conscientious looking and tasting, weighing and haggling, the business was closed down and the purchased provisions brought on deck. Now there occurred an incident that repeated itself year after year, with the same regularity as Riveter Fuss's joke: Skipper Mortensen opened the door to the cabin and invited his guests in for a little refreshment; but Madam Olufsen could not accept an invitation that came so unexpectedly, and the chief boatswain refused firmly because it would take too much of his friend's time, while young Didriksen, knowing all too well about these formalities, calmly dug out the tobacco from his mouth and hid it in his vest pocket.

Soon they sat down in the cozy little mess room around a richly laid table that quickly conquered all the feigned modesty. Per felt thoroughly comfortable in such unassuming company. He never ate with a better appetite than at a spread like this with substantial meats and schnapps and beer, and he found his greatest pleasure in the cheerful straightforwardness of their ordinary talk. Here, he was not—as in the Pot—a silent and critical observer. He plunged energetically into the discussion and chatted about the weather and market prices, about the ferry service and system and current administration.

After the meal, when tea and rum were brought to the table, the conversation moved over to the war years and the succeeding inflation. Of the war, Per remembered only the enemy's first invasion of the parsonage, when the garden and courtyard so swarmed over with soldiers and horses that the whole house had to be evacuated, except for the upstairs, where the large family was packed together in a few rooms. Only seven and eight years old then, he had found all this very entertaining and couldn't understand why anyone would weep over it. Skipper Mortensen, as a Schleswiger, had experienced the war closer at hand, and he enjoyed painting, with a broad brush, the horrors he had witnessed in '64 and in the Three Years' War. He also had the satisfaction of seeing Madam Olufsen cover her ears as she declared war an atrocity.

This stirred the competitive ambition of the chief boatswain. After drinking for a while, he slid easily into a military mood. He was already pensioned in 1864, and though he had not taken part in the earlier war because he was hospitalized with a bad leg, he began to talk disparagingly about these "German wars," which, as a disaster for the country, could not be compared to the wars against England that he had lived through in 1801, 1807, and also 1814. "*Then* we had it nice having to deal with the loss of both Norway and the whole fleet. Now *that* was something to talk about!" In order to trump the skipper, who had gone on about Dybbøl and Frederits, he began to talk about the bombardment and battle of Copenhagen and about the battle in the roads that he, at five years old, had witnessed from the custom house, where he had seen the wounded being brought on boats that "were like slaughter troughs, full of bloody bodies."

Since it was also beginning to grow dark, and Madam Olufsen did not want to hear another word, she expressed the desire to go home. However, it appeared that young Didriksen had fallen asleep under the impression that his fatherland had been humiliated. He sat with his head thrown back and his mouth open; when he was shaken, the top half of his body fell over, and he kept on sleeping with his head and arms on the table in spite of having overturned a beer mug, whose contents spilled onto his knees. After the company, speechless, had taken in the scene, Per lifted the rum bottle, and then he realized that it was empty and that their driver was dead drunk.

Madam Olufsen was grievously offended. Outside, on the quay, the carriage waited with the crooked-legged hack, who in all that time had patiently stood and sighed into an empty feed-bag; it quickly became apparent to all that they had to leave the man on the ship until he had slept off his drunkenness. The big ceremonial day came to a sorry end. The two old folks had to shuffle off on foot in all their holiday finery, each carrying a wrapped ham under an arm, with the sausage and leg of mutton sticking out of their pockets.

Per followed them to the Holmen Bridge, where he helped them onto a streetcar. He himself didn't want to go home; he wanted to get some fresh air after all the laughter and strong drinks. He looked for a moment in the shop windows and went along the canal up to Højbro.

It was that hour in which the sun glides high over the roofs and gilds the spire of the Helligånd Church while the nightlife is already moving energetically in the streets among the lighted shops. Outside in the market it seemed almost daylight. Here and there sparrows hopped around and pecked at the street garbage, and the newly lit lamps burned with a pale and spectral flame behind the glass where the glint of sunset flickered. Per went slowly into Østergade, which was full of people. The sight of so many made him a little melancholy. In spite of the evening cool and the red noses, spring was in the air. You could see it in the eyes of the young and hear it in their voices, which were full of expectation. Crowds gathered in clusters in front of the big window display of women's dresses to look at the new spring fashions. And all the stylish gentlemen wore violets in their buttonholes. Per was walking behind an enamored couple who were so close and moving so rhythmically as one that they seemed grown together from top to toe. He observed the young girl's eyes dwelling on her lover's face with joyous adoration, and he thought of the pleasures of the previous night. He became more and more depressed. He couldn't stop fretting over what he now, without embellishment, called her simple offense. He remembered especially one thing that now reconciled him with the love-happy woman. That was the way in which she had covered up her bosom when he was leaving. It had really been almost touching. And the roses on Neergaard's casket—she must really have loved him. What was there, in truth, to get so upset about? Life paid no attention to such things. It demanded movement, and when it rose up in all its strength, convention was scattered to the winds. In fact, there was something uplifting, something almost religiously touching, in a love drive, that couldn't be subjugated, that overwhelmed all the heart's paltry feelings, even the anxiety over death. Such a dauntless, long-forgotten submission to nature was perhaps really life's highest expression. The "dark power" before which he had trembled when he stood in front of her bed and had felt himself strongly drawn to her white arms, in spite of his pangs of conscience, was the presence of nature in him, his being's original strength, which broke through all the millennial layers of prudery. Yes, that was it. There was no hell other than what mankind, afraid of life's joy and the body's force, created in its monstrous imagination. And the embrace of man and woman was the heaven in which there is oblivion for all sorrows, forgiveness for all sins, where souls meet in guiltless nakedness like Adam and Eve in the garden of paradise.

A half-forgotten memory suddenly surfaced in fiery letters. That was Neergaard's joking remark about that peasant boy in the fairy tale, who ventured out into the world to conquer a kingdom but continually looked back, and when the magic realm opened up for him, with all the glory of the land of milk and honey, he rushed home to the cozy chimney corner and into his mother's lap.

He blushed for shame. He had made such a pitiful mess of his first try. Life had seriously tested his faith and courage. But could the damage be redressed? What if, in the hope of that, he wrote a letter to her, explaining everything and pardoning her?

When he arrived home in Hjertensfrydgade, the wife of the ship's carpenter opened her apartment door to tell him a gentleman was waiting for him in his room.

"That's the man who was also here yesterday . . . I'm sure he's a pastor. He's been sitting there for over an hour." It turned out to be his brother Eberhard. He sat in the rocking chair at the table, the lamp was lit, and the shadow of his head looked shapeless on the bare wall. He still had on his overcoat, and his hands, in woolen gloves, rested on the handle of his umbrella set between his knees. "I had almost given up hope of seeing you," he said, when they had greeted each other. "You know, perhaps, that I was here yesterday?"

Per said nothing. His heart was beating. He understood that his brother had an important message for him, since he had sought him out two days in a row. It wasn't hard to see that Eberhard was aware of the significance of his visit. His whole appearance was clearly calculated to make an impression on Per. But precisely because of that, Per gathered himself together with great effort and tried to seem entirely indifferent.

"Would you like a cigar?" he asked. While, feeling faint, he wondered, Is Mother dead?

"Thanks—I don't smoke," answered Eberhard.

"A beer, perhaps?"

"I have entirely weaned myself from alcohol. That suits me best. And besides, I don't, on principle, take anything between meals."

Per smiled. Though he felt no desire to drink, he fetched a bottle of beer from his corner cupboard and opened it. "See, I am now so self-indulgent as to accommodate the demands of my thirst without reference to the hour," he said.

Eberhard sat awhile and turned his umbrella, while his large, pale eyes watched his brother, who had come to the other side of the table and now quickly poured himself a glass of beer.

"You are certainly, in that respect," said Eberhard at last, "more conscience stricken than is necessary."

"Is it for saying that to me that you have come?" responded Per immediately in a bellicose tone.

Eberhard made a small, dismissive movement with his hands.

"You know, I never mix in your affairs. It's for an altogether different reason that I have come."

Per didn't want to answer. He didn't really dare to. The strong effect the mere hint of an unhappy message from home made on him surprised him. He had thought he had long gotten over that sensation. Anything to do with home had, in the last years, been altogether dead to him, and his brother's presence was far from stirring homesickness in him. On the contrary, as Eberhard sat there with his hands on his umbrella and watched him again from the side with his billy-goat eyes, all the past's unreconciled feelings were incited in him.

That arrogant, accusatory look and manner, that silent expression of wounded family honor, the whole stuffy air of self-righteousness that emanated from Eberhard's buttoned-up figure like the hated stink of peat smoke from the parsonage, reminded him of his childhood miseries, far back as they might be.

But behind his brother's glance lay an expression of real concern, of genuine fraternal compassion. That little cellar-like room with its ragged, worn furniture, the bare floor and blank walls—that dreary spot which, in spite of all the care with which Trine watched over her sanctuary, was the very image of homelessness—stirred in him a sympathy he wanted merely an occasion to express with all his heart.

However, Per gave him no opening, and they sat together silently for some time. "I have, incidentally, just returned from a little trip," began Eberhard, testing the waters. "I went home for a few days."

"So, was it a good visit?" asked Per.

"No, I couldn't say that. Father has been quite ill lately."

"Really?"

"He's in bad shape."

"From what?"

"I'll tell you . . . before I left, I had a long talk with Dr. Carlsen, who confirmed what I had already, for a long time, sensed from the letters from home—that Father's situation gives rise to the most serious concern. I think, in short, we ought to prepare ourselves for his passing quite soon."

Feeling his brother's eyes rest attentively on him, Per kept a straight face, though his heart pounded in his chest. It wasn't concern he felt from the news, not sadness, not even remorse. The unrest that seized him sprang, actually, from an only half-conscious sense of disappointment. It had never occurred to him that his father or mother could die before he could justify himself in their eyes by his life's triumphant work. It was humiliating, now, to feel his great original hopes struck down to earth in a moment's blow by this news.

"It's, in all likelihood, cancer," Eberhard continued, "although Dr. Carlsen didn't use that exact word; but it was obvious and sufficiently clear from his discussion of the case that he was in no doubt about it. Father is up and will go about his work as long as his strength holds out. You know how strict a sense of duty he has. But he won't be able to go on like that for many months, and I think he himself is fully prepared to die. Mother is naturally very down, but, wonderful to say, it looks as if her anxiety over Father's situation has given her new life. She has begun to get up a bit in order to be more with Father now; but I think that curious grace, however grateful she is for it, is her acknowledgment that Father's hour is drawing near."

Though Eberhard was not a theologian by profession, he had a predilection for expressing himself in biblical turns of speech. He was a lawyer, respected by his colleagues for his unusually sharp and clear juridical head. At his young age, he already enjoyed a fine reputation. And he had recently attracted notice for his newspaper article on lessons that could be derived from the state of prisons. He even had gained an appointment in one of the chief bureaus of the administration, and since he was a model of competence and conscientiousness, his superiors held him in high regard.

"I thought you should be informed of this situation," he continued, when Per persisted in his silence. "I think you should not be unprepared if the catastrophe should occur earlier than expected. We—because I speak here in the name of all your siblings and in consultation with them—we have considered that you, after you heard of Father's state, would possibly feel called upon . . . I mean you might feel the desire to seek a reconciliation with Father before it's too late."

"I don't understand—what do you mean?" asked Per bluntly, but he couldn't make himself look at his brother.

"Well, I won't, as I said before, ever mix in your affairs. It was only a suggestion—you can settle with your own conscience, whether you think you can defend the relationship you have, for so long, maintained with your parents. I don't really wish to talk

to you further about it. On the other hand, what I feel obliged
to explain to you is that Father's death will make a real difference
also in the economic situation at home. I know that Father, up
to now—without having met with appreciation from you—has
given you regular assistance that wasn't a large amount, but
which—I can say this with certainty—strained his means. And
he did it so as not to be able to accuse himself of indifference to
your studies—whatever they are—in spite of the fact that he was
not able to judge your talents or what kind of progress you were
making."

"I know that."

"That support will, naturally, stop immediately when Father
leaves this world. Mother's circumstances will be quite limited,
and it will be necessary to practice the greatest thrift on all sides."

"In regard to that, don't have any regrets for my sake,"
responded Per, who now determined to himself that he would
accept Neergaard's legacy in order to achieve complete independence from home. "I was just thinking of writing home that I am
now completely able to manage for myself in the future. I no
longer need help."

His brother was wide-eyed with surprise, but when Per gave
no further explanation, he became solemnly contemplative and
stayed silent for a while, until he could no longer control his curiosity. "But let me ask—how do you intend to—" he began, but
Per interrupted him: "I think, honestly, that you should be serious about your intention not to mix in my affairs. I have told you
before that it is very disagreeable to me."

Eberhard got up. He was pale, and his protruding lower jaw
was stiff with exasperation. "Yes—I see that it's entirely useless
to talk to you. I think it's best we don't continue."

"As you wish."

Eberhard took his hat and started to go to the door, but when
he got there, he turned again toward Per, who had remained
seated at the table, and said, "I might still mention just one more
thing, Peter Andreas, though you, with your feelings, will probably have a hard time understanding. There is nothing, at this
time, that Father concerns himself more than with you. Just now,
when I was home, there wasn't a day he missed talking to me
about you . . . and Mother, for that matter, too. They have long
since given up trying to influence or persuade you. They have
come to hope that life will humble your spirit and teach you what

your duties are. Now Father's time is soon up. Beware, Peter Andreas, that you don't commit a sin you surely—sooner or later—will come to regret bitterly."

After his brother had gone, Per still sat for a while at the table with his elbow propping his hand against his cheek as he stared somberly before him.

"Humble your spirit" . . . "bitter regret" . . . "sin" . . . "grace." How well he knew the lecture. The whole ghostly catechism repeated anew! And how typical it was—an indigenous "Sidenian" characteristic—to use sickness and death as an occasion to try once more to scare him back into the fold of home and church, to use Death itself as a recruiting officer for the solemn crowds of cross carriers.

For what did they want other than to bend him into obedience under the discipline of the family? Who was it they summoned? Was it the man nature had created in one of her bright happy moments? No, it was his subjection they impatiently awaited. His humiliation was urgent now that Father was dying. He knew them! His way of living ought to be curtailed for the sake of their own souls. Their piety could not bear the sight of a straight back and a head held high when grace had no part in it.

He looked up. His room had seemed very cold and somber since his brother's departure. Why couldn't they leave him in peace? He had himself struck a stake through the past's old, grim feelings and buried them. Why did they come to conjure them up again? His father? Well—let him die! Per owed him no love. He owed him a string of years he would rather not remember. Now, in return, he himself had blotted him out of his memory. They were finished.

He finished his glass of beer, then, like someone emerging from a bad dream, rose suddenly, and went to visit the old couple to get his mind back into balance with a chat.

BOOK 2

LUCKY PER
FINDS THE TREASURE

CHAPTER 5

EBERHARD'S VISIT AND the news of his father's sickness meant,
for Per, that there was an end to the mindless rambling by which
he had, in the last weeks, sought to forget his defeat at the hands
of Professor Sandrup. So, that same evening, taking his sketches
and calculations out of the bureau, he stared intently at the
papers, until the lines and strokes danced before his eyes and his
brain was heavy from the multiple numbers that hummed like
bees swarming in a hive. He made himself a sacred promise that
night not to stop working until he was either wholly convinced
of the plan's impracticability or had overcome all the difficulties
and carried his plan to victory.

It was not that many days later that he really succeeded in finding a way to alter his canal line, to remedy the basic mistake Professor Sandrup had pointed out. In order to be certain that he
wasn't letting himself be deceived again by a false measurement,
this time he made a detailed counter-test for calculating the current, and when he saw that the answer was correct, his happiness
and excitement erupted into an earsplitting whistle. He again
felt solid ground under his feet. The work had not been a waste;
the thousand nights it had cost him had not been squandered.
And perhaps there was enough time to achieve a triumph
before Father, at home in the parsonage, closed his eyes for the
last time.

Without further scruples, he quickly resolved the matter of
the Neergaard legacy. He persuaded himself that fineness of feeling could not be indulged when it was a question of succeeding
in the world with only his bare hands.

Furthermore, the amount of money was not as large as
expected. On his visit to the lawyer, he was told that the property
was a bit worn; with that declaration, he was content not to be
thinking about undertaking a closer inspection. The lawyer estimated that he might count on a couple of thousand kroner. This
meant he could provisionally procure for himself the peace to

work on his project for at least a year. An advance was promptly and freely given so he could settle his debts.

Now, to dedicate himself completely to the great work, he could abandon his teaching duties and the other compulsory sidelines. As impatient as a young bear coming out of his first hibernation, he shook off his long, idle torpor and plunged into his work. While springtime spread over the countryside with sun, clouds, and dark blue hail showers, he sat in his little room for the whole day and half the night, bent over his papers, dead to the starling whistling in the trees and the rose-red snow of apple blossoms sprinkling down outside his window. Each morning he awoke to the Nyboder clock's peal and already was sitting at his worktable when Madam Olufsen appeared outside in her flowered night jacket, her nightclothes still under her apron, to water the primroses in the garden.

Despite the improvement in his economic situation, Per in no way attempted to change his mode of living. This, to a high degree, was marked from the beginning by his inborn and habitual instinct for thriftiness. On the other hand, he did purchase various costly trade books and other technical writings that he needed for his work, and subscribed to a German and an American professional periodical. He no longer showed up at the institute. He suspected that his former fellow students knew about his meeting with Professor Sandrup and what had happened—besides, he thought it a waste of time to keep listening to those endless lectures by pedantic scholars who talked about the demands of practical life like a cripple about dancing.

He no longer saw Fru Engelhardt. He was mulling over the possibility of reconciliation, but he had not yet taken the first step. He continued to be embarrassed over his behavior that night, but the experience had also left some mistrust in him concerning the high price of happiness for that gallant adventure. He had asked himself whether it was really worth all the inconveniences, the playacting, and, especially, the huge expense. Every time the temptation came over him to renew the relationship with the worldly woman, all he needed to do was think of the sinful amount of money just that one evening had cost. And, most of the time, it was not hard to forget her in favor of his canal project and water-level calculations.

When the sun shone, he liked to keep his window open to the air. The sight of butterflies and bees straying in from the garden did not lure him into a lyrical mood. At most, he would whistle at work; the chief boatswain would stick his capped head in at the window to express his happiness over Per's good humor, or Madam Olufsen would set a cup of steaming coffee on the windowsill and beseech him to take a little time to breathe in the fresh air. If the good woman feared for a moment that her tenant would be disturbed, she surely would have refrained from expressing her concern.

"Drink up the coffee while it's hot," she would say, in the commanding tone behind which she liked to hide her motherly feelings for him. Per would throw down his pen or tracing pencil, light a little pipe, and lean out the window to have a chat with the old couple while they puttered about in the little miscellaneous garden, which was so narrow that two large creatures could hardly bend over without banging their backs together. With an irreverent allusion to the story of Creation, Olufsen would say, "Right here everything that was left over from the Beginning was slapped together."

It wasn't long before Per would again feel restless. He would then bend over his drawing, and visualize axes and shovels blazing in the sun, how the hills would be leveled and moors and marshes refilled; he imagined he heard the muffled drone of mining, which by the mere pressure of his fingers could shake the earth. He had once more, in various ways, altered and developed his project. In close connection with the canal system, he drafted a plan for a big new harbor on Jutland's west coast, a world-class harbor that would compete with Hamburg and Bremen. And not only that. With this projected scheme, he had hit upon the idea of releasing a great amount of energy from the North Sea with the help of large buoys bound by riveted iron plates lowered into the breakers. From this, energy could again be conducted through lines into the industrial works on the shore. Also, he thought he could utilize wind power for the motors that would be able to gather and store energy, bringing about conditions that could transform the whole land into an industrial country of the first rank.

In the evening, when the weather was nice and his head was dizzy with the day's work, Per sat outside with the chief boatswain on a bench placed by the fence under a pair of laths nailed together and covered with a scrap of sailcloth. This was the so-called Happy House, from which, in the opinion of the old man, the best overview of the garden could be had. Now and then one or another of the house's old friends would peek in, either old Chief Carpenter Bendtz, who came doddering on his cane to complain about his lumbago, or the always cheerful Riveter Fuss, with his cherry-red face and white gorilla beard. Madam Olufsen would whip up a rum toddy for each of them and Trine would have to run down Krokodillegade to fetch the riveter's guitar. A young chief gunner, who played a very pretty hopsflute, lived in the second story of the house behind the Olufsens. Every evening he sat at his open window with his long, homemade instrument, and when the riveter joined in with his guitar, it became a concert that delighted everyone in the neighborhood. Round about the quarter's windows people leaned out to listen; children in the little courtyards stopped their games and climbed up on the fences to see what was going on. And sparrows who had peacefully settled down in the trees flew over to the rooftops and sat there, silent as owls, with heads tipped to the side like small devoted listeners.

On one such musical evening, Per spotted a pretty young woman standing at an open window in the upper story of one of the neighboring houses. With her arms behind her back, she was apparently completely taken up with hearing the concert and looking at the racing clouds in the evening sky. But her blushing cheeks gave away that she was not altogether unconscious of a pair of bold eyes that watched from the chief boatswain's Happy House. *Her* house served as the official residence for one of Nyboder's chief citizens, Meister Jacobæus, whose wife was respectfully called "My Lady," at least by her husband's subordinates. Per found out afterward from Madam Olufsen that the young girl was that man's niece and that she had recently come here to the city to learn dressmaking.

After that evening, he came at sunset more regularly to sit on the bench beside the chief boatswain in order to look up at the windows of that house; it seldom failed that the girl soon appeared at one of them and busied herself with flowers or a birdcage. Sometimes she opened a window, pushed the flowerpot to one side, and leaned out, letting her glance glide over the rooftops or below into the courtyard across the street or up into the sky—in short, anywhere but down to the chief boatswain's garden. No look was exchanged between them, however much Per tried to find a silent language to send over the garden fence. One morning, when he came out of the front door, he saw her outside the house for the first time. She was crossing the street from the bakery to the other side, wearing plush green slippers and carrying a basket. He couldn't suppress a smile when he saw how unhappy, even angry, she was that he should meet her under such embarrassing circumstances. That shame only made her more charming in his eyes, and he decided to raise his hat. She acted as if she didn't see him, but in the afternoon of the same day she gave him a look that made amends. Per was just turning homeward from one of his short, brisk walks on the Langelinie when she came out of her uncle's door in a smart, bright, spring jacket with a large silk bow under her chin and a hat with a veil. For a moment, she stood on the threshold to button the last button on a pair of shiny new black gloves, after which she slowly, with both hands in her jacket pockets, walked along the wall without so much as a passing glance at the side from which Per was coming. But now, again, Per had to smile. He had caught a glimpse of her face in Meister Jacobæus's window mirror before, and he surmised that she had seen him go out and had stayed there, in all her prettiness, to wait for his return.

Per's interest was aroused, and he decided on a bolder approach. He charged Trine with getting him information about the place of her instruction at the dressmaker's shop and when she usually left it; one evening, around seven, he surprised her at Nørrevold right when she was looking into a shop window.

He greeted her with great courtesy and asked permission to introduce himself, and, to his surprise, she did not take offense at his importunity. It seemed as if she, with provincial simplicity, found it entirely natural that two neighbors who met in the big city would converse and accompany each other. However, that artlessness was not wholly sincere. She betrayed herself as they got near Nyboder, when she suddenly stopped and said he could no longer follow her. And Per, who knew that Meister Jacobæus was a jealous man, fully aware of his responsibility for his young niece, declined to ask for further explanation but said goodbye with the wish to see her again soon.

In the following days, they met frequently in the same way and went together part of the way home. With an implicit agreement, they took a cautious route around Kongens Have and Rosenborg-Gartnerierne, where they were less liable to meet

Nyboder people; and when Per lengthened the walk a little each time, she didn't object.

Fransisca (that was the young girl's name) was of middle height, blond, slim, almost thin, but very well built. Most distinctive was her gait, which indicated something fearless and confident in her character. When she went down the flagstone street with her hands in her jacket pockets and her young breasts boldly projected, people instinctively made way for her, and Per was amused to see the covetous looks of the gentlemen. The pink and white face wore a severe expression, the eyebrows darkly drawn together, which was only her way of rising above strange surroundings. She wanted, with that challenging look, to let the good citizens of Copenhagen know that there were people in Kerteminde, too.

Her apparently bold manner with Per stemmed from the same secret anxiety that she would be taken for a naive girl from the country. And Per did not misread that frankness, because it was related to his own Jutland need to assert himself. The fact that they were both from the provinces strongly promoted mutual understanding; even Per's attraction to her could have its origin in the past because her kind of beauty, her manner, and her dialectical speech awakened his memory of the blond, Valkyrie-like daughters of merchants from home with whom his first erotic feelings were connected.

Unfortunately, a row of beautiful summer evenings, light, long, and colorful, were so perfect as to awaken unrest in two young idling hearts. They had gradually lengthened their walks all the way around the lakes and always went home through the romantic stretch of land behind the still-standing remains of the city's east fortress wall, in whose high alley of old wide-crowned trees they strolled back and forth several times before they could resign themselves to parting.

What did they talk about during these long rambles? About the weather and the people they met, about neighbors they both knew, and about the day's news—never of love. Per didn't even attempt to. In the beginning, he held himself back for fear of frightening her. After that, apprehensive of her growing power over him, he avoided the subject for his own sake.

He had originally approached her without any predetermined motivation. He was accustomed to looking for carefree amusement with a young woman. His work had so thoroughly claimed his interest, and his excited, overstimulated brain had so exhausted his body's strength, that he needed rejuvenation, which, in youth, gives rise to erotic urges. But he really set himself against this, because he desired no serious relationship; and this light party mood in which nature bathed him every evening, this shimmering glimmer of gold when they met, transformed the city and the surroundings into a fairyland. Finally, the great secrecy they had to respect for Fransisca's sake, the restlessness and anxiety she could no longer hide when they parted—all this had gradually given their relationship, in his heart, an unknown, unsuspected air of enchantment; and one beautiful day he became aware that he had never really understood what love was.

And he was right.

In fact, he was in love for the first time. Although in some directions he was precocious for his age, in the realm of feelings he lived like a child, a primitive. Now he went around with a pressing sensation growing inside of him, a mystical feeling that a whole new world was about to open for him. Normally, in respect to women, he sought to make the path from word to action as short as possible; in this relationship, he was tenderness itself—so chivalrous in his conduct, so anxious not to wound, that it was a long time before he even had the courage to ask her for a kiss at parting. Since she permitted this and a blush suffused her face, he was not far from repenting of his boldness. It was with a feeling of sacrilege that he touched her maiden mouth and stole the warmth from her lips.

At the end of the summer, Fransisca traveled home to her parents for a long visit. In spite of the constancy with which, in the last days, she and Per had met, and their carelessness in exposing their increasingly tender farewells in the immediate vicinity of Nyboder, no one knew of their relationship—no one but Trine. With this simple girl's nearly clairvoyant instinct about whatever concerned Per, she had long known everything. Once, Per felt compelled to bring her into the secret by having her take an important letter over to the neighboring house, which difficult and dangerous errand Trine had completed as if it were a God-sent mission. Under the devised pretext that she should fetch a clothes peg that had blown over the fence, she entered Meister Jacobæus's well-fortified house and delivered neatly and well her secret missive into the right hands. But when Per was gone, she slinked around so unusually pale and silent and so frequently sought refuge in the privy that Madam Olufsen thought she was sick and, commanding her to go to bed, laid a strong mustard plaster on her stomach.

Upon Fransisca's return in October, the feelings of the couple for each other soon reached such a degree of intensity that Per felt it necessary to do something about it. It would be a decisive end to aim for seduction; on the other hand, he could not really think of elevating their relation to a regular official engagement. But that was without doubt the outcome Fransisca was thinking of and impatiently waiting for. She had a few times—entirely on her own initiative—acquainted him with her family relations; she had, on one occasion, let a little observation about her father's sound estate drop. But to marry a saddler's daughter from Kerteminde—that was entirely foreign to the life goal Per had set for himself. Every time the temptation came over him, he saw Neergaard in front of him and remembered his words about the swineherd prince, which, once before, had flamed up in bright letters before his eyes like a taunting "*Mene tekel.*"

Then something happened that brought about an unexpected and rash outcome. Already, for some time, Meister Jacobæus had mistrusted the reliability of the stories with which his niece explained her later and later returns from her sewing instruction, and one day he resolved to initiate an investigation. That led to an inquiry after which the girl, at last, was forced to make a full confession.

The next day, Meister Jacobæus appeared at Per's rooms and, without first identifying himself, asked him directly whether it was his intention to marry his niece. Per tried to generate some small talk, asked him to sit down, and acted half bewildered, but with a toss of his head, the angry man refused mere talk in favor of a demand for clear information. He wanted a yes or a no, nothing else.

Per hesitated to give an answer. He thought that if he said no now, he would probably never see Fransisca again, and his heart grew heavy at the prospect. He envisioned her in all probability moving around in the neighboring house in anxious anticipation, awaiting a verdict.

The thought hit him in that moment like a bolt of lightning in his heart, that he should leave all his unsure giant dreams to hold fast to this certain little sparrow of happiness he held in his hand, that he should forget the golden birds high on the rooftops and spikes. But once again, Neergaard's bald head popped up before him, and Per rose straight up and answered clearly: "No."

This occasioned a scene that afterward he could not think of without biting his lips in shame. With both hands in his trouser pockets, Meister Jacobæus moved so close to him in two heavy steps that he could feel the hair of his full gray beard tickle his face. The strange man called him an impertinent lout and a guttersnipe, and let him know that if he took one step toward his niece, he would be thoroughly punished and eased out of Nyboder like a mangy dog.

Per was chalk white with fury, but he didn't move or answer. It wasn't the man's threat that silenced him. He had stood up against a pair of clenched fists before, and his first thought, when he saw the man approach, was to grab him by the throat and push him against the wall, holding him fast until he had forced him to drop his rage. But then he stared into that pale, distorted face with the quivering mouth that showed more clearly than all the stammering how much the whole affair affected the old man, how much it had tormented and humiliated him, disturbed his head and heart deeply because of his sense of responsibility, and he kept his hands down and his mouth closed.

Later, when Meister Jacobæus had left, he had to ask himself what his offense really was. He had not wished to hurt Fransisca. If, from the beginning, he had known that love would develop between them, he would have kept away from her, but, in addition, he had not abused her confidence. The kisses they had, in all innocence, exchanged could never really cast a shadow over her future. What misfortune had really happened, then?

It was again "conscience" that had crept upon him, that indefinable, eerie something that suddenly revealed him in a magic mirror in which he saw himself as hateful and distorted. He, who had imagined himself happily emancipated from all kinds of bumps and bruises on the soul, felt as humiliated as a fool. His chagrin almost overshadowed the memory of both Fransisca and his separation from her.

It turned out that Meister Jacobæus's threats had been superfluous. Already, the next day, Fransisca herself decided to go back home to Funen. Two days later, Per received in the mail some small things that he had, at various times, given her as presents. She sent them back without one accompanying word, even of reproach. But each simple thing in the package was carefully wrapped in pink silk paper. As Per held them in his hand, a new sense of humiliation overcame him. His eyes began to moisten. He could not help it. If he had not quickly put the package in a drawer, he easily could have been, to his shame, reduced to tears.

But again, luck was gracious. Not many days later, something happened that made him forget the abrupt expulsion from love's paradise, and, as well, seemed almost like an encouraging wink of fate, a reward for his resolve. For a long time he had been struggling in becalmed, dead waters, awaiting a merciful wind to propel his adventurous voyage through life; now a storm of events gathered around him and bore him out to the open sea.

For some time, Per had come so far with his project that he meant to dare, again, to lay it before an authority for evaluation. This time he had turned to the chairman of the Engineers' Association, a pensioned military engineer he had often heard spoken of as an open-minded man and a perceptive technician who possessed significant influence; in addition, he was the chief editor of the association's distinguished journal. Per had sent him his general plan, together with a letter signed "P. Sidenius, Engineer," in which he had given a summary account of his various ideas and openly expressed his hope that the colonel might recognize the significance of the proposed thoughts and recommend them for publication in the journal.

After a few weeks, when he had waited in vain for an answer, he finally gave up hope that he would receive anything at all. But now a letter came from the colonel, who wrote that he had looked at his plan with extreme interest and asked him to come to see him in his office hours and bring with him a detailed version of the project to which he had referred so it could be discussed more fully. Immediately after Per had quickly perused the letter, he banged with the back of his hand on the ceiling, a signal for Trine to come down. "Ask the old dears to come," he ordered. Then he fetched, from the bottom of his wardrobe, a bottle with some Swedish punch still in it, from which he filled three glasses that he set up on the table.

"What's going on?" asked Madam Olufsen as she stuck her head, covered with curlers, into the room while the chief boatswain was heard tottering down the steep stairs.

"Good news, Madam Olufsen. Come congratulate me."

"My goodness, Herr Sidenius, are you engaged?"

"'Not this time, said the old lady.' Better than that, Madam Olufsen!"

"Did you win the lottery, then?"

"Really you could say that ... the same thing! Skål, old friends! And thanks for everything! Skål, Chief Boatswain! And don't be surprised if you hear about me soon."

The next day Per stood with his drafts under his arm in front of the colonel's door, which a girl opened for him. After having waited a little in a kind of foyer while she took his card in, he was led into a large, three-windowed workroom with clear light from the garden outside. A flushed-face little man, with frizzy hair and a pince-nez in his hand, rose from his desk, and approached Per in a lively manner until he stopped in the middle of the floor. He put his lorgnette on his nose and looked Per up and down a few times, with every indication that he had been uncomfortably taken off guard.

"What's this? Are you Herr Engineer Sidenius?" he asked.

"Yes."

"But good God, you are such a young man!"

"Oh," said Per, a little disconcerted. "I'm already twenty-two."

"But, but ... then the whole thing is ..." He clearly wanted to say "a misunderstanding" but considered for a time before turning on his heels, annoyed at himself for having perpetrated a stupidity and undecided how to cover up.

"Well now, sit down," he said finally, but seemingly against his will. "We can, in any case, talk about this." With a flourish he showed Per a seat on a little bamboo sofa next to the desk, then settled in a wide armchair before he continued in the same tone: "As I already told you, among a heap of absurdities, not to say craziness, there are one or two things in your forwarded plan that might—could—deserve some attention. I will say, to be sure, that I find your idea of a large Jutland canal system and what is connected with it—to put it mildly—too immature. We'll just let that lie. On the other hand, your thought about a straightening of the east fjord inlet, *that* rests, in any case, on a fairly reasonable foundation and, as well, the way in which you have contemplated carrying out the plan certainly reveals, in part at least, new ways of viewing, new ways of observing." While he spoke, he turned a ruler slowly in his hand and looked at Per with a sharp glance over his lorgnette, which was lying horizontally almost on the tip of his red nose. His tone had gradually become less unsympathetic. Per's healthy, broad-shouldered form obviously affected the old military man. He stopped in the middle of his words to blurt out, in renewed surprise and with both hands planted on his hips, "But—confound you! How did you, young man, come upon the crazy idea to do this foolish project? You couldn't think it had any practical significance. And you seem to me, respectfully, more like one who should have pretty girls and that sort of thing on your mind instead of logarithms and mapped calculations."

Per thought it proper to smile at the observation, in spite of the fact that it displeased him. Then he told him openheartedly how he had worked in the past years on his project, which he had, in a way, thought about from childhood on. As he got going, he waxed eloquent and expressed himself with unguarded pride about the project's significance. Among other things, he alluded to a comparison with foreign countries while expressing his conviction that the authorities *here*, since we began building railroads, had neglected, to an unpardonable extent, the development of the country's natural communication routes, the waterways. Unused all over the country, they would gradually become the biggest detriment to the nation's productivity and welfare.

A smile that had been playing on the colonel's face during Per's exhortation broke into laughter after this last tirade. "Well, you are, God knows, a brave soul! I think your project might almost be a challenge to us old fogeys who have so shamefully neglected the country's interests. And you ask, moreover, for permission to criticize and scorn us in our own journal. That, I might say, is the limit! Is that your detailed plan you have with you? Let me see it." Per unrolled his drafts, one after another, and laid them before him on the desk.

"Good God," the colonel exclaimed, taken aback. "This is a whole archive! What got into you? This is pure insanity, my boy. And with all this, I still don't see the draft for the fjord adjustment we talked about. That is what interests me most of all."

Per unrolled his last draft, a huge map that covered almost the whole desk. That chart represented the fruit of half a year's iron discipline. It was an outline and cross section of parallel and internal structures, fascine linings, retaining walls, and so on, all painstakingly and meticulously carried out, even to the scales and the carefully printed headings. The colonel placed his lorgnette more firmly on his nose and took a compass from his case of instruments. "As you perhaps know," he uttered, after a moment of silence during which he reluctantly showed how impressed he was, "a deepening of the fjord passage and rebuilding of the harbor was, actually, contemplated ten years ago. I myself was asked for advice at that time, and, perhaps, those memories have awakened in me, in regard to your project, the sense that it, that I—well, pull up a chair and move closer; tell me how you thought this out."

For more than an hour, the men sat side by side absorbed in measuring and calculating. Time after time the colonel threw the compass down and declared the whole thing a folly; but a moment after, he would speak with warm appreciation in favor of one or another happy discovery, such as a clever use of the terrain or a well-adapted foundation plan. Per was entirely calm the whole time; in contrast to the older man, he seemed even cold-blooded. With shrewd calculation, he yielded on the minor points in order to preserve the integrity of the larger design, where his most challenging concepts were laid out.

The long negotiation developed gradually into a kind of hand-to-hand combat between the young and old engineers, in which the latter, more than once, was reduced to silence and, sometimes, to concessions. At last the old colonel seemed so eager that the previously scorned canal project with its system of locks and its large west harbor was taken out and examined more closely.

Flushed from his effort, the colonel suddenly pushed all the papers from him and said, "Let me keep these things for a week. We might have something by then, be able to separate the wheat from the chaff—the frightful mass of chaff. Before we can talk about publishing it in the journal, the whole thing has to be brought together. I will see what I can do. So that I can under-stand your thoughts better, I grant that the plan ought to be seen in its entirety, should be presented as a whole to be judged correctly. Simply as a thought experiment, in any case, it will cer-tainly entertain and interest the technology circle. You have ideas, young man. How old did you say you were?"

"Twenty-two."

"A happy age! So come back in a week." The colonel shook Per's hand warmly and collegially. "What eyes you have!" he said suddenly, while he held on to his hand. "Where did you get them from? You look at people like a hungry wolf. Well—good hunting!" he finished, laughing, and once more he pressed Per's hand.

When Per stepped out into the street, the world seemed transformed. The air was so mild, the sky seemed so high, and man so amazingly small. Now stay calm, he thought, and forced himself to look soberly upon things. Good God—the whole had developed just as he knew it would have to. When the journal came out, he would send it to no one, not even his parents or anyone else in the family. Surely it would fall into their hands anyway. For now, all this did not mean very much. He had taken only the first little step on fame's track. Now he needed to ready himself for the succeeding bigger ones. What lay before him was the long, more difficult task of bringing ideas to life, creating the appetite for them, winning over followers both among the leaders and the people.

In the following days, he loafed around in the billiard rooms to pass the time and blunt his impatience until he could once again show up at the colonel's. One evening he went into a café in Kongens Nytorv, where he found himself in the company of Fritjof, whom he had not seen since his conversation after the orgy at the Pot when the painter's coarse bout with drunkenness had revealed him to be as weak and trembling as a confirmand. Now he sat here again enthroned in all the majesty of a master artist, the talking center of a circle of young, silent votaries of beauty who, like him, were all in evening dress and sat drinking cognac and water after a big banquet. He had shoved his big gray Rubens hat to the back of his head and rested his hands on the knob of a formidable bamboo cane planted between his outstretched legs.

"What the devil! Is it not Salomon's young Aladdin?" he exclaimed loudly when Per came in, greeting him with a flamboyant wave of the hand. "Where has the lamp's genie kept you for so long? Sit down!"

But Per felt no desire to be included in the circle and instead took a seat at a side table. To Fritjof's renewed questions about why he had been invisible for so long, he answered curtly that he had been occupied with his work. An Olympian laugh thundered from Fritjof's big body. "Oh, that's right! You're one of these modern useful men before whom Nathan has begun to bow and scrape. We thank you! So, you have been busy with drawing off water from one or another of our pure little lakes, right? Or perhaps you have invented a way to cut the Møns Cliffs into scattered stones and make mortar out of them. By what other means have you served the future and contributed to our fatherland's betterment and beautification?"

Per surveyed the circle of young artists who sat in solemn torpor, lounging loosely on the chair backs as if they were brooding over subjective revelations. As he lit his cigar, he threw out, "It's really good that not all of us are born with the genius to create paradise on a bit of canvas."

"No, of course! Long live industry! Up with the stinking factory chimneys and may God improve our sewer system! Tell me, young man, have you ever really seen how modern happiness is generated by the machine? Do me a favor and trouble to go into one of our cramped streets one day and look at the cellar-pale brood that teems like mites in putrid cheese. Or stroll into the rich robbers' quarter with the millionaire Jews and their fat women . . . the whole of it rotten, my friend. Ah, God help us. And that's what's called the future. That will be Science's blessing helping us, I say. No, I prize, rather, an artless fool of a farmer who sings contentedly behind his plow and leaves to his God the task of improving the world. He is still more of a man than all the future's Jewish heralds together." He turned to ask, "What do you think?" to his silent table partners, who responded with an approving mutter.

Because of Fritjof's slightly befuddled condition, Per was not surprised by his tirade that reminded him of his harangue that night at the Pot. On the other hand, he didn't understand this continually scornful allusion to Dr. Nathan, of whom Fritjof had before been such a vociferous admirer. But finding that it was no longer worth the trouble to sustain a conversation, he shrugged and turned to reading the paper.

At that moment the front door flew open and a crowd of ladies dressed for the theater and gentlemen with overcoats hanging loose over their shoulders streamed in and, in a few minutes, took all the seats in the café, which had, just before, been almost all empty. There had been an opening performance at the Royal Theater that evening, and all these men and women were still walking on air, stirred up by the excitement of the five acts. The room buzzed with the name of the author and actors, the roles were discussed, and the play's meaning stimulated a passionate debate. But gradually, Fritjof and his fellow artists, some of whom, despite their youth, were already well known, aroused the interest of the guests. Heads huddled around the tables; there was pointing and whispering. In a corner, by himself, sat a pale young man whose Mephistophelean appearance attracted attention. It was the poet Povl Berger, one of the great Enevoldsen's many disciples, by now viewed as the literary heir of that master of delicate diction, who had recently died in the act of composing a main clause. Per heard some ladies at the neighboring table talk with interest of him and his poetry. He remembered him now from Fritjof's big bacchanal in the Pot. It was he who had jumped onto a chair to toast Dr. Nathan, and in the course of his wild foolishness had crushed a glass in his hand.

With that memory, he experienced deep misgivings as he took in the hullabaloo. He couldn't help thinking how, even if he was lucky enough to distinguish himself in his field, he could never hope to obtain as much fame as this insignificant versifier, whose name was now on everyone's lips. When his ideas were published, his name would scarcely go beyond the narrow circle of engineers. While the papers would give over columns to announce the first love stories that came along, unless he had written a poem about the ocean or painted a river instead of planning a canal project, they would scarcely speak of his work in a little side notice.

As he got up to go, he couldn't refrain from turning toward Fritjof and saying, "It seems to me that your 'beautiful souls' have nothing to complain about in this country. You see what excitement a second-rate play can call out. For a week, the whole city will talk about this great event."

"Well, what the devil *should* our fellow countrymen take an interest in?"

Per felt slapped down by these words. He looked at him silently for a moment. "You may be right," he said. At the same time, he looked over the artist circle with a bitter, challenging glance and added, "Wait, it soon will be different."

"Another crazy fellow," said Fritjof after Per left, and drained his glass. Automatically, his fellow artists also drank up and muttered their agreement.

Although Per, in his impatience, could barely wait out the period prescribed by the colonel, when he once again stood in his office he encountered an altogether different man than that interested colleague who, a week before, had given him such an encouraging goodbye. The colonel neither gave him his hand nor asked him to sit down. With a brusque bluster that obviously covered some embarrassment, he returned all of Per's drafts and said that, upon closer examination, he couldn't find the project suited for publication in his journal. "The whole is too immature. And you're too young to do this by yourself. You are not yet a graduate, from what I hear."

Ah, so that's it, thought Per. He was careful to check up on me . . . probably even asked Professor Sandrup. Well, just wait!

The colonel was standing in front of the porcelain stove at the other end of the room and, from there, critically examined Per's person and clothes down to his boots—cast, even, a scrutinizing glance at the hat he had laid on a chair by the door when he came in.

"Your name is Sidenius," he said after a few moments of silence. "Are you, by any chance, from that well-known family of clergymen?"

As always, when Per got that question, he acted as if he didn't hear it. He began in a directly challenging tone to mock the colonel's sudden change of judgment about the value of his work. The colonel interrupted him quickly, and nervously said that any further discussion was entirely unnecessary and useless. His view of the project couldn't be altered.

It was easy to see that he wanted to be rid of Per as quickly as possible and that he would not allow him to say anything more for fear of again being persuaded. He took a few steps forward and said in a milder tone, "I'm sorry if my words the other day raised false hope in you; but I have no doubts that this refusal will be in your own interests. I don't deny you have talent, but, for the time being, you need, first and foremost, to gain a better understanding of what you lack. At twenty-two, is there any worthier ambition than to learn more? In any case, our journal isn't in the business of accepting the immature projects of the young."

He turned around with a wave of his hand that indicated the audience was finished. But Per kept standing there. "How decrepit, in your opinion, sir, should I be to begin hoping to get my work known?"

His face lobster red, the old officer turned back so quickly that his feet raised ridges in the carpet. "Are you crazy?" he exclaimed. But at the sight of Per's deathly pale, quivering cheeks, he controlled himself. He saw that things might become physical, and for fear of a scandal, he recognized that he must again demonstrate that further conversation would be useless.

"I still have something to say to you, sir," said Per. "You will come to regret that you showed me the door."

"You dare to threaten me?"

"Call it what you will. But next time we meet, it will be *you* who seeks *me* out! You have been mistaken about me, sir, and I about you! Had I known you better, I certainly would not have bothered you. Till we meet again!"

The old officer was boiling with rage at these words, but he didn't answer. He felt torn inside. When the door closed after Per, he gave a start, as if he wanted to call him back. With an "Oh, that boy!" he turned back to his desk, where he rummaged distractedly through some papers. A moment later, his wife came into the room, distressed, and asked, "What kind of a man was that? Good God! He slammed the front door so hard he knocked down a piece of the ceiling plaster! What kind of a man is that, I ask."

"Well, he will do more mischief than knock down plaster, that lout!"

"But what kind of man *is* he?"

"You tell me! A crazy man, I think, or a charlatan—or, maybe, a genius. Time will tell."

CHAPTER 6

ONE SUNDAY MORNING in the beginning of April, a spring day with calm weather and a high sky, Per was sitting in front of a restaurant on the Langelinie and looking at the ceaseless stream of passersby who, after church and lunch, came out to take in the sunshine and breathe in the fresh salt air. His appearance had changed in the course of the last months. He was thinner, which was not unbecoming, and the beard he had grown to appear older gave his face more character. No longer did he have his old careless and somewhat jaunty expression. As he sat there with his head resting on his hand, and stared at the decked-out Sunday strollers, it was not difficult to see by his glance and his furrowed brow that he was a young man to whom life had dealt the first serious disappointment. It had really gone very badly for him. He had, until now, while preparing and building for the future, possessed a strong, self-confident patience, been circumspect, focused, and, often, even smartly concentrated, but after his clash with the colonel, he had lost his composure.

In the hope of getting even with the colonel and Professor Sandrup, or whoever there would be now who stood in the way of his progress, he had not only sought out several other distinguished professionals in the city and showed them his work, but also went around to the newspaper editors to try to get articles placed about his ideas, and even finally made a desperate effort to get an audience with the minister of the interior in order to explain to him how pressing and necessary it was to proceed to a wholesale conversion of the system of waterways. Everywhere he met only smiles and shrugs, if he wasn't shown the door immediately.

It was a misfortune, as well, that he was alone in all this adversity, with no trustworthy companion to talk to about his disappointment, to help him air out his resentment. Bitterness was eating him up, making him as averse to company as to the dark, sickly notion still stirring in him of deliberately and consciously pursuing the chase. He avoided his former fellow students altogether. He imagined that they all thought him a little crazy (and some of them really did). He hadn't visited the Pot in over a year, but had heard that Lisbeth had long ago consoled herself with another.

He had actually come close to despising the artists, the country's darlings, who aroused the same hysterical idolatry of the natural world as the priests of the Beyond and who were also viewed as blessed beings, souls mediating between heaven and earth. When all was said and done, these canvas worshipers and tone-tuning preachers, in all their comicality, were not as innocent or harmless as he had thought; they had contributed to the undermining of faith in men as unique lords and masters of the earth.

In these days of bad luck, the same gloomy, irritable sense of loneliness came back that had oppressed him growing up in his childhood home, where, living with his parents and siblings, he had felt homeless, and now he felt himself a stray alien in conventional society. His countrymen seemed merely like little self-righteous Sideniuses, whitewashing the earth's glitter and glory with their petit bourgeois sense of duty and their arrogant pharisaic scorn. And he often thought what a blessing for Catholics it must be that their priests did not marry; they could not transmit to the people a thorough spiritual crippling, engendered by the false humility of the church that, in Protestant lands, was passed on from generation to generation, turning all ideas upside down as in the country of the Humpback King, where the small are called big and the crooked straight.

Moreover, he had to struggle with new troubles—among others, money problems. Although he had lately been living very thriftily like a poor student, had sought out the cheapest cellar restaurants of the Borgergade quarter and eaten with carriage drivers and messengers, his inheritance from Neergaard was almost used up. He had figured out that his money could be stretched out for only a couple of more months, at best. And what then? Should he resign himself to being a boy-beating teacher again? Or go begging to the manufacturers and artisans for copy work?

In addition, he had love troubles; he could not forget Fransisca. Now and then he was moved when he contemplated some small preserved memorabilia: a dried flower she had fastened in his buttonhole, a silly letter she had written him in mirror writing, a blue silk ribbon he had stolen one evening from around her neck. When he took his lonely walk in the twilight and saw the other young men who, in fine agreement with all earthly and heavenly authorities, were enjoying the sunset and the spring air with their fiancées or other young women on their arms, he was attacked by his old vulnerability and asked himself whether he had sacrificed his happiness for a delusion, whether he could now more easily abandon his proud dreams in order to live like those who made themselves useful in one or another office, to marry Fransisca in the course of time and become a respected citizen and happy family man in the country of the Humpback King.

Still that was not all. As if all the powers had conspired to test his resolution, he was shaken up anew by a disturbing event at home in Hjertensfrydgade: the chief boatswain suddenly died. The old man had, in the morning, undertaken his usual round to Amalienborg Plads, through Borgergade and into Antonistræde and was homeward bound, at the corner of Gothersgade and Adelgade, when without warning he collapsed on the pavement.

He evidently was conscious enough to stammer out his name and address, and he was carried through a curious crowd that had momentarily gathered around, into a closed carriage and driven home. His wife was just then looking in the window mirror for him when the carriage stopped in front of the house. As soon as she saw a policeman stick his arm out of the carriage window to open the door, she understood what had happened and rushed down the steps. Per, who was in his room, became aware of the commotion in the house and went into the hall to find out what was going on. From there he saw how Madam Olufsen, at the carriage door, was resolutely pushing the policeman aside and coming into the house a moment later with the chief boatswain's slack body draped in her arms. All by herself, refusing help, the seventy-three-year-old wife bore her dying husband up the steep steps while the policeman, in all his official dignity, followed, carrying Olufsen's gray hat and brown stick. A doctor was hastily summoned and, while the wife of the ship's carpenter, over-whelmed by the tragedy, of her own accord ran after a priest, Per and the officer helped Madam Olufsen put her husband in bed, where he, in a few minutes, his head on her breast, breathed his last.

Since that day, Per had not felt comfortable in his room. This was the first time death had come so near. The image of the stiff, ungainly, gaping body that was lying upstairs just above his head kept him awake at nights, and in the day, when he sat at the table with his head between his hands, he stared forlornly down at his drafts, those five or six unhappy pages that had stolen all the strength of his intellect and will. It was as if the funereal stillness that brooded over the house, the chill of the grave that pressed down on him through the ceiling, were mocking his troubles by reminding him how poor and trivial was the most triumphant destiny against death's power, how short the longest life in com-parison with the nothingness of eternity.

He had not been home for a night and a day. To kill his thoughts he had gone to the cafés and billiard rooms, had spent the night in the company of a strange woman, one of the street's merciful sisters, and now sat at a café with an empty glass in his hand. He had chased through the city, pursued all morning, as in his childhood, by the hateful clang of the church bell, like a conjuring echo. Never had he felt so exiled, so despondent, dis-heartened as when he would, on holidays, go through the streets' long rows of shuttered shops, looking at all the parks and side-walks full of happy Sunday citizens. Here came a fat-necked gentleman with his nose in the clouds and his hands behind his back—a lawyer, Per thought, perhaps a moneylender, a swindler who had sought absolution in one or another church for his week's sins and now was taking the air as a reborn man with a Havana cigar in his mouth. Another fat-necked gentleman, a twin to the first, came along with a voluptuous blond woman on his arm and a charming little girl holding his hand—a happy family man who had found his calling in life as an agent in tin buttons or had perhaps settled for a beneficial business in toilet paper. Then there were students and soldiers, laughing young girls and old ladies with sour smiles, all airing their little comfort-able, well-arranged snail houses, their whole world. Humble people! Happy people! Honest, right-minded Sideniuses. The hoarse whistle of a ship startled him; a big cargo steamer glided out of the harbor propelled by mighty piston strokes. The sun was reflected on the dark painted hull, and black, woolly bunches of smoke billowed over the brim of the stacks as the captain stood on the command bridge with his hand on the signal apparatus. The English merchant flag flew over the sternpost.

At this sight, a strong longing awakened in Per to leave and start his life anew in another part of the world, among other people ... to make for America, Australia, or go even farther away, to another distant and unknown country beyond the souls of parish clerks and the sounds of the church gongs. This yearn-ing was hardly strange to him, the temptation hardly new. And what, really, was stopping him? Surely not that magic power drawing one home that Neergaard had spoken of—he was its vic-tim. With the imminent dissolution of the Nyboder home he would be losing his last refuge in this country. And wasn't it hopeless to expect any kind of future in a neglected little country that seemed fated for an early end? In these days after the chief boatswain's death, he often would reflect upon what the old man had told him about the experiences of his long life, which stretched from the Battle of Copenhagen on Maundy Thursday, to which he had been witness in his mother's arms, on through the long row of national humiliations. Why keep clinging to a doomed country that, in the course of one man's life, had fallen into ruin, wasted away to a pale and flabby limb on Europe's body swelling with power?

A new life! Another world, another heaven! A new strength seemed to be growing in him at the mere thought. While his eyes followed the departing steamer, all the freewheeling joy of childhood stirred in his blood. He told himself that beyond, far away, that great triumphant happiness awaited him. There, perhaps, his childhood's golden dreams might be fulfilled. There, perhaps, he would win a princess and half a kingdom—even if she were black and the kingdom a South Sea island. Just then a shadow fell over the table. Before him a little, elegant gentleman stood, with a raised hat and a delighted smile—Ivan Salomon.

"I thought it was you! How nice! It's been so long since I saw you. I really think you've been trying to avoid your old friends. How have you been?" Per half rose and mumbled a greeting. This meeting did not make him very happy, but he invited Salomon to join him. Salomon sat down on the opposite side of the table and rapped the handle of his cane a couple of times on the metal top to summon a waiter. "Is there anything I can order for you?" he asked. "I see your glass is empty. An absinthe?"

"Thanks, I don't want anything."

"A glass of beer perhaps? Or wine? How about some English port? Can't I tempt you? The provisions here are first-rate."

"Thanks a lot, but I don't want anything," Per insisted, while he thought, mournfully, that here, really, he had a friend, even an admirer. And he remembered a proverb he once had heard or read that no one is so alone he doesn't have his own fool. Salomon ordered a glass of ice water for himself and offered cigarettes from a silver case.

"You have naturally been buried in your work, Herr Sidenius! In great inventions! It just occurred to me—isn't that why you wanted to be alone? Well, will the bombshells explode soon? Should the world expect a surprise from your generous hand?" Per answered with only a shrug.

"I will tell you confidentially that the world is waiting for you. Waiting longingly. I always say to the complainers who lament that nothing of significance can happen in our country: Wait, there will soon be a new generation growing up in our homeland. And from that, the revolution will come."

Per still didn't want to pursue the conversation. He always felt uncomfortably affected by Salomon's flattery, because often he scarcely had the courage to confess to himself that he also had harbored those immodest thoughts and hopes.

"Have you read Nathan's latest essay in *Lyset*? You don't know about it? Oh, you must read it. It seems written just for you. Altogether excellent, I tell you! He exposes what he terms the milked-out aestheticians in our country, and calls to arms active men of initiative—wonderful!"

Surprised, Per looked up. "Dr. Nathan?" he asked. He remembered the last conversation he had with Fritjof, how the artist kept referring to the Jewish writer in a way he had not, at that time, understood, or hadn't wanted to. Now Salomon's words made him curious. He expressed interest in what the scholar had written, and Salomon offered to lend him the essay.

"Please don't bother," Per said with a gentle gesture of refusal. "I really won't be able to read it." He leaned back in his chair and added casually, "I'm thinking of emigrating."

"You're going to travel?" It sounded almost like a cry of anguish.

"I'm thinking of it."

"Going for good?"

"Perhaps."

Little Ivan lowered his eyes and was quiet for a while. He had heard from someone something about Per's project and about the unsympathetic reception from Colonel Bjerregrav and Professor Sandrup. But he was loath to believe in the possibility that in this day, a man could be exposed to such misunderstandings. "Well, I certainly realize why you feel the need to go away. This is, for the time being, not a favorable soil for you. I just thought of an expression you used once about our illustrious polytechnic education. You called it an 'incubator for hatching office clerks.' I find that absolutely perfect and doubtlessly accurate. In our time, all is arranged to foster mediocrity. There is no longer a place for exceptional talent, no understanding here, no hunger for the unique, the brilliant, for the pioneers. As Nathan puts it, we have all too long been accustomed to a light and loose intercourse with fantasy, which has, therefore, to an alarming degree, weakened the nation's willpower."

"Did he write that?"

"That and much more. But I will send you his essay. You must read it. Are you thinking of going far away?"

"I don't know. I haven't decided."

"Ah, but you will come back, you will *soon* come back! I'm convinced of that. The future belongs to you *here*. But, maybe, all things considered, it's not such a bad idea to make yourself invisible for a little while. That's an intelligent move. And a stay abroad gives you prestige. If you could obtain a post at one of the big English or French engineering firms—Blackbourn & Gries, for example, a firm specializing in bridgework. We have done a little business with them here, from time to time. But maybe you have other plans."

Per answered evasively. Salomon played with his bright-colored handkerchief. He had, the whole time, a burning question on his tongue, but he didn't have the courage to ask it. It was a question about travel expenses. He knew Per's situation much better than Per suspected, knew also of his economic difficulties, and it had been his great concern that Per's attitude toward him so far had made it impossible to offer him friendly help. Now he harbored the hope of finding, at last, the occasion to show Per one of the services he was so eager to offer to those in whose talents and future he had faith. And that generosity was not a mere question of vanity. With his many amusing character-istics, Ivan's deepest self was that of an altruistic, childlike, empathic man with a nature marked by the desire to help and worship and whose only passion was to satisfy his idols.

Suddenly he got up with a bound, as if there were a mecha-nism in his chair snapping him into the air. "I'm sorry I must leave you now," he said. "I promised my mother and sister I would take them to our country house. And I see the carriage coming."

A large, elegant carriage was approaching on the narrow, depressed road that divided the restaurant from the promenade and led under a curved bridge. Behind a pair of high brown horses with a silver mounted harness, a coachman and a servant in blue livery were enthroned; in back of them, two silk umbrellas, one white, one mauve, could be seen.

"Wouldn't you like to say hello to my family?" asked Salo-mon. "It would please both my mother and sister to meet you." Per complied hesitantly. He had no desire to call attention to the introduction in front of everyone. Salomon had already given the signal to the coachman, and a moment later the carriage stopped before the steps that led from the restaurant to the road.

Under the parasols two ladies sat, one of whom, the younger, immediately caught Per's eye. He had, besides, seen her once before, but behind a mask, without knowing who she was. That

was on carnival night over a year ago, when he had encountered
Fru Engelhardt for the first time. He remembered her dimly from
that night as a Snow Queen in a very low-cut white silk costume
gleaming with diamonds. He had, since, always thought of her as
a pale, voluptuous, bedecked Jewess who displayed her charms
and jewels like a merchant his wares. Now he saw before him a
young girl, hardly over eighteen or nineteen years old, whose
Jewish origin could not be in doubt, but who had a fresh, well-
shaped, and red-cheeked face, surrounded by waves of thick,
curly hair. She was strikingly, but not tastelessly, dressed in a
tight-fitting, wolf-gray velvet dress and a lilac hat from which two
large colored silk bows spread out like a pair of giant butterflies.
Just under these wings a pair of lively and lovely dark brown,
roguish eyes looked at him with obvious interest, a bold curiosity
that came close to bewildering him.

The mother, on the other hand, answered Per's greeting with
a little reserved nod. "So you have materialized. My son has
already often spoken of you. You are an engineer, aren't you?"

Per answered mechanically, not turning his gaze from the
young girl, whose eyes did not leave him either, even as she more
and more hid under lowered, long eyelashes.

The whole of the meeting did not last long. Ivan got into the
carriage, and after Fru Salomon had said that her son's friend was
always welcome in her home, they exchanged another formal
greeting. The footman got up on the trestle, and the carriage
rolled away.

Per's cheeks were burning as he went back into the city. He
could not forget the bold look in those gleaming dark brown
eyes. He envisioned clearly the young girl before him, as if she
were gliding by him out of the crowd on carnival night—half
naked, with a gold crown on her dark, woolly hair and the long
trembling veil sparkling with diamonds. It was as if temptation's
voice itself were whispering in his ear, "The dark princess and
half a kingdom."

True to his promise, Salomon sent, the same evening, Dr.
Nathan's much-debated essay, which Per, for lack of any other
occupation, looked into immediately. He was quickly gripped by
both the diction and tone, which were altogether different from
what he had expected. He was reminded of books that, in a similar way, had influenced his relation to the literature outside his

profession, Martensen's *Ethics,* for example, which as a boy he had had to read aloud on free afternoons. Here he saw, clearly and masterfully expressed, what his own experience had taught him about life and people, and he was truly delighted to read the witty and merciless attack on all that petty, self-righteous lot of Sideniuses, who, for this writer also, represented the country's shame and misery. He was especially gratified by the great ending of the essay, in which the author answered the attack his work had attracted from many quarters by reproducing, in poetical form, his first impressions of his homeland on returning from his residence abroad, where he studied foreign cultures for many years. He related how, after an express train ride through the reborn, noisy cities of Germany—Hamburg bustling with ants of industry, and newly built Kiel—one quiet morning he went on a steamer to Korsør and, instantly, upon entering the little town's silent and empty harbor, was seized with the sensation of gliding into another world, a supernatural dream realm. And the impression did not die down when, at the break of day, he rode through the country in a heavy, rumbling train that gradually rocked the other passengers to sleep. It stopped every fifteen minutes at a little country station where a few farmers with Grundtvigian pilgrims' hats and large tobacco pipes sat and waited, not for this train that stopped but for the one that was to arrive in an hour or two. It was as if he had come to a country where time had no meaning, where everyone, literally, seemed to have eternity in front of him. And the impression persisted when he arrived in Copenhagen and moved around the narrow streets; nothing seemed to have changed over the years—the pavement was still worn, the shops still provincial, the carriages going at the same snail's pace as before, and the theater handbills announced a performance of exactly the same childish, hackneyed chivalric dramas he had left behind. It was as if life had stopped here, while out there, in Europe, in all respects, an intellectual revolution, mighty developments, were transforming the social order and giving people higher and bolder goals.

Finally, he talked about coming into the Student Society by chance at the same hour in which, during his graduate studies, he used to have his afternoon coffee with some of his university friends. He thought of the possibility of meeting one or another of these old acquaintances and went in. His surprise was great when he saw almost the whole society gathered around the table in the same corner with exactly the same grouping as when he had been there many years before. They were all, of course, older; one already had gray hair, some had become thin, most had become fat. Their expressions, their movements, and especially their self-satisfied, slow way of talking betrayed an early onset of lethargy of the soul. In addition, they all sat there as if, during the whole year, they had not moved from their place. Their conversation, to which he listened for some time, while sitting unrecognized at a neighboring table, consisted of the same exalted theological and philosophical rambling with which they also had, in the old days, seasoned their coffee and smoking, and it demonstrated that no trace of what had been thought, done, written in the last years throughout Europe had crossed the boundaries of this land. At once, he knew where he was. He had come to the land of Sleeping Beauty, where time had stopped and where the pale rose blossoms of fantasy and the tough, thorny briars of speculation treacherously hid an inner decline and decay. With that recognition (so the story ended), his calling became clear. Like the young man in the fairy tale, traveling back home from far away, who wrested the horn "Cockcrow" from the sleepy gatekeeper's hand to arouse warriors from their stony sleep, so, too, here he would stir whoever was alive in his own country—first and foremost, the young, especially those who were strong and eager to fight, those who had the courage to break through and rip open the tenacious, hard, matted cocoon that encapsulated the nation's soul.

It was the battle signal he heard in his reading of Dr. Nathan that brought the blood into Per's cheeks. He felt that the burning, thrilling call was directed at him—yes, especially at him. His hand pounded the tabletop as he repeated aloud, to confirm his feeling, "Yes! Yes!" He recalled now how the colonel had jokingly called his project a challenge to Danish technology. Well, it *would* be! For he knew now he was born to become, in his domain, the morning horn-herald, the path breaker in this sluggish society of thick-blooded sons of pastors and sextons. Little Ivan was right. This world was waiting for him—just for him. He got up without a thought for the old boatswain's dressed body that was now laid out in his white-trimmed coffin. He marched heavily back and forth over the floor. He pressed his fist against his forehead while he rhythmically repeated, "Yes, yes," to keep himself resolute. He thought as well of the young Frøken Salomon. He saw her big brown eyes, her inquisitive, bold, and (behind the veil of her eyelashes) virtually alluring glance.

Never before had the thought occurred to him that he could further his mission with a good marriage. He had always depended on the sufficiency of his own strength, and, beyond this, there was something in that idea that repelled him. Now, however, he admitted to himself that, in the battle for the large goal, it wasn't necessary to be so scrupulous in a choice of means. A Jewess? Yes, why not? Frøken Salomon was young and pretty and, as far as he could see, extraordinarily shapely. It was time for him to abandon the childish notion of luck as something tumbling down on your head like a lottery win. In fact, in any case, there was no more reliable or worthy luck than that which was wrested from fate. You had to hunt down luck as if it were a wild creature, a crooked-fanged beast, the fairy tale's golden-brush boar, capture, and bind it—treasure for the fastest, strongest, bravest.

A few days later, the chief boatswain's burial ceremony took place. His body had been brought to the chapel the evening before. On the day of the funeral, the old house friends gathered for a silent brunch before the interment. At noon, young Didriksen's carriage stopped in front of the door to take Madam Olufsen, old Bendtz, and their wreaths to the Holmen Cemetery, while the rest of the company went on foot.

It was a summerlike spring day. Around the graves were many small green bushes, and the birds played their love games of tag over the gravestones. The little, aged, silent group of grievers, doddering forms, leaning on canes and umbrellas, who slowly wobbled up the graveyard path in their faded and old-fashioned dress clothes, looked ghostly in the clear sunshine. Only Per at the back seemed in harmony with the vital and blooming nature surrounding them. To be sure, he was, in his own way, affected by the ceremony. But death's power over him was broken. When he, with the others, encircled the grave and saw the sunlit coffin slide into the dark, narrow, and cold hole, his cheerlessness was adulterated by an almost joyous sensation. He still belonged to life and the sun. His blood still sang the song of promise in his ears. Still—still!

After the burial, he went home to change clothes. He wanted to visit the Salomons. But once at home in Hjertensfrydgade, a strange surprise awaited him. There was a visitor's card on his table—a card stamped with a noble crown and the name Baroness von Bernt-Adlersborg. At first he thought it had been sent to him by mistake, but then he saw a few lines written on the back: in friendly, almost humble words, the baroness asked to speak with him; either that very day or the following she could meet him in the Hotel d'Angleterre.

The wife of the ship's carpenter came in and, very impressed, told him about the distinguished lady who had stopped by in a coach and asked for him. She had given her the "slip of paper" and asked her to lay it on his table. Per stared at the card. Baroness von Bernt-Adlersborg! Never in the world had he heard that name! It *must* be a mistake: "Did she really ask for me? Give my name?"

"Ah, yes, she certainly did. She said 'Herr Sidenius.' And she was put out that you weren't at home."

Per ran mentally through a series of bold fantasy pictures. "How did she look?" he asked. "Was she young?"

"Yes, indeed. She is probably about my age," answered the wife, who was getting on to fifty.

"Oh, it was a lady . . . a real lady, I mean?"

"Dear me, she had a luxurious fur in the carriage!"

Per looked at his watch. If he still wanted to meet the mysterious baroness that day, he couldn't waste any more time. He was undeniably impatient to solve the riddle. He gave up his visit to the Salomons, dressed in his Sunday best, and left.

The long-bearded hotel porter was, at first, rather haughty to him; but when he heard Per was looking for the baroness, he bowed respectfully, opened the door, and rang a loud bell, which summoned both a servant and a housemaid. With a ceremonial courtesy that now was directed at Per as if he had been a king paying his respects to the queen, they accompanied him up wide, carpeted stairs and through a long hall, at the end of which he was handed over to a Swedish-speaking lady's maid; she took his card and led him into a small salon furnished with the usual hotel elegance Per found so impressive: some bright red velvet furniture and a chandelier.

Per, who did not allow himself to be easily taken in, could not help feeling, at that moment, somewhat anxious. The thought came to him that he had let himself be lured into a trap and that this was a comedy arranged by one or another of his enemies who wanted to get the better of him. But he had no time for reflection.

A tall lady came in just then from an adjacent room. She was neither young nor pretty. Her face was faded, her nose suspiciously red. Her black dress seemed rather modest to Per. Still, it would be hard to miss that she was a lady from the great world. There was in her form and being—and, as well, in the way in which she gave him her hand and thanked him for coming—so much fine and gentle grace and tact that couldn't be acquired, but came through the blood.

"I hope it didn't confuse you that I wanted to talk a bit with you, Herr Sidenius," she began when they were seated across from each other in red armchairs. "You were my dead brother's last friend and confidant. You're also the one who received his farewell to the world."

Now everything became coherent to Per. He remembered something the lawyer had told him in regard to his legacy: that his benefactor had two sisters, one of whom had married a rich, landed Swede. The baroness continued: "I have long been curious to know the man to whom my only brother felt so closely connected, as if you were a young, renewed version of himself—so he put it in a letter accompanying the stipulations of the will. But the long sickness of my dearly beloved husband kept me confined to a faraway home. I couldn't even grant myself permission to come to my dear brother's funeral." The baroness's strange way of speaking, along with some peculiar facial expressions, betrayed quite a nervous disposition. After her last words, she started to weep and, for some time, blotted her eyes with a lace handkerchief.

Per felt unpleasantly affected and said nothing. He could not overcome a certain discomfort on being reminded of his relationship to the eccentric suicide.

"Oh, I'm so sorry," continued the baroness when she had recovered a bit. "I hope you can give me permission to cry . . . as you might know, the good Lord has taken my noble husband away from my side and left me alone." Per showed his sympathy by bowing his head.

"I will tell you, Herr Sidenius, that I often thought of writing you—also on my sister's behalf—so you wouldn't think us indifferent to your welfare. But I never could gather the courage to do it. And then, you might have felt obliged to correspond with a strange and, perhaps to you, indifferent lady." Per quickly mumbled a constrained demurral.

"Yes, to be honest, I wouldn't have bothered you about coming—I must say this—had I not been at the cemetery today and seen the beautiful fresh flowers on my brother's grave. I know who so lovingly remembered the anniversary of his death. So I felt the imperious need to see you and thank you—because, with a faithful love—dare I say—of a son, you honored the memory of my unhappy brother."

Per stared down at the tops of his boots and blushed. The thought of Fru Engelhardt bobbed up from the depths of his consciousness. He didn't even know where Neergaard was buried.

"But now, let me look at you," continued the baroness. She felt more and more attracted to this silent and shy young man who was embarrassed to acknowledge his own kind deed. "How fresh and healthy you seem! You're obviously not one of these modern youths who waste their days in wanton idleness. How old are you, Herr Sidenius?"

"Twenty-three."

"Oh, so young. I hope things go well with you. I know you had a hard boyhood. My brother wrote to us that you were deprived of a mother early and you never knew your father."

The armchair's velvet began to burn under Per. He hastened to change the subject. "You're only passing through, Baroness?" he asked.

"Yes, I came here yesterday evening and travel, God willing, again tomorrow. I'm on my way to my sister's—the wife of the master of the royal hunt, Herr Prangen. As you perhaps heard, she has lived in the south these last years for her health. Do you know, although we three siblings were never able to live well without each other, I haven't seen her in over two years. It was for a long time my deepest sorrow that I had to live far from my dear homeland; with Alexander, it was the same way. He, too, clung to his homeland, with all the deep devotion of his warm heart. Herr Sidenius has probably heard that His Highness, the Prince of Wales, was once gracious enough to take an interest in my brother, and, at that time, there was talk about a post in our London embassy. Under such protection, a glittering career surely was opening before him. But despite everything that could tempt a man like Alexander to take such an offer, he decided not to accept it. My revered mother lived in Copenhagen then, and my sister was not yet married. Alexander loved Copenhagen and worshiped his home. He could not thrive outside the dear, known place. I think it was from the time when my mother died and he was left alone with the memories that his depression started. And he was also physically ill in the last days. Oh, how could he have done that!"

The memory of her brother's brutal death brought her handkerchief to her eyes again, and Per seized the occasion to leave. The baroness, who remained seated, took his hand with motherly warmth between both of hers and said, "How happy I am now, to have seen you. It's my hope that we will meet often. Will you promise me that you will visit me when I return from abroad? In all probability, I will spend the coming summer with my sister and brother-in-law in Kærsholm, and I know you will be warmly welcomed there."

"Thanks so much . . . if I wouldn't disturb you," stammered Per. In his embarrassment, he couldn't think of anything else to say.

"Don't speak of it, my dear. Remember that you, in a way, belong now to our family. That's how I see my brother's last wish. And you may rest assured that my sister is, in this regard, of the same persuasion. Live well, really well. And, again, thanks for being so thoughtful at Alexander's grave."

Per descended the hotel stairs slowly, almost hesitatingly. It occurred to him how significant this new friendship could be for him if, without pretending to scruples about its origin, he could make use of it with energy and shrewdness.

By a fairy-tale chance, a way opened up for him to people of real influence. If he wasn't mistaken, the estate of the master of the royal hunt was situated in the territory through which he thought of leading his mid-Jutland connecting canal, which would give that man a special interest in his plan. In any case, he couldn't let the opportunity go. He couldn't have too many trumps in his hand. For the high stakes he would be playing for, it now occurred to him that he might not need to come into closer relations with the Salomon house at all. However much he felt attracted to the young woman, he certainly was not desirous of marrying into a Jewish family. And who could tell what possibilities for marriage could open up for him in aristocratic circles?

On the other hand, in Salomon's house he would probably meet the magnates of the Exchange, bank directors, and the city's large industry leaders; in short, the little circle of moneymen who, after all, ruled over the rest of the world. Even beyond the marriage question, it was of prime significance for him to meet these people and to interest them in his work. The baroness was going away—he had no time to waste. Today, tomorrow, in any case, in two or three months, he must win the magic wand that would give him power over mankind and that, in his hand, would become a thunderbolt.

He had come out at the marketplace and looked up at the clock on the tall corner building. There was still time to visit the Salomons, and he decided to go there. But he was still a little confused by his experience with the baroness, and he wanted to drink a glass of beer in a café to calm himself and prepare for the visit. He had never before stepped foot in a Jewish home, and he had heard about the old customs and precepts whose observance had so much significance. It was important to make a good impression, and he was anxious not to offend.

Gradually his thoughts glided back to his meeting with the baroness. He couldn't help wondering what far-reaching consequences the unpremeditated words that had escaped from him that night at Neergaard's had had. For them to be so memorable to the baroness, especially the allusion to his origin, showed how great an impression they had made on her brother. He remembered that he already *then* had regretted his flippancy but couldn't make the effort to undo his lie. But now he wished he had undone it.

No—he drank up his beer—what is done is done. Dubious policies could now and then yield fruit. In any case, whoever would move ahead should not look back.

The family of the wholesaler Salomon was one of the very few who occupied an entire house in the center of the city. The old two-storied building lay in the Bredgade quarter, and from the street it made no great impression at first sight, for it was squeezed between two big tenement houses. On closer inspection, it was evident that a kind of special distinction hovered around it. You could tell that the house had a noble origin from the high, blue-black tile roof and the windows' broad piers. The older inhabitants of the quarter called it "the Palace." The merchant Salomon's father had bought it at the beginning of the 1830s from a debt-ridden aristocratic family. Upon entering the foyer, a visitor went through a glass door into a hall that was so high and large, footsteps gave off echoes. The walls were hung with armor, old bronze tools, and splendid Oriental weapons, giving one the impression of having entered a museum. At the rear, a double-branched staircase with golden railings led up to the main rooms.

The girl who had taken Per's card ushered him into a kind of library and asked him to sit down. Per settled into a leather chair and looked around attentively: at heavy wine-red silk drapes on the windows, a rich, moss-soft carpet extending over the whole floor, gold leather tapestries, an eight-cornered table inlaid with silver and mother-of-pearl in the middle of the room. On the shelves, expensively bound books, paintings on the walls; hanging from the ceiling an old inscribed church chandelier. Along one wall a carved antique counter of old silver with bowls, pitchers, goblets, and, finally, a pair of ancient chalices. If the visit to the baroness and the thoughts it had generated in him had not preceded this scene, all this elegance would have made an even stronger impression on him. Still, he was certainly impressed. Half against his will, he was captivated by this shameless advertisement of the might of money. A peculiar shiver of pleasure seized him at the thought that this power had commandeered so many inherited treasures from so many foreign nations, even the church's holy vessels, to serve as ornaments in this Jewish room.

He smiled a bit self-consciously. He could not deny—the little Princess Salomon had more than her beauty to bring as compensation for being "dark."

The door to the neighboring room opened. A little gentleman with a forbidding appearance entered and bowed deeply. Although he was about sixty years old, he was modishly and youthfully dressed; he wore a short, bright coat with a monocle dangling on his breast. In his hand he held a glossy silk hat.

"My name is Director Delft," he said, with something foreign in his accent. "I am the uncle here in the house." The man's great courtesy reconciled Per to his grotesque ape-like head.

"My name is Sidenius."

"Ah—the young engineer, presumably? My nephew has spoken of you. Please, sit down. Fru Salomon, my sister, is engaged for the moment with her seamstress. She'll be at your service very soon. Please, make yourself comfortable." Per sat down again. The uncle took a chair at some distance. "Dare I ask

... have I had the honor of seeing Herr Sidenius before in this house?"

"No, I met Fru and Frøken Salomon the other day for the first time."

"Ah, my niece Nanny. I think I heard that."

A slight pause followed, after which Herr Delft, with a smile and a tone that would have made anyone but Per suspicious in regard to its excessive courtesy, threw out the provocative observation, "My niece is very pretty, isn't she ... Don't you find her so, Herr Sidenius?"

Per was really surprised and directed an indulgent smile at the funny little man. "I find Frøken Salomon very pretty. A perfect beauty."

"Yes, how true. She doesn't belong to the common lot, I can certainly say ... and I can assure you, Herr Sidenius, she has attracted various young men to the house for some time. For what is beyond the power of beauty? And youth? What's more ... my brother-in-law is not altogether devoid of funds."

The man is certainly not judicious, thought Per, and dropped the conversation.

But the other continued: "If Herr Engineer will visit the house more often, I guarantee you will have the occasion to be entertained. In that regard, you can really make some curious observations. For isn't it true, Herr Sidenius: money is magnetic. These small, round pieces of metal attract the deepest human sensations, bring into the light the heart's noblest feelings: respect, friendship, love. Isn't that right?"

Per began to feel seriously restive. Fortunately, the maid came in, held the door open to the next room, and requested him to enter.

Per entered a drawing room that, even to a higher degree than the entrance hall or library, gave him the impression of penetrating the actual realm of millions and magic. The great room, with an elegant, slightly vaulted ceiling in rococo style, with chubby cherub babies in the corners blowing forth Judgment Day on flaming golden trumpets, was the old palace's gathering salon. Here, where formerly two rows of delicate chairs along a wall and a couple of high pier glass mirrors constituted virtually the entire furniture, a modern superfluity of pieces and decorative objects was now displayed. Deep sofas and large, soft armchairs, tables, footstools, bearskins and groups of leafy plants, columns with statues, shelves with knickknacks, and again, armchairs and small and large tables, more plants, artwork, and a portrait on an easel. In the middle of the room was an open concert piano. From a smaller neighboring room, arrayed as a winter garden with palms, an Indian rubber tree, and singing birds, a splashing fountain could be heard.

At length, Fru Salomon came into view on an ottoman under one of the windows, where she was doing some domestic sewing. She received him with friendliness and reached out her left hand to welcome him. They had scarcely exchanged a few polite words when Per heard a door open in the garden room and a cheerful hum that quickly grew into a bright song. A moment later, Frøken Nanny appeared in the door opening in a coat and hat. When she saw the new guest, she stopped her song with an amusing expression of fright and moved her muff to her mouth, as if she were stopping a shout. Per got up and bowed.

Not for a moment did Per conceive that she had been aware of his presence, so natural was her dissimulation. "Are you still home, my child?" asked her mother. "I thought you had gone out. I don't need to introduce you." To Per she said, "You have met my daughter."

He answered with another bow, accompanied by a glance that patently revealed his feelings. Already, before he had seen her, just with the sound of her song, which rang in his ears like the clinking of gold pieces, he had made up his mind. She was the means. Here was the treasure that must be drawn out. And as she showed herself in the doorway, with the sunroom's light and bird twitter behind her, young and voluptuous, looking temptingly like a beautiful Oriental dancer, she seemed to him to be herself adventure's magic fairy, leading geniuses bearing the palm of winged Victory in her wake.

Frøken Nanny sat down for a moment on a taboret, and one of those usual social conversations began, through which people who hardly know each other, hiding behind a string of commonplaces, seize the opportunity to explore mutual appearances, manners, character.

Per was not a great conversationalist. For that he was too concerned with himself and his own affairs. In addition, he had no interest in the usual subjects of social chatter, knew so little of what went on in the city, in the theaters, in politics, or in the world of literature. He felt no duty to be entertaining. If there was a chance of making an impression on the ladies, he would spring with the carefully calculated pounce of a tiger, out of the silence into the open and free air of confession.

Now he sat there while the young girl was talking and estimated to himself the worth of the huge Salomon fortune. His eyes unobtrusively canvassed the room. It made him dizzy to think that all this might one day be his. Fortunately, Nanny was in form and was entertaining all by herself. While she sat on the edge of her taboret—in a proper posture, but with elbows pressed against her body and her little beribboned muff in her lap—and let her pretty, red mouth run on, her eye was busy, boldly judging Per's person piece by piece from the thick curly hair down to the ankles that showed over the slightly provincial shoes.

Fru Salomon finally became a bit impatient with her loquaciousness. "Dear child, you are forgetting your music practice," she said.

"Yes, little mama." She rose immediately. With a quick glance at her mother and a more telling, lingering look at Per, she flounced out of the room. Per felt absent-minded after her departure. He gave a fairly distracted answer to Fru Salomon, who had led the conversation to his studies. He was entirely enchanted by the young girl. As much as her carriage had dissatisfied him when she came in, by its deliberate and a bit ungainly moves, it entranced him now; it was so feminine, so womanly—an unselfconscious prance. Suddenly he discovered, in the middle of the room, a figure in a black dress—a lady—who must have come in through the door behind him.

"My daughter Jakobe," Fru Salomon said. Per was surprised. It had never occurred to him that there might be children in the family other than the two he knew. A concern about the millions his fantasy had already appropriated stole over him. Maybe there are even more! he thought with alarm.

The young lady seemed to be some years older than her sister, was taller of build, and slimmer; in Per's eyes, she was painfully thin. She reminded him more of her brother Ivan, with those strong Jewish traits: a pale, waxen complexion, a large hooked nose, a wide mouth, and a short, recessed chin. His impression of her appearance that had already been so disagreeable to him was not improved by the silent and cold haughtiness with which she responded to his greeting. A moment later he got up and said goodbye.

"That was the much-talked-about natural genius?" said Frøken Jakobe, almost before the door closed behind him. "He certainly does not make much of a civilized impression!"

"His manners have been a bit neglected," said Fru Salomon. "Ivan says he has always lived in constrained conditions."

The daughter shrugged. "Oh, yes, naturally. They're all poor in this country. Would that God grant just once the emergence of a gifted man here who was born rich. There is something pitiable in the long run about the mark of poverty that disfigures even the best. He is not very attractive! Nanny trumpeted him, the other day, as a genuine Byron."

"Well, not pretty, maybe, but he looks good."

"But the staring eyes! I found him rather repulsive," said the daughter, and slammed shut a book she was flipping through. "He made an unpleasant impression on me, like a horse with glass eyes." She paused, then added with an expression that seemed to hint at a dark memory in her soul, "And he seemed rather brutal."

"I see he annoyed you, Jakobe."

"That he has. I don't know why today's gentlemen look at women with a butcher's eye. It's as if they are sizing up the pounds of meat on our bodies."

"Yes, he was a bit crude, I admit that. But we ought to cut this type of young man some slack," said Fru Salomon softly.

"Yes, so you say. But I do not really understand why we should be saddled with all of Ivan's unhappy geniuses. We know what happens, even in the best of cases. Look at Fritjof Jensen. He never met with anything from us but friendliness. I know that Father helped him a few times with money difficulties. And now he squawks about Jews in the papers."

"Well, my girl, let's not go into that again."

"I think I smell Christian blood!" rang through a half-open door, where the uncle's terrifying face showed itself.

"Is that you?" said Fru Salomon. "Well, come in—we're alone now. Oh, I think I hear the children."

"Here is the brood," said the uncle. And in rushed a crowd of black-eyed children in overcoats, aged four to twelve, no fewer than five of them, all looking healthy and lively, whose presence would have brought Per to despair. For a time, the room was filled with an ear-splitting clatter from all the little red mouths, not one of which was quiet. All of them had something to say. Soon, they swarmed around their mother, sister, or uncle, and all their dark eyes were shining with eagerness to tell their stories. When he could once again hear his own voice, the uncle said, "But I want to congratulate you on the house's new acquisition. I met a young gentleman, a little while ago. What's his name? An unpleasant one. The son of a black-frock, isn't he?"

"Oh, come now," exclaimed Fru Salomon. "I'll hear no more about that man. He is a friend of Ivan's. And he paid us a visit today. Period! Are you staying for dinner, Heinrich?"

"Here? Lea, my sister, have you ever tasted a kosher roasted pig?" asked the little man. Even his family found it difficult, often, to determine whether his words were meant seriously or as a joke. Fru Salomon started to laugh. "I notice you have inquired in the kitchen. Hush, now. I hear Salomon."

Per, meanwhile, was going home dazzled by his impression of the rich house and filled with thoughts of his big decision. Since he wanted to be alone, he took a path through some empty side streets. He had now not only found his way and his goal, but also his means. "Philip Salomon's son-in-law"—those were the magic words that would open up life's winged gates and make him master of men.

And why doubt his good fortune? When he thought back over his life's many curious experiences, couldn't he assume Ivan was right when he spoke of his Aladdin's luck? And wasn't it prophetic that it was Nanny's brother who first discerned the sacred writing on his forehead: "I come, I see, I conquer."

CHAPTER 7

AMONG THE MEN who, each afternoon around two, went up the Exchange's ramp under a broad canopy of trees, there were few whom the uniformed doorkeeper greeted with more respect than a tall, stout, ruddy man with curly black hair, a clean-shaven double chin, and a pair of uncommonly thick red lips between the customary cheek whiskers of a wholesaler. In the brown portico, many hats were lifted as he came by. Especially attentive were the grain brokers in the window embrasures out toward the canal and the skippers looking for freight who sat in a silent row on the long bench to the left of the Exchange. The imposing man was the wholesaler Philip Salomon, chief of the famous firm Isac

Salomon and Son, one of the city's richest men, whose fortune was rumored to be between seven and eight million.

His stay at the Exchange was seldom long. When the security officer rang the loud bell on the floor to signal the beginning of official quotations, he had usually already finished his business and returned to his office. He did not belong with those who looked on the Exchange as a kind of social club where you could meet after lunch to talk about the city's news or criticize the latest play. He did not often appear at the theater and took part in the social whirl only when compelled. He divided his time evenly between his business and his family; for the first, he kept a clear, cold head; for the second, a warm and easily vanquished heart. It was said of him concerning the fact that his house and his office were on the same street: "He never mistook his home address."

Philip Salomon was the only child of Isac Salomon, famous in his day, who gave his name to the firm. He was, in many ways, a remarkable man, a business genius who had raised himself from an itinerant peddler to a prominent position in the Danish money market: "Salomon Goldcalf," he was wittily dubbed by the town. He had some dozen full cargo ships at sea, his own factories and West Indies plantations, and the ingenuity to open new markets for Danish commerce in many overseas territories. During the persecution of the Jews in 1819, he had been among those who had suffered the most abuse at the hands of Copenhagen citizens.

It was also he who had bought the Palace and had it restored to such extravagant splendor. As unaffected by the indignation of the self-righteous as by the envious attempt of mockers to make him a laughingstock, he was never deterred from vying with the great figures of the aristocracy in his mode of living. He had himself driven through the city in a carriage drawn by four thoroughbred horses and, on special, festive occasions, had two footmen standing on the back. He made himself the patron of science, established scholarships, opened his house to artists—and all that in spite of the fact that he was a little, frail, and round-shouldered man who had gradually, by energetic self-instruction, acquired real learning without formal education. It was public knowledge that he had bought his wife for a hundred Rijsbank dalers from a poor, old, Jewish widow with whom he had once lodged in Jutland during his wanderings. From those days, as well, the vestibule's Oriental weapon collection and the many expensive knickknacks that his ships brought back from everywhere on earth were accumulated, filling the Salomon house and making it into a showy and motley museum. The son, more out of piety than personal taste, let it all remain unchanged.

Philip Salomon had inherited only the industry and talent for business from his father, although, perhaps, there was some inner connection between the father's vagabond years and the son's joy in nature, as well. In the summer, Philip stayed longer in the country than most other financiers. The rest of the year, he would, on Sundays, if the weather was tolerable, ride out with the whole family in the early morning. He himself drove, and his wife sat beside him, while a swarm of children—their own and others—filled the back seats of the wagonette. A few miles into the countryside, they stopped at an inn or in the woods, where Fru Salomon and the smallest children stayed with the lunch baskets while Salomon, with as many of the children who were big enough, went exploring the environs. The apprehensive "King of the Exchange," his wide-brimmed hat shoved back on his head and his coat on his arm, uneasily but cheerfully led the troop of beak-nosed children full of the wildness to which those living in cities, and Jewish, to boot, are susceptible in country air. They danced, hit, yelled around him. They couldn't come near a hill without attacking it nor meet a farmer without Salomon chatting with him, nor leave a shepherd boy before he was given some coins. Salomon was an especially eager flower picker—never happier than when, on his return, he could present his wife with a large bouquet, for which she thanked him with a smile and gave him her left hand to kiss.

Fru Salomon, now at the beginning of her fiftieth year, was the famous Lea Delft—or Fru Lea Moritz, as she was called for a short time—whose Oriental beauty had brought to a little dry-goods shop in Silkegade a big reputation among the fashionable gentlemen of that day and made several of them more or less crazy with love. Uncle Heinrich, her impish brother, steadfastly maintained that she had been the only cause for the establishment of the lunatic asylum, Sankt Hans Hospital. The shop belonged to her parents, who had emigrated from Germany, where she too had lived in her early childhood. At eighteen, madly in love, she had married a cousin, Marcus Moritz, a poor, weak-chested German scholar, the father of her two oldest children, Ivan and Jakobe. The girl had not been born yet when he died. Lea moved back in with her parents. Despite their lack of fortune, they were both very proud of being considered one of Germany's foremost Jewish families. When Lea, after a few years of widowhood, became engaged to Philip Salomon, it seemed inevitable that the family would think it a social comedown. The husband's millions compensated, in their eyes, only indifferently for the fact that his father had run about with his box of wares on his back. To the young widow, on the other hand, Salomon's financial circumstances, considering her children's insecure future, were crucial. As she reminded herself, she had once relied fully on what her heart told her; this time, it was good sense's turn. And she wasn't being misled. Her heart was rich enough to yield to what belonged to reason without becoming desolate. It sacrificed only its surplus.

In any case, she had later furnished Philip Salomon abundant recompense for what he, on his marriage day, might have missed of a wife's love. For twenty years they had lived together in a happy marriage. Fru Lea—of whom one of her adorers had said that she had Copenhagen's prettiest face, Denmark's most elegant figure, and the loveliest hands in the whole world—had become, in the course of years, a bit stout, but her creamy complexion was smooth and fine, her teeth well preserved, her eyes dark brown with a golden gleam. Only occasional gray could be seen in her thick black hair, parted into two braided circles over her ears. And she still had, both in appearance and character, the marks of her race immediately evident to the knowing eye. She carried her head, with its hooked nose and double chin, in a lofty way that brought to mind an empress's bust. Philip Salomon was still so enamored of his wife that he now and then forgot himself in his living room, and would press his thick lips against her hand or cheek in such a way that she had to remind him that the children were present.

In only one respect did Fru Salomon feel a lack, which grew larger with the years. She had, in her youth, on her frequent trips to her family and during her first marriage, received too rich and deep an impression of the great world to feel really at home in Copenhagen. She suffered from homesickness for the country she, in her heart, considered her fatherland, although she was careful to confide this only to her husband. Every year she happily undertook a monthlong trip to Germany to visit her family. And it sometimes happened that when she wanted to express herself forcefully in her own way, she would borrow a word from her mother tongue. It was she who saw to it that the most significant part of the oldest children's education—Ivan's and Jakobe's—took place abroad. She did not want (as she liked to say in her uncertain Danish phrasing at that time) her children "reduced" in a provincial town like Copenhagen. As for what concerned Jakobe, there was another reason. She had always been a difficult girl—so impressionable, so susceptible to every affront that alluded to her Jewish origin, so physically weak and sensitive —that her childhood had been one long story of suffering. She had come home one day from school, white as a sheet, merely because some boy had shouted "Yid!" after her in the street. She was sick from worry and agitation each time one of her small, blue-eyed schoolmates—this happened time after time—humiliated her by refusing her trusting offer of friendship, which she, in her passionate longing to find understanding and love, could not help renewing despite all her bitter experience.

She had inherited her mother's rich sensitivity, but not her happy nature, not her healthy equanimity, not her noble and indulgent smile, with which Fru Salomon met the prejudice of the cultivated and the coarseness of the commoners. Nor had she inherited Fru Salomon's regular beauty. She was in her developing maturity almost unfortunate, thin and pale, with large, unattractive features that had none of the quick charm redeeming many fast-growing young girls.

Her schoolmates did not find it very appealing, either, that she vigorously tried to get revenge for her humiliations by outshining them in ways and in situations where she could make her worth felt. Since she had a gifted and industrious intelligence, she could exhibit her wide knowledge, truly unusual for her age, in her examinations.

And, in her misery, she could resort to means that awakened envy in her fellow students with the help of her plentiful pocket money; for example, she would share a bag of the finest chocolates at school, which could buy her a brief popularity. Her relation to her peers and teachers became, finally, so tense that the headmistress herself advised her parents to take her out of the school. Thereafter, her education was completed in a boarding school in Switzerland.

Jakobe's stay abroad, and Ivan's, at the same time, in a German business school, awakened some resentment in Denmark, where nationalist feelings in those years—so soon after the unhappy war—had been greatly aroused. Salomon did not, therefore, repeat the move with the other children.

Anyway, the next in line, Nanny, had an entirely different, easy, and sociable nature. Already from infancy, she was a healthy and plump pleasure to look at, and as she grew up she was idolized by all, petted and stroked like a darling little kitten. It apparently had not harmed her except to engender a bit of coquettishness in her manner and some inclination to fall in love.

Her father called her a "model little girl," because she was always of an even disposition, and was never sick—she never had so much as a toothache. She was, however, a source of anxiety in the Salomon home, always gadding about, spending half the day in her coat and hat. Her voice resounded in the rooms and heralded her return ten times a day. In the evening, her laughter and squeals rang out from the girls' bedroom, and often, a muffled thumping on the floor signaled that Nanny, who had been in bed, was now, in her white robe and loosened hair, dancing the tarantella for her sisters.

There was another disturbing presence that popped into the house daily—Uncle Heinrich, Fru Salomon's brother. That little man, whose appearance was so strikingly different from his sister's, was also, in other respects, a testimony to the irregularity with which characteristics peculiar to the Jewish race emerge. Herr Delft was a bachelor and called himself a director. In his youth, he had committed a "negligence" in regard to some entrusted money, after which, for a series of years, he had lived in America and (as he maintained) also in India and China as an agent or commercial traveler for English firms. He returned home with a little capital that he drew on, at his advanced age, to enjoy life's material goods, without in any way ever tiring of them. About his travels and experiences, as about his holdings, he was always reserved, which made them seem quite suspect. Even to his family, he appeared to have a secret, magical wealth, and he claimed to still be a co-director of a Sino-English steamship company.

However, he lived in a very modest three-room apartment and was extremely scrupulous about those expenses that did not actually contribute to his bodily upkeep. He spent part on his appearance, adopting the newest fashions of the young gentlemen in the city, allowing some for the curling and perfuming of his dark hair at the hairdresser. On festive occasions he wore a beautiful cravat brooch, which he used to say would "make a queen fall in love" with him. His nieces teased him by insisting that it was an imitation. And once he left the house furious and stayed away for a whole week because his sister and brother-in-law dared to doubt the stone's authenticity.

He was not at all a gentle or pleasant person in company, although in general he half-deliberately performed even his indignations with humorous exaggeration. His self-appointed role of watchdog in his sister's home, his joy in snapping at people when, for one reason or another, they displeased him—especially anyone whom he suspected of speculating about his nieces' dowries—all that derived from his *idée fixe* that he had a mission as the young girls' adviser and protector. He took on this task with as much earnestness as was in him. He had his own secret motives for protecting his actively pursued nieces. Behind his boastfulness lay the memory of the shame he had cast over the esteemed family name, and it was to make up for this that he wanted to be a kind of Providence for his sister's daughters—to prevent blind choices and promote good and, above all, noble, matches.

For many years, the Salomons had not had a big social circle. The town's Orthodox Jews held themselves back from them because of their lack of religious observance, which Fru Lea, especially, frankly acknowledged. She had never felt strongly attracted to the Copenhagen social life and had limited herself to opening the house for company two times a month. In addition, she let her friends know that they were always welcome.

A change did come about when Ivan came home from Germany and Nanny had grown up. Though Ivan could not completely realize his dream of turning his home into something like those of Renaissance princes, he had gradually brought in various leading young men of his generation, including authors and artists.

Jakobe meanwhile stayed mostly abroad. She had found another home in an old *pensionsanstalt* in Switzerland where she hoped her body, grown more delicate and sensitive with the years, would become healthier, there in the high mountains. She came home in the summer months when her parents went to the country but longed to be away with the first signs of cool weather and the winter social season. But one day—she was nineteen at the time—just a month after she had last left home, she wrote her parents a short confused letter in which, among other things, she threw out the possibility of giving up her stay at the pension to settle down at home. A few days later, another letter arrived announcing her impending return and, almost simultaneously, a telegram indicating that she was on her way home and would be there the following day. Though this impatient execution of a firm decision was typical of Jakobe, her parents were somewhat disturbed. They suspected that something serious had happened; Fru Lea confided in her husband that she thought there was a love affair in play. Jakobe had, in the summer, spoken warmly of a young lawyer and well-known politician from southern Germany, the nephew of the pension mistress, whom he had visited a couple of times. Fru Lea knew of her daughter's passionate nature, which had already caused her bitter disappointment a few times before. When Jakobe arrived, it was easy to see that her heart was broken, and when she gave no other explanation for her homecoming than that she had begun to feel herself alone among new guests and longed for home, no one was willing to force out a confession—least of all her mother, who, in her own case, always insisted that love secrets must be respected. (She had, for example, never explained to her husband why he was not allowed to kiss her right hand. She had only let him know that she had made a promise to a lover in her youth in a moment that was sacred to both of them.)

Jakobe had now been home for four years. She was twenty-three and still single. There had been offers, in the meantime, even some very flattering ones. She had, with the years, become almost pretty, in spite of her sickliness. Older gentlemen, especially, were attracted to her odd and pale appearance. Some preferred it to Nanny's glowing but more common beauty. In Jakobe's face, with the hooked nose and recessed chin—the face her admirers called an "eagle's profile," mockers a "parrot puss"—were set two dark eyes in which the whites had a bluish gleam that at times seemed almost black. The nose *was* really too big, the mouth too wide, the lips too thin, but those eyes had an unforgettable look, at once proud and shy. They suggested loneliness and deep thinking. She was taller than her siblings, had long, slim legs, an unusually quiet walk with a light and quick step. The few who saw her smile spoke of her pretty teeth. Over her whole dry and nervous figure hovered the uniquely soulful charm that suffering and longing can lend to a delicate female form.

Those who spoke of her mentioned mainly her inner traits. They praised her intelligence, her strength of will, or her broad knowledge. In her loneliness, she had turned her affections to books, studied old and new languages, history and literature, and impatiently sought new fields to satisfy her thirst for learning. Fru Salomon always said of her that she was the image of her father.

Of the younger men who most frequently visited the Salomon house at the time of Per's introduction, most came for Nanny's sake. It wasn't merely because the majority considered her by far the prettiest, but it was also assumed that she, as Philip Salomon's own child, would be the favored heiress of the two, despite the fact that both Jakobe and Ivan, when they were children, had been adopted by him. Jakobe's character did not invite philandering. She was seldom seen, and in her shyness she often showed visitors an insulting coolness.

At the small gentlemen's dinner when Per was the family's guest for the first time, he met—aside from some older men from the business world—the poet Povl Berger; a lieutenant in the hussars, Hansen Iversen; the scholar Balling; and the journalist Dyhring. He had seen only the first of these before, but, in fact, had nearly not recognized him. The fanatical revolutionary and devotee of Dr. Nathan had, since Per had last seen him, not only changed his Mephisto beard, letting it spread all over his face, but had altered his looks entirely; he now resembled most the common picture of a suffering Christ—undoubtedly just what he had in mind. As one of the gentlemen later whispered to Per in confidence, Herr Berger had, in the same day, to his friends' surprise, published some pious verse by which he, in one move, courted both Nanny's mercy and immortality in the Danish Parnassus.

The man who told Per all of this was the scholar Balling, also literary but as a so-called literary historian. He was six feet tall, exceedingly thin and lion-maned, with a face as flat and expressionless as a wafer. The poet converted to piety confided to Per in a corner that Balling was an idiot who wanted to be a genius and path breaker, but so far had just succeeded in studying his chronic gastric catarrh. Balling was, really, immensely well read, had swallowed whole libraries, was full of citations; you couldn't touch him without a stolen piece of wit slipping out of his mouth. In short, he was one of those bookworms who suck on literature like a leech drinking warm and red blood, and afterward become just as clammy. He had, a year before, published a book on classical tragedy, and when it was somewhat praised in the press, Ivan had immediately secured him for inclusion in his social circle.

Per, who had been a little tense over this meeting with his rivals, relaxed as he viewed these men. His confidence did not diminish even at the sight of the lieutenant, although he was really an elegant figure with a pair of bold eyes and a light mustache in a face tanned by the spring sun. What Dyhring—the journalist—was about, Per couldn't fathom, even whether he was a rival at all. The nonchalant way he moved among the ladies indicated that he was not. Per did not understand why Ivan was so eager to bring him together with this man. As soon as Dyhring had arrived they were introduced to each other, and after the meal Ivan attempted to expand their relationship by encouraging Per to speak about his plans. But Per had not the least desire to talk sensibly. He was completely taken up with Nanny, who was looking enticingly charming in a low-cut raw-silk dress with a red rose in her black hair. He had had the honor of leading her to the table; that distinction and the joyous table company, the unusual elegance of the setting, had gone to his head and exhilarated him. In the smoking room, where coffee and liqueur were served to the gentlemen and where Uncle Heinrich, with a diabolically malicious and mischievous pleasure, steadily refilled his glass, Per was on the verge of becoming a scandal. He clapped Philip Salomon familiarly on the shoulder, praised his wine, and profusely expressed his admiration for the ladies of the house. Some of the older gentlemen, amused at the young man who obviously was in such company for the first time, gradually gathered around him.

A middle-aged blond gentleman who did not smoke was in the living room with Fru Salomon and Jakobe. That was a certain Herr Eybert, one of the city's big factory owners and known as a politician, an open-minded and well-informed man with a fine reputation. Among the Salomon family's closest acquaintances, he was expected to become Jakobe's future husband. A widower with two children, he was a bit past his best age, about forty. His love for Jakobe was a well-known fact. He hid it neither from the parents nor from Jakobe herself. Both parents were well disposed toward the match. Herr Eybert was a proven friend of the house and, moreover, a very distinguished man who was above the suspicion of being in the market for a rich marriage. They had various reasons for wanting Jakobe to get married. In this regard, they were under the steady influence of the family doctor, a Jewish professor who openly insisted that "a girl was not made to live like a nun."

With the apprehension that would naturally arise in an older suitor as soon as a new, young, masculine presence popped up in the Salomon house, Herr Eybert had immediately turned the conversation to the subject of Per and asked who the young man was who had become so loud at dinner's end.

"That's Herr Sidenius . . . one of Ivan's friends," said Fru Salomon in a somewhat apologetic tone on behalf of the house.

"Ah, yes—a Sidenius. Isn't he a little . . ." Herr Eybert twirled his forefinger at his temple.

"Oh, I don't think so," answered Fru Salomon, laughing a bit. "But he certainly is a little unsettled."

"At any rate, that surely runs in the family."

Jakobe raised her eyes from the book she had been leafing through with apparent indifference.

"But he *is* a pastor's son," she said.

"Yes, there is a crowd of pastors in the family," the factory owner remarked. "Just because of that, the family tends to deviate from time to time into some bad aberrations. I remember that one of my uncles, who was a farmer in Jutland, told me about a now long dead Vendsyssel pastor who was given the name of 'Mad Sidenius,' and, really, he seemed to have deserved that epithet. If my old Jutland uncle's word is to be trusted, he might have been something of a brigand who instigated fights in the public houses. I also remember a story about how once, in a fit of drunkenness, in the presence of the congregation—you must excuse me—he pulled down the pants of a parish clerk, and in the name of the Father, Son, and Holy Ghost, he dealt him three spankings with the flat of his hand that echoed throughout the church. That was truly a strange kind of edification. After that episode, the good pastor was stripped of his office and locked up."

Fru Salomon smiled at the story, while Jakobe reacted with a dark expression. It was just this look, so full of disgust, that had impelled the factory owner to such an unusually bold performance, and led him to embroider the story a bit to make it even more outrageous.

Per's loud voice was heard again from the smoking room, startling Jakobe. The sound of it made her blood freeze. She returned to leafing through her book, but a bitter memory insinuated itself into her mind.

It was four years ago, in a big Berlin train station. She was on the way to her pension in Switzerland on what was to be her last trip there. (It was shortly afterward that she had surprised everyone with her sudden decision to come home.) Here in Berlin, she was to meet one of her friends coming from Breslau with whom she was to travel south.

She was unsettled and nervous, knowing that soon she would meet that young lawyer again whom she loved and who, she thought, loved her in return. So she could find no peace at home and had left earlier than she would ordinarily. Now, as she entered the big train station under the vaulted glass dome, she saw, some way off, on the platform, a party of pitiable, ragged people surrounded by a circle of curious, gaping onlookers, held back by a pair of police officers. Because of their motley clothes and exotic look, she thought they were an exhausted gypsy troop being sent back by the authorities to their home ground. In her nervous fright at this harsh impression, she started toward the opposite end of the platform to look for a waiting room. On the way there, she encountered two men carrying a stretcher on which an old emaciated man lay barely covered with a cloak, looking confusedly around with large, bloodshot, feverish eyes. Ill at ease, she turned to a station officer and asked for a waiting room. The man looked at her with an insolent smile and said that she could certainly smell it out with *her* nose. Turning her back on him, she hurried away. Before a row of open folding doors, barricaded by the police, a group of curious bystanders had gathered, stretching their necks and standing on tiptoes to see what was happening.

She was, with difficulty, making her way through the crowd when she saw something that stopped her in her tracks. Inside, on the large, half-darkened waiting room floor, hundreds of the same kind of fantastic, ragged forms she had seen on the platform lay or sat—men, women, children, gray-bearded old men, sucklings lying on their mothers' breast. Some were almost naked; many had bloody bandages around their foreheads or hands; all were sallow, emaciated, dirty, as if they had been wandering for days in the sun and dust. What was immediately striking was that the large, motley crowd, where only the women's white headdresses created a certain homogeneity, was grouped by kinship, had gathered around the various family heads, who were mostly small, black-eyed men, dressed in long caftans with belts around their waists. All of them had staffs and one or another kind of drinking cup hanging from the belt. Many of them seemed to own nothing more. Some brought with them a few cooking utensils, and in some places, children faithfully watched over tight bundles that obviously contained the family's entire possessions.

Jakobe was completely confused by the scene until something pierced her heart. She had caught sight of a pair of Jewish gentlemen with white armbands who, together with some women, were going around dispensing clothes and food. Suddenly she understood it all. While she reeled dizzily, she realized that here was one of the many trains of expatriate Russian Jews who had, in the last half year, been going through Germany on the way to sailing to America. She had read in the newspapers, every day through the whole summer, about these crowds of refugees who were half wild with terror over the scandalous crimes perpetrated against them, abetted by the indifference of the authorities. Jewish houses had been burned down around them, plundered and stripped bare, the old stoned, the women raped, the children killed—the gutters were running with blood. She had tried to console herself by assuming the picture to be exaggerated, since such inhumanity, committed by a powerful and industrious populace, would be impossible in this century of freedom and enlightenment.

"Achtung!" she heard behind her. The two men with the stretcher were now coming back and, with difficulty, opened a passage into the room to carry off another of the many sick refugees. Behind them appeared a pair of uniformed police officers, who, with their impassive official expressions, positioned themselves in front of the door and observed the sorry scene for a moment, and then went out to the rattle of their sabers. Jakobe dared look no longer. She saw red flashes before her eyes and staggered into an adjoining first-class waiting room to catch her breath.

The windows faced a marketplace where people were walking around and laughing. Streetcars clanged and dogs were running and playing in the sunshine. She had to hold on to the window frame to keep herself from falling. This was not a dream, but reality! This infamy crying out to heaven could happen right before Europe's eyes with no authoritative voice raised against it! Meanwhile the church bells rang out God's peace over the city, and the clergy, from their pulpits, bore witness to the church's blessing and to the triumph of neighborly love in a country where, with cold-blooded curiosity, even with malicious pleasure, the crowd looked upon this group of miserable refugees, driven through countries like plague-stricken creatures and, in the very name of Christianity, forced into wretchedness and ruin. Jakobe gave a start. Outside in the square she spotted the two police officers. They were genuine Prussian lieutenants, hair parted in the back, swords hanging at their sides. She clenched her fists. In their official indifference, with their arrogant expressions, the two guardians of the law seemed emblematic of the brutal self-righteousness of the whole of a pharisaical Christian society. She counted herself lucky not to have had a murderous weapon before, when she stood a few steps from them. Now she felt that she could have killed them with her own hands.

Later, when her disappointment in love had shaken her, this scene came back to her directly. The one humiliation called up the other from memory, and the impression of the two experiences merging in her exercised a fateful power over her mind.

At the time she had decided, among other things, that she would never fetter herself to a man. She would not marry a Jew and have her children go through what she herself had suffered because of her blighted birth. Nor could she imagine settling into a Christian family. She too relentlessly hated a culture that for centuries had been the executioner of her race. The whole question of race frightened her, worked on her like a raw menace. The sight of a well-built, blue-eyed, full-bodied northerner like Per awakened in her, immediately, the memory of those two broad-shouldered and self-confident officers whom she could not, after all these years, think of without feeling in her fingers the urge to kill.

She had felt like an adult since her eleventh or twelfth year. Now she began to feel old. At thirteen, she had already had her first deep, unhappy, and agonizing infatuation. Consequently, it seemed that her heart now deserved peace. She had known for a long time that her old friend Eybert was very fond of her and wanted her as his wife. As far as she was concerned, she *did* set great value on their conversations. As different as they were, they had many interests in common—political and literary—and had the same despondent sense, for the most part, about home-front happenings and what was going on in the larger world. In fact, she liked him very much. The little, gentle man with the smooth, blond hair and the thin beard had a beneficial, becalming influence on her and awakened in her none of that memory of broad-shouldered brutality stirred up in her so frightfully by so many other men. There was really nothing in him that provoked sexual attraction. Only when she once heard him tell someone else about his two motherless small children did she feel moved deeply in her heart. It brought a fleeting blush to her cheeks. Whenever she felt the need to find her place in life, a calling, she momentarily entertained the thought of becoming a mother for that lonely man's children.

One day, in the early evening, Uncle Heinrich was settled deep in an armchair in the library, smoking one of his strong, sweet-smelling "Manilas" after dinner. He had been sitting for some time, alone, when Ivan came in and sat in a chair across from him.

"Uncle—I have something to speak to you about."

"You have chosen a very uncomfortable moment for that, you know; it disturbs me to talk after I have eaten."

"But you are not fond of talking while you are eating, either, you like to say, so I really don't know when I can talk with you."

"When I am sleeping . . . Well, what is it?"

"Will you do me a favor, Uncle?"

"You know on principle I never do favors for people. Let's talk about something else."

"So, call it a transaction—or what you will," said Ivan, and assumed a favorite posture, with one foot tucked under him. "You see, there is a young man I'm interested in—a man who—"

"In short—one of your geniuses. Go on."

"Yes, but this time I'm not making a mistake, Uncle. This is absolutely an eminent talent. He will achieve something epoch-making in his field. But he is poor."

"Poor? Yes, that's an essential quality of a genius, I would think."

"And, naturally, no one will permit him to prove his worth here at home. That's the usual lot of great talents. But I am not apprehensive. He'll make it. I have talked to Dyhring about him, and he has promised to interview him when he has the chance and write an article about the great plan he is engaged with."

"In other words, Ivan, the man you speak of, who is the self-confident young person with his nose in the air, who appeared here the other day and created a stir, he with the indecent name—just what is his name?"

"Sidenius."

"Herr Gott von Mannheim! Poor man, with such a name!"

"Now, I know he has in mind to travel abroad to study for a while."

"Did he inherit some money?"

"No, Uncle, you see, that's just what I wanted to talk to you about. Do you understand, I would like to offer him the necessary money that I know he doesn't have. But he's a proud man, and sensitive, in this respect; I'm almost sure he would say no if he were offered money. He would consider it an affront. That's the way he is."

"So you should hold back on the money, Ivan."

"Nonsense, Uncle. It's people like us who should help. You must find a way, Uncle."

"I? Are you crazy?"

"I've been thinking that you could be a screen for me. If I ask you nicely, you will do it for me, won't you? You see, the money must be offered him in such a way that it doesn't offend him, absolutely anonymously, or he'll never take it. You can say it's from some friend or admirer who wished to pay some attention to his desire to travel, or you could offer it to him as a loan or whatever you can think of."

The uncle raised his bushy eyebrows and thought it over for a moment. He was not basically opposed to acting as a generous go-between when it cost him nothing. He had, in addition, reserved a small gift for Per, who, of all Nanny's courting philanderers, seemed the one who possessed the best qualifications to pull himself up in the world and become a respectable choice.

"With how much loot are you thinking of lining his pocket?"

"Whatever is needed so that he can make it. I haven't set limits. He would have an account with Griesmann, and he can receive money from me through him."

"You're crazy, Nephew, stark raving mad like your whole family."

"Is there someone there who can give me a light?" asked a voice from the door to the living room. It was Nanny. She stood there leaning in and hugging her waist. An unlit cigarette wobbled between her lips. The uncle made a face.

"There she comes suckling her paper teat! Haven't I told you what a disgusting, loathsome, vile smell that is?"

"Are you in a bad mood, Uncle? That's a pity because there's something I'd like to talk to you about."

"You, too? Go on! My after-dinner repose is now completely ruined for today."

"I have a bone to pick with you, little friend."

"Pick away! And let that be an end!"

"It seems to me that you could be more tactful than to go walking on Strøget with your ladies when proper people are strolling there. In any case, you owe your family the decency to choose a less dreadful companion than that owl I saw you with both today and the other day. We are ashamed that you have such terrible taste, Uncle."

She was standing behind his chair, leaning her arms on the back, while she sent out cloud after cloud of cigarette smoke over the top of his thinning hair. As indignant as he was at what she had said, he didn't stir, but gave himself up, with half-closed eyes, to the modest pleasure of these warm puffs of air from the fresh lips of a girl.

"Didn't I tell you, Nanny, that it is vile, disgusting, to hear a young girl speak so crudely. Besides, the young lady of which you speak—"

"What young lady?"

"The one you must have seen accompanying me once—that is my landlady's daughter, a very well bred and highly respectable—"

"I wasn't speaking of a young lady. I was talking about an old heron with red wool flowers on her hat and thick daubs of rouge on her cheeks. And I tell you, Uncle, you should be ashamed of her."

"And I tell you, hussy, that you should be the last one to speak of who should be ashamed! *You*—what kind of people do *you* drag into this house with your indecent flirtations. A Herr Sidenius! A farmboy who has so much polish he doesn't blow his nose with his fingers! And what a mug that fellow has! He looks exactly as if he had had a saucy maid for a mother and a buffoon for a father.''

"I think he's handsome."

"Oh, you find him handsome," he sneered. "But I tell you, Nanny, if you marry a baptized rube—"

"What then, Uncle?"

He sent her a menacing glance over the back of the chair and said slowly, with a solemn emphasis on each word, "Then you will not get my big, splendid brooch after my death."

"Well, but you promised it also to Jakobe. And Rosalie, as well. And Ivan, I think."

He got up, enraged, and rushed out of the room, shouting, "You are all crazy here! I will no longer put a foot in this house! It's infected! I have had enough . . ."

Ivan and Nanny, taken aback, looked at each other. As usual, they didn't know whether he was speaking seriously or half jokingly.

Jakobe, appearing at the door, asked, "What have you done to Uncle? He's completely beside himself!"

"Nothing," answered Ivan. "You know he never liked my friends—and now he goes crazy on the subject of Sidenius. That's the whole of it! I told him that Sidenius was thinking of traveling and I asked him to do me a favor in connection with that plan— that's all."

"Is Herr Sidenius going to travel?" asked Nanny, and there was something in the tone that made the sister at the door look attentively at her.

"He's thinking of it."

Nanny asked nothing more. She was lost in her thoughts and threw her half-smoked cigarette into a brass basin on the floor.

"I think Nanny's seriously attracted to Herr Sidenius," said Jakobe that evening when she and her mother sat alone in the living room around the lit work lamp.

"Oh, how can you say such a thing!" said Fru Salomon, resist-ing a disturbing thought she too had entertained in silence. "Herr Sidenius is a giddy scatterbrain, and Nanny is not stupid. Besides, he is about to travel, and, therefore, our acquaintance with him will be at an end."

"I've been thinking that he will delay his travels," said Jakobe after a moment of silence. She was leaning back in the sofa corner beside her mother and staring ahead with her characteristic dark, pondering expression.

"Dear child, how do you know that?"

"Ah, I'm not blind, Mother. From the first time I saw him here I was certain of his motive for coming. And he surely is not one of those who will give up so easily what he had in mind. Ivan has remarked on this trait. Whatever faults we attribute to him, and I'm sure there are plenty, he *does* seem to have character."

Fru Salomon smiled a little. "I think you are beginning to reconcile yourself to him, Jakobe."

"No, I'm not. And I never will. Our tempers are really opposite. But I do think he's very unfinished. No one can know how he would develop under favorable circumstances. Perhaps he really will, one day, become a satisfactory mate for Nanny. In any case, I certainly prefer him as a brother-in-law to a man, for example, like Dyhring."

"Well, well, Jakobe, you have become quite a matchmaker," said Fru Salomon. "The other day it was Olga Davidsen you were working on; and today it's your own sister you want to dispose of." Jakobe blushed. Her mother's reproach hurt her.

"Little Mama." Smiling, she bent forward to hide her embarrassment and put her hand on her mother's arm. "You well know that is the weakness of old maids."

In the spring months, Per became a frequent guest in the Salomon home. It was certainly Nanny who regularly drew him there. In addition, this new and unfamiliar family life attracted him greatly.

One evening, when he had gone, Jakobe couldn't help remarking, "God knows what in the world Herr Sidenius is thinking of when he sits staring out and saying nothing." What he was thinking of was his own childhood home. He saw before him his living room as he remembered it from his earliest days: the long winter evening when only one lamp burned lazily on the table in front of the horsehair sofa and his father half asleep in the stiff-backed armchair, with the green visor of his cap shading his eyes, while Signe read aloud from the paper and the younger sisters sat bent over their mending and every minute glanced up anxiously at the desk clock to see if the watchman was about to come and signal bedtime. He heard again that small sigh that, now and then, floated out from the adjoining bedroom to give his bedridden mother's troubled heart a little air. He heard the quiet simmer of the lamp, smelled the peat smoke from the chimney, together with the odor of stain remover and medicine.

What struck him in the comparison of the two atmospheres, the one before his eyes and that of his childhood home, was not just the contrast in wealth. No, it was more a difference in tone, in the warmth of the conversation, the temperature of life in each place. When he heard here the children freely talking almost like comrades to their parents, Fru Salomon discussing spring fashions with her daughter, what colors and what style would become them, as if it were an obligation to look good, where he constantly found lively minds taking up everything that was happening in the world without the least allusion to the dark hereafter that, like funereal breath, permeated his own home, in which the day began and ended with a retreat from the world in prayers and hymns, where to adorn oneself, to dress up, or merely to look good was considered unworthy of a born-again soul—when he made that comparison he felt thankful that he had really found what he had sought in the wider world, nature's children untainted by either heaven or hell.

Wealth seemed even to have a new value for him in the Salomon home. Like a farmer, until now he had always considered money almost a weapon with which, something like an assassin, you could hold your own in life. Now his eyes were opened to another meaning: a good secure condition in life could make for a man's healthy spiritual growth, for his peaceful and free character development. He began to understand that veneration for gold ascribed to the Jews, and that so greatly scandalized all the orthodox Sideniuses. He remembered his father's contemptuous expression, "Mammon worshippers," and his religion teacher, a pale and threadbare theologian who, as he stroked a student's hair with a hand that smelled of his back pocket, insinuated a warning never to go after treasure that "rust and moths can eat away." He thought how, in that little destitute country, generation after generation was disciplined to an almost pharisaical contempt for all "earthly goods" and how a spiritual exhaustion, misery, and cowardice had marked the whole society, and he felt a spiteful desire to cry out over the land, "Respect for money! On your knees to Mammon!—the people's preserver and redeemer!"

But he felt strongly too that the aversion to the gloss of gold had not entirely left his blood. Whenever he looked around the luxuriously furnished room, he often noticed traces of his native troll nature stirring in him. And when, from this eastern-sun-filled home, he thought back on his own life, with its dreary and paltry pleasures and the torment and discomfort of a struggling conscience, he felt the shame of really being what his father had called him: a "child of darkness," a child of the underworld—a Sidenius.

Life in the large rich merchant's home, where so many accomplished and sophisticated men met, acted on him like the soul's mirror and woke in him a renewed self-knowledge. For the first time in his life, he met people here to whom he felt inferior. Even in conversations with the young girls and their friends, he needed to call on all kinds of artifice to cover up the lacks in his culture and hide the big holes in his knowledge. In secret he tried, with as much speed as possible, to catch up with what he had missed in his general education. With special eagerness he studied Nathan's books, which in these circles he had heard so often discussed and disputed. And he sought, also, to improve his woeful knowledge of languages so that he would not be ashamed in a house where there were so many foreigners and where even the young children spoke the three major European languages fluently.

Though he really came to the house on account of Nanny, he liked most to sit and chat with Fru Salomon and Jakobe, whose conversation was as instructive as it was entertaining. He had the highest respect for Jakobe, who, with such ease, could speak of an ancient Greek philosopher and the newest Bismarck policy without sounding like a bluestocking. In spite of a not very reassuring expression she at first directed toward him, and in spite of the fact that she did not often show him her most accessible side, he set a high value on talking to her about what she had been reading or was thinking of reading. And she surprisingly preempted his interest in Dr. Nathan, a man she also saw as the country's strongest personality and the herald of a new day. They had discovered, here, a subject on which they could agree and which drew out of them both their deepest feeling: hatred of the church that had cast a shadow over their childhood. Per did not wear his heart on his sleeve. But with naive transparency he spoke of his feelings and gradually won, if not her sympathy, at least her indulgence. In truth, she was helping him develop himself more than she knew. Yet even Per had no conception of the influence her superior character would have on him. And, with all his respect for her, he was amazed at the extraordinary homage she received from certain quarters—for example, from the liberal party's most distinguished men, who came to many of the evening receptions.

While Nanny, on such occasions, walked wantonly through the rooms attaching herself to literati like Balling and Povl Berger and their foolish followers, Jakobe, despite her reserve, attracted the day's more critical distinguished and famous members of society around her chair, university professors and the most respected doctors, who played a significant role in the progressive party of the capital, already influential in that day. Once Per heard one of these men voice the regret that a woman of so much soul and with so much knowledge would not be inclined to make some man happy. "Besides, whom should she marry?" the man further complained: "With her character, she is so much the queen she should at least have a prince. That tiresome Eybert is, in any case, not for her." These words, though spoken in jest, made a deep impression on Per and changed, little by little, his judgment of her appearance. He conceded that she bore herself proudly and that her profile really was more like an eagle than a parrot. He began to see beauty in her light but sure walk, with its special soundless step of a stalking beast. He noticed the graceful way she had of settling down into an armchair; even the hurried way she wiped her nose struck him as distinguished.

One evening they met by chance for a few minutes alone in the library. Nanny was at a dinner party and was expected back in an hour. Per was specifically waiting for her return. He and Jakobe sat across from each other at the large eight-cornered table, inlaid with mother-of-pearl; the golden silk shade of the lamp between them was reflected in the tabletop. Jakobe sat with her chin resting on her hand and was looking through a picture book. They had not spoken for some time when she suddenly asked him how it was that, belonging to a priestly family, he had wanted to go into a practical field like engineering.

"Do you have something against that profession?" he parried.

"Why should I," she said, and spoke with much warmth about the significance this century's groundbreaking engineering marvels would have for the liberation of mankind: "Where the distances between countries, with the help of trains, telegraph, and steamers, shrink more and more, national differences will too. Then we will have taken the first step toward the realization of mankind's old dream, of brotherly understanding between all the people of the earth."

Per looked at her quickly a couple of times on hearing these words and blushed a little. He had never himself considered his activity from that point of view, but felt himself strongly attracted by this way of seeing his canal project elevated to such a high mission. So it always went with Jakobe. Her words were to him like the books of Nathan, which could in a flash of lightning illuminate ways of thinking that worked on him like an alluring revelation. How clever she is! he often thought when he sat across from her and observed her odd, sphinxlike features, and he could entertain the feeling of a fairy-tale adventure just from sitting face-to-face with a young Sibyl. In such moments she became supernatural, even the unfathomable keeper of all wisdom.

"I wish I had known you for a long time, dear lady." Although he made an effort to inject a little lightness into his voice, he well knew how embarrassing he sounded. Jakobe smiled in a way that couldn't flatter him. Still he went on with, "Well, that was stupidly said. But it's nevertheless true. I really have for the first time the feeling that I am a genuine human being now. And you, mademoiselle, have played not a small part, whether you like it or not."

"What kind of creature do you think you were before?"

After a bit he answered. "Do you remember from your Danish reader a legend about a hill troll who crept up through his mole hole to live among men, but sneezed frightfully every time the sun broke through the clouds? Oh, I could tell you a long story about that."

Just then, as they were sitting there, he began to open up his innermost self to her. Giving in to his desire for intimacy, he told her, though half in jest, about his childhood and his broken relations with his home. Jakobe had heard something of this before from Ivan. She felt a little uncomfortable in the face of this sudden openheartedness and asked him not to continue.

They were interrupted, too, by Uncle Heinrich, who came in from the entrance hall. The old libertine seldom missed an opportunity to observe his nieces all dressed up. His first question applied to Nanny, as well, because a carriage had rolled up to the house and at that moment Nanny swept through the door. As soon as she saw Per, she stopped and, with a slow, calculated move, let her white fur wrap slide down from her bare shoulders.

Per stood up and looked at her a little confusedly. She certainly was a lovely sight there before him in a white, low-cut silk dress, still flushed from the heat of her social round, eyes shining with party pleasure.

But then, when he turned back to her sister's form, darkly dressed, as she sat with her hand under her chin, lit up by the lamp's quiet light, it struck him how favorably Jakobe compared with her sister. Feeling quite strange, he left soon after and went slowly home. Suddenly he stopped in the middle of the street, half frightened as he shoved his hat back on his head and asked himself, Good God! Can it be that it's Jakobe I'm in love with?

BOOK 3

LUCKY PER,
HIS LOVE

CHAPTER 8

IN ORDER TO make his name known to the public, so as, also, to
promote his plans in the Salomon house, Per had, for some time,
resolved in his own mind to publish a little book about his ideas.
That would be his answer to Colonel Bjerregrav, and the booklet
would serve as a challenge to the whole smug lot of engineers
who wanted to gag him and push him down into darkness. Those
gentlemen would be made to realize that there was still life in
the rebel.

He would, among other things, stress the necessity for a complete rearrangement of the country's communication network.
With calculations that could not be refuted, he wanted to show
how simpleminded it was for a little country, surrounded by the
sea and poor in fuel, to favor the development of a costly railway
system instead of attaching the greatest importance to a tentacled
canal system that could bring virtually every single little city into
direct connection with the world's ports. He would first and
foremost advocate his own project, of which his booklet would
contain a detailed description accompanied by drafts and estimates. In addition, he intended to inform a wider circle of his
plans. Spurred by the words that Jakobe, that evening, had let fall
about the role of engineers as the true heralds of the present day's
culture battles, he decided to start his book with some strong,
general introductory remarks on the future tasks of the country.

He began, now, to work on this manifesto. As unaccustomed
as he was to expressing himself with a pen, and though spelling
and syntax were not his strong points, he applied himself inde-
fatigably to the job. In a style and tone colored by the impression
he received from his reading of Dr. Nathan, he established, first,
the situation of deep decline into which the "academic philistines" in the century had steered the nation, and he presented a
dark picture of the helpless poverty into which the country
would sink if, despite the example of healthy enlightenment
and experience of other countries, the people could not tear

themselves loose from the inherited conception of a prosperous butter and pork economy and resolutely create new sources of revenue. As a counterpart, he sketched a lively picture of the marvelous rich realm into which a strong industry could, comparatively quickly, transform the country. While his pen fairly danced over the paper, he saw in his mind's eye large ships steaming through his canal's bright waterways, heavily laden with the raw products of faraway lands. He envisioned proud factories springing up along all the regulated water runs, heard the sounds of humming wheels and roaring turbines. On the barren Jutland heath, where now only some scrawny sheep found wretched nourishment, he foresaw a city swarming with people, busy new settlements, where the midnight church bells would not arouse fears in haunted minds, but where thunderbolts of electricity would rout the darkness and its ghosts.

One day, when he was sitting at work and glowing with inspiration, he received a surprising visit. After two knocks of a cane on Per's door, "Director" Delft appeared in a bright Parisian suit, perfumed and pomaded, with a bluish monocle at his one good, squinting eye.

"You have hidden yourself well, by God," he said, without an introduction, and looked around the dark little back room, flooded with papers and drafting rolls. "So here's where you sit drawing up your false bills of exchange for the future. It's really an ideal counterfeiter's den, by God. Am I disturbing you in the process of manufacturing some hundred thousands? Ha, ha."

Per knew his way of talking too well to take offense. Still, he smiled a little reluctantly. He couldn't stand this ugly man, and his visit made him uncomfortable. What can the old scoundrel want with me, he thought.

"You are surprised to see me?" asked Herr Delft with an assumed air of anxiety, when he had made himself comfortable, at Per's request, in his one-armed rocking chair. "I have been meaning to visit you for a long time, Herr Sidenius, but my business has left me no time. The restless situation in China and complications in India have created incredible troubles for our company. I have to send out telegrams all day. But now I'm here just to chat with you freely."

He stopped with the obvious intention of arousing Per's curiosity, but Per remained calmly expectant and silent.

There was a prolonged pause while Herr Delft again made the

impoverished room the object of an impertinent inspection through his monocle.

"Have you ever been to China, Herr Sidenius? Perhaps to India? Have you had the chance to visit America? All young men should travel, take a class in the art of going abroad in the world."

After another pause, Herr Delft's tone changed and became circumspect.

"Would you, Herr Sidenius, by any chance remember a little conversation we had with each other the first time I had the honor of greeting you in my brother-in-law's house? You were so kind as to express some appreciative words about my niece, for which I thanked you. I allowed myself, on that occasion, to lead your attention to the delight you would experience looking over the many laughable characters the young girls drag into the house. Aren't I right? Has there ever been a more amusing scene? Here come the young fellows strutting and courting without having so much as a red penny in their pockets and with faces as innocent as a newly washed baby's bottom."

Per thought that if it were not for Jakobe, he would throw the old cavalier headfirst out the door.

"Isn't that so Danish? So very Danish?" Herr Delft persevered as he looked again in pity at the room's poverty. "In other countries, something like that would be impossible . . . unthinkable. In America, for example . . ." He embarked on a story about what he had once experienced in New York with a young man who "*machte* a great career" and snatched up a millionaire's daughter right from under the noses of counts and barons, though he was a poor devil who ate his dinners in a saloon.

The young man was called Stadlmann, an Austrian. He was thought to be either a kind of genius or a charlatan. He wanted to make whole milk and butter out of pasture grass without its first coming from the cow. A fine idea! So while he experimented in a laboratory, he became friends with a son of Samuel Smith. "You've heard of that name—one of the stock market's magnates on Fifth Avenue, a man with seven or eight hundred million—dollars, you understand! Now Samuel had an only daughter, twenty years old, and wouldn't you know, she fell in love with the poor wretch and insisted on marrying him. Well, what do you think? The fellow fell head over heels for her—naturally. But if a man like Samuel would simply have handed over his daughter to him, he would have been the laughingstock of the whole country.

"One day, there were a few of us sitting in our club who all had observed and followed this entire affair. We decided right then and there to form a joint stock company."

"A joint stock company?" asked Per, who had started to listen. "For what?"

"For the sake of the young man's future, naturally. We got together our stock capital, first of five, then ten thousand dollars so he could establish himself as a young man about town in New York, rent himself a lavish apartment on Broadway, have servants and a saddle horse, give suppers for journalists and get talked about in the papers . . . In short, after two months his name was known all over town. So he came, one day, to court Samuel's daughter."

"And did he get her?"

"No, not so much as one of her clipped nails. Samuel had his own plans concerning his daughter. He was himself a garbage collector's son and therefore was set on marrying his daughter to a nobleman."

"So how did it go with the stock company?"

"Very well. It paid an interest of two hundred percent."

"I don't understand. If the father wanted to give his daughter only to a man from the aristocracy . . ."

"Well, naturally, we got the young man his title. It cost four thousand dollars. But for one of Europe's oldest and finest names. It was really easy. The young fellow gave us the address of an old poor widow, Countess von Raben-Rabenstein, from his home-town, who managed to subsist by keeping a pension for young girls. We sent her a long letter with a round-trip ticket to New York and requested her distinguished presence for the ceremoni-ous opening of a new orphanage that we had established as a phil-anthropic project. We got three youngsters from the street and an old, drunken black woman engaged for three months, but we didn't mention that, naturally, to the countess. The orphanage would bear the empress's name, we wrote, and be designed for children of Austrian parents. That she could not resist. That was a divine comedy!

"At her arrival on the steamer, the whole partnership met her with bouquets of flowers and drove her in a carriage with four horses to a gala dinner at the Hotel Netherland, where she was presented to journalists as Herr Stadlmann's aunt. All that was reported the next day in the papers. We waved a legally contracted adoption document under her nose along with a thousand-dollar check while she fainted. Six months later, the newly made Count von Raben-Rabenstein's wedding was celebrated with royal elegance in the presence of the aristocracy of the whole country. I can tell you about it because I myself was among those invited and had the honor of leading the young Duchess of Catania, née Simpson, to dinner."

Per sat there, bent over, and fiddled with his mustache. Herr Delft had, with his story, hit his sore spot: his money difficulties. They were bad enough to make his means not really adequate to cover his needs; his head threatened to break open as he thought about how to procure money to print his book. He had been sitting very calmly, with an affected smile, as he listened to the long story, which resembled the cock-and-bull stories Herr Delft was accustomed to telling, for everyone's benefit, after dinner at his brother-in-law's house. He decided that it would probably be wise to appear well disposed toward this old hyena as he considered whether he might, with his help, get a loan with not altogether unfavorable terms.

"In fact, it was not a bad idea," he said, "to make a stock company for a young man's prospects. Do you know, Herr Director, what kind of traffic you would see if you introduced the notion here at home? I have only one objection. Why speculate only on matrimonial chances? That belongs, in general, to the most unpredictable of projections. Why not, rather, speculate on some of the other possibilities that could open up for an industrious and energetic young man? What do you say about an engineer with one or another good idea—an original waterway construction project, for example?"

"I'll grant you that," answered Herr Delft with a merciless smile. "The name doesn't matter much if it sounds good. The partnership I spoke of was called 'The Company for the Artificial Development of Whole Milk and Cream.' An excellent name! It hooked a couple of trusting dairy merchants as guarantors."

"Good! You mean there is a possibility that a similar consortium could be created here if a man published computations and careful estimates that entirely assure that his plan—if carried out with energy—would someday earn millions?"

"Yes, why not?" The answer's surprising straightforwardness

aroused Per's suspicions. He will catch me in a trap, he thought. He knows my plans, and now it is his intention to seduce me into an open confession so he can make a fool of me afterward in front of Jakobe and her family. He withdrew into himself and was silent. But when Herr Delft took his hat, as if to go, he became troubled. He reflected that it would be necessary to find one or another desperate way to get money, and he decided to dare a little more.

But then he was overtaken by disgust. He felt so humiliated by these endless money worries. He resented having to continuously sneak around, lie, and feign to get what he needed. In a kind of desperation, he threw away all scruples and said, "Herr Director—shall we not pretend? I gather from your words that you know of my attraction to your niece, and I am happy to concede that there is something rash in entertaining hopes for a lady with so many remarkable advantages, both inward and outward, given my present situation."

"Very well said, well said!"

"Well, you have, yourself, brought up the subject and given me some justification to ask the following direct question: Will you, Herr Director, set things in motion for my sake to establish a so-called partnership like the one we talked about before?"

"I?" asked the little man, and lifted himself halfway up from his chair in feigned consternation.

"Yes, precisely—*you*," continued Per. "I confess that I am now in great need. I *must* have some money, or I'll have to steal it."

Herr Delft, who thought Per's intentions always concerned Nanny, had now arrived at the place he had planned. He liked Per's last statement. It strengthened him greatly in his trust that Per possessed the qualifications to make a career and gain a social standing that would be suitable for his sister's daughter.

Suddenly he laughed delightedly. "You're no fool. I almost think you are proposing a transaction for my niece! Well, I respect the thought. But I no longer support private business enterprises. Certainly not with young girls. But now I'll tell you why I have come. I have confidence in you, young man! I have faith in your future, and I will help you. You need money. You'll get it. But I say to you directly—there's no question of paying interest or some such thing. Nor of any real business, whatever you call it. Do you know David Griesmann, our barrister? He lives on

Klosterstræde. From him you can get what you need provisionally, with the security of expected proceeds from your eminent
discovery, naturally. But I tell you, I won't put my name to it. If
someone asks me if it's I who is advancing you the money, I will
say no. Do you understand me?"

Per did not answer. Herr Delft's patronizing and supercilious
expression made it impossible to continue the negotiations. In
addition, he in no way had confidence in the reliability of such a
disinterested offer. When the "director" again picked up his hat,
Per did not try to stop him, but said with a smile by way of an
explanation, "Well, naturally, I took your offer as a whimsical
thought. I hope you understood, also, that my words were said
in jest. You really got to me with your American story."

Herr Delft seemed, at first, a little surprised. Then he smiled
his altogether merciless smile. "Well, God keep you, Herr Engineer. You have all too poor a trust in my powers of perception.
There's nothing to find fault with in that. In the meantime, if you
should entertain the notion of continuing your joke, you know
where Herr Griesmann lives. He's in his office between ten and
four, and I can assure you, he has a great sense of humor. I'll take
my leave now."

He was already standing with his hand on the doorknob when
he again turned toward Per, who was by the table.

"One word more, Herr Sidenius. You told my nephew about
a dowager, Baroness von Bernt-Adlersborg, didn't you? Excuse
me for such an intrusive question . . . but do you know her
intimately?"

"No, I knew her late brother a little. But why . . . ?"

"Pardon me—she's an older woman, isn't she? And she's a
little '*morsch*' in the head?"

"Perhaps. But I must ask you—"

"You received a letter from her the other day—a friendly
letter from abroad. Ivan told me that she had asked you to visit
her in her summer house, and she regrets now that she is
undergoing a cure and won't return until winter. Isn't that
right?"

"What the devil," burst out Per impatiently, and banged his
fist on the table. "Why are you asking me all these questions?"

Without being frightened off, the ugly little manikin closed
in on him, lifted himself up on the tips of his toes, and said, "Well,
I'll tell you, it's conceivable that there are people in this country

too who would marry their daughters off only to men with noble names. Adieu!"

By the end of May, the Salomons had already moved to their summer house, Skovbakken, a villa near the coast, an hour's journey from Copenhagen. Per liked to go there on Sunday open house, but appeared also at other times under the pretext of consulting with Ivan about the printing of books and such things that pertained to his own monograph. It didn't bother him that not everyone in the family was equally happy with his visits, especially Nanny, who, after it dawned on her that she was being discarded, turned her back to him oftener than her face. From the moment he realized that it was her sister he was attracted to, and that he hardly hurt his future prospects by following his inclination, he sought out Jakobe's company solely.

Unfortunately, there was no reciprocal change in Jakobe's feeling for him. On the contrary, something of the discomfort his person had inspired at their first meeting again stirred in her after that conversation in Copenhagen when he had confided in her concerning his relation to his parents and siblings. Heartfelt as her own hatred of Christianity was, she was repelled by the apparent calmness and callousness he had manifested when speaking of his background. Because of her Mosaic veneration for home and family she was wary of showing such an implacable attitude toward her relatives.

There was, besides, something in Per's behavior that affected her unpleasantly. Gradually, as he overcame his social insecurity that had, until now, put a damper on his self-confidence, he began the annoying habit of talking incessantly, in any situation. After having read ten or so books of Dr. Nathan and like-minded authors, he felt competent to range widely through an array of knowledge, supporting himself with provincial naïveté, in every discussion about the great coming Age of Enlightenment.

Especially after dinner, when he had been drinking heavily, he became undaunted as he prophesied, almost preached, about the great new age of mankind and of the gospel of science—in such a way that he sometimes induced smiles and embarrassment in those who heard him.

He had by *any* means to distinguish himself. On walks in the woods he jumped over all the road barriers and challenged the other gentlemen in the group to follow him. If they were rowing, he immediately took both oars to show off his strength. He offended the others with his dress, as well. After a coarse style, his suits fit tightly and, almost indecently, showed off his strong body. He had, for summer wear, procured a particular kind of low-cut shirt that exposed not only his muscled neck but also the top of his chest, giving him a kind of unattractive likeness to young men who live on the love of prostitutes. Nanny regularly gloated every time he came to visit. She would say, "When, one pretty day, he bursts open from self-importance, I'm afraid it will start from behind."

Despite all this, Jakobe felt almost sorry for him. But when, finally, it began to dawn on her that it was *she*, and not her sister, he was pursuing—that it was to please her that he was showing off his strength—she no longer knew how to act toward him. She took care never to be alone with him and talked to her brother about seeing seriously to Per's projected trip abroad that he had mentioned. It wasn't good for him to come to the house before he himself realized his lack of cultural refinement; a stay abroad would rapidly help him.

Finally, thinking about his intentions became unbearable to her, and one day things took a bad turn. It was at the beginning of July. The family was sitting on the wide, graveled terrace in front of the villa and enjoying the cool of the evening after a sultry day. They had just come from dinner and were having coffee. The smaller children, in their white clothes and large sun hats, were scampering and scrabbling up and down the huge, forked marble steps that led to the water among the rosebushes. The season was in full bloom; the bushes were glowing with color. At each puff of wind, a wave of perfume wafted over the coffee table and blended with the scent of Philip Salomon's Havana cigar.

Only one friend of the family was there, Herr Eybert, who, the day before, had come back from his yearly spa vacation with a new, almost unnoticeable little hairpiece from Gossec in Paris. The forty-year-old man, tanned by the sun of southern France, looked quite young as he sat there, talking about his excursion to the Alps and the acquaintances he had met on the way. Philip Salomon, who had pushed away from the table a little to look through the evening paper, injected, now and then, a question or shared some news with Ivan. That man could, with no difficulty, follow two or three different strands of conversation at the same time while multiplying, in his head, five or more numbers and writing down answers somewhere in the mental notebook of his amazing memory. Withal, there was no one more than he who could so consciously enjoy the peace and perfume of the evening, the whole atmosphere of domestic warmth and happy trust.

Nanny was not home. Immediately after dinner, she had gone out with a friend to attend a summer concert at Klampenborg to which she had been invited by Dyhring, the journalist.

Around eight o'clock, Per suddenly appeared. He was in a bad mood. Depressed by his destitution and not expecting any help, he had, in the morning, sought out the attorney Griesmann, to whom Herr Delft had alluded in his veiled manner. To his surprise, he had immediately received a large sum just by identifying himself and signing a receipt. But in spite of the fact that he had, by this, been liberated from the most pressing need he acknowledged, he had gone home dissatisfied and edgy. With a sense of unworthiness for having sold himself out, he locked the banknotes in a bureau drawer without even having counted them.

The sight of his rival, returned home, who sat rejuvenated at Jakobe's side, did not improve his mood. In the mix of feelings that went into Per's love for the young lady, one of the most prominent was vanity. Even a less suspicious eye than his would immediately have seen that she was quite interested in Herr Eybert's return.

The calculated carelessness with which he greeted his rival was, because of that, so overdone it missed its intended effect and made Herr Eybert smile. "I think I am unfortunate enough to have become an enemy to this young man," he remarked under his breath and in French to Jakobe, who refrained from answering.

Unfortunately, the words were overheard by Per, and his face grew pale. In spite of a repeated invitation to take a seat, Per remained standing. Even when Ivan pushed a chair over to him, he did not sit down. He merely rested his hand on the back of the chair and, in that position, stood looking insolently at Eybert. The other felt uneasy, but then, fortunately, new visitors came in and a scandal was avoided.

Jakobe did not recover during the whole evening from the exasperated anxiety of that moment. She was positively trembling. And she promised herself that she would no longer expose herself to that foolish boy's arrogance. She had already openly showed him too much indulgence. If he ventured this behavior one more time, she would ask her father to prohibit him from coming to the house. The stupid, conceited boy! What must Eybert think!

When the guests had gone and Jakobe and her mother had been sitting silently alone for a while on the terrace, the latter first spoke of Eybert. "I think he was a bit worried about his little Astrid. She is not altogether healthy."

"Well," said Jakobe, blushing slowly, "I haven't heard him speak of that. Is it really serious?"

"I don't think so, but that was surely the reason he went home a little early. He doesn't have much confidence in his house-keeper, you know. He really has a bad situation, poor man."

Jakobe seemed to have missed this last remark. She was leaning back in her wicker chair, hands folded on her lap, and looking out over the sound, which stretched out shining and milky white under a vast, empty, starless evening sky. On the Swedish coast the windows still reflected the fiery sunset.

It was hardly a secret to her that her parents wanted her to marry Eybert. Especially recently, her mother had betrayed so much eagerness in steering her in that direction that it annoyed her because it had been so superfluous. Her *own* thoughts had, in the last months, turned toward him more frequently than ever before in their long friendship. She had, during his absence, really missed his company for the first time. She had, almost daily, longed not only for their intimate exchanges about all that was wrong with the world at large, but for his personal presence itself—his bright smile, his intelligent eyes, the whole sense of serenity his being gave off and that was so beneficial to her. When she had blushed before it was because of the strong effect the reminder of his little daughter's sickness had on her. She had, then, felt a sort of shy confusion from halfway considering herself already the child's mother.

That she didn't love him as she had loved others before, she well knew, but she had no scruples about that. In her maturity, she now preferred the full trust she felt at his side to a raging fever of passion. She said to herself that if he was not the proud and noble truth seeker to whom, in the rashness of her youth, she had once dreamt she could give peace and happiness, he was, after all, a man of serious conviction. If he was no longer young, he was, by compensation, not disfigured by the raw immaturity and counterfeit pose of masculinity that made young men so vulgar.

There was always a clean, good scent around his person, which meant a great deal to her, who could never endure being tormented by specific sense impressions lasting even a long time afterward—sometimes like insufferable hallucinations. She was aware of Per's scent from a distance of over three feet—the musty smell of poverty, poor hygiene, and old tobacco that hung on his clothes.

Finally, Eybert possessed an advantage that she had thought about before he had become attractive to her. He was from a distinguished family, and with his financial standing and his academic background (a graduate degree in political science), he had quickly emerged as one of the leaders of Copenhagen liberalism, with a seat in parliament and quite influential in his party's politics. Those who amused themselves by comparing possible nominees for minister, in case the liberal view would ever get a representative in the administration, liked to place Eybert in the first rank.

There was always something alluring to Jakobe about the prospect of eminence and power. She considered indifference about social rank and distinction unnatural. They were expediencies, sanctioned by wisdom and pride. In fleeting moments, her dreams of being in the royal audience, on the arm of a king or emperor, raised color in her cheeks and represented long-due reparation for humiliations—a triumph over all those despisers of her race. If it were not for the fact that her sober understanding had so quickly been overwhelmed by such fantastic thoughts, she would never have left poor Eybert dangling for so long, sighing in vain.

When Per realized the significance of his encounter with Eybert, he decided to propose to Jakobe as soon as possible. Now that he had some money he became serious about traveling a year for the sake of practical study abroad—both in Europe and America. Before that, however, he must manage to secure Jakobe for himself. He didn't dare lay himself open to the possibility that Herr Eybert or some other sneaky old fox would snatch her in his absence.

That Jakobe was not exactly encouraging, even was obviously avoiding his company, did not dampen his hopes. He had from the outset been clear that he would go gently to work to conquer her—bit by bit, so to speak . . . already he felt he had drawn so closely to her heart he could hear it beat! He considered the increased shyness that made her, of late, evade him, a good sign. Now he would stay away for a little while and give her peace and time to reflect before he proceeded with his strategy.

One day he got an express letter from Ivan happily announcing that the article Dyhring had promised to write about Per's ideas was now going to press, and *Falken* would carry it the next day. "Indulge me," he wrote, "and pay Dyhring a visit. I know he will appreciate it. Think how important it is for you to overcome the resistance you probably feel about taking such a step. Dyhring can, in many ways, do you favors, both now and in the future. As I previously allowed myself to tell you, dear Sidenius, the press's assistance in our day is an unavoidable necessity."

Per did not sleep well that night. A week ago, Ivan had, once again, brought him together with the respected young journalist, and Per had, on that occasion, finally given in to his friend's entreaties and revealed a little of his secret plan. Moreover, he himself had considered it wise to prepare the way for his booklet; also, he was excited anticipating the announcement of his name and his thoughts for the first time to an admiring world.

But only disappointment and vexation awaited him. Instead of the leading article he had expected, he found a half column printed on the third page of the paper in small type and signed by one of Dyhring's many pseudonyms: "S'il vous plait." That the article was written in a humorous tone, he did not notice, and he even viewed the heading—"Millionaires Wanted"—as completely serious. He was highly displeased at being unable to find his name anywhere in the whole article and with seeing himself referred to indeterminately by epithets like "the plan's young, talented originator." He was also deeply annoyed with the superficial treatment of the question of cost and was especially furious over an erroneous placement of a comma in a decimal fraction that entirely confused the conception of the character and significance of the work.

He had never had the intention of yielding to Ivan's wish that he should pay a grateful visit to Herr Dyhring. He felt it should, rather, be Dyhring who owed *him* thanks for the occasion of a sensational article. But now he considered it an absolute obligation to bring himself to pay that visit, to make him correct, as soon as possible, that compromising decimal mark. The same morning, therefore, he sought out Dyhring at his private address—an elegant bachelor apartment in one of the city's smartest quarters.

Although it was almost noon, Dyhring was still not dressed, and his housekeeper refused Per admittance. But at that moment, the bedroom door opened a bit and the journalist's blond head peeked out with curlers wrapped around the tips of his mustache. "Ah, it's you." The tone seemed a bit disappointed. "Well, come on in. My hairdresser is here with me just now. I'll be with you in a minute."

Per had enough time to look around Dyhring's rooms, about which there had been so many exaggerated rumors concerning their excessive luxury. The apartment was undeniably elegant: silk-covered furniture in the study, Gobelin tapestries, paintings, piles of books and periodicals strewn about on the chairs, a harem of ladies' portraits on the desk. In the adjoining dining room, whose door was open, he saw a festively prepared lunch table with a shiny white cloth, wine carafe, flowers, and fruits.

Per couldn't help silently comparing these rooms with his own two small, dark ones, and an unexpected impatience seized him. It was not that he in any way envied a man like Dyhring, who was in his eyes a half-contemptible person, a kind of pimp of prostituted public opinion and town gossip. But he resented that so wretched a journalist already had reached a state of independence and power that he himself could still only dream of.

Finally, short and bouncing on his toes, Dyhring came back. He was dressed in chocolate-colored pants, morocco slippers, and a short, loud red smoking jacket bordered in black. "What can I do for you, Herr Sidenius?" he asked, like one accustomed to receiving petitioners. "Won't you sit down?"

These two men, approximately the same age, who both sat with crossed legs across from each other, on sky-blue silk-covered armchairs, had, in spite of all their external differences, not a little in common. Otto Dyhring was, like Per, a displaced child. He was the son of an indebted and dissolute officer who, a few years after his marriage, laid his wife in a grave and then committed suicide. Relations in the provinces gave Otto some charity, and when he was eighteen he came to Copenhagen as a student, poor and neglected, but, like Per, full of the boldest expectations and determined, almost at any cost, to gain his good fortune and reparation for the deprivation and humiliation of his childhood. With a military cold-bloodedness that yielded to no distinction, and with a sharp instinct for where Aladdin's lamp was now hidden, he threw himself into journalism just after foreign models had broken through the political monopoly of coverage and attached the greatest importance to a many-faceted, literarily presented news. Without much talent as a writer, but with the deft versatility of the indifferent, and with the help of an outward manner that pleased women, he had soon succeeded in obtaining an influential position at one of the leading newspapers, where he exploited his post ruthlessly without worrying about the condemnation of the citizenry.

Already, from his twenty-first year, he had an income that approached a government minister's. Theater directors vied to put on his farcical adaptations; publishers sought his favor by bringing out his translations (done by one or another poor language teacher), and variety-show singers and actors, young poets and graying anniversary celebrants, brandy brewers and circus impresarios all courted his attention, showed him all kinds of indulgences, and women offered themselves in payment. Like a young god he was enthroned, high up in his undisputed carefree power, worshiped and despised, envied and disdained, living royally on the stupidity, vanity, cowardice, and hypocrisy of mankind.

He had himself written the article about Per's project only as a favor to Ivan Salomon, who, now and then, was helpful in negotiating his investments. Per did not in the least interest him; in fact, to get rid of him quickly, he promised him he would insert the desired correction in the next issue of *Falken*. But when Per began to talk about his work, it was not easy to stop him. Dyhring became desperate and yawned unashamedly behind his white and womanly hand. He found this swaggering farmboy unbearable. In addition, he was expecting a lady. Besides the article about Per, in the last issue of the paper he had put a lyrical eulogy of a ballerina who presently was appearing in the circus, and he was waiting for his expected tribute.

Finally Per left and Dyhring went into his dining room, whose door had been locked during the visit by an invisible hand. On the threshold, a surprise threw him back on his heels. There on a chair at the furnished table sat Nanny Salomon, wearing a broad-brimmed white lace hat on her head and with a half-eaten radish in her hand. Her constant companion, the little misshapen Olga Davidsen, stood by the window blushing in cheerful embarrassment. "May I ask how in the world you two honored ladies slipped in? I did not hear you ring."

"Why should we ring? I have your key," answered Nanny, with a brashness that made her friend fairly gasp for air. "Anyway, the door was open. Your housekeeper was about to sweep outside. She told us there was someone with you and showed us in here. These are really good radishes!" She selected a new one carefully from the plate, dipped it in the saltcellar, and sank her shining white teeth into it.

"You really are bold, Frøken Nanny! Do you know who it was who just left?"

"Yes, it was Herr Sidenius. I could not mistake his voice."

"And you say that so calmly! If you had come two minutes later you would have run right into his arms."

"Oh, that would have been pleasant!"

Dyhring, smiling, pointed a warning finger at her. "Naughty, careless, charming Frøken Nanny! What should we think of you?"

"Ah," she said, inspecting all the dishes at the table. "You should think I'm awfully hungry and that I can have the greatest pleasure dining with you. There are so many delicious things here. Mmm! Pâté de foie gras! My favorite! Well, let's get down to business." She rose as she wiped her mouth with a napkin. "Do you realize that today is the last day Bakken is open for the summer? And aren't you just a little ashamed for not once offering to escort two young, innocent girls? You know, we can't go there alone, for our mothers' sake."

"Good God, why do you want to go to Bakken?"

"Why do we want to go? Olga, did you hear that? Herr Dyhring is really naive. He asks why we want to go! To amuse ourselves, naturally. We want to hear the barrel organ, ride the carousel, eat warm waffles, see the fire-eater and the fat lady . . ."

"Is that all?"

"Oh, we'll also listen to the cabaret singers and dance on the open platform. But first and foremost, I want a squeaking balloon, a bright red, nasty, squeaking balloon that can say 'Bae-aeh!' Now you know."

Dyhring, who with narrowed eyes had observed the young girl's voluptuous bosom and white arms, which could just be glimpsed under the translucent summer cloth of her dress, drew near Nanny and said in a half whisper so her companion could not hear, "It's very thoughtful of you, Frøken Salomon, to always take a chaperone with you. You are really so seductive in that dress that . . ." He stopped there.

"Olga," said Nanny, turning to her friend, "let's go now. Herr Dyhring is beginning to behave improperly." She fastened her coat with two fingers and curtsied. She started to stalk out of the room, with her arm around her companion's waist, but stopped at the door, looked over her shoulder, and said, "Do we have an agreement that we are to meet at seven at the Klampenborg station? But let me tell you, if you talk out of school and tell Mama that we have been here, I'll say you are lying and you will never more be permitted to kiss me, except on the mouth."

"Nanny, you are really crazy today," whispered her friend, and pushed her quickly forward.

While Dyhring enjoyed his celibate lunch, he happily emptied his sherry glass a few times and sank into serious contemplation. The young man about town had lately begun to concern himself with marriage plans. He had, one day, calculated his current holdings and had gradually come to the conclusion that he must look for a good match. Of the marriageable daughters of rich families he had superficially courted, Nanny Salomon was not the wealthiest nor the one he had most attentively considered up to now. On the other hand, she was doubtlessly the most beautiful, lively, and bold—in short, the one who was most like the women he enjoyed going around with.

There was another ringing at the door. Despite having given his housekeeper strict orders not to let anyone in except a certain circus lady with fiery red hair, he heard a man talking loudly in the foyer and sticking a cane in the umbrella rack. The door was opened, and on the threshold stood an old, powerful-looking man with a flushed face—Colonel Bjerregrav—who said, "I *thought* you were still home. Stay seated. I see I'm disturbing you at your work."

"Greetings, my esteemed uncle. Do me the honor of sitting with me at the table."

"You can be grateful I don't like dining at public expense. Besides, I already ate, more than two hours ago."

"A glass of wine, perhaps?"

"Don't trouble yourself. It's not for my own pleasure I've come."

"I can believe that you must really have something serious on your mind since you overcame your resistance to coming here."

"You aren't mistaken about that, my friend! A longing to see you again did not lure me here, in any case. But to come right to the point: I saw by chance this morning, while at the barber shop, in the rag you write for, an article on a so-called waterway construction project, an article that you probably know something about. In any case, I think I recognized your impertinent style. May I ask what the meaning of this is? I didn't think you ever, up to now, busied yourself with serious things, certainly not with waterway construction, and though I don't doubt that you, in general, write about subjects you have a poor understanding of, I must take the opportunity in this particular case to warn you against continuing with your foolish scribbling."

"I've already heard about it—that a few mistakes crept in," said Dyhring, smiling.

"Mistakes? The whole of it is a colossal stupidity, my friend, that for your own sake you should take care not to mess in. And you are very wrong to think that you are doing the young man a service—you will succeed only in making him more crazy than he already is."

"You know him already?"

"Do I know him? The fellow virtually pestered me to death with his wretched project. He's a complete fantasist."

"Don't you think he can do anything worthwhile?"

"I can't absolutely swear to that. But he is wholly immature; he doesn't have the patience to learn anything or in the least imagine that others could criticize him. He feels he has the mission of a savior. He can settle for nothing less. And now, you write, he will publish a booklet."

"Did I?"

"Naturally, there will be excitement, lots of noise! That Jewish critic has put bats in the belfries of the young. The culture will get an airing out, as they say. There'll be reformers and revolutionaries everywhere."

"But tell me, Uncle, don't we need that? I seem to remember that you yourself have often complained forcefully about the national somnolence and the lack of initiative in our native engineers. Isn't that so? And you yourself once published a pamphlet that was rather severe in tone."

"That's an entirely different thing. I won't stand for your comparing me to him," said the uncle, and a blush suffused his bald head. "The charges I, at one time, and after conscientious consideration, allowed myself to level against the administration were justified and well grounded. Then, you see, our opposition was *not* a manifestation of boyish depravity, but a serious and patriotic concern of Danish citizens for their country's future. There's a big difference, my dear sir."

"Do you think the rulers of that day had that same opinion of you?"

"Yes, I think so . . . but it's not my intention to have a discussion with you about these things. I merely wanted to warn you against supporting a fantasist who could make you and your paper laughable in the eyes of those who know what's going on. It's no secret that I am not an admirer of your profession, but I will give you credit for having avoided being a fool up to now. And while we're at it, I'll add this. I've wanted to talk to you a long time, Otto, since I have been reading your articles. It has amazed me that you, with your understanding and your—I will admit it— unusual journalistic capacity, have not realized how much you yourself stand in the way when you continue to work for this dissolute paper."

"Do you, perhaps, have anything better to offer me, Uncle?"

"Not really. But I *could*, maybe. You know, don't you, that the editor Hammer at the *Dannevang* is a good friend of mine. We have often talked about you. Like me, he knows your stylistic talent but laments the fact that you use it in such wretched service. I wouldn't consider it unlikely—well, I have permission to say this: that there could be the prospect of an advantageous appointment on his paper if you could display your talents more reasonably."

"The *Dannevang*! Yes, but that paper is reactionary, Uncle. And it's outrageously patriotic, militaristic, and disgustingly religious. You don't think I can go back on my convictions!"

"Your convictions! Listen, my boy, spare me the pose. I know you. And now I'll say one thing more. I'll make you a new concession. You have chosen your way of life with a deliberate view, if I can trust my assumptions. Journalism seems to you really a springboard that can propel you up the social hierarchy. You doubtless saw that the editor Lille has been appointed as envoy to Washington. And recently another journalist has been appointed an administrative officer. Whether for good or bad, it's a fact that the government recognizes the respectable press with official posts and, moreover, with no prejudice. That's worth thinking about, Otto. Remember that whatever chances your colleagues have, you have to a higher degree. You have a name that is well known in the military and also appreciated at court. That I am your uncle and would be happy to support you in any honest endeavor might also be a plus for you. And finally, you don't lack the characteristics that would serve you well, for example, in a diplomatic career. Who knows? Maybe by your own talents alone, my boy, you could become Herr Lille's replacement in Washington."

Dyhring, who was smiling during this speech, narrowed his eyes and muttered into the air, "Washington? Why not? American women must be enchanting. And the cuisine is more French than English. I'll think it over, Uncle." By now the colonel had had enough. He sprang up with a beet-red face: "And that's how you dare to answer me?"

"Yes, you must excuse me, Uncle. I can't take life so solemnly."

"That's true," said the old military man after a moment, and his voice broke with emotion. "You can't take life seriously. For you and your materialistic, nationless, godless kind, life's nothing other than a good or bad joke. The troubles of the homeland, the needs of the people, political misfortunes, war, pestilence, fires —all of this, for you, is only stuff for entertainment, column fodder, booty for your hired pen. No, you can't take life seriously. But then life will not need you. Be certain of that! Life will reject you, throw you away like useless rubbish that's ready for annihilation. Yes, you can be certain of that."

Dyhring sat with legs stretched out and thumbs hooked on his pockets. He looked steadily into the air with his narrowed, snakelike eyes. "Time will tell, Uncle."

At Skovbakken, Jakobe was the only one at home that afternoon. After lunch, Fru Salomon went to the woods with the youngest children, and Nanny was, as always, in the city. Jakobe stayed, for the most part, in her room. She was again experiencing one of her worst depressions and suffered from severe headaches and sleeplessness. She was kept awake night after night partly by her bodily ailments, partly by restless and painful thoughts, stimulated by unworthy sensual desire. Exhausted after such a night, she lay scrunched up in her chaise longue, with half-opened eyes and her cheeks resting on her hands. Her room was on the second floor, and through the open balcony door she had a view over treetops to a large patch of the blue sky with many small downy clouds. The deep silence around her, eased by the rustling of leaves from the garden, lulled her now and then into a kind of nervous half nap, in which the body sleeps without losing consciousness. At the slightest sound, her eyes popped open and she was awake.

"Jakobe! Are you up there? What the devil, is there no one home in this crazy house?" It was Uncle Heinrich's voice from below in the garden. She got up slowly, her hands pressed, for some moments, against her face, and went down.

She found her uncle in the garden parlor. After having complained with his usual lack of restraint about how long he had to wait, he took out a packet of papers from his breast pocket and threw it on the table. "There," he said.

Jakobe's tired face suddenly lit up. "You've invested in the market!"

"I followed your wishes. But I tell you again: I will not take responsibility for this. I warned you sufficiently against this economic flypaper. In the end it's bound to go bad."

"I gather the market has gone up again today. What did I say!"

"'What did I say, what did I say!'" he mocked. "You women are crazy. If you get lucky once, you immediately think you know what you're doing. Your sister is a bit more reasonable. She allows herself to hear advice so as not to run amok."

Jakobe cheerfully shrugged and took the papers—some risky sugar stocks—and tucked them away. She and Nanny, in all secrecy, invested some of their pocket money in the stock market, and their uncle was the trusted middleman for their business. Both speculated rather passionately, but while Nanny preferred the modest yield from a less risky stock with solid backing before everything, Jakobe liked the tempting excitement of the game, her triumph when she would go against her uncle's or the newspaper's warning, bet on a boom, and come out lucky.

Herr Delft had, in the meantime, taken up the latest issue of *Falken*, which lay on the table together with the other newspapers. He peeked into it and asked, "Have you read Dyhring's article about that boy Sidenius? I think, by God, he's going to rise in the world, that fellow."

"Oh, Dyhring is only making fun of him."

"Making fun, eh? I'll tell you what, my girl; it could happen that the joke turns serious. He has luck with him, that lad. There's already talk of him at the Exchange."

This last remark was pure fabrication, but Herr Delft had lately seized every occasion to praise Per. After he realized it was really Jakobe's hand Per was working toward, he had a high opinion of his courage and sought the means to support him in his bold undertaking. Besides, he harbored a special hatred for Eybert, whom, in spite of his own persistent criticism, he had not been able to displace from the family's favor; the mere thought of seeing that man humbled could make his head spin from malicious pleasure.

Again at the dining table, the article in *Falken* was brought up, this time by Ivan, who had returned from the city filled with fantastic stories about the sensation it had stirred. He had, on the way to the station, been at the editorial office of Dyhring, who, without naming names, had told him of his uncle's visit and, to count on a return favor at the next opportunity, had let him know how hard he had worked to satisfy his uncle on this matter.

"The old bewigged guard is beginning to get frightened!" Ivan enthusiastically burst out at the table. "Now they will try to smash Sidenius before he gets going by forcing the papers into silence. But it will not profit them! How they will howl when he breaks through!"

Neither Philip Salomon nor Fru Lea responded. The latter, especially, was maintaining, lately, a noticeable silence each time Per's name was mentioned. Jakobe said nothing as well, but seemed absorbed in helping one of the small children who was sitting next to her. However, she was neither as inattentive nor indifferent as she seemed! Her brother's version of a potential menace directed against *Falken* editors led her to blush for a moment. She could never bear talk about any kind of force or persecution without immediately heating up. Ivan's exaggerated glorification of his friend quickly cooled her off, and it was with an expression of disgust that she heard his proclamation of triumph.

When they sat at the coffee table on the terrace Eybert came in to visit; and in the same moment, Uncle Heinrich disappeared. He could not—as he used to say with an ugly emphasis—"breathe the same air as the mercury eater." Nanny left soon after as well, to drive to the station, while Ivan, immediately after coffee, was already hurrying off, impatient to find out if the evening newspapers would print something about the article in *Falken*.

Eybert had rented a summer house in the neighborhood and was almost a daily guest now at Skovbakken. Still, his entrance surprised Jakobe. When she had heard the dogs bark, she was convinced that it was Per who was coming. As soon as she read the article about him she was expecting to see him that very day. She could not imagine that he could let a day go by without presenting himself with new vine leaves in his hair. She was thinking of his presence with displeasure in advance and felt only pity. In her happy surprise at Eybert's arrival she pressed his hands warmly.

There were certainly good grounds for the aging suitor to feel, at that time, very hopeful. Every day Jakobe gave him more expressive proof that she considered their engagement a halfway-confirmed fact. Among other things, she had begun to appear with an Oriental ring he had given her once for her birthday and that she had never before worn. And when his two small girls came with him, she sent their nanny home and spent half the day alone with them in the garden.

Today she and Eybert went down to the beach, where, for a time, they walked up and down the avenue along the wharf, talking all the time, as so often before when they were alone, about politics. On this occasion, they discussed the colonial acquisitions of the great powers and the attendant arms procurement. Eybert voiced the hope that *their* homeland would be reasonable enough to resist all kinds of pirate politics. He belonged to the class of sober statesmen. It was his ambition to represent the temperate Danish perspective, and, in spite of his social station and his cosmopolitan education, he felt naturally bound to the broad, liberal people's democracy that had always been a testimony to the cool sanity of his nation. In his conversations with Jakobe, he liked to give his words a rather bold and radical ardor in order to minimize the difference in their temperaments. She had, in all domains, a predilection for extreme standpoints. She found it unwise that the country, as a matter of course, should relinquish competing with the leaders in business and industry of the great world powers and not take the trouble to secure, early, Denmark's own economic place and position in the international markets of the future. She often said that a Lilliputian land like Denmark was, in itself, an absurdity and that such a little, poor country was, in the long run, an impossibility. She desired a movement that could develop Denmark, make the people understand that only with wealth, with abundance, could a small country fortify its existence and elicit respect from the large countries.

A light rain had begun to fall. Toward sunset, with the skies completely overcast, Eybert and Jakobe had to seek shelter in the house. A pair of lamps were lit in the garden parlor, and Eybert sat at the piano, at the request of Fru Salomon, and played "Two Lieder Without Words," her favorite music. Among many other excellent attributes, Eybert had real musical talent. He played well, both accurately and with great feeling. This evening especially, there was such a tenderness in his execution that no one could mistake his intentions.

In the meantime, Jakobe stood there at the open garden door with her shoulders against the frame and looked out at the rain, which now tumbled down in buckets. She was altogether unmusical and quickly became absent-minded when there was playing. Completely without effect, Eybert insinuated his languishing notes of love into her ears. She was thinking that Per still had not come around. She might have done him an injustice, and she felt, on that account, a little ashamed. The day's glorifying talk about him had by no means passed her by without a trace. She asked herself whether she might have appreciated him too poorly and possibly, also, judged his peculiar attributes of character too harshly. Perhaps he really was a natural talent that could clear away the barriers and mount a battle. In any case, he seemed to possess a little of the native capacity of a chieftain who could collect armed followers around him. To think that he has chained even Uncle Heinrich to his triumphant chariot!

Well, she herself was not unfamiliar with that frightful power that shone from his light, sea-cold eyes. He did not lack courage. She could not easily forget that Sunday afternoon when he had alarmed them all with a foolhardy swim. She had then, by chance, again been standing there by the door and looking out over the water when she heard the childlike and playful splashing and yelling of Balling and some other gentlemen down by the bathhouse, hidden by the garden. Suddenly she saw Per's dark head far out in the rough sea. She thought nothing of it at first, not even that it was a man, let alone that it was he. Only when an outcry arose did she understand—and she could then sense a cold flash of fear shooting down her spine from her neck to her feet. She had imagined that the heroes of the future would be made of finer and nobler stuff, had dreamt about a new aristocracy of soul that would, through righteousness and beauty, bring about mankind's liberation. But perhaps it was just these coarse fists and broad shoulders that were needed. Perhaps there was no other way out than a terrible exploding of the criminal and sanctimonious society—vengeance's judgment day—to cleanse the earth with blood and fire.

CHAPTER 9

IN AUGUST, PER finished his manifesto and read it one day to his friend Ivan, who did not understand very much of it but grew pale with admiration and immediately asked for permission to pay for publication.

Still now it was time to prepare to embark on his extensive travels. He had already, for some time, had instruction in languages by the "easy method," and was planning to depart in a couple of weeks, but, in accordance with his plan, he first wanted to propose to Jakobe. He decided to do that on the third of September, a Sunday. To further that end, the tailor had promised him the first of the new suits that he had ordered in the English style, with a looser cut, because Jakobe had once in his presence, probably deliberately, said that she preferred that fashion to the French.

He had originally thought he might wait until his book came out and was talked about in the press. But he grew impatient to put an end to the unrest and anticipation that held him captive to thoughts of what the result of that proposal would be.

Lately, he could hardly sleep at night. He put his whole welfare on the line with this throw of the dice, and he became hot around the ears one day at a café where he met Lieutenant Hansen Iversen, who assumed that Jakobe's engagement to Eybert was definitely settled.

On the appointed day, bright with sunshine, swarms of people crowded the station buildings. He left home before noon in the hope of finding the opportunity to talk with Jakobe in private before the usual flow of Sunday guests began. But then he ran into some bad luck.

This day was a very poor choice. When he arrived, around two o'clock, at Skovbakken, he found the house full of visitors. It was the fifteenth birthday of the Salomons' third-oldest daughter, and some women related to the family, and a swarm of young girlfriends in motley-colored dresses, mixed with various other acquaintances, came to offer congratulations. Among them was the tall scholar Balling, the literary leech, who, after having been rebuffed by Nanny, now had picked out Rosalie to share his future fame.

Another gentleman he had met here before was also present. He was an elderly, unmarried, part-time teacher and tutor, Aron Israel, related to the family on the Salomon side. He was a little, awkward, poorly dressed man, with shy and nervous ways. He invariably stood with his hands tucked inside his coat sleeves, and turned his half-bald head on his thin bird neck now to one side, then to the other, as if he was worried about being in the way. Although enormously knowledgeable about various subjects, he didn't flaunt his erudition. No one who didn't hear him speak (and he was generally his only listener) could imagine that he was the Aron Israel who, in certain circles, enjoyed a reputation comparable even with that of Dr. Nathan. And it wasn't merely his learning that was respected when his name was mentioned. What had solidified his reputation was his generosity, an unselfishness of a rare, noble kind that seems to appear among Jews. He was invited many times in vain to take a distinguished university post; he didn't even want a lectureship, so as not to usurp the place of anyone who might need it. He was himself quite rich, but he lived in extreme modesty and retirement while he secretly gave great sums of money to students, especially poor ones. Together with two older sisters, also unmarried, he inhabited an Old World apartment in Sværtegade, and his little room, whose walls were covered from ceiling to floor with bookcases, was a gathering place for his former students, who sought his guidance, borrowed books from him, and, in every way, carelessly took advantage of his generosity. He was not really a greatly original scholar or teacher. Only people who preferred to judge men by their character could call him as revolutionary a soul as Dr. Nathan. He himself harbored an excessive admiration for *that* notorious critic and often championed him with great passion against the petty-minded, even in Jewish circles, who, partly from fear, partly from jealousy, disapproved of Nathan's visibility. Their judgment of his person fastened on the small, comical human weaknesses that so often accompany a great and famous soul, like the train of tiny pages with tinkling fools' bells holding the end of the king's purple robe.

Per disdained Herr Israel's unimpressive appearance and, moreover, did not possess the necessary information to understand his real worth. Although he treated him condescendingly, the little man always seemed, nevertheless, to be quite a sympathetic and attentive listener when Per, his tongue loosened after lunch, unrolled, in his loud, lecturing voice, his ideas for the future.

He had not been in the room long before Herr Israel quietly approached and initiated a conversation with him concerning his studies. Jakobe still had not appeared. She stayed in her room and waited to come out until most of the guests were gone. She would not run the risk of scrutinizing looks, impertinent questions from those anticipating her engagement to Eybert, particularly because the decisive word in that relationship had not yet been pronounced.

It was she herself who had warded off the ultimate question from Eybert. She wanted to postpone the decision until Per left on his travels. With a sense of shame, she had to confess to herself that she had been thinking about him more than seemed permissible when she was on the verge of pledging herself to another. During the last sleepless night, she struggled not to think of him, convinced that from his day of departure she would be released from his degrading dominance over her fantasies.

As she now looked at him in his new suit, she automatically flinched a little. From the willful searching look he turned upon her, she immediately had a presentiment of the decision he had come to. At first, therefore, she avoided going near him, but when she realized that she hardly could escape from his proposal, and since she herself wished to make an end to this intolerable relation, she decided finally to determine the matter. She went, alone, down to the garden and walked back and forth on one of the paths near the house, suspecting that he would seek her out here where there most likely would be privacy.

Her expectation proved correct. It wasn't long before she heard his quick step on one of the side paths, and suddenly she was overcome with dizziness. She stopped, then took a few steps to seek refuge near a large stone vase standing on an ivy-covered base. She tried to appear occupied, arranging a tendril that had hooked itself high up on the base, but her hands trembled, and gradually, as his steps came nearer, her heart beat so loudly that sunspots on the gravel danced before her eyes. When she heard him just behind her, she turned around and almost shouted, as if taken by surprise, "What do you want from me? Why are you following me?"

He bowed his head respectfully and asked permission to talk with her a moment. "But you seem so tired; don't you want to sit down?" He gestured to the bench positioned against the base of the vase and again asked her to sit. She complied, since she hardly had the strength to stay on her feet. When she had seated herself, Per sat at a respectful distance beside her. He proposed two minutes later.

He said what he thought he should say on such an occasion and added, "You ought to be confident, dear lady, that I would not have spoken to you if it had been possible to remain silent. Don't think that this is merely a fleeting summer infatuation, which you might assume because of the relatively short time I have had the happiness of knowing you. But however short the time, it has had for me, in many ways, extreme significance. I have told you before that from the day I first came into your parents' home and saw you, dear Jakobe, a new life began for me. People say I have some talents—and I myself think so. I fancy that I am really needed here in my country. But at the same time, I feel that without you, I would scarcely be able to fulfill my promise. I well know that because of how much you already have meant for my development. It's not only my personal happiness but my whole future and welfare that depends on the answer you'll give me."

He had asked for permission to speak, and she had not been able to stop him, because she had to admit to herself that it was an unworthy desire to hear these words of love that had actually kept her there. There was, in addition, something in his voice that made her weak. That deep, strong, manly sound staggered and stunned her. In spite of the fact that he had, in his last remarks, been more naively openhearted than he himself knew, it was not obvious to her that, the whole time, he had been more concerned with himself than with her. Made uneasy by her silence and her dark, blank expression, Per continued: "I realize very well that it is rather bold of me to address you in such a way. You are an attractive woman, beautiful, smart, rich—and I a poor, unknown engineer, who can offer only his future prospects. But it's not really a final answer I want from you. What I ask for is merely that you give me a little hope—just a bit of a promise to take with me on my travels. Depend on me, Jakobe! There is nothing I will not risk, nothing I will not do, to gain your approval."

While the first part of his profession had been carefully prepared in advance, the last part he had not rehearsed. It was only Jakobe's continued silence that stimulated him to offer this extensive concession. He didn't know what more to say. He bent forward, as if to indicate that he was prepared to receive her judgment.

Jakobe finally pulled herself together. "I ought to thank you for your good opinion of me. But, then, I am convinced that you overestimate your feelings toward me to a great degree. In any case," she quickly added to ward off his objection, "further explanation is unnecessary since I am telling you here and now that I am already engaged."

"Is that really the case? With Eybert?"

"About that you have no right to ask," she said sharply, got up, and left. As if stunned by a blow to the head, Per sat on the bench and looked blankly after her.

Fru Salomon and Aron Israel's two small, stout, simple, and cheerful sisters were sitting out on the terrace. They called to Jakobe when she passed by, but she pretended she didn't hear them and went up to her room. As soon as she came through the door, she pulled off her right glove and pressed the back of her hand to her cheek to feel how hot she was. Her chest was heaving; her knees quivered under her. That all this should overcome her! She felt like someone who fortunately had escaped a deadly danger. Precipitously, she took off the other glove and her hat and threw them on the bed with a look of relief, as if being freed from something sordid. Exhausted, she sank into her armchair. Good—she had gotten through that and wouldn't see him again. She shut her eyes and pressed her hand against her side. Ah, that wild heartbeat! She recognized it! How many stormy hours, how much tormented happiness it pulsated back from her memory! She tried to rationalize, in some shame, the sensations raised by this alien and uncongenial man; it was not at all a question of him, but of the memories he awakened, that agitated her soul. In order to banish the image of Per, she called out old, alluring, shadowy shapes, relived all her passions from the first time, when she was a little thirteen-year-old girl and felt lust in her heart, up to the last, fateful disappointment that had made her heart close up like a clenched fist.

The dinner bell rang. She jumped up and looked at the time. Almost two hours had passed, and Eybert surely was waiting below! She held her forehead and remained quite still. In all this time she had not once thought of *him*.

The morning guests had long since gone. There remained only some of the birthday friends and, as well, Balling and Aron Israel with his sisters. Balling, with his high lion's mane, was circling Rosalie, who was beaming with joy in the middle of the room, holding her father's arm, and ready to go to dinner as the day's queen, with a place of honor at her father's side. Eybert came in, and, at the other end of the room, stood Per, apparently in a calm conversation with Ivan. An angry indignation welled up in Jakobe when she saw him. But then, she thought, he probably was staying in order not to arouse suspicion and give occasion for gossip about his sudden disappearance. However painful it was for her to be together with him, she had to grant him a private appreciation for his considerateness.

When everyone was at the table, she took care to sit as far apart as possible from Per and pretended he was not really there. But she couldn't help noticing that, contrary to his customary behavior, he did not touch the wine carafes. In a strange and showy way, time after time, he filled his glass with water, which he carefully colored with a drop of wine. There was no mistaking that he had a definite purpose, had planned one or another transgression and wanted to protect himself beforehand against the impression that he was under the strong influence of alcohol.

A wild anxiety suddenly seized her. What had this crazy man in mind? Dinner was over without anything untoward happening, and the company dispersed in the garden, the young girls with cigarettes, the gentlemen furnished with large, dark cigars, the bands stamped with Bismarck's portrait. Fru Salomon, Eybert, and Aron Israel were with his sisters, who had seated themselves in a recessed garden bower where the hostess herself served the coffee. Jakobe also sought refuge there. Suddenly Per's broad form darkened the entrance. His expression was carefree and cheerful, but his bearing was provocative.

"Excuse me, Herr Sidenius," said Fru Salomon, who, lately, appeared to handle the imperturbable friend of her son more resolutely. "You can't smoke in here. Ivan is down by the water, and coffee will be brought there immediately." Per withdrew quietly, and Jakobe looked with surprise at her mother. As thankful as she was to see him leave, she felt a bit offended by her tone. Did she suspect something? It wasn't impossible. Her mother had vigilant eyes. Besides, Jakobe had almost determined that if Per did not stay away from the house in the future out of his own sensitivity, she herself would inform her parents of his proposal. She wanted, at any price, to keep from being with him. As she leaned her tired and aching head against the wall of the bower, she closed her eyes for a moment, in the sweet expectation of the peace she would again enjoy when she could be sure of not seeing him again.

At that moment she heard his name mentioned. It was Aron Israel, who, in all his artlessness, was speaking about the two-week-old article in *Falken* about Per's ideas and, in an enthusiastic tone, about the "bold and magical future plans for the country and its people. Of course, I'm not in a position to say . . . to judge, how practical they are . . . how doable," said the little man, in his curious stammering and self-conscious tone. "But Herr Sidenius seems to think seriously that, in consideration of our peculiar geographical situation and our . . . as one might say . . . hitherto unused . . . or, rather, hitherto disregarded natural resources . . . we have the provisions we need to become a first-rate industrial power when the modern machines he speaks of . . . those wind and wave motors, or whatever he calls them . . . have been fully developed. As I said, I cannot pretend I have any understanding of the technical side of things; but there seems to me to be some-thing very engaging about these thoughts . . . to transform, like this, the forces of nature we, until now, have considered our enemies, destroyers of our country. The west wind, pounding waves, atmospheric turbulence . . . to transform them into an endless source of wealth and power that will make out of our presently poorest attributes a true Eldorado. That sounds almost like a fairy tale."

His words awakened some unrest in those listening to him. Eybert smiled a little nervously. Fru Salomon ordered more coffee. Balling, who had also come into the bower, looked with compassion on the speaker. Even Aron's two old sisters gradually sensed that their brother had ventured onto a risky road.

When he stopped talking, there was a long silence. Eybert felt called upon to break it. "Yes, a fairy tale, dear man—we have no lack of them in our land."

"Hear, hear," roared the lion Balling, whose bloodthirstiness rose whenever he heard someone praised.

Encouraged by that approval, Eybert went on: "The desire to fly with the wild geese has, unfortunately, always been our national weakness and, politically and commercially, a costly passion. Nathan once hit on an eternal truth when he wrote in an obituary notice for an unfortunate man he was acquainted with, 'We are born, live, grow old, and die as fantasists, in this country.'"

Aron Israel sat there picking at his thin goatee. Then he said, as if excusing himself, "But isn't that really just illusory? I mean, don't our young people keep—altogether—strikingly close to the ground? I have, as a teacher, had occasion to know our young thoroughly, and it has often surprised me how seldom their imagination gets hold of something that lies outside the narrowest frame of daily life. In nine out of ten cases, their dreams of the future don't get higher than one or another well-known position in our society, one you would find in a bourgeois administration, a lucrative medical practice, a comfortable country parsonage. It seems to me, therefore, very interesting and engaging to meet a young man who, like Herr Sidenius, sets his goal so high—so fantastically high, if you will."

"I won't argue with you about words," Eybert broke in sharply, while Fru Salomon again called for more coffee and the two Israel sisters surreptitiously tried to signal their brother that he should stop talking. "Perhaps we should, rather, be called a dream-afflicted people than just fantastic. But unfortunately, the result, in any case, would be the same."

This reply inspired Balling to quote from his collection: "Well, we are a wool-gathering people with foggy minds and weak wills," he flung out, without crediting the author. Instead, characteristically, he gave himself airs.

Aron Israel humbly waited a moment to see if someone else would speak, before he said, "Is it such a bad thing for a young man to dream? I mean . . . haven't the greatest men really proved their worth for us out of their dreams? Has anyone accomplished a great deed on earth without first having dreamt it? In fact, every actuality comes out of our fantasies."

"God spare us!" laughed Eybert. "That's another matter. When we are not content with fantasy alone, but also want to realize it . . ."

"Well, I don't know. For the individual, in any case, is there a real distinction of value between the two things? I mean, couldn't we say that dreams, like wishes and hopes, are the father and mother . . . the sign of a secret magic power that can help an individual to break out of the boundaries of birth, upbringing, habit, heredity, and other conditions that hem us in . . . and so, in a way, seemingly in every case, burst nature's barriers. Even if, for example, Herr Sidenius would not be able to realize his bold fantasy, which is undeniably possible . . . it could have the greatest consequence for his personal development, and that, ideally, could be the most important consideration."

"Excuse me, dear gentlemen," interrupted Fru Salomon, a little nervously. She had observed Jakobe, who was listening with a strained look in her eyes. "I hope you don't mind; it was our plan to have an outing and the carriage is at the door. I can hear my husband snapping the whip."

Aron Israel felt embarrassed, and everyone got up to leave. Jakobe followed, but more slowly and at a distance. When she had come up the broad marble steps and reached the terrace in front of the villa, she stood a moment with her hand on the balustrade and thoughtfully looked out over the sea.

The carriage, a wagonette, stopped before the entrance steps, and Philip Salomon, in all his glory, was sitting on the coachman's seat with two of the bigger children at his side. When it came to leaving, Rosalie and her friends preferred staying home to play croquet; Balling therefore stayed as well. Likewise, both Aron Israel and Uncle Heinrich excused themselves, because they didn't want to risk going out in the cool of the evening. Philip Salomon was inquiring after Nanny, who was nowhere to be found. She had gone out earlier to meet Dyhring at the station. So, contrary to the plans of Fru Salomon, there was plenty of room for both Per and Ivan. At the last minute, she tried to get rid of them by suggesting that they follow Balling's example and be attentive to the young girls. But Per pretended not to hear her and sat down forcefully on one of the outer seats.

The sun was going down, and the sky glowed red over the woods. There was not a breath of wind. First they rode a bit out to the beach path, then turned into the gloaming of the woods, where Philip Salomon let the horses go at a walking pace on the sandy path.

The chatter in the wagonette was very lively the whole time, and Eybert especially was quite entertaining. Per, on the other hand, uttered not a word. He sat stiff and straight in his seat. Only his eyes seemed to be moving restlessly, and the color of his cheeks came and went. From that time in the morning when Jakobe left him behind in the garden and just after the first effect of her answer had died down, he had repeated the same sentence to himself: I will not give up. He had built too much on that expectation to suddenly give in. It seemed to him that the foundations even of his life's work would crumble if luck deserted him here.

All this concern for his future was more and more pressing on his mind and mood because of the sorrow and disappointment over not having Jakobe's love. He had not quite realized how much she meant to him. Though he could see she was no great beauty, the thought of someone else getting her was unbearable. Egoism and his wounded vanity had in these past hours aroused in him the sense that he really loved her. For the first time in his life he seemed to understand the word *adoration*. As he, just then, saw her before him, with her small, pale face, framed by her dark, wavy hair against a background of a glowing red sunset and black, solemn tree trunks, she became a sacred being for him, and he was driven crazy by the thought that any one but him should make the look in those pitch-dark Sybil eyes break into an earthly delight of love! He couldn't let that happen. With clenched teeth, he repeated to himself that he wouldn't lose. His life's motto, "I will," would now be tested. It would be all or nothing.

What particular path he had in mind to take in order to capture Jakobe's favor he did not yet know. He would, in this matter, let chance lead, give himself blindly over to the power of inspiration. He did have, though, a small triumph to build on in the midst of his defeat. Both at dinner and now on the outing he noticed that Jakobe was a little annoyed by Herr Eybert's obliging attentions and had to restrain herself from becoming impatient over the intimacy of tone he had already assumed with her. He noticed something else, as well. A poor woman selling flowers stood on one of the red forest paths that opened before them. Eybert bought a bouquet and handed it over to Jakobe with a few gallant words. She accepted it but without thanking him, and Per observed that she held it in her lap the whole time without once smelling it.

In the meantime, they had reached Raadvad and now came out of the woods. For a while they drove on along the Lundtofte road. Then Philip Salomon turned to the left into a byway in order to head home across the Eremitagesletten.

The evening was already quite advanced. White mist gathered down in the valleys and around the small ponds. Everywhere across the wide plain, it was still; the only sound was of a distant song of a group making its way through the woods. The horses began to snort, and the ladies drew their shawls tighter around their shoulders. The conversation, which had died out, came to life again at the sight of a herd of red deer grazing near the road. The two old Israel sisters seized the occasion to tell a story about a Swedish student from Lund who had bet he could outrun a flock of deer from the royal game preserve and catch a specific deer, but after an hour's wild chase through the woods the student suffered a heart attack and fell to the ground.

"Do you ladies really believe that story?" asked Eybert, laughing. "I remember hearing it already when I was a young fellow. But even then, I had my doubts."

Both ladies, as if from one mouth, swore to the truth of the story. They had read it in the paper. "But with all due respect, I doubt its veracity, anyway," teased Eybert. "Even a half-crazy Swede would hardly come upon such a maniacal idea. In any case, during the run he would surely have come to his senses and spared his heart."

Per felt personally moved by the story, and these words seemed to him a throwing down of the gauntlet. "I think the story sounds quite plausible," he said.

Because of his previous protracted silence and the challenging tone in which he spoke, he stirred some surprise.

"So, Herr Sidenius, in that case, you, too, belong to the believers," remarked Eybert.

"I think that what a man with any self-respect resolves, he should follow through with at all cost." With the last word, he looked at Jakobe, who, when she noticed it, looked the other way.

"That sounds very pretty and quite manly," answered Eybert, smiling to the ladies. "But merciless nature has undeniably set boundaries that even the most virile will respect. And remember, God once equipped such a graceful and tasty deer population with four long, nimble, galloping legs, while we have to be content with a pair of posts that, at best, are adaptable to a more thoughtful way of life."

"In that case, it's not only a question of speed, but also of perseverance. And this latter works wonders in the world. As the proverb says, Herr Manufacturer, 'He who laughs last, laughs best.'"

Eybert raised his eyebrows as he began to understand the hidden threat in Per's words. With a sympathetic expression, he turned away and did not answer.

"Besides," he said, once again addressing the ladies, "I realize that I myself, in my younger days, was part of a story that reminds me a little of that Swedish student's, though it had a lot less tragic outcome. I remember that I was on the way home from an outing in the woods with some of my friends. We had hired a carriage at Klampenborg to drive home by the coastal road, and one of my friends wanted to make a bet. He would run the last five miles at the side of the carriage the whole time, no matter how fast we let the horses run, and would get to Copenhagen at the same time as we. The bet was on, naturally, and when we reached Konstantia, the man got out and started to run. We had a pair of stiff-legged coach horses, so there was really nothing unreasonable about the race. But when my friend had run only five minutes, he groaned like a pair of bellows and then was silent. Suddenly he stopped. He explained solemnly that he didn't want to run anymore, out of consideration for the horses. Then, really moved by pity, he made various pointed remarks about how morally reprehensible it was to misuse dumb creatures, and got back in to the carriage."

The story was a success. The old ladies laughed, and Philip Salomon turned around and said, "If that man is still alive and I were director of the Society for the Protection of Animals, I would grant him a medal of honor."

Per was in a cold sweat from fury. He felt convinced that the story was aimed at him. And though Jakobe had not taken part in the general entertainment, he was tormented by his rival's triumph and meditated revenge. When the old Israel sisters finally finished laughing, he said, "I'm sorry, Herr Manufacturer, that you have lost confidence so early in the power of the will. I would like to ask you if you could hope to regain it if someone else would redeem those words of that friend of your youth."

Eybert again raised his blond eyebrows. "What? I don't understand you."

"I'm asking whether there could be hope for you to regain confidence in the power of the will if someone else made good your friend's bet. If such is the case, I'd be happy to undertake it. And immediately, here on the spot!" Without waiting for an answer, he swung himself over the tailboard and started to run at the side of the wagon.

Philip Salomon stopped the horses and said with some determination, "Herr Sidenius ... I beg you ... sit down in the wagon."

But Per shouted gaily, "Herr Wholesaler! I assure you, it just feels good to stretch the legs a bit. Remember how valuable this can be? There's no way to know what it can mean for God, King, and Fatherland if a member of the parliament from Holbæk's Seventh District regains his trust in the power of the will. And don't worry about my heart. It's in good shape."

"No matter, Herr Sidenius," said Philip Salomon in an almost dictatorial tone: "I cannot allow you to run at the side of the wagon."

"It's best that I get a head start." And then Per pressed his hat onto his head and set forth at a furious pace. Although Philip Salomon immediately whipped the horses in order to overtake him, after a few minutes, Per was out of sight—vanished into the mist.

"This is really crazy!" muttered Salomon, red with anger, and gave the horses a flick.

Then Fru Salomon spoke up: "You really don't need to strain the horses," she said to her husband. "Herr Sidenius was obviously not feeling comfortable with us and has, in his own way, found a means of escape. From here he has the shortest way to the station by cutting through the woods."

This explanation seemed sufficient; though the horses were still running, no one could see Per. He couldn't have taken some other way, since he ran in the direction of Skovbakken, and, besides, the Deer Park was completely blocked by a fence.

The Israel sisters were thunderstruck over Per's behavior and couldn't help whispering a remark to Fru Salomon about the young man's lack of manners. Ivan found his whim very badly timed, and the smiling Eybert allowed himself a bold observation about the possible cause of Per's sudden "evacuation."

Jakobe was quiet and was looking at the moon that had risen blood red over the Swedish coast. It appeared as if the whole episode had not affected her in the least. Nevertheless, she felt at one and the same time thoroughly vexed and so curiously liberated that she was on the verge of laughing out loud. As pained as she was over Per's behavior, still, after she realized that it was evidence of a consciously pursued plan, she was really happy in her heart at the ungoverned outbreak of a man's passion she had longed for. The power of that passion, nature's force, had discharged itself in a wretched boyish prank!

They had, meanwhile, reached Springforbi and turned in again onto the beach road. Here, by the sea, a lighter breeze was blowing away the mist, and swarms of giant flies hummed around the heads of the horses.

They had almost reached home when, suddenly, Philip Salomon stopped the horses. "What's this? Isn't that Louise over there? Something must have happened!"

One of the housemaids was running toward them, and before she reached them, Philip Salomon shouted, "What is it? Has something happened?"

"Yes—there is, there is ... ," stammered the breathless girl. "It's Herr Sidenius!"

"Is he at the house?" three or four voices asked together.

"Yes, and he has been injured! I'm running to fetch the doctor."

"Good God, what's wrong with him?" asked Ivan, grown pale.

"I don't know—Herr Sidenius has fainted! Herr Dyhring gave him some of the mistresses' drops, but I don't think he has come round yet!"

Philip Salomon bit his full lips and cracked the whip around the ears of the horses. Everyone was silent and pale as they headed for home in haste.

Already before they got to the door, they were greeted by a group of alarmed young girls, and, as they drove up to the entrance steps, Aron Israel appeared with Balling and Nanny. Just behind them came Dyhring and, finally, Per, his face still somewhat colorless and his shirtfront rumpled, but with a big, happy, and self-satisfied smile.

"You see, Herr Manufacturer, I have redeemed the bet!" he shouted triumphantly, even before the wagon had stopped.

"Was there a bet?" the young girls cried out together, and crowded around the wagon.

"And may we dare inquire what was at stake?" asked Nanny. She stood alone on the lowest step, and her artful eyes, full of suspicion, went back and forth between Eybert and Jakobe.

Ivan immediately jumped from the wagon and, with a look of concern, grasped Per's arm: "Good God, Sidenius, you have been sick!"

"Oh, it's nothing. Just a little dizziness. I was foolish. I obviously didn't need to run so fast."

The others, all in silence, got out of the wagon, and a scowling Philip Salomon merely said to the groom, as he tossed him the reins, "Get Kristian to run after Louise. We met her on the way. Tell him to tell her the doctor need not trouble himself to come." In the following minute the whole company gathered in the half-dark entrance hall, where the young folk loudly discussed the happenings with the exuberant liveliness that often relieves a residual fright.

Ivan carried on. He suddenly became wild with enthusiasm over Per's exploit and had to hear again and again the story of how Nanny and Dyhring, who were coming back from the woods, had met Per on the stairs, incapable of speaking, and how, a moment later, he had fainted in the living room. Eybert stood by the coat rack and helped Jakobe take off her coat. His eyes seemed to rest suspiciously on her awhile; with a lingering movement, he took the fur stole from her still-quivering shoulders.

"I think I got thoroughly cold on our outing," she said, to explain her irrepressible nervous trembling, which fairly made her teeth chatter. Immediately, she started up the steps to her room.

Although Per laughed and was talking loudly, as if he took no thought of her, she had not strayed from his attention for a moment. In his feverish agitation, he had sworn to himself that he would again speak to her this very evening, even if he had to break into her room from the balcony. Then he noticed Eybert's bouquet, forgotten on the window ledge. That gave him his opportunity to approach her.

"Jakobe! Your flowers!" he cried after her. In two or three leaps he bounded up the steps with the bouquet, but he didn't get all the way up. Jakobe had just reached the top step and, from there, without turning around or thanking him, stuck out her hand for the flowers. Instead of giving them to her, he clutched her hand and, after making sure that no one could see them, kissed it violently. She sank to her knees without the strength to tear her hand away. When he realized that, he was quickly next to her and took her in his arms.

"You love me," he whispered to her. "Don't you? Will you be mine?"

Her willpower was exhausted. In his embrace a sensual shiver seized her, and, instinctively, her hands sought his.

"You will be mine?" he repeated. "Won't you?"

"Yes, yes," she whispered, driven mad by the sweaty smell of Per's overheated body. Her head dropped onto his shoulder.

"I'll come again tomorrow morning," said Per. "We'll talk more about it then." He pressed her again to him and was down the steps in a few bounds and into the hall with the rest of the company.

The whole episode had not lasted more than half a minute. From the moment Per knew he had won out he was again entirely himself. He talked freely, as if nothing had happened, and followed the others into the garden room, where tea was now served.

Little by little, the aftereffects of the wild excitement made themselves felt. When the death-defying run had succeeded, he almost couldn't comprehend that he had dared it. Looking back, everything seemed dark to his eyes. And when he looked to the future, he was seized again with vertigo. He couldn't believe what had happened. Was it really possible that he would forever be free of money worries, that he, Per Sidenius, the poor son of a pastor, would be joint owner of a million? But that was the reality of the situation! He held the magic wand in his hand! The world opened up for him with all the wonders of a fairy tale.

Despite the fact that he had succeeded well in hiding his excitement, some of those present, especially among the older guests, seemed to have a perception that something unusual had happened on the steps. And the fact that Jakobe was not to be seen strengthened the suspicion. The general mood became more and more strained and, finally, uncomfortable. Eybert was silent and went around with a gray face. He approached Per a few times in a way that awakened unrest around him. Balling strutted around with his usual insensitivity and spoke loudly about literature in the hope that he would be asked to entertain the company by reading something.

Finally, the maid came in with the anxiously awaited announcement that the carriage to the station had come to the door, and the party quickly broke up. Only Eybert, who didn't want to go to Copenhagen, remained seated, in the small hope that Jakobe would come down now that it was quiet. But after having waited in vain for ten minutes or so, he got up and, in silence, took his leave.

"Now, Philip," said Fru Salomon when she was finally alone with her husband. "What do you have to say?"

"You're right, Lea. We can no longer put up with this. He is entirely out of control."

"I have been saying that for a long time."

"I'll talk about it tomorrow with Ivan. He must be made to see that we cannot possibly have this man here again."

"I'm only afraid it is too late! Have you really looked at Jakobe?"

Just after the carriage drove away, Nanny went up to her room. She had crept up to Jakobe's door to listen. Since it was still inside, she peeked through the keyhole and saw that there was no light. She then concluded that her sister had already gone to bed and, disappointed, walked softly back to her room.

But Jakobe was still up. The door to her balcony was open, and she stood outside in the moonlight following the sound of the carriage that took Per away. Her face seemed to have aged in the last half hour. Its expression was darkened with sorrow, but she stayed outside like a statue until the last rumble had faded into the woods.

Then she went back in and shut the door behind her. She paced back and forth a few times, then sat in her chaise longue and pressed her face into her hands. For some time she remained in that posture, a prey to the deepest despair and shame. So, then this was the end! This was where her hard-fought renunciation had led her! That her young dreams of heroic love should be realized in such an ignominious way—in such a caricature! She did not try to extenuate the feelings that had thrown her into Per's arms. Nor did she attempt to deceive herself that she would be able to break loose from her sensuous waywardness. She knew only too well: she was in his power. And her humiliation only became greater as she was forced to admit that she had so helplessly yielded to him. There was no saving release. Her fate was sealed. Though their meeting had lasted only a minute, she had lain in his arms, his lips had touched hers, and, in his embrace, a presentiment of rapturous love had shaken her. She was already half his.

There was a light knocking on the door, and Nanny stuck her head in. "Oh, I'm sorry. You are dreaming in the moonlight!"

"What do you want?"

"Pardon me. I heard you still up. Can you lend me a couple of hairpins?"

"Look and see if you can find some."

Nanny was in her nightgown and, with her characteristic cat-like moves, went over to Jakobe's dresser and searched through one of the drawers. Suddenly, she turned around and sat on the half-opened drawer. The moonlight fell upon her thin gown and illuminated the whole form of her body. With an ingratiating way of leaning forward, she said, some anxiety in her voice, "Dare I congratulate you?"

The question shot through Jakobe with a cold shudder. "What do you mean?"

"Oh, forgive me. Perhaps it's still a secret. But maybe I should say it hasn't been very well kept."

"Secret? What secret? I don't understand what you're saying."

"Ah, so you want to pretend innocence? What was so important before that you had to discuss with Herr Sidenius on the stairs?"

Jakobe was sickened by the sound of that name—"Fru Sidenius"!

"And the racing wager . . . ," continued Nanny. "That seemed to me, right off, a bit suspicious."

Jakobe resolutely recovered herself. "Well, you might as well know this evening that I am engaged to that man you name. That's the whole of it, if it really interests you."

There was a moment of silence. "If that interests me? What do you think? Naturally, I'm happy for you . . ."

"Are you?" asked Jakobe.

"How oddly you are talking! Why shouldn't I be glad on your behalf . . . Oh, now I understand. You think, perhaps, that I, myself . . . I remember you once teased me about Herr Sidenius. But in that regard, you have no worries. I don't deny that I have always been attracted to your fiancé, but now I think that you two are much better suited to each other."

Jakobe looked up attentively. "What do you mean?"

"Well, you both are in a higher intellectual class, while I—and you have reproached me with this—am only a poor, thoughtless, superficial worldling. Well, people will now have something to talk about! Oh, poor Eybert."

Jakobe got up impatiently. "Listen, Nanny, it's late. And you must be cold sitting there."

"Am I being a nuisance? Well, then, of course I'll go, I'll go."

She stayed, nevertheless, for a bit. And then, in her characteristically artful way, she finally glided again across the floor in her bare feet. At the door she turned around once more and said, "You are really trying, Jakobe. You are never willing to talk about something like this with genuine interest. I would have enjoyed having a real conversation with you and profited by learning from an older and more experienced sister, in case I myself should ever fall into that dreadful situation of having a man with a mustache touch my mouth."

"Well, you'll have to excuse me—I'm tired," said Jakobe, and began to undress.

"How noble you pretend to be! Don't try to make me believe that you're going to bed! You'll still write to him this evening, pour out your heart in the lonely night, embrace the beloved in violet ink, and send him ten thousand kisses by the morning post. But I warn you, old girl! Hold yourself back a little in the beginning. Be a little cautious in the whole affair. Do you remember Rebekka when she was engaged? She had to wear lip pomade in the early days because he kissed her so violently. And if I have any understanding of men, your groom belongs to those who take what suits them. Goodnight, happy sister. And may your dreams be not altogether agreeable."

CHAPTER 10

NOT MANY DAYS passed before it was clear to Per that despite the acceptance he had wrested from Jakobe, he had not come further along, really, than he had in the past. In the first place, both Jakobe and her parents demanded—the latter in the most decided terms—that the engagement should provisionally be kept secret and, in any case, known to only their closest relatives. And, secondly, Jakobe's behavior to him was marked by the kind of capricious mood that had often tried his patience. More than once it happened that when he came to Skovbakken she avoided seeing him, staying up in her room under the pretense of not feeling well. And that was recompensed only a little when, at other times, for example, they were alone in the twilight and she would yield to his passionate caress.

He had enough knowledge of women to understand the relationship between such an ungoverned outbreak of tenderness and the regularly succeeding attack of irritated coldness. And he realized that a continuous indulgence on his part could be dangerous for him.

After a week, he gradually changed his behavior toward her, appeared a bit indifferent, seemed less consistent, and, finally, stayed away for some days. With hunger shall the obstinate be tamed, he thought. Now he needed to demonstrate that he had the power to lead people and to make their wills submit to him.

The first day Jakobe felt his absence as a liberation. The second, she was surprised, and the third day, a little uneasy. She decided, finally, to write, in order to find out if Per was sick. But just as she had taken pen in hand, she heard his voice down in the garden. Instantly her feelings changed. Her heart started to pound, but she wished he was gone again. She didn't want to see him. Her mother immediately had one of her small sisters tell her of his arrival, but she stayed up in her room. On the sheet of paper she was going to address to him, she wrote an indifferent letter to a friend abroad.

Only after half an hour did she come down. Per met her with his happiest smile and gave no explanation for his long absence. Most of the evening he stayed with Ivan and Uncle Heinrich in the billiard room and seemed to be enjoying himself greatly. He left immediately after tea; the engaged couple had not spoken to each other.

That night was decisive for her relationship with Per. For hours she paced back and forth in her room and struggled with herself. She said that now she would, must, break that unnatural and unworthy connection that not only had disturbed her relations with her parents and old friends, but was on the way to robbing her of her last bit of self-respect.

Toward morning, she seated herself at her desk to inform him of her decision, but when she tried to write, her hand resisted, and the desire for love flared up in her blood. She flung down the pen and sat motionless with her hands on her face.

From that moment, Per was her master. From that night, she gave herself up to her misfortune, sinking down into the tide of the inevitable. Per continued to come and go at his pleasure. When he stayed away, he sent a letter with a few lines of apology and, on one occasion, flowers, as well. But, in general, he gave no clue as to the reason for his absence, and Jakobe never asked for any.

One day, she was in the boudoir of her mother, who was sitting on the sofa sewing. She herself was seated at the window with a newspaper. She was entirely uncommunicative and didn't look up from her paper as she indifferently leafed through it.

"You had a letter this morning from Sidenius," her mother said after a long silence, and searched for something in her workbasket.

"Yes."

"Is he coming today?"

"I don't know."

Again there was a pause. But then Fru Salomon, with an air of decisiveness, laid her hands on her lap and looked at her daughter. "Jakobe, sit down here, my girl," she said. "Let's talk a bit."

Jakobe lifted her head with a startled expression and, with some hesitation, went over to her mother. "What do you want to talk about?" she asked, as she leaned back in the corner of the sofa, as far as possible from her mother, with her cheek resting on her hand.

Fru Salomon took her other hand and said, "Will you answer an indiscreet question?"

"What do you mean?"

"Now don't get offended right away. I won't force myself on you. Will you just—openly and honestly—answer one question from your mother. Are you happy?"

"That's a strange question," said Jakobe, who seemed puzzled and tried, finally, to laugh. But she became very pale.

"Oh, not so strange. You know I'm not in the habit of demanding my children's confidence in love matters. But in this case, I think I have some right to ask ... and to get an honest answer."

"How wonderful you are, Mother. It's of my own free will that I have become engaged, so I must be very happy!"

"Well, if you deal with it like that, my girl, I may as well speak my mind. An hour ago I looked for you up in your room. I thought you weren't well, since you didn't come down for lunch. You had just gone out for a moment, and I happened to see, by chance, that Sidenius's letter lay out on your desk. There is, perhaps, nothing very remarkable in that, except it isn't usual to leave that kind of letter lying about. What did seem very strange to me, on the other hand, was that the letter had not been opened."

"And so?" Jakobe asked after a short silence, while the hand her mother was still holding turned cold as ice.

"And so? Listen, Jakobe, I'm not young, but not so old that I can't remember how it feels to be in love. When you leave a letter from your dearest one unread from eight until two, all is not as it should be."

"You don't understand. There's a reason for that I can't explain."

Her mother looked at her a moment, full of doubt. "Yes, yes, my child. I won't push you if you simply tell me forthrightly if you are happy. Are you?"

"Yes, naturally." She said it unwillingly, took her hand back, and stood up. Her mother followed her with her eyes, but then in romped Nanny in her overcoat and full of town news; any further conversation was impossible.

Fru Salomon again took up her needlework, and Jakobe soon left to go to her room. Her mother's question and, especially, the sympathetic tone in which she spoke had hurt her and filled her with new unrest. She would not be pitied—not by another, not by herself. She had linked her fate to that strange man of her own free will; she had nothing to complain of.

Quickly she cut open Per's letter and began to read it. She had not really been able to tell her mother why she couldn't bring herself to do it before. Nothing humiliated her more than the indifferent, youthful casualness of tone in the fault-free letters Per sent her. She herself interpreted her reluctance as an anxiety that one of them would make reference to those moments when they had met on the stairs and she had given herself entirely into his power; she now thought back on that with shame and disgust—but that was really a kind of self-deception. When she read through the letters without finding the least dreaded allusion to that episode, no sign of gratitude, no expression of longing, she could indignantly and contemptuously have crumpled them up and thrown them into the oven.

This time the letter contained nothing but a few words saying he wouldn't be able to come out to Skovbakken that day. Together with this information, written on the back of a visiting card, he had sent some papers—proof sheets of the manifesto Ivan had spoken so much about and trumpeted as a world-historical event.

She picked up the papers reluctantly. What was it to her? She never had much confidence in his capacities, least of all in his ability as an author—he couldn't even write his mother tongue well.

She had not read many pages before her cheeks began to glow. Though most of the material he wrote about was foreign to her, it was not difficult to make out the general design, and by the way he fashioned it, it quickly became evident to her that here was something new and fresh, grand in its special grasp of how to use the power of nature in the service of culture. She recognized some of these ideas from his oral remarks, which, because of his diffuse, didactic style of delivery, she had never been able to regard seriously. Some other parts she could recall as ideas and insights that she herself had occasionally voiced in their conversations on this subject. But that in no way diminished the impression she had now—quite the opposite. She was especially struck by his capacity for originality and natural intellectual power in his presentation of thoughts that in *her* mouth had almost seemed trite. Here they appeared surprisingly important. The casual notions that she had scarcely offered as serious ideas had, in him, become a lucid model, had shaped themselves into a full sense of the future that struck her both by its boldness and by the powerful conviction behind its expression.

After she finished reading, she stayed for a long time with her cheek resting on her hand and stared out thoughtfully. Who really was this strange man who had become her fate? In truth, she didn't know him, knew nothing other than the most untrustworthy facts, only what he himself and Ivan had told her. What was hidden in his past? For example, what lay under that dark, cold hatred of home and family he had once revealed to her?

Often, in these days, she felt the urge to talk with someone in his family, to shed light on all that obscurity that, in the meantime, disturbed and discomfited her more than anything else and that his own confession merely made darker. She knew that one of his brothers, a lawyer, held a public post in an office in Copenhagen. Per had mentioned that he had recently met him in the street and that, in the course of conversation, he had confidentially told him of their engagement.

As shaky as she was over the thought of presenting herself to a complete stranger on such an occasion, she decided, nevertheless, to seek out that brother, who might be able to give her some information. Already, the next morning she went into the city.

The government office of prison administration where Eberhard Sidenius had his post was in a big, sinister, filthy gray building near the canal. Jakobe lost her way in a labyrinth of empty passages but eventually found a messengers' room where two sleepy men sat with their backs propped against the wall looking down at the toes of their boots. To her question about where she could find Herr Secretary Sidenius, she got the laconic answer: "First floor, third door on the right." And just as she turned to go, one loudly added this remark: "What a beak!"

"Sure," said the other, "she's a Jew girl."

She found the indicated door on the first floor and went into a divided half-dark room that overlooked a courtyard with some green trees. There, at one window, stood Eberhard, writing on a pinewood writing desk that, together with a pair of wooden stools and a bookcase with ledgers, constituted the room's furniture. He wore a long, black, tight-fitting coat with narrow sleeves, shiny at the elbows, and, as it had rained a little in the morning, his trousers were carefully rolled up at the bottom and revealed a bit of his coarse, dark gray woolen socks folded over his double-soled ankle boots.

Though he had answered Jakobe's knock with a "Come in," he did not look up and continued his work for some moments, unaffected. Partly because of this and partly because of his clothes, Jakobe took him for a clerk and asked if she could see the municipal secretary. At that point, he put aside his pen with a dignified air, and met her gaze with his pale, cold, watery eyes, a look that resembled Per's. She said her name and added, "I know that your brother, that Per, has spoken to you about me."

Eberhard remained silent and, with an official air, gestured to a chair.

"The reason I have looked you up you can surely understand," continued Jakobe after taking her seat, her voice uncertain. Her heart hammered in her chest, and she clung to platitudes to ready herself for a conversation. "I know that your brother, my fiancé, has been, for some time, estranged not only from you but from his whole family. Naturally, I can't judge what lies behind these bad feelings. I don't need to assure you how genuinely sorry I am about it."

Eberhard remained standing at his desk, where he had assumed an affected posture, with his open hand shading his forehead. He patiently let Jakobe speak. Not one aspect of his face revealed his feelings, and yet he was thunderstruck with astonishment. He well knew that his brother had been introduced into the rich merchant Salomon's house. He knew that Philip Salomon was a man whose fortune was in the millions. Nevertheless, he had not, for a moment, believed Per's words that he was engaged to that man's daughter—even less since Per had expressly asked him to keep the news secret from others. He had assumed the story was a shameless joke to cover up some sort of defeat.

His first conscious thought was that this connection must be prevented at any price. It was not malice that motivated him, and even less some hidden envy. But he foresaw that with the future prospects that would open up for his brother with this marriage, he would wander deeper and deeper on the path to perdition and any hope for his conversion would once again be out of the question. Eberhard had, more carefully than Per imagined, followed his brother's life in the past years, from a distance. And just now he had believed the time was near when Per, pressed by need and disgrace, finally would repent and recognize what he owed his home and parents.

"Dare I ask you," he said when Jakobe stopped talking, "is it only you who wants this conversation about my brother's relations?"

"Yes."

"My brother does not know at all that you would be seeing me in this regard?"

"No."

"You ask exclusively on your behalf?"

Jakobe, unpleasantly shaken by the interrogating tone, quickly pulled herself together and answered with cold dignity, "As I said—only I wanted this conversation, not Per."

"I can believe that. Unfortunately, it's all too true that my brother, in the last years—really, from his childhood—has divorced himself from his home. You could even say that he has systematically hardened himself in this regard and has manifested a shameful satisfaction in resisting every obligation to those to whom he first and foremost owes gratitude and respect. This detachment has been exhibited down to his change of name! I see you call him Per. Maybe you know that is an assumed name?"

"I think I heard that."

"I won't hide from you that, in my opinion—and you expressly wanted a frank talk—his engagement to you is a premeditated rebellion against home, a conscious denial of its religious spirit . . ."

Jakobe looked up with a furrowed brow. "I don't really understand you," she said.

"I shall try to make myself clearer. It's scarcely news that Peter Andreas came from a Christian home. He well knows that for his parents, Christianity is the only true source of life, and that there can be no happiness—however tempting and exceptional it might appear—if it is not grounded in Christian piety."

"Oh, I understand." Jakobe bit her lips until they hurt. Throughout Eberhard's calm and careful speech, she picked up the same vulgar taunt she had just heard in the messengers' office and that had persecuted her her whole life long. She would have liked to get up to show him her contempt. But the desire to hear more about Per was too strong; she mastered her feelings and remained seated.

"That Per does not share his family's view of the religious life, I know," she said. "But I confess—that does not condemn him in my eyes."

"That doesn't surprise me . . ."

"I mean that if Per has not in any other way broken with his home, it seems to me he can be forgiven. That he has another vision of Christianity does not mean we should presume ill-will in him, and that he has openly admitted it instead of being hypocritical—which, in many instances, could have been advantageous for him—that is only to his credit."

"I don't think, Frøken Salomon, that we need to initiate an exchange of opinion on that subject. I'll limit myself, therefore, to saying for my parents, on whose behalf I speak, that there can be no excuse for anyone to close his ears to the voice of truth—least of all, naturally, for someone like Peter Andreas, who has come from a home where he has heard it from his earliest childhood."

Jakobe did not respond. She had bowed her head, and, as always when she was strongly stirred, her cheeks changed color with each heartbeat. Meanwhile, Eberhard, propelled by the Sidenius narrow-minded self-assertiveness, misunderstood her posture as well as her silence. He thought he had provisionally succeeded in what he intended by his words: humiliating that proud daughter of a millionaire, whose eyes, from the beginning, seemed to express contempt and whose silk dress and light gloves, the delicate scent of perfume, had further incited his evangelical zeal.

Then he changed his tone a bit. With a spark of sympathy, he said, "I am wounding your feelings reluctantly, but I consider it my obligation to tell you that my brother's life, in other respects, gives sorry testimony, to the extent that he has gradually lost every moral standpoint. It is really a common and major delusion to think that the religious life should concern itself alone with the heavenly and not deeply imprint the whole personality. I shall not say more on this point concerning Peter Andreas. These are things that are difficult to say to a woman . . ."

"I imagine so. But Per's unfortunate relations to his home and—perhaps partly because of that—the nature of the society he was reduced to in the past years both explain and excuse, I think, his behavior. And even apart from that, it seems to me that in what concerns us here, there is nothing that justifies so harsh a condemnation."

"You're mistaken, Frøken Salomon. We don't judge our *brother*, only his deeds, his way of living."

"But also in this regard, there are various aspects and attitudes that speak in his favor. He certainly has both talent and a serious will to excel in his profession. Under difficult circumstances, he has, at a young age, awakened attention among his fellow engineers and is on the way to making a name for himself."

"I think I am hearing that you yourself do not have that much confidence. I do know that a newspaper has written something about a canal project, or whatever it is, and has tried to give it some importance. I also know that he even thinks of himself as a pioneer, a prophet of a new age. Just now there is rising in several of the young an urge to be revolutionary that could be merely smiled at if great misfortune did not come out of such immature and unstable souls. There is something alarming about that kind of intellectual storm now sweeping through Danish youth—because it is always the most superficial and unoriginal who—like chaff from a winnowing fan—whirl highest into the air and spread out the farthest. And as for what especially concerns Peter Andreas, the undeniable and depressing truth is that now, after seven long years of study, he still has not taken his examination nor given any proof of development that would compensate the great sacrifice his parents have made. But I repeat—we neither condemn nor reject Peter Andreas himself, only his actions and choices in life. On the contrary, we have all the compassion in the world toward him, and, in spite of everything, we haven't given up hope that one day the good in him shall win out. As to how he could redeem himself in his family's eyes, I don't need to explain more clearly. If it matters to you to know—and I still assume you have turned to me for an open and frank answer—I can tell you in advance what you probably will not be surprised about nor misunderstand: that on his parents' side, no approval at all is to be expected of his engagement to you."

Jakobe rose. In a half-averted posture, she stood a moment behind her chair and looked down at the tip of a shoe, against which she pressed the knob of her parasol. Then she lifted her head and looked at him over her shoulder. Her gaze was marked by vehement agitation. A little smile played secretly around her mouth, and in her dark eyes there gleamed a newfound happiness.

"I came here in the hope of some reconciliation," she said. "I see that was very naive of me. Still, I don't regret having looked you up. I have obtained the information I was missing. And now—I can't help telling you—I am going away happier than I came."

Unsure of what she meant, Eberhard was going to respond, but Jakobe was already on her way out the door and left without saying goodbye.

When she stood out in the street, she was seized by such an overwhelming desire to see Per that, after a short struggle with herself, she hailed a carriage and went out to Nyboder. She felt she couldn't find peace of mind before she had apologized for her mistrust and asked for forgiveness for the betrayal her visit to his brother (she realized it now) really was.

Ah, how well she now understood him. How vividly she felt what he had lived through in his father's house. She had, from the self-righteous words of his brother, gained an impression of that home that made her blood freeze.

She reached Hjertensfrydgade just five minutes after Per had left. Gray streaks of smoke from his cigar still drifted under the low ceiling in his little room, where Trine let her in and left her alone at her request.

She stayed standing there in the middle of the floor and looked around at the bare walls, at the broken rocking chair, at the little black oilcloth sofa, and for a moment she almost forgot her disappointment because of her dismay over the dark room that looked like a prison cell. She had not thought he lived in such inhumanly depressing poverty. And, again, a novel clarifying and reconciling light spread over him and his reckless craving for life's sunshine. Given the disheartening poverty and the joyless childhood behind him, how could he be anything else than a hunter of happiness? And she felt, now, a new and loving satisfaction in the knowledge that, rich, she could make him happy.

She took up some small things that lay by his worktable and laid them down again in their place after having examined them for a moment with the curiosity of devoted love. She moved around in the room pensively, pausing here and there. In her desire to be near him, she handled everything that belonged to him. When she came upon an old bathrobe hanging on the door, she stroked it lovingly, and when she came around to it again, she laid her cheek on it and closed her eyes, to take in the characteristic smells of Per's body. Though she had, before, been put off by the tobacco scent, now it made her passionately long for him.

But then Trine came in, and Jakobe sat down to write on a visiting card, "My dear! Why have I not seen you for three days? I await you this evening. I have a lot to talk to you about." That was her first letter to him. She stuck the card in an envelope she found on the table and wrote his name on it.

As soon as she drove away, Madam Olufsen knocked her stick against the bedroom floor to call Trine up for a report. The old lady spent most of her time now in bed. After her husband's death, her strong body gave way, and she moved around with difficulty. But she couldn't control her curiosity when she heard a stranger speaking downstairs. She got out of bed and limped to the kitchen door to listen. And, then, at the window mirror in the front room, she followed the carriage rolling away until it disappeared around the corner of the Store Kongensgade.

When Per came home a couple of hours later and read Jakobe's note, he smiled in satisfaction. My treatment seems to have been effective, he thought, but it was still too early to show himself compliant. A little more time with the bridle!

In the afternoon, Jakobe went twice to the station when a train from Copenhagen was expected. The second time she returned, disappointed, and found a telegram in her room in which Per, in his usual way, brusquely regretted he wasn't able to come that evening to Skovbakken. She stood there with the telegram in her hand and pondered. Something's going on here, she said, suddenly, to herself. It's not likely that work would keep him in the city every evening. The color drained out of her face. Was it all over? Had she lost him? No, no. That must not happen. She would write to him. She would confess everything, clear the whole thing up, and beg his forgiveness for her mistrust and coldness. She sat down and pressed her head between her hands to concentrate. Yes, she couldn't let him go. She had to win him back, even get down on her knees.

At that moment the door opened a little and her sister Rosalie stuck her head in. "I'm to ask you to come downstairs. A gentleman has come."

Eybert! Jakobe thought in a rush of apprehension. Her old suitor had begun to show up again at the house. Was that an unlucky omen? And that he should come just now!

At first she didn't want to go down, but changed her mind when she thought her mother would be suspicious if she stayed in her room, since she probably knew she had received a telegram and that it was, once more, an apology from Per.

Downstairs in the dusky garden room, she found both her parents together with a gentleman whom, in the dim light, she didn't immediately recognize because he sat with his back to her. But now he got up, and she saw that it was Per.

Overcome, she covered her eyes with her hand as if blinded by the sight. He had regretted his hard-heartedness and took pleasure in surprising her. With a loud cry she threw her arms around his neck. "It's you!" In half a minute she lay abandoned on his chest. Then she pulled herself together, ashamed of having given herself to him so unguardedly in front of her parents. But she continued to hold him tightly by the hand, as if she were afraid to lose him again. Between laughter and tears, she finally took him under the arm and led him out to the garden.

Philip Salomon and his wife looked at them as they went out, and then at each other. "We have to let fate have its way, Lea," he said. Fru Lea nodded silently.

In spite of the couple's decision to keep their engagement secret, it wasn't long before it was generally talked about. It was now only a nuisance for Jakobe to restrain herself when she was no longer ashamed of her feelings. She went around with the sensation of a woman who had given birth clandestinely and who suddenly dares reveal her happiness to the whole world.

Per noticed also that certain circles were showing an interest in him. When he went into one of the cafés in Kongens Nytorv, which he visited exclusively, a few guests would stick their heads together and start whispering about him. Throughout the social scene, the amazing connection awakened the acutest attention. It was the stuff of fairy tales—the young fortunate knight who first had inherited money from Neergaard and now had bagged some of Philip Salomon's treasure for himself.

This news reached the ears, as well, of Per's former fellow students at the college. They had already read the article about him in *Falken*, and the announcement of his manifesto awakened an especially lively expectation. Per had been neither so isolated nor so misunderstood among his comrades as he thought. Not only did the more independent thinkers like him find the air in Professor Sandrup's lecture hall too stuffy, but also all the good-for-nothings, who seized every criticism of the school as an excuse for their laziness, and who had long expected that, by one or another dramatic way, Per would make his name. On the other side, however, the first fame created a line of unreconciled enemies among the hard and decent workers, who, until now, had viewed him with sympathetic condescension. Among them was a certain Marius Jørgensen, who was the apple of Professor Sandrup's eye and to whom Per, on one occasion, had given the nickname "a God-delighting index." That future pillar of society was prepared to launch in secret a terrible revenge against him by providing *Industribladet* with a mocking critique of his book when it came out.

The Salomon family gradually began to reconcile itself to the conception of Per as the house's future son-in-law. Now it seemed that it was Uncle Heinrich who was the least satisfied. Although Per had long since realized what the deal was with his consortium, Herr Delft continually felt the need to act as a protective father and let him know in confidential conversations that he had taken just the first and only moderately significant step toward his future. He often spoke suggestively about the Dowager Baroness von Adlersborg, and Per, who had smelled blood, now understood that suggestive song and quietly entered into his way of thinking. He knew that the baroness had gone to a spa in southern Germany, and it was his intention to plan his trip in such a way as to pay her a visit. He had, for the time being, no other purpose than to maintain a connection with the distinguished lady, to keep alive the possibility that something might come from that quarter. In reality, he would have nothing against putting the hateful Sidenius name in perpetual exile, that laughable troll-token of parish provinciality that betrayed his origin. Baron von Adlersborg! Why not? That would look good on a visiting card.

He told nothing of this grandiose dream to Jakobe. He thought her altogether indifferent to the signs of social status and assumed, therefore, that she would not approve of it. He did not suspect that she was building, in her thoughts, still more high-flying plans for him and their future.

One evening, he had, at her urging, read out loud his whole manifesto. And now that she listened to him with love's ears, each sentence sounded to her like a ringing fanfare. She was wise enough to keep this impression to herself. In spite of her love, she was never really blind to Per's many frailties and well understood that there was much to work on before he stood adequately armed for the battle he now, in her eyes, had chosen as his own destiny.

On the other hand, she gave herself more and more unreservedly to him in her passion. The elevated sense of tenderness in her breast, the burning devotion that from childhood had caused her such bitter humiliation, could now, finally, find an outlet. Her thoughts were of him day and night. Each morning she sent him fresh flowers to enliven his sad little rooms. She overwhelmed him with all kinds of presents, strained her ingenuity daily to find something that could make him happy. Finally, she persuaded her parents to return to the city earlier than usual so she could see him more often, await his presence every hour of the day, know that at night he was merely eight hundred and thirty steps from her side—she had secretly measured the distance. But even that was not all. One hour after he had left her, she would sit down to write or telegraph him. There was always something she just had to tell him immediately, or something she worried about having said in the wrong way, or something she had said but now regretted and wanted him to forget—an altogether half-conscious pretext to tell him, one way or another, that she loved him and that she counted the minutes, the seconds, of her heartbeat's clock until she saw him again.

"Bonjour, monsieur," she wrote in the morning when the sun was shining in at her window. "Will you come, perhaps, today? In that case, I could be spared writing this letter. But you are so unpredictable. Why didn't you come last evening? I waited until ten, went to bed in awful spirits, and hated you with my whole heart until eleven. Today I forgive you for the sake of the marvelous sunny weather. Couldn't you, for this one day, leave your drafts and proofs and come here around two? Only Mother and I will be home. Remember that soon we will be parted from each other, and, when you are far away, I'll go into the cloister and live out the eternity until you return."

Per felt happy and contented with all this and gained twelve pounds in a month. Nevertheless, the erotic atmosphere in which Jakobe wrapped him was sometimes too tropical. He himself could, on occasion, blaze up, especially when they were alone together after dinner. But Jakobe's perpetual flame was alien to him and, finally, exhausting. With his life of feeling stunted since childhood, cut off from all emotion other than what thrives in shadows and is loved by the harsh wind, he felt almost put off by the sunshine of her rich love. He was really embarrassed by her ungoverned outbreak of tenderness and made a fairly awkward lover.

One day, when they sat together in the twilight, Jakobe put her arms around his neck and said, "Do you realize, Per, that you have never told me you loved me?"

"But you know that."

"Yes, but that's not enough. I want you to say it, at least one time, to hear how it sounds when my dearest tells me he loves me. Do it now, Per."

"But, dear, I have really often told you that—"

"But you haven't said those words, Per. And it's those words I want to hear. Remember, those are the words we women hear in our heads day and night, waking and in our dreams, from the time we come home from our first dance. Say it, Per! Shall I help you? Listen, now—you just repeat my words so it will be a mutual acknowledgment: I."

"I," he repeated.

"Love."

"No, this is really too stupid, Jakobe," objected Per, red in the face and with his hand on her mouth. And when she continued to beg, he became angry and disengaged himself from her arms.

Though he often felt relief when he came out into the street and lit a cigar after an evening of stormy parting in the hall like this last, he never desired to go home immediately to his work, and even less, as in the old days, to a café. He had come to enjoy walking around in the streets when they were still and empty, yielding to a new mood he didn't really understand. Like the first time he, unawares, drank at eternity's springs, he had a thrilling, half-terrifying sense that a magic world was opening inside him. But while the paradise of love he had been led to by the good Fransisca had been a comfortable little herb garden with mignotte, stock, and well-tended vegetable beds, now he was looking in at a whispering palm grove, large and solemn as a temple! He began, in these night wanderings, to have a presentiment of a higher happiness, a bigger and purer earthly joy than what he had, until now, desired. He started to understand that life could be rich just with a woman's love, and that there was a deeper truth than he himself had known in his loose allusion to the embrace of paradise, where there was oblivion for all sorrows and forgiveness for all sins.

One night after coming home from an hourlong stroll, he wrote these lines to Jakobe:

> There was a man who, in jest, once called me "Lucky Per." And I have never really considered myself a stepchild of life. Oh, perhaps in certain moments of discouragement I could complain about my fate that let me be born into a country where, long ago, a pastor's son named Adam married a parish clerk's daughter Eve and gradually filled the earth with these million Sideniuses. But when I now

look back over the past years, I feel that a guardian angel has followed me through life, and, although I have often been wayward and chased after false glitter, I am here now with the golden crown of triumph in my hand: you and your love.

I feel the need to hold you again in my thoughts and to thank you before I go to sleep. You have been my dear guardian angel from the day I first came into your parents' house, the day that was the great turning point in my life. What I could not, before, manage to say when I sat with you and you asked me to, I now will whisper to you in the still of the night: I—love—you!

When, in a solemn mood, he read through the letter the next day, he thought it affected and burned it. He wrote her another letter, instead, in which he mostly spoke about his book. "The printing is taking a devil of a time. The sketches are holding it up; they must be cut out of wood. And, you know, I'm thinking about another title for the book. 'The New Age' sounds commonplace. I think I'll call it 'The State of the Future.' Does that sound good?"

It was October, and Per had finally finished preparing his travel plans. It was his intention to spend some time first in Germany to visit some of the well-known technical institutes there. Later, he planned to seize the opportunity to see one or another of the large waterway construction projects, enterprises of an Anglo-American international firm—Blackbourn & Gries—to which his father-in-law had promised to recommend him. In addition he planned to see Paris, London, New York, and a couple of other large North American cities. He would be away altogether for two years. Although Jakobe could not conceive of how she would pass such a long time, she made no objections. It had been she, after all, who suggested a year. Per himself thought he needed only half that time. But she begged him earnestly not to hurry, and she was, on that point, in agreement with her father, who, one day, asked Per to come to his office, where he handed him a letter of credit for five thousand kroner with the rider that would renew it at the end of a year.

In the middle of his packing and planning his wide-ranging travels, Per received a letter from his brother. Eberhard wrote that he had heard Per intended to travel abroad. He did not want, therefore, to fail to inform him of his father's situation, which now was such that a crisis was at hand. He himself would go home almost immediately, where all the children, as might be expected, would gather.

After the reception of that letter, Per paced up and down in doubt-ridden thought. The letter's tone had been unusually considerate, and happiness had disposed Per to be conciliatory. No one could believe anymore that he could return as Per, the prodigal son, he thought. But his triumph, after all, was still incomplete. If only his book had come out!

Finally, he burned the letter, together with some old papers that he cleared out of his drawers, and didn't mention this to Jakobe. The day after he set off for Germany.

BOOK 4

LUCKY PER ABROAD

CHAPTER 11

But now I must tell you about my peculiar debut in the Great World, which had a touch of comedy about it. You know how traveling to Berlin is not very pleasant. I confess, frankly, that I finally collapsed into sleep and didn't wake up before we rumbled into Stettiner Station. I staggered into a carriage, delivered up my suitcase, and gave the order to the driver: "Hotel Zimmerman, Burgstrasse"—that's the hotel your uncle recommended to me. But the driver stared at me and repeated in his Berlin dialect, "Bu'straasse? Bu'straasse?" He shook his thick beer-barrel head: *"Kenn's nicht."* A couple of other drivers came up. "Bu'straasse? Bu'straasse?" they repeated, and, all together, shook their heads. *"Kenn's nicht."* And there I was.

Then, one of them stuck his finger in the air and cried out, "Ah! Burrgstrraasse!" And with that brusque roll of the drum, I first woke up. Now I felt I had really come away from home, and with this initial foreign experience I realized that a Dane who intends to move about and abroad should develop his sense of consonants.

But listen to this! When the carriage stopped in front of the Hotel Zimmerman—incidentally, an old dilapidated box with an ancient outside staircase that reached all the way to the sidewalk—a porter wearing a leather apron received me. And what happened? Scarcely had he opened the carriage door when, terribly upset, he ran back into the hotel and shouted, "Herr Zimmerman! Herr Zimmerman! A gentleman with a decoration!" The whole house came running out, and the manager dashed up to me bareheaded. What a tableau! I had, in the meantime, cast an astonished look at my coat lapel. In the buttonhole was a little remnant of the rose that you stuck there in the morning when we parted. Dearest: that your last gift to me should raise such a ruckus! You can certainly imagine the reception I got when a connection was made. But believe me, I got even for both of us! When I went to my room, I rang and blew up like a veritable Knight of the Grand Cross, and when the waiter came with the register, I could not help putting an elegant "von" before my name. Don't shake your head! You should have seen how *that* helped! When I went out, the manager stood at the entrance and bowed. He opened the door personally for me with a most respectful greeting: "Herr Baron!" That's the other experience I had on my first day of travel, and a noble name is nothing to sneeze at. That's what your uncle told me earlier. Of course, the whole thing is laughable, but one of the ways of gaining power over people is, certainly, to have the courage to exploit their folly.

I have now looked around Unter den Linden and am sitting in the Café Bauer writing to you. Outside, in the streets, there is a humming and a roaring that leaves no doubt I am in a world capital. I have the sense that I am sitting in the middle of a giant waterwheel. This huge city is like a monstrous turbine that sucks up a stream of humanity and spits it out again after having consumed all its energy. What a concentration of living power! There is really something uplifting in feeling the floor under your feet vibrate with the discharged energy of two million men. What won't we be able to achieve in the coming century when we have learned to gather together a productive force in comparison with which what we have now is mere child's play. But enough for today.

OCTOBER 17

I have rented a couple of rooms in 25 Karlsstrasse (Frau Kumminach: *Zweite Treppe links*). I have decided, provisionally, to stay here in Berlin. There is something in the life and noise here that energizes me internally. *"Herrrrrich!"* It feels as if I have been charged by lightning and thunder. You can imagine what kind of a stormy rebuke I would like to send home, over the sea to our stifling shores. From this vantage point, relations and people there seem doubly provincial. Everyone here, down to the street sweepers, has an altogether different style. By contrast, call to mind our salon lions of Østergade, who drape themselves like little innocents from the country. In comparison with a German officer in his long cape with the large, blood-red trim, our lieutenants look like, God help us, uniformed seminarians.

I paid a visit today to Dr. Nathan. He lives very comfortably in the neighborhood of Königsplatz and—in spite of his various rather bitter pronouncements—seems to be doing well in his life of voluntary exile. He greeted me in a most friendly fashion, but I'll honestly confess that he didn't please me. I tried to give him an introduction to the contents of my book, but he hasn't the faintest notion of technical issues. Every minute he interrupted me with the stupidest inquiries. He didn't even know what a turbine was used for. The whole of the conversation was for the birds! It was a big disappointment. It's strange how some people like Nathan, who want to create a new critical culture out of the romantic ruins of the Middle Ages, do not really understand, themselves, what they have put in motion. They remind me of the kind of untrained academic architects who, as far as artistic concerns go, can draft, perhaps, a highly attractive plan for a new building but can't bother to think about where to get the wood it will take, where the bricks are fired. This demands different skills; men like Nathan are only in the way. I remember that, in one of the books you lent me last summer—maybe even one of his—there was an "irrefutable" contention that the foundation of the fifteenth-century Renaissance was the discovery of the compass. It made possible, as well, the discovery of America and the utilization of the established colonies, whose riches streamed into impoverished Europe and renewed the courage that mankind, made timid by priests and monks, had lost. It brought to life commerce and the passion for adventure, and so forth. But really, in the same way, I think the development of the power machines is the next big advancement of civilization. Whoever lacks this understanding and prophesies about the future is blowing soap bubbles in the air to the delight of poets and other babies.

OCTOBER 19

Well, I have not yet paid my respects to your mother's uncle. I have deliberately put it off until my German gets

stronger. The other day I went by his villa in Tiergarten-
strasse; it's a regular castle! They say he is a millionaire fifty
times over. You might let me know how I ought to behave.
What is *"Geheimecommercienrath"*? I mean, do you address
him as "Your Excellency"? Catch me up in detail on the
family relations. He has a wife (*Gemahlinn*?) and daughter.
Does he have other children?

OCT. 21

When I came into the Bauer today, who did I see sitting
there with a robber's hat shoved back on his head and a
gnarled walking stick between his outstretched legs?
Fritjof! I almost didn't recognize him, he has become so
old since I last saw him. His beard is gray, his eyelids red
and swollen. Nevertheless, he still looks like a proud fellow.
Even here in Berlin, he attracts notice and is having success.
The occasion is an exhibition in an art gallery of some of
his paintings. The newspapers write a lot about him. I don't
understand much of it, but he took me there to admire
them, and there certainly are many brilliant things among
them, especially a couple of larger pieces of the North Sea,
with powerful waves. While I was looking at them, I
couldn't help thinking forward to the time when my
thousand-ton iron buoy (you remember from my book)
will be moored on Jutland's west coast and will rock out in
the breakers milked for their power.

I asked Fritjof whether, when he sat on the beach and
painted those giant waves, he ever became sad at the
thought of so much utilizable power being wasted, lost to
mankind and its civilization for a thousand years. He began
immediately to spew forth his old wretched jeremiad
against the vileness of industry's soul and its desecration of
nature. I inquired if he really never found anything interesting in the thought of making all this wasted horsepower
useful for society, of conducting it through wires into the
whole country, distributing it to Jutland's towns, into every
home, so, for example, a seamstress in Holstebro could start
her machine as a mother in Viborg begins rocking her
baby's cradle, from the power of the North Sea's waves.
You should have seen his face; he sat up and roared,
"What?" so loudly everyone in the room turned around.

"Will you, scoundrel, change my sea into a beast of burden?" Although he is altogether incorrigible, I had some
sort of sympathy for him. When I saw him there with his
floppy hat and gnarled walking stick, his loosely tied cravat,
and the indignation of a wild man, I said to myself, The
last artist. In twenty years, they will stash such men in a
madhouse and, when they die, stuff them and put them in
a museum with the mummified beasts of the past and the
three-humped camels.

OCTOBER 23
Yesterday was a big day. Recently I had read in the papers
about an experiment in the presence of some invited engineers involving a new kind of river blockade near a little
town, Berkenbrück, a couple of hours from here. Since I
felt a desire to witness the enterprise, I went to the Danish
legation office, trusting that someone would be helpful in
getting me an invitation. But never have I seen a pair of
eyes so round with shock as those gaping at me when I put
forward my request. The man was obliged to lean back in
his chair to catch his breath. He remembered, he said, that
once there was a visiting actress who was given a free pass
to the royal playhouse and that the way was eased for some
Danish scholars to visit the library's manuscript collections—but this! An older man entered from the adjoining
room (he was certainly a high-ranking minister), looked
me over with great consternation, and let me know, in a
fatherly way, that I couldn't expect such favors in a foreign
land. In any case, the legation, before it could do anything
for me in this matter, would have to confer with the home
minister, and therefore I would have to send off two copies
of a written petition delivered with the requisite recom-
mendations, verifications, and certificates from the relevant schools that I had attended from my seventh year, and
so forth. In short, I realized I was suddenly, once again, in
my dear old Denmark, in that twaddling paradise. So I
decided to take things into my own hands and, yesterday
morning, took the first train to Berkenbrück. The chief
engineer immediately issued a permission card, thanked
me for my interest in the experiment, and made all information about the preliminary work available. I shall try to

give you a summary of what I saw. Let me tell you that what it involves is draining a section of the river to the bed in order to repair a pier. First, they tried, in the usual way, to lay the blockade at an angle across the water, but the current was too strong to anchor the dam without a diversionary canal, which, under the circumstances, would be too elaborate and costly. So they decided (and this is the new ingenuity) to let the current itself do the closing off. A huge wooden chest, steered with a suitable weight from the shore, and exactly the size of the dam opening, was allowed to float down against it. The whole thing was a remarkable performance. Just as the wooden chest hit the dam planks, clashing a bit alarmingly, the water rose sharply; but the current carried it nicely to the right place and, at last, drove it into the dam opening like a cork into the neck of a bottle. It was really a gripping moment. I only wish you could have been here. The effect was heightened when, at some distance, a couple of blasting shots resounded. There they were providing a temporary diversion of the river into a moor and its lake.

Afterward, champagne was served in a tent that was pitched on the spot, and, for the occasion, there were a lot of speeches. Finally (don't fall off your chair!), I *also* proposed a toast to the German engineering profession, which has, here again, given the world a shining proof of its brilliance. It went over well. Naturally, I had some difficulty with the language, but when I was missing a word, I resorted to warmly expressive hand movements. The speech provoked great enthusiasm, and I was surrounded on all sides by those who wanted to shake my hand. A reporter subjected me on the way back to an interview. My name is in today's *Tageblatt*. In addition, on this same occasion, I made the acquaintance of a man, a Professor Pfefferkorn, who could be of great use to me here. He is a teacher in Berlin's technical college and appears—the earth is so small—to be a good friend of Aron Israel at home; because of that, he has some interest in Danish affairs. When we were parting, he asked me to visit him.

OCTOBER 24

You reproached me, dear friend, for my words about

Nathan, and you seem a bit vexed, on his behalf, that I cannot think of him as a leader. I will readily admit to you that I have much to thank this man for. But as the academic he is, he will always be an incorrigible aesthete with no understanding of or interest in the demands of the practical life. When I recently tried to give him a conception of my project, I could hardly make myself heard. He persisted in talking about a drama he had read and about the political relations at home and God knows what. All he had to say about my project was that he found it "fairly fantastic." *Please!* And this is the man I should recognize as our leader? He is, in reality, not more farseeing than Fritjof, without the least spark of presentiment about what marvels the future is carrying in its lap to turn the world upside down— its politics as well. I'll say this: by living here, I am fortified in my belief that, for us, nothing could be more fantastic than how we, at home, with our natural wealth, continue in our narrow and pinched Cinderella existence that our governors consider the best security for our national identity and culture.

I maintain that we, in our smallness, can have only one means to lift us up among the great countries: money. As I have written in my book: "Such a Lilliputian country as Denmark is in itself an absurdity." So little and poor a country is, finally, untenable in our day. We must engender respect by our abundance. The solution will be money, money, and more money. It's the glitter of gold that will shed the "light over the country" Nathan and the others talk of. A culture of poverty is finally food for the priests. I think, often, of Venice, which was only a poor city and then raised itself up to become a world power. Cities like Hjerting and Esbjerg have, in regard to the present north European traffic spheres, a central situation similar to the ancient floating city. Here, abroad, I dream about a future Hjerting, where business palaces with golden domes rise over broad wharfs while small electric gondolas sweep like swallows over the canal's bright water.

OCTOBER 25
Today, only a few words in haste. I have just come from the *Geheimecommersienrathen* and brought him greetings. I met

his wife and young daughter in his house, and they received me warmly. Your half cousin is a full-blown beauty but strikingly simple in appearance and a little shy. But she is still so young. In general, the tone was somewhat formal. There was a servant who stood at every door I entered and I was received, as you might have guessed, in the winter garden. We talked mostly about you, though I naturally did not mention our relationship, but said I was a good friend of your parents' house.

The day after tomorrow, there will be a big musical soiree here, to which I have been invited. Three hundred invitations are being sent out.

I have my coat on and am about to go out to meet Fritjof. We spend quite a few evenings together and, in spite of our differences, get along well. He can really be very nice. He has taken me along with some of his German fellow artists, half-crazy fellows like himself, but clever and jolly. Isn't it laughable how many times it happens that these people find a likeness between Fritjof and me? Once I was asked if I was his younger brother. Can you believe that?

OCTOBER 27

Once again, a rich day. I haven't written to you, have I, about Professor Pfefferkorn, who is a teacher in a technical college and who invited me to visit him? Today I was at his house. He lives outside of Charlottenburg right next to the school, a palace with pillars and statues that cost at least ten million. Professor Pfefferkorn showed me around the college, lecture halls, and interesting research laboratories connected with the college. Most of all, I was fascinated with a collection of brilliantly crafted models of the world's most important engineering enterprises, bridges, sluices, foundations, and so on, and a museum that has no equal. Pfefferkorn promises to get me a pass to study there, which otherwise would be hard to obtain. Naturally, I'm delighted. It's a real storehouse! I think, in addition, I can attend some lectures here, of Professor Freitag, a younger man, who has won a big reputation with his work in electric motors.

All told, my friend, I won't be idle. My fingertips are

itching to get back to logarithms. My book is nothing—in any case, all too little. But wait! Pedant Sandrup and his small, clammy drones can soon go home to bed. In ten years, things will look different in Denmark.

Recently I was with Fritjof all the way up the tower of city hall, next to the flagpole, two hundred and fifty feet over street level. It was just sunset; the air was clear. I dare say I could see a couple of miles on all sides. Everywhere there were high houses and long streets where the lights were already lit, and there were telegraph wires, chimney smoke, and the electrically illuminated railway station corridors, where the trains go in and out—and, farther, the factories spreading out to make the city seem endlessly extended. I thought that here before me lay what, only a couple of generations back, was a comparatively unimpressive small town with train-oil lanterns, stagecoach conveyances, and so forth. I was filled with pride at belonging to the human race, and, to Fritjof's indignation, I waved my hat. Dear Jesus! These fellows with their "art," their painted canvases! I say that the sight of such lit-up train stations is more thrilling than all of Raphael's *Madonna*s put together. If I believed in some Providence, I would kneel every morning, dirtying my trouser knees, in gratitude for being born in this proud century when mankind, at last, has become conscious of its power and begun to create the world after its own desires, larger than any God's wildest dreams.

After Per's departure, Jakobe, now that she was no longer influenced directly by his person, and when the prospect of a yearlong absence had stretched her nerves to their uttermost, experienced a little passing dip into dejection over their relationship. Immediately after she received his first letter, but especially when she herself would write, she noticed how alien, in the course of a few days, he again seemed to her. She suddenly had so little to say to him. Her critical sense was reawakened, and her scruples. Once again, reading his youthful letters was humiliating and painful. They spoke so much of things she was indifferent to, so little of his love, and not at all about his longing. But after a few weeks had gone by, it happened that Ivan met Aron Israel on the street and Aron showed him a letter he had received that morning from an old friend in Berlin, Professor Pfefferkorn, who spoke very highly of Per. Ivan asked permission to borrow the letter and, after having read it out loud to his parents in the living room, sent it up to Jakobe, in a large, closed envelope with the phrase inscribed: "Vive l'empereur!" Here was part of it:

> Furthermore, I'm living now in complete, intimate communication with your country through a young man, an engineer Sidenius, who, from what he has told me, is a personal acquaintance of yours, a remarkable natural talent from whom the whole Danish nation has a right to expect something unusual. I have conversed with him a few times and have had the opportunity to familiarize myself with the ideas that obsess him and that have interested me. I have seldom met a man who possessed such an unmediated, fresh, and vivid conception of nature and her phenomena. I wouldn't claim to have a strong affinity for his point of view. It is, for me, too earthbound. But it belongs, surely, to the future, and it scarcely helps for us old men to sigh over it. Every age has its ideals. And when I hear your young countryman, with no flailing or hesitation, put forth the boldest plans for a conversion of our society achieved through an always growing control of natural forces, then I believe I have before me the prototype of the active man of the twentieth century.

With flaming cheeks and a swelling heart, Jakobe read these lines, and then she had an unusual reaction. She started to cry. She cried not only out of happiness, but also out of shame that she had been filled with doubt and uneasiness, and had again betrayed him in her thoughts. "Man of the twentieth century." Yes, these were just the words that illuminated the larger contradictions in his character, excused the weaknesses, accounted for the strength. He was like the first, formless draft of a coming giant race that—as he himself had written—finally could seize, as legitimate masters of the earth, ownership of it and mold it to its needs. He was a forerunner, grown up in a stifling atmosphere, oppressed by all kinds of petit bourgeois faintheartedness, superstition, and subjugation, and, therefore, intractable, self-willed, and without respect or belief in any other means of happiness and success than what makes a steel wheel whirr. And was that so strange? The nineteenth century's dream of a Golden Age, the beautiful faith in building a glad and righteous realm with the authority of only mind and soul and the word's persuasive power—how pale that seemed!

Already, before Per's travels, she had tried to procure an insight into the mysteries of mathematics and mechanics. But that was, on her part, only the lark of a woman in love, an expression of her restless longing to accompany Per in all his journeys. The difficulties of the application had fairly quickly made her give up. Now she threw herself, again, into the study of natural science with all her Semitic energy. It became clear to her that, without a sound knowledge of these things, the necessary assumptions for understanding modern society and the laws for its development would be missing. Her table, which, before, had overflowed with "belles lettres," and where Enevoldsen's *Creation* had often lain open with the poet's picture tucked into its pages, now was loaded with books on physics, geometry, dynamics. In her letters to Per, she threw out careful accounts of her progress and sought his advice and guidance. The relationship between them was thus reversed. Jakobe, who, until now, had thought of herself as intellectually superior, whose slightly embarrassing obligation it was to stand by her inexperienced fiancé, to help him with his neglected development, had suddenly become the pupil who needed his assistance and indulgence. As in the first days of her love, she wrote him ten times a day, either jotting down a single line or exclaiming with a burst of pleasure at having suddenly understood a difficult geometric problem, or sighing with sorrow for not having him with her when she needed help. And love played a bigger part in her eagerness than she herself realized. Everything that happened in the course of a day, even the most casual thought that raced through her head, she wanted to tell him, and this despite the fact that Per's letters to her always left both confidences and affection unanswered. On that point, she had gradually resigned herself. She understood now that she asked of him what nature had denied him; and she was even thankful he had not tried to pretend, but honestly showed himself to her as he really was.

She wrote him, as well, of her favorite subject—politics—in her letters, especially about the different labor movements that had such close ties with modern technical development. She had, until now, never wholly understood her own interest in these continual wage disputes and power struggles, which went against her aristocratic predisposition. She had felt insecure in the face of these grumbling millions of workers whose demands often seemed to endanger all that she most treasured in life. But along with her slowly developing understanding of Per, she had now arrived at some clarity about these dark, reluctant feelings of alliance with the sooty, subjugated army of workers craving light, air, and humane treatment: the twentieth-century men.

Meanwhile, the days flew by for Per in Berlin. He divided his time and efforts about equally between his studies and the big city's amusements. Every day he made new acquaintances and was well received by all. As at home, his apparent openness won over all their hearts. He first became completely conscious of his capacity to attract people with his personality here in Berlin, and, without thinking about how it became manifest, Per managed it with an intelligent sense of command. At the same time, he dedicated himself with attentive energy to looking more and more like a man of the world in his outer appearance. It went with him as it does with many people traveling abroad: his private bad habits were perceived by foreigners as national characteristics for which he couldn't personally be held responsible, and taken along with the attractive immediacy of his lack of sophistication he awakened a sort of ethnographic interest.

At the big musical evening at the house of the privy councilor of commerce, his outward form was lost in the crowd of shining uniforms and decorated lapels, but there was a moment when he became the object of general attention as the hostess, during a pause in the concert, called him over to her and did him the honor of conversing with him until the music began again. The aging lady, wearing a very low-necked dress and heavily rouged, had a weakness for young men with well-developed builds and took no pains to hide it.

Per himself had, meanwhile, eyes only for the house's daughter, a nineteen-year-old redhead who was in every way the opposite of her mother—a quiet, fine, charming little creature who looked shyly at the men who approached her. She was, like her mother, gorgeously dressed and shamelessly décolletée, as fashion demanded, but she seemed embarrassed by her exposure and covered her bosom as much as possible with her fan.

Per had only had the chance to bow at meeting her, and he wasn't at all sure she would recognize him now. Since then, she had been continually besieged by uniformed and distinguished-looking gentlemen, and he had at last given up trying to approach her. But during the concert, he twice caught her looking at him covertly, and the hurried manner in which she withdrew her glances suggested that they did not happen to rest on him by chance. Per was fairly certain he detected a slight blush.

When he went home that night, high on champagne, away from the social whirl, his head was spinning with daring thoughts. Would there be a chance for him? He remembered Uncle Heinrich's story about the poor Austrian in New York who conquered the American oil baron's daughter and now was one of the New World's reigning moneymen. The young girl here was heiress to at least fifty million, and a charming bride! . . . That could tempt him to try. Nonsense! Craziness! Still, up till now, he was successful in everything he had seriously tried for. He had not yet disappointed Ivan's prophecy: "I come, I see, I conquer."

Of course, there was Jakobe to consider. He had in no way forgotten that, and it was naturally a serious problem. But, then, he could ask whether it was absolutely necessary to let oneself be bound to the past when an undreamt-of glittering prospect opened up for a man. Did he have the right to renounce such a future? When he had dedicated all his powers to something, could he be responsible for how it turned out? God knows he was very fond of Jakobe. He understood and fully appreciated her remarkable attributes, and it would be very painful to give her up. But all personal feelings must be subordinated for the sake of a larger good—even Jakobe herself would realize and sanction that! Fifty million! A sum like that would procure for her husband, in a little country like Denmark, a royal power. What couldn't he accomplish at home with that kind of money! What a help for the large battle for freedom that no one more than Jakobe wished to see move forward and succeed. He had no desire to go home, so he sauntered down Unter den Linden, where there was still life in the cafés and wine bars.

Normally, as much as possible, he tried to avoid these elegant restaurants on the great boulevard that cared so devilishly little for cost. With all his desire to appear like a man of the world, he had an ingrown resistance to spending and always felt most comfortable in Fritjof's artist pubs, where he could get a half pound of beef with a fried egg and a large roll, a slice of cheese, two tankards of beer, and a friendly smile from the waitress, all for two marks. But in that night's champagne mood he defiantly pushed all his petit bourgeois predilections away from him and went into one of the most fancy officers' wine bars in the neighborhood of Neue Wache.

With a half flask of iced Vix-Bara and among a lively coming and going of rustling silk and saber-rattling couples, he kept up his self-fulfilling daydreams. Before everything, the noble title that Uncle Heinrich had recommended was still haunting him. Now it could *really* be a benefit! Without a distinguished name, he could gain virtually nothing in these circles, but with a baronage he would have to fear no rivals. To be sure, he had only a little to build on—a mere stolen glance. But did he have any more than—even as much as—when he had eyed Jakobe earlier? He needed merely to rely on his pact with luck and his motto would prove accurate: "I *will*."

It was past three when he reached home, and, in his preoccupation, he couldn't fall asleep. He tossed around in his bed, drank one glass of water after the other, and couldn't pacify his thoughts. These fairy-tale fantasies that kept him awake could not be expelled. Here, alone in the darkness, other thoughts emerged and stirred his blood. During his entire stay in Berlin, he had been pursued by an anxiety that, like the shadow in the fable, showed up only when it was quiet and deserted around him. He could not lose the thought of his father and his possible death. That is to say, when he was active during the day or sat in the cafés with his friends, the subject didn't bother him; but as soon as he was alone in the foreign city, especially in the evening when he came home to his empty and unfriendly rooms here in Carlstrasse, the shadow appeared. Every night when he stood in his shirt at his bed and wound his clock, he asked himself, Could Father be dead today? So it was that night.

Toward morning—just as he was ready to fall asleep, he was quickly startled. From one or another place in the room he heard a noise that sounded in his ears like three knocks. He was once again wide awake. And, in spite of his assumption that he was free of all kinds of superstition, he couldn't escape the thoughts that at that moment his father had died.

In the morning, he telegraphed an inquiry home to Eberhard, and toward noon received this short answer: "Father is dying." He looked at his clock. In two hours, the express train to

Hamburg would leave. He could be home the next morning, and in the evening he could leave again. Only two days' absence—and his conscience would be at peace. He stayed a moment with his clock in his hand, nodded his head decisively, and started to pack a suitcase.

He did not himself have a clear understanding that what drove him home was not solely the fear that he would be sorry if he hadn't said goodbye to his father. Another motive was obscured by those thoughts that had kept him awake that night: now here would be a little peace from the play of a persistent haunting. Like the first baptized pagans, in face of their great conversions, who secretly made offerings to their old gods, he felt the desire, on the point of arming himself for the last daring battle for the golden crown of happiness, to reconcile himself with his father's God by a sacrifice.

A couple of hours later, he was sitting in a train going north.

CHAPTER 12

WHILE PER, DURING the night, rolled on through Jutland, he thought often of the unhappy Christmas journey almost seven years ago when he last was on the way home. He remembered, in all its particulars, his homecoming in the dark winter evening when a cold, yellowish, foggy rain shrouded the town and made the sleepily burning lanterns still more sluggish. He saw his sister Signe standing on the wet platform in her short, old-fashioned coat with black wool gloves on her hands and, under her dress hem, a pair of large feet in galoshes. He summoned up his father's dissatisfaction that he had taken this vacation without asking per-mission, and, especially, his own disappointment at hearing the floor of the dining room being scrubbed—realizing that the others had already eaten.

He wondered why he retained such a living memory of these old incidents that meant nothing to him anymore. He wasn't, in any case, willing to admit that home and its sad memories had any power over him. He was conscious of reliving the past only on rare occasions. In the course of the years it had dipped below life's horizon.

He reached the little town in the clear October sunshine of early morning. His fashionable clothes caused quite a sensation on the platform: he wore a long, mouse-gray silk traveling coat with broad velvet facings around the collar and cuffs. On his dark, close-trimmed head sat a Scottish traveling cap. His suitcase, hat box, and other travel gear were of the finest quality and shining new.

A couple of coarsely dressed and intimidated peasants made way for him. He heard, with satisfaction, one of them whispering to the other, "Hey, I wonder if that's him, the young Count Frys?"

Though he had, by telegraph, announced his arrival plans, no one was there to greet him. It's better that way, he thought; I have a free hand. He decided to go to a hotel, where it would be more comfortable in every way, but just as he was climbing into one of the two hotel buses that stopped outside the station, he caught sight of Eberhard coming slowly from the little park opposite the station. Per understood immediately that his brother, who was careful of his dignity, had been waiting there for the train's arrival to make it look as if he half chanced by on a walk. For that kind of superciliousness, which would have, in the old days, provoked him, he now felt only pity.

When his brother saw Per dealing with the hotel attendant, he became visibly alarmed and hastened his steps.

"You're not going to the hotel, are you?" he asked almost before greeting him.

"Yes," said Per. "I think that's best under the present circumstances in order not to cause any trouble at home."

"But a room is ready for you there, and we have plenty of space. Mother will surely take it badly if you go to the hotel."

"Well, if you think so—will you get me a porter?" He directed the last words to the hotel attendant. Then he asked Eberhard about his father's condition.

"Father has been sleeping since yesterday evening. Mostly he just lies there and dozes. In the last twenty-four hours he has become conscious only now and then."

Then a porter came out of the station together with the hotel attendant, who bowed expectantly to Per with his cap in his hand. Per tossed him a krone and gave the other instructions as to his luggage.

Meanwhile, Eberhard, stealing an uneasy glance at Per's clothes, stepped a little to the side. "I suggest that we go back around the gardens," he said, and turned into a path that led to the parsonage, along the town's outer fringe where people did not customarily walk.

Per demurred: "That path is much longer, and I'm really tired."

"Well, as you wish," answered Eberhard, with the tight mouth he displayed when he had to negotiate his dignity. The brothers walked silently side by side through the main avenue. Seeing his childhood town made no great impression on Per this time; its small and crooked streets, its one- or at most two-storied houses with endless gutter planks seemed to him almost comical play toys compared with the cosmopolitan city from which he had just come. It was the same with the town as with his family home. In the course of the years, it had glided out of his life, dipped beneath the horizon. And he began, suddenly, to smile at remembering how much it had once been his most ambitious dream to be the most celebrated magnate in that hole of a town that had witnessed his humiliation.

He recognized almost every person he met. Each of the small houses with street mirrors at the window, each name over the shop doors, every old sign over the gates, brought back one or another part of his past. This was especially true of the grammar school, whose broad gable and playground with a high brick enclosure faced the street. As they walked by, it was recess time. The shouts of boys that, as in his schooldays, resounded over the wall brought before his eyes a swarm of half-forgotten childhood memories. And surrounding the town were the hills he had loved as a boy and the fjord. Here was the mile-wide meadow, the summer-day playground where the first tender shoots of his canal project were seeded in his mind, and this was where he had also gained his first inkling of what wind power could mean, when he loosed his giant kite Heljo into the air and it pulled a little, attached stone-loaded toy wagon across the ground.

Eberhard asked about Per's journey, but Per's thoughts were immersed in the past and he didn't hear him. He felt humiliated by his continuous, helpless sense of dependency on the little provincial town. What especially disturbed him was that his connection was so unreciprocal. The bowlegged shopkeeper, Hjerting, who stood in front of his door in a white linen coat, wooden slippers, and a meerschaum pipe mounted on silver; the flabby, redheaded barber, Siebenhausen, who—just as in the old days—leaned out of the open window to ogle servant girls. The public street criers, drummers, and old fishwives gossiping in an alley across the way—all affected him, while he meant nothing to them.

They turned into a side street where the parsonage was. The first glimpse of the peculiar, large wall with the prison gate, especially, the sight of the bark-strewn pavement, made his heart beat. He had not been prepared for the way the prospect of seeing his mother again, of standing by the deathbed of his father, would affect him. His sister Signe received him in the hall. She was very moved at seeing him again but took his hand in silence and, with downcast eyes, half turned away, as a reminder that something else was happening in the house.

"Mother has gone to rest a little," she said when they came into the dining room, where Per could hardly recognize a couple of his youngest siblings, the twins, who had half grown up in his absence. They shyly received his handshake while Signe continued: "Mother said I should call her when you came; but I think it best not to disturb her. She was awake all night long."

Though her father's quarters were off on the other end of the large house, Signe talked the whole time in that subdued voice that gradually becomes habitual when someone in the house is sick. Per agreed that his mother should in no way be disturbed.

Just as at his homecoming seven years ago, a tray with open sandwiches was brought out to him. Signe poured him a cup of coffee, and, in order not to hurt her feelings, he forced himself to eat, even though he could hardly get food down from anxiety. Meanwhile, the twins regarded him with big, inquisitive eyes from the other end of the room. "I know you'd like to see Father," said Signe. "He's lying there in a doze and hasn't been awake since yesterday evening. The nurse is in there now, washing him. I'll go ask when you can go in."

She quickly left, closing the door after her with both hands in order to keep the lock from clicking. Eberhard had already left the room, and, so as not to be alone with their strange brother, the twins slipped away through the kitchen door.

Per got up and mindlessly paced back and forth. Then he stopped at a window that looked out on the little grass lawn with some stunted trees that constituted the parsonage garden. His heart was beating and his thoughts wandered wildly seeking vindication.

But as he stood there and looked at the little sunless plot, surrounded by the high firewall, his thoughts turned gradually to his conduct, and it became clear that he had found the self-justification he was looking for. His acquittal lay in this chilly atmosphere where he again saw his childhood's first playground. Not one good memory, not one bright recollection was connected with this enclosure, all the way back from when he had felt a prisoner at fifteen.

Suddenly, a strange, flitting sensation of frenzied and wailing sadness took over his mind. How the shadow of this walled prison had darkened his existence and soured his happiness all these years!

His nerves were on edge. The door behind him was gently opened by Signe. "You can go in now. Just come in."

Per went through a little, almost empty room, into the living room. The door from there into the bedroom was half open. Signe approached on tiptoes, soundlessly pushed open the door, and led Per to the foot of the bed that stood free from the side wall. It was so dark he had trouble, at first, finding his way.

Gradually he distinguished the outlines of a shriveled head with closed eyes, in a deathlike sleep, lying deeply sunken in a large, soft pillow. A cold shiver shot through Per's body, but was not caused by anything beyond the naturally stirred sensation of discomfort at the dreaded sight of deathly dissolution. Actually, the fact that his father's condition obviously made any reconciliation impossible calmed him down. What he most feared was the family zeal to bring one about before the end. He knew what he had, for his part, wanted to say to his father would have given occasion for a very unpleasant scene.

As his eyes got used to the room's darkness, the face of the sleeper and the whole of his emaciated form stood out more clearly. He saw that his father still had his full hair, but the sickness had robbed it of its color. The face, therefore, looked dark, almost bronzed, and there was no sign of life in it. A couple of flies circled round and now and then crawled on his forehead or cheeks. It was as if, already, the peace of eternity was settling on his eyelids.

The nurse, who had stayed in the room at the washstand rinsing the sponge, now went out with the basin, and the brother and sister were left alone with the sick man. Neither of them talked. Signe was seated in a low armchair by the side of the bed. She was leaning over with her hands folded on her knees and observing her father with a patient expression of love and pain. Her big, bright eyes were full of tears that ran down around her mouth. Now and then she waved her hand gently over her father's face to keep the flies away.

Just then, there was a scratching sound near the wall. A hidden door that led to a back guest room opened and the mother's little, bent form appeared in the small opening. She stood there for a moment as she supported herself against the doorframe with a trembling hand. With the other she leaned on a dark cane. It was a little while before Per understood it was she. He remembered her as almost always bedridden and hadn't thought of her as this little. She had also aged markedly in the past years. Not only was her hair gray, her features sharper, but from such a strong effort of spirit, during the father's long sickness, almost a supernatural force that kept her upright, a kind of strange austerity had come over her face, especially in her deep-set, almost clairvoyant, staring eyes, that surprised and confused Per. The look that now met him, the way in which his mother came near with an outstretched hand that seemed to be warding him off, puzzled him even more. It was as if she were expecting a repentant confession from him, and, for some time, they stood facing each other like two pillars. Then mother-love gained the upper hand at last. As tears rolled down her cheeks, she took his head between her hands and kissed him on the forehead. Signe, who had stood up, helped her over to the armchair at the side of the bed.

"So, you have really come, Peter Andreas," she said, bowed over and half turned away, with her hand above her eyes as if she still couldn't really bear, yet, to see him. "Why didn't you come before now? Now it is probably too late." There was something in these words that roused Per's suspicion.

"Too late," he repeated to himself. They had all been hoping for a final reconciliation. They had viewed his homecoming as a penance journey. His mother began to speak, but then the nurse came in from the living room with an older man. He was the doctor on his daily morning visit. Per and Signe left at a sign from the mother, and the nurse closed the door after them.

Per did not see his mother again that day, and, generally, his homecoming was not the occasion it might have been under other circumstances. The father's condition naturally absorbed minds and hearts, and, in spite of the quiet, a great busyness reigned in the house. Soon the warm compress, then the doctor had to be fetched, not to mention the arrival of inquiries from the townsfolk about the patient's situation. In addition, in the course of the day, two of the children had still not come and were awaited—the brother who was the curate of Funen, and a sister who had married a doctor in one of the small towns around the Limfjord. Their rooms had to be readied. So everyone had plenty to do.

Per was given his old loft room, and there he spent most of the day, partly in a futile attempt to sleep and refresh himself after his trip, partly occupying himself with writing to Jakobe. For the sake of decency, he had decided to abandon his original plan and to stay here until his father died. It would not, after all, be long now. He felt anxious and depressed. He did not regret that he had come here, but he wished it would be over with. He had, only one time before, seen a man die. That was the day in Nyboder when the old boatswain was brought home half dead from his walk. That unpleasant memory seemed connected to this death. The chief boatswain's dread and the alarm of the others pursued him now.

Toward evening, the awaited brother, Thomas, and sister, Ingrid, accompanied by her husband, came. Thomas was a ruddy theologian with a staid manner behind which was hidden a strong but starved ambition. Ingrid was a little, self-assured, provincial wife, a full-blooded Sidenius for whom Løgstør was a first-class town because she, her husband, and her children lived there.

The father had, in the course of the day, opened his eyes and seemed clearheaded. But he could make himself understood only with difficulty, and after a few minutes again sank into unconsciousness. The doctor was just then paying his evening visit. When he came out of the room he told Signe to follow him into the hall.

"I won't hide it from you; your father will probably not live through the night. I expect you to call me if you want me here."

His prediction proved correct.

It was a little past two when everyone in the house was awakened. The hour of death had come. Per, who, travel weary and confused after almost two days and nights of wakefulness, had fallen into a heavy sleep and did not immediately know where he was. In his dreams he was socializing with Fritjof and some of his artist friends in Berlin. They had just driven in a carriage to their favorite pub on Leipzigstrasse when the door opened and Signe came in with a light in her hand and asked him to come down.

In that second he realized where he was and what his sister's words meant, and he shivered with cold. The transition from a joyous cosmopolitan gambol to his sister's quiet death summons was too strong even for his mental constitution. For some time after he had dressed, he had to pace back and forth to recover his composure.

When he went downstairs he found all his brothers and sisters assembled. Most of them had not been to bed but had napped in armchairs and on the sofa to be as near to the father as possible and with him as soon as something happened. The living room was lit, and the folding door into the bedroom was open. Inside, only a little night lamp was burning. It was on a table at the head of the bed and threw a weak light on one side of the father's white body. The other side still lay in darkness.

To ease his breathing, he had been raised up a little and supported by pillows. He was almost fully conscious, but couldn't talk, nor could he lift his dark blue eyelids. The children were saying goodbye. One by one they drew up to his bed, and when they had taken his hand that lay heavy and powerless on the bedspread, the mother named the children for him. She sat in her low wicker chair near the headboard, away from the night lamp on the opposite side of the bed.

Per felt ill at ease during this ceremonial leave-taking he had hoped to be spared. He held back as long as possible, but finally he too had to approach the bed. When he felt his father's already deathly cold hand and heard his mother (as it appeared to him) naming him with a stronger voice, an icy shiver of discomfort rose up in him, an oppressive sense of being called forth for divine judgment. Only his consciousness of all his brothers and sisters, standing together around the bed, gave him the strength to master his expression.

It was now between three and four. The watchman was walking through the still streets. Because of the litter of bark chips outside, his steps could not be heard, only his toneless song, which sounded in the room like a supernatural announcement of the impending death:

Now black night is here
But dawn's drawing near
May God keep away
What can harm us today.
O Father we pray
Look on our face
And send us your Grace.

After the father had finally taken leave, as well, of the house's servants, he indicated by a movement of his face muscles that he wanted to say something. With a whisper that only the mother could make out, he asked to have a hymn sung. The children went into the living room and gathered around the piano; while Signe played, they sang with subdued voices some verses from the psalm:

For thy mercy is great above the heavens
And thy truth reacheth unto the clouds.

Per was the only one besides his mother who stayed behind in the bedroom. After his farewell to his father, he had seated himself in a dark corner where he could let his guard down. While the song of his brothers and sisters was borne in to him, filled with the peaceful power and joy of an unshakeable assurance that heaven was opening—God's radiant form floating there with outstretched arms to receive their father's pure soul—Per sat all alone and struggled with himself so as not to be carried away. It was all so different from what he had imagined. With a quivering mouth and moist eyes, he stared at his father's shriveled head, which lay there so peacefully on the pillow encircled by the full, white hair like a saintly halo. And with the chief boatswain's terrible death scene in his mind, he said to himself, So this, then, is how a faithful Christian dies! When the singing had ended, the flock of brothers and sisters returned gradually to the bedroom. Their father's mouth had, in the meantime, opened a bit, and his eyes were sunk even deeper in his head. Not long after, the death throes began.

The mother held his right hand and, now and then, wiped the sweat from his brow with a cloth. On the other side of the bed, Eberhard and Signe stood ready to serve if help was needed.

An hour passed. Waiting for the last breath, the other children sat around the room wherever they could find a place. The youngest stood at the foot of the bed watching their father with compassionate eyes. Once again the watchman's monotonous song sounded in the silent street:

> Praise God who waits for us
> With a heavenly chorus
> Be our watchman on earth
> And bring morning to birth.
> As night fades away
> Pray safeguard the day.

Except for the steadily weakening sound of the father's tired breathing and now and then a half-suppressed sob erupting from the children, it was completely quiet in the room. Things remained like this until approximately four. The mother sat in a collapsed state and pressed her forehead against the dying man's hand, bathed with her tears. Eberhard touched his father's left hand gently, feeling the slow, diminishing pulse, while Signe intently watched the expression on his face. The hour was just about to strike in the living room. Shortly after, Eberhard went quietly around the foot of the bed to his mother. "Mother," he said, as he touched her shoulder lightly, "Father has passed on."

At that moment, all the watchers rose and circled the bed. Only the mother remained seated. She had, at first, looked up at Eberhard with a beseeching expression of helplessness. Again she bent over the dead man's hand and hid her face—it was as if she did not have the courage to meet the sight of the glazed eyes. But she lifted her head and looked at him for a long time in silence. Then she said, "Well, children, now Father has left us. But let us thank and praise God. It is not a farewell for eternity. He has gone to our heavenly home before us, where we shall, one day, with God's grace, be with him again."

With moving words she thanked him for everything that he had been for all of them, praised his steadfast faith with her and the family, thanked him for all his love and sacrifice, and, in a touching way, the tenderness with which she spoke as she stroked her husband's white hair and kissed his forehead, seemed to suggest a reawakening of the feelings of her youth.

For still some time the children stood around the bed in quiet prayer and contemplation, but with the first obvious sign of death, Eberhard and Thomas spread a sheet carefully over the body and Signe took her mother away. Per left shortly after and went to his room. A lamp was still burning on his table. Through the bare window came the first gleams of day. For a long time he remained standing there and stared out over the town that was about to awaken. Some pale stars still twinkled in the sky while work wagons and the heavy slap of wooden shoes could be heard round about the streets. He arrived at the conviction that what he had experienced that night would mark a distinction in his life. But he had no clear sense of his feelings. He was, for the time being, too gripped by the ceremonial occasion to be able to think at peace. At last he sat down at the table and took out his travel case. He felt the need to communicate with somebody, to write to Jakobe. The day before he had sent her a short notice of his homecoming, and now he wrote, "Let me say right off that my old father died a short while ago. And I won't pretend I'm not happy I decided to come here. However much there was between Father and me, he always acted according to his best convictions. His death was very affecting. He was conscious almost to the end, and he confronted death with a wonderful spiritual strength." Here his hand stopped, and as he read through what he had written, he became embarrassed. For a while, he sat there biting the pen, then suddenly tore up his letter and began another:

"Dear Jakobe: I have the sorrowful task of informing you that, this morning, my father died. I came just in time to take leave of him, which is what I desired. He was fully conscious and peaceful till the end. But—naturally—his life was really an unbroken preparation for death. These lines in haste. I'll write soon, again."

After having signed the letter, he sat still for a time with a troubled look and reflected. Then he added a postscript: "Perhaps I'll stay here for the burial."

Five days later, Pastor Sidenius was buried. Already from early morning, the flags hung at half-mast everywhere in town, and on the long stretch from the church to the graveyard, the street, at noon, was strewn with sand and spruce twigs. Young girls had even decorated the church with green plants and hung black crepe on both the altar and the old, richly carved pulpit. The lights in both twelve-branched chandeliers were burning under the ceiling, and a soft lament came from the organ when, a little after noon, the congregation began to fill the church.

That it wasn't at all just curiosity that drew the crowd was evident from the stillness in the church and the many solemn faces. It went with Pastor Sidenius as with many strong leaders: the resistance, finally overcome, is converted to reverence. And, as also often happens, the traits that had originally most offended —his air of authority, his disdain for the town's inherited customs, his strict simplicity in the way he lived and dressed—were now highly esteemed as witnessing a true, apostolic zeal and piety. And, in fact, in the course of the years, he had somewhat changed. Gradually, as people submitted themselves to the church's guardianship, the gentle and endearing qualities in his character emerged.

In addition, there was the long sickness and the noble peace of mind with which he had borne his suffering and awaited his death. He had lain in bed over half a year, fully conscious that he was a man marked for death. Not only did he never complain; he did not allow others to pity him. "We don't talk like that here," he had once said sternly to someone who wanted to comfort him with the hope of recovery. "Are we not God's children and should we not be grateful when our Father calls us home?"

On the church's chancel stood the black casket, which, according to the deceased man's wish, bore no other adornment than a simple wooden cross lying on the cover. He had always been zealously opposed to what he called the people's effeminate desire to beautify death and "decorate the worm trough." Around the casket sat about fifty clergymen in vestments, as guards of honor, and, in the most esteemed seats in the congregation, the town's most outstanding citizens: public officials in uniform, councilmen, even many garrison officers with shiny silver bandoliers and gleaming helmets on their laps.

Per looked around with mounting surprise. He had, by various impressions, gained a sense of the triumph the priestly rule had achieved in this previously worldly town. But here and now his conception of his father and his personal significance was turned upside down in his mind. One pastor after another came up behind the casket to speak, and the church echoed with their loud praise and gratitude to God for the great service and rich deeds of the departed. Afterward, eight young pastors lifted down the casket from the catafalque. Then the whole congregation followed the hearse on foot, the long way through the streets, to the graveyard.

Per felt conflicted.

Was this really his father—he of whom, in his boyhood, he had been ashamed because he was the target of ridicule through-out the town? Was this the man who was getting a funeral fit for a count and who was being followed to the grave by a grieving throng? He couldn't grasp this. In an unexpected and humbling way, the noblest dream of his childhood from the time he imag-ined himself the mistakenly exchanged son, an abandoned prince, who would someday find his way home to his father's glorious realm was coming to pass.

On the way back from the burial, he found himself walking beside his brother Thomas, who had officiated at the graveside and was in vestments. Of all his siblings, Thomas was the one, despite the difference in their ages, from whom he had found the most understanding, perhaps because in his growing up, Thomas, too, sometimes felt himself oppressed by their father's one-sided authority. In his student years, he had experienced freer currents in the Christian parish life than his father would have sanctioned. Not without effort had he crawled into the uniform of the Dan-ish established church, the funereal robe that did not suit his ruddy cheeks and bright blue childlike eyes.

Per had noticed that Thomas had tried these last days to break the ice between them, but he had not wanted a reconcilia-tion. He was on his guard against the somewhat pharisaical goodwill that was in his brother's nature and that had often attracted Per's trust in the past. Nor did he allow a conversation to start up between them. An inner anxiety had seized him, and he instinctively feared taking up with this well-meaning brother.

Thomas gave up trying for a rapprochement, and the two brothers walked silently side by side the rest of the way home. When they arrived, they all went to see their mother, who lay in her bed and had not been able to attend the burial. Immediately after the immense effort she had been expending, a frightful weakness came upon her and the doctor had ordered the most rest possible. Per had hardly seen her at all these last days. He had been called in only once, and had then sat a few minutes by her bed. But she had only enough strength to ask him a couple of questions about his health.

This time, as well, there was nothing more than a word and a handshake, and Per went up to his room to pack. He was burning with impatience to leave and had decided to take the evening train.

He certainly did not have any reason to complain over his reception at home. As if there had been a silent understanding, not only Thomas, but also his other siblings endeavored to be as considerate to him as possible, or as much as would let them settle with their conscience. In addition, he had spent most of his time in his room and in long walks around the countryside. Once he had been gone a whole day and night away from the town and had used the occasion to travel out to see a newly built cement factory near the Limfjord coast.

Neither his mother nor any of his brothers and sisters had so much as alluded to his engagement. He couldn't imagine that Eberhard had not told them about it; he felt the silence was provocative to some extent. On the other hand, he wasn't unhappy that Jakobe's name had not been mentioned, though he no longer thought about breaking with her. The effect of the last days' experience was, already, to make him sane and sober. The champagne mood in which he had made the great decision to win the throne of one of Europe's money barons had vanished in that earnest and thoughtful night in his father's dark death room. And, because he was now ashamed of the crime of faithlessness toward Jakobe he had committed in his mind, he avoided speaking about her.

In the twilight, when his siblings again went to the churchyard to see the father's grave and when he knew his mother was alone, he went in to say goodbye.

"Sit here awhile with me, my child," she said, and spoke once again with the depressed and lamenting voice he knew so well from his childhood. "We've hardly talked together. And now you're leaving, your brothers and sister tell me."

"Yes, I have to get back to my work." His mother waited for him to continue, but when no further clarification came, she said, "Your work? Yes, we know so little about what you are busy with, Peter Andreas, and where you are moving about. You were in Germany—in Berlin, I think."

"Yes."

Again his mother waited awhile before she continued: "Your father and I thought you must have procured wealthy patrons to live as freely as you do, because, as far as we know, you don't have a post."

Per pricked up his ears. He realized now that his mother knew nothing about his engagement. His brothers and sisters had kept it from her to spare her grief. Or, perhaps, Eberhard had told nothing either to his parents or his siblings. That would be like him. And, in that case, it was hardly only out of consideration for the feelings of others.

While Per was mulling this over, his mother had turned around toward a little table near the headboard and taken something out of the drawer.

"You'll not go away, Peter Andreas, without knowing what Father wanted to say to you, before he closed his eyes. He had such an unshakeable confidence that you, one day, would find yourself and return to the path of humility. Not a day went by that he didn't speak of this and remember you in his prayers. Some time ago, when he heard you were traveling abroad, and thought he must give up hope of seeing you again, he asked us to send you this remembrance from him, after he died."

She handed him the little object she had taken from the drawer. It was his father's old silver watch that he had always valued and worn until the end. He used to call it his only earthly treasure. "This watch," continued his mother, "has a history. And Father would have told it to you if he could have talked to you again. Now I'll do it in his stead. And when you have heard it, you will understand on your own why he decided to give the watch to you."

She left off, for a moment, and from time to time closed her eyes as her husband had done in his sickness. "Once, when your father was a half-grown boy, he had spent his Christmas vacation at home in the parsonage and had to travel back to school. His father asked for the suitcase key so he could, as he said, examine the case before the carriage came, to see if everything was in order and nothing was forgotten. That outraged your father, and he left in anger without having said a proper farewell to *his* father. When, in the evening, having arrived at school, he opened up his suitcase, he found his clothes just as he had packed them. Nothing had been moved. But in a corner was a little wrapped packet. It was the watch you now hold in your hand. That was a gift from your grandfather. And then your father understood that he had used a pretext to place it in the suitcase when he wasn't looking, so it could be a pleasant surprise for him in a place away from home. When your father realized that, he burst into tears, and when he had cried himself out, repenting of his rashness, he put on his coat and, the same night, walked almost twenty miles on foot and wouldn't stop until he had thrown his arms around his father's neck and asked for forgiveness. That's why, my son, your father kept this watch his whole life like a sacred thing. I remember he called it, once, God's special gift to him. Because that night when he had humbled himself and given himself over to this heartfelt penance toward his earthly father, he also found his way home to the light, peace, and blessing of his heavenly Father."

While she spoke, Per sat there with the watch, which felt heavier and heavier in his hand. When she had stopped, he said nothing. It was dark in the room. His mother had opened her eyes, but she could no longer make out his face.

There was nothing more to say. Per left shortly after, and, as his mother kissed him goodbye on the forehead, she whispered to him, "God send you His merciful peace."

Not much time after, Per drove to the station. His brothers and sisters had, in the meantime, come back from the churchyard. But he went alone, having refused all offers of company.

When Signe, an hour later, came up to his room, she found her father's watch lying in the middle of the table. It was obviously placed there on purpose, and could not have been overlooked or forgotten.

CHAPTER 13

PER CAME BACK to Berlin, but was no longer so happy there. Fritjof had, in the meantime, traveled home, and he felt all alone in the big city. It was now autumn. Lights burned the whole day in many shops and cafés and rain poured down at all hours. After a heavy drenching, the water was an inch high over the asphalt. Most of the time, he stayed home alone and studied. He hoped that, with energetic work, he could overcome the despondency he had brought with him from home, but he couldn't find any peace or comfort in his rooms. His landlady, Fru Kumminach, a small, flabby, dirty woman with a fist-sized tumor on the side of her neck, cooked sauerkraut the whole day on a smoking stove, and the monotonous hum of a dozen machines in a sewing room on the floor above him would, at times, almost drive him crazy.

Susceptible as he was to impressions, he gradually discovered the dark side of modern life in the big cities. Not long after his return, he experienced a series of small but very unpleasant incidents, giving him an intimate look at the habits and living conditions of the larger population.

When he had first rented his rooms, he had laid down the definite condition that there would be no other lodgers to disturb his work, and his landlady had solemnly promised, and even showed him a police document that stated she was not permitted to rent out more than just his two small rooms. In addition to these, the entire apartment consisted only of a little, dark, tomb-like room behind the kitchen, just big enough for a small iron bed, where the landlady lived. Nevertheless, it wasn't many days before it became clear that there was at least one other person in the dwelling. Per was often awakened at night by coughing and finally discovered that it came from the front hall, or, more accurately, from a tiny space between its ceiling and a cupboard-like cubicle that served as a cloakroom. He had interrogated the landlady, but the saucy old woman swore up and down that he was mistaken, and she had an explanation at hand even when he had, one Sunday morning, surprised a young, pale-faced fellow sitting in the kitchen in his shirtsleeves, fixing his hair in front of a mirror fragment. After that, he gave up trying to get to the bottom of things, though he wasn't sure she hadn't stashed more night guests in the apartment's nooks and crannies.

One night, he heard, along with the coughing, a deep rough snoring that, as far as he could judge, did not come from the landlady's room. He discovered, after asking around, that the legitimate lodger, in many places, served simply as a cover in an unauthorized shelter for the kind of vagabonds the city swarmed with, often relatively proper young men: shop clerks, factory workers, barbers' assistants, waiters, and the like, for whom having a home was a superfluous luxury. They spent their free time in the streets, in beer joints, in dance halls, and in houses of prostitution, and had access to one or another place to sleep at night for a few hours. They owned only what they wore and flitted from quarter to quarter without notice. It was the kind of life that was, in part, forced upon them by the struggle for existence in the big cities. Those who were accustomed to live the haphazard street life, free in their comings and goings, procured jobs easily. For such people, the comforts, peace, and safety of home were altogether strange notions that they didn't even miss.

One day, he happened to hear his landlady talking with a man in the front hall. He turned out to be a police officer seeking information about a barber's assistant who, having been brought to one of the city's hospitals during the night, had given her place as his "sleeping quarters." The man had hemorrhaged in a beer joint and had died shortly after he was admitted to the hospital. When Fru Kumminach, at first silent, heard this, she suddenly became garrulous: What nonsense! The police officer must surely know that she wouldn't have that kind of lodger. A barber's assistant! And no one could imagine that she, who was an upstanding woman with the most distinguished lodgers, could house such rabble. A filthy beggar with a weak chest who croaked in the street!

Per felt a shiver down his spine at hearing that disrespect for the body of his unknown fellow lodger. He was convinced that the man concerned was really the same one who, during the night, had his haunt under the front hall ceiling; last night he hadn't heard the familiar hollow cough. He couldn't help thinking what would await him if, for example, he got sick here and had to have a nurse. There was good reason to worry just now since he hadn't been feeling well. He had caught a cold on his trip back from home and thought he really shouldn't go out in the moist air. For that reason, he stayed in as much as possible. He discontinued socializing with Fritjof's brother artists at the pub on Leipzigstrasse. He ate in a neighborhood restaurant, and no longer went to the privy councilor's house.

In this time of loneliness, he wrote almost daily to Jakobe. Though he tried to hide it, his letters were marked by the anxiety that was overwhelming him. Contrary to his custom, he wrote almost nothing about himself. He talked, instead, of this and that in the life of the city, whatever he had, by chance, observed.

At the end of November, he received, through Ivan, a note from Blackbourn & Gries, the big English engineering firm, to which his father-in-law had recommended him. There was no question of an appointment to the firm. He was only invited to follow from a closer view the daily work, a large realignment project that could have the greatest significance for him; he decided to leave Berlin immediately. He knew, at this point, only that the town where the work was going on, Dresack, was a little mountain village in the Austrian Alps. He planned to winter there until the thaw, then go to Vienna and Budapest, to the mouth of the Danube, and look over the big dredging work there, then on to Paris, London, and New York.

On the way to Dresack, he stopped in Linz to see the nine-hundred-foot-long railway bridge. He arrived late in the afternoon and observed, for the first time, on the horizon, the airy, white row of Alpine peaks. In the glow of the sunset, they soared over the evening mist as if on the first morning of the world. The next day, he was walking in the mountains where the air was bright, but because some obtrusive, babbling German hikers were annoying him, he took a train out of a little country station and, despite the season, spent the rest of the day under the open sky. It was as if something in the huge wilderness of stone and snow were calling to him. He was being lured higher and higher, out into the wide-open spaces, as if by a secret promise of freedom from everything that had oppressed him, had weighed him down.

Without a guide, he followed a mountain path twisting up to a sheer cliff side. He had been warned at the station not to go alone, but, suppressing the anxiety he unquestionably felt in these vast and strange surroundings, he climbed briskly. And what a mountain scene spread out before him! He inhaled in long, refreshing breaths the snow-cold air while the clouds sailed away, deep under him in the valley. In these hours he entered into a relation with nature he had never known before.

As a boy, woods and meadows were the playground in which he sought to frolic freely and forget the oppression of home. Since then, he had never had the opportunity to engage in a more intimate fellowship with nature.

He had been sitting in his back rooms in Nyboder, studying nature on topographical maps, disrespectfully making her plunder for his creative urge. She consisted there only of stone and earth masses that could be calculated. At the sight of a field, his thoughts immediately would swarm with leveling instruments and tape measures. He could never sit at the window of a train compartment without his imagination ceaselessly tinkering with the landscape he was moving through, constructing new roads, drying out the bogs, building bridges, and digging canals.

Now his vision was not captured by the mere lines and colors of maps, but by the vastness, spirit, the mystical powers of nature to which he was made susceptible by his anxiety. These were masses of immeasurable extension, the immense power of forms and the deep stillness of eternity that called out strange and new feelings and moods in him.

He had gone some thousand feet up and saw before him an enormous snowfield opening above him from a sun-soaked, bare, reddish, and rocky crest. Winded from the steep ascent, he had to stop to catch his breath. And when he stood there, leaning on his stick, looking around in the silent and wild wilderness, he experienced a protracted astonishment. He asked himself how it was possible that there could be something so wonderful, so uplifting for the mind, as moving, hour after hour, through a completely lifeless stone wilderness in monotonous silence. How did it happen that something so negative as the fact that nothing could be heard be so completely liberating? Perhaps, after all, something could be perceived? Were believers, in certain respects, right when they spoke of "the world beyond the known, natural world"? Was it to be found in the vibrations of sound in space that could not be heard by the mortal ear? What we called dead was, perhaps, only another form of life that could be discerned by the "soul's senses."

Per remembered how one of the pastors who spoke over his father's coffin had called stillness in nature "God's voice," and he had, by this term, wanted to remind the congregation how the old prophets, in moments of doubt and weakness of will, invariably sought out the isolation of the wilderness. "God's voice!" No, the truth was that face-to-face with the empty and soundless universe the mind was seized by the "horror vacui" that the ancients saw behind everything. Anxiety created hallucinations and hallucinations new anxiety, and so it was through all time until God was created and heaven and hell populated.

He climbed, still, some hundred feet and stopped anew to draw his breath. Always, the same frozen waste, the same passionless peace! These huge snow-covered rocks really gave a sense of the powers that had moved them the first night of Creation when Mother Earth was born. And while he was looking at them, he was overcome by a dizzying perception of drawing near to that distant, still-living event. Time seemed to shrink so amazingly at the sight of these stiff clumps of rocks resting in eternal indifference, so naked and untouched, just as they were a few million years when "issuing," as they say, "from the Creator's hand." The Creator? You mean the burning cloud and the dissolving solar system? And behind that? Emptiness! Emptiness! Ice cold—the stillness of death.

It was evening before he again reached the station. There, people had begun to worry about him. In the inn, where he had left his luggage, they were already talking about sending out a search party. Tired from the exertions of the day, his head heavy with so many thoughts, Per wanted to go to bed immediately, but already when he had arrived in the morning he had noticed that something special was happening. Over the door of the inn hung green braided fir trimmings. The staff were so busy they could hardly find time to assign him a room. It turned out that there was to be a wedding there. The place was swarming with people, and he was invited to the party. At first he declined, but scarcely had he slipped into his room when there was a knock on his door. In came two young girls, arm in arm. They curtsied and, speaking at the same time, with much giggling and elbow jabbing, recited a long verse from which he was able to infer that the bride and groom requested the honor of his presence. So he was persuaded and had to spend the whole night eating, drinking, and dancing until he was giddy.

Out in the vestibule was a space as large as a barn floor, where the hammering of hobnailed boots could be heard to the music of zithers and harmonicas. Two long well-stocked tables were in the room, on one of which was a roasted goat with gilded horns. The wine was presented in large pitchers, and, in the course of the night, drunkenness and looseness in the relations between the sexes developed markedly, seeming to clash strangely with the many crosses and holy pictures that ornamented the place and were to be seen everywhere along the roadsides of the country.

Gradually, Per felt pleased with the country bacchanal. He thought about what Fritjof had always preached—that such nature folk were, essentially, the happiest. With a curtsy before a pair of sticks nailed together to form a cross, they solved all the riddles of life and death and let the fiddles wail on.

It had been his plan to travel on the next morning. But he let one, two, more days pass. At the wedding party he had made the acquaintance of a young girl who captivated him, a full-bodied peasant girl, a little heavy and awkward, as Alpine women tend to be, with a delightful snub nose and the kind of corn-blond hair that had always especially attracted him. They had, by chance, been sitting on a bench next to each other, watching the dancing, and they started to chat. He didn't understand much of what she said, and she did not understand him at all. Therefore they laughed a lot and quickly became intimate. She was twenty-two and lived a little beyond the village with her mother, whose indulgence Per won with a couple of twenty-guilder pieces. He had submitted to that relationship with a wild carelessness and, at the same time, with a certain sense of shame about being unfaithful to Jakobe. But he had to get out of the futile pondering that had been plaguing him since his father's death and was almost at the point of making him crazy. He understood that he needed to beware, especially of loneliness, and when he wasn't with this girl, he passed the time in the taproom with the innkeeper and other townsfolk. The wine and conversation flowed, and the smoke from the pipes made the air blue, while the circle around them gradually grew, stirred by the most fantastic rumors about his origin and princely fortune. After the passage of a week, he suddenly left. A crowd, high on wine, accompanied him to the station while the blond girl sat on her bed at home and cried. But his father's ghost followed him.

Dresack lay in a narrow, sunless two-mile-long ravine at the bottom of which a mountain stream rushed out and created an unbroken row of small waterfalls. On both sides of the ravine, the mountain slopes were forested up to the summit. But to the south, the view was blocked by a huge, completely bare, reddish-gray mountain, Hoher Goll, whose snowy back, most days of the year, was hidden by clouds. The town lay around the foot of that mountain and consisted of two rows of tightly built, wooden houses in an S contour on a very steep street adjoining the main road that ran along the river's right bank. A bit below the town, on the top of a little projecting summit of a hill around which the river bent, lay the old ruins of a castle shaped like a molar, that served as a law court. On the other side, a blood-red, speared church spike rose above the town.

Until nine months before, fruitful meadows stretched out on both sides of the river, and a couple of sawmills and a gristmill were near the largest of the waterfalls. Now the bottom of the valley was a chaos of splintered logs, gravel mounds, rock heaps, and an accumulation of uprooted trees. The whole of the woods was lying there, the roots turned upward and the tops buried in mud. Between the rocks and tree roots, the remains of buildings were manifest—here a splintered girder, there some rusty machine parts. The entire deep-lying part of Dresack, the station buildings, were leveled in one night when Hoher Goll, after eight straight days of rain in the spring, shook its white locks. The flood came on so suddenly that the people had to escape from their houses in just their nightshirts. Five men and about fifty head of cattle were carried off by the flood and shattered on the cliffs.

After eight months, the work of clearing had so progressed that the railway line was in running order again. The torn-up parts of the roads had to be provisionally spanned by wooden bridges. In addition, the riverbed had begun to be regulated by dynamite blasting. The plan called for the creation of a kind of exigency discharge behind the projecting hill on which the ruins of the town were stranded and whose positioning was partly responsible for the inundation. A hundred workers were laboring here every day, and three engineers from Blackbourn & Gries had been quartered in Dresack.

Per found lodging with an old saddler's widow who lived in the middle of the town in a brown, tarred log house with a stone roof and a half-covered gallery that looked out over the valley. Here he had two rooms, dark and low, in the upper story, in which he had arranged his entire field gear; this did not add to the rooms' comfort. In spite of his almost petty love of order and his desire for well-being, he lacked the talent for creating around him a sense of home. It was as if his inner restlessness immediately marked the rooms he had moved into. A door led from his work-room to the gallery, where he often stood in the early hours of the evening in his traveling cloak, looking over the dark, somber mountain ravine up to the moonlit fields of Hoher Goll. Deep under him, in the darkness, the river roared. He could clearly make out its uneven run through the large chaotic mass of stone, here and there illuminated by the bivouac fires marking the spot that had been, during the day, the place of dynamite blasting.

That solemn and dwarfing feeling of powerlessness in the face of nature that had seized him at the first sight of the colossal Alpine rocks was not diminished here. In his booklet he had proclaimed, with a confident sense of victory, that the mankind that had been, before, a dreadful slave of the elements soon would harness thunder to its triumphant carriage and use the storm as a cracking whip. In the face of this wild destruction, he realized that men would always live here on earth at nature's mercy. After a couple of weeks, he wrote to Jakobe, who was impatiently waiting to see him forcefully defend his finally published manifesto against a spiteful attack appearing in a professional paper: "You ask me if I have seen the *Industritidende*, and you seem to wonder that I haven't responded, at this point, to the belittling judgment about my book. But how should I really answer? What does criticism matter? You wrote that you would be happy to see me counterattack my enemy and shred his false assessment like a moth-eaten stocking. It seems to me you are taking this whole thing too seriously. Good God! It is only a book, and one, furthermore, I'm no longer fully satisfied with. There is some youthful foolishness in it that should have been edited out. Unfortunately, as humiliating as it is for us, we are forced to admit that our mastery over nature is, for now, only slightly strengthened. And with this, we should, in all probability, try to account for the fact that so many people, and fairly enlightened ones, can see in nature an expression of an eternal governance of ceaseless will and power."

Jakobe never answered the letter, and Per never again referred to his book or its fate. He wasn't, in fact, at all dissatisfied with the silence and indifference that greeted the book everywhere else but the little-read *Industritidende*.

In general, his letters, during the winter, were fewer and shorter. He wrote mostly about the weather and the progress of the work of clearing—that sort of thing—or he told little stories about town life, most often in a humorous tone that could hide the mental crisis he knew he was having, now fully aware of how significant it was.

In reality, he was experiencing nothing other than what he was ashamed to write about. He was with the engineers of Blackbourn & Gries every day at work, but he had almost no communication with them. They were three cold-blooded whisky drinkers who had gone about in all parts of the world and who had treated him, from the first, with offensive condescension, partly because he expressed himself so poorly in English. But after he spent Christmas Eve with them in the Good Neighbor Inn, their hangout, there was a change in this regard. On that occasion, he drank them all so thoroughly under the table that two of them had to go to bed at the inn and the third was taken home in a wheelbarrow. With that exploit, Per considered his honor restored, and the three fellow workers really changed their behavior toward him from that day on.

Nevertheless, he did not seek out their company and appeared only seldom at the Good Neighbor.

He spent the long evenings by himself reading in his room, and it was often late when he put out his lamp. With all his Jutland obstinacy, he was applying himself intensely to the kinds of knowledge that went beyond his studies—not, as in the previous year, to satisfy his idle desire to master the contemporary social culture, but from a deeply felt, genuine desire to find his way to a firmly based life perspective.

He went far in his systematic reading plan. Accustomed as he was from his study of mathematics and natural sciences to look for proof in an emerging series of conclusions, he went continuously from one book to another. His way of reading would lead him on by references mentioned here and there, and then he went to still other writings in order to find the original premise, to get to the simple, final truth that would silence all doubt. So that Jakobe wouldn't hear of this, he had a Copenhagen bookseller send his books directly without, as before, using Ivan as a middleman. Gradually he had a whole library of philosophic, aesthetic, and theological writings that were stacked on his worktable.

But the more he read, the more confused he became. With his persistent search for the ultimate word that would annihilate forever all superstitious fantasies about the "Beyond," he spun around in the dark like a continually fooled victim in blind man's buff. Every time he thought he was nearing the final proof, an "Over here" sounded from the opposite end of his echoing, intellectual universe, or he banged his head against a wall over an inaccessible work of an old Greek or Latin philosopher.

Still, he didn't give up hope. With an implicit faith in the book that gradually evolved in him in the course of his self-education, he often stayed home even during the day to force out a result. It was a matter of life or death. Weeks, months went by; he had promised himself that he wouldn't leave Dresack before he had reached absolute clarity and peace of mind.

One evening, at the beginning of March, he came home from a workplace on the other side of the river. He was tired from the day's exertions and walked with a dragging step in his high boots. Spring had been in the air in the last few days. Up in the mountains, the sound of avalanches could be heard, and the river had risen several feet. As the anniversary of the great catastrophe approached, Per was made very nervous, not only by his many fruitless ponderings, but also by the whole of his isolated life here among the threatening mountain walls in front of him. He was infected, as well, with the tense unrest of the populace. The papers had already announced several big avalanches in the high hills.

The sun had recently gone down behind the crests of the mountains in the west. Hoher Goll's white top glittered, and snow ran like a river of lava down the sides. On the provisional beam bridge that spanned the river, there were, as usual, a couple of men with long angler spears, with which they harpooned and fished out the tree debris that cluttered the water. Per was accustomed to standing for a while watching these spear fishermen, whose pointed poles were thrust with amazing sureness into even the smallest tree stump that rolled by in the whirling and foaming river. But this evening, he passed by them indifferently and returned in his absent-mindedness a Danish "Good evening" to their German greeting.

His thoughts were of home. He was wondering, among other things, whether there would be a letter from Jakobe at the end of the day. He hadn't heard from her in over a week and could not grasp the reason for her sudden silence. True, he himself had not written for some time. It had gradually become a kind of mental suffering to compose those indifferent epistles, so full of dissimulation. But *his* silence had, it occurred to him, been one more reason for *Jakobe* to write. He could have been sick or have suffered even worse luck, which might make it impossible for him to write.

"Is there a letter for me?" he asked his landlady, the old Frau Babi, who had hurried out to open the entrance hall door when, from the window, she saw Per coming.

"No, sir," answered the little woman in a timid tone. Still, when he came up to his room, he couldn't help peeking down at the worktable where Jakobe's oblong envelopes with large, stiff writing ordinarily lit up his homecoming every other day. Shrugging, he moved around the room, softly whistling in an unsuccessful attempt to shake off his heavy mood, and sank silently into an old armchair in front of the open fireplace where a couple of big logs were blazing. Twilight was closing in swiftly. The darkness advanced from all corners of the uncomfortable room as he sat there with his arms on his knees, gazing into the fire.

Jakobe's silence had begun to upset him. Could she be sick? No. In that case, he would surely have heard from Ivan. Maybe there's something I'm not seeing, but what? he thought. He pictured her as she probably would be at home, sitting at the festive dinner table together with her parents and siblings. He saw that broad table under the large, gleaming chandelier, the lovely spread, the flowered centerpiece, and the ever-present fruit bowl . . . Philip Salomon at the head of the table in his high-backed gold leather chair with a napkin under his chin . . . Ivan, Nanny, and the other children seated at random, without regard to age or gender, and talking all at once in a carefree manner. Only Jakobe was silent, as always, and apart, pale and earnest, a "wise owl," as her father jokingly used to call her; a "strict institute director," as Nanny, less charitably, dubbed her. Suddenly, a new shape glided into the picture: Eybert. Per knew that Jakobe's old suitor had again infiltrated the Salomon house. She had, some time ago, mentioned it herself. Actually, she had never wholly overcome her attraction to the slicked-down Apostle of Temperance. When he thought about it, there had also been a certain reserve in the last letters, almost some irresolution—concealment. Was she thinking of breaking off the engagement? Or could her silence, in a gentle way, be preparing him for that? Was that the meaning? Well, the feelings that had brought them together were, for her as for him, of a special and elevated nature, but they did not bind harmoniously their separate characters. Especially in these last days, it was becoming uncomfortably clear how very different they were in every respect. He knew this: if he had been compelled to reveal to her what his mind and thoughts were occupied with during this winter, she would never have understood it. He remembered Jakobe's various condescending observations about the religious temptations of mankind. Perhaps, for both their sakes, it would be best if they split up now before all this caused greater harm.

While he sat there buried deep in these twilight thoughts, the door to the steps opened and in crept Frau Babi. In the small woman's face, and also in her quick, timid movements, there was something mouselike that had reminded Per, from the beginning, of the simple Trine in Nyboder. It was, therefore, difficult for him to free himself from the superstitious fantasy that this was that servile spirit from his years of poverty, in the form of a little old mother, puttering about, caring for him.

She had come to turn on his lamp and set the table for his supper. But when she saw, by the light of the fire, that Per was still wearing his dirty high boots, she fetched his slippers out of the bedroom. "Perhaps you would like to put these on, sir," she said, and placed them in front of him. Per did not answer. Not until she had lit the lamp and closed the window shutters was he really conscious of her presence. In a few minutes, she left.

Per continued sitting by the fire. With his arms resting heavily on his knees, he stared into the dying flames and quickly reverted to his dark brooding. It was no longer Jakobe he was thinking about. Inevitably, when his thoughts were left alone for a moment, they wandered back to his mother, restlessly circled around his childhood home and his father's grave. He felt a twinge, as he regularly did every time when, either in waking or in dreams, he remembered his father's watch. He now understood full well that there had been as much fear as spite and scorn behind his behavior at home, and, pushing away the memories surrounding his visit, he moved quickly on to thoughts of other things.

He got up as Frau Babi, who had been down in the kitchen, came in with his evening meal on a tray.

"What have we got today?" he asked.

"A little ham, sir."

"Always ham," he grumbled, and gave vent to his bad mood: "You could have been more imaginative!"

While the landlady set the table, he went out onto the gallery to get a breath of the icy evening breeze that swept down through the valley from Hoher Goll. It was, by now, completely dark. Over by the workplaces, a couple of watch fires flickered, and out by the new station building a row of oil lamps were burning with a sleepy glimmer.

Stillness reigned over everything. Only the river could be heard and the thudding rumble of a distant train. Once, a booming avalanche echoed. Heavy, dark masses of clouds lay on the mountaintops, but right over his head, Per saw a clear field of stars.

He had stood there many nights in the last months, worn out and depressed by his fruitless reading, and stared up at the bright swarming sky. Then he could fantasize that the golden, heavenly script might hold the solution to the riddle of life and death for those who understood how to interpret the signs. And what mysterious signs! As in the most ancient ideograms from mankind's childhood, there were, here, all kinds of animal shapes plainly outlined in punctuated flowing lines: Lion, Bear, Snake, Bull, mankind's first ABC. And in the midst of all these wild creatures was the sign of the cross, a clearer and stronger light than any constellation, surrounded by the halo of the Milky Way.

He was suddenly startled by a long-drawn-out whistle cry from the valley. It was the express train from the north that was announcing its arrival. The locomotive's red fire-eyes glowed already through the dark. The brake steam could be heard, and a few minutes later, the short train, like a tired horse, clattered up to the front of the station building.

It stopped there for only a few moments. Some compartment doors were opened and shut, a bell sounded, and the conductor gave the signal for departure.

Per followed the lighted train with his eyes until it slithered with a sharp serpent's hiss into a tunnel under Hoher Goll. At this sight, as so often before, he thought he needed only to *wish* it and in a few hours he could find himself hundreds of miles from this stone prison in which he had been locked up for almost three months. The next day, he already could be rolling through the free and light air of northern Italy, bathed in the summer sun and the scent of flowers. He was his own man, in no way bound by obligations. But where would it get him? How would it help him to travel farther out into the world, as long as he hadn't shaken off the nightmare that imprisoned his thoughts in his sleep and drained his blood, courage, energy. No, here where he was giving battle, he must fight to the end. Here, in the gloomy grave of a mountain dungeon, he had to conquer his frightful ghosts or be conquered himself.

When he came into the room again, the table was set. Frau Babi waited humbly at the side of his chair in order to slide it in under him as he sat down.

"Well, now," he said, with a renewed attempt to work himself into a more cheerful mood, "let me devour the ham, in God's name!"

"You mustn't be angry, sir," stammered the little, repentant woman. "It's very difficult to get fresh meat here."

Altogether Trine's voice, thought Per. "Don't take it too

hard," he said, not entirely softened. "I well know I'm a little unreasonable these days. I'll tell you, then, I haven't felt right, lately."

"I thought so, sir. You have looked poorly these last days."

"Yes," he remarked, and immediately felt less well. After a little while, he cleared his throat and said it was raw. It was probably the cold from Berlin still settled in his body. He was certain he should call a doctor and let his lungs be examined.

Just then there was a knocking at the front door, and Frau Babi went down to open it. Shortly after, she returned with burning cheeks and told him that a lady was downstairs who wanted to speak to him.

"A lady?" Per put his fork down. "There must be a mistake. I don't know any women here."

"She's also a foreigner. She doubtless came on the train."

"On the train," repeated Per, perplexed, and he looked at her in bewilderment.

Then he heard footsteps on the stairs, and a moment later, a dark lady dressed in traveling clothes was smiling at the door. An expensive fur coat hung loosely from her shoulders. "I heard your voice," she said. "Good evening! Don't be so frightened!"

Per leapt up: "But . . . Jakobe!"

"Yes, it's really me," she answered, apparently completely calm, with an air of self-mastery she affected, to provide cover for her delicate nerves in the midst of strong emotional agitation.

"But what—how?"

"I really should have telegraphed, but I didn't have an opportunity anywhere during the whole trip. And then I thought it would be amusing to surprise you. I counted on finding you at home. But help me off with my coat. You're not very gallant." Only when she had taken off her traveling coat, and her hat, as well, and straightened her hair a bit did she let herself be embraced in the hesitating arms of her entirely dumbfounded fiancé.

Though her whole body vibrated with impatience to throw herself on his chest, she settled for taking his head between her hands and kissing his forehead in a friendly fashion. "One usually says 'Welcome'—or aren't you happy to see me?"

Per really was not entirely clear what this feeling was that so powerfully moved him at seeing her. His first thought—that his bad conscience prompted—was that she had come to spy on him.

But now, when he held her in his arms and saw the large, dark eyes beaming with a desire to give herself to him in love, he understood it all at once. It was as if an iron shackle had burst that had been squeezing his heart. Since his first, naive love for the saddler's daughter from Kerteminde, he had never felt an emotion so strong as to make his eyes misty like this.

"Why didn't you write?"

"You didn't understand that?" At the sight of Per's wet eyes, tears filled her own. And when she heard the door close behind Frau Babi—who, finally, had understood that she was not wanted—Jakobe could no longer control herself, and with a wild burst of passion threw her arms around his neck.

"You have, all the same, longed for me a little. And now, it's true; I'm finally here with you! It's no longer a dream." With her eyes closed, she pressed herself against his chest. "No, it's not a dream! I hear again the loud heartbeat. Oh, Per—darling. A thousand times my darling." For a long time they stood like that, with their arms tight around each other. Per silently moved his hands over her hair—he could not find a word to say, he was so overwhelmed. So many questions raced through his head. At last, he composed himself enough to begin to ask and answer in clearly arranged sentences.

"Why didn't I write that I was coming?" said Jakobe when they were seated side by side on a wooden sofa between the windows, holding hands and every moment breaking off talking in order to kiss. "No, I couldn't, dear. Remember, I didn't know until the last minute what I would do. For a long time, I had the complete plan in mind. I felt that I should come here before you traveled farther off. I thought—you had been away from me during the whole long winter, and you wrote so little about yourself. I didn't really know what, in the end, I should think about you, Per! Finally, I said to Father and Mother that I wanted to visit Klara Hert in Breslau. You know, she is a friend of mine from the old days. They found that entirely natural, but still I didn't dare write to you about it . . . I did not have, as it were, the courage for that. A hundred things could have come in the way and—think of my terror—at the last minute, Ivan suddenly thought of coming with me to keep me company. But I put an end to that. And now you have me here."

During her story, Per lowered his eyes a few times. He knew her love of truth and understood (what was clearly involuntarily betrayed in her tone as well) that it had cost her a great deal to overcome her resistance and entangle herself in so many lies to her parents and siblings; she had sacrificed all that, endured all that anxiety, defied so many dangers and prejudices only because she understood that he needed her.

He hardly dared to look at her for shame over what he had just a little while ago thought about her. "And now?" he asked, with uncertainty. "Now are you going to stay here?"

"For two days, yes. I don't dare let home be without letters for longer than that. Then I'll travel to Breslau. Is there an inn here in town where I can stay?"

"No, you can't do that. It's unpleasant. You stay here, and I'll move to the inn. You saw my landlady before. She's a decent woman who will take good care of you."

"Well, all right, as you wish. But now, my darling," she said, and stroked his hair with a motherly touch while she tried to look him in the eyes. "Now it's your turn to confess. How are you? Not so good? You seem to me a little tired."

Per was uneasy and looked off to the side to avoid the look. "No, really, I have had it good here. Naturally, it's not been too amusing. But the countryside is magnificent in its way, and the work really interesting and educational."

Jakobe had slowly withdrawn her hand, and a few minutes of silence followed. Then she turned again to him and put her arm around his neck.

"Per," she asked. "Why don't you have confidence in me? Do you really think you could hide something from me? No, no, you needn't apologize. Just be open with me. Or how can we talk frankly about things? Even if I can't understand, I still know that those raised as Christians, whether believers or not, are not free from temptations, and I have been entirely prepared for the fact that you haven't been able to escape them. But I have also been entirely convinced that you would overcome them."

"You're right," he said, blushing for shame and freeing himself in order to get up. "I have really been a little at a loss." He walked across the floor. "It's laughable! Rather laughable! But it's been lonely here and . . . so my accursed pastor-blood, that whole clan of stiff-collared forefathers, has started to haunt me. But that's all over now, I assure you . . . I'm entirely myself again."

Jakobe was silent for a moment and looked thoughtful. Then she got up and went over to him. Instead of answering, she patted him calmly on the cheek and said, "Let's not talk anymore this evening about all this, my darling. Listen, Per. I see I have surprised you in the middle of your supper. That's fine, because I realize how very hungry I am. I didn't eat during the whole journey. You'll have to share your meal with me."

"Of course, dear," said Per, happy to have escaped the subject under discussion. "But now I'll call my landlady. I'm sure she can rustle up something good for you."

"That's fine. When I am this hungry, I'm like a fire or a pig— I consume all. Talk with the landlady, and meanwhile I'll clean up a bit. Can you get my little handbag? I set it down at the bottom of the stairs."

While Per had the table set anew and drove Frau Babi dizzy with all his orders, Jakobe stayed in the neighboring bedroom. When she emerged, she had arranged her little curls at the temples and decorated her dark gray traveling dress with a high and broad collar trimmed in black lace and a lilac silk ribbon. She took a small bunch of violets from her belt and put it in Per's buttonhole, and after she had again taken his head between her hands and given him a series of hot and tempestuous kisses, she sat down at the table.

Despite Per's sincere happiness and gratitude for Jakobe's presence, there was something inhibited and restrained in his bearing toward her. He felt oppressed by the disproportion between her generous, devoted, and defiant love for him and his own for her. He had never fed on fancies in regard to the nature of his feelings for her. He had, with each step forward in their relationship, been very clear about how much she meant to him. She had once awakened a sense in him of love's paradise, but her thin and susceptible body, her whole strange appearance, held little attraction, in general, for his senses. And his passionate temper, which had been released in the relationship, actually had the effect of cooling him off more than exciting him.

While they sat at the table, where the poor surroundings had been made festive with a bright, clean tablecloth, a couple of old copper three-branched candlesticks, she awakened, for the first time, his full desire, though her large collar did not really become her. Living in his stone prison like a monk in his cloister, lost in the shadowy world of his thoughts, he had not been so near a young woman in a long time. Now a life passion was again warming up in his blood. Courage and strength streamed back into his swelling heart.

He drank one glass after another of the strong native wine. Jakobe's cheeks became rosier, and, despite her hunger, she often forgot to eat for all the clinking and toasting of glasses, kisses, and embraces. When they finally rose from the table, Per said, "You've seen how I live. Now come and look at my view." He draped her coat around her and led her out to the gallery. Both in the town and below in the station buildings most of the lights were already on, but up in the sky, the field of stars spread out. The clouds had glided in from the mountain ridges and settled down in the gorges for the night. Only over Hoher Goll's snow-fields, some dark, brownish smoke floated. Per was talking about how many nights he had stood there and heard nature speak to him through the dark rustle of the river, feeling like the last living human being on a deserted planet. But Jakobe no longer was listening to his words. She was pressing against his chest and interrupted him every moment by touching her lips to his. And, finally, he, too, was silent. They stood there for a long time, rocking in each other's arms, and spoke only with looks leading to long, long kisses.

Once, the drawn-out roll of an avalanche thundered from Hoher Goll. Per lifted his head to listen, but Jakobe didn't move. Even when he called her attention to the rumble, repeated a moment after, she didn't answer him. All she heard in the whole wide world was the beating of their hearts. When they had come again into the room, Per said it was late and she really needed to get some rest. She didn't answer. Somewhat flushed, he went into the bedroom to gather up his toiletries and a few other small items. When he came in again, she was standing at one of the windows with her back to the room.

"Now I'll be going to the inn," he said, and went over to her to say goodnight. She didn't turn around, and he kissed her twice on the cheek without her returning the caress. But when he was ready to go, she held him back with her hand—silent and determined.

He looked at her, questioning. Then she turned her head toward the bench couch and said, "You could sleep there. I would have you near and could watch over you. I don't like hotel life." Per leaned over her. Still not sure he had understood her rightly, he wanted to look her in the eye. Then she leaned against him and pressed his hand to her heart.

The next morning, the sun shining through the window slats woke her up. She raised herself on her elbows and looked around with surprised, wide-open eyes. The door to the other room was half opened, and when she heard someone cautiously puttering around, she smiled.

"Per," she called out cheerfully. At the sound of his steps the blood rushed to her cheeks. But already, before he opened the door, she was reaching out for him. He came in quietly and kneeled at the bed. "How well you slept!" he said, and grasped her hands.

"Yes, and you know what? In the last half year I haven't slept a night without taking my sleeping drops. I was aware of almost nothing from the moment you left me. But you? You're all dressed and have already been out, I can see. Your hair smells of the fresh morning air."

"I've just been pacing up and down on the balcony for a while. I didn't wish to go any farther away from you."

"Ah, I understand now! Those were your steps I was hearing the whole time in my dream. So you certainly must have been outside for a long time. Haven't you slept at all? Poor dear! Was the bench couch too hard? I told you it would be!"

"No, it wasn't that. But Jakobe—"

"What is it, my darling?" She saw clearly now how moved, how shaken he was, and she became anxious. "What has happened?"

"Jakobe, I'll confess something to you because I won't have any peace before I do, before I have told you that—" She laid her hand on his mouth.

"I know it all, what you want to say, and I won't hear anything of it. The past is now forgotten."

"And you can forgive me? Will you forget that I talked to you about love and won your heart and received your kisses before I even knew what love was? Because it's true, I'll admit, only last night did I learn what it is. And I am ashamed at how wretched I was and how little I understood about life. Will you forgive me?"

"Ah, my darling," she said, and, with a rather sad expression, took his head and pressed it to her chest. "That I did a long time ago."

* * *

Some days after, Jakobe and Per were climbing on a steep footpath that wound up over an alternately bare and scrubby mountainside. It was somewhere around noon. The sun burned on the red-gray cliffs, and in the air around them, spring was carrying the strong and fragrant resinous perfume of spruce and fir. They found themselves in the Laugen mountains on the south slopes of the Alps. The very day after Jakobe's appearance in Dresack they had climbed up to get closer to the summer, and now, in eight days, they had roamed about on both sides of the Etsch valley like two happy vagabonds, had slept in Alpine inns, bought bread and eggs in the villages, quenched their thirst in forest springs. On the third day of the journey, Jakobe had written home and calmly announced to her mother where she was and explained that she couldn't resist the temptation to greet the spring and therefore had changed plans on the way to Breslau, turning south toward the Alps. Without expressly mentioning Per, she had also written that her mother shouldn't be concerned, since she had secured a competent escort.

Now she was stumbling slowly and unsurely up the rough path with a long alpenstock in her hand and her skirt tucked up. Per steadily followed, carrying on his back a simple green rucksack, their entire baggage. Jakobe stopped often and turned to hold him in her arms and give him a kiss. Both were tanned by the spring sun, and Jakobe's usually neat curls fluttered wildly like a gypsy's around her ears. Her eyes sparkled, her mouth was hot with the delight of love.

She did not prove to be an able mountain climber. Every half hour she had to rest, and Per had to carry her over spring water and support her on all the steep descents. But he was far from complaining about it. She was as light as a bird, and he loved the feeling of having her in his arms. The many small rests in the woods or among the mountain cliffs were, as well, happy occasions for idyllic and giddy love scenes that for both of them would be the most cherished memories when the day's wandering was over.

For Per, these days really signified a new birth and baptism. His life had suddenly come into a charged richness and beauty he had never dreamt of. He went around in an intoxicated state of revelation, as if he had developed new senses.

What he had demanded of happiness before seemed to him indifferent and insignificant compared to the degree of joy to be found now in merely one kiss. Jakobe was transformed for him. He loved her now as a woman who had given him a new life, who had widened the boundaries of his world, and whose embrace had exorcised the threatening shadow of death from his path.

But now the days of happiness had come to an end. For the sake of her parents, Jakobe dared no longer postpone the terrible moment of their separation. She had decided to be in Botzen by the evening, and from there to take the night train to the north, while Per would go back to Dresack in order to arrange his things and set out on his world travels according to his original plan. They were, on account of this, very quiet on this last day. When their looks met, Jakobe tried to smile, but in her caress there was something unrestrained that betrayed the painful anxiety in her mind. At last, she could no longer leave him alone but went slowly to his side, her arm around his waist and her head pressed against his shoulder. When they stopped to kiss, she closed her eyes to grasp with her whole soul the happy present and register it deeply in her memory. They had again reached the spot where the path turned; there were a couple of small chestnut trees that threw a bit of shade over the stony ground, and they decided to rest. Per spread out a travel shawl for Jakobe, who was tired and sat down immediately. Suddenly they remembered that they had forgotten to eat their lunch in the rucksack. That made them laugh, and they forgot their sorrow for a while.

Per unbuckled the green canvas bag from his back and began to unpack the food. Then his eye caught sight of a cross that was stuck among the stones over on the side of the path. It was one of the common four- to six-foot-high crosses with a crude, dismally painted picture of the crucified Christ. "The devil with it!" exclaimed Per. "Shall we have a ghost to look at? Let's move!"

"Oh, let's stay," pleaded Jakobe. "I can't go farther without having something to eat."

"Well, all right. We can turn our back to it! Do you see how beautiful it is here, Jakobe?" They were turned toward the valley, which sloped downward deeply and was full of haze, enjoying their frugal meal of some dry bread, a little cheese, and a couple of eggs. Per moved to Jakobe's side on a barren rock. When they had eaten and he had lit a cigarette, they sat, hand in hand, immersed in small talk and looking out into the golden mist.

Suddenly Per cocked his head as he listened. "Do you hear that?" he asked.

"What?"

"Don't you hear it? A church bell!"

"Where?"

"Somewhere down in the valley."

"No ... well, maybe—but to think you could clearly hear it!"

"Doesn't it sound hideous? Imagine that up here, in a magic realm, we are to be persecuted by that ghostly ringing!"

"You have an amazingly sharp ear for church bells," answered Jakobe, laughing.

Per told her how, already as a boy, he had hated and feared that sound that chased him everywhere on his forbidden adventures and echoed in his ears like a menacing incantation. Jakobe tenderly squeezed his hand and said that for her also, that eternal bell had sounded like an arrogant threat. She could still remember how, as a little girl, she had hidden on Sunday when the bell began to ring so no one could see her cry for indignation. And when she got older, she would often, on the way home from school, direct a defiant look at the bell up in the garrison church where two of her classmates' families had permanent pews they boasted of.

"Think of it, Per. Already so young we had the same ideas and feelings. Isn't it wonderful that we have found each other?"

He put his arm around her waist, and they talked together about the future, envisioned the coming century that, eventually, would give mankind back its spiritual freedom, reawaken the courage to act and the instinct for adventure, erect altars to strong and great deeds on the ruins of the church.

"Do you know," said Per, "lately I have often thought about a story I once heard at home in the parsonage from our old one-eyed servant girl. It was about a farmboy who wanted to be a magic marksman. Perhaps you've heard it?"

"A magic marksman? What's that?"

"You don't know! That's a man who shoots with charmed bullets and hits everything he aims at, however high over his head it might be suspended. But to accomplish that, he must, on a moonlit night, go to one of the cross-laden paths and shoot a bullet through an image of Christ—right through the heart."

"Aha—the story *Der Freischütz*," said Jakobe.

"That's it! But when it came to the climax of the story, the fellow's courage failed. Every time he lifted his gun to aim at the crucifix, his hand shook, and as soon as he wanted to press the trigger, his arm was paralyzed, and, for the rest of his life, he remained a common Sunday hunter. It seems to me that the story is a kind of picture of the impotence of the whole of mankind in the face of the ghosts of superstition. The courage to kill off idols with a vengeance just isn't there. Damn if, at the last minute, there are always scruples." He turned himself around toward the picture of Christ behind them and continued, with growing excitement: "Look at that pale man hanging there! Why don't we have the courage to spit from disgust right in his face. Look calmly at him, Jakobe. Such a shameless humility. How wretched a display of his misery. Well, his time will soon come to an end! We'll all be magic marksmen! With charmed bullets we'll shoot him. Look here!"

He leapt up recklessly and drew a heavy revolver out of its leather holster he was carrying under his coat. Before Jakobe could stop him he had cocked his firearm with this shout: "Now I shoot in the new century!" He sent a shot into the crucifix that hit one side and sent some splinters flying into the air. At that moment, a sigh seemed to go through nature. From the valley, a hollow boom sounded that, while growing quickly louder, was tossed back and forth between the mountain walls like a long-drawn-out infernal thunder. Per turned around. He had become completely pale, but when he realized what had happened he broke into a ringing laughter. He remembered now that, at many places on the ascent, he had seen a sign in three languages: "Take notice of the echo!"

"Yes," he snarled, then cried wantonly, "Ghosts!" and raised his revolver, discharging the rest of the bullets into the air so that a renewed and amplified roar and rattle filled the valley, as if a legion of mountain spirits had been loosed.

"But Per—you're so wild!" Jakobe, who was now standing up, cried out. Half resisting, half attracted, she threw herself around his neck. "What's going on with you?"

"I was merely scaring away a shadow from my path. But come! We must move on. Time is precious. In two hours, we'll go to the mail coach. And in about five hours, Jakobe, we'll have to leave each other's embrace."

As she laid her head on his shoulder and closed her eyes, she said, "Oh, Per, I don't want to think about it." They went slowly on, arm in arm, climbing up toward the flaming sunshine and surrounded by the wild and strong smells of spring.

BOOK 5

LUCKY PER, HIS GREAT WORK

CHAPTER 14

A WHOLE NEW powerful sense of life had been developing for some time in the Danish capital. People from the provinces or from abroad, who hadn't seen the city in some years, could hardly recognize it now; it had grown and changed so much in all respects. The European wave of culture that had swept over the country, carried by Dr. Nathan, had not only awakened a long-untapped intellectual ferment and fostered a series of revolutionary writers, scientists, and politicians, it had also inspired a breakthrough of young, bold energy in the practical domain seeking its own playground. Per Sidenius was merely one of many ambitious and vibrant young men stimulated by the progressive spirit of enterprise and the half-magical development of the large industrial countries that had, as the petty and peevish put it, "golden flies in the head."

While Per was whistling, bent over his drafting table in his little dark Nyboder back room, everywhere—on the revolving stools of businesses, at the cloth-covered desks of the bankers, and in the last row of the university's law auditorium—sat other daring dreamers who secretly were preparing themselves to seize positions of leadership in their country; and, in fact, already several of the most clever and ingenious of them had succeeded in winning a prominent place in public life that, until now, had been dominated wholly by the reactionary party and a stupid royal court.

In truth, Copenhagen was well on the way to opening itself up to the new times and their spirit. Not only had the capital's size and rapidly doubled population now moved it to the rank of the world's greatest cities, but the life of the street, entertainments, the tone of the press, and the social whirl became more European every day.

In the provinces, however, especially in the market towns, life was still lived virtually unchanged in its worn-out forms. Here the officials still ruled by means of academic breeding. Here the poetically inspired student was still the hero of the day when he came home for vacation with his silk hat swelling like a balloon on his curly head. It was unthinkable in the provinces that a man of business or industry, however mighty, bolstered by a title like "councilor of state," could be seated in the ranks of the city's gallooned officials.

Nor was there, in the countryside, any decisive break with the past. To be sure, smokestacks had begun to appear over the dairies, and threshers and mowing machines gradually replaced the flailing whips and scythes. But despite all the technical improvements of a progressive enlightenment, the countryfolk had become even poorer. Mortgages of estates multiplied, and so did the debt to foreign countries by many millions a year.

Nevertheless, the broad-backed Danish peasant stayed on his land with a stubborn sense that he was the marrow of the nation, its churning power and hope for the future—a notion that, sanctified by the Grundtvigian folk high schools, had become a national faith in the course of the last century. From Skagen to Gedser, the Danish cities and counties were united in a glorious cultivation of butter and pork.

In the meantime, the country's rivers and fjord mouths had become more and more sluggish. The old commercial streets in which, in the last century, there had been such a lively navigational bustle that individual citizens could fit out twenty ships, now served chiefly for a little, poor fishing business. Finally, only windmills caught the enormous energy of the restless winds that blew over the land. Along the coasts, the waves rose and sank, exhausting their roaring power in empty space.

While other nations in the world poured out streams of blood and gold to acquire a piece of shore or merely a coal depot, the forty-mile stretch from Skagen to Esbjerg, the breadth of a great international canal, lay blank—a wasteland of drifting sand without a port or even a city.

Then, too, in various places in the country, man-made projects augmented time's work of destruction—draining straits and inland lakes, reclaiming inlets to produce more cattle fodder. Where, in the past, fully loaded sailing ships came in from the sea with a breath of wind from faraway lands, now, green meadows with full-uddered milk cows created a deceptive impression of prosperity.

Even an exceptional attempt to do a real job of clearing on

the Jutland heath merely opened more fields, fostered still more cottiers, still more welfare for the poor—all that Per had so strongly ridiculed in his little manifesto.

The fact was that Copenhagen had taken the wind out of the sails of the rest of the country that dwindled more and more to mere outskirts of the capital. The country's energetic manpower, like the province's principal, flowed into the city, attracted by the high profits in speculation.

Lately, only what concerned Copenhagen and its development had held the general attention. That was also one of the reasons that Per's booklet, although it was expressly intended to create a sensation and rouse unrest, had stirred absolutely no interest either in Copenhagen or the countryside. His generous friend and brother-in-law, Ivan Salomon, pestered the editorial offices in vain with requests to sound the alarm. Everywhere he was met with indifferent shrugs. A channel project availing Jutland! Wind and wave motors at Blaavandshuk! The stuff of sensation? Even Dyhring, who had certain reasons to show himself obliging, excused himself with the claim that he had already caused himself great difficulties with the little article he had, at his friend's request, written about the subject. Ivan hadn't had much better luck in interesting financiers and speculators, even though he had spared neither his legs nor his eloquence in trying, personally, to influence the leading businessmen—first and foremost his own father, who, thus far, had firmly refused to involve himself in the plan.

Philip Salomon still had no confidence in his daughter's fiancé, and his wife, as was her wont in most cases, shared his feeling. Neither one would directly admit it; they still had not given up hope that Jakobe would come to her senses and, in time, break a connection that, by all human calculations, could only bring disappointment and sorrow.

One evening in March, after a meal in which he had been unusually quiet, Philip Salomon asked to have a talk with Ivan. That very morning Fru Salomon had received a letter from Jakobe, who everyone thought was in good hands at her friend's house in Breslau, but who now wrote from a little Austrian border town. She casually mentioned that she had met her fiancé and at present was going on a mountain excursion with him.

Philip Salomon said nothing to Ivan about what Jakobe had confessed, but immediately, in a businesslike way, brought up Per by asking his son how his endeavor of putting together a stock company to exploit his friend's projected plans was going. He had, he said, heard nothing about it for some time.

Ivan made a face and gestured defensively with his hands. "Let's talk about something else, Father . . . How is it going? How do you think it can be going when those who should be taking a close interest in it are indifferent? I have told you that the first thing people ask me, when I approach them about it, is your position. The whole Exchange knows now that Jakobe is engaged to Sidenius."

"I have thought about that," said Philip Salomon, always mild in spite of his son's excited, even disrespectful tone. "Tell me, how great a sum are we talking about?"

"How much, you ask? Have you read his book?"

"Yes, certainly, but I already told you I didn't care for it. Perhaps I read it through too quickly, or, perhaps, I didn't even understand it. He has his own way of writing about that sort of thing. I have thought of asking you whether you couldn't, straight out, give me again the main points of the book—a cohesive, more or less consecutive account of what your friend's ideas and plans really are aiming at."

Nothing could have pleased Ivan more. He quickly gathered together the relevant maps and papers and held his father glued to his chair for over an hour with his stream of words. Per's project, sketched in his book, as outlined by Ivan, went essentially like this: "Just before the Grådyb, where it flows into the Hjerting Bay, is an empty, almost uninhabited island, Langli. When you come into Skallingen, it appears as a long, gray-green row of dunes with a straw-covered fishing hut peeking out here and there. Along the east side, an old waterway runs to Hjerting, the original port of disembarkation for southern Jutland and now a poor little fishing hamlet where a couple of large, empty merchants' manors and a customhouse still recall a former splendor.

"It is one of Per's allegations, that the 'Stupidity Office' chose Esbjerg as a port toward the end of the sixties, a decision made, partly, just because of its unfavorable situation and also—and this before anything—because it could be connected to the rest of the country only by railway. Per's proposal is to move the South Jutland landing back to the old place, or rather, a bit north of that, namely Tarp, at the mouth of the Varde River. From there, traffic

could go farther inland. This waterway, deepened and straightened with the help of a couple of locks, would be connected
with the Vejle River, and together they would form the more
southern of the two channels that, according to his plan, would
unite in conjunction with the Belts, the North Sea. and the
Baltic.

"He writes that only the completion of at least one of these
lines of connection could bring a competition with the north
German ports, especially Hamburg, whose growing business
power, he contends, is the real danger that threatens Denmark's
independence. Denmark's defeat in the battle for business markets that, secretly or openly, is the concern of international politics, will be more and more fateful; on the other hand, a victory
would be a golden triumph and, gradually, Denmark would
become the center point of Europe, moving Russia's rising
developing might and culture farther and farther east.

"That Langli, in all this, would have great significance as a
trade center is easy to imagine. But, in addition, it is Per's intention to create even more favorable conditions for the development of little Klitø. His plan aims to make the island duty-free.
In his book, he has given a marvelous picture of wharfs, docks,
and mighty warehouses rising out of the sterile sand; as well, on
land, at the river delta, a great city would quickly emerge, the
Venice of the North. Everywhere, the necessary energy would
be produced through better wind motors or borrowed from the
breakers of the North Sea, and, with the help of mechanical
adjustments of Per's own invention, it would travel through wires
over Skallingen."

It was, for the time being, only the industrial part of the great
plan of the future for which Ivan had tried to procure the participation of the Copenhagen business world. He had even begun to
fancy that the construction of the actual channel project might
be taken up as a national cause that only a state had the capacity to
realize. On the other hand, the industrial activity and acquisitions
related to little Klitø, together with guarantees of the necessary
area around the river mouth, might be managed by a private consortium. Per had estimated the complete cost for this part of the
layout at five million.

While Ivan reviewed all this for his father, Philip Salomon's
face grew more and more attentive, really even surprised. But the
son was speaking too long, and he interrupted him at last to say,

"Thanks a lot, for now, my boy! We can talk about this thing more thoroughly another day. But I just have one question. What about these inventions, frankly speaking, that Sidenius claims to have made? Has he obtained a patent for some of them?"

"We have submitted applications both here and abroad. I'm waiting every day for an answer from the Patent Commission."

"It seems to me, Ivan, that you have brought this thing to a head before you are ready to take it public. Before a patent is granted, you are missing the whole foundation you need to build on. All the rest you spoke about sounds very interesting, but is only castles in the air. When an invention is patented, on the other hand, you have something immediately solid, however great or small the significance ascribed to it."

Ivan shoved himself back in his chair and, with hands clasped behind his head, stared hopelessly up at the ceiling. "You haven't understood a word of this, Papa," he said. Leaning again on the table with his arms covering Per's drafts, he continued, almost shouting, "The factories must be established before the value of the inventions can be proved. And, then, there are other requirements to be satisfied: docks, wharves, dwellings for the workers, at the mouth of the river. The whole hangs tightly together. That's precisely the beauty of the plan."

"I understand only too well, my boy! But it's still a good rule to follow in the building of a house, to start with the foundation, not the roof or the towers. You won't get anyone to believe that so many preparations are absolutely necessary to prove the value of an invention! The first thing to do now is to get the project going and, if you're successful, the developments will come of themselves."

"Yes, that's how it always is! How well I know, that when a really great idea is born," said Ivan, "it will inevitably be ground to dust before it is acknowledged. What you say doesn't mean much, Papa, because you don't believe in Sidenius. That's all there is to it."

"Believe! Believe! Dear Ivan, can *I* understand about channel and port construction? Do *you* know about windmills? I repeat, you have gotten things all wrong. To begin with, you are misguided in your connecting of dissimilar projects, and then in not having the patents in order. If your friend had been able to submit his plans to recognized experts for examination, he would have had the kind of backing he needs to carry the project forward.

But that people, as a matter of course, should take a young man's allegations on faith—that's naive, my child."

"Frankly, Papa, isn't it rather naive to request reputable testimonials from the same people the whole project is meant to challenge? There is, for example, the old bureaucratic dead end here at home that Sidenius wants to break; his book is a priceless complaint against it. In addition, I can tell you that, for some time, he did turn to our so-called 'outstanding' authorities, both individual experts and professional institutions, but, naturally, he met everywhere with scorn and, at best, with indifference. Colonel Bjerregrav, you know—Dyhring's uncle—had once promised to publish Per's project in the journal of the Engineers' Association, but when it came down to it, he didn't have the courage. Those kinds of people are all alike. Because Sidenius exposed their shortsightedness, they have conspired to knock him over. I know, with certainty, that they are furious with him."

"Well, one way or another, you must try to overcome the opposition—that's all you can do. Can't your friend seek out Colonel Bjerregrav again, since he's a man of such great influence?"

"That's not possible. I know that they clashed on the first occasion I mentioned and Sidenius offended the colonel personally."

"He could offer an apology. Colonel Bjerregrav is certainly not a vengeful man."

"Sidenius apologize? That shows how little you know him. You might as well ask the emperor of Russia."

"You could try another angle. I can tell you beforehand—dispensing with that kind of person's approval is not tenable."

"Listen, Papa, what is really your intention here? What does all this talk mean when you won't support us? I have told you that the basis of the general indifference toward the project is first and foremost your position in relation to it."

"That's what I wanted to talk to you about. I will say straight out: My behavior toward the whole concern has not and cannot change. If you were a little less bewitched by your friend, you yourself would see that I cannot possibly involve our firm in a speculative enterprise of this kind; at any rate, not the way things stand now. But I'll make you a proposition. I thought of putting some money at your disposal. Then you can manage the whole thing independently and in your name. You have often said how much you would enjoy engaging in more self-reliant enterprises. On several grounds, I think this undertaking might be just such an opportunity."

Ivan screwed up his eyes and examined Philip Salomon with unconcealed mistrust. While father and son customarily manifested the greatest confidence in each other, as soon as the talk was about business they were both on their guard.

"Is it a loan you are offering? Would I reimburse the firm?"

"You can arrange it any way it suits you. I leave you free in every respect. What alone counts for me is, as I said, that the whole thing get started. I think we have talked long enough. Let's try it out."

"Are you sure you realize it's not about a small sum? We need at least a couple of hundred thousand just to start."

"I imagine less would probably suffice. But that's enough talk for today. You can think about my offer. We'll discuss it more thoroughly tomorrow."

Ten days later, at the beginning of April, Jakobe returned from her journey. After having spent a week with her friend in Breslau, she had become irresistibly homesick. She reached Copenhagen in the evening in a furious snowstorm, and she stayed shut up in her room the whole of the next morning, to write to Per:

"Here I am home and can finally write you again a real letter. Did you get my two hurried ones from Breslau? I could almost wish you hadn't because I'm a little ashamed about them and you must pardon me both their confused form (I had to steal off and write them at night when I was dead tired after company or the theater) and also the content that, to a great extent, was just a miserable complaint instead of what it should have been, an endless, unutterable thanks to you, my darling, for all we had together. My week in Breslau seems to me now like a misty dream. I almost have to ask myself if I was really there, and I feel some remorse toward my friend and her husband, who did everything to amuse me—invited guests, took me to a concert and to something I abhor, a riding exhibition. But my thoughts were always with you. There I was again in Dresack and in Ausserhof, with all I had experienced and lived through once more returning in lovely dreams. Yesterday evening when I came here, I was met by some news that had a bit of a depressing effect on me, although I was not unprepared for it. The day before yesterday, Nanny got engaged to Dyhring. I'm not at all happy with the match. I have always quite disliked him, both as a journalist and a man. But Nanny seems very happy. And he is certainly, for the moment, as much in love as he is able to be. He was here last evening when I came in, and, as you can imagine, it was a little strange for me to see them sitting together in the little room where we so often sat and to hear them whispering and laughing.

"But I won't fall again into depressing thoughts. *Our* time is coming also, Per. I take consolation in the thought that nine days and nights of God knows how many hundred before I hold you in my arms have already passed since we parted. I wonder where you are today. In Vienna? Budapest? I see you before me, all too clearly, in your brown traveling jacket and with your blessed red cheeks that I kiss in my thoughts again and again. Do you know, I dreamt once more last night about the big woods in the Laugen valley. Never will I forget certain moments in that long, lovely day we spent together. Do you remember the bird that perched over our heads and sang? And our rest by the spring where you (as you put it) drank from my hands the waters of forgiveness for your youthful sins. But not a word more about that.

"I'm glad to be home again, sitting in my own room, surrounded by your picture and the other small mementos of you I so missed. Together with our books, they shall be my consolation and refuge in my loneliness. Can you guess which book I'll take up first? It will be Poulsen's little textbook on hydrostatics. You remember that I read in the winter, on your recommendation, his *Dynamics* and I was enthusiastic about its clarity and imagination. He is a kind of poet, really the only completely modern lyricist in our country. There were parts of his discussion on the velocity of falling bodies that could be enjoyed as much as Goethe's epigrams in his day. I have the impression that here, in regard to you and your interests, something is brewing. Already yesterday evening, Ivan referred to an 'emerging partnership,' and this morning, when I went down for tea, he rushed past me with an air of mystery and a shiny new briefcase under his arm. As soon as I track down his secret, I'll let you know more precisely.

"I don't have any other news to relate for the time being. Mother and Father are, as always, gentle and good, though I can tell they weren't exactly happy about our encounter. But that's as may be. Today the sun is shining, the birds are singing, although yesterday we still had wintry weather and I came home in a heavy snowstorm, the kind that, in this northern country, blows in the spring. I was worried for a while that the train would get stuck in a snowdrift.

"I won't tire you with scribbling about the trip, but there is a little experience I want to relate. I well know how trivial it is in and by itself, and since I'll admit that beforehand, you can just smile at my prattle. I told you once about a scene I witnessed some years ago in the Berlin train station that had a shattering effect on me—one I have never, really, been able to overcome. I keep thinking about the miserable procession of Russian Jews, industrious and law-abiding people who, solely on account of their origin, were being hounded from place to place after being plundered and beaten, even mutilated. Like a convoy of prisoners they were driven to seek a refuge among half-wild tribes in America under the eyes of the police and derided by the citizens of Europe's civilized countries. You remember that I spoke of them.

"On this trip, and again at the Berlin train station, I was reminded that I belong to that same damned and persecuted race. I was in my compartment, together with another woman, and, when the train was about to leave, an elderly gentleman entered the compartment accompanied by a young officer. When he looked at my unhappy face, he went out again, followed by the lieutenant, who burst into laughter. To the conductor, who was about to close the door, he said clearly and so loudly that it was impossible for me not to hear: '*Pfui! Hier riecht ja entsetzlich nach Knoblauch!*'

"Well, that was the whole episode, and you might reasonably ask why I wanted so much to tell you this. It isn't the incident per se to which I attach such significance but the surprising way it affected me. It didn't really make any appreciable impression on me. I felt, at most, a little melancholy. When the lady, after the exit of the two men, sought a rapprochement with me, obviously with the intention of making amends for the afflicted insult, I refused her tender, as I had earlier, but I did enter into a conversation with her as if nothing had happened. Do you understand what I'm saying? I, who, already in my childhood, was called unforgiving, cannot now stay angry. That's how happiness has changed me. The feeling that now fills me when I think of the great, blind, misled mass of mankind is one of endless pity, an all-embracing forgiveness.

"I've already begun my third sheet of paper and it seems to me that I haven't yet said all that is in my heart. But I'll stop for today. I ought not to keep you longer. You need your time. But it's not easy to let you go. I know how empty I will feel when I have brought my letter to a close. Just a last kiss, and, then, still a very last one. And so farewell!"

A couple of weeks after his conversation with his father, Ivan succeeded in arranging a meeting of some financiers at the office of the attorney Max Bernhardt, whom he had earlier, without any luck, tried to interest in Per's project. The attorney had agreed to gather together his business partners one evening to afford Ivan the opportunity to present his friend's project and to discuss more thoughtfully its possibilities.

Although he was only forty years old and of Jewish origin, Max Bernhardt was already a man of important influence in the capital. He was recognized as the organizing and implementing power of that branch of bold speculators who, in the course of the past ten years, had razed Copenhagen and built it up again, converting it from a provincial town to a great European city. By virtue of his activity, he had created many enemies; but even they had to admit that he was a brilliant businessman with a lightning-fast mind that, for clear thinking and juridical or commercial knowledge, had no equal. On the other hand, his friends generally conceded, without serious contradiction, that he was as empty as a worm-eaten nut in the place reserved for conscience and that he cold-bloodedly abandoned every higher considera-tion for the sake of his personal ends.

Whenever the Danish citizenry became alarmed in those years by one or another large bankruptcy, unsuccessful speculation, or unlucky investor's suicide, and raised a threatening and indignant protest against the new times, it would be directed against Max Bernhardt as the symbol of European corruption, which was, in the prevalent opinion of the last generation, marked by Jewish selfishness. Bernhardt was unperturbed by the opinion others had of him. On the contrary, he took a particularly deep pleasure over the compulsive curiosity with which people—and not least the women—regarded him when he, at predictable hours, went to and from his office. Everyone recognized his little, exotic form that was caricatured so often in the illustrated humor publica-tions. He was invariably elegantly dressed, a little bent over, with his hands, sensitive to the cold, in his coat pockets while he looked at the passersby with a half-dead impassive glance under lowered eyelids. In reality, he was not altogether what he seemed to be. People who had known him as a child remembered him as quiet, reticent, and fainthearted, his nose always in books, and avoiding the games of his peers, fearing rough handling because of being Jewish and physically slight. His father, a small shop-keeper in one of the city's side streets, had been very displeased with him because of his distaste for a life of business the father attributed to his constant reading.

When he was seventeen, he passed his school exams with dis-tinction and began the study of law. It was at that time his inten-tion to enter the civil service. He wanted to become a judge. The persecution he had suffered growing up had created in him a pas-sion for justice. To wear the dark red velvet cloak of a high court justice was from early on the secret ambition of the shopkeeper's little boy.

One day, however, it became obvious to him that, unbaptized, he could not possibly attain to the judiciary. There was, of course, no specific law against it, but in spite of the established law's rul-ing about the equal rights of citizens, a Jew had never risen to a judgeship in Denmark. Since he had been a law student, he could see how, soon, one or another of the blond fatheads among his fellow students would travel the academic highway of honor, power, and regard, while he had to go into the business world he hated. His Jewish self-esteem, his proud aversion to being an object of pity, had already furnished him with a striking self-mastery. When he moved among the people, he wore the cool, ironic mask of a man of the world while his heart secretly beat as nervously and anxiously as that of a young girl entering a ballroom.

No one was surprised when, immediately after receiving his attorney's license, he flung himself into a series of daring specula-tive ventures. His specialty was cultivating business associates and starting up joint stock companies. He had aroused a sense of scan-dal among his colleagues by using means that, until then, had not been legally sanctioned in the business world. Among other things, he had, in line with international models, established close connections with the press. He had bribed auditors and members of the board of directors of his various stock companies and so, gradually, had created a secret alliance of interested confederates through whom he could influence public opinion and mercilessly persecute every opponent.

Now, after merely ten years, he had risen to the ranks of the
city's biggest taxpayers and was recognized by all as a power in
the capital. However much citizens grumbled about the means
he used, the world of business finally bowed before his capabilities and the amazing luck that accompanied them in almost
everything he took on. With the exception of a couple of the
oldest and most aristocratic business firms and a single bank that
steadily refused to enter into relations with him, no one dared
any longer to oppose his influence, growing day by day.

Still, his ambitions were far from being fulfilled. He, whose
early hope was the comparatively modest honor of a high court
justice, now had an entirely different overall goal. The wrongs
endured by a small and rather dispirited child had created a
powerful will, a strength hardened by anger that continually
thirsted after a greater extension of power.

It was clear to him that, because of his birth, he would never
reach the highest social position, the only thing that seemed
worth fighting for. But in the large alliance of his hangers-on, he
knew, in the course of time, how to procure and develop obedient agents of his will; several already occupied entrusted positions. It was his plan to gather substantial power in the country
through this mechanism. It was understandable that Ivan would
be especially eager to win over the man to Per's cause and that
now, sensing that he might succeed, he might anticipate an
almost certain victory. Of the seven gentlemen invited by Max
Bernhardt to discuss the project, one was the stockbroker Herløv,
Max Bernhardt's personal friend and indispensable partner, a
large, fat, ruddy man with a strange, sluggish, and sleepy expression. In their dealings, he was not far behind his companion and,
in fact, really superior in ingenuity and cunning. At the
Exchange, it was said of him that he was Max Bernhardt's imagination. It was he who conceived their joint ventures and
planned them with a calculating care, while the other was the
constant, manly, strong implementer.

Their personal interests were quite different as well, and
explained in large part why they worked so smoothly together.
The stockbroker was altogether devoid of ambition. Unlike Max
Bernhardt, who would spend anything for the possession of
power, he had no goal other than profit, no other aim than to

hoard money, no inkling what to spend it on. Unmarried, he had only one, relatively inexpensive passion—to go, after the day's work, to one of the finer restaurants' private room and with merely a couple of newspapers for company, consume a dinner of six or seven courses, during which, for reasons of health, he drank only water.

He stood now in Max Bernhardt's large, expensively furnished conference room, stooping like an ox, hands clasped behind his back, under his long coattails, with a lifeless look behind his glasses, as if his insides were asleep. He was having a conversation with one of the other guests, a young, showily dressed, blond man of fashion, well known throughout Copenhagen, in Østergade, and the theater world, by the epithet "the Golden Lamb's head." His real name was Sivertsen and he was the only child of an eminent coffee wholesaler at whose death, he, at twenty-seven, inherited a very significant fortune. One of the city's many stagestruck theatergoers, he talked only of the cast, the gossip in the wings, and reviews. He was a friend of Dyhring, whom he—as he put it—"admired both as a gentleman and writer"—and it was through him that he was brought into connection with Max Bernhardt. It was not long before he became one of the latter's bondsmen whose fortune Bernhardt managed to good effect. That helped greatly to keep the young ne'er-do-well from harm, since his theater mania would probably have quickly ruined him, as he would pay through the teeth for the honor of calling one of the children of the stage a friend.

In addition, a Herr Nørrehave was there, whose name, as well, was often seen among Max Bernhardt's solicited business associates. He called himself an "erstwhile farmer" and had, in fact, once owned a farm in Jutland, but that was twenty years ago; he had since led a very stormy existence in Copenhagen, first, for a time, as a pawnbroker and secondhand dealer, and later as a real estate agent, until he launched into speculation in high style and became a venture capitalist. He had originally been called Madsen but adopted a new name when he exchanged his basement shop for an office. He retained, however, the title of "farmer" because it inspired trust, as did his Jutland roll of the *r* that, to Copenhagen ears, suggested reliability and sincerity. Max Bernhardt used to confess privately that he was the craftiest fox in all Denmark.

When the company was seated at the table in front of Per's

spread-out drafts and calculations, Ivan took the floor. The gentlemen, at least during the first half hour, listened attentively and
agreeably to his well-planned presentation. Later, they became
somewhat restless and the "erstwhile farmer" looked, several
times, with rural shamelessness at his watch. When Ivan, at
length, stopped, there was a long pause. They all turned to Max
Bernhardt, who still seemed expectant. At last, the stockbroker
Herløv took the floor and asked Ivan various questions, wherewith, little by little, a more general discussion took place.

These men—like Philip Salomon—considered it absolutely
necessary, first, to obtain a solid judgment of the undertaking
from technical experts whose opinions would be available to the
public. Some names were mentioned in that connection and,
finally, that of the engineer Colonel Bjerregrav was selected as
someone whose word, in this affair, would carry great weight in
the country.

Ivan emphatically repeated what he had already maintained
with his father—that it would be unfair to expect a judgment on
the project from a party who, not without reason, felt abused by
Per's past insults. He knew for certain that Colonel Bjerregrav,
on purely personal grounds, was set against the plan—an enemy
both of it and its author.

To this the stockbroker merely replied that the colonel could
be offered the directorship of the prospective project with compensation for the management of the affair. Then he would easily
overcome a little personal animus. "And," he added dryly, "in
case no more serious difficulties emerged, the matter could be
effortlessly settled."

The company showed no confidence whatsoever in Per's
machines to harness power and the other inventions that Ivan had
called epoch-making. In contrast to Philip Salomon, they spoke
only about the harbor project and, especially, about the possibility of getting little Klitø recognized as a toll-free territory. Max
Bernhardt emphasized that he considered only this part of the
proposal suitable for discussion. On the other hand, he spoke
heatedly against a few of the other gentlemen who suggested
further curtailments in Per's plan to make the endeavor easier to
manage. "A more extensive amputation would be equivalent to
murder," he said. "For my part, I strongly maintain that the full
realization of the free port project should be attempted as a
national enterprise for which it is important to awaken the

general interest, as Herr Salomon rightly mentioned before . . .
or that we give up the whole affair right away as undoable."

Ivan's eyes opened wide. In consideration of Max Bernhardt's
previous, protracted resistance to having anything to do with the
project, he had not expected such a positive decision from that
side. Many of the others were equally surprised at the unusual
warmth with which Max Bernhardt championed a business that
seemed so questionable in their eyes; but the sudden interest of
Max Bernhardt and the stockbroker Herløv in Per's work had a
hidden cause. They had gotten wind of plans for another free port
project, connected to Copenhagen, being worked up at the
present time, by one of the chief banks in the capital—the very
one whose management they most competed with. Their intent
now was to waylay the rival with a West Jutland project completely delineated so that, in twenty-four hours, the campaign
could begin in the press. In addition, they were not really convinced that an active enthusiasm for the project could be built up
in the business world. Their thinking was that their publicity
could be used as dynamite to split the public's interest in a free
port currently evident in the countryside on which their rivals
counted for support of their Copenhagen project. After further
debate, the meeting was adjourned, with the decision that Colonel Bjerregrav should be approached and persuaded to take on
the initial management. As soon as an answer was available, a new
meeting could be called, in consultation with the colonel, to
determine in detail how the project should be handled.

During this time, Per was in Vienna. He had spent a couple of
weeks in the swampland around the mouth of the Danube to
study the larger regulatory works of the river and harbor. He had
gone about in all kinds of weather, on horseback or in an open
boat, or even in a precarious barge, and, at times, had difficulty
finding a roof over his head for the night. Worn out by these
unaccustomed hardships, he sat in an outdoor café the day after
his arrival in Vienna, feeling a strong desire to talk to someone
about anything other than pile drivers and dredging. Since parting from Jakobe, he had been circulating only with engineers—
not engineers of the well-cultured sort, but, rather, technicians
with an extraordinary, if often quite narrow, expertise created by
international demand, with barely any knowledge outside their
specialty and, in general, with no interests other than their

immediate existence and personal welfare. He had gone around with these colleagues as he had with the three cold-blooded English whisky drinkers with whom he had spent the winter in Dresack and with whom he could not, in any way, discuss the great questions of existence that had so occupied him at that time.

He remained a stranger in such society. However much he admired their special abilities and expertise, and although their sense of superiority often tempted him to imitation, a feeling of pity stirred deeply within him for these kinds of men whose thoughts never rose higher than the smoke from their cigars. While he sat with a newspaper in an outdoor café, thinking of Jakobe, whom he doubly missed in this large, strange city, he scanned, according to an old habit, the hotel list, searching for names from Denmark, and was startled to discover the name of Baroness von Bernt-Adlersborg. During the course of the winter, the old lady had gone completely out of his mind. His development had, in the meantime, led him so far from the desire for social glamour and status that he could scarcely remember how much he had, before his travels, been tempted by Uncle Heinrich to use that poor lady's friendship toward the goal of gaining a title.

In his longing to talk again to someone in his native tongue about general human subjects, he decided to look her up. He found her in one of the city's most elegant hotels, where she was staying, together with her sister, the wife of the master of the royal hunt. The two women had come here a few days earlier on their way to Italy.

The baroness did not seem to have received much benefit from her yearlong stay at a German spa. Her face had certainly lost some of its glowing color. True, her expression was more controlled and her hands steadier, but her speech was rather con-fused and betrayed a weakened mental capacity. She still pre-served her odd attachment to Per. In her happiness at seeing him again, she almost embraced him, and time after time during their ensuing conversation, she seized his hands in order to show her gratitude that he had come. About her time spent in recupera-tion, the old lady said nothing. She merely noted that her dear little sister had come to fetch her and they intended to go to Rome—as she explained in a mysterious, low voice—to seek a private audience with the pope. She tried to persuade Per to follow them to the south, and when she heard that it was already his intention to leave the next day for Paris, she entreated him so persistently that, at last, he promised to stay in Vienna for the week that she and her sister planned to be there.

That afternoon, he escorted the two ladies on an outing to the Prater. He described the baroness's sister in his letter to Jakobe telling her about this meeting:

"She is a very tall and large lady. I estimate she must be five feet ten and correspondingly broad. About fifty years old. She was certainly quite beautiful at one time. She still displays, today, a pair of bright eyes. In temperament, she is approximately like the baroness, but, by contrast, she doesn't talk very much. Obviously deeply religious. Already, yesterday evening, we got into a long and heavy discussion about the Christian teaching concerning immortality. I have the feeling she wants to work on me. It will amuse me to again take up arms. She seems to have read, thought, lived through quite a lot and, despite religious feelings, at least she is not, remarkably, a hypocritical devotee. All in all, an interesting acquaintance."

The letter made Jakobe a bit anxious. In a quickly returned answer, she wrote without once naming either the master's wife or her sister:

Something about our meeting that now I'm a little sad about is that we never got to talk more together of that winter, after your father's death, when you were a little disquieted. What occupied your thoughts so much? But the days were all too short, the time ran away from us, and love claimed its rights.

Perhaps you'll say, as well, that there wasn't anything to talk about, that it was your loneliness that made you nervous, and I myself believe that. In addition, isn't it true, my darling, that now we have full confidence in each other in all things and you will never more try to hide from me what you're thinking about? Promise me that, Per!

Here, at home, we are living, at present, through a new outbreak of theological desperation and persecution pathology. As I recently wrote you, Nathan is now back in the country, and that's what has stirred panic in the priestly caste. Every opportunity is seized to thunder against the new times and new men. Yesterday evening I read in the *Berlingske Tidende* a three-column-long account of a funeral sermon given by one or another archdeacon at the service for one or another conference councilor in Frue Kirke. I wanted to send you the paper. Seldom have I read anything so infuriatingly stupid and arrogant. Naturally, the pious man melted into tears of pity for the unfortunates who have lived their lives without the hope of eternity and for whom death is only a terrifying door into a bottomless nothing. And there was the usual self-congratulating delight over faith without which "life would be unbearable." How does he know that? Has he, perhaps, tested it? My old half uncle Philip used to say about himself that he had a kitchen-stove faith, namely, that life was flames, smoke, and crackle, but that "there was nothing above the chimney." Still, he went all the way into old age a very happy and jolly man. When he was lying on his deathbed and the doctor couldn't discover what was wrong, he joked about it and said that it was terribly annoying not to know what you are dying of. And that is far from an isolated example. Both in my own family and among my acquaintances there have been many without the least religious faith, yet they went to their deaths as proudly and fearlessly as any archdeacon. I often think about Christianity's exaggerated anxiety about death, deriving, doubtlessly, from the teaching of Judgment Day, not to speak of the fact that Christianity—unlike other major religions—had its origin and development out of a common and, moreover, cowed people. There is, then, a link between the fear of death and slave anxiety. Never will I forget the impression that some plaster casts of bodies excavated in Pompeii made on me. There were, among others, a master and his slave, both evidently caught by surprise in the rain of ash and choking to death in the course of a few minutes. But what a difference in the facial expressions! On the slave's face, you could read the most confusing puzzlement. He was overturned on his back, his eyebrows were raised up to his hairline, the thick mouth open, and you could virtually hear him screaming like a stuck pig. The other, by contrast, had preserved his mastered dignity unto death. His almost-closed eyes, the fine mouth pressed shut, were marked by the proudest and most beautiful resignation in relation to the inevitable.

My primary complaint against Christianity's hope of

eternal life is that it robs *this* life of its deep seriousness and, with that, its beauty. When we imagine our existence here on earth as only a dress rehearsal for the real performance, what remains of life's festiveness? But even if I were not personally fully and finally convinced that life's great and noble goal is annihilation and that it is the sign of a really spiritually developed person to be reconciled with such a selfless thought and to feel it as a harmonious ending to life that we give back to the natural universe its power that moves through us, while all Christian dreams of immortality and heavenly joy are only a transformation of the popular, uncivilized, coarse representation of an eternal joy of war and the hunt—what was it now I really wanted to say? You must forgive me, but I have to put off until next time my conclusion . . . No! I have it. I wanted to say that even if I didn't see death as an absolute giving up of the self, a full yielding to the universe and indissoluble union with it, I would refuse to know anything about what would become of me when I leave this earth and all I have held dear. Good God, here we are, all afraid to wish to have some foreknowledge of our earthly future and actually glad that the eternal wisdom has hidden from us the content of things to come. If we could, with some certainty, guess the future, what awaited us in life, wouldn't that, however happy its shape, be altogether intolerable? How much more when it is a question of eternal life?

Isn't that true? Oh, that ineradicable theology! It's all part of our "heritage from the fathers"—that watchword of the enemies of culture here at home. Isn't it frightfully depressing and humiliating, to the point of despair, that a war still rages today around the simplest question, a war that wastes both time and strength? Who could any longer doubt that it is just this heritage in all of us, Jews and Christians together, that obliges us to overpower it, if not on some other ground, because it is only the working of chance. We could just as well have inherited something else altogether, something entirely opposite! How much time shall pass, how much harm shall we do to one another before this is really understood and we can make of religion that only permissible dogma, something on which we could build our own life and that of our nations, not on

what is accidental, peculiar, but on the common humanity
in all of us.

At the meeting at Max Bernhardt's office, Ivan was delegated to
make inquiries of Colonel Bjerregrav and to try to conquer his
resistance to the new project and its young originator. Ivan was
not normally lacking in boldness when it came to working for
Per. He had, a couple of times, let himself be kicked down various
stairs for Per's sake. But the old colonel inspired a certain respect
in him. He was familiar with his small form and flushed face and
he had heard about his testiness and ruthless manner. His nephew,
Dyhring, had laughingly told him that he still became furious
whenever he heard Per's name. Discomfited, Ivan confided in
Uncle Heinrich, who was usually his adviser in difficult situations
and who, after some fussing about, promised to help him. "I
know Bjerregrav a little. I have done him some small favors now
and then. I'll give him a nudge so he might be more tractable.
Can you ask for more?"

There was a grain of truth in his preening claim that he really
had a kind of connection with the colonel. Although he never
himself would admit it and left his family in the dark about it,
this counterfeit rich man carried out modest commissions for the
colonel that helped to support him. Among other things, he was
his agent for an English firm that produced iron and steel girders
and in that capacity had regularly reported a couple of times a
year to the colonel with his price current.

A few days following the conversation with Ivan, he looked
up his patron. After having spent half an hour in the foyer, he was
finally shown in and caught the colonel all flushed after eating,
in a gay mood. Feeling free and easy, the old officer smiled at the
ugly little Jew coming in with gray gaiters, holding his top hat
and gloves in one hand.

"Well, good day!" he said, and sat down behind his desk without inviting his guest to be seated. "How are you doing, my good
erstwhile 'wanderer in the wilderness'?" Herr Delft fixed his bluish monocle on an eye, neighed, and assumed a pleased look. He
sensed a favorable mood for business and was much too sly to
destroy his chance by showing himself offended. After some discussion, he succeeded in moving the colonel to assign a commission. He had already collected his things and stood with his hat
and gloves, ready to go, when suddenly he cocked his frizzled

chimpanzee head and said, "Dare I ask the colonel a question in confidence?"

"What is it?"

"Have you heard something about the new national under-taking under consideration?"

"I don't know anything about it."

"Really, nothing?"

"I have enough to do with just my business. I keep myself apart from the commotion, you know." Herr Delft looked away with an insidious smile. Now that the business was under way, the opportunity had come to pay back the colonel for the epithet "wanderer in the wilderness." "Oh," he sighed, and shook his ugly head. "The times have changed. Now it is the young every-one is screaming for. The old professional powers have been shoved aside *'ganz und gar'* ... simply ignored. Youth has the word."

"What is it you want to say to me?" the colonel impatiently interrupted in a commanding tone.

"There's a large free port project that is about to be launched ... by a very young man, a mere stripling named Sidenius."

"Not that ranting ape!" exclaimed the colonel. "I know him, as it happens. At one time, he pestered us with his 'National Works.' People would be foolish to waste their money on that. But I don't think the project of a boy fantasist will tempt anyone."

"The undertaking is secured ... as far as money is concerned. I know it's completely confirmed."

"What are you saying?"

"The thing is lined up. Only the sanction of the legislative powers is wanted. Yes, it's as you say. Danish money has polka fever these days; it has begun to dance and can't stop as long as the music is going. In addition, Herr Sidenius now has good con-nections with the banking world."

The colonel said nothing. He lowered his brows, shaped like a handlebar mustache, and it was as if all the postprandial flush had been drawn from his cheeks and absorbed by his eyes, which began to glow like a bull's.

"So is it really true that the young Laban is engaged to a daughter of Philip Salomon?"

"You must know, Delft. Aren't you Salomon's brother-in-law?"

"Colonel, my mouth is shut! I'm not an agent for love affairs!"

"You're a diplomat, Delft . . . Well, I don't care. If people want to roll their money into the sea, it's all right with me. It would really be a sin to deny them the pleasure. Here's a toast, gentlemen! There's room for barrels of gold in Hjerting Bay!"

"That's a blessedly true observation, dear Colonel!"

"As I said, I'm keeping myself out of the whole swindle. I won't hear of it! Adieu, Herr Delft."

"I respectfully take my leave," said the little Israelite, and drew back with his most deferential bow.

The colonel remained seated, hands under his cheeks, and agitatedly chewed his mustache. The choleric old man was seized by pure rage at Herr Delft's news. He himself once, in his young arrogance, had thrown the gauntlet down before the stagnant national temper and dreamt of becoming a revolutionary leader in his domain; now he belonged to the new day's bitterest adversaries. Like most of the country's other old liberals, he abhorred the young, triumphant pioneers with an envious hatred that, in Per's case, had almost the cast of a mania. The thought that a provincial lout who had insulted him in his own room had achieved what he himself had not been able to saddled him like a nightmare.

But since, for some time, his name had carried a reputation for unbiased and independent thinking, Philip Salomon and Max Bernhardt immediately thought of him when they needed to find a distinguished expert who might be willing to vouch for Per's ideas to the public. Besides, they knew he was a vain and money-loving man.

The following day, Herr Delft had occasion to again visit the colonel. In order to have a reason for returning, he had pretended, on the first visit, that he didn't have the relevant statistics with him to supply the information the colonel had requested about the stress capacity of some steel rails.

The colonel predictably led the conversation again to Per's project and wanted to know which financiers and bankers stood behind it. Herr Delft seemed not to understand him, at first. Then he smiled and shook his head: "Oh, Colonel, you mean that Sidenian amphibian! I don't have much confidence in the whole thing. It's a still birth."

"I beg your pardon! You stood here yesterday and told me the undertaking was secured. You knew it was already decided, you said."

"I beg you, sir, to remember that I said it was secured as to *money* matters. I emphatically added that the state's necessary sanction of the plan was missing. And that has never been received."

"Why not? When money can really be provided, why should the government oppose the enterprise?"

Herr Delft shrugged and squirmed, as if in embarrassment. "I would hope Your Excellency understands me—even without words."

"What, then? You are a devil of a secrets merchant. What do you mean?"

Herr Delft remained silent and shook his head self-consciously from one side to the other. At that moment, he really looked like a trained ape.

"Good God, man," shouted the colonel, "tell me, now!"

"Well, I mean, sir ... the government doesn't dare ... that's the problem."

"Dare? On account of what? I don't understand a word you're saying!"

"I won't keep you longer, sir. I'll take my leave ..."

"Nonsense! You must tell me, openly, Delft! What do you mean? Why does the state withhold its consent in a case where money can be procured—when the plan is, otherwise, sound and good?"

"Just so, sir, the plan is sound and good."

"Oh! Now I'm losing my mind! What is the meaning of all this?"

"Well, to speak plainly, do you really think, dear Colonel, that our neighbor to the south will look on peacefully while such a dangerous competition to Hamburg is being hatched? I don't think so. Never in the world!"

The colonel shoved himself back in his chair and put his hands on his hips. His dark red face looked skinned.

"I have never in all my days heard anything so foolish. Good God, man, where did you get such a crazy notion? Do you really mean to say that the Germans would declare war on us for that reason?"

"Oh, well, war! That certainly isn't necessary! Just a little, firmly formulated note from Berlin to Copenhagen ... You will grant me, dear sir, that such a thing has been sufficient before in similar situations."

The colonel remained silent and lowered his eyes. Herr Delft shrugged. "Such is the lot of small nations! They must bow . . . and be silent in the face of injustice. It's pitiful, very pitiful, but those are the facts of life. The small must accommodate the large . . . accommodate and be prudent . . . extremely prudent." He was about to repeat this when he saw the effect of his words on the old defender of the Fatherland whose body still carried the scars of German bullets. The colonel remained silent, and Herr Delft seized the moment to take his leave. It was just in time. He had barely left when the colonel jumped out of his chair like a bullock stung by a horsefly. As always, when there wasn't anyone there and he could let his feelings spill out, he went from his office to the living room to give vent to his emotions in front of his wife. He had to call her in, this time, from the kitchen. Without paying attention to her being on the verge of tears because her soup pot was about to boil over, he went on raving for half an hour against the cowardly and petty spirit that had descended on the Danish people since the war.

That day, Uncle Heinrich, as so often, ate his midday meal at his brother-in-law's, and when the family got up from the table, he took Ivan aside and said with an air of surly shyness he assumed when, uncharacteristically, he did a difficult, unselfish service, "Now you can go to the colonel, my friend! He's been set up."

In order not to raise suspicion, Ivan waited a few days before he went to work. Then he wrote the colonel a letter in which he asked for the honor of a meeting and briefly explained the purpose.

There was something in the letter's tone that disarmed the colonel. Ivan had, to a large degree, that Jewish talent for ingratiating himself, tickling vanity, and the colonel had thin skin for flattery. In addition, there was, in the name "Salomon," the clink of gold that sounded seductively in the ears of the money-minded man.

But, above all, it was against his nature to sit idly by and look on while others busied themselves. In spite of his seventy years, he still had too much restlessness in his blood to voluntarily become a pensioner. He had never been a reliable ally of the reactionary party in the country. Despite all the favors from their chief ranks, the old revolutionary spirit had never been extinguished in him. Hidden under his bitterness against the new, beneath his envy and an assumed indignation, a secret sympathy moved within him. While his outer conduct continued to be one of a disquieted, straight-talking hothead, all the young, strong, and daring life forces still had power over his mind. In reality, he concealed a good deal of attraction toward Per.

Still, when, some days later, Ivan sought him out, the colonel received him rather ungraciously, but when Ivan clearly declared that the whole affair would rise or fall according to his support, he softened. He insisted on various conditions, among others, that Per be immediately called home to make the needed changes in his draft before it could be used as the basis of a detailed plan. Furthermore, in order that there could be the possibility of a fruitful cooperation between them, he demanded that Per personally solicit him to take the project into his own hands and make the first move toward an understanding.

Ivan urged him to withdraw that demand, but the colonel was unbending on that point. He had not forgotten those words of Per on the day he left his office: "Next time we meet, it will be *you* who seeks *me* out." That arrogant prophecy must not be allowed to come true literally.

Ivan still sought to persuade him, but the colonel, who during the whole meeting had been considerably nervous, interrupted him finally, and in a flash of anger said, "No more discussion, now, about the affair! I consider all the business between us finished." Ivan got up and left dejected.

CHAPTER 15

PER WENT TO Rome in the middle of April. He had finally yielded to the baroness's pleas to follow her and her sister, or, rather, to the allure and excitement of being in the company of the latter. He wasn't himself clear about the kind of pleasure he felt in the society of this large, middle-aged, gray-haired woman. Since any kind of erotic attraction was out of the question, he felt free to write to Jakobe about the impression this woman's personality and character made on him, without noticing that Jakobe, for her part, never mentioned this friendship. It was the motherliness of the master of the royal hunt's wife that drew Per to her. And, as well, it was her solicitous concern for his spiritual welfare, gratifying feelings he himself wasn't conscious of. Add to this the strange discrepancy between her genuinely deep piety and her fashionable dress—the whole of her style of exquisitely fine elegance—between the solemn Bible language she was fond of using with him and a certain almost stealthy and earthy glint of a smile he noticed playing around her mouth or in the depths of her still bright, dark blue eyes. In her mix of worldliness and piety she was a provocative puzzle.

Among their countrymen in Rome, there was quite a bit of talk about the two noblewomen and their young travel escort. Per's relation to the baroness especially roused their curiosity. The feelings of that old lady for him had risen, during their journey, to a hushed, romantic devotion. Every time someone told her something, she would cry out with tear-filled eyes, "Oh, you must tell that to Herr Sidenius" or "How it would amuse our dear friend to hear that." Right after their arrival in Rome, she commissioned a bust of Per. He was well aware that the old lady was putty in his hands. He had to tell her, in detail, his future plans, and she had immediately offered him her support. When she heard about the consortium that was forming around the project, she became so enthusiastic that she even spoke of selling one of her properties in order to secure the undertaking. Per could not think of taking any personal advantage of his power over this poor, sick creature, least of all when he realized that she thought he was the illegitimate son of her brother—a delusion he was not innocent of fostering.

In addition, every day he was engrossed in the new and strange life he saw around him. As a sun-loving northerner, he enjoyed the clear sky and the warm, soft air. Never had he felt himself so healthy and strong in body and soul as now! His face, with his little dark goatee, had, in a few days, taken on an almost bronze color against which his eyes looked doubly blue. It happened more than once, when, in the afternoon, he walked with the baroness and her sister at the Monte Pincio, dressed in a new, light gray summer suit, that a black-eyed beauty sent him a burning glance over the edge of a fan. He did not stay in the same hotel as the two sisters, but he escorted them every day on walking tours or accompanied them to the Scandinavian Society, where, each afternoon, they read the newspapers. He basked in the glow conferred upon him through his intimacy with these noble ladies. He enjoyed the eminent titles people like the hotel attendants bestowed upon him; but, in the long run, his spurious baronial dignity did not deceive his own countrymen.

Although his intimacy with the master of the royal hunt's wife had put the finishing touches on his manners, a provincial Jeppe lurked, undeniably, under the worldly fashionable demeanor. If, at the beginning, his countrymen had some doubt about what to make of him, gradually, by Per's own indiscretion, many of them came to know enough about his goals and plans to tax their patience. It was really the life of the street, especially of ancient Rome, that attracted him in that eternal city of cities, the mausoleum of the world's soul. But it was far less the architectural beauty that occupied him than the massive walls, the solid connective plastering, the whole of the gigantic power that emanated from the huge two-thousand-year-old ruins. He could entertain himself for hours in the Colosseum's desolate interior with thoughts of rebuilding it from the ground up. He would surround a monstrously big workplace with a wickerwork of scaffolding and, within, cyclopean stone blocks, ox-drawn carts, and hundreds of sweating slaves would raise it section by section from the base, like the foundation of a Tower of Babel.

Such fantasies led him back again to books. These ancient giant walls awakened in him a desire to know something more about the people of Rome and their fate, which he remembered only dimly from school. He borrowed Mommsen's *Römische Geschichte* from the Scandinavian Society, and, with the concentrated energy he could display by fits and starts, he worked through the thick volume in a short time. For the first time in his life, he was drawn into a historical frame of mind. His vision had, until now, always been expectantly projected toward the coming great future. The past had never interested him. Now he could positively relish sitting up among the ruins on the Palatine Hill and, with his back leaning against a sun-warmed stump of a column, reading about the men who, from that very place, had ruled the world. In addition, for the first time, he was being led into a culture earlier than his hateful Christianity and entirely unaffected by that spiritual power that was the curse of the present age.

He found in the Republic's heroic figures the model character he had previously missed. In all these men of a practical turn of mind, boldly active, clever, and unsentimental pagans, he saw mankind in its original state of health, a race of Titans he had

vaguely dreamt about and with whom he felt allied. In one of his
letters to Jakobe he wrote enthusiastically:

> Never have I felt so strongly as now what a crime against
> humanity Christianity has been. Never have I understood
> with such shame how far we still have to rise merely to
> reach the shoulders of this race whose great manhood was
> impudently rendered suspicious by that pale eunuch from
> Nazareth. Do you know the story of the Hunchback King?
> When fate determined that the king should be born with
> crooked legs and a bent back, an ordinance was issued that
> turned all notions in the country topsy-turvy. What had
> been small was now called big, and what was crooked,
> straight. An erect back was called humped, a giant a dwarf.
> That's the crazy country we live in today.

After a ten-day stay, the master's wife received a telegram from
her husband; he had fallen sick and wanted her home. The two
sisters left, although the baroness whined a bit over leaving Rome
without having had that audience with the pope she had raved
on about during the whole stay. The farewell to Per was very
heartfelt on the part of both ladies. The baroness's sister made
him promise that he would visit her and her husband at
Kærsholm, where the baroness would be for a while as well. From
the compartment window, the baroness, with tears in her eyes
and waving her handkerchief, cried out, "Till we meet again!"

Per still had to stay some time in Rome because of the bust
that his motherly patroness had commissioned and in which he
was uninterested. But, on the whole, he was not impatient to
leave. He felt unusually well here, and continual reports of the
steady cold and wet spring north of the Alps hardly tempted him.
Feeling anxious, however, from loneliness, he was always looking
for company. He had received, as well, word from Ivan that he
should prepare to cut off his travels because his presence at home
might be necessary for the advancement of his project. In his
last letter, Ivan had asked outright if he could be ready to leave
with a day's notice. Per did not answer him. He had begun to
weary of these almost daily communications arriving from his
brother-in-law, with their endless inquiries, suggestions, and
admonitions. From the moment in which the possibility of
a breakthrough had materialized, there had been, almost

unnoticed by him, a change in his relation to what he had called his life's work. It had not seemed less valuable in his eyes, but his interest in the project diminished when it was transformed from a revolutionary idea to some kind of object fingered by financiers and speculators and devolving into matter-of-fact debate. The business gibberish alone, in which Ivan wrote, that half-incomprehensible shopkeepers' babble, made him disgusted with the whole negotiation. In addition, almost every one of Ivan's letters contained new reservations or a proposal for new reductions or for radical adjustments and adaptations; from sheer aggravation, he let them lie unanswered for days on end.

The contrast between the dispiriting place in the present and his impression of those great ancient days in which his thoughts were living increased his indifference and sense of dejection. In his last letter, Ivan had even had the nerve to suggest a rapprochement with Colonel Bjerregrav—with the man who had, at one time, cold-bloodedly tried to push him down into darkness.

All these annoyances from home heightened the attraction of the carefree, easygoing life in Rome. He had come to know several of his Scandinavian countrymen and -women, in whose society he was quickly compensated for the loss of the master's wife. He regularly spent evenings together with them at one or another inn in the city's outskirts, where, according to an old custom, the Scandinavians met in order to give themselves over unrestrainedly to the bohemian life of enjoyment. Here was the cheer of the full glass, songs and arguments, warm days in shirtsleeves, and Per felt remarkably happy in this easy atmosphere. He was always in sparkling good humor. The spring air Jakobe had breathed into his disposition with her generosity now was coming into full bloom. Seeds of light and joyous feelings were sprouting in him, and he gradually found himself engaged in everything. When the company would be wending homeward singing into the night, Per was to be seen at the head of the troupe, crowned and adorned with flowers, with a couple of charmed ladies—young or older—on his arms. One evening, he met, in this society, a full-bearded German artist Fritjof had introduced him to in Berlin in the autumn. At the present moment, he was very fashionable in Rome, a small, dwarfish man with a heavy Victor Emmanuel beard and two-inch-high heels on his shoes. With the customary festive toast they renewed the old acquaintanceship, and Per was invited to visit the famous man's studio on the following day. There he encountered a surprise. On an easel in the middle of the room stood a just-completed life-size portrait of a young woman, a strawberry-blond Jewess, whose fine features and shy deer eyes he recognized immediately. It was Jakobe's half cousin from Berlin, the privy councilor's young daughter—sole heiress to fifty million.

"Is she here in the city?" asked an astonished Per.

"She was. She went home yesterday. You know her too?"

Per told him he had been in her parents' house a couple of times. "How are things with her? Is she married?" he asked, unable to take his eyes off the lovely face that looked at him with the same stolen, searching side glance as that evening at the concert.

"She is married, yes. She was here with her husband—the lucky beggar!"

"What's his name?"

"Bieber—Dr. Bieber."

"Yes, right. I remember I saw him there in the house. He was hardly distinguished by good looks. He seemed a kind of walking belly."

"Oh! Good looks," exclaimed the dwarf, and twisted the tip of his bushy warrior beard with a hand sporting a sparkling amethyst.

"Is he himself very rich?" asked Per.

"Rich? No, he was a poor devil. Didn't you know that? A priceless story! The concerned parents filled their house with indebted barons and officers so the daughter could make a good match. All the middle-class young men were kept at bay. Only they didn't think of the stout Dr. Bieber. He was secretary to their doctor—and so he won the prize, naturally."

"Yes, to be sure," murmured Per, suddenly preoccupied. His eyes, as if bewitched, were fixed steadily on the young woman's features.

"I dare say you saw it was a gilded hell for the young lady when you were a guest in the parents' mansion in Tiergarten. The mother shamelessly kept a whole staff of paid paramours, and the father is simply a scoundrel. What is clear is that the daughter wanted to get out of that life at any price. I think she would have taken just about any tolerably presentable and inoffensive man who had the courage to take her off."

Per turned away from the painting and looked piercingly at the talkative painter. "Did he take her away?"

"Well, not literally, really. But he certainly had an eye for his chance. In spite of his ugliness and poverty, his very bourgeois origin (his father was a kind of secondhand dealer in fine goods), he had the requisite courage—or self-confidence—we could really call it conceit—to grasp his happiness. Perhaps he thought himself an Adonis. He conquered by means of his foolishness. Have you, young man, realized the ironic wisdom that hides behind this? Do you understand that, in reality, it matters less what you are in life than what you imagine yourself to be? Do you think, perhaps, that Lieutenant Napoleon would ever have become France's emperor if he had not had the crazy notion that royal French blood flowed in his veins?"

With these words the world-famous dwarf artist rose on his high-heeled shoes and again twisted his military mustache, but Per diffidently lowered his eyes and sat for a long time silent and distracted.

Meanwhile, back home in Copenhagen, Nanny and Dyhring had gotten married, and Dyhring had left *Falken* to take over as chief editor of an older, respected paper, *Borgerbladet*, which had extensive circulation in the business world. His father-in-law played no part in that promotion, owed entirely to the influence of the attorney Max Bernhardt. Dyhring belonged to that man's long train of followers. Because of his pleasant appearance, his adroitness, and his early developed contempt for all human laws and conventions, Max Bernhardt set great store by him. Owing to the great man's patronage, Dyhring, at twenty, had risen to a prominent place on *Falken*'s staff and had, in that post, by total deference to his patron's wishes, won his confidence, even his friendship. However, Max Bernhardt had clearly been very unhappy when Dyhring announced his engagement to Nanny. The deep wrinkles at the base of his nose were accentuated as he said, "A Jewess, Dyhring! That really surprises me. I thought you'd make a better assessment. For some time now, I have been drawing your attention to Councilor Lindholm's daughter. She is both pretty and rich. And you would certainly be the man to make the right impression on her."

For the first time, Dyhring refused to obey his lord and master. He was really in love with Nanny, and as his inability to resist that kind of woman was his only weakness, Max Bernhardt realized he had to resign himself to the match. He himself was not impervious to pretty women, and the only failings he could forgive were those committed for the sake of a lady. He merely made Dyhring promise that he would keep the engagement secret until he could procure him a more esteemed and independent post in the press. By this move, Max Bernhardt wanted to anticipate Philip Salomon. He was afraid of losing something of his power over Dyhring if the latter had to thank his father-in-law for his editorship.

A week later, the road to the most coveted editorial position at *Borgerbladet* was opened for Dyhring, and Nanny and he proceeded to get married. They did it with the smallest amount of fuss possible. One fine day, Nanny returned home from the city with the newly appointed editor on her arm, curtsied to her parents, and introduced herself as Fru Dyhring. In the morning they had been officially joined at the mayor's dusty office and had—she glibly related—the most appalling trouble staying serious during the ceremony. Afterward, they had gone to a restaurant and eaten lunch with a couple of Dyhring's acquaintances they happened to meet there.

At the table, which was now as festively set as possible in such haste, Philip Salomon toasted his darling girl and her bridegroom with an involuntary solemnity that contrasted with the cheerful equilibrium of the newlyweds. The mother was equally affected. Although the parents, aging in the last years, had, under the influence of their children, tried their best to keep step with the new times, on an occasion like this their innate feelings broke through their sense of etiquette. Neither of them was really confident about the future. The willful behavior of the girls, especially, aroused a hidden anxiety.

Gradually, however, they were carried away by the general cheerfulness and the joy that, with the younger children at the table, became altogether boisterous. Jakobe alone remained silent and seemed distant. She was also the only one who hadn't dressed up. She was so disturbed over Nanny's giddiness and over the profanation of love that the wedding and the marriage dinner represented in her eyes that only her mother's insistence induced her to take her place at the table. She had, at first, excused herself on the pretext of feeling indisposed—and, really, she did not feel well. Many times during the meal she was overcome by dizziness and her whole body quivered with nervousness.

Shortly after everyone had left the table, she went up to her room and was no more to be seen. She decided to write to Per— she knew no other way to soothe her longing for him and to deaden the wild, consuming jealousy almost devastating her body and soul.

It wasn't so much that she, in any way, mistrusted Per. She was so far from any thoughts of unfaithfulness that she was not even disturbed by the brevity of his letters and the difficulty he, once again, had in finding an intimate tone. Since their tender meeting, she felt him to be an integral part of herself. With her proud and chaste nature, she couldn't think of the possibility of betrayal. And she had not forgotten the expression of happiness and gratitude that glowed in Per's eyes the first time he rested in her arms. She hid away that memory as a sacred possession.

At those moments, she was certain about what she had, sometimes, almost doubted, that she was a woman who could give Per the bliss of love; but when she thought of all the people through whom Per moved daily, who enjoyed the happiness of living near him, taking his hand, hearing his voice, seeing him smile, there rose in her something akin to hatred for these strangers who had all that she longed for. She was envious of the pavement he walked on, of the air that brushed his tanned cheeks. She was jealous of the café waiters who served him, of the girls in the hotel who, in the morning, made his bed that still retained the warmth and scent of his body.

Below, in the living room, her mother had, meanwhile, tried to excuse her to Dyhring and Nanny when the latter made a sarcastic remark about the cause of her disappearance.

"Jakobe is overwrought these days," said her mother. "I'm really anxious about her."

Nanny smiled without responding. But later in the carriage with Dyhring, driving home to his bachelor flat, where they were spending the night, she said, nestling against him, "Do you know what's the matter with Jakobe? You surely noticed her at the table. She is envious, the poor girl! She is angry because it isn't she who can now go home with her husband."

The following morning the newlyweds traveled abroad, where they planned to spend some weeks. It was their intention to move mainly through central Europe and down to Spain because Nanny insisted on seeing a bullfight. The trip was essentially a continual stopover between trains and hotels. But just this kind of variable life among all kinds of people was what they both wanted. Even in this honeymoon stage, they had no desire to be alone. There was no question, on either side, of real passion. Dyhring's love expressed itself, after a while, mostly as a kind of impudent affection, and, despite the comparative meaninglessness of this inclination, Nanny showed herself willing to accept his provocative kisses. In fact, it was really the exigent satisfying of their mutual vanity that bound them together. Dyhring enjoyed the sensation Nanny's Oriental beauty stirred, everywhere, especially because he was convinced people didn't think they were really married. He well knew that, both in her fashion and manner, she resembled a fine demimondaine. That was precisely what her attraction had always been for him. Now, it massaged his ambition to notice how men, even in wicked Paris, cast envious looks at him.

Nanny, for her part, was proud of her husband because of his elegant and modish appearance. His dapper figure, with his golden hair, attracted notice in the hotels. She herself would say of him that he looked like a German prince. Moreover, she was glad he wasn't Jewish. Although she had always insisted it wasn't so, she did feel from time to time oppressed by her origin. She confessed honestly that now she was thrilled to be finally finished with the Salomon name and to be called Fru Dyhring.

Then, too, she prized her husband's capacity as editor to procure on occasion free entry to the great exhibits that others would have to pay for or be unable to get into. Despite her fine clothes, her head for values that she displayed even as a young girl had not forsaken her in marriage. Dyhring's liberality already had caused her some latent unrest. She was habitually seized with anxiety every time a payment was expected. After stays in hotels, when she must have rung for a maid ten times to help her dress, she could calmly depart without giving a tip, or she left behind on the washstand no more than half a franc.

The spring chill and rain quickly drove the young couple south. From Paris they were going directly to Madrid, when they heard, on the way, that cholera had broken out in that city. They immediately traveled back over the Pyrenees and crossed the Riviera to Italy. Per was still in Rome at the time. Jakobe had prepared him, in a letter, for her sister's arrival, which, really, had been superfluous. The Danish newspapers, which he invariably read at the Scandinavian Society, contained daily notices about the young pair and their travels. Dyhring, the often mentioned but, hitherto, not especially respected theater and music hall critic, had suddenly become a famous man back home. Until now, it was unheard of that such a young man, without an irreproachable reputation, should be entrusted with the management of a concern like *Borgerbladet*, and, in reality, it wasn't easy for Max Bernhardt to get his way in making this appointment. Meanwhile, his pet rolled through Europe in a velvet-lined compartment coddling his beautiful bride while, in the name of morality, a battle was mounting against him in all the papers Max Bernhardt had been unable to corral.

Dyhring's appointment was the signal for a fresh outbreak of the standing quarrel between the representative men of the new and old days. His name marked the battle line where the active men of power and the powerless, the arrogant and the envious (disguised as virtuous), collided. The small papers printed long articles about him with his portrait; the large papers came out with color caricatures, while thousand-legged gossip ran through the land and provoked fantastic rumors of his decadent habits, his satin-upholstered rooms, his orgies with women, and the legendary lavishness of his daily existence.

Consequently, it was not surprising that the anticipated arrival of Dyhring and his young wife in Rome had stirred some excitement among their countrymen. The way women, despite their moral indignation, interested themselves in the couple especially annoyed Per. He had never been given to envying others their success. He had felt himself too clearly chosen—an exception favored over any rival. But the last half year's life of traveling had in so many ways developed his self-knowledge. The comparisons that his acquaintance with so many strangers among the world's cultured citizens had given rise to—and now, recently, the visit to the dwarf painter and his news of the amazing triumph of the poor and ugly Dr. Bieber—all that had deepened his understanding that his character had weaknesses that must be overcome. The mood that arose in him that day in the painter's studio, now renewed by Dyhring's growing reputation, had already dominated his unconscious life for some time. A hidden feeling of powerlessness had burdened his soul on his journey—a sluggish sediment of melancholy.

When, one day, at the Scandinavian Society, he by chance
found out that the newlyweds were expected in Rome by the
afternoon train, he decided, after some hesitation, to meet them
at the station. He told himself that, when he and Dyhring became
brothers-in-law, it would be best if they could be friends. He was
particularly concerned that in being distant, he might betray
those envious feelings that humiliated and preyed on him. He
met them at the station with a little, inexpensive bouquet for
Nanny and welcomed the couple to Rome. The slick editor was,
as always, very obliging. He muttered some grateful words and
took Per's hand, offered as a gesture of magnanimity, with a smile
that, luckily, only Nanny noticed.

She showed an unreserved pleasure at seeing him again, calling
Per her brother-in-law and bringing greetings from Jakobe and
everyone at home. Later they met for dinner at one of the town's
French restaurants. After the meal, Dyhring quickly became
unsociable and yawned uninhibitedly behind a carefully
groomed hand. By contrast, Nanny's mouth never stopped talking. Her chatter, fortunately, so engaged Per that he failed to
notice her husband's careless behavior. They had their coffee at
an outdoor café at the Piazza Colonna, and here, as everywhere,
Nanny's beauty, her free carriage and dress, attracted attention.
She wore all white from her lace hat down to her shoes adorned
with bows, and the airy clothes rustled around her ripe body like
swan feathers.

Per couldn't get over his surprise at how glowing she looked.
He had almost forgotten how pretty she was. While he sat across
from her at the little round coffee table, he stole frequent glances,
in the course of the conversation, at her exposed neck and her
overflowing bosom, and he began to recover the memory of how
near he had come once to proposing to her, and it wasn't altogether improbable that she would have said yes.

When the threesome separated for the evening, it was
arranged that Per should fetch Nanny at the hotel the next morning, and entertain her while Dyhring paid a visit to the Danish
consulate to garner material for a travel letter he intended to send
to his new paper about commercial concerns in Italy. It was
Nanny herself who suggested that arrangement, and, with his
usual courtesy, Dyhring gave his approval.

The only condition the couple had made, which was determined when they married, was that each must preserve full and

unabridged freedom. They were, as well, agreed that the slightest attempt from one side to constrain the other would be considered sufficient grounds for divorce.

When, the next day, Per came to the hotel at the prescribed time, Dyhring had already gone. Nanny, very smart in yesterday's white dress, met him and was ready to set out. She rose from her breakfast (consisting merely of chocolate and cakes) and immediately exclaimed without so much as a "hello" or any other greeting: "Where shall we go? Today I want to be entertained." Per told her that at a nearby marketplace he had just passed on the way over, there was a monthly fair in progress with all kinds of old stuff gathered from the hidden corners of Rome; when Nanny heard that, she absolutely had to go there first. The conception of such a large rubbish heap excited her. Later, she said, they could take a carriage and drive around the city to consider all the sights worth seeing.

She made a final circling survey of the rooms, and stuck a macaroon in Per's mouth while passing. Then they commenced their tour. When they neared the marketplace, whose noisy buzzing could already be heard from a distance, she took his arm. Suddenly she did not feel so bold at the sight of the packed mass of people and the narrow, tented streets. She stole an anxious glance at the ragged figures who descended from everywhere, filling the marketplace or standing in clusters around the large heaps of green copper wares, iron junk, and old clothes heaped onto the pavement at the entry. Unnerved by her sense of the filth of the Roman rabble, she gathered her skirt tightly around her, and, gradually as she entered the swarm, lifted it higher and higher over her white shoes.

Per found her still more alluring than on the previous day. He was altogether giddy at walking with her arm in his and feeling the form of her soft body as she pressed closely against him for protection when she was frightened by one or another half-naked or especially ragged individual pushing forward to offer wares for sale. He had been a little unsure how to act toward her, feeling some embarrassment in the face of her unreserved familiarity as a sister-in-law, but now he resolutely shoved all thoughts of Jakobe aside and yielded to the moment's mood.

It was impossible to preserve one's bearing in such a crowd. He tried to protect her against all the pushing and shoving—first with his arm, then with his whole body. He suggested, at last, that they should withdraw from the crowd, but she wouldn't hear of it. In the midst of her intense anxiety over the lively ragged forms that steadily pressed nearer her, in the midst of the noise, the scent of garlic and the harsh smell of sweat, she was thrilled and laughed constantly and convulsively as if she were being tickled.

"I'm really enjoying myself," she cried out from a tightly compacted throng. "This is something Otto would never in the world agree to." Suddenly a tumult broke out in front of a tented booth at some distance from them. Two young men started quarreling and instantly had attracted a circle of interested spectators, who opened up a kind of boxing ring for them. Per wanted to take Nanny away, but, without saying anything, she held him back, pulled him some steps nearer to the battleground, and stood on tiptoes to be able to see.

In an excited Italian manner, the two fighters faced each other in a crouching posture. With wild movements, one, then the other, raised a clenched fist while their black eyes flashed and their red mouths discharged oaths and curses that sounded like wild cries in the midst of the market din.

Per was a little surprised at Nanny's absorption. She was, by turns, red and pale, and her lips trembled. As she pressed close to him every time those clenched fists were raised in the circle, it was obvious she had gradually forgotten that it wasn't Dyhring whose arm she was holding.

"Will they, perhaps, stab each other with a dagger?" asked Nanny. Per laughed. He had more than once, here in Rome, been a witness to such street scenes, which seemed as if passionate men were on the point of fighting a life-or-death battle while, with a kind of artistic pleasure, they would get drunk on heroic gestures and then separate without having exchanged anything other than a mouthful of dirty invective.

The same thing happened here. Just when the tension seemed at its highest pitch, suddenly it evaporated, and the two men went to their corners like a couple of actors after the applause of the spectators.

"What? Is it over?" asked Nanny, and turned toward Per with an expression of disappointment.

"Yes, that's it—I really prize our good Danish hooligans!" he said, and resolutely drew Nanny away to get out before the packed crowd of spectators dissipated. After much difficulty, they reached the outskirts of the marketplace, where they could move rather freely.

Then Nanny stopped and cried out, "But we didn't buy anything!" and she mercilessly dragged him back into the crowd. Hooked on his arm, she pushed forward to a dilapidated wooden booth where there was a sale of supposed antiques. An old man, who looked like a bandit with white chin stubble growing all the way down his naked bird neck, greeted her with Oriental humility. And without haggling she bought, for an extravagant sum, a little silver tumbler and a gilded buckle and then, as a matter of course, left the payment to Per.

At last she declared herself ready to follow him on a tour of the city. Per hired a carriage, and they drove away.

First they went to Piazza del Popolo, which Nanny insisted on seeing because she had once read a novel by that name. After that, they drove to Monte Pincio, through Gregoriana Street to the Quirinal, and, again, up and down hills, past the Diocletian Baths, the Capitoline, the Forum.

The coachman had instructions to go quickly. They didn't stop anywhere. Nanny was satisfied to see what could be viewed from a carriage through a pair of binoculars. She did not forget to make the compulsory exclamations, but was, in reality, exclusively concerned with herself, or, rather, with what kind of impression she was making on her escort. Her feelings for Per still carried a good deal of resentment from the old days. She had never forgiven his rejection of her, and she had been on the watch for a chance for revenge. When she thought that opportunity had finally arrived, she let loose all her artful charms, starting with the previous day's meeting at the station.

Consideration for Jakobe didn't bother her. With her spoiled nature, she could not forgive her half sister for, unlike all the others, not being taken in by her but rather often openly admitting that Nanny's false and coquettish ways offended her. Nanny was never scrupulous about her means when it came to satisfying a desire or merely a whim. Although her father, in good faith, because she was from the beginning a picture of health, called her his "normal child," she always had given herself an unnatural pleasure in provoking unhappiness. Already in her schooldays it had amused her to make trouble for her comrades by cunning means, and she was only half grown, just rounding into mature form, when, as a sport, she would generate bad blood between engaged couples by arousing female jealousy. Her malicious enjoyment seemed even more pernicious because, with her weak empathic imagination, she seldom suspected the extent of the harm she wrought. She was like a child, who in half-innocent exuberance might set fire to a neighbor's house to watch flames spread to the roof, and afterward be shocked by the resultant destruction.

Meanwhile, it went the way it always did for her when she was with Per; she was still not boldly confident with him. The recollection that he, of all men, had been the closest to becoming her master made her behavior a little tentative. She was especially on her guard after he had, on his part, become daring—really seeming to be making advances to her. She thought it surely could not be by chance that he had squeezed her hand so firmly when he helped her into the carriage. While it jostled them, he was, a couple of times, thrown so near to her that she had to move a little to keep their bodies from touching. As much as she felt great satisfaction in his courtship (especially when she thought of Jakobe), it troubled her to realize how their roles, in relation to each other, were about to be reversed, so that she, who began as the pursuer, now was almost becoming the pursued. In spite of this, she talked incessantly, agitated her swan-down-trimmed fan, and laughed wantonly.

The Pantheon, Trajan's Column, the Arch of Titus—all glided by without her really seeing anything. The sight of the amphitheater made her, for the first time, attentive again. Here she overcame her desire for comfort and got out of the carriage to go into the arena.

"We should now be in Madrid, watching the bullfights," she said in her Østergade dialect while, on Per's arm, she disappeared into the half-dark, cold walk that led inside to the enormous hollow stone basin, "but that stupid cholera got in the way. That was terribly annoying!"

While Per was involuntarily seized by the historical atmosphere of the place, she was ready to chat. Even when they stood at the bottom of the huge sacrificial bowl that had witnessed so many bloody hecatombs, she was not silent. With her binoculars in front of her eyes, she looked up and down at the rows of seats rising up to the sky, while she was thinking she should have worn the flowered muslin dress with the red silk jacket. That outfit had driven Lieutenant Hansen Iversen altogether crazy when he saw her in it at the theater one evening, shortly before she left on her travels.

Per attempted to explain to her the arrangement of the construction, showed her the elevated seats of the emperor and the vestal virgins, described how the arena had deliberately been built lower than the water pipes so that when flooded, naval battles and fights against huge river monsters could be performed, and Nanny gradually became really attentive. Her interest especially grew in the grated gates through which the gladiators came, rattling their weapons to either kill or be killed for the pleasure of the crowd.

She remembered a picture that represented just such a Roman swordsman in a filled amphitheater—a warrior figure with bulging muscles, altogether naked except for a scanty loincloth, and a metal helmet on his head. The picture had hung in a bookstore window in Østergade during one of her last years at school, and she had always taken care to go past it on the way. She thought, now, that here, on the very spot on which *she* stood, there had stood such a large, naked, powerful, muscled man with his heel on the conquered opponent's bloody throat and smilingly receiving the theater's applause—both the emperor's and the crowd's. Her nostrils flared involuntarily, and she felt the same sensual, cool breath on her neck and back as did the white vestal virgins of that day when they began to smell blood in the air.

When, in a little while, she again took Per's arm to return to the carriage, her eyes stole furtively over his form and she was silent for some time. Per suggested that they should forgo sightseeing and drive a bit on the heights to get some fresh air. After some hesitation, Nanny got in, and the coachman was ordered to drive over the Tiber. By this famous, snaking drive, they reached the Janiculum, with the wonderful view of all of Rome and the mile-wide vista from the Campagna to the shining Albanian mountains in the distance.

It was now Per who was doing most of the talking, while Nanny, with her face averted, seemed mostly to be paying attention to what he explained to her about the buildings, whose spire and domes rose high through the golden haze that hovered over the city. The restiveness she felt the whole time began up here in the solitude to turn into fear. Every time Per moved on his seat, her nerves sent shivers through her. And suddenly, she realized she was tired, and said she wanted to go home. Per protested, but she was unyielding and insisted on being driven back. They parted at the gate of the hotel.

Dyhring had long since come home from his visit to the consulate. He was writing at a table in his shirtsleeves. As soon as she came through the door, Nanny could see only the part in his hair and the vest on his narrow back, and it struck her how old, yes, how really old and thin he looked when seen, like this, from behind. "Well, is that you, my dear?" he asked, and nodded over his shoulder. His calm tone irritated her. She answered a curt "Yes" as she took off her gloves and tossed them on the sofa.

"Did you have a good time?" he added coolly.

"Splendid, wonderful! I was almost never going to come home again!"

"Well, fancy that! How nice. Excuse me a moment."

"Of course."

Dyhring continued silently with his work while Nanny, after having removed her hat, flopped into an armchair at the opposite end of the room. She thought she would not be noticed there, and didn't suspect that her husband could observe her in a corner mirror without changing his posture; he was dividing his attention just about evenly between watching her face and writing a well-crafted article in an expert and seriously learned tone in which he gave the readers of *Borgerbladet* a general view of commercial concerns in Italy.

For almost half an hour, the room was very quiet. Nanny could not deflect her thoughts from a sense of defeat she felt once again in her relation to Per. She did not understand her impotence—an intolerable humiliation. Beyond that she had already noticed in Paris that she was no longer herself—there was decidedly something wrong with her. If she didn't know for sure that it was impossible, she would have thought she was pregnant. She would wake with a dreadful headache and be dizzy the whole morning. And all the strange desires she was having! Oh, the horrible dreams, so shocking she didn't dare tell her husband about them.

In the four to five days the young couple was still in Rome, Per was often together with them; and apparently his philandering made no impression at all on Dyhring. The latter acted with his usual affability, but Nanny, cautious about scandal, saw to it that she and Per were no longer left alone.

Only when the couple was leaving and Per came to the station to say goodbye did she boldly renew her advances. Not only did she squeeze Per's hand with unmistakeable warmth, but when the train started to roll and she was standing at the open compartment window, she artfully let her lovely shimmering eyes rest on his face with a passionate expression. It appeared as if now, in the moment of leaving, she could release a suppressed feeling she had been secretly struggling with.

She held in her hands some very pretty and expensive flowers, a farewell bouquet from Per. As soon as the train started moving, she let one of them, a rose in half bloom, fall to the platform. It might have happened inadvertently, but it could also be interpreted as a sign, a quiet confession, a shining promise.

Per picked up the flower, uncertain what he should dare to think. When he looked up again, the compartment window was empty. His eyes followed the train, but it disappeared behind the corner of a building still without her face in the window.

When, in the evening, after a long, distracted wandering in the environs of Rome, he returned to his lodgings, he had decided to break it off with Jakobe. The thought had for some time been smoldering in him. His day-by-day development was leading him away from her. He realized how essentially different they were and how poorly Jakobe, with her peculiar, forbidding character, would be adapted to the free and easy exuberant life of pleasure that now was before him as the goal of a new Renaissance. With a joyous flare and the clang of cymbals, the troll attire could be buried in the earth at home. Women of Nanny's sort were distinctly better suited to assist him with sustaining such a festive mood in his own life.

Then there was the fact that Jakobe was already no longer young. It had always bothered him that she was a year older than he, and her sickly and delicate constitution did not make her look any younger. It annoyed him as well to think of her distinctly Jewish features. When he had read in her letter about how she was affronted by a couple of gentlemen on her way home from Breslau, he himself felt highly embarrassed, despite the condescension with which she related the story.

That a break would offend and hurt Jakobe deeply he well understood. But he could not be obliged to ruin his life for the sake of a single thoughtless mistake. In addition, there really was more at stake here than some womanly tears. With the life task he had, he didn't have the right to renounce what spurred men on: to have power over other men and, even more, over women. He could no longer be bound. Until now, he had been very wrong not to use his natural sources of strength fearlessly. That was why he hadn't come farther on his fairy-tale voyage than he had.

But now—unfurl the sails! He had just received a new express letter from Ivan earnestly requesting him to come home and personally participate in the negotiations over his project. As usual, he had left the letter unanswered for a few days. Now he telegraphed his intention to return. The promise in Nanny's eyes drew him back. He realized, as well, that the time had come to act.

First he had to prepare Jakobe, as mercifully as possible, for the unavoidable break. He would try to make her understand that, given his disposition, it would also be best for *her* that their engagement should be canceled. It wouldn't be at all easy for him to say that farewell. He owed her so very much. But he couldn't sacrifice his freedom to her—jeopardize his future. He must show that he had not been sitting in vain at Caesar's feet, but had learned how to go manfully over the turbid Rubicon of irresolution with a firm will: *"Jacta alea est."*

CHAPTER 16

IN THE EARLY morning, some days before Per's return was expected, the same little circle of financiers gathered once again in the office of Max Bernhardt to discuss the possibilities of carrying out the West Jutland plan for a free port. Ivan was also present, with a very preoccupied expression on his face. While the other gentlemen engaged in a lively conversation at the window, he walked distractedly back and forth in the room and flipped through the newspapers and books lying around. He was very depressed about his unsuccessful attempt to mediate between Per and Colonel Bjerregrav. The way in which Per had talked about the colonel in his letter seemed to block all hope of a reconciliation. He didn't understand the indifference Per had manifested lately toward his own work and its destiny. When he, on his part, had announced to him the happy news of Max Bernhardt's support and, later, his fundamental hope to see a financial consortium develop soon, Per had answered with laconic irony:

"A certain man went down from Jericho, and he fell among thieves . . ."

After the company took their places around the table where the drafts, maps, estimates, and so forth had been laid out beforehand, Max Bernhardt began the meeting by announcing that, unfortunately, Herr Salomon still had not succeeded in settling the dispute between Colonel Bjerregrav and Herr Sidenius, and that was a provisional obstacle to the first stage of cooperation. Consequently, a more determined posture might be taken in regard to the question so they could reach a final decision about the nature of the eventual direction of the association. Ivan immediately reminded them of how, at the first meeting, he already had been doubtful about the possibility of cooperation between the project's young, brilliant originator and the technicians of the older school. He beseeched them not to be less hopeful about the undertaking despite his failure to reconcile Per and the colonel. He was convinced that if the press's participation could be assured, the extraordinary significance for the general public would be realized even without the assistance of the older and envious authorities.

Max Bernhardt responded that he had great confidence in the press's influence, but less in the public's capacity to judge—a remark that made the others smile. Next, he declared himself entirely at odds with Ivan's conception of the situation before them. The colonel had patiently promised his cooperation and only set up certain conditions—very reasonable, in and by themselves—that still had not been complied with. He would, therefore, suggest a new and more decisively formulated approach to Herr Sidenius in order to dispose of his purely personal problem with the colonel as quickly as possible.

Ivan unflaggingly opposed this position. He maintained that it wasn't a question of smoothing out the consequences of a personal quarrel. The conflict lay deeper. It was a repetition of the ever-constant argument between the older and younger generations. Colonel Bjerregrav and Herr Sidenius supported, technically and temperamentally, altogether different points of view that could not be reconciled. Max Bernhardt interrupted him to suggest that the gentlemen there certainly did not want a theoretical debate to continue.

After the colonel matter was decided, they began to discuss the present state of the money and stock markets, and Bernhardt concluded the meeting by proposing that they consider the association sufficiently established to inform the press. Despite the fact that the company—with the exception of the broker Herløv, Bernhardt's confidant, and the young Sivertsen, his echo—expressed strong misgivings, already the next morning the various Copenhagen papers contained, under the headline "A New National Project," an enthusiastic notice about Per's plan.

Per's name did not appear in the notice that, on the whole, had a decidedly provisional character and only repeated a "rumor in the banking circles." However, the next day the same newspapers announced that "a group of important men and highly distinguished financial houses backed the project." Max Bernhardt was in a hurry to attract the attention of the public to the undertaking, although he himself had little or no confidence in it, and intended to let it fall through as soon as his goal was reached of nipping the competitive Copenhagen free port project in the bud. And, as well, in his announcements to the papers, he avoided naming Per, to keep quiet whose plan was under discussion as long as possible. He had no faith in any offspring of a Danish parsonage as a conquering power. He had once met Per at a party in the Salomon house, where Ivan had been eager to bring them together; it was soon clear to him that this loud, conceited young seminary fellow was not made of the kind of stuff he could use.

He played with the idea of shoving Per aside, if necessary, and replacing him with another, more serviceable person. He already had in his sights a certain engineer named Steiner, who had recently come out in a provincial paper with another West Jutland project, doubtlessly borrowed, not to say stolen, from Per, but could, in its details, stand on its own and was, in any case, good enough for Bernhardt's purposes.

Already, by the first days of May, the Salomons had moved out to Skovbakken, though the spring had been wet and stormy. It was because of Jakobe's expressed desire to go to the country that the departure from the city was accelerated. She wanted to be there not only to have some peace, but also for the fresh air and the chance to take long walks. She had always neglected her health because she had no confidence in the possible improvement of all her bodily ailments, but lately, she seemed exaggeratedly careful with herself. Now that she had so much to live for, she nurtured hope for the renewed strength and well-being of her delicate, sensitive body. Among the many hetero-geneous books and periodicals invariably piled up on her table were medical works and health journals that she was eagerly studying. She suffered heroically through a Spartan toughening cure with ice-cold baths and hour-long hikes. Already in Copen-hagen she had begun to go on early-morning walks out to the Langelinie in spite of the weather and state of the roads—to the great amusement of the family's acquaintances in Bredgade, who watched her from their windows when she was returning home around nine o'clock, striding in a disciplined march under a wet umbrella.

All that persistence bore no fruit despite the strength of her longing. Finally, she could almost not bear the sight of people. The nights were sleepless and as endless as eternity. The buzz of a fly could awaken her from her deepest sleep. Still, she was seldom depressed. Like her letters to Per, which contained not the slight-est complaint, she herself in her weakest moments was full of hope. She was so used to bodily ills from childhood that they no longer affected her mind. She was, as it were, on good terms with her suffering. Her hidden anxieties troubled her the most. She was more and more convinced that she was pregnant, but the signs that strengthened her suspicion were at variance with her respectful responses to her mother's increasingly intimate ques-tions. She had not mentioned anything of this to Per. She knew nothing for sure because her natural cycles had always been very irregular. The notion that she would be a mother alarmed her only to the extent that she was fearful she wouldn't have the strength to bring a child into the world; but, in general, her mind was less worried in advance than she might have thought. For every time her thoughts turned to her situation, they circled a hundred times around Per. Her constant and uncontrolled jeal-ousy was much more harmful and destructive for her.

She was living with increasing tension and anxiety since there was talk about calling Per home. She had not tried to influence his decision by any communication, though Ivan often prompted her to do so. She didn't really understand the reason for his con-tinuous stay in Rome, where he could hardly have anything special to do. If it really (as he wrote) was only because of his concern for the commissioned sculpture of the bust that held him back, it seemed to her unpardonably thoughtless. Moreover, he had, in the last days, sent her a couple of strange, incoherent letters that were not at all unkind—quite the contrary—but had given her something to think about. But all these anxieties disappeared when the telegram came announcing that he would be in Copenhagen in a few days. To be entirely alone, she went into the woods and, for the first time in her life, missed having a God to whom she could send gratitude and a hymn of thanksgiving.

The day Per was expected, she was already up at daybreak, and dressed with the slow and calm thoughtfulness that was character-istic when she was under the sway of a strong emotion. Several hours before the carriage would drive to the station, she was ready to leave. Per was to come to Copenhagen on the morning express train, and she was worried about getting there too late. The weather had been beautiful the last few days. It was that same kind of sunny summer day when she would come into the city on the school train.

Per, meanwhile, had set foot on home ground and was travel-ing up through Zealand. He was in a depressed and distracted mood. On his departure from Rome, he still was strongly deter-mined to dissolve his engagement, but he had been unable to write the decisive words. He really had not had the necessary peace and quiet, what with the packing and pressures of getting ready to leave. He had decided to make a stopover on the way home either in Munich or Berlin to collect himself for a final explanation.

But gradually, as he journeyed north and, especially, when he approached the wooded mountains that only a few months ago had framed his holiday of love, that memory had more and more power over him. The night he traveled over the Alps, he sat dis-heartened at the compartment window and stared out over the moonlit mountain slopes. Here he recognized a wooded ridge, there a glittering snow peak that they had viewed on their happy love journey—and his heart grew heavy.

He began to debate with himself. He asked himself whether it was wise, just now, to break a connection that could be of invaluable use in the coming battle. All things considered, did he dare renounce the support that had always been assured him by his relation to the Salomon house? That consideration might well be, for the time being, the most important one. A life-or-death struggle was now to be fought out, and he longed to begin. While he traveled through Germany's hammering factories, with their enormous station buildings and forests of smoking chimneys, an impatient energy awakened in him a kind of work fever after his long bout of idleness in Rome. He asked himself whether it could be defensible to put the destiny of his life's work at risk or merely, even, to delay it, simply for the sake of a woman's beautiful body?

He had plenty of time for reflection during the next three days and nights, and he rode first through Munich, then Berlin, without stopping over. He had now decided, for the time being, to avoid all that could impede his project's advancement or render difficult the final triumph. Provisionally, at least, all should be sacrificed for the great work of the future—including the joys of love. Even if Jakobe were no longer the one who best suited him, common sense bade him continue with the choice he had made. It had to go as it would with domestic happiness. For men whom fate has called out for great work, the common, bourgeois law did not really count for much. In affairs of the heart, so-called royal individuals had the obligation to sacrifice private feelings for a higher purpose.

As the train roared into the main station of Copenhagen, he found himself still in a conflicted and agitated mood. But then, something unexpected awaited him. When he caught sight of Jakobe, who stood on the platform searching the passing compartment windows, his temper suddenly shifted and he was flooded with warm feelings toward her. He leaned spontaneously out of the window and waved his hat.

Jakobe looked uncommonly good. She had a new, wide-brimmed summer hat that was especially becoming, and her emotional state and the fresh morning air had given her cheeks color. Per leapt out of the compartment. Though the platform was full of people, he shoved his arm under hers without reflecting that their engagement was still supposed to be secret. He couldn't get over his surprise at finding her so much younger and prettier, so much less Jewish looking than a contrast with Nanny had led him to believe. Jakobe couldn't say a word from sheer happiness, but on the way through the hall's crowd, her heart was beating so fast Per could notice it. He smiled and looked into her eyes. She aroused so many intimate memories that he drew her arm tighter to him and whispered, "Dear love!"

They snuggled in a closed carriage, and when Jakobe threw herself on his chest he surrendered utterly. The carriage rumbled on, and before they realized it, they had stopped in front of the hotel. Jakobe stayed seated in the carriage while Per went in and ordered a room and hastily freshened himself. Afterward, they drove straight to Skovbakken without using the train. They had too much to talk about to be surrounded by curious ears. They stopped on the coastal road to have the carriage hood pulled down. Now, at noon, without an iota of wind, the sun felt hot. He drew a deep breath, his whole being expanding with a happy feeling of liberation after the long torment of being in a straitjacket of irresolution. His heart was full of gratitude toward Jakobe, who, through her beauty and joy at seeing him again, sanctioned his surrender. In addition to this, he felt peace of mind at being home again and hearing his mother tongue around him. As he sat there with Jakobe's hand in his and looked out over the well-known countryside with the forest bursting into leaf and the Sound filled with sails, a wave of patriotism swept through him. The sight of the flag that fluttered over one of the country-house gardens moved him instantly. "Dear old Denmark!" he exclaimed.

But now Jakobe began to talk to him about the Dyhrings. "They came home yesterday," she said. "They have traveled so very much. Oh, yes, that's right, you met them in Rome. What impression did you really have of their relationship?"

"Impression? I don't know anything about that."

"I think they are already through with each other. Nanny, in any case, has the same fluttering manner she always had. She is probably coming out, moreover, for midday dinner. She talked about how happy she would be to revive her Italian experiences with you!" Per tried to smile and deftly turned the conversation to other things.

Nanny appeared half an hour after the family was at table, and left again before coffee because she had an evening party. She seemed to be in excellent humor and looked glowing in a yellow flowered dress with a Spanish blood-red silk jacket.

Per felt a great relief when she had gone. He no longer felt satisfied. Although he had no grounds for complaint over the reception he received at Skovbakken (Philip Salomon had even had champagne poured out for the occasion), his homecoming pleasure had, bit by bit, and in hidden ways, dissipated and left a little residue of melancholy—an emptiness, some lack—he didn't know what.

He had known this feeling somewhat in the past and had never really had a comfortable, intimate sense here in this house of his future parents-in-law. There was so much in the family's way of life and conventions that alienated him. The breath of modern Europe that blew through the atmosphere hit him, at times, like a cold draft. When, for instance, in the afternoons, friends came to visit from neighboring villas—mainly Jews—he had, in spite of a common language, the sensation of being in a foreign land.

He went down into the garden together with Jakobe. Arm in arm they walked back and forth along the path by the water, where they were least exposed to being surprised by visitors. Jakobe didn't want to hide their relationship from people anymore, and in a couple of days, there was going to be a big party at Skovbakken in honor of the marriage of Nanny and Dyhring; she knew it was her parents' wish to use that occasion to announce her engagement. Her mother was especially eager for it and added that it soon would be time to be thinking about setting a marriage date. Jakobe had led Per out into the garden, now, to talk to him about that and, at the same time, confide in him about what she could no longer doubt: that she was pregnant.

For a while, she didn't say much, but walked with her head leaning on his shoulder, while Per, with a concealed embarrassment, returned her caresses. Every time Jakobe's lips were raised to his the picture of Nanny glided between them and confused him.

Involuntarily affected by his reserve and not quite sure how Per would receive her secret, she was a little inhibited about imparting it. At last, she decided to wait until the next time they were together. Stopping, while she laid her hand on his cheek, she said that he should stay at home the next morning and she would come to visit him. Per pretended, at first, not to understand her meaning and said, "That's unfortunately impossible, dear. Ivan just summoned me for a business meeting at Max Bernhardt's tomorrow morning at ten. Well, it's time for work now."

"But later in the day, when it best suits you."

"No, that won't do, dearest. We must be careful now."

She looked at him in surprise. Something was in the little laugh that accompanied these words that hurt her. So they went farther on and no longer talked about it. They left the path and went onto the beach. There was a bench under a cupola near the water. The sun had just gone down, and the Sound lay like shining metal under the red clouds; out by Hveen, the gravelly shore glowed. The seething, rushing noise that stayed in the woods long after all the wind had died down came in from the game sanctuary. Otherwise, it was completely still except for the plash of oars in the water that could be heard from a long, long way out.

To avoid more questions, Per started skipping stones. As a boy, he had been a master at it, and it amused him to notice that, after the passage of so many years, he hadn't lost his skill. Jakobe sat on the bench, bent forward, with her hands under her chin, and watched. Every time he got off a good throw, Per turned around to get her applause as she smiled and nodded. But in the meantime, her face looked serious, thoughtful, distracted.

"Did you see that? Eight hops!" shouted Per like a boastful boy. He had become animated and searched the open beach, with great care, for the stones he wanted, and, finally, took off his coat. Here, he found again that pleasure of being home that had died away up in the villa. The soft thump of the waves on the broad shore, the sound of the rustling woods behind him, those dull strokes of the oars from an invisible rowboat way out on the water—all this made him happy. It was as if he was hearing the intimate and confidential "welcome" from his country he had missed.

Per had agreed to meet Ivan the next morning at the hotel, from which they would go to the arranged gathering at Max Bernhardt's. Dead tired from the day's many successive, conflicting impressions and from the previous day's hardships of travel, he left Skovbakken early, went straight to bed, and fell into a deep sleep. The next morning the ringing of the streetcar in the street awakened him.

When he realized where he was and what a significant thing was imminent, he became wide awake and rose immediately. Despite the discomfort he still felt at the thought of those alien businessmen whom he now had to take into his confidence and to whom he must virtually surrender something of his innermost self, he was impatient to begin. There was the hope that by his personal presence, he would inspire more courage in the patently anxious and sober potential investors and give them a larger sense of the task they had before them.

He hung his shaving mirror on the window post and gazed down at the marketplace outside. He stood there for a while with his shaving brush in his hand and viewed the people going by. This was the so-called Halmtorv, an extensive space that with its irregular form and neglected condition was a model of the unfinished nature of the whole city. In the midst of a row of quickly erected deluxe buildings in the modern European coffee-house style, the ruins of the city's old ramparts could be seen with a piece of an avenue of broad-topped one-hundred-year-old trees. A windmill whose rotating blades cast shadows on the market's pavement soared out of the surrounding country.

Glaring sunshine lay over the big marketplace, still dirty and wet from the night's dew. It was the busy morning hour in which the inner city, with its shops, offices, schools, and sewing work-rooms, attracted the population of the suburbs. A stream of people hurried in from Vesterbro over the two rows of flagstone that made a path through the mud.

The Danish people! My own Sideniuses! thought Per, and smilingly observed that these square forms all seemed to resemble each other like brothers and sisters.

He fell for a moment into a meditation. After the wearisome contemplation of so many lonely years, after so many prepara-tions and fruitless attempts, this would finally be the day, the four-teenth of May, for the laying of the foundation stone for the new realm he had, bit by bit, built up out of the chaos of his thoughts, counting really from the time he was a boy of eleven.

And down there, the unsuspecting crowd—that raw stuff of Denmark's future, the dead clay that he, like God, dreamt of creating in his own image, breathing into it the life of his emanci-pated soul.

He smiled again and, finally, started to soap up his cheeks. There was a little madness in this—he saw that clearly, but it did not frighten him. On the contrary, he felt a satisfaction and com-fort in knowing he was in possession of this little bit of madness, without which—the small worldly-wise painter in Rome had declared—no victory could be won in all mankind.

After he finished shaving, he rang for a maid, who brought him the morning coffee and the day's newspapers. He was hun-gry, and the cozy board greatly sharpened his appetite. What a pleasure, after so many months' passage, to again have rye bread and Danish salt butter. He quickly finished with the papers, having no interest in the domestic politics of the country, and from habit jumped over the many articles about the theater, literature, and painting exhibitions.

Suddenly, he started. By chance his eye had fallen on an advertisement under which he found his sister Signe's name: "Beginning pupils wanted for first elements of music," the heading read, and her address was given under her name. It was somewhere in Vesterbro on one of the small side streets near the beginning of Gammel Kongevej.

During his stay in Italy, he had again shut his family out of his life. A few times in Rome, to be sure, and in Dresack, too, he would be awakened by a jarring dream of his family at home in the parsonage; but in his waking state, he had, in the last months, not troubled himself about them. As in his youth, he had again deliberately made himself indifferent to their memory, and had justified himself with the notion that, in this small respect, he was emulating Christ himself, who unconditionally bade us leave our fathers and mothers and follow the inner calling.

His eyes remained fixed on the small-type notice. He now recalled that at his father's burial, there was talk about moving here in April in consideration of the younger brothers—the twins. One of them had just found a place at one of the city's pharmacies; the other at a bookstore. His mother and most of his siblings were also in Copenhagen.

There was a knocking at the door, and, as if shot out of a cannon, Ivan rushed in with his large briefcase under his arm. He brought flowers and greetings from Jakobe and added, on his own part, a greeting from his parents; he took the occasion to give Per the pleasure of hearing that they were quite happy to see him again, which, as a matter of fact, was not untrue. Philip Salomon, especially, was surprised at how much Per had matured.

"But now to our business!" interrupted Per a little impatiently as he got up. He was still only half dressed, in shirtsleeves and slippers.

"Yes, to our business!" repeated Ivan dully, and threw himself nervously into a chair, while he fingered his neck as if something were suddenly squeezing his throat. He couldn't imagine how he could tell Per how badly his project's chances looked at the moment and prepare him for the unconditional demand that would be made at the impending meeting. To gain time, he started to give a profuse account of what he had mentioned in his letters—the first board meeting and the various comments that were dropped concerning the project.

Now and then Per contributed a grunting remark. He was again standing in front of the mirror on the window post about to knot his tie, and was thinking continuously about his mother. He couldn't get used to the idea that she lived here in the city, even in his immediate neighborhood, perhaps not more than a thousand steps away.

"May I ask you something?" began Ivan after a moment's pause. His tone sounded quite submissive.

"Please!"

"Tell me—would it—could it—I mean would it be impossible for you to resolve to reconcile yourself with Colonel Bjerregrav?" Per turned his head to him slowly. He didn't know for a moment whether to laugh or be enraged. He chose the first. "Listen, little child," he said as he again turned toward the mirror. "I think the old fool has made you crazy! If he has persuaded you that we cannot do without his assistance, you can approach him for me and say that he can—well, you know what. Don't get nervous. When the beast yelps it's because he doesn't dare bite."

"I'll grant that, in a way, you're entirely in the right," answered Ivan. "It's obvious—from a certain point of view—that it's absolutely preposterous to attribute such a crucial significance to his consent in any case. But, on the other side—when our dear cohorts cannot free themselves from the idea that he is indispensable, and when he himself has declared himself willing, with certain conditions, to support the undertaking, well . . ."

"Well what?"

"Well . . . I mean . . . well," repeated Ivan, and twisted himself up, as if he had a stomachache, "it will undeniably facilitate the progress of the project significantly if you could bring yourself to the kind of—kind of—concession he wants."

"Nonsense, my friend. You don't know what you're talking about. But now let me take charge of the much-mentioned dear cohorts and insist that they could not be more benighted than to imagine that I either can or will be persuaded to settle for some kind of trusteeship."

"But it's not at all a question of that, dear friend! It's only a question of the public, and they want to use his name. And I can guarantee you the most excessively friendly reception by Colonel Bjerregrav. Since the papers have announced the undertaking, he has been going around like a hen about to lay an egg. I got that from my uncle."

"It's all the same to me. I won't hear anymore about it."

"May I just say one more word? However much I acknowledge the superiority of your point of view, I think—pardon me—that you are miscalculating in this case. What concerns, especially, Max Bernhardt . . ."

Per lost all patience at the sound of that name. He turned around and said, "Leave me alone with your everlasting Max Bernhardt! For God's sake, I'm the one who decides here. Stop worrying about it; let's get going."

When, a half hour later, they entered Max Bernhardt's elegant reception room decorated in the Parisian mode, the group—except for the broker Herløv and Max Bernhardt himself—was already assembled. The men were clustered around one of the high windows and greeted Per with the brutal condescension characteristic of financiers. It took Per a moment to compose himself. He was altogether unprepared for such a reception. He had, rather, dreaded an oppressive kindness from these men who hoped they could enrich themselves on his project. But they, really, hardly deigned to answer his bow. The "erstwhile farmer" stared at him coolly from a pair of small, white-fringed pig eyes, and nodded without taking his hands out of his pockets. Per took his measure with a resolute glance and turned to Ivan, who had managed the introduction: "I didn't hear the gentleman's name."

"Herr Nørrehave," whispered Ivan, who shuffled his feet, taken aback by Per's provocative behavior toward these men who were to decide the destiny of his project.

"Ah, so," said Per slowly, and continued staring at the stout farmer until the latter, finally, grew red and turned his back with a haughty sniff, taking his hands out of his pockets and placing them behind him under his wide coattails. The fact was that these gentlemen were all, more or less, uneasy at having promised their names to the undertaking in which they had no confidence; only the firm trust in Max Bernhardt had prompted their participation. Most of them weren't far from suspecting Per of being a confidence man who had had singular success in hoodwinking Max Bernhardt. In reality, they were just thinking about how they could find a delicate way of withdrawing from the project without making an enemy of Max Bernhardt.

The latter and the broker came in from an adjoining room, and the men seated themselves around the large, centered table, where, with some difficulty, the discussion commenced. To begin with, the conversation had little or no relation to Per's project, but, rather, was a rehash of their previous meeting, or, entirely off the subject, raised questions about other businesses in which the various participants were interested. They passed around financial news and street gossip; the young Herr Sivertsen entertained his neighbor with an anecdote he had heard about one of the city's popular actresses.

Max Bernhardt had to bang on the table with a ruler a couple of times, and request his colleagues to stick, as much as possible, to the business at hand. "Sirs, here we are on Hjerting Bay, and we should be trying to convert our much-celebrated North Sea into stock."

Ivan sat on burning coals. He stole a desperate glance at his brother-in-law, who sat leaning back in his chair with a storm gathering on his face. Per did answer the questions that, from time to time, were directed at him—curtly and reluctantly; he could not, in the long run, control his bitterness. He still exhibited some nervousness over the discovery of his family's move to Copenhagen. Even if he wasn't dwelling on them, the mere awareness oppressed him and made him irritable. The whole time, he had a great desire to get up and leave without further ceremony. As he viewed these bank bandits sitting there carelessly and condescendingly chatting and turning topsy-turvy the work that had been his only thought for so many years—even the very meaning of his life—he felt disgusted, as if he were personally being sniffed and pawed by them.

He was unaware, in the meantime, of being sharply observed from the head of the table, where Max Bernhardt, supporting his dark head on his pretty, white hand, sat with an elbow on the arm of his chair. His large, puffy eyelids, surrounded by blue shadows, were, as usual, half closed, so that no one could see where his glance was landing. It rested uninterruptedly on Per.

Per's tight mouth and the swollen veins in his powerfully cut forehead captured this man who used to say he would, by the time of his death, have put a premium value on every head of tolerable character in the mass of meatballs that constituted the

Danish race. He was, on the whole, surprised by Per's imposing and sophisticated appearance, which didn't at all fit the picture he had preserved from that social meeting at Philip Salomon's house, where Per seemed an unsavory, characterless creature, half seminary student, half prostitute's john. Could he have been mistaken? Could the Danish clergy class have hatched an exception, a real man with a strong will in his body?

He considered Per's stubbornness regarding Colonel Bjerregrav in a whole new light. He began to think it a bit risky to have involved himself with him. Like all bullying natures, he was frightened to make an adversary and rival of someone who wasn't immediately willing to be under his yoke. Yes, the more he observed Per, the more he was convinced that he could become dangerous and, therefore, should be gotten rid of.

Questions were raised about the press's assistance. Broker Herløv said to Per, in a fatherly tone, that, really, he should immediately visit the various editorial offices here and in the provinces. He named a series of major newspapers and added that it would, naturally, be best if he would promise a guaranteed sum for advertisements. He concluded, with his dry wit, "This tends to be looked upon favorably in many places."

Per pretended that he had heard nothing and turned his head aside. Max Bernhardt took the floor, and in support of his friend's remarks brought up the question of Colonel Bjerregrav for discussion. Turning to Per, he said in his invariably joking tone, "It's very unfortunate that the colonel and you, from what we hear, got in each other's hair—though not literally, since the colonel, as a rule, is bald." There was spontaneous laughter at the table, while Herr Sivertsen brayed like a donkey.

"As I said, I find that unfortunate," continued Max Bernhardt, "because Colonel Bjerregrav is definitely one of our most prominent experts who can best serve the project, not to speak of how difficult and dangerous it might be to have him as an enemy. Now, in the meantime, as you know, we have procured the colonel's promise to support our undertaking under the condition that you take steps toward a reconciliation—which is not an unreasonable demand when you take into consideration his age and social standing."

During these words, all eyes turned expectantly toward Per, whose manner gradually had awakened puzzlement in the group. He did not make them wait for his answer: "I absolutely protest against any kind of trusteeship," he said. "I have worked out my plan without outside assistance and do not require any associate in the future."

Ivan collapsed quietly into himself like a bird shot through the heart. Among the other gentlemen, there was a shocked confusion, so unusual was it that anyone—never mind a young, unknown man—would palpably venture to oppose Max Bernhardt's wishes. Bernhardt himself was not far from letting his smiling mask slip, but he kept it intact and, in order to give Per the opportunity to remedy his blunder, said with some humor, "Herr Sidenius obviously got up on the wrong side of the bed this morning." Turning to Per, he continued, "How can you have the heart to show yourself so implacable toward such an honorable man as Colonel Bjerregrav, an old wounded war veteran, a defender of our country! He should be embraced!"

The slavish sycophant Herr Sivertsen again showed off his screeching laugh, but stopped suddenly when he noticed that the others remained serious. At this, Per completely lost his composure; with a bang of his fist on the table he got up, gray in the face, and said, "I will remind you, gentlemen, that it is you who sent for me, not the other way around. I think, therefore, it is up to me, and not you or anyone else, to set up conditions."

He sat down to ice-cold silence. Everyone looked at Max Bernhardt, who again supported his head with his hand and stared down with half-closed eyes. His bloodless face had taken on the dismal, stiffened expression that always surfaced when he was in the act of pondering a death sentence. He had, in the meantime, exchanged a pair of quick glances with Broker Herløv, who sat with both arms on the table, his large, fat, red head bent over as if he were inwardly asleep. In fact, he was wide awake, and his little assenting nod sealed Per's fate.

"Is it also your intention," resumed Max Bernhardt with apparent indifference, "to refuse the concessions desired by Colonel Bjerregrav and us?"

"Yes."

"And that's your final answer?"

"Absolutely."

"Well, my friends, we're done here. Our proposal has not been accepted, and, therefore, we will let the undertaking die. I'm hardly mistaken, I think, in believing that there has not been a strong feeling for it among you, so I shall refrain from expressing any regret over the results."

Bernhardt arose, and one after another the company stood up, mostly with a feeling of relief at such an unexpectedly quick liberation from what, in their eyes, was a stillborn project. Nevertheless, a few of them were dissatisfied with this cool-headed conclusion, especially Herr Nørrehave, who was strongly affected by Per's performance and now continued to watch him with his small pig eyes, while Per, after a rapid and careless bow, stormed out of the room, followed by Ivan.

As soon as the door had closed behind them, Max Bernhardt called again for attention and said, "It's superfluous to add that I have not given up the free port idea. I can already announce to you gentlemen that, in the near future, another plan with, as I believe, a better-reasoned foundation, will be considered. We'll get together soon again, dear sirs."

Out at Skovbakken, Jakobe went around that morning in a rather depressed mood. The very tense expectation with which, during the previous days and nights, she had counted the hours until Per's arrival had taken its toll; it was inevitable that fatigue should follow. He had disappointed her a little—even more than she was ready to admit to herself. She couldn't help thinking he had changed. The self-control, almost reserve, that had come over him, and that pleased her parents, did not make her happy. She remembered an anxious tone in his last letters from Italy. It was perhaps merely a front he had adopted, a cooked-up posture of a man of the world, but in her eyes, that did not become him. She loved him as the naughty bear he was when she was getting to know him and as he was when he said goodbye, two months ago in the Laugen woods. She was used to having her heart in her mouth when they were together in company, for fear he would, in one way or another, offend or provoke a scandal, and she did not want to be freed from that little martyrdom at all. It was almost as if she feared coming to love him less when he was no longer subject to a lack of appreciation.

Just as she was filled with these thoughts, Ivan came home with his piece of bad news about the meeting with Max Bernhardt. She was sitting in the garden with her mother when he stormed in with his briefcase. At first, the impression his report had on her made her laugh, because the incident seemed such an amusingly emphatic protest against all she had been worried about. Ivan's face, verging on tears, and that of her mother, with its guarded expression, momentarily filled her with satisfaction. Now she again recognized her wild bear.

But it wasn't long before she, too, became alarmed at the story. When she had put the whole of it together, and especially when she understood, through Ivan's account, with what rashness and futility Per had behaved, she was almost more vexed and ashamed than the others. She thought little about what he and, as well, she would be exposed to—although the prospect of again having to live with uncertainty in relation to their future did not cheer her. But her anger was aimed specifically at the thoughtless indifference that his behavior had shown, for all that her father and Ivan had done for the project.

Per telegraphed that he was coming in the afternoon. She went through the forest path to meet him at the station, and already from a distance he called out to her with a smile on his face: "I guess you've heard the news; I have plagiarized Christ and chased the money changers out of the temple!"

The braggadocio made Jakobe extremely dispirited. If only he had taken her in his arms and defended against any reproach by closing her mouth with a kiss. But Per made no such move. Already before they came together he read disapproval in her face.

He had been so convinced that she, at least, would understand him and acknowledge the significance of his challenge to the financial speculators; she had always spoken with aversion of these kinds of unscrupulous exploiters. She had complained, as well, about the role, as one of the leaders of the new day, a man like Max Bernhardt was playing in the public consciousness. But on that point, he thought bitterly, when it came down to it, she was not any better than the others. The shopkeeper's soul was in her and was waiting for the first opportunity to ambush his pride—yes, in truth, the Jews also had their ghosts!

They were coming close to the edge of the woods, and Jakobe, feeling tired but reluctant to get home immediately, sat down on a bench under one of the trees. Although, by the way she drew her skirt to her, she invited him to sit beside her, Per didn't want to. With the tips of his fingers stuck in his vest pockets, he paced up and down in front of her, absorbed in thoughts of how to explain and justify the motives behind his behavior.

Jakobe leaned silently against the back of the bench, her arm resting there. She followed him with an intent watchfulness while he paced up and down. It hit her again how much he had changed. A flicker of suspicion shot through the searching glance of her dark eyes. Could the reserve of yesterday and the irritability of today have the same hidden cause?

She brushed her hand over her darkened brow to forcibly chase away all ugly thoughts.

"I feel almost worst for Ivan," she said as she looked away. "It was moving to see how eager he has really been about the project. I don't think he could have worked harder had it been a question of his own future."

At first Per didn't want to answer. It was beginning to annoy him that it always had to be about Ivan's self-sacrifice.

"Yes, naturally, it's tedious. I feel bad about your brother, but there's nothing to do about it. But then, Ivan must have said to himself that it would be useless to get me together with those kinds of people."

"You yourself accepted the invitation."

"I didn't know them and their great plebeian arrogance with which they sat there, as if they were doing me a favor to be willing to enrich themselves by my work. If it's people like that who will become the new men here in this country, we have jumped from the frying pan into the fire."

"What are you thinking of doing now?" asked Jakobe after a moment of silence.

"Very simply continue as I have begun. Agitate, write, and ring the storm bells until the people hear. There must be others in this country to talk to beyond just the bank bandits. Can you believe they had the gall to demand that I should pay my respects to the newspaper editors? What do you think? Should I dance in attendance with the philandering boors of the press, of Dyhring's caliber?"

"Oh, for heaven's sake . . ."

He stood looking at her, patently surprised. "Then that suggestion meets with your approval, I gather."

"If it could be for the benefit of the undertaking—and it could well be—how could you really not do it?"

"Do you actually believe that? I must say, you surprise me today."

"I think that when you need to think about procuring yourself the necessary influence, it's wise to yield, for the time being, to a well-known power without losing too much time scrutinizing how it came to be."

"Well, please excuse me, but I have a somewhat different conception of what you owe yourself. I don't see how it is less disgraceful for a person to humiliate himself before a golden calf than, for example, before a crucifix. What I have experienced today has given me such a bad taste for the whole swindle of the business world that I don't know if I can overcome it."

Jakobe did not answer. It pained her that Per was devoting himself so intensely to justifying himself in the affair. She wished he would stop his explanations, which, in her eyes, were rationalizations and a willful attempt to elevate himself by posturing.

But Per seemed about to speak. Jakobe's continuing and total disapproval of his behavior, added to her complete incomprehension of what had driven him to this collision, and, finally, his own inability to clarify for himself and for her the inner urges that made him behave like that—all this exasperated him and made him belligerent. "It amuses me, really, to see the admiration you have for Max Bernhardt and his company. That's new. That seems to have been invented for the occasion."

"I'll disregard that last remark, Per," answered Jakobe with studied calm, and very seriously. "In addition, I don't know that I have expressed my admiration at all—not for Max, although I think he is a bit better than his reputation. I happen to know that he has quietly done a lot of good and supported many poor Jewish families here in the city."

"Obviously penance for all the misery he has visited on hundreds of families in the country. He must have a very considerable number of ruined households on his conscience."

"Well, he is a fighter: 'War is my business,' he once said. He is merciless and unforgiving, cruel, as well. I, too, was once uneasy about his growing influence—on that you are right. But I think, perhaps, I have not estimated him fairly and have, on the whole, undervalued the significance of those kinds of people. Perhaps we need just such a person here in our country, where we are close to forgetting how a really purposeful man looks."

"You mean an ideal, a teacher for all of us?"

"Perhaps."

"Tell me how many suicides we can count up that, to date, can be ascribed to his honor?"

"Oh, you're speaking nonsense."

"But you are obliged to concede—"

"Yes, well, I think the fuss that is raised each time he uses his power to disarm an opponent or push one of his allies forward more noticeably than some others shows how difficult it is here for us to learn to understand that if you have a goal, you need, as well, the means—and not always to hassle over it—with yourself or others."

Per looked at her a moment in silence. She had, with these words, hit him in an entirely different way than she had intended or could suspect.

"You are bold, on that score," he said, and some strong words burned on his lips. He wanted to say to her that if *he* had followed the rules of conduct she advocated, they now would have spoken for the last time. He settled for assuring her that, as far as he was concerned, he had had abundant occasions to weigh ends against means, and for more significant decisions. In addition, he would not particularly object to the axiom—it only amazed him that she would go so far as to defend a fellow like Max Bernhardt with goals of the basest kind, who was pathologically arrogant and power-hungry, or, perhaps, merely greedy, and who had exposed himself as an uncommonly pernicious little—. He was about to say "Jew," but suppressed it for "money badger." "But I concede," he added, turning away with a shrug, "that you have hereditary reasons I lack for appreciating a character like his."

Jakobe darted a flashing glance at him. Then she looked away again and was silent.

"But as we have said before," continued Per, "I do not find the whole affair worth all this fuss. It seems to me that you are ridiculous to take this so seriously; you have, in general, an unfortunate weakness for wearing the conturn of ancient tragedy."

"You mean 'cothurn,' Per."

"Oh, please, spare me your airs!"

"But you really must respect the way you use words. It won't do to extend your reforms to learning and language themselves."

They stayed like that for an hour, one bitter and wounding word chasing the other, until Jakobe put her hand over her eyes and pacified herself. No, no. She would not mistrust him. She would stop her ears to shut out his vain hooting, not think of any danger. Quickly she got up, took Per's face between her hands, and forced him to look her in the eyes.

"Per," she said, "doesn't it seem that we should be a little ashamed of ourselves? Kiss me now and let's forget all the ugly words we have spoken. You have my permission to say it's I who am to blame if only you'll be sweet again. And so, let's promise that nothing like this will pass between us again. All right? Let's promise!"

Per was quickly appeased. These days he could not bear to resist loving words. "You're right. This is stupid. But I was so convinced that in every case you would sanction what I did, and I feel that now more than ever I need you to understand and support me."

"You'll never lack that support, Per," she said. And they sealed their reconciliation with a long kiss.

It wasn't a very pleasant mood that reigned at Skovbakken during the midday dinner. Philip Salomon, who had already found out in town what had happened, did not utter a word. There would have been no conversation at all had the younger children not been there with their freewheeling chatter, which slightly dispersed the tension among the rest. Per sat as if in armor, with his face braced for battle. After the way in which Ivan and Jakobe had taken his behavior, he was prepared for his parents-in-law to demand an explanation, perhaps even a kind of accounting, because he presently lived on their support.

But there was no need for any self-defense. Philip Salomon, who had made up his mind about Per and his future prospects once and for all, successfully overcame the temptation he undeniably felt to instruct him on what passed for permissible in the business world. Nor did his mother-in-law refer at all to what had happened.

After dinner, Jakobe and Per went into the garden, arm in arm, but in spite of the reconciliation in the woods, the old mutual confidence was not there. For fear of saying something that could again awaken the former dissension, they kept their thoughts to themselves and talked of incidental things. Jakobe could not, therefore, raise the question of the announcement of their engagement, still less confide in him concerning her conjecture about her condition. And Per, on his part, could not bring himself to tell her about his family's removal to Copenhagen, with which, in spite of the morning's weighty events, he was more and more occupied.

In addition, he was concerned that Nanny would pop in. At dinner there was talk that she would come already that evening for the next day's gathering and stay overnight. The whole time, therefore, that he was listening carefully for her arrival, he had to take care not to let Jakobe notice his distraction.

At last they sat on the bench down on the beach where there was shelter from the strong wind. It was about the same time they had tarried there the day before, but the atmosphere was entirely different. Today, way off in the north, the coastlines were sharply outlined. The island of Hveen was so clearly visible that you could see the waves breaking on the sun-drenched sloping shore. The wind blew in from the west, but, along the Zealand coast, the water's surface was calm, and in spots where the land rose up behind the beach, it was so glassy that the bathing jetties and villa gardens were reflected in it. Out in the Sound, on the other hand, dark blue waves were flecked with white foam. Some yachts pitched about at half-mast while a green freighter glided through and warned the boats with its hoarse steam whistle. The thick coal smoke that hung over the scene like a cloud caught the gleam of the sunset and threw a long, somber shadow over the water.

This fresh sea picture reminded Per of Fritjof, and those thoughts took him back to Berlin, to the cheerful evenings with the mad painter and his crazy artist brothers in their favorite pub on Leipzigstrasse. He did not really understand what it was that had attracted him to this crowd so much that he could now feel a definite longing for their company. He took Fritjof, in a certain sense, for a fool and, in addition, had no understanding of his large and powerful paintings. It didn't in the least flatter him that these friends saw a likeness between the two of them and had taken him for Fritjof's relative.

He vaguely sensed that it was Fritjof's notoriously careless behavior that had attracted him, something in the capriciousness of his opinions that was just the opposite of the one-sided, stolid, narrow life view of Jakobe and the whole Salomon family. While they had their opinions and judgments directly prepared beforehand in a clear form that reflected the bright, stylish, but sterile atmosphere of the house's rooms, Fritjof championed a new outlook every day about the same things and always with what seemed like great conviction and undiminished passion. While the Salomon family, despite a certain inclination to extravagance, nevertheless always remained on the same side of life—namely the side that fostered reasonable and measured judgment—Fritjof's vagabond soul obviously had, several times already, circumnavigated existence both on the day and night side, and had suffered shipwrecks before finding happiness in restlessness itself.

When Per began to talk about him, Jakobe told him that she had seen Fritjof on Østergade several days ago.

"So, he's in town!" said Per with a lively interest. "But he said in the fall he was going to Spain and wanted to live there. He hated Denmark—'the new Jewland,' as he called it."

"He has wanted to travel all over the world and live in every city on earth—but he seldom goes more than a day's distance from Copenhagen. Perhaps you don't know that he is, for the present, once again an inspired progressive, indeed, a revolutionary and incendiary spokesman."

"What?"

"Since Germany made so much of him, he has again become fashionable here at home. He's altogether done with his anti-Semitism. Markus Levi has recently bought a whole series of his paintings for his collection—I think for twenty thousand kroner—and he has now become, simply, a eulogist of Jewish enterprise and of modern industry's blessings."

Per laughed loudly. "That sounds like him! I met him in the fall in Berlin, and, in spite of all his bombast, I have become really fond of him. But it is undeniably a little difficult to explain where the real man in him begins and the comedian, twaddler, speculator, and windbag end. It's as if there are a dozen people in him who live their own independent lives. But, perhaps, to a certain extent, it's that way with everyone—in any case, with us northerners."

Jakobe didn't want to answer him. She had already during Per's stay in Berlin been a little vexed by his fascination with Fritjof, who, in her eyes, was both a fool and a beggar, a tragicomic Falstaff whom extravagant nature, in a derisive mood toward mankind, had inspired with artistic genius. She acknowledged his great ability and unique virtuosity, but she would not allow that talent could excuse the defects of his nature. On the contrary, she thought that rare talent came with obligations; and she thought the tolerance with which people in general spoke of Fritjof's faulty character was an insult to real greatness and a degradation of art.

As on the previous day, Per left early. He felt tired, and

therefore Jakobe did not try to keep him there. Nanny had not yet showed up. She could still come by the last train, and Per wanted to leave before that.

It was late in the evening when he reached the city. A faint twilight still hovered over the Halmtorv, but the street was dark. On one side of the space a long row of café windows in a newly built, synthetically fashioned deluxe building was lit. On the other side, the old windmill rose up like a ghost against the sallow horizon. Viewed from the market it resembled a large, fat witch with outstretched arms raining down curses on the modern city.

Per did not go straight home. However tired he was, he followed an impulse that was waiting to ambush him under all that day's shifting thoughts and moods and now was ready to catch him off guard. Slowly, half reluctantly, he went out to Vesterbro, stretching out between rows of streetlamps and full of the usual noisy evening traffic.

At Bagerstræde, he turned away from the city into the quiet quarter around Gammel Kongevej. Soon he stood at the corner of the street where his mother lived. In order not to be recognized if he should meet someone in the family, he had pushed his coat collar up and pressed his hat down on his forehead. For the time being, there was not a person in sight. First he went over to the side of the street where the house should be; but when he had found it, he crossed the road diagonally and stood on the opposite pavement, where it was dark. He looked up and down a plain, shabby, three-story building with small apartments of three to four rooms. His eyes had immediately gone to the windows of the first floor to the left of the door entrance, but there was nothing to see other than a row of painted-over windowpanes. He must have remembered wrong. This apartment was obviously uninhabited and under repair. Then it occurred to him that, in relation to the entrance steps inside the house, an apartment to the left—as it was described in his sister's advertisement—would be to the right of the entrance door when the building was viewed from the street.

He now directed his gaze there and saw a weak light at one of the windows. The blinds were not pulled down in the neighboring room, and he could observe a ceiling with a streak of light that must have originated from a half-open door to a lighted room. He tried in vain to make out something inside. In addition, he could not get himself to believe that his mother really lived in that strange house until he noticed an object that stood between a couple of flowerpots on the windowsill—in an instant his heart beat violently. He had recognized his mother's little red wooden tub for her balls of yarn, which had seemed to him a veritable well when he was a little boy.

A moment later, a shadow glided over the blinds. Maybe it's my mother, he thought, and began to shiver from the evening chill. After a few minutes, a shadow again appeared but so fleeting and unclear he couldn't determine whether it was a man or a woman. At that moment, when he heard voices from a noisy group of people coming nearer in the street, he left.

Slowly he went back into the city by the same way he had come. When he reached the hotel, he felt, despite his painful fatigue, such displeasure, almost fear, at the prospect of confronting the loneliness of his strange room that he turned around at the main door and rushed over to a café on the other side of the marketplace. There he sat in a corner with a glass of beer and tried to collect himself.

Only now—while taking final stock of the day's happenings, while confessing that he could no longer defer with platitudes the question of what he should do with his life—did he fully realize the great difficulties he had fashioned for himself. He felt once more at rock bottom, in the middle of a large, empty, menacing room, with no way out. Yes—there *was* one—Colonel Bjerregrav . . . well, as a last resort, still one more: the crazy baroness.

To put it in another way, he must, like Dyhring and so many others, sacrifice his independence, castrate his "ego" and make himself a public eunuch; or, he must learn from Max Bernhardt to carefully choose a defenseless victim and cold-bloodedly plunder him. Jakobe was also right in this respect; there was no other way out. "If a man desires a goal, he must also accept the means." No, he was obliged to concede—he did not have in him the stuff of a world conqueror, as he had imagined. He could not bring himself to pay the cost of such success. Or, rather, it was with fame and power as it was for him in the past, with all the other highly celebrated temptations in life: they lost their worth as he got closer to them. He considered the price they demanded too ridiculously high. In this regard, he found himself thinking of the blessed Neergaard. What was it he said in those prophetic words the night of his suicide?

Just then, the glass door out to the marketplace opened, and in strode a two-mile-high, gray-bearded form in a light cloak with a walking stick held like a broadsword on his shoulder:

Fritjof!! Per came near to shouting his name in his happy surprise, but as he was about to get up to greet him, he had misgivings and stayed seated. He took up a newspaper and diffidently hid behind it while Fritjof stalked by into the adjoining room. It was now clear to him that he could no longer bear to stay here in the city, where, everywhere, he was exposed to these painful meetings. He thought with positive terror of the big party arranged for the next day at Skovbakken and to which almost all the Salomon family's social circle was invited. He could not, under the present circumstances, look forward to the daily association with his parents-in-law; he really had nothing more to do here. The agitation he decided to stimulate again, whether with a new manifesto or a series of newspaper articles, he could just as well do, perhaps better, from abroad. And, then, there was Nanny . . . and that other thing, the unforeseen move of his mother to the city.

Yes, he had to travel again. As soon as possible. The very next day he would talk to Jakobe about it. At any rate, it had always been his intention to stay here only provisionally.

He drank up his glass and left. When he had emerged from the café's noise and strong light into the large, empty open spaces, his eyes fell upon the old windmill. He stood in the middle of the marketplace, transfixed by the melancholy mood that hovered over this ghostly remnant of the past—then he walked slowly back to the hotel.

BOOK 6

LUCKY PER,
HIS FIANCÉE

CHAPTER 17

IT WASN'T THAT often that Philip Salomon hosted a real party, but when it happened it was always done in grand style. Ivan—the family's designated master of ceremonies—would prepare, a good while beforehand, a veritable program that he showed his parents for their approval. He always provided for one or another surprise by which he—as he said—"could assure success"—whether it was an especially elegant floral arrangement in the rooms or a novel choice of postprandial sweets, or a cotillion, in case there were plans for dancing. He had made special efforts this time in the hope that the party, in addition to being in honor of the newlyweds' return, could be a celebratory inauguration of Per's great project. He had proposed to light up the garden and shoot off fireworks, to which Philip Salomon, in the meantime, had strongly objected. He had, however, given permission for some Chinese lanterns to be hung in the trees out by the water, which, in his opinion, would have a brilliant effect. Ivan had, as well, kept a great surprise in reserve. He called it the party's "pièce de résistance."

Before the decorating of the rooms was entirely completed and while the family's various members were still in their bedrooms getting dressed, Per appeared. He had forgotten to ask what time the party started and had the misfortune to arrive an hour early. He was already in a very bad mood. When he had returned home last night, he had found a large roll of papers on his table. It was from Max Bernhardt, who had sent back the drafts and calculations he had received from Ivan. In spite of his fatigue and the lateness of the hour, Per had, with a hesitant curiosity, opened the roll to look at the multiple sheets, already yellowing with age, that he had, for so long now, not had in his hands. And soon he became entirely absorbed by them. The whole work that in the last year he had chiefly assumed as a sketchily outlined idea suddenly appeared newly illuminated—all these half-forgotten detailed plans, painstakingly worked out,

of sluice work, bridgeheads, fascine embankments, all this belab-
ored calculation of numbers and labyrinthine diagrams—the
sober sediment of the dreams of his revolutionary years.

What particularly seized him was an almost solemn sense of
surprise. He was impressed with himself. What a fertile conception, what a display of imaginative power! Each new page he
unrolled increased his admiration, but also a crushing perception
of decline. He sat there with the last sheet in front of him,
plunged in dark thought. He pictured his little Nyboder back
room, the bare work cell of his young years, where he had labored
and whistled cheerfully over his drafting board, in spite of the fact
that he hardly had enough money for bread, and there stirred in
him a kind of homesickness for those busy months of indomitable
courage when the trolls of conscience did not bring down, by
night, the castle of happiness he had built up by day, when adversity was only another spur, increasing his defiant satisfaction at
being misunderstood and misjudged. That was a time when, in
spite of hunger, debt, and patched trousers, every day he slept
like a king and woke like a god.

When he again took up the drafts in the morning, the astonishment he had first felt diminished on closer examination. With
the knowledge he had gained during his travels, it was not
difficult for him to find points open to criticism, even plainly
impossible things in them, and that discovery gradually made him
anxious. His self-confidence, which had lately taken so many
nasty hits, grew wobbly. He stayed in his rooms the whole day,
more and more feverish in his eagerness to change the work for
the better. There was, finally, nothing that was immune from his
criticism, and, despite all his efforts, he did not succeed in coming
up with one good conception. Those crawling ants he had always
felt in his head in front of his work or on his fingertips, when
thinking, had completely disappeared. For the first time, impotence took hold of him and awakened a horror that tasted like
death. Impatiently, with a dark expression, he was pacing back
and forth on the terrace in front of the garden room. He really
looked elegant in a modern dress suit with a white satin vest and
an ornate shirtfront on which a pair of diamond studs (a present
from Jakobe) were gleaming. The barbered hair that covered his
head like dark velvet was, after the new European fashion, shaved
at the back of the neck and showed off his muscles. His small
mustache was, in the military style, turned up at the ends, and his

goatee, which had gradually been reduced during his stay abroad, consisted now only of a tiny point under his lip.

Suddenly he heard the rustle of a silk train sweeping into the garden room. When he turned around, Nanny was leaning forward in the doorway and looking around eagerly. She well knew he had come. She had seen him driving up to the gates and had hurried her preparations in order to come down a little before the others. She appeared only fleetingly at the door, signaled to him by an apparently bemused nod, and drew back again immediately, as if she were going to search for something. Per stood there looking after her. She had been so infinitely far from his thoughts that day. After some hesitation, he followed her.

"Are you looking for something? Can I be of help?"

"Oh, thanks, it's nothing," she said, on the verge of leaving but still looking. "It's only my glove studs. But it doesn't matter. I went in to borrow Jakobe's. It seems we have come early," she added after a pause.

"Yes, I came a whole hour too soon."

"Oh, poor thing!" she sympathized as she looked over her bare shoulder.

Per was momentarily irresolute. Then he approached her with a determined step, bowed, and said, with playful courtesy, offering her his arm, "Well, now, as the company starts to gather, I can perhaps dare ask for the honor . . ."

She looked up quickly at him with a shy glance, as if frightened that there would be a concealed hint in his words. Then she spread out her fan with a tired air of resignation, as if she couldn't be bothered with misgivings about all that, took his arm, and said with an averted face, "You're right! Let us act as if we were having fun."

"It doesn't seem as if our gracious lady is in good humor this evening," he said when they had entered the adjoining room, small, white, lacquered, and gilded in rococo style. "Is there something wrong?"

"Nothing at all. I only wish that this disgusting day was over."

"Why?"

"I hate parties."

"Well, that really surprises me. Is this something new?"

"It might well be. But I am not the same person anymore. First you become 'Madam.' Then, before you know it, you are a grandmother."

"Well, you know, the last title of honor doesn't come without a tradition of expected formalities. Shall we sit down?" He had stopped in front of a little silk upholstered sofa and gestured toward it. "Or are you afraid to crumple your dress before the company comes?" he added when she hesitated.

She confused him again by looking at him as if she suspected a bold and hidden meaning in his remark. Without answering, she spread out her dress to the side like a fan and sat down in the corner of the sofa.

"Can you understand," he said, after sitting by her side, "can you really grasp that it is only a week since we separated in Rome?"

"Well, why not?"

"Don't you have a sense that it is a little eternity since we said goodbye to each other that morning . . . you remember . . . at the train station?"

Nanny stared into the air awhile as if entirely uncomprehending, and shook her head decisively. "No—I haven't thought about that!"

"Really not?"

"No—and then it was horrible in Rome, wasn't it?"

"Is that what it seems to you? I couldn't tell you were depressed there."

"You couldn't? That may well be."

"So, in other words, you are happy to be home again?"

"Happy?" Nanny looked off with a kind of bored, resigned shrug. "It seems to me it's dreadful everywhere. And worst of all at home."

Per started to laugh. "You really are impossible today. Who in the world, then—"

"What I wanted to say," she interrupted with a pretense of nervousness, "was that Rome seemed to you exceptionally good, didn't it? You certainly were enthusiastic."

"In a way, yes. But I'll tell you the truth. The city lost not a little of its interest after you—and your husband, of course—left. Therefore a few days later, I did, too." After these words, Nanny was silent and looked down at her fan while a sad smile artfully crept across her face. She slowly lifted her lovely eyes and gave Per one of those soft, telling glances he received as a secret caress.

Per, once again captivated by Nanny, began to feel anxious. And she had tried her utmost to display her beauty that evening with unreserved boldness. She was wearing her favorite color, the glowing golden yellow that went so well with her Oriental complexion and black hair, and, in the Japanese fashion, she had combed her hair straight up from the neck and fastened it on the top of her head with a high tortoiseshell comb. At her bare cleavage, she cradled a couple of large, dark red roses.

Per really had to restrain himself to keep from taking liberties. Nanny noticed that and was on guard—against herself, as well. She knew this game was risky for her, but that no longer troubled her; she only wanted to heighten her pleasurable excitement. She didn't want to believe that there was imminent danger for the time being. If there boiled up in her a moment of intense desire to throw her arms around his neck and kiss his red mouth, she wouldn't dream of actually doing it. For that she held her sense of pride too dear. The thought of seriously being unfaithful to Dyhring was far from her intention. Certainly she had many times been furious at him for his assumed or genuine indifference and, occasionally, was not afraid to tell him that. But she was still too proud of him to want to run the risk of being cast off. Her heart swelled every day with delight to notice how the whole city, from government ministers to nightclub singers, courted his favor, and she had the highest hopes about what she could gain, one day, in her capacity as wife to such a man.

But her continuing game with Per was not entirely without purpose. She could maintain that there was a rational, justifiable basis to it. She knew, from similar occasions, how great a mastery a man could have over her, and she was mindful that if she could succeed in thoroughly seducing him up to the dangerous abyss and then let giddiness seize him, at that very moment, her own infatuation would dissolve. Her desire would be completely satisfied and she could witness his defeat with peace of mind.

They were interrupted by the housekeeper and a maid who had something to arrange in the room. Per moved farther away from her, and they talked for a while about this and that.

Suddenly, with servants still in the room, Nanny exclaimed, "But where can Jakobe be? She certainly knew you had come. And she was almost ready when I was in her room."

Per remained silent. He didn't want to go into that subject.

But Nanny continued: "And you'll be happy to see her. She looks so good in her new dress. Perhaps it was you yourself who chose it for her?"

"I? No," murmured Per reluctantly.

"Oh, that's right. Jakobe must have ordered it before you came back. But she selected it according to your taste. Didn't she tell you about it?"

"No—I don't, in any case, remember that."

"Then it shall be a surprise!"

Per didn't answer. He suddenly became distracted, absent-minded even, while he stared at her with a look all the more telling. The impression of her beautiful body raised in his mind and heart a latent rebellious and pillaging passion. His bad mood as well, his dissatisfaction with himself that he wanted to put off for later reflection, spurred him on to plunge into a new adventure. He was drawn to her as a kind of anesthesia to calm his mind, and he felt that only she could give him the hot and potent potion of oblivion he needed. Every consideration for Jakobe would have to make way. She had herself given him the motto: "If you want the goal, you must also be willing to use the means."

When the servants left, he again moved closer to Nanny. He started, then, to talk about Rome and about their parting, intimately resting a hand on the sofa back behind her. That made her feel the way she did that day on their sightseeing tour over the Janiculum; the unexpectedly bold approach rendered her less sure of herself, and she anxiously moved away.

There was something, as well, in his look that evoked a memory of a dream she had had one night during her journey home from Italy—one of those strange, unpleasant, voluptuous dreams from which she always awakened with a dreadful headache. A few days before, she had visited a zoo and been very taken with a large, flaming yellow tiger. In her dream, it came creeping over the floor to her bed and started to play with her, brushing affectionately against her with its soft coat. Finally, it lay with all its weight on her chest; and, suddenly, she recognized Per's piercing glance in the beast's eyes.

"Can you remember that a rose fell out of your bouquet when the train left?" asked Per. "I picked it up and hid it, and I still have it."

"Good God! Surely it wasn't worth the trouble—"

"That depends. It fell, in any case, from two pretty hands."

Without knowing it, Per had said something that she wanted to hear more than anything. Her hands were her vulnerable point. They were, to be sure, by no means ugly; but she had difficulty hiding from herself that her fingers were too short.

"It seems to me that you should save your compliments for Jakobe," she continued, shifting her seat in a vain attempt to avoid his penetrating gaze.

"But why?" he asked, and rushed on at random. "Is it against the law to say to a beautiful woman that she is beautiful? Should I, perhaps, lie to you, dear sister-in-law, and say I don't consider you the most perfectly beautiful, the most criminally dangerous woman I have met? What good would that do? You know that anyway. Once, I presumed to have vain hopes . . . something you certainly couldn't have avoided knowing. Well, let's not talk about that old painful history. You wouldn't have me, and I had to give up. You were doubtlessly too beautiful for me."

He was afraid, now, that he had heedlessly gone too fast. He seemed—and he was right about this—to have caught a passing gleam of hatred in her eyes, and his ears grew hot at the thought of what could happen if his offense miscarried.

Then he suddenly felt her arms around his neck and a pair of warm lips on his mouth. It only lasted a minute, and before he could collect himself, Nanny had quickly hurried off to a window. There she stood with her back to him, nervously holding a hand on her cheek as if she had received a slap in the face.

At that moment, Ivan's assertive voice was heard in the entrance hall, and, directly afterward, he himself came gliding through the room on his small, busy legs like a mechanical windup toy. With the expression of an army officer ordering his men into battle, he rushed by, closely followed by his staff: a couple of hired waiters in gallooned uniforms and a full-bloused decorator.

But when he looked at Per and Nanny hiding here in this small room outside of the party plan, he stopped for a second.

"The reception is in the salon!" he announced, and glided off again with his helpers, who were grinning to each other behind his back.

Neither Nanny nor Per had moved, but then Per got up, still half bewildered and bemused. At the sound of his steps, she turned around and stopped him with a look that was certainly unhappy and guilty. But she very decisively, even sharply, forbade him to come nearer. And when more voices were heard in the garden room, she seemed, for a moment, to turn white with anxiety as she hurried past him with her head bowed.

She stopped again at the door, looked back, and said in a soft voice, as she held her folded fan up in front of her mouth, "If you dare to say anything to anyone of the liberties you took here—"

"What? . . . Then what, Nanny?" asked Per, who was now simply ablaze.

"Then," she continued with a hypocritical pledge in her lovely eyes, "then—we two can never be good friends."

The voices they had heard were Philip Salomon and his wife, who were going into the garden room, arm in arm. The great, clever money magnate was simply and entirely enchanted by his Lea, who was wearing an expensive, wine-red dress trimmed in elegant lace. But when he saw Per, coming into the room, his smile disappeared. He was remembering the painful commission facing him: to openly announce his daughter's engagement to a man who was, in his eyes, entirely unfit and useless. He had in mind to talk to Per about this already on the previous day, but, after hearing of his exploit at Max Bernhardt's, he could not bring himself to do it. He felt no different now. He couldn't even manage to hold out his hand to his approaching son-in-law, nor did Per's expression invite him to.

Ivan came motoring in again like a toy, this time to convince himself that everything was set. The first carriage had driven up to the door. The small children came hopping out in their white dress clothes; Rosalie, as well, was there, but Jakobe was still missing. A problem with her dress was holding her up. Unaccustomed as she was to fussing with her clothes, her efforts to make the bodice right were badly managed, and finally, in despair, she had to call in the maids to help.

Half of the guests had already arrived when she appeared. Nanny, who had tried to stay near to Per in order to observe his face the moment he saw Jakobe, was greatly anticipating her artfully planted little bomb. Per went suddenly gray with chagrin. Jakobe had had the unfortunate idea of having her dress tailored with a fairly deep décolleté, for which she decidedly did not have the right figure. Her erotic feelings, roused by her impending meeting with the bridegroom, together with certain happy memories of their love-holiday, had led her to this folly. She hit Per, here, in his most sensitive point. He noticed that a couple of gentlemen were smiling when she came in, and he didn't want to turn toward her.

In the meantime, the guests started streaming into the large entrance hall, where ladies' maids and hired servants were busy helping people with their coats. Carriage after carriage drove up to the carpeted steps, while out on the beach path a long line of elegant equipages and rented coaches formed, which, bit by bit, with endless halts, moved toward the villa. In the end, about a hundred people gathered in the garden room and two adjoining rooms. Naturally, most represented the financial world, evidenced by the value of the ladies' jewels, but there were also university professors, doctors, artists, and writers.

Most of the very young ladies arrived in ball dresses because they knew there was to be dancing. Several of the older ones, especially among the Jewish ladies, had shamelessly let their seamstresses reveal as much of their beauty as the occasion and the time's fashions permitted.

As to the members, all invited, of the failed free port consortium, most sent excuses, something Ivan expected after yesterday's events. Only the "erstwhile farmer," Herr Nørrehave, appeared, and his rustic attire—a thick gold neck chain and double-soled boots—proved quite remarkable in the elegant gathering. Ivan, who, by chance, had seen him driving up in his carriage together with the Copenhagen social lion, the lawyer Hasselager, was taken aback by that partnership and wondered whether the two had plans for Per. He remembered that Herr Nørrehave, at yesterday's meeting, had shown some displeasure with the cool conclusion of the discussion; and, as for the lawyer Hasselager, since he belonged to the group of young, fiery, aspiring businessmen who had adopted Max Bernhardt as their model, it wouldn't be surprising that he should feel tempted to go through with what the master had to drop.

Among the family's usual guests, the so-called Sunday visitors, were Aron Israel and, towering over all the others, Balling, literary historian, citation sponge, who, like the biblical lean cow, devoured his colleagues without becoming fatter. Aron Israel had placed his little, nervous body in a corner, where his many friends immediately found him anyway. Balling, on the other hand, had placed himself in a conspicuous spot in a doorway, but despite his fantastic height and his interesting, sickly pallor, he had here, as on the literary scene, the misfortune of remaining entirely unnoticed. Even Rosalie, the small, slight, not yet sixteen-year-old girl who already dressed like a woman and was honored by his courtship, walked past him, arm in arm with a girlfriend, not noticing him, though in most situations, she made good use of her eyes. Per had gradually become the subject of a great deal of attention, more than he liked. His erect, tanned physique made a good impression here among the many wintry faces of the sedentary stay-at-homes and office shut-ins. Most well knew how he stood in the Salomon house, though many of those present were seeing him for the first time. Those among them who had heard something of him, and might have known of his book, were surprised by his youth. They had imagined he was more a poetic type and were amazed to meet a man who had the look of a pioneer and herald of the future.

But no one in the company attracted more attention than Dr. Nathan. He was standing outside on the terrace, surrounded by a flock of admiring women and men who were all laughing and talking loudly. He was being asked his opinion of a newly published book that had stirred some notice, a long poem called *Wrestling with the Angel*. The poem's author was Povl Berger, the young poet with the ugly face who had once been a frequent guest in the house and one of Nanny's many unsuccessful suitors. He had, up until now, belonged to the circle of free thinkers who gathered around Dr. Nathan and sought the protection of his authority. His poetry had displayed a linguistic elegance that recalled Enevoldsen himself, but, as well, an unearthly, spectral absence of voice. He had learned from that master to wait patiently and polish a rhyme, fuss over an adjective; and, in a series of very small books that, year after year, had become thinner and more anemic, he had continually repeated the sad story of his youth in the form of a poem, whose tone swayed limply between whining and a forced titanic defiance.

A year ago, he had published a book that even his friends and patrons could not praise, and that was more than the titan could bear. He suddenly disappeared from Copenhagen, and for a long time no one heard anything from him. But one fine day, it was rumored that he had hidden himself in a little Jutland town where he lived like a hermit in a shabby room, far from the world and occupied only with pondering his fate. From there, he had also sent out his startling book in which he had directly, in a preface, rebuked his rebellious past and explained that, after a long spiritual struggle, he had found peace and happiness in suppliant Christian humility.

While his former friends had little faith in the sincerity of his conversion, Nathan maintained that that kind of religiosity derived from an offended literary vanity, vindictiveness, and unsatisfied sexuality, but could, certainly, still be genuine. In fact, in his opinion, this genesis of that conversion was typical and he cheerfully tried to prove it by dragging out a series of illustrative examples gathered from confessions of the most famous church fathers, right down to Grundtvig.

Further, the poetry clearly showed signs of that breakthrough the poet, as well as the man, had experienced. Every page of the bulky book testified to his spiritual passion, to a newly minted strength and depth of feeling that found expression in a careful and authoritative art. In the dozen poems of his collection, there was a series of moody scenes of the empty and dreary Jutland landscape and the colorless life of the people. And though they were done in such a way that reality, outwardly rendered, seemed natural on the surface, a kind of light from an invisible world behind it was shining through. That was, for everyone, the remarkable and surprising thing. Until now, he had fingered his soul so crudely. But now, when he had regained his childhood faith, he found his personal tone and his poems were marked by a manly strength of heart, a voice like rich, dark ore, from the deep—from the underworld.

There was movement in the rooms. The doors to the dining room were opened, and the company began to take their seats at the table.

Directly before the company went to eat, Philip Salomon had let Per know through Ivan that he considered this occasion to be fitting for the announcement of the engagement. He had spoken to Jakobe at the same time, and, when she didn't answer, he assumed her silence to be a self-evident consent. In truth, she had heard nothing. She had thoughts for one thing only: to discover the cause of Per's change of behavior toward her. It wasn't long before she was on the right path.

Although Per was partaking freely of the wine, he didn't succeed in hiding his anxiety. Nanny sat across from him and was amusing herself in a carefree manner with another man. Natur-ally, she had her husband as her dinner partner, but she had arranged to get one of her former suitors, the cavalry lieutenant, now the insurance agent, Hansen Iversen, on her other side. She was flirting with the latter now. On and off she laid her head amorously on her husband's shoulder with the clear intention of keeping him indemnified. Dyhring, apparently, did not feel aggrieved, and answered her tender gestures with a gracious glance.

It was not because he was as deluded as she thought, but because he was fairly certain that she would not misuse her freedom to secretly transgress the limits of what he would allow. When he had come to know her nature and character more thoroughly and, especially, after he had cleverly stirred her ambition by picturing a perspective of the future for her that climaxed in the court itself, he felt convinced that she would guard against even the mere appearance of scandal. However much temptation there might be for her, it would go the way it did in the shops she continuously visited, where she sensuously fingered one thing or another that roused her pleasure. She would inevitably let the enticement lie as soon as it became a question of paying for it herself.

Not once did she look over to Per. He sat waiting in vain for a secret glance. He was and remained mere air to her. The notion that her preoccupation with the lieutenant could be dissimulation—a blind—he could certainly entertain, but he really felt outraged at her seemingly guileless gaiety.

Then something else occurred. Immediately after Philip Salomon had toasted the newlyweds, he asked for silence to announce the engagement. He made it as short as possible, but nevertheless, and despite the fact that most of the guests already knew, his words stirred a lively commotion around the table.

Per rose, with his glass in hand, to receive the company's congratulations, and, while the air around him suddenly was filled with his name, he couldn't help thinking that it was not for his sake that he was being toasted, but for Jakobe's future husband and Philip Salomon's future son-in-law. That thought oppressed his Sidenian pride and did not dispose him more favorably toward the whole gathering.

Though he wasn't altogether conscious of it, he had never so strongly as now reckoned his family's hereditary aversion to this kind of worldly, open, happy, unconstrainedly rejoicing society that called itself superior. The hundred-voiced conversation in which every individual joined, in some instances in foreign tongues, sounded like a concert of parrots. The time was long past when he, as a country boy, let himself be dazzled by that rich man's league. He became more and more ill-tempered about everything: the table's elegant floral arrangement that must have cost many hundreds of kroner, the heavy silver candlesticks and the rest of the beautifully crafted table service brought out for the occasion, the uniformed servants and the incessant change of plates—all, merely, in his eyes, ostentations of the Jewish need to show off.

Unnerved by Nanny's laughter, which seemed to get more and more exuberant through all the noise, he finally said straight out to Jakobe that he found the whole party showy and stupid. Jakobe did not answer. From the moment her suspicion of her sister was roused, she had not talked to him at all. Nanny's apparent interest in the former lieutenant did not deceive her. She knew her sister, and that her enjoyment consisted of games of flirtation chiefly to make her suitors jealous. She also was aware that Nanny, from a certain cowardly fear of being overpowered by her feelings in dangerous situations, always sought cover in the admiration of other men.

She did not conclude that things had gone as far as they really had between Per and Nanny, but she had no illusion that sisterly concern about her feelings would apply. She imagined that it would give much pleasure to Nanny to entangle her fiancé in her seductive yarn. And she understood, now, that it was triumph she had read in Nanny's eyes on her homecoming when she began to talk about her meeting with Per abroad. There was no way Jakobe would air all this; she would bravely carry through the role of the happy bride. Since childhood, her sickness had trained her to exercise an almost superhuman capacity for self-control. Although she saw and heard everything as through a fog and had the sense, the whole time, that she was on a rolling ship, there was nothing so different about the way she looked except that she was a little paler than usual and seemed a bit tired.

It was only with Per that she could not dissimulate. Every time he said something to her, she turned her head away. She almost couldn't stand to hear his voice. Even when his arm touched hers, a shiver went through her. Fortunately, for the time being, there was no leisure for thinking. Every minute she was torn away from her dawning doubts, as friends and acquaintances wanted to drink to her and her fiancé. Among them was Nanny, who wished to toast them; she looked at Per, on that occasion, for the first time. With an openness that chilled his spine, she nodded and smiled at them both over her lifted glass. "Skål, dear brother-in-law. Skål, Jakobe!" She really is too shameless, thought Per. He was blushing and could not bear to meet her gaze.

On the other hand, without drinking, Jakobe, apparently calm, moved her glass to her mouth. She forced herself to return her nod, to avoid seeing again the triumph in her sister's eyes.

Meanwhile, Per and his future projects became a general sub-ject of conversation at the table—at any rate, among those who were not sitting in his immediate vicinity. The ladies were very busy observing the house's new son-in-law, and Per's stern and dark expression, the measured way with which he received the friendliest invitations to drink up together, heightened, in many, the respect previously awakened by his manly appearance.

"Yes, these Sideniuses are characters!" said someone near Philip Salomon, a comment he seemed not to hear, despite the fact that it was especially said for his ears. However, the remark made a certain impression on another man—older, with a pro-nounced stoop, and a gray beard—among the guests at the upper part of the table. It was the well-known titular councilor of state, Erichsen, one of the city's wealthy men—perhaps, even, the wealthiest—and a philanthropist on a grand scale. Already, before dinner, the attorney Hasselager had talked to him about Per and tried to interest him in the project Erichsen had only heard of. Now, with a searching look, he was paying close attention to everything said around the table about the young man and his well-respected family.

At the end of the meal, Philip Salomon tapped his glass for silence for the third time, but not—as he explained immediately in the midst of the social gaiety—to again give away a daughter. He wanted, instead, to propose a toast to Dr. Nathan and to wel-come him back from his long stay abroad that, fortunately, could only have bound him closer to his country and its youth. Glasses were lifted with great enthusiasm. Many of the guests, including women, got up from their places and gathered around the doctor to touch glasses with him. "He has not changed at all since we last saw him" was heard around the table.

"Well, his hair is beginning to lose its color."

"But he still doesn't look old."

How did he really look, that very celebrated and censured man, who was more energetic and purposeful than anyone in the

service of clearing a path for Denmark's future and of stirring in
the land a great revolution of heart and mind scarcely paralleled
since the Reformation? He was small of stature and deemed ugly
by most—in any case, quite anomalous. But it would be difficult
to judge that, because he was always in motion, with an endlessly shifting expression that reflected his inner emotions; a
spontaneous, convulsive play of his features was becoming almost
deliberately exaggerated with the years. His face was most
attractive when he was listening, exhibiting all that was best in
him: his thirst for knowledge, an insatiable intellectual delight,
even lust.

This didn't happen very often in general social conversation,
since he decidedly preferred to talk. He possessed a counter-
weight to his unlimited absorptive mind—an urge to communicate, that, even with his graying years, was as strong as that of a
young girl; his tone could become a little gossipy and not entirely
free of malice.

His liberal liveliness had contributed more than he himself
realized to the resistance and reluctance with which he was
received. It had, time after time, alienated friends and natural
fellow travelers because it offended their conception of
Scandinavian-Germanic virile values. His disposition was so
entirely estranged, so unreconciled with the national Danish
character, that he inevitably had to insult it, all the more since, in
blatant contrast to the Jewish writers who had appeared before
him in Danish literature, he tried neither to adjust his incom-
patible character to his surroundings nor to make himself
interesting by setting himself up with a pharisaical: "What have
I to do with you?"

He had never doubted his right to speak. He had very early
felt himself called upon to play a special role in the nation, and
that, precisely on the grounds of his origin as an outsider, allowed
him to observe the life of his country from a distance and judge
it without prejudice.

His education, as well, was not of the usual Dano-Germanic
kind. His Romance culture and a predilection for French
refinement that he, as a young man, advertised by a certain outer
elegance made him immediately suspect among his countrymen,
to say nothing of the intellectual circles. In truth, he met his
bitterest resistance within the walls of his own university. With
his attractive and well-groomed hair, and his always snow-white

shirtfront, his whole neat and trim appearance was so perfect that the old theology professors thought him a charlatan.

Still, all this was not sufficient to explain the extraordinary effect his appearance made. He certainly possessed glittering talents, but was not what is generally understood as a "genius." He did not have a creative intellect, or an inventive imagination. Compared with original thinkers like Grundtvig or Kierkegaard, he seemed to lack the deeper attributes. He had been too impatient to incubate an independent, universal perspective, too taken up with life's claims and joys to spin a sticky, tenacious, secret spider web out of his own personal passion by which even minds poorer in gifts could discover and develop more or less unique designs.

With his restless appetite, he could better be compared to a golden worker bee that in sun and storm sorts through all the intellectual fields of flower and faithfully returns to the hive with honey hidden in its stinger. As with a hundred eyes he flew over the literature of all lands and times, buzzed down with an unerring instinct on everything in the world that could serve to stimulate those at home, and mixed up, with the most ingenious art and energy, sometimes with bitter, sometimes sweet spices, a special life-giving nectar for the Danish youth. He understood how to unroll and turn on its sides the whole of a period's intellectual history in a way that seemed to give it the vigor of a vivid drama. He illuminated the darkest of philosophy's secret passages by sending out from his mind a few, charged lightning bolts that could galvanize even the dullest brain into a sense of what he was talking about.

A deeper secret was hidden behind this synthesizing art and its unique power over the minds of the young. Not only were they immediately captivated, but they reached out to him because of a characteristic of the Danish people that could never be exhausted and that Nathan himself energetically battled against: indolence. Never before had the young students in Denmark been able to seize upon knowledge in such an easy and entertaining way. While stretched out on the sofa, a long pipe in the mouth, they could envisage the great personages vividly stride past and the contents of their work presented with such emphatic lucidity that, afterward, it felt as if they themselves had read and thought through the books and they could consider it entirely unnecessary to really do it.

Nathan's judgments and viewpoints were learned without qualification because they were absorbed as one's own. His readers filled themselves with his purely personal feelings and dispositions, sucked up his hot, Oriental sympathies and antipathies in the conviction that they had been magically enriched. Never had so much boldness and enthusiasm for freedom fermented among the young university students. Even the most thickblooded and provincial among them were intoxicated with the urge to live heroically a life of achievement when, after a few hours of reading Nathan's writings, they bounded off the sofa to pack a new pipe full.

This sense of excitement didn't, for the most part, last that long, and, in many instances, a later recoil was the most powerful effect. Povl Berger was far from the only one for whom Nathan's baptism of fire was a preparation for a religious rebirth. How could it be otherwise? Where a spiritual life was awakened and seriously, deeply, pursued, there was no cultivated soil to take root in other than theology. What there was of culture in the people virtually derived exclusively from the church. And, once past the surface, there remained only the medieval or the void.

In an ironic way, the extent of Nathan's influence could be provisionally measured best by his enemies. He had really been able to awaken an active passion in them, a dedicated fervor he had all too often sought in vain to inspire in his sympathizers. If the religious reaction was not so noticeable in Copenhagen, where interest was consumed by the stir of newly created businesses, in the provinces, especially in the country, it grew with quiet strength and centered itself around the parsonages and folk high schools like an army around a fortress.

After the company had risen from the table, Per and Jakobe held court in a corner of the garden room where the large crystal chandelier was lit. Among the first to come up to greet them and press Per's hand was Herr Nørrehave, "erstwhile farmer"; with his all too naive burr of the *r*, this canny Jutlander was expressing his extraordinary regret about what had happened the day before at Max Bernhardt's, and that he had not agreed with that "opinion of the situation."

Per was only half listening. His attention had turned to Nanny, who was standing at the other end of the room flirting with a circle of fawning philanderers. Although he was almost determined to let her sail on her own turbid sea, he couldn't keep his eyes off her. He saw how Lieutenant Hansen Iversen, who had been out in the hall fetching her ermine wrap, laid it with lingering tenderness on her shoulders, and how, when he wanted to fasten it under her chin as well, she would not permit it and slapped him on the fingers. But immediately afterward, she dauntlessly took his proffered arm and walked off with him through the room and out into the garden, where some of the young guests had already retreated to the Norwegian garden house to drink their coffee.

Herr Nørrehave was, in the meantime, still chatting, and Per realized that it was his intention to talk to him about the events of yesterday and to learn what new plans he had for the future of his project. In order not to betray that, in fact, he had nothing new, Per became more taciturn and reserved, which only heightened the curiosity of the Jutlander and made him more eager to reach an understanding with him.

Finally, Nørrehave drew back, but was immediately replaced by another, who detached himself from the congratulatory group encircling Jakobe. It was Aron Israel, the little, timorous, and awkward scholar with a naive appreciation for everything he did not understand, especially in the realm of practical activity. He had been part of the circle around Per, awaiting a moment when he could come up to greet him without getting in anyone's way. When at last he could grasp Per's hand, he did not want to miss his chance, and went on to press it warmly between both of his. "And may I use this occasion, Herr Sidenius, to express to you my sincere thanks for your little book of last winter. It was a dynamite bomb—a terrorist explosion . . . but in the *service* of mankind. I well know it can have little interest for you to hear what I—completely ignorant—think of your book, but I can't keep from telling you that, despite its very fierce message, which certainly shook things up a bit, it made me very happy."

Per looked down at the little man uncertainly. He was not, to be sure, the only one of the guests who had talked to him about his book and told him agreeable things about it. But while Per had considered the other words of praise simple, courteous compliments, he could not easily doubt Aron Israel's sincerity. He had heard too much about the quiet scholar's enthusiastic passion for truth and his struggle in the name of the ideal. This wasn't, as well, the first time he had showed his partisanship toward him and his ideas for the future.

Per answered, and this was true, that he was surprised his book had come to his attention. It had not, after all, received much notice. The press had not talked about it, and all the Copenhagen newspapers, on the same day the book came out, seemed very concerned only about a plan for a future relocation of the Tivoli.

"I noticed that," said Aron Israel. "And I was torn by the desire to write you. It seemed to me that you should not remain ignorant of the fact that there were people here who were made enthusiastic and edified by your proud and bold faith in the possibilities for mankind's development and your visionary sense of the future, the taming of nature. Yes . . . I use those words purposely. In my opinion, your book belongs to the true works of enlightenment; it was, to me, like a breath of spring—a little dizzying but fresh and salutary, like ocean air. I hope your nature gospel will be taken straight to the heart by our dear youth here at home, who blindly disregard real knowledge, and, probably, that is why they are so pitifully dispirited in the face of life." Per was blushing and gently withdrew his hand. That was always the way with him. Despite all his bumptious conceit—all his ardent hopes for praise and glory—as soon as someone took serious notice of him, he became self-conscious. He also had, for the moment, a natural reluctance to go too deeply into these things and tried, therefore, to turn the conversation in another direction.

But Aron Israel was too interested in the subject. He began to talk about Nathan, to whose critical activity Per had alluded in one place in his book with some of the disdain for all aesthetes he had still harbored when he wrote it. Aron Israel said that, in spite of the almost unlimited admiration he had for that man, he could concede that his lack of knowledge of natural and technical science was something to lament and could be of fateful significance for that part of Danish youth whose educator he had been. "It would, undeniably, have been more beneficial if his mission had appealed to more active men and fewer beautiful souls. Here was doubtlessly a neglect to make up for, and to accomplish this task—perhaps the greatest one of our time—it seems the author of *The State of the Future*, and I say this without any flattery, possesses the outstanding qualities that are necessary. The youngest generation has clearly been waiting for its herald and future leader. It is on the watch for the chosen one, the royal prince. The throne is empty."

He had to stop. Suddenly the whole room grew quiet as a dark-maned gentleman seated himself at the big piano and played a few chords, while Ivan, his face shining like a freshly minted twenty-krone coin, led a tall, full-bosomed lady to the side of the pianist.

This was the unveiling of the big surprise Ivan called *"le clou."* The lady, a famous singer from the royal stage, had the kindness to accept an invitation to the party and, for a generous compensation, to sing two lieder and a *da capo* number after dinner—a favor that, until now, was granted only to a few very highly placed and well-to-do aristocratic families.

Per, who had no ear at all for music, tried to leave. He noticed how some other gentlemen, lured by the peace of the smoking room, successfully slipped off along the walls. Unfortunately, he had too far to go to get to the door, and was forced to stop, when he got near, by a theatrical shriek that resounded throughout the room, immediately followed by a dying pianissimo.

He did not heed the song, however, because Aron Israel's words buzzed in his ears and made him strangely giddy. Was it not Providence that he should receive that kind of enthusiastic confidence just now when he was beginning to lose faith that he was specially called out? A shiver went through him when the strange little man, in his prophetic way, told him of the "empty royal throne." These words recalled the proudest hope of his youth—that he had, for a long time, given up—and they rushed into his heart like a scared eagle back to its nest. He chased away his thoughts when the song stopped and applause, led by Ivan, rippled through the room like a shower of hail.

Then he thought about Nanny, who still had not come back with her escort. She's still amusing herself, he said to himself, and a nasty desire seized him to go out to the garden to discover what they were doing, alone and in the dark.

At the door, he bumped into Uncle Heinrich. The old man of the world had had his hair curled for the occasion, and shamelessly showed off his large, false, brilliant pin that gleamed on his shirtfront like a royal badge. Per wanted to go past him. Since his return, he had, as much as possible, avoided the bad demon of the Salomon house, who continually had the air of being his patron and whose jesting liberties Per had put up with during his courtship because he feared his poison tongue.

The uncle, in the meantime, stopped him and drew him aside with a mysterious look. "One word in passing, my dear friend! But, first, my most respectful compliments. It seems to be going excellently this evening."

"What do you mean?" asked Per, unable to hide his impatience.

"I beg your pardon? No . . . you're playing out a comedy for me, too. You can spare yourself, good friend; I know you, by God, all too well. But don't be embarrassed. Just stay in your role—that's the best thing, perhaps. Your serious mask makes a grand impression, I can tell you. 'Herr Gott von Mannheim'! How I am amusing myself. People talk about you as if you were a kind of he-man. Isn't that comical? Stay that way, by all means. Only go further. Lead them all by their long noses; blow snuff in their eyes; slash and burn so I can have a little glory from you."

Per looked down at the hateful little man with an expression of disgust. He was obviously a little drunk, and his half-lidded lizard eyes positively shot forth malice. The sham director was never more furious than when there was company in his brother-in-law's house, because none of the guests paid any attention to him. The moneymen, especially, were patently contemptuous. "What nonsense you are talking," said Per. "If you have something to say to me, out with it!"

"Your most obedient servant! Do you know you remind me of a play I once saw here in the Royal Theatre—a stupid play, of course—a fashionable chivalric romance in verse and all twaddle. A young man comes forth, a good-for-nothing, a country clod, with whom everyone falls in love whenever he appears. All the women hang on his neck, and the king himself becomes so delirious with admiration that he appoints him to a minister's post. And all that happened with the help of a *kleines Ding* he kept hidden on his body that had some magic power, obviously. The charm lent him beauty in the eyes of everyone. I dare say, haven't *you* inherited the ring, sweet sir? What do you think? You came back from your trip and immediately created a scandal, so everyone is ashamed of you. Yet, today, you are no less fortunate, this evening's hero, a great success! And you, sir, find it all very natural!"

Per thought, I would like to shut his jaw up. Instead, he had a more delightful fancy: No, let him keep up his banter. He could be my court jester, whose pure malice could spice things up now and then during a dead hour in life's blustering masquerade.

He placed his hands magnanimously on the simian man's padded shoulders and said, "Let's leave it at that, venerable Uncle. If you have anything else to say to me, come out with it. Don't keep me here if it's not necessary."

"Well, then, hear this. Do you know that a new consortium is being contemplated in your name? You see the fat farmer who is here this evening stinking the place up with his sour, greased boots—his name is Nørrehave. I saw him talking to you before. Didn't you notice anything?"

"No, nothing special."

"Well, all right. But it's still as I say it is. He and that tall humbug, Hasselager—the lawyer—have their antennae extended. I saw it—they were standing there talking to that buffoon, the titular councilor of state, Erichsen, with the mug of an ox, whom everyone makes such a fuss about and calls a man of honor and a patriot because he has a way of getting himself to cry as soon as anyone screams out sentiments about the Fatherland, national redress, and the cultivation of the Danish spirit. I immediately surmised that it was you they were discussing, and I stayed near them to overhear a bit. I think the fish was biting. The councilor listened to the gentlemen very carefully and looked completely witless. Now, I warn you, don't do anything stupid again. Seize the moment and hammer down the nails. Such a favorable opportunity probably won't come soon again."

Per was quiet for a while. He didn't invest a lot of confidence in the significance of the other's observations. But, excited as he was after his conversation with Aron Israel, the uncle's words did make an impression on him. "Was that all you wanted to tell me?" he asked.

"No."

"There's more?"

"Yes—but you certainly won't be able to guess what it is," he said, screwing up his eyes and pausing for a moment to provoke Per's curiosity. "When I was walking on Vimmelskaftet this morning, I met—who do you think?—Colonel Bjerregrav." At the sound of the name, Per felt a spasm go through his body.

"So you talked to him, I suppose."

"Naturally."

"Did you, perhaps, tell him what happened yesterday at Max Bernhardt's?"

"Of course."

"Well, what did he say about it?"

"He already knew of it."

"Oh, from whom?"

"He didn't say, but I have since guessed. He let fall a word about Nørrehave and asked me—a bit surreptitiously—whether I knew something about him and what kind of a person he was. The *schlauer Fuchs* had already been with him yesterday and had talked with him. I tell you, the colonel knew everything about what had happened at Max's, and you better believe that he was very impressed with you. God strike me if he didn't downright gloat that you had dared to rebuff Max. He said he would like to see 'all our young Jewish rebels hang—so God bless him for that.' His eyes fairly shone. 'I take my hat off to the fellow' . . . and I understood what he intended to say. He wanted me to tell you afterward. He wants to make up with you, do you understand? He still hopes for a reconciliation! 'That's a man after my own heart,' he said. 'There goes our sound Danish youth that wants a seat at the table and will chase off all the foreign brood that has given itself airs in our land!' Those were exactly his words. Comical, isn't it? Amazing!"

Per was lost in his own thoughts and didn't respond.

"So don't I have a reason to call you a lucky dog? The more stupidities you do, the more success you have." Some people standing by were trying to shush him. The songstress had taken up a new sheet of music, and the room had, again, become as still as a church. Per turned away and slipped out. Slowly he went through the small room and into the front hall. The doors stood open to the library and the billiard room behind it, serving as smoking rooms. A dense cigar smoke spread out from the front room, where some loud gentlemen were having a lively debate. Per couldn't see them from the hall, but their voices drowned out the music from the main room. He stopped short a few steps before the door when he heard his name mentioned; he stood there motionless with burning cheeks and a beating heart. The argument was about him, about his project that had set all their passions in motion. Two of the men were talking at once, one saying that, for the sake of the country, Copenhagen's interests should not be challenged, whereas the other, with a stronger voice, answered that for him it was just this new and appealingly progressive thought that could decidedly break through the conventionality that had done irreparable damage, given our location, by pushing us farther than was necessary from the central business of Europe.

Per did not want to hear more. He circumspectly turned away and went back to the small, empty room. There he stood for some time by an open window that looked out on the road, woods, and the still faintly colored evening sky.

So, now his time had come! It occurred to him (and he smiled with self-irony) that this moment was actually in line with his old calculations, if he merely took account of the likely effect of what had happened today. With the announcement of his engagement, his luck had been sealed. He now had the right to fame's golden crown of thorns.

In the living room, a new hailstorm of applause broke loose, after which the company dispersed into the other rooms. Per's head was heavy from the overheated, perfume-saturated atmosphere, and he had no desire to be swallowed up by the swarm. With a quick decision, he turned back to the hall, found his hat and coat on one of the rows of wardrobe pegs, and went out onto the road. It was a mild summer evening. He looked out at the woods on one side, and, on the other, the Sound covered by a smoky fog. He stopped a few times to breathe deeply the dew-filled air that refreshed and cleansed his whole body. He held his hat still in his hand and had thrown his long overcoat loosely over his shoulder so it hung down like an artist's cape. It now depended, he thought, on his getting serious about carrying through his work on the project. He would succeed in fixing the mistakes. The despair that had filled him in relation to it just that morning could be ascribed to indisposition. The next day, it would go better.

At the turn of the road, when he came very near the water, he stopped again. The Sound's whole expanse spread out between the receding coastlines, overarched by an almost cloudless sky. He stood still for several minutes and listened to the soft splash of the water along the beach. As on that evening after his homecoming when he had stood there below Skovbakken together with Jakobe, he was moved by the strange way that monotonous reverberation in the deep stillness became eternity's intimate voice in his ears.

The stars, as well, seemed so wonderfully alive to him. One little bright star was shining over the island Hveen; it blinked so familiarly it seemed to be trying to remind him of something. "Don't you remember me?" it asked. "Aren't you reminded of that time—long, long ago—and far from here . . ."

A pair of carriages with departing guests brought him back to reality. An illuminated phenomenon that, at first, surprised, then almost frightened him was out here on the beach. He quickly realized that Ivan's Chinese lanterns, reflected in the smooth water, created a shining row of columns of light. A little higher up, he dimly saw the fully lit villa itself through the garden's dark trees. The whole sense of it in the still evening had a fantastic effect, as if it were a gleaming fairy palace.

Just then, he remembered that he had had it in mind to spy on Nanny and her lieutenant out in the garden. He had really completely forgotten her and was not at all sad about it. "Let him have her!" he said, and with these words he irrevocably and entirely took leave of Nanny and that love adventure. Here, face-to-face with the endless space, mankind's tireless games of love tag seemed deeply disagreeable, even filling him with disgust.

He went farther along the road, past a place from where he heard music, and automatically stopped to look over the high hawthorn bushes that fenced off the road. He saw a little house with a thatched roof and an old garden where some young women and men were playfully rushing around. Obviously a party going on. He contrasted the personality of this group with the one he had left. The ladies here were all brightly dressed; but in their choice of clothes, they showed no sign of the influence of European liberality, and the game they were playing was the good old child's game of hide-and-seek. A student had just placed himself under a tree with his white hat in front of his face and had begun to count while the others scurried around over the lawn and garden paths to hide behind the bushes. Through the open house door could be seen a half-cleared family table and a pair of older, tobacco-smoking gentlemen, one with a skull cap—a complete picture of country simplicity and coziness. The music that had stopped him was coming from there—thin, off-tune piano notes from one of those aged instruments his sister Signe played at home in the parsonage and that he could never hear without being moved.

Two young girls with their arms around each other's waist

came out from the courtyard behind the house and stopped on the steps in front of the garden door, where, in a romantic attitude, they began to gaze at the starry heaven. Some breathless ladies who had been playing the game sat with them; gradually, they formed a cluster of white-dressed figures looking up at the heavens and fanning themselves with their handkerchiefs.

"Maybe we'll see a falling star," said one.

"What do you want to wish?" asked another.

"I won't say in front of the whole world."

"Won't you confide in me, Frøken Jensen?" asked the student, who, together with the other gentlemen, had settled down on the lawn opposite the group.

"I don't know—well, maybe—if you will promise not to say anything about it to anyone."

"I swear it!" he cried out, and laid his hand on his heart.

"What are you wishing?"

"I wish I won't burn the porridge tomorrow morning." Hilarity and clapping from the gathering.

Then someone asked, "Can we have a song?"

"Yes, sing, dear children," said an older woman who had come out from the door opening. "And, meanwhile, we'll set out the dessert."

Without his knowledge, Per himself was being watched by one of the solitary couples still moving around the garden. A man suddenly popped up in front of him on the other side of the hedge, lifted his hat with an ironic courtesy, and asked whether he was waiting for someone. Per slipped away, but after a couple of hundred steps, he stopped again and listened. The company had begun to sing in the garden, and he recognized both the words and the melody—it was one of the main evening songs his siblings used to sing outdoors in the summer:

> Peace reigns over all the earth
> No sound in all the land.
> The moon now smiles in cloudy mirth
> And stars blink in a band.

He listened and held his breath. Never before, it seemed to him, had he heard so many beautiful voices. The evening's deep peace added to that. Despite his distance, every word of the song rang remarkably clear and rich in his ears. There was something almost supernatural in it. The song seemed to rise up directly out of the earth around him from the naked fields—a chorus from the underworld:

> The shining, peaceful, spreading sea
> Holds heaven in its embrace.
> The watchman far upon the lea
> Praises the Lord's sweet grace.

He closed his eyes, and a dull pain shot through him. The sound of these notes awakened a weeping echo in the hidden depths of his soul:

> The night has brought a hushed surcease
> Of pain in all the earth.
> O restless heart may you find peace
> Great calm, and, then, rebirth.

At Skovbakken the dance was beginning. For the time being, it was mostly the young guests who had the courage to move so energetically after the heavy dinner. The older folk distributed themselves through the room or sat as witnesses along the walls. The general mood, which, after the concert, had threatened, for a moment, to ebb, had again livened up when the dance music started playing and strong drinks were served in the smoking rooms. On his way to the dancing, Dr. Nathan came rushing in through a side room with two of the evening's youngest and prettiest ladies on his arm. In no circumstance was this remarkable man more amazing, perhaps, than in good company. However long his workday or night had been—and the lamp in his study often burned all the way to the dawn—he did not become irritable, but leapt into the entertainment, always with a young, springing step and accentuated vigor. He never had to be artificially stimulated. However much his sincere and deep disdain for mankind had grown during the last years of intellectual warfare, it had never gotten the better of his life force. A brightly lit party room, pretty women, laughter, and flowers kept him going. Whenever and wherever he would be seen, he would always be busy talking, explaining, and persuading.

In social life as in his literary work, he was a conqueror and an enchanter, but with all his bold provocation, he really cared

about what people thought of him. Even the most insignificant
young student's opinion, in this respect, mattered. In his writings, he could often speak jokingly about life as a masquerade,
but when he confronted it, it still had power over him. Even in
its least attractive form he could not resist it, so indomitable, so
excessively rich was the essential nature of this man of the capital,
born in the heart of the city, growing up on its sidewalks, and,
like the southern cactus, flaming into bloom out of the rocky
ground.

It was just this radiant absorption with life that made him such
a curious phenomenon in a dull, provincial country like
Denmark. Where all kinds of instruments were heard, from the
bassoons of the court to the trumpets of country fairs to the pious
play of the church bells, he sounded his natural notes that at once
attracted and disturbed in the midst of the time's literary concert.
Hurrying, despite one leg lightly limping, onto the dance floor
with his two blushing young women on his arms, his gray and
goateed form was a living model of what he represented to the
youth of the times: a Pan of the wide woods who, with his magic
flute, had lured the dispirited out to the waters of rejuvenated life
and the parish prisoners of Denmark to the dance.

Among the many spectators in the room was Jakobe. She
remained seated there because the music and general noise of the
dance did her good by keeping her from thinking. At her side sat
Balling, who was talking about Povl Berger. She was not listening
to him, but looking around the room for Per. She couldn't find
him anywhere, whereas Nanny's gold-yellow form continually
appeared among the dancers. She thought he had settled in the
smoking rooms and only wished he would stay there. She was
anxious that he might come in and ask her to dance, and she
did not trust herself to keep cool if he should try such a
rapprochement.

The tall literary scholar did not notice how distraught she was.
He himself, as always, was distracted and stopped short several
times in his comments, turning a donkey ear first to one side,
then to the other, to catch something of what his neighbors were
talking about. Balling was one of the original good-natured
young Danes who sprang up, under Nathan's influence, like lions
hungry for battle, but who later recognized their mistake without
being able to admit it—still less, like Povl Berger, to achieve
a Judas celebrity in the enemy's camp. He was among the

conquering army of pale scholars who, out of fear, still followed the flag, while in their hearts they rejoiced over every defeat.

That he was in a way a martyr to his integrity made him seem to himself a tragic figure, and a dark red blush suffused his face when Nathan—the conqueror—showed himself in the door with his women. In the midst of the dancing whirl, Nanny's gleaming, gold-bayadere form could be seen. She too was looking everywhere for Per; she had been on the watch for him because she wondered what he was up to. Despite her carefree expression, she had been restless the whole evening, squeezed by anxiety about the episode in the side room. Her whole behavior since had been calculated to confuse Per's impression of it and enable herself to forget the whole affair, but she began to worry that she had gone too far and that he, out of vindictiveness, would begin to talk out of school. Meanwhile, Per had just come back. He was in the entrance hall, hanging his coat on a wardrobe hook. As he looked through the open door of the packed smoking room he saw, by chance, Dyhring, sitting in a circle of well-known financiers.

Dyhring had, originally, established his reputation by stirring scandal among the good citizens, but now he was feathering his nest with the same shrewdness by saying and writing just what those citizens and, especially, the financiers wanted, for the moment, to hear. His travel letters about French and Italian commerce had gained, for that reason, great recognition in the business world and given him a big reputation for having at his disposal a surprisingly wide business knowledge.

He had continually stressed the soundness and solidity of Danish commerce, in contrast to that of foreign countries, and it was acknowledged everywhere that, through him, the position of editor of a great business newspaper had grown significantly. In his articles, there was a seriousness and a sense of responsibility that no one had expected of *Falken*'s former entertainment editor.

His appointment, which, at the beginning, had been so strongly criticized, was evidence, once more, of Max Bernhardt's ingenious capacity to choose his people and put them in the right place.

It was Per's intention to mingle with the smokers in order to chase away his lonely thoughts and, with the help of a glass of whisky, try for a sense of harmony with his surroundings, but the sight of the much-courted press Junker immediately took away all desire to fit in, and he turned around to move into the other rooms. A kind of faint, otherworldly reflection played on his features, but, gradually, as he worked himself through the crowded and overheated room, filled with so many flushed faces and feverishly waving fans, he assumed once again the haughty and harsh look he had had at dinner.

The glaring light of the chandelier hurt his eyes. The transition from the evening stillness on the road to the billowing, roaring social whirl confused him. He had a sensation that he was entering into a powerful machine running and groaning under high pressure.

When he reached the living room, he remained standing at the door to watch the dancing. In the meantime, it had become very lively. Even many of the older folk felt the desire to dance. He was touched to see Jakobe in the midst of that hubbub, sitting across the way against the opposite wall in the same place he had left her over an hour ago. Yes, he thought, it was and remained only with her that he felt at home here. It had not been a deceiving instinct that had drawn him to her before he was able to judge her true worth, but the deepest life force.

It struck him, as well, how out of place she looked in these circumstances. She had not, obviously, taken part in the dance. Both her fan and her gloves lay in her lap.

Seeing her again was something of a revelation to him. Never, until now, had he so strongly felt how inextricably they were bound together, how Jakobe's love was, in reality, the only worthwhile prize he had won so far on his hunt for happiness in the magic realm of adventure.

Hereafter, he had to take more care, he thought, while he stared at the wise, fine, and pale face with the heavy eyelids and the strongly marked, yet feminine, mouth. The disastrous dress now moved him precisely because she had been so unfortunate in her choice. He wanted to make his way over the floor to be near her, when Nanny, red and warm from the dance, steered straight for him with her partner on her arm.

"Well, where have *you* been, old boy? We ladies wanted to dance with the future bridegroom and then—*psst*—you disappeared. Is that proper behavior?"

Per looked at her coldly. "I'm sorry, but Jakobe is tired this evening, so I won't dance either."

As he turned away, Nanny began to laugh to hide how much his words and looks had made her tremble. "Shall we go in and get some refreshments?" she asked, and marched off with her escort. "It's a dreadful boor my sister has caught. Doesn't it seem that way to you?"

Jakobe had spotted Per as soon as he appeared at the door. While she deliberately was looking the other way, she had well noticed the little scene between Nanny and him; when she saw him coming toward her, she suspected that there had been some kind of showdown between them. He greeted her tenderly and sat down beside her in the seat just vacated by Balling. A little afterward, he moved nearer and quietly laid his hand on hers as it rested on the chair. She did not remove it—she was unable to. She was overcome by his quiet request for forgiveness, but her pride was still too great to render her defenseless, and she could not respond to his hand squeeze nor meet his eyes, for which he was clearly waiting.

"How cold your hand is," he said. "You're really freezing. Should I get you a shawl?"

"No, I'm fine."

"Is there a draft from the door?"

"No, I don't notice anything."

"But still . . . won't you . . . ?"

"No, let it be."

"As you wish, my dearest."

There was something impatient and troubled in her voice, which he didn't notice. He patted her hand and drew it toward his chest so that her arm rested on his. At the same time, he leaned a little more against her; their shoulders touched intimately. When she seemed about to draw away her hand, he held it fast, and whispered in her ear with the cadence she recognized from their nights of love, that sent blood into her cheeks: "You dear . . . dear love."

After a while he asked, "Have you danced?" She shook her head.

"Would you like to?"

"No, not really." After a short pause, she added, afraid that he would misunderstand her refusal, "I'm too tired."

"Then let me propose something to you. This evening, the weather is so fine—not at all cold. Like a summer evening. What do you say to a little walk in the garden?" When she hesitated, he continued: "I think the fresh air will do you good. And, besides, I have something to tell you, Jakobe."

Now, for the first time, she looked at him, purely by instinct, because, in fact, her thoughts were wandering. But she could detect the sincere and intimate tone of his voice.

She got up, and after he had fetched their coats, they went through the garden door. Out on the terrace the dancers gathered around some tables to cool themselves off; there were cold drinks and other refreshments. Here, under the starry sky, Nanny had also retreated with her escort. She was about to consume some sherbet when she saw Per and Jakobe going past, arm in arm, and disappearing down the marble steps.

Now he will tell her everything—thoroughly shock her! she thought. Her mouth was white with hate and lust. She set her half-emptied dish down and went with her partner back into the living room, still thinking about it while she danced. Jakobe will not be allowed to triumph for long! She'll be sorry. Now there will be war!

Per and Jakobe went all the way down through the garden and sat on the covered bench near the water, where they would sit when they wanted to be left in peace. Here, in their solitude, Jakobe surrendered herself entirely. Per put his arm around her, and she lay so close against him that her head rested on his chest. They sat quietly like this while, in front of their feet, the sea rippled as if it were sleeping; the reflections from Ivan's Chinese lanterns shimmered in the water like a throng of gold-fish. "Aren't you cold?" asked Per, and drew her fur wrap tighter around her.

"No, not really," she answered once again, a little irritated.

In connection with what they had talked about the day before in the same place, Per began to explain how, when he saw the company this evening, he became even more convinced of the developing decadence of the so-called leaders of the future here at home. The spell that, up until now, had held him, had, in any case, been thoroughly broken. He had to give her full credit for what she once wrote to him, that a society in which, for example, a person like Dyhring is allowed to play a prominent role has condemned itself. It was altogether clear to him that if there were to be hope for victory in the name of free and visionary thinking in Denmark, other powerful agents must come into the front lines—*men*, in the real sense of that word, of an earnest and high-minded nature, who could raise their goals above the wild daily chase after money, women, or personal fame.

He developed his perspective with habitual eloquence, but Jakobe wasn't listening to him. The serious and heartfelt words glided past her ears in a dull hum, but when, at last, as a sign of their mutual understanding, he asked her for a kiss, she heard him clearly. She quickly lifted her head and offered her lips like a languishing, parched wanderer with no thought other than to slake her thirst.

CHAPTER 18

WHEN PER AWOKE the next morning, he felt sick. He was often a restless sleeper, but he had thrown off his blankets during the night and felt quite chilled. When he sat up in bed, he felt a sharp pain in his chest and anxiety in his soul. He recognized the pain; it was the same that had disturbed him a few times during his travels—the last time in Vienna after the trying boat ride on the Danube.

Because of his lack of confidence in foreign doctors and, perhaps, out of a reluctance to learn the truth, he had not, as yet, undergone an examination. Now, however, it was high time. He rang for the housemaid and had one of Copenhagen's best-known doctors called, but it was some time before the doctor came. In his solitude, Per had time to deliriously imagine that these stronger and stronger attacks could be the interdiction of death.

Die already at twenty-four with his life's work unfulfilled—not even begun? That would be senseless, entirely illogical—as life often was. To be sure, he no longer boldly stormed forth in all his health and defied death in his assumption that life couldn't do without him, that his capacities and strengths were vital for the maintenance and development of his fatherland's business. He now was aware that nature, with its limitless wealth, could afford to waste great talents and send them unfulfilled to their graves. Death did not ask permission. As the sun shone alike on the just and unjust, so, he realized, did the dark figure with the empty eye sockets blindly move through the called and uncalled without the slightest regard for usefulness. But the terror he earlier had felt at the thought of annihilation was no longer so strong in him. As he lay in his luxurious bed under a radiantly colored silk bedcover and prepared himself for his death sentence, he was relatively peaceful and composed. Even when he had no pain, there were moments when, in his fatigue, he almost reconciled himself to leaving this world in order to be free from the vain sorrows of life.

The sound of the wagons that rose from the marketplace, the perpetual clang of the street trolley, the thought of renewed negotiations with foolish and shameless speculators—all that filled him, during these moments, with unspeakable disgust. The longer he waited, the more difficult it was to suppress his discomfort. An oppressive sense of loneliness possessed him, and his body broke out in a cold sweat. Think of lying here dying without anyone at one's side! He decided to read to distract himself. The previous day he had unpacked the books he had brought home from his trip, chiefly big, expensive, technical works, but also a collection of writings of a more general nature that he had procured during the long winter stay in Dresack and later added to in Rome. Among the latter, he chose a particular edition of the works of Greek and Latin philosophers in German translation, a book that, once before, under similar circumstances, had been a consolation to him. He hadn't been reading long when the doctor arrived. He was a small, gray-bearded man who, without many words, sat down on a chair next to the bed. After asking some questions and tapping Per's chest and back, he asked, "You think it's your lungs that are giving you trouble? I don't really think so. They are a completely sound pair of bellows. Where do you especially feel pain?" Per showed him a place on the right side of his body, near the lowest rib.

"Is it there? But, before, you indicated it was on the left side."

"Yes, the pain changes."

"Aha—hmmm. Does it hurt now when I press here, like this?"

"No, I can't say that it does."

"You don't notice anything strange?"

"No."

"Perhaps you don't even have any more pain?" Per had to confess that the tormenting, oppressive feeling in his chest and in the area of his diaphragm now had almost disappeared. He could breathe deeply again, without a stitch.

The doctor also examined his lower torso and legs. "There is nothing wrong with your lungs," he repeated when he was done.

"You should not trade them away. But your frame is a little weak. Your heart could also be a little less lazy. Tell me now: What is the routine of your daily life? Do you exercise? Do you take a cold shower every morning? You should certainly be doing these things. And weight lifting. There is nothing so beneficial as some brisk arm swings with a pair of twenty-pound weights on an empty stomach. You could make your noble blood circulate a bit more efficiently. Nothing else is really wrong with you, but this is enough for someone of your age. Stay in bed a few days and try to bring about a kind of equilibrium in your nervous system. I can't recommend highly enough your paying attention to your health. In spite of your unconditionally manly body, you tend, apparently, to . . . hmmm—what shall I call it—a little of the sort of indisposition of the kind you had early this morning. On the face of it, it's easy to see why you had it now. First of all, you were thoroughly shaken up by a three- or four-day train ride during which you got neither regular sleep nor meals. Then—as you yourself say—you came home to business and all kinds of nonsense, to social life, and that is enough in itself to explain your problem. We all have a constitution as weak as our national sweet soup, even if you belong to the stronger class."

He said these last words with a particularly mischievous gleam in his small, squinty eyes. Per was scarcely listening now. After having been assured that he wasn't going around with the beginning of a lung disease, he felt entirely well and merely wanted to get rid of this chatty man. When the doctor had gone, he got up immediately. With a sense of rejuvenation, he walked up and down in the room, humming, got dressed, ate breakfast with a pretty good appetite, and settled down at his worktable. The passion for work had suddenly been reawakened in him. He took out his drafts, together with his measuring instruments, tables, and other tools. He thought, Now we'll stoke the fire: Full steam ahead, as the English say.

He had arranged everything to get down to work when he discovered the book he had begun to read when the doctor came. He had thrown it onto the table among the rolls of drafts, and now he couldn't help peeking into it before laying it aside. The book was marked where he had stopped reading, at Plato's account of the frank conversation between Socrates and his disciples on the subject of death, just before the great teacher's execution. His glance fell on the place where Socrates speaks of the body as heavy and sticky dough into which the soul is kneaded, and that is what causes us never to have the satisfaction of possessing what we desire, unless it is base and ignoble: "The body causes us a thousand troubles. It fills us with lust and longing, with fears and many kinds of illusion, vanities . . . The acquisition of money is the cause of all the wars on earth; but money can be used only for the body's sake and we must get it to serve it. When we, finally, have satisfied ourselves in this respect and prepare ourselves to consider things of importance, again all kinds of difficulties arise. Anxiety and confusion come to disconcert us and, on account of that, we don't understand how to find the truth . . . While we live, we will come close to it only when we have as little as possible to do with the body and have no more association with it than is absolutely necessary and if we don't comply with its whims."

Per let the book fall and stared out with a troubled brow, lost in thought for a long time. Strange, he thought, these words, uttered four hundred years before the birth of Christ, could have come out of a Christian book of devotions. He read to the end of the page, then the next and the next. He couldn't stop. The profound play of the imagination with the supranatural set in motion the deepest and most secret parts of his soul. It was late in the morning before he took up his measuring tools and tables, but he had no more luck with his work that day than on the previous one. Before, he couldn't examine any scrap of the charts without being seized with work fever; the difficulty, until now, had consisted primarily in choosing with circumspection between the swarming ideas that pushed their way up from the project like germinating seeds. Now, however, he had trouble concentrating on what lay before him. All kinds of irrelevant things—every shout in the street, every bell in the hotel, disturbed and distracted him. And since, as on the previous day, he found, with morbid exasperation, the project misconceived, he sat in the dark, with his head in his hands, in utter despair.

Then he called to mind Professor Pfefferkorn in Berlin, who had taken such an interest in him during his stay there. Per had sent him a requested written account of his ideas, and, in gratitude, the professor had written him a lengthy letter. Now he dug it out and read it:

I'll comment, first, cautiously on what concerns your

hydraulic motor. You're opening up a new road and it's only logical that your first steps are unsure. During our conversations I already told you that, in America, experiments in a similar direction are under way and that there, they are continually working to solve that huge and tantalizing problem of bringing the ocean's infinite power under the control of human ingenuity. It's to your credit that you, as well, have been obsessed by the thought, but how far toward your goal your idea will lead I cannot really say. On the other hand, after becoming acquainted with your new system for regulating wind motors, I think you have, here, a workable plan.

The idea of inserting a balance bar, and your method for equalizing, especially appeal to me. Here you certainly point to means that deserve attention, but even you cannot think you have found the solution to the great and difficult problem that is of such significance, especially for all countries poor in mountains and streams. The principle that perfection is reached only through endless little ameliorations applies more than anywhere to the technical. And you surely cannot be satisfied just with the knowledge that has already been gained in the name of progress. I will always follow your development with interest as far as my circumstances allow. Before everything, I await with excited expectation the results of your continual research in the field. About your rich capacities for this, you yourself can have no doubts, and you will certainly go far, especially if you succeed in doing more than you have up until now about bringing together your remarkably wide view of the larger pattern with more thoroughness in details, which the young are inclined to scorn, but on which, in reality, the overview depends. I seem to remember that you intended to go, on your travels, to America, and that's a worthy goal. There you will, better than anywhere, have the opportunity to complete your education in the purely practical aspects of the field. And I mean, by this, not only the technical means. In other fields as well we have become apprentices to the New World. In that country of significant inventions we can learn, above all, that powerful effects can, very often, be achieved with apparently unimpressive means.

This old, half-forgotten letter had not meant much to Per when he had received it because it had not seemed sufficiently appreciative, but now it elevated his self-confidence. In addition, the idea of continuing his interrupted apprentice journey, breaking off his stay at home, became fixed in his mind. He would, once again, put his affairs in Ivan's hands and trust him entirely to start up possible new negotiations with speculators. In the meantime, he would quietly set out, and this time directly, to America. It was not worth running the risk of exposing himself again to the temptations of the Old World.

That afternoon, he went out to Skovbakken to talk to Jakobe about it. When he arrived, she was in the garden, sitting on a sunlit bench by the big log summerhouse. Although she very well heard Per's voice from up on the terrace, she remained calmly seated and gave no return shout to indicate where she was. When he finally found her, she offered only her cheek to kiss, though he sought her mouth. Nor could she even say thanks to him for the flowers he brought, particularly because she saw how clearly he expected it.

She had spent the whole day in a constrained and exhausted lethargy, attempting to forget what had happened. A lover of clarity, she had, in her relations with Per, begun to be unfaithful to herself in this way, that, as much as possible, she closed her eyes to the truth where her happiness in love was threatened. Like one who has been awakened from a sweet dream and turns onto the other side with the hope of dreaming again, she gave herself over, with a kind of lust, to her self-betrayal.

Per was reluctant to tell her that they already had to part again. It had not been that easy for him to decide now to travel. He was tired of the wandering life and of the difficulty of making himself understood in foreign languages, of which German was his only fairly fluent one. Besides, he was sorry to have to leave Jakobe when they finally had arrived at full openness with each other and a reciprocal understanding. But that didn't matter. He had to go.

He was too busy at first with his own feelings to notice the change in Jakobe's attitude, but when he sat next to her, he saw her quickly wipe away a tear from her cheek, as if she were brushing away a fly with her hand. He was completely taken aback. He had never before seen her cry. "Dearest," he said, "what's the matter? Has something gone wrong?"

"No, not at all. It's just nerves," she answered, and pushed the arm that he had started to put around her waist.

"But are you feeling sick?"

"Oh, I'm all right. As I said to you, it doesn't mean anything. Let's walk a bit. I'm getting cold."

She quickly stood up—his solicitude pained her—and they went down to the beach. Now Per noticed how sad and pale she looked, and his travel plans began to waver. Then a bright thought came to him in the midst of his concern.

His inspiration illuminated a whole new existence for him, as a single sunbeam breaking through the clouds can suddenly transform an entire landscape. Jakobe could go with him! They could get married immediately and travel together before the eyes of God and men. How could he not have thought of that before? The journey's difficulties, the discomforts of lodging, the loneliness that had always made him despondent, suddenly changed at once to joy and happiness. He knew from experience how exceptional a traveling companion Jakobe was—so intrepid, so unassuming, so maternally solicitous, and so easily at home in foreign languages!

"Jakobe! Jakobe!"—he stopped in the middle of the garden path, and before she could prevent him, put his arms around her. He told her everything he had lived and suffered through since the day before and what mutual plans he had for them.

Jakobe went on a little farther, still silent, her head on his shoulder, in a kind of happy numbness that drained the blood from her cheeks and lips. She well knew that she neither would nor could go with him. It was impossible for her, in her present condition, to travel so far. Per was talking about being gone half a year. Any shorter time would not really give him a return for his efforts. She would only be a burden and an anxiety to him.

"You say nothing," he said, when they had come down to their favorite place on the beach with a wide view of the Sound, all the way to the sunny Swedish coast. "Don't you like my proposal?"

"I don't really know what to say," she answered. She was sitting, bent over and half turning away, with her elbow on a knee and cupping her chin in a hand. Per would not let go of the other hand.

"I understand very well that you have to travel again. I was thinking about how necessary that is for you. But, my dearest, you can't take me with you over the Atlantic Ocean."

"Why not? With me, you can feel entirely safe. I will take good care of you ... or is it the sea journey you're afraid of?"

"Well, yes, that too. So I'll stay home ... and wait for you. I shall be very patient. But you are right to propose that we get married before the trip. That makes sense for a number of reasons."

"So when we really are man and wife, we shall immediately be separated? Are you making fun of me? That would be the worst kind of barbarism! I don't know you at all anymore, Jakobe. How could you think of something like that? That can't be your meaning, can it?" She nodded silently.

"I don't believe you, Jakobe. You have been acting strange lately. What's going on? Are you hiding something?"

"Nothing, really, dear," she said, and nervously squeezed his hand. Now, especially, she would be unable to tell him the full truth. She dared not. She no longer was a fantasist about his character and was frightened that he would use her condition as an excuse for putting off his travel plans or giving them up altogether. She would not have that on her conscience for anything. She realized fully how significant a stay in America could be for him and how, more than ever, she must see to it that he push forward. If she had thought herself satisfied earlier with just his love, now she instinctively sought a direction that would be a compensation for what value that love, of late, had lost. She said at last, "Listen. I have an idea. You can travel to England and I can go that far with you. We can spend a week in London and a week in a place in the countryside or at the shore. Then we separate in Liverpool. What do you say to that?"

"Well, of course, that's better than nothing. I can always hope that in Liverpool you'll change your mind."

"You oughtn't to think that. At least, not for your own sake, dear. Remember, also, that we can't live in a hotel when you return. We'll have our own apartment. And I'll have plenty to do arranging that while you're gone."

"That's true. You're right, as always, Jakobe. Oh, you darling! How happy I'll be to come back. Think! Our own home! It doesn't need to be especially splendid. And it will be a little out of the city in open surroundings with a view of the woods and shore. What do you say? We two!" He had, in his delight, drawn her closer to him, and she laid her tired head on his shoulder and shut her eyes. "Ah," he continued, "how meaningless and empty everything else is in life compared to the good things that are, in truth, the same for all, rich and poor—and that grow as naturally out of our lives as fruit on the tree. There is something backward in the way life's values are ranked—even in our modern society. I count myself lucky to have realized that in time, because I was almost stuck in the mud."

Jakobe felt a little uncomfortable again. Although these words were, in fact, a repetition of her own, even those very ones she had once dreamt of hearing out of his mouth, something alarmed her. She had changed, in the meantime. Especially, during these last days, the so-called "true values" in life had altered in her mind.

"I think you are miscalculating the state of the world," she said with a strange hardness in her voice. "Just look around and tell me if selfishness, vanity, brutality, imperiousness, and so on are as firmly planted in our society as in the old."

"Yes, why shouldn't they be?"

"Why? These are the kinds of characteristics that push the world forward. Therefore, it can't be so reprehensible that society promotes them." Per laughed. He took her words as mockery.

"Well, do you mean to say, really, that these qualities are commendable?"

"I don't know. Man's welfare does depend on them."

Now Per understood that she was serious, and he looked at her with surprise. But he was not in the mood to quarrel and treated it all with good humor.

"Yes, today you will contradict me and force your words into battle even against your own opinion."

Jakobe was silent. She felt no desire, either, to renew their quarrel. They began to make travel plans and map out the journey.

The public war that Max Bernhardt, strongly supported by Dyhring's *Borgerbladet*, had waged against the originators of the Copenhagen free port project now had a surprising conclusion—it succeeded in making them nervous. They had undertaken a bold enterprise and were obliged to bring a lot of capital to it. The reputation of *Borgerbladet* in the financial world, in addition, was, against all expectations, steadily rising under its new direction. Other papers, as well, with which Max Bernhardt had influence, acted as if to throw suspicion on the business side of the project. In order not to risk a defeat in the approaching subscription of shares, the originators—these powerful men—were compelled to humble themselves in front of the hated attorney and invite him to take a seat in the management.

Max Bernhardt had planned this outcome of the affair the whole time, and it determined his tactics. He accepted the offer without showing any surprise. During a great jubilee celebration that was going on that day, the reconciliation between him and his old adversary, the former mighty bank director, was officially sealed. The latter conspicuously begged for the honor of toasting to Bernhardt's health—an event that was publicized in all the newspapers of the city the next day—in *Borgerbladet* under the heading "A Historical Moment."

The victory was decidedly important for Max Bernhardt. He succeeded in firmly establishing in the public consciousness the recognition that no one, not even the financial magnates, could do anything without securing his support. Ivan almost stopped breathing when he heard the news. He considered that, now, any hope for Per's project was irretrievably lost for a long time; in a hysterical outburst of bitterness, he screamed something about treason and assassination. Per contemptuously shrugged.

"I told you," he said to Jakobe, who was also upset by the news. "Do you admit, now, at least, that your Herr Max is a bit treacherous and that it was lucky I didn't let myself get trapped into appeasing the old fox? I would now be standing there like a bamboozled fool! No—I say a movement must rise here at home to eradicate that kind of noxious animal from public life, or, in the end, all integrity will be ground under." These words nettled Jakobe, but she didn't try to answer. It wasn't necessary to continue the discussion for the time being. She set her hopes on his trip to America, and was able to control herself and subdue her newly provoked criticism, determined to continue to love him as he now was.

Ivan's gloomy estimation of Per's prospects was premature. Max Bernhardt's new and decisive victory gave added life to the resistance of his envious and secret enemies—not least of all Herr Nørrehave, "erstwhile farmer," who considered himself betrayed in this affair. He, in addition to the attorney Hasselager, suddenly becoming intently involved in Per's plan, unreservedly, on their own initiative, solicited Colonel Bjerregrav.

A feeling of justice and love of the Fatherland had gradually overpowered the old man's jealousy. An instinctively potent anti-Semitism was enflamed in the blunt old soldier, for whom patriotism had become a religion. In his eyes, every Danish Jew was only a half-naturalized German with secret sympathies for the hereditary enemy. He claimed—which wasn't altogether untrue—that the largest part of the Jewish wholesalers in Copenhagen were simply agents for German firms, and it was mainly with the money from Jewish bankers in Hamburg and Berlin that the whole modern transformation of the capital was being carried out. In the provinces, even to the country's indebted farms, German money had found a surreptitious way to complete the conquering of Denmark their gunners had begun. On account of this, Per's harbor plan had especially attracted him. Here, finally, was an attempt to support the country's commercial independence in relation to the great neighboring nations, while a free harbor in Copenhagen, in his opinion, never would be able to attract world business because of the city's situation on a narrow, shallow channel.

He had firmly decided to take the first step toward a reconciliation with Per. He wanted to resolve the old scores. The arrogance with which Per had walked out on their original fateful clash a year ago was now almost more of a spur to him. Because, with full conviction, he saw the country's deliverer in him, he had something of a religious gratification in enabling that prophecy to literally come true.

Meanwhile, Per was in his hotel room, getting ready for his trip. Among other tasks, he was still working diligently on his drafts in the hope of completing the necessary alterations, at least of the harbor project.

He rose at dawn and remained home almost the whole day. But the old inspiration wasn't there. He thought slowly and with difficulty, vulnerable to disturbance from any sound in the corridor or marketplace.

One morning, around nine o'clock, he was sitting at the worktable, reading, when there was a knock on the door. He recognized Ivan's rap and quickly hid his book under some papers. It was, again, one of the Dresack books that had tempted him. "What's new," he asked his brother-in-law, who rushed in with an air of confusion.

"A new dirty trick! A treason of the first rank! Look here—"

Ivan took from his briefcase, which had gradually become an inseparable part of his body, a copy of one of the city's least significant and least read papers. "Read this." Under the heading "A New Country," there was a lengthy, matter-of-fact lead article about Denmark's navigational problems. It was, as it immediately claimed, an abstract of some article from a provincial paper by an engineer named Steiner and concerned a plan that, throughout the piece, was called the "Steiner project," but was, with a few immaterial changes, Per's. "What do you say to that?" asked Ivan, and, expectantly, looked at Per, who, during his reading, became more and more pale. "This is pure plagiarism! Do you know this person?"

Per shook his head.

"He must be exposed instantly. What do you think we should do?"

"Nothing," answered Per after a moment's thought, and handed him back the paper.

"You don't mean that! The man must be held liable. You must defend yourself. You need to claim your rights!"

"Defend myself?" asked Per heatedly.

"Yes. Pardon me for saying this, but you cannot take this so lightly. It could be dangerous for you. Remember, you have many who envy you and are your enemies and who will rejoice to see you pushed aside for another who takes all the credit for your work and ingenuity."

"Oh, there's no need! It's not so easy to usurp me! And even if it were ... ," he added, back under the spell of the mood he was in before Ivan's arrival had disturbed him, "I've had enough of dealing with that rabble. If it really is necessary to ally oneself with such mean pettiness, you have to ask if the whole game is worth the cost and trouble. To change the subject, do you know your sister and I are thinking of getting married *now*?"

"Father and Mother have been talking about it."

"Speaking from the heart, this is worth more than all the world's newspaper nonsense. And tell me, since you are here, do you know something about what kind of certificates you need to get decently married in this country?"

"Haven't you taken care of that? I thought—"

"Yes, it's been irresponsible of me. I forgot ... or, really ... couldn't bring myself to run around from civic office to civic office. I always go crazy when I meet with so much arrogance and mean gossip everywhere. Could you do me the favor of taking care of this business for me? I know, for example, that you have to apply to the magistrate's office and, as well, register something. It's a devilish bother!"

Ivan, who was used to Per in all circumstances using him as his errand boy, agreed without further deliberation. In return, he made Per promise that he would be vigilant about the suspect Herr Steiner and take measures if, even once, he were to be mentioned publicly as the father of the West Jutland free port project. He had already thrust his briefcase under his arm and was at the door, ready to leave, when he turned once again to Per, who remained seated at his worktable.

"By the way, is there someone in your family named Kristine Margrete? A pastor's widow here in the city?"

Per gave a start. That was his mother's Christian name. "No," he said, staring blankly ahead. "Why do you ask?"

"Oh," said Ivan, a little embarrassed, as he always was the few times he had spoken to Per about his family. "I happened to see the name in this morning's death notices in the *Berlingske Tidende* under 'Sidenius.' Well, goodbye for now. We'll see you this afternoon."

Several minutes after the door had closed behind Ivan, Per was still sitting motionless in his chair. When he finally got up to ring the electric bell for the maid, he noticed that everything went dark before his eyes. At the same time, irritated thoughts were going through his head. That's all I needed to be hit with! he thought. And just now I really am a man persecuted by bad luck!

"Will you bring me the morning *Berlingske Tidende*?" he asked the housemaid when she came in. Shortly after, he held the spread paper between his hands; he became dizzy when his eye caught his mother's name in bold print in the long row of death notices. "Our dear mother, Kristine Margrete Sidenius, widow of Pastor Johannes Sidenius, entered, today, into eternal peace." The announcement was signed: "The bereaved children."

Per stared at the words until the letters dimmed into mist. He had, just a few days before, repeated his night visit to his mother's dwelling, and he shuddered to think that, perhaps, she was that day at death's door. There had been a light behind one of the windows, and he had seen shadows moving on the blinds. Well, what would it have mattered if I had been there? he thought in an attempt to pacify himself. A genuine understanding, to say nothing of the only kind of concession that would have satisfied his mother, would not have been possible. It was good, perhaps, that she had believed him to be so far away, just as it was fortunate for him that he had known nothing of her condition. He could, perhaps, have feigned a scene for the sake of her peace of mind, but he would have been ashamed of it later. Poor Mother! She was one of those souls intimidated by life. The long years before in her dark sickroom had gradually changed her into a simple vessel of anxiety. For her, death surely was a liberation.

He began to pace up and down the floor to settle himself. He wasn't used to this kind of mental turbulence, which inherently frightened him. Then he began to think of Jakobe waiting for him at Skovbakken at the usual hour. What should he do? He felt he would not be able to sit peacefully with her and talk about preparations for the journey or about whatever else they shared. In addition, he had a bad conscience because he still had not told her that his family had moved to Copenhagen.

He wrote a few lines to her: she shouldn't wait for him, and, as was his custom, he used busyness as an excuse. At the letter's close, he curtly announced that his mother, according to a notice in the *Berlingske Tidende*, had died here in the city. After he again rang for the maid, to take care of sending off the letter by messenger, he was seized by a strange restlessness. Time after time he went back to his drafts, only to get up again. It was impossible for him to sit still, to say nothing of gathering up his thoughts about shapes and numbers. Although he finally sat with his hands pressed against his head to force himself to work, his thoughts would not come. The image of his mother, memories of childhood, his complete lack of knowledge about his mother's last days, the desire to talk to someone who knew her—all that finally overwhelmed him.

He gave up working, got dressed, and went out into the street. He ate lunch at one of the best restaurants and then walked to a public garden to distract himself by looking at people and listening to a military band playing there. When he returned to the hotel in the afternoon, the porter told him that there was a woman waiting for him in his room. He felt his blood rush vehemently to his heart, and he immediately thought that it was one of his sisters who, in one way or another, had found out that he had come home and had tracked down his address to tell him about the death.

It hadn't occurred to him that it could be Jakobe. She had, at that moment, been so far from his thoughts that he found it difficult to recognize her when, as he entered, she rose from a chair by the window. Surprise and disappointment showed so clearly in his face that Jakobe could not help seeing it. But she had been prepared for an inhospitable meeting. She knew him well, had met before that moody brusqueness behind which he hid when anxiety-ridden. She knew, too, how carefully and subtly she had to insinuate herself into his confidence in such a situation and how terribly difficult it would be to make him open up to her with complete sincerity and trust when the conversation was about his family. Without any sign of vexation, she took his head between her hands, kissed him, and said, "You can understand I couldn't stay at home after receiving your letter. I had to see you. Oh, dearest, how much I feel your misery. I had to cry because it seems to me this is a grief that hits us both." Per looked suspiciously at her and mumbled some words about how his mother had, in reality, been dead to him for a long time, that nothing in their relationship had ever changed.

"Well, dearest, that's something we say to console ourselves. I well know what you have lost. How can we conceal it from each other? And you didn't tell me! Oh, Per, when will you stop hiding yourself from me when we need each other so much. Or don't you know that?"

Per replied, as he freed his head from her hands, that he had always in mind to tell her of his mother being here, but every time they were together, there were always other things to discuss that made him forget.

"So let's talk about it this time! Let's sit down," she burst forth. "It seems to me there is so terribly much I have to find out from you."

She took off her coat, gloves, and hat and settled herself in a corner of the sofa. "Did you know your mother was sick?"

"I knew nothing. But she was in a weakened state for many years."

"Didn't you look her up or see anything of your brothers and sisters?" she asked, looking searchingly at him.

"No," answered Per as he hung her coat on the doorpost.

"But how did you find out they had moved to the city?"

"I saw it one day, by chance, in a paper where my sister had advertised for piano students. Besides, the family was already talking about it at my father's burial. They wanted to move to be with a couple of my younger brothers who had found jobs here."

He sat down at a little distance from her. With her cheek resting on her hand, she stared straight ahead. "Do you know what," she said, after some moments of silence. "I think that if I had known your mother was so near—I couldn't have helped going to see her. Especially when I had just come home from my journey and felt so terribly alone; I needed someone to talk to about you. Do you think she would have received me?"

"I don't know."

"Ah, she would have. I'm convinced she would have and finally understood us."

"Do you remember that you thought the same thing when, with similar intentions, you paid a visit to Eberhard? It would only have been a disappointment for you."

It was awhile before Jakobe answered, but not because she didn't remember her meeting with Per's brother. The memory of that scene in the unpleasant, cold, and bare office had quite recently popped up in her mind and awakened a hidden anxiety because she more and more noticed a family resemblance between Per and his brother.

"Well, yes, but siblings are something else," she said, and brushed a curl from her forehead as if chasing away a painful thought. "I know that from our family. But some affection always is retained for the mother, no matter how far we feel distanced from her. Because of this, I can't believe your mother and I would have been unable to speak to each other, even if we were in every way as different as two people could possibly be."

"You're right about that."

"And I also think that, finally, we would have understood each other. At least, from the little you have told me about her, I have constructed a picture that I have come to like. It's as if I see her clearly before me. She was small, wasn't she? And didn't she have the same eyes as you and your brother, only darker? But you children resemble your father more closely, don't you? And she had a cane when she was out of bed. My grandmother did, as well. That's possibly why I see her so clearly. And what a strong will she must have had with all her bodily weakness. It seems to me that it is amazing and so moving that, for years, she ran the whole house from her bed and, in the middle of her own frightful unhappiness, watched over all of you with such care that nothing was lost or wasted. Think of what a fate it was for a mother with so many small children to lie fettered to a bed for eight years. Also, your father was a difficult man, you said, and it certainly was not a prosperous house. Yet never a complaint! I can remember you once told me what your mother had said to someone who was feeling sorry for her: 'Don't feel sorry for me; feel sorry for my husband and children.' That was so beautifully and nobly said."

While Jakobe was talking, Per sat bent over in his chair, elbows on his knees. Restlessly he drummed on the knuckles of one hand with the fingers of the other.

Then he jumped up impatiently and walked across the room. "Yes, yes—let it be," he interrupted. "The past is past. It's useless to talk about all that could have happened." He stood at a window and looked down at the marketplace, where the shadows of the houses were already lengthening; and gleaming in the evening sun was the old windmill in the midst of the remains of the fortress, as if it were greeting the sunset with open arms.

"You're right," said Jakobe, heavily, after more silence. "The past is past! Just tell me, have you some of your mother's old letters to you I can read? We have so seldom spoken about your family; I feel the loss of not knowing more than I do, especially about your parents."

Per pretended, at first, that he didn't hear the question. When she repeated it, he said curtly, "I don't have any letters."

"I well know that you haven't, in the last years, exchanged letters with your family, but I'm thinking about the first years you were in Copenhagen. Then, you said, your mother wrote to you. And those are the letters I want to read over together with you."

"You cannot because I don't have them."

"Where are they?"

"Where are they? I burned them after reading them—"

"Oh Per—how could you . . ." She didn't finish the sentence. Per wiped his face with his handkerchief as if perspiring. However, she had seen something wet glittering on his eyelashes, and she understood that he had begun to cry and wanted to hide it.

Her first impulse was to go over to him and throw her arms around his neck. But her understanding and experience told her, just in time, that she should pretend as if she hadn't seen anything, and she remained seated until Per left the window. Then, she went to him and took his arm. For some moments, they silently walked back and forth over the floor. And now she recognized that, at present, it wasn't really possible to give him any more comfort.

She herself felt so unsure, so feckless. Her steadfastness disappeared when she thought of the long separation. If only she were able to confide wholly in Per! She had a desperate daily battle with herself in order not to betray anything to him and had to remember how much was at stake if she shared her secret before the Atlantic Ocean came between them.

It wasn't just the upcoming birth that made her anxious and restless. She was nervous, as well, at the thought of the rumors that would arise on the occasion of the early date of delivery. In that regard, there had been a change in her since Per had come home. She had been all too proud of her love to care very much whether her prenuptial surrender could be concealed; now that she looked more soberly at the bridegroom, it was that very pride that suffered from the realization that their relations would become the object of common gossip.

It was less for her own sake than out of respect for her parents that she decided, rather than returning home after following Per to England, to find some place in Germany, perhaps with her friend in Breslau, and have her baby there. But when she began to think about having to wait yet more than half a year for the event, she was again close to despair. Still, she would have borne it all without a murmur if she had the same confidence in Per that she had had just two and a half months ago when they had parted in the Tyrol; since the play with Nanny, she was insecure and suspected dangers everywhere. She couldn't possibly think of leaving him. With all the human weaknesses she saw in him, she loved him no less than when her critical insight was still sleeping. Because she could make herself sick with her longing for him, she had become, in general, more careful in hiding her feelings. Her attitude toward him was more subdued, even when they were alone. She could, at times, even seem capricious. But he had mastered her so completely, so absolutely, that it often seemed there was no longer anything she wouldn't forgive him for.

Per stopped suddenly and looked at his watch. "But are you paying attention to the train? Not that I want to chase you away.

I really am grateful that you came. But you don't like to get home too late. And it is eight o'clock now." She looked at his face, still pale and distorted.

"What are *you* going to do?"

"I have to get back to my work. As you can see, this table is full of things that need to be done. I have to use my time well."

"No, no," said Jakobe, and put her arms around him protectively. "You can't be here alone. Let the work go this evening. What good would it do to stay here? You won't be free of your sad thoughts as long as you sit here by yourself."

"Will you stay with me, then?"

"No—not today—and not here," she said, blushing. "It's too uncomfortable. But you shall come home with me and stay overnight. You know the guest rooms at home are always prepared. You won't be the least trouble, and Father and Mother would appreciate it if you told them, yourself, about your mother's death. It seems to me, as well, that you owe them that. Come, Per. In the morning we'll take a long walk in the woods and forget all our sorrows."

Jakobe and Per awoke to a glorious, sunny day at Skovbakken. Neither of them had been able to sleep the night before. The consciousness of being so near each other kept them both awake in the light, spring night. Finally, they came together while the others in the house were sleeping.

It was fairly late when they came down for tea in the dining room. After a quick breakfast, they disappeared, arm in arm, into the sunny, green garden, where dew dripped from the twigs and leaves. In the morning hours, when the rest of the family, except for the mother, went to their offices and schools in the city, the place became a paradise of peace and quiet. In the woods, to which they had retreated, there was an entirely different atmosphere than there would be later in the day, when the road would be dusty from vehicles and all the benches filled with chatterers. Now there was no noise other than birdsong. During the whole walk, they met only one old man, who greeted them in a fatherly way as he went by. But Per gradually became more anxious, distracted, and hinted that he had to be in the city before two o'clock—an untruth—because he needed to get some information for his work from one of the public offices that closed at three.

Immediately after lunch, he left. When he reached the city, he took a carriage to the administrative office where his brother Eberhard had a post. He gave the driver orders to wait for him and disappeared through the doors. Since a year ago, when Jakobe had gone through the same doors in the big, dirty gray building, Eberhard's competence and firm sense of duty had been rewarded with a little promotion up the hundred-step ladder of municipal authority. At his former desk in the front room was another young, aspiring keeper of the flame in the solemn state machinery, while Eberhard himself had his own little private office adjoining, with a desk and armchair. He could not part with the noticeably narrow-armed, black coat, shining at the elbows and on the back from years of honorable wear, and neither his tie nor his shoes were more refined since his elevation.

Eberhard was busy sharpening a pencil with the meticulous care and conscientious fervor that marks work habits in public offices. But as soon as he heard someone utter his name in the front room, to which his door stood half open, he hastily hid his knife and snatched up a large document. Holding it before him, in an authoritative posture, leaning back in his chair, he awaited the entrance of the stranger.

"Come in," he said sternly at the knocking of the door, and lifted his eyes just high enough to look over the paper's edge. His surprise at the sight of Per was so great that he couldn't even pretend to hide it. With an expression of someone who thinks he is seeing a ghost, he got up slowly from his chair, and, for half a minute, the two brothers faced each other without saying a word. Per was struck by how much Eberhard looked like their father as he stood there, slightly quivering with emotion, and supporting himself against the tabletop. The tightness around his beardless lips, the old-fashioned, close-cropped cheek whiskers, the red-rimmed eyes, and, then, the cold glance and the stiff posture—all this reminded him of their father's form and figure as they were burned into his childhood memory.

Per closed the door in order to talk without distraction and sat down on a sofa across from it. Eberhard sat down as well.

"You can imagine the reason for my visit," Per began. "I saw in the paper that Mother died."

"Yes," said Eberhard after a pause and with evident reluctance.

"I have been back for a week," said Per.

"Really? You have been here so long? Perhaps you didn't know that Mother had moved to the city."

"Yes, yes, I knew that," said Per, and looked away. Then he asked him if their mother had been sick for very long. Eberhard made him wait a bit for an answer. Finally, he said, with a resolution that seemed the result of a long series of reflections, that their mother had died suddenly and unexpectedly.

"She was spared, God be praised, bodily suffering. Other than her chronic weakness, there was nothing remarkable to notice before she died so quickly. She had, for some time, talked about a little difficulty in breathing and some restlessness at night, but that was only the same condition we knew her in for many years. In the morning, when Signe was combing her hair, she asked her, a little impatiently, to please hurry. She felt so tired, she said, and wanted to try to sleep a bit more. When Signe looked in on her in twenty minutes or so, she was already unable to speak. She merely opened her eyes a couple of times as if saying goodbye and sunk into her final, quiet sleep."

Eberhard was speaking as if preoccupied. After the surprise and the first shock had settled, he was concerned, in his customary, secret manner, with examining Per's appearance. With short, oblique glances, he inspected his silk-lined coat, his gloves, his pointed, Parisian shoes, and the diamond stud in his shirtfront. "Naturally," he continued, "we were not entirely unprepared for Mother leaving us like that. It was clear that she had been weak for a long time, but she seemed, recently, to have had a presentiment of her coming death. Not only did she painstakingly leave stipulations concerning her burial and the distribution of household effects, she also wrote farewell letters to all of us whom she didn't see daily. There's a letter for you, in addition to a sealed box."

He uttered the last remark after an artful pause. At the same time, he was trying to observe what effect this information had on his brother. "Signe is holding them, for the time being, in safekeeping," he continued. "We thought you were still abroad. Now I don't know whether you will want to come to get them. In these last days, we have been all together. Ingrid and Thomas, as well, have come to lay Mother in her casket. Of course, Mother will be buried next to Father. We plan to put her on a ship that leaves tomorrow afternoon. Before that, we will hold a little family ceremony here, around the casket, and now that we know you are here in the city—and I confidently speak for us all—it would disappoint us if you missed this occasion. In the evening, we'll travel by train to the country. Mother decided this, because Signe and Ingrid don't tolerate sea journeys well, and she wanted all of us together. That way, we'll have plenty of time to meet the ship and arrange everything for the interment. The casket will go directly from shipboard to the chapel, and, from there, the burial will quietly take place the day after. That's how Mother wanted it."

Per said nothing. Even his face did not betray anything of what he was feeling. When, a little afterward, he started to leave, Eberhard asked him, "And how are you? Is it your intention, now, to stay in Denmark?"

"No, shortly I'll be traveling to America. I have something to do there. In addition, before that, I'm getting married. As you know, I have been engaged to a daughter of Philip Salomon."

Now it was Eberhard who didn't answer. He suddenly lowered his eyes after he, once again, involuntarily, looked at the diamond stud in Per's shirt. Per stood up. "I didn't tell you," said Eberhard with renewed self-control, "that the little ceremony I spoke of has been set for three thirty. If you also want to gather with us . . ." Per shook his head.

"I think it best, for various reasons, that I don't come," he said. "I wouldn't want to come without my fiancée. And she, on the other hand, would scarcely fit in. Perhaps she wouldn't even be welcome." Eberhard answered nothing. His face, once again, wore a mask of stiffness and did not betray anything of the horror he felt at the mere thought of the presence of a Jewish woman of the world at the singing of hymns of gratitude around his mother's bier. Per said goodbye and left.

Down at the gateway, he encountered a couple of young men who attracted his attention because of the suddenness with which they moved aside for him, interrupting their almost military march. They were two adolescent lads of sixteen or seventeen who appeared rustic and provincial with full heads of hair under broad-brimmed Grundtvigian woolen hats. He knew them immediately; they were his two young brothers—the twins—who were on their way up to Eberhard. When they also recognized him, they clearly gave themselves away as they looked at each other with frightened faces and blushed.

Per stopped them. There was something in the shy way they

stepped aside for him that touched him, even made him feel ashamed. He was still disposed to conciliation and, despite his visit with Eberhard, desirous of a rapprochement with his siblings to atone for whatever guilt he had toward his mother.

"Hello," he said, holding out his hand. They took it hesitantly and self-consciously. "Are you going up to see Eberhard?" asked Per.

"Yes," they answered together.

"I have just been there to find out a little about our mother's death."

At these words, the brothers lowered their eyes silently, and one of them started to scrape the tip of his shoe between the paving stones at the gate entrance. Per sensed some sort of accusation in that embarrassed silence. But whatever there had been of resentment and revolt in *his* mind during his conversation with Eberhard, it melted away in the face of these two young brothers who met him with the artless expressions of a childhood home's innocent and happy simplicity. Despite their half-rustic appearance, even *because* of it, he had to struggle against the wish to take their heads between his hands and kiss them. But with all his desire for intimacy, he could think of nothing to say to them. And they, on their part, stood helplessly estranged from him and felt uncomfortable in his presence. He took them once more by the hand, made a remark about his busy preparations for an upcoming journey, and said goodbye. When he was in the carriage, his feelings overpowered him completely. Instead of immediately going to the station so he could be out at Skovbakken for midday dinner as he had promised Jakobe, he went back to the hotel. He was full of confused sensations, and Jakobe couldn't help him in this case.

Once in the hotel, the porter handed him a visitor's card that read "C. F. Bjerregrav, retired Colonel in the Engineering Corps."

"Was that man *here*?"

"Yes, perhaps an hour ago. He wrote something on the back of the card, too."

Per turned over the card: "An old veteran wishes you luck and success in your patriotic battle." With the card in his hand, he was smiling weakly. Though he himself had long forgotten that arrogant prophecy he had once flung out, in his collapsed and half-despairing state he received this greeting like a supernaturally renewed confirmation of his demonic pact with luck.

"Do you remember," he said that evening to Jakobe, "that you and Ivan reproached me for my behavior at Max Bernhardt's, especially with regard to my relation with Colonel Bjerregrav and the way that—"

"Let's not talk about that again," she interrupted impatiently.

"Well—read what he wrote on the back. What do you say about that?"

Jakobe really didn't know what to say; she was too numb from surprise. "But you are a regular wizard, Per!"

The next morning, Per went down to the harbor and looked for the ship he thought would be taking his mother to Jutland. When he inquired of the mate, he learned that, indeed, a body was expected as cargo and he gave him the approximate time. In the afternoon, some time before the anticipated hour, he was sitting at a table in a run-down café across the way, with an unobstructed view through the window. He ordered a glass of beer and, hidden behind a newspaper, waited with beating heart for the arrival of the body.

Outside, a steady summer rain was falling. Nevertheless, there was a lot of busy activity on the broad harbor square, filled with packing crates, barrels, and sacks. There were only a few hours before the ship's departure. Heavy wagons were pushing forward to the ramp from all sides, to get unloaded. The steam winches clattered and hissed, large wooden boxes, iron girders, and barrels were swept up out of the deep wagons, held swaying for a moment in the air over the cargo hatch, then lowered into the all-devouring belly of the ship.

A large pig was being hoisted aboard and was causing a lot of trouble. Two men pulled the ears while a third, like an organ grinder, persistently turned the curly tail. And still they couldn't get it off the ground. The rain and bustle made everyone cheerful, and they were quite amused by the obstinate pig that screamed as if calling on all the heavenly and earthly powers for protection. Finally, they got the pig on the gangway, and in a short gallop, it disappeared under the foredeck. Then there arose a row between two drivers, who, in the meantime, had collided in the middle of the piled-up heaps of commodities. They could move their wagons neither forward nor backward, and they were fighting when a policeman came up and got some barrels rolled off to make room.

Meanwhile, the rain had slackened, but the air was still heavy and dark over the city. The red warehouse roof over on the Christianshavn side could be seen dimly. Suddenly Per spotted a one-horse hearse of the kind that is sent to carry a body from homes to churches and chapels. It came rolling up with a man in work clothes sitting on the coach box beside the driver and stopped a little way from the ship. Behind it, a closed cab followed from which four people now stepped out—his brothers. First came Eberhard in a silk funeral hat, his black trousers rolled up at the cuff and an umbrella that he immediately opened although it wasn't raining anymore. After him came the red-cheeked Thomas, the curate, and, last, the two young brothers.

Preparations were under way with the winch to raise the last bale from a cart. When that cart went by, the hearse coachman began to move up his horse.

The mate who had been supervising the loading from the command bridge stopped him with a shout. He ordered him to wait a bit. First, a young, unruly horse had to be brought aboard, and that would take time. The men attempted to lead him over the gangplank like the pig, and it seemed at first that they would succeed. Although the horse shook and snorted from anxiety until blood was coming from his nostrils, both his forelegs were now on the plank; unfortunately, one of the small tugs that cease-lessly darted back and forth in the harbor tooted its steam whistle, and the horse became altogether ungovernable. The only thing to be done was to lift him on board in the same way as the commodities. The ship's crane was directed out toward the quay, where the beast was pressed into a crate with strong boards, as high as a man. Two tough iron rings on the rims of the box were fastened onto the crane's chain. When that was accomplished, the winch was set in motion, and the beast, who was lifted off the ground, stiffened into an anxious paralysis as he was slowly looped over the heads of the gathered workers and set down on the ship's foredeck.

While this was taking place, Per was watching the hearse. He was hardly conscious of the whole scene that had attracted a crowd of interested spectators. But now the driver got the signal to move forward, and Eberhard and the brothers followed on foot. The man in work clothes who was sitting on the coach box had already gone to the ramp in front of the loading hatch, where, with a couple of other men, he set out a twelve-foot-long trunk-like crate whose lid was marked with a large lading stamp. The hearse was quickly opened, and the humble, flowerless coffin came into view. Two harbor workmen wanted to help, but Thomas held them back. He and his brothers carefully lifted the coffin and lowered it into the open box that it almost filled. The space around it was stuffed with straw, the lid closed and firmly screwed on. As the unpainted, rough box sat on the harbor pavement with its precious content, it could not really be distinguished from all the other cargo that was spread out on the wet quay. Especially after the departure of the hearse, it would be hard to imagine that any of those boxes with the painted lading marks contained a person, a mother, an extinguished world whose life had been more richly and deeply felt than most. The workers wrapped an iron chain around the coffin as if it were flour sacks and petroleum barrels. And when the mechanic in charge of the winch gave a signal, it was lifted up. It swung for a while in the air over the loading ramp, until a new command was given. In the midst of the rattle of chains and loud hissing, the old Jutland pastor's widow was lowered between beer barrels, brandy casks, and sugar sacks.

Behind the café window, Per's face became more and more pale. The waiter, who had, all this time, been looking at him because he was so quiet and had left his beer untouched, rushed up to him, alarmed, and asked, "Are you ill, sir?" Per turned around with a confused expression. He had forgotten where he was. Suddenly, he felt the floor lift him up and the walls collapse into the room.

"Give me some cognac," he managed to say. He drank two glasses, one immediately after the other, and a little color came back into his cheeks. He had just seen his mother hanging there and swaying in the air like a bale of goods, and he felt night closing around him; at the same time, a flash of lightning revealed the foundation of existence: it was that cold and silent, ever indifferent, pervasive wilderness of ice he had seen on his first journey through the Alps. When he again looked over at the ship, the work of moving bales and barrels was in full swing.

His brothers stood with the man in work clothes in the middle of the wharf, as Eberhard conscientiously counted out some money into his outstretched hand. After having received the sum, the man continued standing there for a while, evidently hoping for an extra tip that was not forthcoming, as the brothers left in a line with a uniform, measured stride.

Per stayed seated. Despite the fact that the other guests had begun to make him the object of attention, he couldn't get himself to leave. He wanted to stay near his mother up to the last moment. It was extremely unpleasant to think that she would be lying there, all alone, so completely abandoned. And, suddenly, a redeeming thought shot through him. He did not need to part from her here. He could follow her on her journey without anyone knowing about it, could accompany her like a secret guard of honor during the overnight run through Kattegat, and go ashore at one of the stopping places at the mouth of the fjord at home, where the ship would be in the early-morning hours of the next day. He could go from there to a station for the East Jutland train in the course of the morning and be back in Copenhagen by evening.

He looked at his watch. Just two hours until the ship's departure. Consequently, there could be no question of going out to Jakobe, who was the one who needed to know about his journey. He had to settle for writing to her. But when he was home at the hotel and had dipped his pen in ink, he felt how difficult it would be to explain himself decently in a letter. He therefore sent a very short telegram that told her only what was absolutely necessary.

Then he began to pack his suitcase, but suddenly stopped, holding a pair of boots in his hand—he happened to think of Colonel Bjerregrav. In all probability, the colonel expected his return visit that very day. To put it off, even for a couple of days, would be a discourtesy that could again ruin the potentially invaluable relationship. What could he do? . . . No, he had to content himself with writing to him: "Because of an unavoidable journey . . . ," he wrote.

Shortly afterward, he was sitting in a carriage on the way to the steamship. Meanwhile, it occurred to him that, when he came to Jutland, he might as well pay the promised visit to the master of the royal hunt's wife and the baroness in Kærsholm. There was good cause and expedience for renewing his connection with the two women. Since his return, he had constantly felt oppressed by his dependency on his parents-in-law, who seemed alien to him and always would. Philip Salomon had never alluded to money accounts, but it was, nonetheless, a pain to owe the man gratitude. In the meantime, it was again necessary to get a loan to be able to travel to America, and it was now his intention to get that from the baroness, who, on her own, had urged, almost begged him, to call on her for support.

When Per's telegram reached Skovbakken, Jakobe was up in her room. Without suspecting what Per was busy with during the day, she had gone into the city to make some purchases after lunch and had also looked for him at the hotel. When she found out from the porter that he was not there, she was ashamed and departed without leaving a note. For a time, she walked through the streets in the wild hope of meeting him, but with some anxiety because she knew Per did not like such chance encounters. Finally, the rain drove her home.

She found no peace even at home. She felt, in the last days, a certain restlessness that impelled her to a futile and fretful busyness. And then, she was occupied with preparations for the trip to England. Whatever was on the other side of what she secretly named "the second wedding journey," she blocked out as much as possible to prevent anxiety, unrest, or worry from throwing a shadow on their renewed union. In those two short weeks, she wanted to live only for her love. Deeply, deeply would she drink and slake her burning thirst for life before the days of distress arrived. When she read the telegram, she was instinctively seized by a troubling presentiment she could no longer grasp the very next moment. Actually, there was nothing so remarkable in what Per had done. She assured herself that it was natural and nice that he wanted to pay his mother this last respect. In a few days, she would have him back.

Still, when she read the telegram a second time, she again felt frightened. And every time she looked at his curt message, she seemed to be able to read more into it. The twenty words raised so many questions in her. Where did he get such an idea? The day before he hadn't said a thing about it. Had he, perhaps, spoken to someone in the family? And why had he telegraphed at the last minute? Why had he gone off without saying goodbye? She remained seated with her cheek resting on her hand and the telegram in her lap. It had begun to grow dark, and the twilight that gathered in the corners of the little room seemed to inject an even heavier and more threatening severity into her mood of misgiving.

She was thinking about how much he still held back from her, despite all her entreaties for candor and trust. She was aware, from time to time, how little she knew about what he was planning, thinking, occupying himself with, and she had to ask herself whether she would ever succeed in overcoming the hidden, inhibited, mistrustful nature of his character that caused her so much pain.

But down in the garden room, it was cheerful. The family was hosting some acquaintances from among the neighboring summer residents, and Nanny, who always brought little stories back with her from the city, led the conversation. She sought to cover her disappointment over not having come upon Per with incessant, somewhat strained, laughter.

She had, in this regard, really been unlucky, because her visits to Skovbakken, of late, had been irregular. Although she had, in the meantime, meditated all sorts of ways to prevent Per from escaping her, she couldn't figure out if he had just left or if it would be necessary to take her leave before he was expected. Because of this, she was sick with impatience to see him. She no longer was thinking of vengeance. She had been able to gather from Jakobe's attitude toward her that Per had betrayed nothing, and she had to admit to herself that she was in love with him. By his concealment, which she ascribed to consideration for her, presuming a hidden tenderness, he had conquered her shallow heart. The thought of hazarding her marriage and its invested hopes for his sake no longer seemed so strange. Nor would she draw back from seriously engaging in battle with her sister over him. Hearing of their marriage preparations only made her more passionately determined to get him. She begrudged Jakobe that attractive, strong man with the red mouth. The remembrance of his full lips could, at times, drive her wild with longing.

And then, not to come today! Nanny was not the only one who had expected him impatiently. For a while, Ivan was restlessly walking up and down the terrace, looking at his watch every second. He had something very important to tell him. The attorney Hasselager had asked for Per's address in a letter because he and Herr Nørrehave, with several others, wanted to meet with him tomorrow. Ivan was sure he would see Per this evening. But when he heard that a telegram had come for Jakobe, it was clear to him Per was excusing himself, and he hurried to the station in hopes of finding him in the city.

Meanwhile, it had become almost dark in the garden room. The maid came in to shut the door, after which lamps were placed around the tables and consoles. Though she was expressly called, Jakobe had not yet come down, even when tea was served. Nanny, who had learned about the telegram, took it as a good omen. This couldn't bode well for the marriage! Her parents spoke as little as possible about it; they had no great faith in it.

There was music for an hour or so, and when it was eleven o'clock, the guests prepared to go. Nanny, on the contrary, ventured to defy Dyhring's decided objections and stayed there overnight in the hope that Per would come the next morning. Just then, Ivan came back from the city with a very distraught expression. When the visitors had left, he turned to his parents and Nanny to ask, "Hasn't Jakobe been down this evening?"

"No, why?"

"Sidenius is traveling."

"Traveling? Where to?"

"Just to Jutland. They said at the hotel that he would be gone for a couple of days."

"Yes, he is going to the burial," said his mother. "That's why he telegraphed to Jakobe."

"Well, it's still so strange . . . to leave without telling anyone. And just now!" said Ivan, mentioning his letter from Hasselager and the colonel's visit that would remain unreciprocated. Fru Salomon looked questioningly at her husband. But he said nothing. He had made it a rule not to speak about his future son-in-law. He merely shook his head and said, "Come on, children. Let's go to bed."

Per had already, for some time, been shipboard on the open sea. Like a giant, floating sarcophagus, the ship's large, dark body glided over the peaceful surface in the twilight while smoke billowed over it like mourning crepe. The sky was covered with clouds and hung heavy and black over the horizon. Here and there was a rift in the clouds through which a few pale stars peeked down like angel eyes watching over the solemn journey of the corpse.

Per sat alone up on the mid-deck, enveloped in his cloak, and looked out over the water. He had chosen a spot as near as possible to his mother's casket below. All the ship's other passengers had gradually gone to sleep. No voices could be heard from the rooms on the foredeck or from the cabins. The pilot on duty was pacing back and forth on the command bridge with quiet strides, and from the sternpost, at intervals, the short clangs of the log clock sounded. There was no utterance on the whole ship other than the persistent pounding of the machines and propeller and, now and then, from below, the clanking of a stoker's shovel.

In the southwest, the beacon fire from Hesselø came up over the horizon. The watch on the bridge and the pilot were relieved shortly after. Per noticed that the first and second pilots were, on their switch, negotiating something that made them lower their voices. Immediately afterward, everything fell again into deep peace and stillness around him. He didn't even think of resting. He would continue to stay as near as possible to his mother, and, besides, he knew he wouldn't be able to get any sleep.

So many pictures from his childhood home glided before him that night while he stood there staring out over the radiant sea surface. He had never before really managed a whole and consistent sense of his mother. Because she was, while living, put into the shade by the authoritative father, his remembrance of her remained darkened by the absolute dislike that still clung to that man in his mind. He recalled her most vividly from her long time in her sickbed. When his sleeping or waking thoughts were taken up with her—and that happened more frequently than he himself realized—he always saw her in bed in the dim room with the dark green blind pulled down, with him or one of his siblings sitting at her feet massaging her painful legs. But, of late, more memories than ever were crystallizing from those days and nights when she moved through the house, washing and dressing the children, helping the oldest with their homework, and going round to the children's rooms in her long, white gown, straightening a pillow here, patting a quilt there, stroking their hair with a remarkably soft hand just as they were closing their eyes and turning over.

He remembered most clearly the war year, though he was too little to understand its misery and, therefore, could be amused by the disturbance and disorder. The town had been occupied for months by German troops who, daily, marched through the streets with music and pompous drum majors at the head of the review, stopping at the marketplace or riding grounds for the roll call. Even the parsonage had always been full of soldiers; often up to twenty men were in the yard, with seven or eight horses stabled in the peat stall, driven out every morning to the garden to be curried under an officer's supervision. Only a few rooms, into which so many children had to be crammed at random, were left for the family. He had found all this entertaining. And they had syrup at meals instead of butter! When he thought about it afterward, he realized his mother was awaiting, then, the delivery of her twelfth child—the twelfth painful battle against death. And more. The children got sick; one of them, a three-year-old girl, died, after terrible suffering. Later, he gathered from stories, she breathed her last in her mother's arms just as a Prussian regiment was marching out of the city and another was expected.

Was it so strange that his mother became, finally, nothing but her anxiety? Perhaps the younger generation that grew up in such apparently peaceful and reassuring times seemed to judge unfairly the insecurity and fearfulness of the parents, especially of those who had endured the war's pains and humiliations. Wasn't it rather surprising that his mother wasn't entirely overcome? Jakobe, who had herself gone through some suffering, had also recently marveled how his mother, with such a weak body, had called upon an almost supernatural strength to bear all of fate's heavy vicissitudes without complaining. Yes, how did she manage that? What inner fortitude more or less saved the elder generation in that time of miseries, through the war years' fearful agitations and the deadly paralysis that followed, through all the bloody collapse that made his mother's suffering story so movingly emblematic.

For her own part, his mother had never been in doubt about the answer. He remembered the lines she continually came back to in conversations:

> Not my honor, Christ the Lord
> But Thine, who save us by Thy word.

Per got up, chilled to the bone, and began to walk up and down the long runway mat that was laid on the deck. But his legs felt like sandbags and his head was so heavy with the emotion of the day that he had to sit down again. The pilot came down from the command bridge and stopped near him with the clear intention of initiating a chat. He called Per's attention to a row of boats, rocking on the waves with loose sails, and said it was flounder fishermen who were now going home to mooring on the southern current from the banks around Anholt.

"Oh, I see," said Per curtly. He happened to be thinking about the letter his mother had left for him and of the box that probably contained his father's watch. He did not know how he would gain the courage to read the letter. He wanted to believe that his mother had not altogether misunderstood him—but there had been something in Eberhard's look the day before that seemed to portend nothing good. He again got up, so chilled by painful anxiety that he couldn't stay still.

"You really should go to bed," said the pilot, and drew himself together, his hands in his pockets. "Damn if it isn't cold enough on deck to freeze the balls off a brass monkey." The tone of disrespect made Per stiffen. He had an answer on his lips, but then he began to realize that he had been suspected of contemplating suicide and that had been the question discussed by the two pilots before, when they quietly exchanged words at the relief. He asked the man straight out whether he thought he was going to jump overboard.

"Since you yourself say it, I won't deny we thought of that up there. Those things happen now and then. And we're not spared 'cause it leaves behind nothin' but trouble—legal inquiries and everythin' else. Just last fall we had that trouble with a man who jumped into the sea in these very waters!"

"And what kind of man was he?"

"A steerage passenger from Horsens. He said somethin' had gone wrong in his world. His hat was the only thing we saw of him again. And he's never been heard of since. So now he's gone with the mackerels."

Per instinctively lowered his eyes. Then he said goodnight and went below deck. For some hours he lay there in stuffy quarters in the midst of snoring, groaning men and could not fall asleep. His thoughts would not leave him in peace. He felt that, during this night, a long-developing spiritual rebirth was coming into being. It was as if, out of the darkness and mist, a new world was opening to which, up to now, the path had been hard to recognize. What was behind him sank into nothingness. In the story of an old, infirm pastor's wife, a power opened for him compared to which even a Caesar's triumph now seemed poor and paltry—a power and greatness in suffering, renunciation, and self-sacrifice.

He lay with his hands behind his head and with wide-open eyes, looking into the semidarkness with the anxious presentiment of an imminent spiritual struggle. Still, he was not depressed. To his own surprise, he didn't envy the peaceful conscience of the people around him, snoring and snorting under the influence of a sleep potion. In his awareness of remorse and grief, there was something of the wonderful thrill of a woman's labor pains that signaled a new life about to be born with new hopes and promises.

At daylight, Per disembarked at the first landing in the fjord's mouth where the ship stopped. From the top of a hill, his eyes followed the slow journey around the fjord's many windings through the wide stretch of meadowland, the same way he himself, eight years ago, set out to meet the world with such young courage and sunny hopes. Eight years. And he really had had "luck" with him. He had conquered the kingdom he had desired and the crown he felt he had been born for. With dew hanging on his eyelids like rainbowed tears, he kept staring over the flower-filled meadows at the sarcophagus steaming away until it disappeared in the morning mist like a vision for which the realms of heaven open up.

BOOK 7

LUCKY PER, HIS VOYAGE TO AMERICA

CHAPTER 19

IN ONE OF East Jutland's most fertile hollows, a manor lay that, with its red-brown walls and broad, rising gables, reminded one of a cloister. That was Kærsholm. It was situated on the border of a flat meadow range that wound through the country like a mighty, green river with elevations of fields and woods on both sides.

In the middle of the meadow flowed a lazy stream, the dwindling remains of a proud expanse of water that once had covered the almost five-mile-wide valley. Walking along the meadowland, away from the bank, you could not even see the river, only an endless surface of gleaming green sward, broken here and there by a ditch or by a puddle with some still-standing water. It was strange, then, to think of the fresh, massive body of water that, in the old days, had splashed between these peaceful hills. Now, where small brown and gray songbirds timidly flew up from the reeds, there had once been large herring gulls crossing on their sunlit wings; where the ditch diggers and dung spreaders reverently munched on their lard sandwich snack, battle-drunk freebooters had once come ashore from their blood-stained ships, joyfully carrying home their booty.

Up on the elevations, where light-filled and friendly groves rose above the cornfields, thick, gloomy, wild woods once brooded, where wolves howled on frosty, moonlit nights. The woods still remained a refuge for the exploits of the daring and spirited, long after the land had risen up and the former sea was cultivated by peaceful labor. From there sounded the shrill hunting horn of the landed masters delivering death from their saddle bows and dragging the bloody prey through the woods. There storms screamed, a thousand-voiced roar, which sounded like a ghostly echo of the ocean's organ tones that had once filled minds with solemn terror.

But, gradually, the woods as well were pushed back by the arable land. A crowd of weaponless strangers settled here, planted gardens, and lived on the fruits of the earth. By one route, marked by erected crosses and holy pictures, they came up from the south in long cowls, and sandals on their naked feet. Soon, the first prayer bells rang "Peace on earth" across the old land of the Vikings. As the years passed, the farmers' oxen gnawed their way, from all sides, into the dark woods, where crows already cackled from abandoned eagle nests.

Centuries went by. The riches of Mother Earth, accumulated in barns and stables from the blooming fields and meadows, streamed out across the thresholds of the chosen children, filling the cellars of the cloisters and storerooms of the estates with plentiful meat and honey-sweet beer, finally congealing behind the cowls and shining knights' armor as thick blood. Then, while the holy monk was rendering fat from kidneys, he was seized with carnal temptations. He wanted to marry, felt the simple Christian duty to become a father and submissively to share life's riches with the rest of Adam's sons. The first Pastor Sidenius with a starched collar and a flock of children emerged out of the coarse penance robe, stiff hemp rope, and sandals, as from a cocoon. At the same time, the masters accommodated themselves more and more to the bourgeois social order. With their inherited material comfort protected by friendly laws, they felt less inclined toward adventure and the miserable life of the warrior. The offspring of the Vikings were cattlemen or proud landowners with velvet trousers and waving plumes on their hats. Large and fleshy, flabby from atrophied muscles, they rode out on farting steeds as carriers of the homely blessings of the earth.

These were men like Herr Lave Eskesen Brok, who was involved in feuds and lawsuits with half of Jutland, or like Knight Oluf Pedersen Gyldenstjerne, whose own sisters, Fru Elsebe and the spinster Lene, accused him at Viborg Landssting "of doing great damage and injustice against them, namely, by hitting them and the servants with weapons and drawn swords, overturning their houses, and brutally taking their property from them." These were men with a lively willfulness and a lust for adventure in their pirate blood, who were marked by stubborn arrogance and a passion for pursuit. Or there were individuals like Jørgen Arnfeld, in whom an ancient savagery expressed itself as bloody religious fanaticism—who, with a voluptuous faith, set up secret pipes to carry sounds from the castle's cellar prison up to his room so that his soul could gloat over the wretched screams of witches

and other diabolical rabble he had tortured to death in those dark
pits and mud-filled caverns in the blessed name of the dear Lord
Jesus Christ. . . .

A rich, gleaming meadow, monotonous and silent, stretched out
between the hills like a wilderness, without a path, house, or tree.
If it wasn't harvest time, you could follow, by the hour, the snaking brook without meeting a person or hearing any sound other
than the murmur of the stream and, now and then, the dull drone
of a train in the distance going over a bridge.

The old cargo-boat traffic, the last remains of the navigational
commerce that up to a dozen years ago still generated some life
on the river, was now as good as stopped. Weeks could pass by
without seeing any of those long, wide-bowed vessels that, when
loaded, stood so deep in the water that the crew, pushing with
sturdy poles against the current, could keep their feet dry only
on gangway planks along the gunwale.

You could often bump into people who, with good Danish
philosophic calm, sat on the bank with long angling poles and
smoked. Sometimes, there was eel fishing, where both men and
women waded into the water over their waists and poked up eels
from the slimy, muddy bottom.

And then, you might meet a particular hunter whom the district folk seemed to avoid, a tall, lean, gloomy-looking man with
high shoulders and a pair of long legs in big boots. He had a rather
reserved expression and, generally, didn't return greetings. His
face was sallow, his nose flat, and a coarse, dark beard covered his
mouth.

This was the proprietor of Kærsholm, Herr Prangen, master
of the royal hunt. While his two spotted hunting bitches ran
around the meadow and, now and then, disappeared in the
watery ooze with a splash, he himself walked slowly and straight
ahead. His gun usually hung over his back, and his hands were
buried in the slanting pockets of his tufted shooting jacket. It was
clear that he was walking here not so much to shoot as to be alone
with his dark thoughts.

People often spoke about what it could be that the master was
always pondering. It was difficult to make it out. It was as if more
than one man lived in him. The silent man with a scowl could
sometimes be a talkative, sociable man, a Munchausen, puffed
up with foolish self-regard. For some time, it was thought that

relations with his wife disposed him to pensive moods. Now, people inclined more to the explanation of countless lawsuits in which he was uninterruptedly entangled and that, almost without exception, ended badly for him. And there was talk of digestive problems. It was well known that frequent dispatches had to go out in a hurry from Kærsholm to town in order to procure drops from the apothecary.

Curiously enough, even the master was unable to understand the cause of his moodiness. While he sat comfortably in his room and amused himself with watching puffs of smoke from his pipe sail into the sunshine, depression could rise up like a black cloud to blight his existence. When he struggled in vain to think of the cause, he always sank deeper into despair. The word would quickly spread around Kærsholm's stables and barns that "the humors" had come over the master, and there was a general move to sneak off when his long-legged form appeared. With his dark, blue, hollow eyes and his bowed head that gave him the look of an ox with a board in front of his forehead, it wasn't at all pleasant to look at him. His wife, an intelligent woman too proud to submit openly to his moods, always pretended not to notice anything. She realized that any attempt to influence his temper could only make it worse. The nuisance had to play itself out and disappear as mysteriously as it came.

At their lonely meals, where the master didn't open his mouth except for eating, she took over the conversation and, at the same time, tamed him by seeing to it that he got his favorite dishes. The master was, in fact, a big eater, and even the blackest mood never influenced his appetite. Huge portions of rice pudding with sweet beer, pork loin with apples, sausage with cabbage in white sauce, and the like disappeared into him as into an alms bag. After the meal, he would withdraw into his own room, separated from the living room by a small sunroom. The master's wife always cleverly took care that the doors between them were not shut, to shield her husband from too obvious an isolation in the eyes of the servants. She knew that there was talk about their marriage—another reason to keep the appearance of intimacy open between them.

The master's wife had been over thirty years old when she married Prangen, then only a landowner. The connection had caused some surprise and snickers among her contemporaries, because Herr Prangen had become known to them only by his reputation for lack of intelligence and his untrustworthy tall tales. But the most provocative rumor in the district had been concerned with *her* past. It was said that her beauty had early excited a very high-ranking gentleman's interest, but whether this had led to any more intimate a relationship, no one could reliably say.

There was a general, hidden amusement when the proprietor, in a high, spirited mood, would brag about his wife's connections at court. And later, her conduct had given rise to prattle and gossip as well. Her name had been connected with this or that Danish aristocrat because of her frequent trips to Copenhagen and her often extended stays in European spas. But there was no real proof. She understood how to frustrate all inquiries with clever tact. And her husband, who was so taken up with the demands of his processes and indigestion, was never, or just passingly, suspicious.

She herself in her younger years took this sin of dalliance very lightly. She had married Prangen because he was suitable to serve as a screen for her passions. And, in addition, she justified herself by procuring him, as ample compensation, an appointed title that was, certainly, higher than he could have expected from his birth, education, and financial circumstances. Meanwhile, when she had grown older and her blood had ceased boiling, her conscience excused itself with a claim on her credit plus usurious interest. The wife of the master of the royal hunt had, in her later years, become very religious. A certain Pastor Blomberg from a neighboring district had, in this regard, a great deal of influence over her. He did not belong to those fanatical preachers who, in other regions of the country, conjured up the Middle Ages from the grave. He was, on the contrary, a very mild and humane pastor who avoided all excess and bombast—a cheerful, consoling preacher of a peaceful and pleasant everyday gospel that did not demand impossible sacrifices of life's comforts and, therefore, attracted many followers.

The master's wife was grateful that her conscience had gained a comparatively painless release. She fell in love completely with this Christianity that was so movingly undemanding. If she found it, from time to time, a little difficult to remember her devotional hour and to find just the right childlike, trusting tone in her private intercourse with the Highest, she made up for it by her intense loyalty to all of the church's functions. Her rooms were overflowing with godly books and journals, and in private circles she sometimes took part in debates while she more and more openly acted as a missionary for the Blomberg faith.

It was to that house, with this couple, that Per sought refuge after his secret night journey over Kattegat with his mother's corpse. Both bodily and mentally exhausted, he reached Kærsholm around noon the same day on which he had, early in the morning, left the ship at the mouth of the fjord. He received a warm reception not only from the master's wife and her sister, the baroness, who was still visiting, but also from the master himself, who had just heard that he had, quite exceptionally, won one of his court suits.

In order to acquaint Per immediately with the process's detailed history, he led him into his room and devoted some time to telling him of the other two legal disputes he had won in his life. One, as he described it, turned on such an astonishing, amazing, and complicated situation that the high court devoted three full days to the case. Per was happy to be permitted to sit quietly with his own thoughts, which were still following his mother's coffin. The master, who wasn't used to having such a patient audience, afterward confided to his wife that he found her young friend very appealing. When Per, at lunch, brought up his plans for departure, the master eagerly sought to persuade him to settle at Kærsholm for a while, now that summer had finally arrived. It wasn't hard to convince him. He didn't have the slightest longing for Copenhagen, and where, he thought, could he find a better place in which to fight through the spiritual crisis he felt coming on? He was given a peaceful and pretty room that overlooked the park on a side of the main house. A row of thick-leaved chestnut trees let in a mild light. In the middle of the room, on the white, scrubbed floor, stood a four-cornered oak table with heavy, sphered legs and four high-backed chairs. The bed was hidden behind a folding screen and, as well, by a tall, old-fashioned iron stove that seemed to guard it like an armored knight. On the wall between the windows hung a shelf full of books.

He felt immediately at home in this room, which was so pleasant in contrast to the various, uniform, numbered hotel rooms he had been condemned to live in. The green half-light corresponded to something in his own, expectant mood, and this was just the hidden, cloistered retreat he now needed. In particular, he was happy to have the books, on whose backs he had already read the titles, edifying and theological works that the master's wife had often talked about to him with some warmth. He telegraphed to the hotel in Copenhagen to send some of his clothes. To Jakobe he wrote an explanatory letter telling her of the sudden impulse that had led him to follow his mother's body and use the occasion to redeem a promise to visit his old traveling companions from Italy. About his reasons for staying at Kærsholm, he confessed, for the time being, only that he needed to rest and gather strength for the impending new journey. He said to himself that he still lacked the necessary understanding of what he should and could explain to her in such a letter. That must wait. There was now an irremediable problem in their relationship: they were not rooted in the same spiritual soil. However much goodwill there was on both sides, the difference in their natures precluded, in reality, any deeper intimacy.

In the evening, after he had sent off the letter, his mind immediately felt more at peace. At sunset, when he sat with the ladies in the living room, he had the genuine sense of being at home, even in such foreign surroundings. He didn't try to figure out precisely why this was so. But when the last of the sunlight played over the broad windowsills, there was something ghostly in the large, somewhat low and dusky atmosphere of the room, even in the slightly stuffy air in which hung traces of peat smoke from the kitchen that held him in a motherly embrace.

The master, who had settled down with them, suddenly got up with a great hullabaloo and went humming through the sunroom back to his own room, leaving both doors open behind him. A while after, a rummaging and rattling were heard and the sound of a window opening—then the shrill tones of a hunting horn echoing in the hills and woods.

Among the many quaint fantasies with which the master kept up his self-esteem was this one: that he was a virtuoso of his brass horn. First, he played some hunting signals that came back from the answering woods with a kind of musty sound from olden times when his forefathers made their bloody way through the thickets. Then he played a couple of patriotic songs, after which he felt more and more the warm feelings, the simple poetry of the heart.

It sounded frightful. And then he played the melody to "It's Lovely to Be Here for Each Other," and he injected a really languishing, heartfelt tone into his delivery of the old song in praise of married life. He made his unsure notes tremble in such an elaborate way that Per didn't dare raise his eyes from the floor for fear of laughing. The master's wife, on the other hand, sat with her cheek resting on her hand and looked out the window with a tender and gentle womanly smile.

Per spent some days in the pleasant company of the inhabitants of the estate. The master seemed in good humor now and showed him around the property. Per took a carriage ride with the ladies in the afternoon in the pretty surroundings and, in addition, went on small outings on his own or with the steward, a young man of his own age. It wasn't long before his body felt strong again and his cheeks as becomingly tanned as when he had returned from Italy. He spoke as little as possible about his relations with the Salomon house, which was quickly noticed by the master's wife, who, accordingly, never brought the subject up. Because he still assumed that the two ladies were taken in by his desperate version of his mysterious origins, he was wary about mentioning his mother and the real reason for his flight to Jutland. But after a while, he realized that the master's wife, at least, must have procured some intelligence about his family. He was convinced that she had gotten her information from Pastor Blomberg, of whom she had spoken a few times with such respect.

He quickly had to give up the thought that had led him here, to borrow money from the baroness. He was really a little afraid to be alone with her because her tone was so uncomfortably intimate. With her dried-up little lace-capped head supported by two fingers, she would begin, immediately, to speak of her dead brother and regularly end by reciting verses from her favorite poets, Hertz and Paludan-Müller.

Determined not to go again to his father-in-law for a loan, Per invested all his hopes in the master and his wife. It shouldn't be said that he was living endlessly off the favors of Philip Salomon. Up to now, he had not been able to find a suitable moment to bring up the issue. There was so much else that occupied him, not only in his inmost being but also in the outer world around him. Before everything, there was nature. After three days, he had only told the master's wife that he intended to go to America soon to continue his studies.

The weather stayed summery, and spring dressed the environs in their best. Fields and woods were fresh and green, and the meadow was one big, flowered carpet. Per was already chummy with the steward of the estate. He liked to spend the quiet time after the midday meal with him in his room, which was in an independent wing of the administrative building. From here, on one side, could be seen the dairy where milkmaids, with their skirts tucked up, moved in and out with clinking tin pails. On the other side, the view from a window was of the open yard behind the dunghill where Kærsholm's most valuable prize bull was fulfilling his assignations with the cows. Stretched out on the sofa with a cigar in his mouth, Per entertained himself here with all kinds of country chatter, or he played with the steward's dog, a black poodle with puppies. The steward himself was a gentle Jutlander of the kind that, in all good nature, shows his lack of regard for everything others make a fuss about. Above all, he always had some funny story or other to tell. And he didn't do it out of malice, but only out of comic delight.

Per found pleasure in his company and these hours of happy companionship in the midst of the lively busyness of the farm helped to drive away the moody discomfort he had come with. The river had a strange, mystical attraction for him. It was the same smooth-flowing water that, only nine or ten miles away, had gurgled along the decaying bridge in his childhood town and that, with its magic reed bank and hidden muddy bottom, had been his great love as a boy. When, one day, he discovered a small boat in a shelter on the bank, his old passion for fishing seized him. With the help of the steward, he procured the necessary tackle and sat daily, by the hour, on the river with his line.

And so some days passed and the crisis he had anticipated with so much suspense and apprehension failed, at least for the time being, to materialize. The explosive spirituality that was gathering in him that night on the steamship had dissipated in the outdoor life he was enjoying here. The edifying books of the master's wife were left, up until now, virtually untouched in his bookcase. He was out all day. When he finally came into his room in the evenings and lit the lamp to sit down with a book, he read only a few lines before a pleasant sleepiness descended on him like an earthly blessing and put him to bed.

He began to miss Jakobe a little. When he sat in his little boat and let himself bake in the sun, or when he stretched out in his favorite spot in the shade on the fringe of the woods, he wished she could share these days of summer joy with him. It certainly would have done her good to get the dust of the beach path out of her lungs. She had lately seemed so high-strung. But then he began to think that she would certainly decline. She had no taste for the kind of plant life he was leading. She couldn't at all understand the pleasure of lying still with your hands under your head and letting your thoughts drift through the clouds in the limitless blue with a sense that your whole being is melting and floating into eternity. He remembered how, once, in one of her love letters to him, she had used the expression, concerning her disposition, that she was as restless as the ocean. That was like her.

A lack of constraint contributed to the sense of well-being that marked his life at Kærsholm, even to his clothes. The master himself stalked around the rooms with his long boots and didn't dress until the midday dinner. Nor was his wife very particular about her toilette at home. And that rustic relaxation immediately worked infectiously on Per, for whom the strict observation of form in the house of his parents-in-law and the continual changes of clothes demanded by modern traveling were, often, really oppressive.

One warm, sunny day, when Per returned from the river with his pole over his shoulder, he met the master's wife, accompanied by a young lady, a blonde in a bright and light, blue-striped dress. The two ladies were going up the long poplar lane that led from the meadow to the park in front of the main house. They walked with their arms around each other's waist and something special in the young woman's manner made one think of the two as a pair of lovers.

The master's wife introduced them in passing: "Engineer Sidenius from Copenhagen—Frøken Blomberg," and added, merely, that Pastor Blomberg was visiting her husband inside and would certainly be glad to meet him. Per swore to himself as he went on through the park and into his room. He was convinced that his beautiful peace was about to disappear, so he was hostile, beforehand, to that pastor who seemed to play a special role in the house. In addition, he had gradually realized who the man was. He remembered that he had, now and then, seen him mentioned in the papers as a talented advocate for one of the day's many ecclesiastical movements, and he also faintly remembered that his activity had been the subject of debate in his parents' house because his brother Thomas—the curate—had been more taken with his preachings than seemed right to his father.

He would have preferred to stay in his room during the visit, but the invitation of the master's wife to meet the pastor was so amiable that he really could not disregard it. He found the strange man, sure enough, sitting opposite the master in a tobacco mist with a coffee service between them. As soon as he entered, their conversation stopped in a way that suggested they had just been talking about him.

Per was mildly surprised by Pastor Blomberg's appearance. After all he had heard at Kærsholm about this church reformer and his battle for the so-called more human side of divine affairs, he envisioned him in the form of an exalted Nordic apostle—a Christian Viking; instead, he saw before him a little, plump, and chubby-cheeked man who in no way could be distinguished from the typical, affable, Danish pastor. Clear, blue, soulful eyes, which seemed like two large drops of water in which a peaceful heaven was mirrored, shone from his large head, which was covered with wavy, flaxen hair and a beard. From his clothes (he wore a skimpy, summer jacket of black twill) to the way he sat back in his chair and puffed on a chewed cigar, it was evident that the pastor was trying to cast off the signs of his distinction, to shake off veneration—a move by which, to his colleagues' vexation, he had attracted many irreverent jokes. In spite of this, no one was ever in doubt that here was a spiritual man. In that regard, his whole person unmistakeably bore the characteristic stamp of self-righteousness, the patriarchal sense of nobility that hung on the men of the cloth like that moldy smell that always rose, despite all the modern mechanical adjustments for heat and ventilation, from the old floors of churches.

Pastor Blomberg got up with some difficulty from the chair and shook Per's hand with rustic heartiness. "Well, look at this," he said, and gazed at him in an entirely unconstrained manner. "Welcome to our neighborhood, Herr Engineer." There was something in the tone that seemed condescending or patronizing and made Per stiffen. "Yes, the name Sidenius is, naturally, not unknown to me," he continued. "For one thing, your father was a man of fine reputation in our profession. Although we were serving for years as neighbors, so to speak, I never knew him personally. Our church views were, in many respects, quite different. But I esteem him in death. He was a zealous worker." When Per did not answer, the pastor sat down, and for a moment no one spoke. Pastor Blomberg turned again to the master and began to talk about affairs of the district. Per sat down by the window and lit a cigar. Half turned away, he was viewing the expansive lawn, with a gilded sundial in the middle, that stretched out from the main house. He was looking at the master's wife and the very young woman, who were coming back on the path and just sitting down on a bench in the shade of a big beech tree on the other side of the grass. The master's wife put down her parasol, and her companion laid her broad-brimmed summer hat on the bench and brushed a curl from her forehead.

Per started to look more carefully at the pastor's daughter. She seemed eighteen or nineteen years old, and, except for her blond hair, she didn't resemble her father. She was tall and lanky, with a slender, fine figure. From his distance, he could not clearly distinguish her facial features, but he found her form very attractive. As she sat there in the dark shade of the tree, a little bent forward, and with one knee over the other, she was twisting a plucked flower, and now and then sniffing it. She affected him like a dreamscape. She made an almost bodiless impression in her light dress, especially next to the massive form of the master's wife, whose shiny gray silk bodice stretched over her chest like steel armor. She reminded Per of someone. Already before, on the pathway, the same memory had flitted across his mind.

That deer-like slenderness, the thick blond, almost silver hair, the sloping shoulders—in all this there was something he once knew that made him sad. The pastor got up from the table to go. It was his intention, he said, to visit a man in the neighborhood, one of his former parishioners, injured by a mad bull. He and his daughter would drop in again on the way back. When he said goodbye to Per, he looked at him once more with unreserved candor and let him know that if his way ever passed by the Bøstrup parsonage, it would please him if he looked in.

"I well know," the pastor said cheerfully, "that today's young men of Copenhagen view the church as a temple of ignorance, the parsonage as its vestibule. But perhaps we aren't really so bad as your Copenhagen press and litterateurs make us out. Now you yourself can come and see."

Despite the condescension in his tone, Per returned the handshake and thanked him with a polite murmur. The impression his daughter had made rendered him unconsciously more accepting of the self-satisfied little man. The master followed the pastor out. Per, on the other hand, took up the large straw hat he had brought with him from Italy and went back through the sunroom out to the veranda steps, where he began to look into the air as if he didn't suspect the presence of the ladies. The master's wife called him and asked, "Can you guess what Frøken Blomberg thinks you look like?" The young woman, whose hand she held in her lap, blushed a hot red and wanted to cover the mouth of her hostess with her other hand.

"My dear, why can't I say it? I think it sounds so amusing. Frøken Blomberg says you look like a nabob. And she's really right. There's something exotic about you today."

"A nabob!" Per repeated, and looked down at his light yellow velvety suit that came from Italy and that he was wearing now for the first time on the occasion of the very warm, sunny day. "That flatters me, naturally, only I, unfortunately, lack the necessary millions," he replied.

"But you'll be getting them," the master's wife observed casually. The words fell out of her mouth half against her will. She regretted them immediately and began to talk about other things. Per well understood the meaning of the little remark, and it annoyed him. Obviously she had been talking about his engagement, which was indistinguishably joined together with his father-in-law's money in everyone's mind. In addition, he himself had understood that Frøken Blomberg's nabob simile was not meant as a compliment.

He sat down and inspected the young lady. Now, when he could judge her figure soberly, like a connoisseur, he did not see much to find fault with. Despite his irritation, he had to marvel that he had not already noticed, when meeting her on the path, how very pretty she was. What clear, innocent eyes! What a lovely, softly curved mouth, perhaps a little too tender and pale, but as fresh and untouched as a wild rose.

The two women had begun to talk about the unhappy case the pastor just touched on in the master's room. In turns of phrase that suspiciously resembled her father's, the young woman told how "the pitiable man" had had his whole abdomen ripped open and the doctor didn't think he would live. But Per suddenly became inattentive. He realized who it was the young woman had reminded him of the whole time. It was Fransisca, his Nyboder love. Good God, he thought, and his heart melted. How long has it been since I thought of her! While the women continued their chat, he sank into his memories. He looked continually at the pastor's daughter, who didn't look back once and, seemingly, was unaware she was being observed.

Yes, he said to himself. There really is a likeness. Their stature and carriage are about the same. Undeniable! Frøken Blomberg made a more distinguished picture than Fransisca and, with slimmer lines, a more delicate edition. There was also something that played around the mouth that reminded him of her. Every time Frøken Blomberg smiled, the tip of her tongue would run over her upper lip with a pretty little move, as if she wanted to lick her smile away.

"It's beginning to get cold. Don't you want something around your shoulders, dear girl?" asked the master's wife. The sun was going down behind the park, and humidity, rising from the ground, could be noticed in the air under the leaves.

"I'm not in the least cold. It's so enjoyable sitting here," she said, pleased that the master's wife had again taken her hand and patted it.

"Still, you should get your cape. I'm sure you left it in the living room."

Per stood up. "I'll get it," he said, but at the same time, the young woman rose from the bench. "No, you won't be able to find it," she said hurriedly. And, as if scared he would follow her, she strode quickly across the lawn.

"Isn't she sweet?" asked the master's wife when she was gone, and Per sat down again.

"Yes, she's very pretty," he said a little curtly.

"Yes, that too. And she has such a good disposition, so open and natural. Unfortunately, her health is not really dependable."

"Is Frøken Blomberg sick?"

"My dear fellow—she was in bed all winter—from typhus. As she herself says, for three months she belonged more to the dead than to the living. Can't you see it in her?"

"No—well, she does make a kind of ethereal impression. But that she is frail—"

"Well, thank God she is over the worst. And the summer will, I hope, do the rest. The dear child is so happy here, and she is so thankful for her life, as only someone so young can be who has been close to losing it—and, yes, who knows how to receive life as a gift of grace from God, Herr Sidenius."

Per looked away. He had lately become somewhat embarrassed when the master's wife touched on religious subjects.

"Frøken Blomberg feels a special affection for you," he said, to turn the conversation in a new direction.

"Oh, she likes to come here, the dear little creature. She feels so comfortable at Kærsholm, she says. Around the parents' home, it's perhaps a little monotonous for such a young girl. But, otherwise, it's lovely at Pastor Blomberg's. You really should pay him a visit. He would be so glad to talk with you."

The gardener approached on the path and stopped some distance away.

"What is it, Petersen?" she asked. Hat in hand, he advanced a few steps, and asked her to come into the vegetable garden when it was convenient.

"I'll come presently," said the master's wife, whose Christian feelings of fellowship evidently failed to apply to her own subordinates.

Shortly afterward, she got up and left. The young woman had, in the meantime, come back and looked very unhappy to be left alone with Per. She sat with both hands squeezing the edge of the bench and changed color a couple of times. Suddenly, she called out to the master's wife, who had not yet disappeared from sight, that she would like to accompany her. Almost before receiving an answer, she hurried off.

"Remember—no running!" the master's wife cautioned her.

Per cast a glance at her over his shoulder—and, at that moment, a shadow glided over his face. There was something in her shyness that conjured up a dark memory. His siblings had fled from him like that in his childhood, especially when his father, in the morning or at dinner devotions, directed one of his great punitive preachments at him. Even recently, he had again experienced this when he met the twins; they were so self-conscious, they seemed unsure whether or not to look at him. Nabob! That was, of course, meant as a contemptuous term. The girl had fled from him as from the devil himself. Well, what of it? Since when had he become so feeble that he had to anxiously assess everyone's opinion of him? Or was there something else? Was it true that he himself was beginning to feel his tempestuous chase after happiness as a disgrace?

Well, he didn't need to resort to those kinds of speculations. He had to battle against the inflated feelings that left him such a defenseless prey to his shifting moods. It was high time to put an end to his idleness here and to get back to his work. If he had done harm to himself, as to others—still, in his diligent struggle, in a strong and honest drive to establish something good and useful here on earth, there's where he could find justification, even if a great triumph would elude him.

A window was opened in the main house. The baroness had arisen from her long nap, and a short time later she appeared on the veranda, romantically draped in a lace mantilla fastened at the back of her head. She was heavily powdered, as she was wont to be, to hide the inflamed blemishes that, in the course of the day, appeared on her face. Per quickly disappeared. Rather than having to remain alone with the crazy old lady, he had sneaked out to the park, and now was walking on the road that led along the meadow up to the woods.

It was one of those very light and still summer evenings that, in spite of their peacefulness, seem so sinister. The shadowless earth stretched out silent and empty under a blank sky with neither sun nor stars. The sun had disappeared unceremoniously, leaving only a little, reddish hazy patch on the horizon. There was not one cloud in the sky that might have caught the rising rays and thrown them back over the earth as a reflection of the day's splendor. Here and there on the hills, a windowpane glowed —that was all. Still, down around the river, as soon as the sun disappeared, a kind of spiritual life awakened. The fields began to blend in with the gray clouds. Soon, the wide valley was hidden in undulating vapors. It looked as if the fjord, in a ghostly move, was taking possession of its old bed as night came on. Like smoking surf, a phantom ocean, the pale mist rolled through the hills.

And then a sign of life emerged. A horned head popped up out of the sea of fog and bellowed. A little after, the top half of a man's body came dimly into view; it seemed to end in a dark bottom of a beast with a high tail. Soon, a flock of horned heads appeared, crowding around the man with raised muzzles and pushing vapor out of their nostrils. The man shouted off and on, swinging something over his head. He might have been a centaur in battle with a pack of sea monsters.

It was Kærsholm's three hundred head of cattle being driven home by a herdsman cracking his whip. From the road, they looked as if they were swimming beasts. You couldn't see more than heads and dark backs that moved with a peculiar rocking and swaying motion as the smoking mist rolled over them and erased all outlines.

Per sat for a while on a bench under a tree behind the road ditch. With his head resting on his hand, he followed the herd wending home until it was again swallowed up in the mist. Small flocks of crows flew over, and he could hear how, with joyous croaks, they settled down in their nests in the forest behind him. Nearby, a frog sat in his water hole and gurgled contentedly. Otherwise, a vast silence surrounded him.

A despondent feeling of loneliness stole over him. He thought of the biblical saying: "The foxes have holes and the birds of the air nests," but he didn't know what place he felt bound to by strong and good memories. As he thought about his imminent journey, he reflected that he was, in reality, indifferent about where he was in the world. He couldn't feel more homeless on the Atlantic or the American prairies than he did in the heart of his own Fatherland.

Another saying came to mind, and a little shudder went through him. It was the biblical curse his father had applied to him: He who defies God will be "a fugitive and a vagabond" on earth. The words now seemed to be fulfilled. Cain's fate hung over him. Once again, the alluring image of Fransisca came into his memory, framed by a small yellow whitewashed Nyboder house with a tiny green garden behind tarred fences. How dear she had been to him! It had not been an easy thing to let her spring-fresh love go. Of course, he well knew he had not lost his treasure. Jakobe was a much richer human being, whose significance for his development he could never overestimate. But he had to ask himself whether they belonged together by anything more than the physical. When, on the other hand, he thought of his quiet walks in the twilight with Fransisca around Sortedamssøen's golden water—of the always sweet and sad farewells under the trees up on the Østervold—all that glowed, now, in his memory as a momentary paradise in his dreary and storm-tossed youth.

Perhaps she had married. If anyone deserved to find a good man, it was she. Perhaps she was now living somewhere in the provinces as a happy bourgeois wife with a babe at her breast. It occurred to him that he might find out through Nyboder neighbors whether she was still at her parents' in Kerteminde or what had become of her. The old home in Hjertensfrydgade had, doubtless, been broken up. Madam Olufsen, he knew, had followed her husband in the autumn into the "black barge." But there were surely others who could give him information.

A new flock of crows flew over his head and disappeared into the woods with their high, joyous croaking. At that moment, he became aware of hoof beats and the rattle of a carriage that was on the road from Kærsholm. A pair of large roans were pulling, at a walking pace, an awning-covered barouche and coming up to a steep hill below the place where he was sitting.

When he realized it might be Pastor Blomberg's vehicle, he got up and went out on the road in the same direction as the carriage, hoping no one would recognize him. But he miscalculated. When the carriage caught up to him, the pastor stopped and greeted him with a cheerful wave.

"Look! Herr Prophet of the Future is daydreaming in the evening calm. Isn't that so? It's beautiful here. And, as I just said to my daughter, it's no wonder that our old folk poetry, in which nature sings in its own way, is so crowded with all kinds of fairy creatures. There is something really so fantastic, something magical about an evening like this. And we seem not yet to have lost our sensitivity to the mystical in nature when a modern engineer in our advanced, realistic day can let himself be captured by it." He said this with a roguish smile that ransomed the ingenuousness of his words. And, at the same time, he turned toward his daughter—who, sitting beside her father, seemed more self-confident in front of Per, almost looked haughtily at him—and continued: "Look here, my girl ... the engineer has really infected me. I have a desire to stretch my legs a bit. You go to the store and fetch the goods. Drive on and wait there till I come. Do you have anything against my accompanying you for a while?" he asked Per. Per muttered an "Of course not," and, with a little difficulty, the pastor descended.

"There is too little healthy movement in our precipitate steam-driven age," he said, and marched firmly forth on the path, as if to kick up the slumbering might of youth. "Our railways, which I sincerely admire otherwise, are leading us astray, betraying nature, making us disobedient to its fatherly commands. When I see a long, black rail monster whizzing over God's green earth, I always think of the snake in paradise. In the old days, when I had errands in town, I often took 'the Apostles' horse' in order to spare my tenant farmer's. It was five miles out and five

miles back in the same day. Yet the time never seemed so prolonged as now. I roll in on the train in half an hour, and I am
beside myself with impatience for only a five-minute delay. In
the past, the watch was left in the pocket and the time was read
by the sun, which doesn't have a second hand. And when you
had trudged five miles, how tasty was a little snack in a haystack
or at the edge of a ditch. Nowadays, young men will never know
what a wonderful—I can say even a *spiritual*—joy comes from
merely the earth's company with some cheese and bread while
the larks, starlings, and lapwings furnish table music. Now I have
become old and fat. But still a real longing for the country road
comes over me. When you have been sitting too long in the
house and brooding, when you have gathered so many silly and
capricious thoughts from the newspapers and books, what a
blessing it is to go out walking. You can easily sense how delicious
it is for the soul to stretch out as if awakened from an ugly dream
when now the sun is shining through the window and birds are
singing in the treetops. Listen!" he burst forth, while he stopped
and laid his hand on Per's arm. "Hear the larks up there? They
are still singing in honor of the sun." He stood very still, with a
charmed expression. "Isn't it delightful! It reminds me of a
woman who, after her beloved leaves, begins to hum in order not
to cry. Have you really noticed, Herr Engineer, what deep life-
wisdom a little singer in nature can express? You never listen in
vain to its sorrow or joy. I must honestly admit that, for my part,
I have received more edification from that clear, little warble than
from the many collections of sermons on my shelf. But you must
promise not to tell anyone," he added, laughing spontaneously
and shaking Per's arm. "My dear colleagues would never forgive
me such a frightful heresy." He laughed again, loudly, at his own
words and started to walk on. Per, who felt flattered by his confidential tone, also began, in other ways, to be fascinated by his
personality. He had to concede that the master's wife was right,
that Pastor Blomberg did not seem like the usual Bible funda-
mentalist, but like his own man.

After just a few steps, the pastor stopped again and swept his
arm over the whole landscape. The evening was already far
advanced; a few stars glimmered here and there in the blue-green
heavens. "Will you tell me something honestly and sincerely,
Herr Engineer? When, on an evening like this, you look out over
our lovely green land, can you really seriously wish it covered

with soot and coal dust? Yes, I know of your view of our national idyll. I will confess that I have still not read your book. But Fru Prangen told me about your ideas, and I find them especially representative of our time. I ask you, then, does it really seem to you that it would be more appealing to see some soot-belching steamship-monster here on the river and the flowery shores covered with smoking factories? I am not, of course, thinking exclusively of aesthetic concerns. I'm not a fantasist, and well know that they have to be subordinated to practical demands. But aren't there other and larger values at play? See the little house over there on the hill with the light peat smoke coming out of the chimney? A family I know personally lives there. They are humble folk of the kind we have in this country—about a quarter of a million of them. They work hard to get enough for food and clothes. But if you knew them, you would, nevertheless, envy them their happy and cheerful existence. The husband and wife work together in the field while a flock of children tumble around them in the fresh air. They have an old horse and a cow and feel themselves rich. Can you really, in all confidence, wish to put a father like that in a dark and stinking factory to toil like a slave on a machine while his wife and children are confined in a six- or seven-story barracks? Now be honest."

Per was somewhat irritated by the aggressive tone of the pastor's question. Because of that, and because he had become less certain lately, his answer sounded rather defiant: "I don't know what significance there can be in what I or any other man can personally wish in such a case. Development goes on without asking our permission, and, whether we want it or not, we are forced to adapt our own life and habits to its demands. To seek to fight against it is merely a waste of time and energy."

"You say that so categorically. But even if you are right, won't we always arrive soon enough at that progressive future?"

"I don't think so. On the contrary, I believe that it is high time for us to move, if it isn't already too late. Statistics show clearly that the welfare of the country is waning from year to year. Whatever you may call the idyllic happiness that you, Herr Pastor, speak of, it rests on very unsure ground that immediately makes it much less idyllic."

"Well, yes," the pastor responded, a little put out and starting to walk again. "This is, perhaps, not a favorable time for our farms—I know that. But, therefore—"

"The times are as good as can be expected for European farmers. But this work can no longer be what is needed in a modern civilized country. 'Farmer' will become, in the not-too-distant future, an obsolete category in Europe."

"But how can you say that? That sounds crazy to me. The standard of our agriculture arouses the highest interest and admiration everywhere abroad. We read it every day in our papers!"

Per answered, smiling a little indulgently: "That's an admiration entirely free of envy. It's a fact that we—in this beautiful, green country, as you call it, Herr Pastor—no longer own, in reality, more than half of our cattle and buildings. The rest has, in the last twenty or thirty years, been taken over by the capital of industrial countries, especially Germany. And it's a fact that in our whole country, there can't be found many farms or significant enterprises that foreign investors don't have a warrantable part of. Through our banks and credit unions, our country has been pawned piecemeal to foreign capital in a way that, as I wrote in my book, reminds us of our humiliation under Christopher II."

"Hey, slow down," the pastor burst out with a somewhat forced smile. "In your eagerness, you're going too far!"

"Not at all! You only have to take one of the larger German financial newspapers in hand and go through the stock exchange investors to be convinced how great an interest German capital has in us and how vigilantly it watches us. I was really struck with horror when I recently saw a paper in Germany with daily quotations from even the smallest Jutland joint stock company and savings bank union. That gives you cause for reflection!"

"To think it has really come to that," said the pastor after a little pause that could be regarded as a concession that this state of affairs was getting the most earnest attention from a concerned listener. "You mean, in other words, that the Danish people materially live by outmoded rules and conceptions that have crippled our powers. Yes, that could well be. Perhaps, simultaneously with the struggle for spiritual liberation here at home, should go a struggle to advance our economic development. That's basically a very pretty thought. And in that case, it's not necessary to ask for mercy. I am really not afraid to air things out. Whatever no longer can serve life we should give up, however dear it is to us. And, in addition, we must console ourselves that no overturning, however violent it seems, will be capable of shaking the genuine values we live by. I don't have to speak of how we are still God's children during this frightful steam-driven age—whether or not we recognize the paternity; all our other deeper feelings, as well, remain unaffected by outer circumstances. Thanks to God, life can grow green and blossom in gloomy garrets. The joy of love and domestic happiness follows us into our sooty backyards. What is happening is merely a change of scene in the endless play of the world. We ourselves remain what we are through all time and eternity."

The confidential tone in which the pastor said this again made Per smile, somewhat indulgently. He knew, for sure, that the pastor's words did not pertain. He had followed the development of modern culture sufficiently to understand that when the outer circumstances change, the "humming steel wheels" made for man gradually change him as well. Then he talked a bit about his impressions during his travels and, especially, his stay in Berlin, of the struggle for survival in a great city's populace. He told about the hordes of roaming workers, men and women for whom the words "home," "family," "security," and "comfort" already were as good as meaningless; these were people who, in one place or another in the monstrous mound of mankind, found sleeping cells just big enough to accommodate their bodies and who, when not working, lived in the streets, in beer halls or other public places, until they passed out of the world as a mere number in a hospital. But Pastor Blomberg was no longer listening. He felt that the conversation was moving onto an unfortunate track, and he customarily turned a deaf ear to a subject he was not used to dealing with or when, in a discussion, he confronted information with which he couldn't cope.

He stopped and said that he didn't wish to lead Per farther out of the way. He was just at the boundary of his parish, so it was convenient for him to say goodbye here. At parting, he repeated, once more, his invitation for Per to visit him soon. "We could perhaps continue this conversation. But you must really hurry home to dinner. You probably have already noticed, ha, ha, what a jealous lord the master is when it's a question of his meals."

CHAPTER 20

PER HAD NOT once heard from Jakobe during the week he had been at Kærsholm. Although he wrote every other day and went into fairly detailed accounts of what he was experiencing, she continued to remain silent. Finally, he became somewhat anxious. He had to concede that she had some reason to be annoyed over his absence, all the more because he no longer had an excuse.

True, he still had not gotten his financial needs in order. Every morning he meant to appeal to the master or his wife, but when it came down to it, he couldn't persuade himself to do so. He talked to them a bit about his future plans and they both seemed to be interested, but he still couldn't force a request out of his mouth.

It occurred to him, too, that such a petition could easily awaken their suspicion; it wasn't impossible for them to suppose he found it uncomfortable to receive money from his father-in-law.

So, provisionally, he would let the question ride until he was about to leave, and that day was continually postponed. As far as his health was concerned, he felt so unusually well at Kærsholm that the thought of the imminent turmoil in a strange land made it doubly hard to tear himself away. He spent most of the day in nature, where there were always so many new things to attract him and so many old things to interest him in a new way. He always had a predilection for being out on the river with a fishing pole—not so much for the fish themselves as for the sheer pleasure of sitting in the middle of a wilderness of stillness and hearing the water slapping the bottom of the boat, of staring down on the large, broad-leafed greenish-brown vegetation silently and gently moved about by the swift eddies—a slumbering world, an enchanted life, that seemed tormented by anxious dreams. He felt himself thinking often of Pastor Blomberg's words about the life-wisdom that could be gathered from nature just by listening to the song of the lark. In moments like this you could really feel spiritually connected, in a mystic way, with all the living earth. Losing oneself in nature's aura brought on a sensuous feeling of pregnant sacredness. Fantasy became so active, ideas poured out. It was as if life's original power was gently and quietly loosed within the body as a golden mist of teeming germs of thought. The sound of nature seemed to carry a message from the eternal and imperishable in existence. The race of man could die out and the world's cities disappear without a trace. But the water would gurgle under the boat the way it did under the first man's canoe, and the sound would be repeated until the end of days, not only here on earth, but in the whole endless expanse of the universe, wherever there was water and an ear to hear it.

One day, he received a letter from Ivan, who knew of his whereabouts from Jakobe. His brother-in-law wrote that he awaited his return with impatience because, despite everything, he still cherished the hope of favorable results for his plans. Herr Hasselager and Herr Nørrehave were still discussing them, he wrote, and bad feelings toward the Copenhagen project were spreading wider and wider, especially in the provinces.

He thought Per should seize this occasion to give a series of public addresses on his plan in some of the larger Jutland towns where there were so many requests for information; he understood that the mysterious Engineer Steiner presently was traveling around Jutland and talking to the industrial associations.

The words pierced Per's mood like a knife a boil. He remained completely determined not to have anything to do with commercial interests. He was an inventor, a technician—not a financial speculator. In a letter he wrote that evening to Jakobe, he spoke fully of it. At the same time, he told her that, under these circumstances, he considered it best to stay away from Copenhagen until, in a couple of weeks, the term for the legal marriage registration would be up and then they could immediately get married. "As for what concerns my joint canal and harbor project," he wrote, "I consider that I am finished with it and hereby hand it over to the nation to do whatever it wants. I myself will turn to my next task with undivided strength—the further development of my wind and wave motors, as Professor Pfefferkorn recommended—for which I expect to gain good experience in America. Perhaps you will maintain, as you have before, that such disrespect for the financiers will do me damage; that's as may be. I confess that I certainly do not possess either a sufficient vanity or ambition to go against my nature on this point. That's, of course, a fault, but still not something to really complain about. So I will write to your brother tomorrow and legally delegate to him the care and concern of my interests during my absence. They are, with him, in the best of hands."

This time, she answered. The reason she could not write up to now was that, from the moment she had received his first letter, Jakobe was convinced she had seen the last of him. She had asked herself whether it would not be best for both of them to decisively break up with each other. She was terribly tired of battling against that strange, secret, ghostly power that, time after time, stole him away from her just when she believed him to be held fast by love.

She was not at all sure she would be able, this time, to win him back, and she could count less and less on her own power to hold out. She saw him now as he really was. She now knew thoroughly that side of his character she *could* examine and judge. With all his natural strength, he was a man without passion and without the instinct for self-preservation, or, more to the point, he possessed only the negative traits of passion—its cold, night side: defiance, selfishness, and obstinacy—not its stormy desire, its devouring longing, its hard and purifying, glowing flame.

Was it hopeless to continue struggling? She had, in these days, often remembered how he once, jokingly, compared himself to that mountain troll from the fairy tale who crawled out from underground through a mound in order to live among the children of the earth, but, suffering from the sun's rays and from the continual fear of the light, took refuge again in his little mound.

She understood now that there was a more profound self-understanding here than she had suspected or believed he was capable of. Yes, he belonged deep in another world, under another sun. However different he seemed to be and always felt himself to be from his contemporaries, he was the country's genuine son, a full-blown child of the passionless Danish people with pale eyes and a timid soul, mountain trolls who couldn't look at the sun without sneezing, who lived originally and naturally in the dusk sitting on thin little mounds, their glowing eyes casting spells in the evening mist as a comfort and support for their oppressed senses, a dwarf race with large, pensive heads but the weak limbs of a child. They were a twilight people who could hear the grass grow and the flowers sigh, but burrowed back into the earth as soon as the cock crowed.

Without naming in any way a reason for her long silence, or saying anything about their preparations for marriage or their travel plans, she criticized, in a joking tone, the decision to which his "development" had brought him. "You speak of your lack of vanity," she wrote. "You beat your chest and thank God you are not like other sinners. Good Lord, must we now throw suspicion on the poor remains of our pride? I once chose to be a genuine revolutionary on that score, but, with the years, I have become more sober. My view of mankind has become more and more conventional. I have even changed toward such despised things as forms and titles. I began to understand the significance of this foolishness for the well-being of mankind. Decidedly, the Danish people, above all, cannot afford to sacrifice whatever spurs on 'the development of their power,' a phrase you, in earlier times, always had on your tongue and that I myself was fond of. Were I a poet, I would write hymns of praise to it. And if I were a priestess, with or without a collar, I would root out vanity from the official list of sins that is, already, quite long enough."

Some days after Pastor Blomberg and his daughter had been at Kærsholm, the master's wife proposed to abandon the usual post-prandial excursion in order to make a reciprocal visit to the parsonage at Bøstrup. Per really had no desire to go, but made no objection.

The master promised to be in the party, but when the carriage pulled up before the door, he declined to get in. He had another attack of thick-blooded melancholy, and his wife needed all her ingenuity to smooth over his ill-natured capriciousness.

Per was prepared in advance, by the steward's stories, for his host's sudden mood changes. Still, he was a little doubtful about how to interpret those scowling looks. He began to get anxious that, perhaps, he was abusing the family's hospitality, and he used the ride to feel out the master's wife in this regard. But she insisted straight out that if he was thinking of going away now, she and her husband would think he had not been happy at Kærsholm and they would certainly even regret having invited him to stay. Per was very relieved by this firm assurance, especially since it helped to exonerate him in relation to Jakobe.

The distance from Kærsholm to the parsonage in Bøstrup was about three miles. The route went over steep rising hills and then through a bending stretch of meadowland. The weather was calm, and, since the sky was slightly overcast, the sun did not bother them. A green valley with a winding river could be seen on one side, while on the other were many small woods with endless flocks of crows.

Charmed by the sight, the baroness declaimed:

> See, a bird is flying there so high
> Its dark wings set against the sky.
> Through clear blue air the beauteous scene
> Sings with him in motley green.

Not far from Kærsholm, they rolled through a little village, Borup, with that manor's parish church. Here, also, was a profusion of birds surveying the rich fields. Crowds of sparrows played in the road's dust; starlings by the hundreds sat in the treetops.

Along the road, a series of thatched huts shamelessly exhibited the poverty of their owners. The farms, surrounded by old apple orchards, with stork nests sitting on the roofs, were pushed back. Per already knew almost every house and inhabitant of the little village. He came through every day on his walks and had, now and then, chatted with the people. This was the first time in his life he had the opportunity to be in close contact with the country folk, and it interested him to hear them speak of their circumstances. It struck him that their high farm mortgages did not seem, particularly, to oppress them. They led him with friendly and satisfied smiles around their farms as if they did not realize that the whole splendid field was only loaned and leased. While several of these people descended from fathers who had saved up to a hundred thousand silver dalers in their chests, now the talk everywhere was about how much or how little a man owed.

A bit below the slope, out by the meadows, lay a dilapidated parsonage. From the path, only the sooty chimney and the garden treetops could be seen. An older man lived there, Pastor Fjaltring, about whom many derogatory things had been said at Kærsholm.

The master's wife had contended that the "mildest interpretation" of the man's appearance and whole way of life was that he wasn't quite right in the head. Most of his congregation had, like the landowners, left their parish obligation to go over to Pastor Blomberg.

Per started to discuss Pastor Fjaltring and wondered why he had not met him on his walk. The master's wife answered that that wasn't so remarkable. Pastor Fjaltring very rarely came out of his cave and, in any case, not usually before evening. He had an owl's nature and shied away from the light; he was really a soul that belonged to the dark, much to the indignation of the parish.

"Isn't he a believer?" asked Per a little cautiously. "It occurs to me that I even heard he was strictly orthodox."

"Yes—on the pulpit, but in his heart, he is a mocker and denier. He once was supposed to have said to someone: 'I believe fully and firmly in both God and the devil. It's just that I'm not really always sure which one most offends me.' Have you ever heard the like?"

"But how can such a man stay a pastor?"

"It's really a scandal, but he is cunning enough to hide his abominable talk until he is alone with people. In his sermons, he is, as I said, very orthodox, almost terribly commonplace and boring."

Beyond the village, the path again descended, and after a ten-minute rapid ride, Bøstrup came into view, lying prettily at the foot of a wooded hill. They found the pastor's family gathered behind the garden, where a playing field had been created for the young folk. Three golden-haired boys from ten to sixteen were playing football in shirtsleeves and the pastor himself cheered on the players and shouted out most excitedly when a ball swiftly found its mark. His wife stood off to the side, holding the hand of a little girl, and watched. Frøken Inger, who was the oldest of the pastor's children, was sitting apart by the low garden wall, reading a book propped on her lap. None of them heard their guests coming, and the visitors, wanting to surprise the family, went directly from the carriage in through the garden.

The first to spot them was Frøken Inger. Instantly she got up with a little cry of delight and threw her arms around the neck of the master's wife. Then there was a general reception with hearty expressions of pleasure and surprise. The pastor slapped Per on the shoulder and welcomed him. "Do you go in for sports, Herr Engineer?" he asked, while he took off his large straw hat and wiped his forehead with his handkerchief. "Oh, it's a blissful thing! On that score, my generation missed out, and now I'm too old to start. I have to be satisfied with being a spectator here on the playground. But even that is wonderful when you see how the young romp around. It's as if your own muscles were stretched. I simply can't dispense with motion!" With a cheerful laugh, the little man, majestically striding in a white linen jacket and a pair of trousers too short at the ankles, led the company back through the garden.

They all sat down on a bench and some chairs in the shade of the house in front of the garden door where there was a country coffee table set with a copper tea urn and fragrant pastries. It was Frøken Inger who undertook the arrangement, which she did very prettily, though Per allowed himself the criticism that she, perhaps, felt this herself.

As it often does when countrywomen sit together around a coffee table, the conversation gradually turned to domestic affairs. Even Pastor Blomberg put in his oar with a few joking remarks about baking and pickling until he was called away because a man had come to talk with him. When it was revealed that the cakes on the table were Frøken Inger's own handiwork, the baroness and her sister vied with each other to eulogize them, while the pastor's wife showed her appreciation by patting her daughter's cheek and saying she really was very clever.

The young girl pretended to be fairly indifferent to the praise. She could not even keep from sulking a little when her mother caressed her. Per thought to himself that she certainly was very spoiled. But she was undeniably pretty. He found her even more appealing today than before when he saw her in Kærsholm's park at twilight. She really looked better as she stood there in full daylight in her little white apron and poured tea. He could no longer see a likeness to Fransisca. Out of consideration for Per, the master's wife tried a few times to shift the subject and began to talk about Copenhagen. But Per was not very forthcoming, and the pastor's wife quickly led the conversation back to the domestic sphere. She was a tall, slim woman with a distinguished air about her. It wasn't difficult to see that it was from her the daughter inherited her attractive appearance. In contrast to her husband, she seemed very reserved in relation to Per. Without really being rude, she still had not once directed a word to him, and it was just to remedy this that the master's wife continually tried to draw him into the conversation. But now the company got up at the request of the hostess to look about a little in the large and well-maintained garden.

The three women went ahead in lively chatter. Per followed behind with Frøken Inger. He felt a little uncomfortable, because he didn't know what to say to her. Ordinarily an easy talker, he couldn't find the right tone for this little country girl. She, on her part, was on home ground and altogether more relaxed with him than before at Kærsholm.

She seemed more grown up, more a woman. Of course, she

was patently aware of her social obligations as the oldest daughter of the house, and she attended to them quite graciously. "You come often to Kærsholm, don't you," said Per, just to say something.

"Not as often as I would like. But the trip is fairly long, and I can't always get a carriage."

"You seem very fond of the mistress of Kærsholm."

"Yes," she answered curtly, as if the subject were too exalted to be touched on between them. "You met the baroness and her sister in Italy, didn't you?"

"Yes."

"That must have been amusing to travel like that," she said, and then talked about how it had long been suggested that she should go on a tour in Switzerland together with her parents. But her father could never find time; his congregation could not do without him for so long. It was hard enough to get leave to go to Copenhagen for a week.

Per noticed that she seemed to grow more erect when she spoke of her father. There was something there that reminded him of his sister Signe, and hardly knowing why, he smiled. Just then, he saw an iron hook painted red and placed at eye level on a tree trunk on the side of the road. "Is that intended for hanging oneself?" he asked, and stopped to look at it.

Frøken Inger couldn't help laughing. She called his attention to a little iron ring fastened on a long rope that hung down from a tree on the other side of the garden path. "That's part of an amusing game," she explained. "The art consists in flinging a ring at the hook so that it catches there."

Per wanted to try it. It will pass the time, he thought. He was not lucky. "I'll have to practice," he said after some vain attempts, and asked her to show him how he should manage it. "You are doubtless an expert?"

Inger hung back, a little irresolute, but she could not resist the temptation to show off her proficiency. She tossed the ring, which described an elegant loop in the air and came down onto the hook with the concentrated fervor of a young woman who catches her lover's arm during a game of "forfeits." Per was impressed. He had to try again, but was still unlucky.

"No, I can't do it. You try it again, Frøken," he said, and handed her the ring. Inger let herself be talked into it, although she already had looked several times after the other ladies, who had gone some distance away. Whether from anxiety about this or something else, her skill abandoned her. She missed the next toss as well. She blushed and aimed carefully, but still misfired.

Per had no inclination to gloat over her catching his bad luck. Even though, to a certain extent, Inger felt this considerateness as a new humiliation, he won, at that moment, a little piece of her heart. When, in her agitation, she continued to misplay, she finally laughed at herself, called herself a bungler, and became more and more zealous.

In the midst of this scene, the ladies returned. Neither Per nor Inger heard them before they stopped behind them. "Inger!" the pastor's wife called out sharply. "Go see to your brothers and sisters, my child." And, turning to the others, she said, "Let us go inside now."

At the garden door, Pastor Blomberg, puffing on a pipe, greeted the company. "I was just looking for you, Engineer. You must be tobacco-starved. Come, come into my room—that way we won't embarrass the ladies with our sensible talk," he said humorously, and turned around with the heartiest laughter.

It was necessary to go though the whole, large house to get there, and Per had a vivid impression, on that walk, of the solid comfort that suffused the Blomberg home. It was a real Danish pastor's dwelling, a symbol of permanence; large, immovable mahogany furniture lined the walls with its dark, heavy mass that seemed built for eternity.

Fru Blomberg belonged to an old family of public officials that was quite well-to-do. It was made evident in the house that one member had been a prefect and chamberlain. Pastor Blomberg's family, on the other hand, was not often mentioned, least of all by the pastor himself. The most people knew was that he was the son of a provincial teacher and that something in his pronunciation betrayed him as an islander.

The pastor's room was completely separate, on the other side of the entrance hall, and was an authentic clergyman's study with a few large, book-filled shelves that contributed so much to upholding the church's reputation among laymen (though, in so many cases, they were merely screens for ignorance). Here it was genuine. Pastor Blomberg was far from an erudite man, but he did read a bit and was more susceptible to book learning than he was aware of. It was his ambition to know about every place where something new was in play. On the other hand, he appropriated only what could feed his spirit without disturbing his Christian faith. He was, in this respect, a kind of Jesuit. In the end, his thought was not ruled by logic. He was a feeling man and, because his external life was always extremely harmonious, there was no reason for a stricter self-examination. In his youth, he had been somewhat bothered by hardship and poverty. Later, he had a few disappointments in relation to possible posts, and, although he was an idol to his congregation and had a name known throughout the country, his ambition still was, to a degree, unsatisfied. But life, on the whole, had not dealt him serious blows, and those he had met glided off him because of the happy soundness of his nature.

When Per was seated on the sofa and had lit his cigar, Pastor Blomberg settled into an armchair at the corner window with his pipe and started talking. He related some entertaining stories from the parish, and Per immediately felt a little flattered by the straightforwardness with which the pastor talked to him as to a contemporary.

He would have been less pleased had he known that the conversation was part of a plot between the pastor and the master's wife, insofar as the latter, in her missionary zeal, had recommended Per to him as a man who certainly "was not impervious to religious awakening." It wasn't long before Pastor Blomberg took up the earlier discussion he had discontinued because of his lack of preparation.

Now he was better armed, and began by asking Per how it had happened that, at such a young age, he had thrown himself into tasks of such a civil and rational kind for the improvement of the country's economic condition. Per confessed candidly how his interest had been kindled for his project all the way back to his childhood, probably by impressions from his home, especially after the war. In addition, his studies had, very early, made him familiar with foreign developments in industry and communications, and so a comparison was automatic.

"Yes, yes," said the pastor. "These comparisons between our narrow homeland and the great world with its many glories so often bring on depression in our youth. I'm thinking that, in addition, Nathan's writings also have had some influence on you, in this respect, as they have had in our day on so many others of our young, ambitious men. Am I right?"

Per objected: "Nathan was simply an aesthete. He brought to

a close a period of culture, and in that sense, only, was a maker of modernity. He had cleared the way for it. In actuality, he didn't at all understand it."

"Hmmm," the pastor mumbled, puffing forcefully on his pipe, and was silent for a moment. That Nathan's perspective could be considered passé was something so surprising that his thoughts were thrown into confusion. And though he still had the desire to discuss that subject more deeply, he refrained, for fear, again, of being led beyond his range of knowledge. "Yes, yes. I assume, however, you consider Nathan's influence on modern youth's spiritual development significant," he continued, in consonance with his laid-out plan of discussion. "Naturally, for my part, I think most intently about relations to the religious. I think, for example, that you yourself, though a pastor's son, have kept a decided distance from the church and that this can be attributed to Nathan's works, which must have played a part."

Per conceded that Nathan's writings had strengthened and undergirded his life views, but insisted that he had already adopted his personal perspective growing up in his home.

"To think you were so early a stranger in the house of God!" The pastor shook his head good-naturedly. "Well, that's unfortunate. As I told you recently, I didn't know your late father personally, but I was aware that he had an old Lutheran and curiously narrow and one-sided sense of many aspects of life. Oh, that benighted orthodoxy! It hovers over us like a nightmare, over church and home, and renders many of the best and most vibrant of the youth of our day spiritual orphans. When such a capable and eloquent man as Nathan comes forth and confirms the young in their belief that God's church is a dilapidated house—yes—it ends in a full repudiation; I understand it well."

Per didn't answer. He was a little anxious over the direction the conversation had taken. But the pastor began to speak of Nathan with much appreciation. He only regretted that such a gifted and knowledgeable man had set himself up in a decidedly hostile relation to Christianity, and he confessed that the excessively orthodox here at home and abroad certainly had a part in it.

"But, of course, Nathan himself was not without blame in that error of judgment on the most powerful spiritual force the world had ever known. It's with him as with the others who fight

Christianity from a scientific viewpoint—they can't free themselves from one-sidedness but have become negatively dogmatic. Their fault is not so much that they let reason prevail as that they haven't thought things out thoroughly. When, for example, the scientists of our age call themselves naturalists and mean, by that, that existence can be known only as what lets itself break up into atoms with certain mechanical or chemical attributes, that is really a very inadequate conception, a student's laboratory postulate that, finally, explains nothing. We, who really live with nature, cannot possibly endorse such a deficient point of view, because we know and have felt, countless times, that nature has a soul and that behind the visible and mechanical forces that work on our senses, there lives a spirit that speaks to our heart. If we just first open our ears to that spiritual voice, we finally hear only it, perceive it in the crashing storm and in the faintest whisper around a blade of grass. And we not only hear it; we understand what it is saying. For it is the same spirit of eternity that lives and works inside us. If we go one day into the woods and hear the leaves rustling over our head or listen, in solitude, to the murmur of a spring—yes, a modern physicist can explain to us how these voices emerge naturally from the movements of leaf masses and from the fall of water drops; but if he thinks that explains it all, we say, 'No, stop, my good man! Something is missing. The most essential thing is missing. With all these calculations, you can reveal nothing about the peculiar intimacy, the almost sisterly warmth with which such a little spring can chat with us in our solitude.' Because—isn't it so—it is not forbidding to us that a seemingly dead thing has a voice. And we are not offended that a little spring suddenly makes itself familiar and says 'dear friend' to us. On the contrary, there is something very comforting and homey in such a strong feeling of companionship with nature. But what does all that really say except that behind the multitudinous visible world a oneness flows that is the common source of all things. The curious, dreamy feeling that moves us at such moments is a longing for home. And if now the learned physicist defines this feeling as a mere mechanical and chemical power working in us, a dependence on or connection to original matter, I recommend to him, again, that he leave his books and laboratory and gather his wisdom from nature. Let him look to the little spring in the woods! Let him sit there in the evening when his heart is anxious, and if his spiritual senses have not become altogether dull, he will perceive the spring's little song as a path opening to the depths of the infinite, a stairway to heaven that connects time and eternity, dust and spirit, death and everlasting life. He will become aware that the umbilical cord between us and our celestial source has not been cut, but through it, we are always supplied, in moments of devotion and prayers, with renewed power from our eternal spring we Christians call our God and Preserver and All Merciful Father.''

Per remained silent. He was a little annoyed by the pastor's tone, which had gradually become rather didactic. But he could think of nothing to advance against his argument, especially since, on many points, he had touched on something he himself had lately dimly felt during his renewed companionship with nature.

The pastor wanted to continue, but just then, they heard steps at the door and Inger stuck her head in to announce that the master's wife and the baroness wanted to leave. ''Well, so we'll stop for today,'' said the pastor, and got up. He warmly put his hand on Per's shoulder and added, ''It has really been a pleasure to talk with you; perhaps we'll have the opportunity another time to continue our debate. I have the feeling that, essentially, we aren't so far apart that we couldn't come to an understanding with each other.''

Just as they entered the living room where the ladies were, a carriage rolled up to the house. ''That's the councilor of justice,'' said Inger, who was standing by the window. ''Gerda and Lise are with him.''

Councilor Clausen, who was a land agent in the neighborhood, belonged to the district's most zealous Blombergians. As such, he was one of the closest companions of the master's wife, and she and her sister were persuaded to stay as well when it was evident that his family had in mind to spend the evening at the pastor's home. Per, who was also invited, dared not refuse, though he was himself impatient to leave.

The councilor was a slight little man with white cheek whiskers and gold-rimmed glasses. His wife, on the other hand, was a mountain of flesh, who even a fair amount of time after she had stepped down from the carriage still groaned audibly from the effort. The two daughters were young women about Inger's age.

At the evening meal, which was served out in the garden, the conversation was very lively. Among other things, the talk was of Pastor Fjaltring. The councilor had just heard a new, outrageous story about that priestly doubter and mocker who lived a wretched life with his invalid wife. One of the parish's most reputable young farmers of the Blomberg persuasion had returned to him on the occasion of some official business, and Pastor Fjaltring, in the course of their conversation, is supposed to have recommended that he surrender himself more to debauchery: "You should sin a little more," he had said. "With the life you now lead, you will never really become a genuinely devoted Christian."

While the ladies expressed indignation and disgust, Pastor Blomberg shook his head indulgently and said, "He is a poor, unhappy man!" Just then, the evening bell rang out in the white church tower, reddened by the sunset behind the garden's tree-tops. The peal almost frightened the guests, who weren't used to being so close to the sound. Pastor Blomberg, who apparently wanted very much to get away from the subject of Pastor Fjaltring, laughed and said that the din of the bell was, in fact, inexcusable. The commissioner of health should forbid it straightway!

The master's wife protested that the evening bell sounded beautiful from a distance and that really it served a good purpose in reminding us to settle our minds after the day's unrest. Pastor Blomberg did not appreciate being contradicted, especially by one of his own followers. Although he had thrown out his remark without meaning anything except to hazard a little joke, with which, in the Lutheran style, he liked to season his conversation, now he took up the question seriously for discussion.

He didn't like that kind of reminder by the bell, he said. He wouldn't himself have ordered a call to devotions by demand. There was something too Catholic about it that he disapproved of. God did not have consultation hours like a doctor or an attorney, and as for the symbolic implication, it was as childish as looking on the sun as God's golden watch. It was really almost ridiculous.

His point gradually developed into a whole lecture in which the question swelled up to a case of the most serious significance for a man's healthy and sincere relation to God. Supper was now over. The young ladies got up and were walking in the garden. The Clausen girls were both pretty, lively brunettes; the older

one, especially, was a luxuriantly sensuous daughter of Eve with
a pair of eyes that sparkled with a love of life. When the table was
cleared, Pastor Blomberg suggested that they sing an evensong.
The girls were called back, and the pastor's wife went into the
sunroom, where the piano was located.

> Peace reigns over all the earth
> No sound in all the land . . .

It began to grow dark in the garden. From a hazel hedge a
blackbird blended its nature notes into the company's somewhat
uneven singing:

> The moon now smiles in cloudy mirth
> The stars blink in a band.

The girls had camped on the steps in front of the garden door
and sat there in their light dresses singing out boldly in clear
voices as the pastor and the councilor accompanied them with
their bass tones. The councilor had crossed his arms on his chest
and was humming with furrowed brow and a flounder mouth.
The three women guests at the table participated as well, with a
little humming, while the pastor's wife, with a strong and well-
trained voice, gradually dominated the singing:

> The shining, peaceful, spreading sea
> Holds heaven in its embrace . . .

Per was the only one not singing. Nevertheless, no one was
more deeply affected by the moment. He remembered under
what circumstance he had last heard that song. He was standing
then outside a garden hedge and longing to go in. Now he was
in, but did that matter? He felt superfluous, like an unbidden
guest. That was his fate, to remain an uneasy stranger in every
place, haunted by the ghost of his childhood home.

When the song came to an end, the pastor folded his hands
and recited the Lord's Prayer. A few more songs were sung, and
then the carriages drove up to the door.

After the company had departed, the pastor sat in the sunroom
with his wife and pipe and began to talk about the departed
guests. Inger was there as well. She had already said goodnight,

but when, on the way to the door, she heard her father mention Per, she found something to do at the music cabinet.

Pastor Blomberg spoke very appreciatively about Per and his capabilities. He even praised his appearance quite warmly. But then his wife suddenly became anxious because of the presence of their daughter. "Why are you lingering here, dear girl? Now, off to bed!"

Per kept quiet all the way home, and the master's wife, who suspected the reason for his withdrawal, let him remain undisturbed and talked with her sister about domestic matters. When the carriage had gone some distance past Borup, a tall man passed by on the roadside. Per didn't see him, but the master's wife grabbed her sister's arm and cried out, "There's Pastor Fjaltring!" Per leaned out of the carriage and caught sight of a tall, slim form just as its outline was blotted out by the darkness. "Was that the crazy pastor?" he asked.

"Yes—this is his hour. They say he sometimes goes back and forth on the road during the whole night."

Per sank back into his former silence and, as his thoughts followed the lonely, restless night wanderer, a shiver went down his spine. The biblical curse, "a fugitive and a vagabond shalt thou be on earth," sounded again ominously in his ears with his father's voice of authority. It was as if he had seen a symbol of his own fate.

The next morning Per earnestly resorted to the little library of edifying books with which the master's wife had stocked his room. He took down one of Pastor Blomberg's collections of sermons, *The Way to God*, and although the weather was windy, since he didn't want to stay inside he took his book to the woods. Here he settled down in his favorite spot, under a hedge, and turned his back to the woods for its shelter while he had before him a wide-open view over the river and meadows to the thicketed slopes on the far side.

The surroundings suited the reading he had now begun. Something in Pastor Blomberg's preachings reminded him of a Danish meadow scene in the cool of a summer day: high wind, blue sky, sun-trimmed clouds, birdsong, here and there a calf bellow, and overall the most luxurious green, soft lines—an open perspective and a plain, flat horizon. Pastor Blomberg expertly used a poetic and unassuming language in his sermons. He was faithful to his church's tone and teaching, borne into the world on the wings of a Grundtvig hymn, and never losing the stamp of its lyrical origin.

This was not, however, a style of representation that especially attracted Per. His susceptibility to the enchantments of figurative language had been fairly stunted by his education in mathematics and natural science. He was always looking for a proof behind the beautiful words; his thoughts pursued clarity in regard to life's mysteries, which were becoming despairingly obscure for him.

His conversations with Pastor Blomberg had already given him a sense of a Christianity very unlike the one in which he had been raised. Now, for the first time, he realized how far men in this ecclesiastical circle had come from the past's grumbling orthodoxy, with its branding of the flesh, crucifixion of the understanding—its whole medieval soul torture that could seek respite only in a misty dream of paradise's glory. Here there was nothing of terrifying thoughts or shocking feelings, nothing that disappeared into clouds of speculation or faded into fogs of foreboding. Here, above all, there was no resistance to overcome. The mystery of existence opened up into the simplest clarity. Everything seemed so straightforward, so natural, and, withal, in a wonderfully practical way, to really suit man's nature. With good humor, the devil was viewed as an aborted, fearful, monkish fantasy and taken to the woodshed; and, as to belief in eternal damnation, this was simply called barbaric and terrible, contrary to the Christian representation of God as an all-loving Father. About the Beyond, there was generally as little talk as possible. What mattered most, in this view, was primarily that man should cheerfully and piously put an end to the former way of life with childlike confidence in the love of the Heavenly Father.

For Per, all this was something like happy tidings. He could recognize the truth, always claimed by the master's wife for Pastor Blomberg's preachings, by how wonderfully reassuring they were. The grinding oppression that had hovered over his mind since the evening before and pursued him into his night dreams seemed, now, to have been removed.

He closed his book, finally, and lay back awhile with a hand under his head and looked out over the meadows. He felt like one who had been troubled by the thought of a long and agonizing night voyage over a stormy sea to an unknown country but was waking in the morning to the realization that the danger was over, the storm exhausted; the land was greeting him warmly with sunshine and green woods.

He admitted to himself that when, in earlier days, he had struggled against the outbreak of a spiritual crisis, it was not only because he was concerned to protect his conscience, but also because he was vaguely anxious about a new and untried life view into which that kind of inner change was leading him. But now he felt at peace. What was required was really only the same strong and honest self-discipline, which he had already, for some time, on his own initiative, been practicing.

At breakfast, the master's wife told him about a folk festival that was to be held that afternoon in a nearby woods at which the pastor would speak. She had, she said, already made an arrangement with the councilor and the pastor to all meet there. The baroness would probably be going as well. Did he have any desire to accompany them? Per answered, and this was true, that he really wanted to hear Pastor Blomberg. Also, the prospect of consorting with the young ladies attracted him. He didn't mention this, and it was really something he hadn't yet realized. He seemed not to have had them in mind since the previous night, and, even on that occasion, he hadn't, he thought, very much heeded them. Nevertheless, without his being conscious of it, his eyes had, the whole time, followed the brightly dressed forms when, after the evening meal, the girls had walked around on the lawn; so that, despite his preoccupation with himself, he was continually receptive, in a hidden corner of his being, to an impression of them, and even now retained a very vivid picture of the three.

Toward four o'clock, the landau stopped in front of the door and, after some delay—the baroness, as usual, was not ready—drove off. The master had, at the last moment, decided to go and, during the drive's tolerable discomfort, tried to make up for his social offense of the previous day. They arrived at the spot after an hour's drive, a green at the bottom of a deep-forested basin where there was shelter from the wind. A couple of hundred country folk—both men and women—were standing in front of a flag-ornamented platform and already singing. The arrival of this distinguished, noble company stirred a sensation in the gathering, but certainly no sense of awe. Rather, the master's long-legged form in his Junker-like buckled jacket with a black rooster feather in his hat seemed to arouse some gaiety here and there as he led the ladies up to some seats, directly in front of the platform, that were reserved for the district elect.

Per held back. He had become a little confused by the sight of the large gathering and didn't want to mingle with the crowd. He saw the councilor get up in front and greet the master and his wife. He also spotted Pastor Blomberg's brown velvet hat and his wife's high-held head in the front-row seats. On the other hand, the whole time, he was looking in vain for Frøken Inger and her friends. But when he noticed the master's wife turning a little to the other side and nodding toward the forest slope, his eye caught three young forms in summer dresses seated there as on a balcony.

The singers stopped, and Pastor Blomberg mounted the platform. He started to discuss the mother tongue, about its significance, in contrast to foreign tongues that, at most, are a tool for communication. "As the language of the heart," he said, "it is the spiritual breast from which we suck the national milk. Our language contains, as in a vessel, the people's spiritual legacy that our forefathers, through hundreds of intimate links, transmitted to us; they shaped it in their image, and therefore we should honor it and hold it sacred. As we have fenced in the springs from which our bodies drink so they do not get polluted, we must, even to a higher degree, protect our spiritual source—the word. If you look at the everyday speech of the people, you will, unfortunately, find much that is unclean, even rotten, in it, and, in that respect, the country people are no better than the city folk. There are those who can't open their mouths without improper words, filthy allusions tumbling out. Here is our great task, then."

He called, especially, on the young, in whom the habit of indecent language still wasn't too deeply rooted. "A movement must be created to develop a sense of spiritual hygiene that is as important for us as the care of our bodies. All the virtuous powers in the people must be called out to protect the young against the pollution of the word to which they are daily exposed."

Per listened with interest, but gradually, as the pastor began to moralize directly, his attention wandered. The presence of the young girls and the fact that everything was so new to him contributed, as well, to his distraction. Because this was the first time he had participated in a popular gathering, the audience interested him as much as the speakers. He surveyed the close rows of solid, homespun forms, of open and attentive faces listening intently, and this was the first occasion that made him realize fully what a spiritual movement he was being led into.

He had often heard talk of the Grundtvigian awakening, with its chief idea of a folk culture, in contrast to the orientation of international education, but since even the central conception of the newly instructed farmer was old-fashioned in his eyes, he had, on that basis alone, never thought it worth the trouble to familiarize himself more with this movement, widespread as it was.

In the Copenhagen circle in which he had moved, it had been condescendingly looked upon, but when, instinctively, he drew a comparison between this gathering of Danish country people and the Austrian and Italian farm communities he had come to know on his travels, he concluded that he had no grounds on which to be ashamed of his countrymen. He discerned a big distinction between these wide-awake, sympathetic listeners and the sleepy herd of Tyrolean mountain folk the pastor drove in procession through Dresack on Sundays, like bleating sheep. As well, compared with the old farmers of the district whom he remembered from his childhood when they appeared on market days in the towns, this circle seemed very progressive. Clearly, here was a development, a kind of liberation that was parallel to what he himself was supporting, and it had, patently, brought much happiness with it.

When Pastor Blomberg had finished his speech and some singing began again, the festival's organizer, a young, blond, smiling farmer, came forward to announce that there would be a half-hour intermission, after which the high school principal, Broager, would speak. The gathering dispersed slowly over the grounds, and those who had had to stand up during the address sat down on the grass. Per approached Inger and her friends. The girls had just risen to go down to the others when Per proposed that they should use the intermission to see a little of the beautiful woods. The Clausen girls were very willing, but Inger hesitated. She glanced irresolutely at the space in front of the platform where her mother was talking with the master's wife. She took after her mother and her provincial patrician family in this respect, that she was very attentive to proper form. But the oldest Clausen girl, the full-breasted Gerda, grabbed her firmly under her arm, seized her sister with the other, and walked off with them both.

Frøken Gerda found it difficult to keep her lively brown eyes off Per. Her boyish manner was a screen for her womanly appreciation. Her sister, who was only a child, adopted her tone and hung on her arm laughing like a playful schoolgirl. But Per had eyes only for Inger. He found the others, on closer acquaintance, rather common, and couldn't help assuming that Inger felt somewhat embarrassed for her friends. In any case, she lowered her eyes, and the more the others exhibited their vulgar dalliance, the more taciturn she became. It had already struck him the previous evening how distinguished her manner was in comparison to the others, how self-assuredly, with a fresh, young pride, she carried her head, as if she wished to lift it high over all that was crude, commonplace, and dirty. It occurred to him, then, that it was more by this chaste composure, rather than by any particular outer traits, that she resembled Fransisca in his eyes. That cool modesty, like the scent of wild roses, had hovered around her form. He could remember how the least allusion to love's mysteries brought the blood to her cheeks, while Jakobe—no, with her, it was otherwise. He couldn't deny that it had, now and then, struck him that there was something unsavory in the reckless passion with which she lovingly devoted herself to him.

They had emerged from the woods. In front of them rose a huge gravel hill, almost entirely bare except for some scrubby grass and dark patches of heather. This was the famous Rolhøj, the district's highest point, from which you could look over a twentieth part of Jutland. Although the two Clausen sisters gradually understood that they were superfluous, they pretended not to notice it, or, in any case, not to show they were offended. On the contrary, like the Jutlanders they were, they avenged themselves with a constant abandoned cheerfulness.

"First man to the top!" shouted Frøken Gerda, and rushed up the slope, followed immediately by her sister, whose hat flew off her head while she ran, and precipitated a wild chase down the hill after it. Inger made as if to follow them, but Per, who remembered the warning given her by the master's wife—that she should not run—counseled her earnestly against it. "Remember, you were just recently sick, Frøken! You shouldn't overstrain yourself." With this solicitude for her person, Per, unknowingly, again conquered a little piece of Inger's well-fortified heart. She was still enough of a convalescent that it was satisfying to her to be thought weaker than she was. But now she insisted, with a little toss of her head, that she wanted to climb the hill. When Per proposed that she should, at least, support herself on his arm, she wouldn't hear of it. "I'm not the least weak," she said. "There's no cause for alarm."

Per stayed close in front of her during the climb in order to be able to grab her if she should stumble. In one place, where it was especially steep, she actually took his outstretched hand. That did not happen without hesitation, but she could not see anything improper in it, especially since he was engaged. And it was not at all unpleasant to feel almost as if they were soaring together up the steep slope.

The whole time, Per wanted to tell her that he had spent the morning reading one of her father's books and how much pleasure he had from it. But he was afraid she would think he was just being polite and let it be.

He contented himself with saying that the visit to her house the day before had made him very happy—something she seemingly took for granted. The effort of climbing had made her warm, and she stopped to catch her breath. She held her hat in her hand, and her light, fine, curly hair ringed her head like a halo. At that moment, she was once more Fransisca, Per thought —Fransisca transfigured.

The Clausen girls had, meanwhile, long since reached the top. They stood there holding their hats while the wind rushed at their skirts with invisible hands as if to tear off their clothes. At the sight of Inger and Per again moving up, the youngest said, "Look how they're creeping!"

"It's so annoying about Inger," said Frøken Gerda. "When someone pays her a little attention, she gets all worked up."

"You certainly have to admit he is very handsome, fusspot."

"Handsome! I think he's horrible!"

"You don't mean it, Gerda. You told me, yourself, last evening—"

"Are you crazy, girl? Have you really looked at his peepers? A pair of milk pails!"

Inger and Per finally reached the top and were able to look at the celebrated view. The girls began to count the church towers. When the air was clear, you could see thirty-five. The sisters knew the names of all of them, but Per was interested only in the ones Inger could point out. "Is that really Tepperup? What are you saying? Oh, Ramlev!" he exclaimed, as if the names awakened cherished memories in him. The two sisters poked each other surreptitiously with their elbows.

It was hard to hear each other because the wind made so much noise blowing their clothes. It wasn't long, therefore, before they decided to go down. When the woods had, again, closed up around them, they stopped for a moment to fix themselves up. The wind had thoroughly ravaged the girls' hair, especially Inger's. She had to take both gloves off to smooth it into shape, and while she stood there, with her hat pin in her mouth, she asked Per to hold them for her since her friends were busy with their own grooming. She thought nothing of it, but the two sisters looked at each other and, more than once on the way back through the woods, had occasion to nudge each other. When they reached the festival grounds, the meeting had again begun. A tall, serious-looking man with dark hair and beard stood on the platform. It was the principal Broager, the head of a neighboring high school and Pastor Blomberg's rival in popularity throughout the district, especially among the young. The girls quietly took their former places under the trees, and Inger glanced down at her mother. She felt a little anxious about her absence, which had lasted much longer than she anticipated, and was relieved that her mother, sitting calmly and entirely absorbed by the principal's talk, did not seem to have missed her.

The pastor's wife watched jealously over her husband's reputation as a lecturer, and, although no one could in any way notice it, she was nervous every time anyone, especially the school principal, spoke. That explained why, despite Per's presence on the scene, she did not think of looking after her daughter during the intermission. Something similar was the case with Pastor Blomberg. To be sure, he was always the first to applaud other speakers approvingly and to laugh the loudest at their jokes. But the blood that rushed to his cheeks as soon as he noticed someone else's success betrayed him. When the meeting ended with a few songs, and while they were waiting for the carriages parked a bit farther up in the woods, the master's wife, with Inger on her arm, moved off a little from the others. Then she said, "You were with Sidenius, I noticed."

"Yes, we took a little walk out to Rolhøj. There wasn't anything wrong with that, was there?" she asked, and looked at the master's wife a bit anxiously.

The latter started to laugh. "No, not really. Especially since he is engaged."

"To be sure. It's strange how little he seems to be engaged, isn't it?"

"Well, I don't think the engagement has a serious foundation . . ."

Inger stopped and looked a little panicky at her. "What are you saying?"

"Well, naturally, I don't really know anything. But I suspect he is not so happy with the connection. She's a Jewess."

Inger remained silent. She should have known that. She felt, suddenly, deeply ashamed of how free she had been with him. There was a call from the carriage, which had started forward. Pastor Blomberg and his wife already were settled in the open barouche, and the pastor was a little impatient, so there was time only for a hasty farewell.

When Inger got in and wanted to put on her gloves, she could not find them. A new embarrassment seized her; she had forgotten to retrieve them from Per, who probably had tucked them away. There was still time to get them back. The master's carriage had not yet started out—but so guilty did she feel that she didn't want to say anything that would betray her to her mother. In her confusion, she didn't even dare to look back when they drove off, and during the journey, she anxiously hid her hands under the lap blanket. When they had driven a little way, Fru Blomberg said to her husband, "I don't think Broager was really so good today."

"No, he was really dull," answered the pastor, shaking his head. "He definitely was not in good form." After some minutes, he repeated, "Absolutely not," although in the meantime they had been speaking of other things. For his part, Per spoke warmly on the way home of all that he had experienced during the outing, except that he didn't once mention Inger. The master's wife noticed it and was thinking it over.

The sun had gone down, and it was almost dark when they reached home. As they drove through the gates of Kærsholm with the hollow, rumbling echo Per already knew so well, and when he saw the light from the windows shining so invitingly, he was seized with a new and wonderful feeling. For the first time in his life, he had the sense of being connected to a place that felt like home. As if to confirm this, the steward's dog came leaping out and danced around him, licking his hand in sheer happiness at seeing him again. The poor beast had transferred her love to Per since her puppies had been taken away. Touched, Per leaned down to pat her head. When he came into his room, he was jarred by the sight of a letter for him placed on the table. Fearful it was from Jakobe, he hesitated to pick it up. But when he recognized Ivan's scrawl, he breathed easier, though a feeling of discomfort persisted. His brother-in-law's handwriting reminded him painfully of the continually unresolved money problem that, every night, generated anxious moments as he was falling asleep. He shoved the letter aside, unread; business must wait until the morning. On the way back to the living room, he found in his jacket pocket a small, light-gray little bundle, Inger's gloves, a brand-new, supple, but rough pair of so-called Randers gloves.

He had not altogether thoughtlessly kept them in the woods; he had felt happy to be carrying something that belonged to her, and, at the rushed farewell, he had forgotten to return them. Now he unfolded them gently and inspected them for a time, carrying them up to his face and greedily breathing in their perfume. He smiled pensively. He had the necessary pretext to visit the pastor's house the next day, he thought, but wasn't it, perhaps, advisable for him to let things be? Didn't he run the danger of falling in love if he saw her more often? The old Adam was aroused in him again. But where could it lead? He had no right to a new love. He had, for the rest of his days, shut himself off from life's flower-strewn paths . . . if ever, really, he had known them.

CHAPTER 21

IT WAS THE season in which the Copenhagen summer life at the villas along the coast of the Sound displayed brighter and more festive colors day by day. Miles of strong railroad tracks transplanted the big throb of the capital into the silence of nature. Large ships, weighted down on one side by their living cargo, steamed up to the gangways. Trains about an eighth of a mile long pulled into the stations to belch forth a swarm of people going by wheel and foot, dispersing the capital's mighty restlessness deep into the North Zealand woods.

A heavy mood clouded life at Skovbakken. Philip Salomon

and Fru Lea were having long and depressing discussions about their children. It wasn't only Jakobe whose future filled them with anxiety; now, also, Nanny's situation gave them cause for reflection of the most serious sort. She had sought reparation with her old suitor Hansen Iversen for the defeat that her vanity had suffered at Per's hand. Since she really wanted to forget, she had resorted to her bold flirting with a certain passion.

But it became evident that the former cavalry lieutenant with the elegant mustache was not such a sturdy character as had been supposed. One day, he went home and put a bullet through his head. In addition, he left behind a letter in which he explained to the world his motive and solemnly cursed Nanny. Thankfully, her husband's position kept the affair out of the press, and, in the following days, to cover up his wife's transgression, Dyhring liked to exhibit himself with Nanny on his arm and would jokingly tell his acquaintances that it really was a dangerous thing to have a wife whose eyes not only flashed like a pistol shot but actually could set one off. Privately, he subjected Nanny to a thorough inquisition climaxed by a box on the ear, which she received calmly. She thought she had escaped cheaply from the affair, since she had been scared to death, and, what was more, she became from all this really attracted to her husband and, for the first time, his humble slave, who willingly, and with more experience, submitted to his sexual intemperance.

Meanwhile, inevitably, rumors leaked out about the cause of the lieutenant's suicide. Copenhagen gossip infiltrated the country, carrying the suggestion of a letter left behind. When Philip Salomon and his wife took their usual evening outing on the beach road with their best team of horses, greeting and greeted by friends and enviers, ardent whispering circulated in the village gardens. Some people had never forgiven Nanny her beauty, and, on that ground alone, her virtue was always under suspicion in the little closed circle of the Bredgade quarter, where, as in the provinces, everyone knew each other down to the underwear.

The parents themselves judged their daughter's behavior very severely. Philip Salomon felt impelled to offer apologies to Dyhring on the family's behalf. The only relative of Nanny's who stood up for her a little was, oddly enough, Jakobe. She, who had always been rather merciless in her judgment of her sister, only shrugged in regard to the whole affair. She didn't think it should be taken so solemnly. When it is really lived, life demands blood, and whoever partakes of it, she said, must be prepared to shed it.

Jakobe had greatly changed in the last days. Not only had her appearance again deteriorated badly, but there was, in her bearing, something of the old tired and unnatural indifference that had been so characteristic in the past. When anyone asked her about her health, she answered calmly that she was well. About her fiancé she seldom spoke, and made no objections when her parents talked to her of the imminent marriage. But she was talking, now, too, about the possibility of visiting her friend in Breslau, and no one was really wise to her plans.

There was one who understood her a little. That was Rosalie. Her room was next to Jakobe's, and she was awakened one night by her sister's sobbing. Since she thought Jakobe was sick, she got up quickly, but found that her sister wouldn't let her in. The next morning, Jakobe explained that she had had a toothache. But Rosalie was no longer a child, and following in Nanny's footsteps she had begun to hunt in love's secret forest. She had already some success in bagging prey. The scholar Balling had confessed his love for her, and it amused her to pretend to be indifferent and to see her tall, literary piece of work tormented by apprehension and uncertainty.

What made Jakobe so despairingly depressed that she thought about taking her own life was that she could not decide on a final break with Per. She had well understood, for some time now, how the whole thing was going, and though she suspected that there was another woman in the picture, she put off her decision from day to day. Love was actually so degrading; that very feeling she thought life's most sacred was shameful. Under all this, there was a consolation, even a little revenge, in the fact that she had not confided in Per about her condition. She had not given up to him her dearest secret. In her maternity, she would remain inviolable. She would be spared the utmost humiliation of becoming an offering to his sympathies. She had, once again, left his letters unanswered, and it was only with great effort that she managed to read them. His interest in the pastor, moreover, filled her with pity. In one of his last letters, he had plainly recommended that she procure that man's writings (which she had already done), and when he again mentioned these sermons in the obvious hope that they would win her over to that Christian perspective, she was induced to answer him.

It presented an occasion in which she could bare her heart without humiliation. And though she had not, in her previous letter, written a line about their personal relationship, she felt that now she could prepare the final break:

> I have, up till now, felt no desire to follow through on the challenge you made in your last letter, to go into the subject you are obviously thinking about so much—I mean your relation to Christianity. That my silence is not owing to a lack of sympathy you, perhaps, have understood. But it is more and more my conviction that this is a question that is useless to discuss. What, especially, counts when the talk is of matters of faith is that we not allow ourselves to be influenced by rational argumentation. We get our faith as circumstances give it to us. Our religious organ develops as naturally as the heart and kidneys, and any artificial interference to counteract an inherited disposition has only the consequence that the whole organism weakens.
>
> In your last letter, I read between the lines a direct question to me that demands an answer, if for no other reason than that you do not ascribe my silence to an implied concession. My own relation to Christianity is, naturally, no less than yours, determined by birth and upbringing. From the time I was a little girl, and up to the present day, the persecution that the Christian church has directed against my race has awakened desires for vengeance in me. I almost believe that I would be able to forget all this if I could discover the church's beneficence to the rest of mankind; but wherever I read in the two-thousand-year history, I find, under the mask of compassion, the same treacherous and tyrannical persecutory lust, the same cold-blooded indifference to means when the hunger for might must be appeased.
>
> Never has any other spiritual movement been able, to such a degree, to take the worst traits of mankind into its service. And, therefore—an exclusive therefore—the Christian church has enjoyed such widespread influence.
>
> It's entirely incomprehensible to me, most perplexing, that upright men, able to read and think, are not disgusted with that society of faith under whose wings the most hideous suppression, the darkest ignorance, the most beastly

atrocities have found protection or, in any case, indulgence, while all of time's efforts to lead mankind forward to more light, greater righteousness, and more happiness by healthy, proud, and courageous endeavors, have been opposed by its unreconciled and envious enemy, the church. Even if the Reformation might have called forth some progress, it is not of great significance. Nor do the various modern movements that seem to aim for a comparatively benevolent understanding of a different kind of thinking pacify me.

On the contrary, Protestantism also has its Jesuits who in difficult times seem to be moving the church toward a kind of freedom of thought that serves only as cover for compelled concessions. That's a phenomenon as old as Christianity itself.

As it procured, from its beginning, a cunning foothold in the country in order to appropriate pagan customs and conceptions it could not overcome, so it clearly understands today how to adapt to the demands of science and the humanities at once, whenever a defeat threatens. And through all this, continually to claim to represent the only unchanging, God-inspired truth is a hypocrisy of which the world has never seen the equal.

With all that, I would not be unreconciled, I could still believe in the possibility of an understanding with Christianity, if it possessed some independent aspects of truth significant to mankind's welfare. But only on one condition could I offer my hand—that it repent and become honest, and that as a testimony to its sincere conversion it impose on itself the same penance it demands of its members.

Let the old sinner veil its countenance, as it is written, and, in front of the world's eyes, acknowledge its guilt. That might be a beginning; on its knees before mankind, whose simplicity it has deceived, the church should atone for its sins! On its knees before the truth it has subdued, before the righteousness it has blinded, it should ask for forgiveness for its past. Then, for the first time, but not until that move, can it expect to win the trust of those who really are the keepers of Life and Light.

At Kærsholm, the days glided by in the rustic simplicity that makes time pass so fleetingly and makes life seem so short. It was already Sunday, and the family drove, as usual, to Bøstrup to hear Pastor Blomberg. From Per's previous pronouncements after the meeting, the master's wife expected that he would go with them. The urge to go was certainly not lacking, because he would probably, on that occasion, again meet Inger. But the prospect of taking part in a formal service with hymns and the Lord's Prayer and benediction dissuaded him. He had received Jakobe's letter beforehand, and her passionate tone had made a strong impression on him, rendering him again uncertain.

When the carriage had left, he felt himself quite alone at Kærsholm. He went into the garden to an artificially constructed outlook hill on its border, where he sat on a bench and looked out over the district. All around, the church bells called to devotions. In the still air, the sound went forth far and wide over the meadows. He could clearly hear the church in Bøstrup. It did not call in vain; out on the road that curved around the property, one carriage after another carrying farmers in Sunday clothes could be seen, all going to Bøstrup. Per's eye followed them until they disappeared behind the high Borup hill. When the last one had passed, it was as if the district had died before his eyes, with its inhabitants being drawn forth to a strange country and leaving him behind, all alone. He hadn't felt this Sunday sense of unease he remembered so clearly from the past since the day his parents-in-law opened their house to him and introduced him into a world where no church bells rang. But even so, he didn't at all long for Skovbakken. He thought without envy of the crowd of happy, dressed-up, worldly party guests who would be there.

One after another the bells stopped chiming. The uncomfortable sense of abandonment seized him ever more strongly. The sound of a carriage far away on an unknown road evoked a powerful and fantastic premonition of the hereafter. He felt like a dead man who in the realm of the shades could hear the living walking over his grave. He thought once more of Jakobe's letter—he now knew how he wanted to answer her. That still and solemn morning, the farmers in their Sunday best, their fine, polished carriages, the thousands of homes all over the world from which people at that hour trustingly sought out churches to gather renewed courage and strength in the struggle for existence—that was surely life's own convincing protest against her words. It may be that the church has frightful sins on its conscience, he would write—and he himself thought that—but it was certainly compensated for abundantly by the good it brought to people. In any case, as Pastor Blomberg just said in his talk in the woods, we inhabitants of the northern Germanic world had a special reason to, at least, show Christianity respect, since it had freed us from barbarism, formed the soul of the race, so to speak, from childhood; it was the spiritual mother's milk that never could be entirely drained from the blood.

But why do we need historical proof? That's what he had already realized that night on the steamship going over Kattegat —that Christianity was a new source of strength for people since it was able to give his old, work-broken mother such a powerful spirit of self-sacrifice. Didn't he also, for his own part, feel more and more strongly the impossibility of sustaining his courage and vigor without help from heaven? And didn't every day bring around new testimony from lonely souls of the common desire for a God, a Heavenly Comforter?

Among the books and journals with which the master's wife had continually furnished him was Povl Berger's *Wrestling with the Angel*, which he had heard so much about in Copenhagen but now read for the first time. The great and famous confession deliberately cast in the style of the Old Testament moved him deeply. In one of the parts, in which the author directly took aim at the intellectual movement principally imported by Nathan from abroad, he compared it to a spring rain that makes the barren cornfields come to life, giving the sandy ground a deceptive look of luxuriance. "When, however, the summer drought arrives and harvest time grows near, where are you, then, you wild, rootless sprouts that preened along the way and spread a thousand colors over the earth like a promise of paradise's glory? Alas, your empty blades curse the corn. The sun that granted healthy growth to the original germ dries up the ears, and, before the harvest, the storm blows the corn away, for the fruit of sin is death. Blessed is he who, in the springtime of growth, humbly sinks roots in Mother Earth, where the stream of eternal life flows."

It was these words, especially, that had made such an impression on him he knew them by heart. When he had read them for the first time, they affected him as if they were an epitaph on his gravestone. For it was just such a spiritual warning that he had been feeling in the last year with a gradual exhaustion of strength and power. He had never really been willing to confess this to himself.

"So, farewell, you barren season; my years of wandering in the wilderness are over. My Father's paradise has opened up for me, and, blinded by the light, I kneel on the threshold in prayer and penitence." He laid his head in his hands and sat for an hour altogether still. He asked himself whether it was, now, anything but false pride that held him back from seeking a reconciliation with his father's God. Was it merely that he could not bow his stiff neck to acknowledge a power he had once denied?

Humility: that was one of those weighty Bible words whose decisive significance for life he was just beginning to understand. To be humble—that was the final difficulty. That was heaven's price for gaining peace of mind.

He raised his head. The bell was still ringing in Borup's church. It was only a little over a mile away; there was time enough, he thought.

He remained seated a few minutes more, but then got up resolutely. Quickly he went out behind the garden and park and succeeded in reaching the church before the pastor mounted the pulpit. Through the porch door, he heard hymn singing wafting out, and he stood there awhile to listen. He felt a peculiar excitement that did not, in truth, have much to do with devotion, still less with humility.

When he had his hand on the door latch to open it, he hesitated. He had to exert his will to make this last movement—to brave, as it were, his conversion in order to put an end to it.

He went for the bench farthest back and closest to the door, and, after he had found his seat and the dispersed churchgoers had satisfied their curiosity by turning around a few times to look at him, he quickly felt at peace. But it was not the kind of gathering geared to sustain his reverent mood.

The pastor stood on the altar and blew his nose elaborately. He turned his back to the congregation, which, all in all, consisted of only a dozen people, primarily older citizens, who did not look very bright. Hardly any men were seated there. Not even the hymn singing could really animate the service. Besides that of the parish clerk, only the whining voices of a few old ladies could be heard. The church's interior was a low, cellar-like room with large spots of discoloration from moisture and green mold on the walls that smelled sour from whitewash. On the pulpit before him lay a thick layer of plaster dust.

Then the pastor stepped up to the pulpit, and only at that moment did Per realize that it was the notorious Pastor Fjaltring he was going to hear. He stood there under the blue-painted sounding board—a handsome, pale man with regular features and silver-gray, slick hair brushed back from his forehead. He seemed not the least diabolical, as Per had assumed he would be. His cheeks and chin were smooth shaven, with a wide and well-formed mouth, large and dark eyes. His movements were measured, his bearing distinguished. Only once in a while an involuntary and, as it seemed, painful tremor shot through his shoulders into his face.

After a short beginning prayer, he took up the Bible to read the day's text. When he caught sight of Per, he stopped to observe him with obvious surprise. In a moment, he recovered from his distraction and began the reading. The sermon followed and lasted almost an hour. It was delivered in the usual preacherly tone and was filled with nothing but the conventional commonplaces about sin and grace and redemption and, again, about sin and hell's eternal torment. Per became more and more impatient. His mood was irreparably ruined. He realized now that when he had chosen not to go to Bøstrup, he should have stayed home.

He was happy when the service finally was over and he could slip out. Annoyed and ashamed, he hurried home. He felt deeply embarrassed by the result of his first church foray and promised himself not to tell anyone about it.

Wanting to shorten the time until the family returned, Per visited the steward to chat a bit and smoke a pipe. Among the country customs he had adopted here at Kærsholm was a taste for a long pipe with a big bowl that could be smoked for an hour without refilling. A humidor was hanging in the steward's room, where he regularly spent some time after the midday meal.

"Tell me what it is you find fault with in Pastor Blomberg," he asked when they had been talking about other things.

"I?"

"Yes, I seem to remember something. You once made a nasty remark about him."

The steward laughed into his curly beard. "God keep my

mouth from saying anything against him! Why should I say anything about the Reverend Infallibility? I'm not crazy!"

"Well, you did say something!"

"Well, maybe I wondered a little how he could neglect his old
father so much."

"Is Pastor Blomberg's father still living?"

"To be sure. Somewhere out in Zealand. And he goes around
as unkempt as a poorhouse beggar. He is full of lice and mange.
It seems to me that Blomberg could well take him into his home
and do a little for him in his old age."

"There must be something wrong here! Perhaps the father is
a drunkard, or Pastor Blomberg can't afford his upkeep."

"Blomberg is not so scrupulous about money. He always
knows where he can get some if he happens to need it. People
around here hang on him like a babe on the breast."

"How—get something?"

"Well, for example, some time ago, when he wanted a new
team of coach horses, he just let a word fall: he could no longer
answer to his children if he stayed here. He would have to look
for a more lucrative post. The people got scared and pitched in
to get him a landau and a pair of horses. And he barely thanked
them. He considered it his due—what was owed to him. Haven't
you heard what Pastor Fjaltring calls him?"

"No."

"The Wholesaler."

"What does that mean?"

"Well, I don't entirely understand, either. But it sounds so
funny, it seems to suit him."

Per was quiet for a while and watched the smoke from his pipe.
"How do you like the daughter?" he finally asked.

The steward laughed again. "She's very pretty."

"Nothing more?"

"Well, then, say, also, nice."

"Isn't the expression you always use 'blue-ribbon'?"

"Well, in my opinion, Frøken Blomberg is a trifle too
stuck-up."

Per involuntarily frowned. The steward's tone jarred him
today. The fellow was certainly more malicious than he thought.
His story about Pastor Blomberg was pure slander. At that
moment, the house carriage drove up through the gates. Per got
up and left without even saying goodbye. The master's wife met

him in the living room with a loud outburst: "You don't know what you missed, Herr Sidenius! Pastor Blomberg spoke wonderfully today."

But Per was not listening. Inger was standing by her side, and his surprise and pleasure over seeing her were so great he became embarrassed. "Now to the table," said the master's wife as she put her arm around Inger's waist with a glance at Per, as if she wanted to provoke his jealousy. "My husband is already seated here."

Uncharacteristically, it had been very difficult to persuade Inger to come back to Kærsholm. The reason she finally decided to go while Per was there was simply because she did not want to send for the forgotten gloves, but to get them herself. It had become tormenting to share a secret with the strange man and to know that something belonging to her was in his possession—on his table or hidden in his pocket as a pledge of intimacy.

To pacify her mother, who, after the folk meeting in the woods, had spoken to her about Per in a way that clearly was meant as a warning, she agreed to be home again by early evening. It was arranged that the pastor's family itself would fetch her in the course of the afternoon.

She was alone with him barely a minute when she blurted out her request. Per studied her awhile; he really had intended to ask her permission to keep the entrusted property as a souvenir, but he couldn't get his question out of his mouth. She looked so earnest, and there was something in her manner that nipped all sentimentality in the bud. So he bowed silently and went to his room to fetch the gloves.

When he came back and found her still alone—the master's wife had made herself invisible after the meal—he ventured to propose a walk in the garden. Inger considered this for a moment and decided that she couldn't refuse without being rude. In the meantime, she was anxious not to go so far from the veranda that the master's wife could not see them if she reappeared.

They did not have a real conversation; for that, they were both too taken up with their own thoughts. As soon as Per had seen Inger, it had become clear to him that he was in love with her, and that inhibited him, made him almost a bit grim. For her part, Inger was thinking over something that the master's wife had said during the drive back, namely that Herr Sidenius seemed in poor

spirits lately, and that his depressed mood was doubtless connected with his unhappy engagement.

A few times during lunch she had looked at him, and he did
not look well. Things must be going badly for him. She could
not think of anything worse than to be bound to someone you
didn't like or, perhaps, even respect.

"Do you think the air would be fresher out in the field?" asked
Per, and stopped at the gate of the garden fence that led out to
the open. "It's so oppressive under the trees today. The flies are
bothering you also, I see."

He was right about that, and Inger did not contradict him.
She had really given up thinking about the master's wife. Besides,
there was something in the courtly manner with which Per
opened the gate for her and stepped to the side that she
couldn't resist.

They came to a little stretch of grass that sloped down to the
meadows. Here there was a bit of breeze. A whirl of dust blew
back and forth over the road. The clouds had dispersed, but the
air was still sultry.

"Aren't you tired?" Per asked. "Do you want to sit down? The
grass is quite dry. And here there is a little air."

Inger, who discovered that she really was somewhat tired,
thought it over a bit, and then sat down on the slope, carefully
covering her feet with her skirt. That little chaste move fed Per's
infatuation like air fanning a smoldering fire. At that moment, he
realized how absolutely her light, young, virginal form dominated his fancy. With a blade of grass in her mouth, Inger looked
out over the meadows. She had tied her large, soft straw hat down
around her ears so that it framed her head almost like a bonnet.
She did that because of the breeze, but also because she well knew
it became her. Her own father had once said, in jest, that with a
hat like that, she needed only a garlanded staff and a little white
lamb on a leash to look like a pinafored princess in a pastoral
scene, and she always remembered that kind of compliment. Per
had seated himself a bit apart from her. He forced himself to look
quickly away. I have to get up immediately, he said to himself, or
I'll become ridiculous, sacrificing myself on the altar of a hopeless love.

After they had settled down, the conversation stalled. On
Inger's side, she really was not nervous about being alone with
him; she no longer had scruples of conscience. When she thought

about her mother's warning, she even felt a little nettled by it on Per's behalf. He was behaving with admirable correctness. But the situation was so unusual and dangerous she had the sensation of floating in air.

Per began to entertain her with his travel experiences, which he seized on when he couldn't think of anything else to say. But Inger wasn't listening. She was thinking, again, about something the master's wife had said once about him: he was certainly a big ladies' man, and it was his passion that had led him astray. She understood, by these words, that his fiancée was not only very rich, but also pretty—which she herself had imagined. She didn't know why, but she could not believe that he could have chosen her only for her money.

Per again stole a glance at her. She still had a blade of grass in her mouth and was staring over the lavishly flowered meadow. Leaning forward a little, she had lifted one knee a bit so she could rest her arm on it, and, squinting from the sun, her eyes were half shut.

"Am I boring you?" he asked, after a period of silence. She was a little startled by the sound of his voice and blushed. At that moment, they heard a carriage drive up to the manor house.

"That couldn't already be your parents," he blurted out in dismay.

"It certainly is," she said, and got up. "I must go in."

However, she exhibited no particular haste returning through the garden. When she spied a pair of beautiful marguerites by the side of the gate, she tarried in order to pick them. A little spite toward her mother was hidden in this gesture, but first and foremost, it was an assertion of her good conscience. She was aware of no transgression, but she must, in any case, not conceal the fact that she had been walking with Per.

Per did not have the slightest desire for social conversation now, so he left her at the veranda steps and went into his room, which had its own entrance on the gable side. There he paced up and down in order to calm himself. He was serious, now, about leaving. But where should he go? After what had happened, could he go back to Jakobe? Wasn't it his obligation to confess openly to her that he loved another? And then what? Was he ready for a break with Jakobe and her family? But he must get some money. He needed money—stupid, accursed, dirty money! He had to give up his plan to borrow a sum from the master. He hadn't been able to ask directly for a loan, but had alluded so clearly to his troubles that, if he wanted to, the master could have understood. Per stood by a window, his arms behind his back, staring out at the shimmering light in the dark leaf clusters of the chestnut trees.

In any case, he had to return to Copenhagen. And there—this now occurred to him—his relations with Jakobe would be threatened by another danger from a different direction. He would see Nanny again. And what then? Nanny had not often been in his thoughts at Kærsholm. But his flesh had not forgotten her. More than once he had awakened at night with a head heavy from sensuous dreams, and, to his shame—he had had to confess to himself—it was in Nanny's arms that he was embraced.

The wanton kiss she had planted on his mouth had stayed in his blood, and he had no basis for trusting his powers of resistance. When he thought of her, how she used to come toward him with her shameless, provocative gait, her lascivious womanly hip-wagging, with a smile full of promise, looking to the side with a glance like a brazen caress, he could already hear her silk petticoat whispering to him, with bold confidence, that with her the oblivion of a love he couldn't name would be found. He pressed his hand over his eyes and foresaw rows of foaming, black waves rushing toward him from the days ahead and, finally, closing over his head.

He turned away from the window and began, once more, to measure the floor with his shaky steps. His arms were again resting behind his back, his head bowed. There was something tired, slack, resigned about his form. On the table lay an open book, Povl Berger's confession, to which he was continually drawn because it seemed oddly to him to illustrate his own situation.

He picked it up, threw himself into one of the big armchairs, opened it to a place he had marked, and read:

"I am like a hungry man who cannot be satisfied, a sick man who will not call for the doctor. It is evening and the wind is still, but my heart is anxious. I am sitting on a hill, looking at the sun slowly sinking into the sea like a golden bell hanging there over the bluish reflection of light and filling the air with its clang. Listen, the very heavens are ringing. It's an angel's song! Why do I not bow my head? Why do I not fold my hands? Why do I not kneel and pray—'Father'? But I can't. And, nevertheless, I think, even know, because my soul has told me, that in God alone is the source of all comfort. You feel that everything in your life is joy-less and sterile, but He will grant you rich fruitfulness. When you sigh so downheartedly under the day's burden, He will change the world's heavy yoke to wings on your shoulders."

It had been the intention of the pastor and his wife to make only a short visit, but the master's wife persuaded them, without much difficulty, to stay for dinner. Then they all took a walk through the fields to look at the corn. Inger was with them; she had, the whole time, contrary to her custom, accompanied her mother, even holding her arm.

Per did not show up, and neither Pastor Blomberg nor his wife had yet talked about him. This was not because they had forgot-ten him. Per's continued stay at Kærsholm had finally begun to awaken notice in the district. There was gossip that the young man had gained great influence over the master's family, not alone with the women, but also with the master himself, and there was some truth in the last assumption. Here was the evi-dence: for many years, the master had entertained plans to drain a large swampy section that lay between the hills on his property. One day, during a coffee chat after dinner, he happened to men-tion it to Per and had claimed he was now serious about getting a surveyor to measure and level the terrain. Out of desire to occupy himself and, as well, to give a small return for the hospitality he enjoyed, Per offered to carry out the work, and the master, who was still farmer enough to want to economize, especially when it came to money, had gratefully accepted the offer. The neces-sary tools were already available and, in the course of a couple of mornings, the comprehensive work was completed. Then Per hit upon the idea of undertaking a thorough regulating of the draining, not only on the Kærsholm property, but also on the surrounding territory, thousands of acres of meadowland. Half playfully—but with the hidden motive, as well, of preparing for a request for a loan that would later be successful—he laid out, one evening, his plan before the master, who, despite his sluggish comprehension, did not need long to be convinced of the value. With the fertile inventiveness that was the fruit of Per's talents and that at happy moments made him ingenious, he had grasped that by a few cleverly conceived alterations in the river's channel bed, the conditions could be created for lowering the meadow's groundwater level by many inches and large stretches of foul and spongy swampland would be transformed, at comparatively little cost, into fertile fields.

Like a wily dealer, the master at first refused to think further about it, although he was so preoccupied with it that he slept poorly at night. The more deeply he thought about the idea, the better he understood what it could mean, not only for Kærsholm but for the whole district. What particularly attracted him to the plan was the conviction that he had once had a very similar notion, and that, should the occasion arise, he could justifiably take credit for it.

Exactly at the stroke of six, the company was called to the table by the sound of the bell. Mealtimes here were stamped by the same lack of formality characterizing the whole of Kærsholm life. Despite the presence of the pastor's family and although it was Sunday, the master sat at the table in his usual shooting jacket with his high-necked vest. His wife was, to be sure, wearing a silk dress with many ruffles and bows, but it was evident that it was an old party dress past its prime. Nor was the table service particularly festive—scarcely, in fact, proper. There were no flowers, and the glassware and porcelain were of a most modest kind.

At first, the master didn't talk much, but ate all the more and drank lots of wine. In addition, he mischievously enjoyed filling Pastor Blomberg's glass every time he turned away and wouldn't notice. The result was that the two gentlemen gradually became red-faced, along with the baroness (who liked to appear completely sober), whose face, even before the meal, was glowing suspiciously through her makeup. She "allowed herself to be persuaded" to empty a couple of glasses of sherry. The talk around the table was very loud and lively.

Under cover of the conversation, Per was permitted to sit fairly unnoticed with his own thoughts. Only Inger could not avoid remarking his absent-mindedness. She was seated next to him and, with her father on her other side, was, so to speak, reduced to Per for conversation. Diagonally across from her sat her mother, who was watching them covertly until the pastor's high spirits redirected her vigilance.

Per's distraction awakened an involuntary cheerfulness in Inger. She suspected nothing of the reasons for his altered manner and couldn't help amusing herself in a childlike way over the apparent effort it cost him to gather his thoughts for such a simple thing as passing the saltcellar or receiving the jam dish. During the whole first part of the meal, she was very animated, and the tip of her tongue darted often over her upper lip with the quick and subtle movement that characteristically accompanied her smile.

Then it occurred to her that, perhaps, Per, in the meantime, had received unpleasant news in the mail, obviously from his fiancée. And the tip of her tongue suddenly disappeared.

Toward the end of the meal, Per tapped on his glass, to general surprise, and asked for a moment of silence. He wanted, he said, to take the opportunity to express gratitude for the generous and indulgent hospitality that for so long—too long—he had enjoyed at Kærsholm.

"You're not leaving!" interrupted the master's wife, rather alarmed, with a glance at Inger.

"Unfortunately, I dare no longer ignore the voice of obligation that calls me to the other side of the Atlantic. Besides, I have doubtlessly tried the patience of my hosts."

"Oh, nonsense! How can you say that! You must stay on," the master's wife said eagerly, supported by a mumbled echo from her husband, who had already become fairly intoxicated.

Per thanked them with a nod but continued: "As hard as it is for me to leave this house that has become so dear and intimate to me, I must now be serious and depart. Nevertheless, I cannot separate myself from this place without expressing how much I will always treasure the memory of my stay at Kærsholm. And, in this respect, I must also thank the Bøstrup parsonage. Allow me, especially, to thank you, Pastor Blomberg, respectfully, for the rich conversations whose significance I can't speak of now, but which I will never forget."

In spite of this last assurance, the master's wife was suffering a serious disappointment. It was not the kind of conclusion she had counted on. She must stop him from traveling. She would talk later with him about it. She would not renounce a triumph of the Blomberg faith she had worked on for so long and would feel satisfied only with a great conversion here at Kærsholm.

She had prepared a countermove, she reminded herself, looking at Inger with a new and loving glance. Per's little speech had made a good impression on the pastor's family. It put his wife in a milder mood. She automatically judged him less harshly and grew calmer when she realized that he would soon be gone. Inger was very disconcerted that Per was leaving. What now? she thought. His dark, meditative mood had gradually made her a little nervous. She had been seized by the kind of discomfort one feels standing next to a loaded cannon. When she realized that he was going to give a speech, she became more tranquil, since she thought she would better understand why he was distracted. But she was, then, prey to another anxiety. During the whole first part of the speech, she sat with her heart in her throat worrying that he would break down, so a warm wave of relief washed over her when she recognized with what tact and taste he chose his words.

Per's announcement itself did not surprise her. She had long thought that he would certainly have to be leaving soon. Still, she felt entirely convinced that it was a letter from his fiancée that had initiated that sudden decision to break away. Perhaps he had simply been instructed to return to Copenhagen. That Jewess had him entirely in her power. She was probably not only very pretty and rich, but also flirtatious, as that kind of woman typically was. She remembered how the master's wife had once hinted that he surely had fallen, innocently enough, into an unhappy relationship.

The master's wife said she hoped the guests had enjoyed the dinner, and they got up from the table. Per bowed courteously to Inger, who returned his gesture with apparent indifference. Then she turned to her father and, entirely contrary to her custom, threw her arms around his neck and kissed him. During the general postprandial contentment, no one paid attention to this unusual sign of affection. But her father tenderly stroked her hair and said, "Bless you, little Inger." Per was the only one upset enough to feel his heart stop for a few seconds. Never for a moment did he imagine that his love could be answered, but this little incident awakened a suspicion that, at once, opened the gates of both heaven and hell.

Coffee was served in the garden, where, soon, something happened that caused the pastor and his family to depart hastily. The master had ordered cognac and liqueur brought out and, though the pastor realized, to his shame, that he had imbibed more than he really could tolerate, and refused another drink, the master filled his glass and treacherously shoved the tray over to him.

When, some time later, the pastor saw his glass empty, he clucked contentedly; he was unaware, in his befuddled state, that it was he himself who, in the course of the conversation, had downed another glass. His delight was so great that he fairly giggled, and his pale eyes searched out Per, with difficulty, on the other side of the table to find a sympathetic witness to his triumph. But Per neither saw nor heard what was going on around him.

The pastor's family ordered their carriage to be readied, and, since the master's wife was unsure of her husband and knew how it would all end, she did not request them to stay. This the pastor seriously resented. If he still pretended not to take notice of anything, it was because he, once and for all, had assumed the position that he would close his eyes to the moral flaws of the master. He did this partly out of regard for the master's wife, and partly because, as a practical man, he was not unaware of the significance he had for him and his standing in the community; namely, that he had the reputation of being a kind of Providence for the master's household.

The servant announced that the pastor's carriage was at the door. The ladies had already climbed in. Inger had not showed up for coffee. She had stayed in another place in the garden with the excuse of looking for four-leaf clovers, but really from a lack of desire to be with company. She seemed very impatient to get home. Although Per had helped her into the carriage, she did not once look at him. Nor had she given him her hand when she said goodbye, though both her mother and, especially, her father bid a heartfelt farewell. At the point of departure, the master stood on the highest step and steadied himself on his long legs. He waved his handkerchief gaily and smiled with extreme satisfaction because he thought he saw that the pastor was wobbling.

Per withdrew to his quarters. He was dizzy from the whirl of his mind and had to sit down immediately when he got to his room. There it was already dark and a blood-red evening sunset could be seen through the chestnut trees, throwing a reflection onto the ceiling and the walls.

He sank down in one of the large armchairs at the table and laid his head on his hands. His mind was more agitated than at any time he could remember. At first he tried to imagine that he had been mistaken, that the whole thing was one of his wretched fantasies. But he couldn't calm himself down. The mere notion that he might be loved in return by Inger drove him wild. It was like catching a glimpse of paradise's glory just as eternal darkness was closing over him.

He pressed his hands on his eyes and had to struggle to keep from crying. Yes, the hour of punishment was at hand. The judgment of God was descending. Cain's wandering, lonely, wilderness life—that was the hell to which he was reverting. But he had nothing to complain about. He had sold his soul, with full foresight, for earthly treasure. His pact with luck he had been living by was a pact with the devil, with Satan. And the fiend had honestly warned him at the agreement. Gold and honor and sensual joy—he had strewn all the world's glories at his feet. He only needed to reach for them and grab them. He jumped up, his hands on his head. No, no! God could not be so merciless. Had he sinned that deeply?

He knew he had transgressed, and he was ready to do penance. With cold deliberation he had sold out his heart's peace and trust, his mother's love, his father's blessing, the rights to his soul's homestead. He had sacrificed his entire spiritual fellowship with his country, its people, his family at the blood-splattered altar of vanity and greed. And that was not the whole of it! He had, on his wild chase after delusion, cast a shadow over the lives of others, been a trial to his parents, a worry to his sisters and brothers, a disappointment and a shame to his friends and patrons. And he had betrayed Jakobe.

He could no longer resist the deadly, terrifying haunting of his conscience. He sank down on the edge of the bed and hid his sobbing face in his hands. Oh, God, I have deserved all this, all of it, all!

That evening and night, he broke decisively with his past. The whole night he lay sleepless, and when he reviewed his life, he felt more and more guilty. His consciousness of sin brought on the sense of humility that he had not yet felt that morning. And from this, at last, came prayer. Only toward morning did he feel a little peace. When the servant came in with tea, he was sleeping.

His first thought, when he awakened, was of Jakobe and the letter he now had to write her. For it had become clear to him that night that it was now his absolute obligation to break off the relationship, which could never bring anything but grief and anguish to both of them. A long explanation was not really necessary. Jakobe's last letter had plainly revealed that she was prepared for the break, even wanted it.

As soon as he dressed, he sat at the table and took out his

writing materials. It wasn't so easy for him to put his confession on paper. He could not make himself write in detail about his relation to God; it was still so new it had to be kept sacred. He contented himself with some commonplaces about a lack of harmony in their perspectives, without which no happy union could be possible for long, and, as well, he asked her to believe that it was only after a long struggle and with a heavy heart that he could break the bonds that had been so dear to him. In order to spare her from any unnecessary sense of offense, he chose his words with the greatest care and put the entire blame on himself for the fault of bringing them together.

The letter sent, he sat deep into the afternoon in the garden's summerhouse with the master's wife, who was busy with her embroidery. She had given him a skein of yarn to hold, and after they had talked awhile about minor matters, Per felt the need to confide in her, to tell her right out that he had broken his engagement.

She wished the best for him and said that was only what she had expected. "And what are you thinking of doing now?" she asked after a pause. "You are surrendering a significant fortune, aren't you?" Per answered that this circumstance would naturally affect his situation in many ways and require certain changes. Among other things, he had decided to give up his trip to America, at least provisionally. "That's wise," said the master's wife. "I never thought the trip was really a good idea. You have moved about sufficiently in the last year. Do you know what I thought of proposing to you? You have spoken to my husband about a new water draining system for the district . . . a re-regulating of the river flow, or what have you. As far as I know, my husband is drawn to your thought and it would not really be impossible to realize. Wouldn't you, in that case, be interested in undertaking the work and also in settling down here until something bigger or better shows up for you? You like the district, and you have friends who would be glad to keep you here."

Per glanced at her with shining eyes. He understood her words as an implicit confession of Inger's feelings for him. She was her confidante and would scarcely have proposed something if she knew Inger would rather not see him here. "If you will permit me," continued the master's wife, "I will talk to my husband about the project. I think it best that you don't involve yourself in it before the various interested parties agree. Until then, you can travel. I hope, as I said, that all will go as I wish so we can see you here again soon."

Per decided to leave the next morning. He did not want to go straight to Copenhagen yet. He needed to visit his birthplace in order to spend a devotional hour of reflection at the graves of his parents to confirm, to himself, that he was serious and sincere about his conversion. As well, he made a decision about something else that had occupied him for some time. It had begun to weigh on him that he had never taken his exam. He realized that without a professional degree, it would be very difficult to gain the sure and secure position he wanted in order to work in peace on his inventions. Especially now, when he no longer basked in the light of the Salomon millions, he couldn't do without the standing the exam would give him.

In order to remedy, as much as possible, his former neglect, he decided to take the surveyor's exam or, more particularly, the exam his partial education at the Polytechnic half prepared him for in order to gain his commission as a chartered surveyor. He surmised that he could get ready for that exam in about six months with a little effort. As for his means of maintenance, he thought he could get a loan or an advance from the attorney Hasselager or one of the other businessmen interested in his plans. During the afternoon, he took a long, lonesome farewell walk through the district. It had been sultry for some days, and a storm was expected. The sky was overcast, and, in the North-west, the sun was sinking, burning red behind the black clouds like a smoking flame sputtering on a candlestick.

While he stood on a hill from which he could see the Bøstrup church and the parsonage garden, he was surprised by the rain. A few large, heavy drops plopped suddenly on the crown of his hat. He looked up, and, with a crackling explosion, a bluish light-ning flash tore through the cloud cover and seemed to shake the earth under him. A moment after, the water streamed down, as from a sluice. There was no question of outrunning the storm; the distance to Kærsholm was too great. So he sought refuge in the half-opened barn in the meadow used during haymaking. The storm chased at his heels as he ran across a field, and he got to the shelter just as a new thunderclap crackled in his ears.

It appeared that he was not the only one who had sought ref-uge here. In the darkened shelter he bumped into a tall, thin man in a long, gray frock, his head covered with an old-fashioned, high-crowned hat with a wide brim. It was Pastor Fjaltring. Per greeted him in his surprise, and they exchanged a few remarks on the weather. The pastor was obviously not well disposed to this meeting. The whole time he was standing half turned away, and he rubbed his chin with the gesture characteristic of those who feel self-conscious about not having shaved. Gradually, as Per's eyes got used to the dark, he discovered that the pastor's cheeks and chin looked almost moldy with stubble. He seemed to be, altogether, ill-kempt. Per was especially surprised by a black, silk handkerchief wrapped around his head that could be seen under the borders of his hat.

Out in the West, the clouds again became black-blue, shot through by another bolt of lightning, and then the earth, once more, shook from a mighty thunderclap.

"It's coming down over Bøstrup," Per exclaimed somewhat anxiously.

"You're not unfamiliar with the district," said the pastor.

"I have been here only a few weeks."

"Was I mistaken or did I see you in my church yesterday?"

Per introduced himself and said he was a guest of the master's family at Kærsholm.

"I think I heard that. You are an engineer, aren't you?" Per confirmed that. "Yes," the pastor continued, "we live now in an age that belongs to the engineers, 'millennial artists,' freely translated. It's surprising how railroads and steamships have already made our globe seem insignificant. The distance between countries is being reduced day by day and will, finally, be wiped out."

"Probably."

"Perhaps we shall succeed in reaching both the moon and stars with our machines. It's not such a physical impossibility, and then the world's space will be as intimate as our trouser pockets. But we still can't change the distance between our nose and mouth," the pastor added, after a little pause.

Per couldn't help laughing. He felt some sympathy with the man, whose way of speaking seemed a little crazy. They talked again for a while about the weather, the suddenness with which it had come up, about the barometric reading and so forth. When the subject finally was exhausted and the rain continued to splash down, the pastor again spoke of the contemporary supremacy of technology.

"There were once plans being promoted for a railroad through the parish. In our day, we might see a pair of rails run up to every man's door. I don't think the plan has yet been abandoned, as far as I know."

Per answered curtly that a progressive development of communication was *now* a vital necessity. The pastor pondered this and then, still half turned away, looked out at the rain.

"A vital necessity," he said with a singular, seemingly blanched-out smile. "Well, just what is *not* a vital necessity in our day? Doctors and engineers, teachers and the military—they all come with their claims. I hope it doesn't go with us as with certain apoplectics who die from too much blood."

"Well, first of all, we Danes hardly run that danger. We have not yet replaced what we lost in '64."

"Replaced," repeated the pastor slowly, and stared stonily away, with a look as fiery as the lightning's continual flicker kindling the clouds in the West. "I think, to the contrary, that we still have the soul's power to sustain us, to call out as in those troubled days. That was really a moment when it was almost clear to us that there is no vital necessity other than God's grace."

Per answered, a little embarrassed, with an old proverb: "God helps him who helps himself."

But the pastor shook his head: "God's help—that really is *no* help."

"Then how did we overcome that crisis?"

"Who said it was with God's help? If you follow that chain of reasoning, what has happened in this country since then could well be ascribed to the devil's help."

Per found it really senseless to involve himself in a discussion with a half-mad man. But there was something in his judgment of the times that moved the new man in him, and he again felt the desire to bear witness.

"The fear of God," he said, "that had sustained the Danish people in those bad times and turned the feeble into heroes"— and here he was moved, once more, thinking of his mother— "had not abandoned them in peaceful days, but it has energized the country's rehabilitation, in any case outside the capital."

But the pastor, rather brusquely, interrupted in order to say that terms like "fear of God" could not be applied to the Christianity of our day, in which God is taken as a comrade by the arm, and, with a patronizing expression, or when it feels serious, hugged and embraced in childlike love. With a clear allusion to Pastor Blomberg, he mocked "our jovial old wives' Christianity" that was about to become the country's national religion and that, with its babble and lyrical sentimentality, was really suited to a people like the Danes, who, in the religious realm, were still looking for idylls and were replacing faith's passion with poetry.

"You mention the war year. But although you might, now and then, think of it, perhaps with a little, longing sigh for the great days of adversity and countless pale faces, you are, nevertheless, too young to remember that time. If you had experienced those days—really been a witness to the courageous faith, the spirit of sacrifice, the willing and unselfish martyrdom, that the terror of ruin engendered in lukewarm souls . . . then you would understand or guess what the country's spirit could have developed into and you might only regret that we couldn't really stay as serious as we did in the face of the obliteration of our nation. Now we must wait until God, in His mercy, dissolves the whole Germanic race, into which, I dare say, we are gradually disappearing. For it is with the soul of the nation as with the soul of man: only death liberates it. Once the Greek soul appeared as God's chosen translator. Then we listened to the shepherd wisdom of the Jews as God's blessed tongue. Someday, I dare say, the north German race, with our Lutheran barbarism, will lift up a corner of eternity's raiment."

Per looked startled, and the pastor noticed it and stopped talking suddenly—as if a little anxious and vexed at having let himself be carried away by such an incontinent outburst. So he abruptly broke off the subject. Although it was still raining fairly heavily, he uttered a curt farewell and hurried off.

At the evening meal, Per was still thinking a good deal about that meeting and asked the master's wife more explicit questions about Pastor Fjaltring. Among other things, he wanted to know what was the meaning of the strange handkerchief around his head under his hat.

"He suffers a lot from headaches," the master's wife explained. "And he imagines he has a brain tumor. In every respect, he is a poor wretch."

CHAPTER 22

HAVING SHUT HERSELF up in her room, Jakobe was sitting at her little writing desk, her hand supporting her head, and looking through the window at the garden treetops swaying in the wind. Her eyes were large and shiny, and she was breathing heavily. In front of her, on the desk, lay Per's letter, which she had just received by the morning post.

She didn't know what most disgusted her: the apparent effort it had cost him to craft his considerate turns of speech, or the hypocrisy with which he sought to hide both from her and himself the actual cause for the inevitable break. That he, until the end, should display such a lack of means and courage to see the truth right before his eyes! What she would not have given for him to confess, with complete sincerity and frankness, that he had become enamored of another. But no! His troll nature too thoroughly poisoned his blood. He couldn't overcome his need to hide from the light. It was the characteristic Sidenian habit of concealing feelings. As once the significance of his plan for the nation's future had disguised his egoism, now religion served as a cover for his cowardice, his pitiful homesickness.

Well, good! She stood up and pressed her head with her hands. Why torment herself any longer with such brooding? Her thoughts could now let him go. They no longer had anything to do in the dusky realm in which his soul moved. She was free. Her heart's aberration was over. Love's wretched, exhausted fairy tale was almost at an end for her. It remained only to tell her parents. Then, away from here. The earth was burning under her feet. In all probability, Per would return to Copenhagen to order his affairs, and she did not want to risk bumping into him on the street. As well, she could scarcely hide her condition anymore. She surmised that her mother was beginning to suspect, and she absolutely had to avoid any explanation whatsoever—at least for now. Therefore, she would take off, already the next day. All had been prepared, so there was no reason to tarry.

Then she remembered that it wasn't only her mother she would have to deal with, but Rosalie, who was bathing the small children, and her father and Ivan, who had long since gone into the city.

Down in the living room, her mother sat at her sewing machine with a mountain of sheets that she was busy hemming.

"Always working, dear Mother," said Jakobe, and kissed her on the forehead. "If you aren't occupied with your accounts, you are busy with something else." Her tone made her mother immediately suspicious. But, without letting her notice anything, Fru Lea patted her daughter on the cheek and said, "Yes, dear girl, work was my generation's means of bearing up in life. And, really, I don't think there are any others more effective." Then she started the wheel spinning, and the machine clattered on. Fru Lea had markedly aged in the last year and now needed glasses.

Jakobe walked back and forth for a while, peeked into a newspaper, laid it down again, and seated herself in an armchair near her mother.

"Mama," she said, "I've told you before that I would like to visit Rebekka again in Breslau. I have decided, now, that I'm going to do it. But my money has been prematurely depleted this year. Can you ask Papa for a little advance?"

"Of course I can," answered her mother, somewhat hesitantly. "When are you starting off?"

"As soon as possible. Perhaps tomorrow."

Her mother stopped the machine and looked straight at her. "Are you traveling alone?"

"Yes."

"And the marriage?"

Jakobe leaned forward. She could not bear the look in her mother's eyes that seemed so uncannily large and dark behind the polished lenses. "Well," said Jakobe as she nervously closed and opened her fingers, "I might as well say at once, my engagement has been broken." There was a long silence.

"Is that why you have been so unapproachable lately?"

"Have I been? You'll have to forgive me."

Her mother rose, went over to Jakobe, and took her head between her hands, lifting it so that their eyes met.

"Is there anything else you are hiding from us, dear child?" she asked.

"You have no right to ask that," answered Jakobe with tears in her eyes. "About matters of the heart, one should be silent. You yourself taught me that."

Her mother remained irresolute. Then she pulled back her hands and turned away. From the other end of the room, where she had begun to clear a tabletop, she asked, "How much money do you think you need?" It was as if she no longer was calm enough to stay seated. Jakobe named a large sum. Her mother looked up once again. "Do you think you will stay away a long time?"

"Well, you can understand, Mama, that it won't be very comfortable for me here at home after what has happened. A canceled engagement always offers occasion for so much gossip. I'm so sorry to cause you and Papa all this unpleasantness. You must once more forgive me."

"We have never been particularly happy about your engagement. Still, it seems that now . . . ," began her mother, but, noticing signs of impatience in her daughter, didn't continue. They talked for a while only about practical things pertaining to her trip or her preparations.

As soon as Jakobe went up again to her room, she began to lay out her things for packing and to gather and store away what would be left behind. A good deal of that work had already been done. She had, for some time, covertly made preparations for her new departure from home that, perhaps, would be her last. Among other things, she had neatly put in order her letters from friends, wrapped them up, sealed them, and written the sender's name outside so they could not fall into the wrong hands if she didn't come back. Then she did the same with Per's letters. And when she wrote the name "Sidenius" on the packet, she smiled despite her sad mood. She had been spared from having to bear that barbarous name!

Shortly before dinner, her father, who was waiting for her in the library behind closed doors, called her down. He kissed her gently on the forehead and began immediately to talk about her financial situation without saying a word about Per.

"How much do you think you'll need?" he asked, and took out his accounts book.

Jakobe named a sum that was considerably less than what she had told her mother. She didn't have the courage to expose herself again to questions about the duration of the trip. Her father said nothing and entered the sum, which he voluntarily doubled. "I'll bring you the letter of credit tomorrow." At dinner, Jakobe tried her best to be lively, and, in fact, she was happier and more cheerful now than she had been in a long time. The oppressive cloud of uncertainty that had weighed on her consciousness was in the process of disappearing. If only she had been able to free herself from the notion that she was traveling off to meet death, she would have felt almost happy.

The presentiment of death had now taken possession of her imagination. Like a rising fever, successive chills invaded her body. She didn't want to make her mother anxious by confiding in her. It was her hope that her liveliness would remove any suspicion. Both her father and her mother seemed fairly calm. But Ivan was altogether brokenhearted. He, who usually spoke of twenty things with each mouthful, did not say a word during the whole meal. Afterward he went into the library to see his father, who was writing.

"Am I disturbing you?"

"No, you are coming just at the right time. I was going to send for you. Do you have something on your mind?"

"Perhaps the same as you. I have received a letter from Sidenius—just a few lines—on the subject of your financial support. He asks me to tell you that, naturally, it is his intention to pay back the money. He asks only for some grace time."

Philip Salomon said nothing. He couldn't bear to utter Per's name.

"There is something else I wanted you for," he said, and took up the note he had just finished writing. "Do me the favor of taking this immediately to the city. See to it that you have it printed up as quickly as possible. As you see, it is an announcement to our social circle—you can, on the way, estimate, yourself, how many of these we need. But they must be ready in time to send around, by the latest, tomorrow, with the evening post."

The note read as follows: "Philip Salomon and his wife wish to announce that the engagement between their daughter Jakobe and Herr Engineer Per Sidenius has been canceled."

Per went back to his childhood home by the large, still meadow the same afternoon that the news was dispersed through the Salomon family's large circle of friends. Unrecognized and uninterested in seeking out any of his old friends, he spent a day and night there alone with his memories. He was not struck, this time, as he had been when he last saw the town at his father's death, when it had appeared to him in a half-comic light, stirring his pity by its provincial lack of distinction, its crooked streets and paltry shops. As his childhood impressions, by degrees, came to the fore to nourish and shape his feelings, his relation to the town took on a half-religious character. From Berlin and the Tyrol, from Rome and Copenhagen, his thoughts had made pilgrimages back to this remote corner of the earth where the threads of his destiny ran together and lost themselves in eternity. The little meadow village at the foot of the high hills had become for him the earth's beginning and end, through which the path to the source of all things ran. When he came back in the evening from the churchyard and sat with some sandwiches in the hotel's café, the waiter brought him various newspapers, among which was the local paper, whose name and nature he remembered from the parsonage and which he therefore looked at first.

On the paper's first page was a rather long column called "Letter from the Capital," which passed on the latest assorted items in Copenhagen. In the midst of news of court and theater, the Tivoli and the circus, he found a detailed account of a "sensational suicide" in higher society. A promising young man, a former cavalry officer, had taken his life under very romantic circumstances. He had, it was posited, loved and thought himself loved in return by a young, recently married woman who belonged to the moneyed Jewish aristocracy. And when his hopes were dashed, he had gone home directly and put a bullet through his head. Per's face became alternately white and red. Although no names were given and although he had not heard that Lieutenant Hansen Iversen was dead, on reading this, he was sure the story concerned him and Nanny ... Nanny, whose bare arms, just a few weeks ago, had encircled *his* neck. He read the article to the end with the sense that a poisonous snake was crawling up his back. The whole bloody incident was graphically depicted. The conscientious journalist did not spare the readers from a picture of the stained floor, how the body had been found, a description of the sofa from which it had rolled off, or a tablecloth splattered with brains. Even the content of a letter the dead man had left behind was deftly hinted at, without violating the legally protected right to privacy and peace, in the service of satisfying general curiosity.

Per went up to his room, where he paced the floor; he couldn't recover from his shock. He got dizzy when he thought about how near he himself had been to getting tangled up in that wretched woman's net, that it could just as well have been him who was offered up to a scandal-mongering journalist's pen, if he hadn't ... if ... He stopped, suddenly, at this thought. It was as if a shutter had opened up in the depths of his soul and light had streamed in, chasing out half-hidden shadowy pictures from his past life. He saw himself that night, long ago, when he had fled from Fru Engelhardt's bed, seized with disgust at the pleasures that slut gave him. He remembered another time, still earlier, from his boyhood, when he was tempted by his dark-eyed sledding partner from the Riisager house, but in a crucial moment was rescued by the shame he felt in the face of the depraved child's brazen words and manners. And he thought of the many other times when he would have become a self-destructive prey if he had not had, in his soul, an instinctive horror of sin, or if, through his parents—and, above all, through his father's legacy of generations of pastors—he had not had a surreptitious pact with the life-saving force he had wanted to defy in the arrogance of his youth.

The Sidenius inheritance he had called his life's curse was really his amulet, a blessed sign he had secretly carried in him and that he could thank for the fact that things had not gone worse than they had. That drive for liberation, that instinct for self-preservation that had developed in his soul entirely independent of all theology—what was this other than the breath of God, the Bible's Holy Ghost, the Angel of Christianity that invisibly watched over him and kept his foot from stumbling and led him safely through all aberrations?

He sat at the window that overlooked a quiet, deserted alley. He was lodged fairly high up and could view a swarm of red roofs and white chimneys behind which the sun was just sinking. It was as if he fully understood himself for the first time and what had happened to him in these last days. Certainly he had already become conscious of his Christianity at Kærsholm; but that had really been more a frightened warning of an alarmed conscience than the testimony of a believing heart and mind. For the first time, here, his faith rose up in him as a sanctioned light breaking through the mist of black moods. While he sat there, his hand under his chin, and looked out at the golden-red evening sky, his soul opened to a large sense of wonder, the coming into being of a "new man" that had been long in the making.

Early the next morning he again went to the cemetery. He sat down on the little bench by the hedge around his parents' graves. It was a pretty, sunny, calm August morning, and he was alone. No one could be seen or heard in the whole, walled-in cemetery.

All through the air gossamer webs shimmered. Hedges and bushes were overlaid with silver threads and each blooming calyx and blade of grass was heavy with golden drops. There was a soft rustling overhead in the old, towering poplars that formed a broad alley through the graveyard, but down by the graves, not a blade of grass moved. The stillness was so deep it spread out like eternity itself.

For over an hour, he was privileged to sit altogether undisturbed in a mood touched with joy and solemnity, generating a strange and wonderful sense of repose and inner peace. Even thoughts of Inger were pushed to the back of his mind. Instead, he was thinking about Jakobe. Now that he himself had found the way to salvation, he had to think of those who knew no remedy for their pain. For Jakobe there was little hope. She belonged to a people that had deserted and denied the vital principle, but the time was soon coming when the wayward Danish youth would be seized by the kind of glowing, buoyant mood that now spread through him. He remembered some prophetic words from Povl Berger's great confession:

"The black night and darkness have disappeared; God's day is coming again with peace and happiness for all who want it. Like a flock of wild ducks that stretch their necks when, on their long flight over barren mountains, they spot the sea in the distance, like soldiers grown faint from a daylong march, burned by the sun, white from the dust of the road, who throw themselves down to drink at a brook—so you, mankind, will slake your thirst at the recovered springs of Grace!"

The break between Jakobe and her fiancé stirred the greatest sensation in the family's large circle of acquaintances. Even at the Exchange, the event was discussed. For the second time, Per succeeded, by his connection with the Salomons, in being a personality talked about in Copenhagen. Nanny, who had begun to recover from her horror over Lieutenant Hansen Iversen's suicide, was busily on the go, letting herself be heard. She had quickly sized up the situation and took sincere pleasure in saying that it was Jakobe, the poor thing, who had been shamefully betrayed. In a heavenly summer dress with virginal, white, long full crepe sleeves and angel wings on her hat, she would troop into the homes of friends and acquaintances to entrust them with a secret that must not go further: her sister's fiancé—the

scoundrel—instead of traveling to America, had fallen in love
with a country girl. Think of it! A common dairymaid! With eyes
turned toward heaven she declaimed:

> He cast off his woes and found his comfort
> At the bottom of his sago soup.

Among those reached by the roundabout rumor was Colonel
Bjerregrav. The old warrior had almost decided to support Per
in his battle for his great future project, and, if necessary, to take
up cudgels for him against the Copenhagen plan. But gradually,
as the days went by without his seeing anything of him, he
became once again alarmed. He was indignant over the foolishness with which Per had put himself out to graze just when his
presence was most essential. In the beginning, he had presumed
that it was a new symptom of his youthful arrogance. But gradually he realized that there must be something serious going on,
and when the note about the canceled engagement reached him,
he became even more upset.

Jakobe had, in the meantime, quietly left. Before Per arrived
in Copenhagen, she was on her way to Berlin. After her long,
prison-like loneliness in the country, she felt even the tiresome
train ride as a liberation. And when she drove, in the evening,
from the Stettiner station to the Central Hotel, it was with a
feeling of sensuous pleasure that she felt the cosmopolitan city
closing up around her like roaring waves. The crowds in Fried-
richstrasse, under the magic of electric lights, the long rows of
carriages, the clopping of horses' hooves on the asphalt, the
illuminated store palaces, the rattle of the metropolitan railway
over her head, and, finally, the gigantic hotel itself, people rushing in and out, swarming like bees in a hive while, on the steps
and in the corridors, every possible foreign language was heard,
all that made her tormented heart swell with a painful longing
for life. She felt like someone coming home to her native land.
In this bubbling, kindled crowd, she felt safe. Of course, she knew
how much evil was hidden here in the dark depths, how many
poor, shipwrecked wretches were ground down and buried
under the city's slime every day. She was aware of the helpless
troop of poor in the great world capital, that gray, pale, hollow-
eyed indigence that made the red-cheeked poverty of the small
town and country look, by comparison, like prosperity. And still!

Even this homeless and exhausted beggared life in the capital seemed to her, then, a hundred times richer than the peasants' safe mole-like existence, and she understood so well why, despite hunger and misery, they clung to the pavement until death washed them away. Such a huge city had something of the sea's magic, its billowing fairy-tale attraction in the murderous struggle for existence, in this wild tossing about, in the ceaseless rocking that, up to the final destruction, lures one on with new and boundless possibilities.

And, always, Jakobe's thoughts came back to the child she was bringing into the world. She hoped—if it took after its northern ancestors—that it would not belong to those mole men, to those chained to their home towns like slaves, for whom the world and, even, happiness stops when they can no longer see the smoke of their mothers' chimney. He should be a son of the sea, with a Viking nature, filled with the joy of painful and distant fighting. The instinct to wander and an uneasy but determined aspiration that had made so many of her tribe's men and women into leaders of mankind was in her own restless, Jewish blood.

She more and more held to the final wisdom that happiness lay only in struggle—if on no other grounds than by granting the deepest oblivion. It was with life as with war. There were always those in the retinue who would have colic, and it was on the pale faces of marauders that the fear of the battle showed up. Those who found themselves in the middle of blows and turmoil thought less of the danger—did not dread blood.

BOOK 8

LUCKY PER,
HIS LAST STRUGGLE

CHAPTER 23

IMMEDIATELY AFTER HIS arrival in Copenhagen, Per set about
arranging lodging and his financial affairs so he could take up his
work again with peace of mind. It was his intention to turn to
the attorney Hasselager for a loan of fourteen or fifteen hundred
kroner that could secure him support for at least a year. As painful
as it was for him to have to make himself dependent on the kind
of man whose methods of exploitation and whole way of life he
now despised more than ever, he knew, for the time being, no
better resource.

For security, he thought of offering two patents he finally had
obtained for his wind and wave engines—one Danish and one
from abroad. To be sure, no would-be purchaser had turned up,
and he didn't want to pretend that he himself attached any special
value to them. He considered his invention only half finished.
But he assumed that Hasselager, who was such a cunning businessman and who had some understanding of the significance of
his invention, could recover expenses if he supported him with
an advance. The lawyer received him with irreproachable courtesy, but he had, just the day before, learned that Per's engagement had been canceled, and he was, therefore, rather restrained.
They talked for a while about Per's plans and hopes, especially as
they concerned the development of his invention, and Per felt
himself obliged to speak frankly. When, at last, he came to the
question of a loan, the lawyer turned very reserved. With the
most polished Copenhagen charm, he regretted that he was not
in a position to oblige him on that point. He confessed that he
never gave a loan, on principle, for which there could not be
established bankable security. That was a business rule that every
lawyer had to uphold strictly in order not to be suspected of
having something to do with money deals that could not bear the
light of day.

Per asked him whether he then thought it would be possible
to get a loan elsewhere from business-minded men who weren't

bound by that kind of consideration. To which Herr Hasselager, after a short reflection and against his better knowledge, answered that he thought there surely was. The large, blond, plethoric Dane who otherwise imitated, and not without success, Max Bernhardt's wild temerity as a speculator did not possess the fearlessness of that pale man in the face of an assassination, but handed over to others the job of giving his victim the deathblow. In this case, he referred him to Herr Nørrehave, whom Per also had thought of. The next day, Per sought out this grand swindler dressed like a farmer who lived in a well-furnished villa suitable to his station in Frederiksberg.

This thick, paunchy Jutlander, who had heard the rumor about the canceled engagement but had not wanted to believe it, greeted him with his most ingenuous smile and a warm, sweaty handshake. But Per had not been talking long before the gentleman farmer grew silent, and his small, white-lashed pig eyes were busy peeking at Per's ring finger. The plump farmer became wider and wider in his gilded armchair the longer Per talked. Finally, he crossed his arms over his chest and declared emphatically that he would have nothing to do with this business.

Per began to feel restive. He remembered that this man, together with Hasselager, had, in the spring, proposed an alliance with him on terms that entirely justified Per's present application. And now, unmoved, he shook his head and repeated in his Jutland market-town accent: "I'll have nothing to do with it!"

When, unwilling to accept this response, Per demanded an explanation, Herr Nørrehave responded with the rustic straightforwardness that his potential business partner doubtlessly expected, that the "situation" (his favorite word) had totally altered since Per—he could understand this—was no longer Philip Salomon's future son-in-law. He expressed his surprise at the break with the rich businessman's house, even tried to pump him about it. But when Per got up looking as if he wanted to punch him in the mouth and said, "Short and sweet, this is really your decision, that you will not give me the loan I am asking for?" Nørrehave seemed a little unsettled. That peremptory tone reawakened the awed respect Per had inspired in him by his performance in Max Bernhardt's office. His thick arms slid down his sides, and he folded his hands over his belly, his thumbs twirling round, while his small, white-fringed eyes looked up at Per with a reflective expression. Meanwhile, he was again calculating and weighing the possibilities against the risks.

Finally, he concluded his consideration with an answer like the kick of a wooden shoe: "No, I'll have nothing to do with it!"

Almost before these words were uttered, Per had grabbed his hat and left. Outside, he felt calmer. He said to himself that he had no right to complain. He himself had taken part in the cannibalistic sacrificial dance around the Golden Calf. Was it any wonder that the beast butted him when he no longer wanted to play the game? But what should he do? He must get some money! He owned scarcely a hundred kroner in cash.

He walked into the Frederiksberg Gardens and, for a long time, sat on a bench and wracked his brains to find a way out. The ingenuity that was his strength as a technician did not fail him. When he got up an hour later and went home, he had a plan ready. He would turn to Colonel Bjerregrav, whom he already owed a visit. But it wasn't his intention to try to get a loan from him; the colonel would merely be a middleman between Per and Councilor Erichsen, the well-known patron he had once seen in the Salomon house and who, as far as he knew, had supported others in their enterprises. Just because he had met the councilor in the home of his former parents-in-law, he could not bear to solicit him directly. And, besides, it was really not easy to turn to a strange man in such a concern.

On that very afternoon, he was sitting in the colonel's study on the same little cane sofa where, so full of hope, he had presented his plans three years ago. The colonel leaned back in his desk chair and observed him attentively over his level pince-nez with a half-compassionate, half-curious look. From his nephew, Dyhring, he had learned that religious differences had caused Per to break off the engagement, and although he—God knows—certainly was familiar with that motive, he looked upon Per as one who, through an unfortunate chance, had taken leave of his senses.

Per began by apologizing for returning his host's honorable visit so late; but he had felt the need to stay away for some time from Copenhagen for, as he put it, "personal reasons." The colonel honored this confession with a considerate silence. Without beating around the bush, Per informed him of his financial difficulty and how he thought he might get through it. He had reason to believe, he said, that if he could dare to count on the colonel's benevolent assistance, he could get support from Councilor Erichsen—all the more since he knew that man was already favorably disposed toward him.

Although it was clear to the colonel that he wanted to have nothing to do with the matter, his response was very obliging. He promised to take the request under consideration and to let him hear further from him. He looked upon Per as a sick man whom it was best to string along.

And, undeniably, Per appeared somewhat overwrought as he sat there and talked more effusively than he realized. The last days' agonizing soul struggle and the joy he now felt at finally having conquered his old self had stirred some desire for confidentiality in him. He had changed in another respect, as well. He had become pale and thinner, with deep shadows under his eyes, and, while at Kærsholm, he had let his hair and beard grow.

When he had gone, the colonel sat still for some time in his chair and fell into a melancholy musing. Poor fellow! he thought. There he goes, irretrievably under. To be sure, it somewhat satisfied his vanity that, like his own reformation, which had miscarried in his day, nothing would come of this. But for the sake of the Fatherland, he couldn't rejoice. He had lately had great hopes for Per. He had seen in him a sign of the restoration of the hidden Danish strength by which the country could finally free itself from the brood of Jews and other half Germans who had been necessary to help the nation get on its feet after the postwar exhaustion. His thoughts now dwelled on his sister's son, who, earlier that day, had scored a new coup. In order to secure support from his paper, one of the country's largest joint stock companies had elected Dyhring to its board, and this would throw thousands of kroner annually his way without his lifting a finger. Soon he would, in all probability, have a seat in Parliament. That boy's luck was close to making him skeptical about a just Providence. With no business acumen, without faith or patriotism, he was continually gaining power, significance, and distinction, while the really chosen ones, the born leaders, were pushed down. But it was always like that in Denmark. Generation after generation grew up red-cheeked and clear-eyed, bold and strong. And generation after generation went to the grave, broken and bowed— always defeated. It was as if a hidden sickness ate into the nation's strength, wasted the best of the youth, and exposed the country to the conquering foreigners.

Per had rented himself a room at an old widow's house in one of the small side streets behind the Frederiksberg Gardens. He had chosen that outlying district of the city not only in order to live near the agricultural college where he could hear the lectures, but also in order to be as far as possible from the Bredgade quarter and other places linked with oppressive memories of the past. His room was a little, poorly furnished attic space, and, as usual, he did nothing to make it more comfortable. He merely thought of the quickest possible way to get himself ready for his exam so he could, again, leave the city.

Trusting in the colonel's promise and convinced that his money problems would be arranged, he had his books, drafts, and other possessions fetched from the hotel, where they had been in storage during his absence. He already had some good ideas for improving his wind and wave motors; the big advantage a plan like that had over the canal project was that he could develop it independently by himself. Happily, no help from the likes of Max Bernhardt and Nørrehave would be necessary. Out in the country, he would, as well, have the chance to set up practical trials that were in need of space. He would probably have to build a couple of small test motors.

But all these thoughts had to wait for a while. One of his professors, to whom he immediately turned to lay out a plan for his experiments, had recommended that he count on a year and a half of study. He himself decided he could do it in half that time. And he assumed for this occasion the bold watchword of his youth: "I will."

So he sat in his little room and fought for his life and future happiness. As in his time in Nyboder, he got up in the morning with the factory whistles, and his window was, in general, the last to show a light when night fell on the quiet little lane. Although his goal, as big as it was, no longer had anything of a romantic aura of shining gold about it, he got down to work with an unmatched eagerness and perseverance without being held back by the sudden, painful attack of impotence that formerly overcame him so frequently. He expected no great material success from his invention; he didn't even want it. It would be reward enough if he knew that it would work for the benefit of mankind. All that he personally hoped from this work was that it would make it possible to lead a peaceful, happy, useful life in harmony and consonance with his heart's desire.

He didn't really hazard to build his future, yet, on his love for Inger. As often as his thoughts began to return to the Bøstrup parsonage, a sword-brandishing cherub stopped them. He had to wait; he was not yet worthy of paradise. Now when he was thoroughly aware of his sinfulness, it seemed to him often that he did not have the right to hope for such a rich happiness. In the face of such an innocent and pure heart, he had to lower his eyes; that was his punishment. He had to hide his hope like a thief his lamp, and he dared only to look forward to seeing her again. At his departure from Kærsholm, the master's wife had asked him whether he had not thought of spending Christmas with them, and, with a rather cheerful little smile, she had added that it would make those in the parsonage happy, as well, to see him again.

The first Sunday after his return to Copenhagen, he went into the city to the Vartov Church. It was a beautiful sunny day, and he started out early from home because he wanted to walk the whole way to save expenses. But when he entered the avenue and met the stream of happy people coming out to spend Sunday in the fresh air, he felt self-conscious and got into a streetcar. A quarter hour before the start of the service, he reached the little oratory in Løngangstræde. The church was already full, even overflowing. While in the city's other, large churches, preaching was to half-empty pews, here in the Grundtvigian congregation's maternal home there was always a crowd. It had been a long time since the great founding father's voice had sounded there, but his soul brooded over the place and people came here from around the whole land as to a holy place where God had revealed Himself again to them as in the parabolic burning bush.

With some difficulty, Per succeeded in finding standing room against a wall. The sun was shining through a row of windows on the opposite side in broad streaks and, like a holy light, circled the heads of those who sat in the center. Among these many haloed heads, there was one that, during the first part of the service, often turned toward him without his noticing it. Only in the middle of the second hymn did it catch his attention. He saw a light pair of eyes under dark, joined brows, and he was startled to recognize his sister Signe. Next to her were his younger brothers, the twins. They sat shoulder to shoulder as they followed a single hymnbook and had not yet seen him.

He felt his cheeks burning, and he could barely respond to his sister's nod. It hadn't occurred to him that he might meet anyone from his family here. He had not even thought he would be exposing himself to an acquaintance. Signe, on the other hand, hardly seemed surprised. She nodded calmly to him without interrupting her singing, as if, sitting there Sunday after Sunday, she had been expecting him.

Immediately after his return to Copenhagen, Per had looked for his family in his mother's old apartment on Gammel Konge-vej, but he had actually been relieved to find no one at home. He had not, up to now, repeated his visit. He did not know how he would tell them everything that had happened to him, and that he was no longer engaged.

The singing was finished, and the pastor appeared at the pulpit above the altar, but Per was no longer in a state to concentrate on the sermon. This church visit did not go any better than his first, unhappy one in Borup. However much he tried to collect himself, he felt, once more, despairing before all this.

In addition, he was experiencing a bodily sickness. He had not been feeling well lately. He had vestiges of his old pain in the diaphragm, and his sleep had been restless—shot through with confusing dreams. The bad air in the overstuffed church, the sun hitting him in the eyes, the strain of standing for so long, in addition to the stress of an imminent meeting with Signe and his brothers, all that made his head swim. There was a moment during the prayers, after the sermon, when he thought he really would pass out.

He felt seriously ill when, at the end of the service, he met his brothers and sister outside the church. Signe spied him immediately and asked what was wrong with him. Then the sunlight flickered before his eyes and he fainted. When he came to, the brothers put him into a carriage. He heard Signe give the driver the order to go to the family apartment, and Per made no protest. He felt so terribly weak he thought he was dying. As soon as he was put to bed, he fell asleep.

Some time afterward, he was in a half-darkened, low-ceilinged room with a single window, its blind rolled down. It took a little time before he realized where he was, and he looked around timidly. There was his mother's mahogany desk with the round, ivory keyhole plate. It stared at him with a surprised, wide-opened eye. There was the basketwork chair that he remembered from his father's death room. And the ottoman with the hand-embroidered seat that his mother so anxiously cared for. There, on the mirrored console, lay the large, African shell in whose blood-red interior you could hear the song of the ocean, that enchanted, ghostly roar, to which he listened as a child with so much wonder, and that, perhaps, first provoked his dream of a far-off and strange fairy-tale splendor.

He breathed deeply with a happy feeling of liberation. He was home now! The wild flights of his dreams were finished. He had come back to reality with a foothold, again, on Mother Earth. The door to the next room was half open, and he heard his family chattering away. It sounded so warm, so comforting. And then the old table clock chimed ... three clear, delicate, silver-tongued chimes. How well he knew that sound. It was as if his whole childhood were born again out of the womb of time. He remembered how, as a little fellow, he had devoutly listened to that clock conscientiously ringing out the death of every hour like the church bells the passing of a body. Later, he wondered whether it was the dying hour's soul that was released, rising to heaven on the silver tone. Even after his fantasy had turned from the Beyond and landed on the earth's playground, these regular, grave, admonitory chimes could put him in a solemn mood. In fact, he had never really freed himself from the feeling of devotion at the passing of the hours. However old he had become, he could never hear the chimes without the sense that it was a secret message brought from deep inside eternity.

He began to think of his mother's letter. It had lain the whole summer in his mind like a large, anxious anticipation. Though he was longing to read it, he had not had the courage to write for it. Now he felt he was ready and would ask his sister for it. He was going to call her when the front doorbell rang. A little after, he heard Eberhard's voice in the neighboring room.

He lay there awhile listening to it and thought about how much it resembled their father's. And the way his brother paced up and down the floor while he talked was so completely like their father's habit that it was uncanny. He heard Signe tell him what had happened, and, although they both spoke with hushed voices, he could more or less follow their exchange. Eberhard scolded his sister in quite an irritated tone for what she had done. "It would have been better," he said, "to drive him immediately to the hospital. When we can't know the cause of a condition that is always the thing to do. Perhaps it is, as well, a contagious disease. At least a doctor should have been called right away."

Per turned over on his side. He didn't want to hear any more. For a moment he struggled with a feeling that, again, challenged his mood of reconciliation. He said to himself that his brother was right. In any case, now that the work of expiation had begun, it was time to show that he was, in fact, serious about his penance. "Eberhard," he called out. His brother came in and a little after, Signe, too, who stationed herself at the foot of his bed.

"I don't think you need worry," he said so quickly he seemed to be willfully outrunning himself. "There's really nothing wrong with me. I have merely been a little overstrained these last days. I feel completely recovered."

"Well, you don't look in bad shape, either," said Eberhard as he offered his hand. His tone was entirely friendly and sympathetic. "But fainting is, nevertheless, always a serious thing."

"I was simply a bit under the weather—it was nothing but that. And, unfortunately, I happened to be standing with the sun in my eyes. I never could tolerate that. But I feel quite strong, now."

"I still am convinced we should send for the doctor. If he is home, he can be here momentarily."

"Well, if it would put you at ease, naturally. But, as I said, I don't think my ailment has anything to do with a real sickness. It was merely the sun . . . and, perhaps, the bad air."

"Well, I won't give an opinion on that," Eberhard said rather brusquely. "But even in that case, the doctor can best analyze it."

Despite all his good intentions, Per couldn't keep from being on the watch for the expression of triumph on his brother's face that he dreaded more than anything. But Eberhard was standing with his back to the light, so his face, with its underslung jaw, even more prominent than his sister's, was a rigid, leathery mask, its life confined to his eyes. Per repeated that he, naturally, would yield to his wishes, but he asked him only that he send for Professor Larsen, whom, once before, he had consulted in a comparable situation.

That request was not well received by either Eberhard or Signe. They looked at each other, and Per's brother said, "We have our own doctor. It's not the professor, to be sure, but he is a man in whom we have full confidence."

"Mother would have no other," added his sister.

Per didn't understand their resistance. He said it would be uncomfortable for him to be seen by a doctor other than the one who had examined him before and, therefore, was best geared to judge his condition. But Eberhard would not give in: "I won't say anything about your relation to Professor Larsen, but we, for our part, cannot insult our own doctor, all the more since we have no reason to be dissatisfied with him. It's probable Professor Larsen wouldn't even come out at this time of day—in any case, not for those who do not belong to his regular clientele. So, on that ground alone . . ." But Per realized they were treating his wish as an untimely pretension, an attempt to show off his aristocratic customs, and that misconception annoyed him. He replied that if they were so much against Professor Larsen, he would rather get up and leave.

When Eberhard understood that he was serious, he withdrew, displeased, to tell the servant girl to send for the professor. Signe wanted to follow him, but Per held her back. "Signe," he said, "you have the letter Mother wrote to me, don't you?"

"Do you want it now?"

"Yes, thanks, even though it will seem very strange to read it here where it was written."

Signe silently took out a bunch of keys and unlocked a desk drawer, coming back with a sealed letter and a little packet with their father's watch.

Only when Per was alone did he look at the letter. A tear rolled down his cheek when he saw the address written on the envelope by his mother's trembling hand: "To my son Peter Andreas—to read in a quiet hour." He broke the seal and read:

> In the blessed name of Jesus Christ I write this to you, my son, for the last time while my eyes can still see to try to appeal to your heart that is closed not only to your mother and father, sleeping with the Lord, and to all the others near to you, but also to God the Almighty and His Grace through Jesus Christ. I write you although I do not know, anymore, where you are living and traveling. You always hid yourself from us, and I'm sure you have your reasons. Your brother and sister say you are far away, either in France or America. But wherever you are, I know one thing: you are not on the path of God. You have chosen to

harness yourself to the world's yoke and it is written that from him who hardens himself in spite and sin, the Gospel will be hidden until the end of time. In one of his sermons, your father once used this image for the life of a godless man: that he is like an inmate in a prison cell without the smallest opening through which the light of heaven could enter to comfort him and without any exit other than a trap door deceitfully fastened over a bottomless abyss. My unhappy son! May the truth of this frightful picture be impressed upon you. May you understand this truth: that if we live for the body, we shall surely die, but if we die to its temptations for the sake of the soul, we will live forever. May you learn to *fear for yourself*; there is still hope that you can find the path to your Redeemer and turn your mind away from evil and pray for grace and forgiveness of your sins in the name of Jesus' blood and wounds.

I have much, still, to say to you, my dear son, but my hand is weary and my eyes dim. So let these words be your mother's last to you in my frail mortality: "Kneel before the Lord your God with a crushed and broken heart so that the Holy Ghost can redeem you in the name of our dear Savior, Jesus Christ. May God have mercy on you so that you shall not awaken on Judgment Day from the sleep of death to these most terrible words: 'Go from me, wretch. I know ye not.'"

Per was still lying with his mother's letter in his hand when Eberhard came in half an hour later to bring the professor's answer. At his brother's unexpected appearance, Per could barely hide the letter under the sheet. Eberhard was standing at the door, in a hurry to go. "It is, naturally, just as I said," he informed him with satisfaction. "Josefine brings the answer that the professor no longer will go out today if there is no impending danger. He would, on the other hand, be happy to come tomorrow morning if you wish." Per answered merely with a nod. He scarcely understood what his communication was about. Nor did he realize immediately that in Eberhard's words was hidden a renewed suggestion to him about giving up the request. Only when his brother turned around and almost slammed the door behind him did he really become fully conscious.

He couldn't fathom the uncomfortable and oppressive mood

he was left in by the reading of his mother's letter. He had been prepared for very censorious and merciless words, but the whole letter left him entirely cold. His first thought, after reading it through once, was a wish that these farewell words had never come into his hands.

He placed the whole fault for his disappointment on himself. He reproached himself for not paying closer attention to the admonition his mother had given him on the envelope. He should not have read it just after his mind was overheated from the little family argument. He now wanted to hide it and to read it again in a calmer hour when he was home by himself. He was also depressed by the fact that first Signe, then one of the twins, had come into the room on some errand but clearly with the intention of studying the effect the letter had on him.

The clock in the living room struck four and he thought anxiously about how the day was ending. Although in the course of the afternoon, both Signe and the twins did their best to care for him and to entertain him, he longed to get back to the peace and quiet of his own little lonely room. Toward evening, Eberhard appeared again. He did not live here with the other siblings and came only for the family meal at three o'clock, just as he had when his mother was alive. It moved Per that, despite their quarrel, he had come a long way from Christianshavn just to check on his condition.

There never was a question of a more confidential conversation with him or Signe. He couldn't even find out whether they knew of his break with Jakobe. He had, in the afternoon, tried, a few times, to lead the conversation there with Signe, but in her apparent anxiety she always started to talk about other things. Eberhard, too, seemed entirely indisposed to take up that subject. With their solicitude and sympathy in their relation to him, Per had a sense that they were especially inclined to interpret the most innocent utterance from him as an attempt to boast of his past and his connections.

In that regard, he wasn't mistaken. Neither Eberhard nor Signe had for the time being put great reliance on the sincerity of his conversion—for this, it seemed, he still was far from being humble enough. They had heard from others that his engagement to the rich Jew's daughter had been canceled, and on this they rested great hope. But how things would develop, they didn't exactly know, and Signe wished, for her part, not to know, because she didn't want to learn anything about his life except what was related to family and faith.

The next morning the professor came to examine Per. The little man with the curiously modest, even slovenly, appearance and the remarkably colloquial speech was, at first, quite peevish. He hardly wanted to acknowledge seeing Per before, and he began by saying that he himself was sick and really shouldn't have come out, a pronouncement that was rather unpleasantly supported by his lead-colored face and the large, dark blue bags under his eyes. After his examination, he became somewhat more accessible. He sat on a chair at the side of the bed and said, "What do you want to know from me? Your food cupboard takes up too much space in the house of your body and you have bad circulation—but I told you that last time."

Per mentioned that he thought these sudden nervous disturbances must have a specific cause. He did not feel sick and had, one had to agree, still an uncommonly solid and strong body.

"A solid, robust, earthy body? Indeed, if you are convinced. I would, nevertheless, advise you not to put too much trust in your primal strength. It won't sustain you. I already told you that the last time I saw you. We Danish men, our stomachs distended from meal-pap and water soup, are not fit for the modern rush. It's with us as with the farmer's horses and their swinging tails. They are good enough for the old-fashioned level jog and trot, but by God, in a race, they would break down. It's not merely a question of broad shoulders, my fine fellow! Or a pair of well-formed thigh muscles. Now it's a question of iron in the blood and phosphorous in the brain. And, then, of the nerves, that are not protected by excessive fat, dear boy. As I said, don't bank too much on your constitution. It's nothing to boast of."

"But just now I need all my strength for my work," Per said, and asked the professor to prescribe whatever would be best under his circumstances to boost his strength and vigor. The doctor shook his head sadly.

"I don't know any remedy for that."

"When I last talked to you, you advised me to take cold showers, work out—a total hardening routine."

"Yes, well, you know it's just something to say. I'm sorry it's like this, but, undeniably, it would have been better if I had prescribed something to your honored grandfather and great-grandfather. For it was our blessed forefathers' thick eiderdowns and sweaty woolens, the legacy of sweet soup and tobacco smoke, the whole of the pious life of the study that is now wreaking havoc on our bodies. You are actually a pastor's son, aren't you? I gather that from your name, you know. And I do know from personal experience the menu in our idyllic parsonage with large families, where table prayers have to fill in for solid meat dishes. Have you, at least, been taking regular showers?"

Per answered that he had recently been in circumstances that made a systematic toughening up difficult.

"Say, rather, that you don't like cold showers. And that is very understandable. They are far from comfortable if you are not accustomed to them from childhood. Permit me, dear sir, to peek down your throat." Per opened his mouth. "I thought so. Most of your molars are gone. You really must have been fairly old before you were introduced to that little secular tool of grace, the toothbrush. I myself was over twenty. Until then, I contented myself with confidently rinsing my mouth in the evening, like my parents, with the Lord's Prayer. But let's not go too deeply into these old wretched abuses," he interrupted himself suddenly, and pressed his hand on his side with a gasp of pain.

Per would have felt seriously offended by this chatter if he had not understood that the doctor was a deathly ill and suffering man who, in his agony, could hardly know what he was saying. For the same reason, he wasn't particularly anxious about his forlorn pronouncements. He could see that the man was more concerned throughout his examination with his own condition than with his.

But he still had a question to ask him. Wasn't city life and city air, as far as he could observe, not really healthy for him, and did not the professor think it would be sensible to arrange to live, in the future, as much as possible in the country?

"Yes, by all means! Go to pasture! That's what we should call home. This generation is not suited to pavement. And, perhaps, the next as well. Stay in bed for a couple of days and give your noble nerves a little rest. I can also give you a tablespoon of potassium bromide. And so, fellow sufferer, let us bear our compressed guts with patience. We shall, I hope, ascend to heaven without them."

Per had no patience to stay in bed longer than the next morning. In twenty-four hours, he was home. Shortly afterward, the lectures and exercises at the agricultural college began and he was swallowed up by his work. Except for the Frederiksberg Gardens and the paths around it, he seldom went out, save for Sundays, when he rode into the city to go to church. He had a continual aversion to the city proper and avoided, as much as possible, any meeting with old school chums, or other acquaintances. Once, in a streetcar, he happened to be seated across from a former classmate whose gaping surprise and uncertain smile, an expressed acknowledgment, made him so nervous that, out of sheer anxiety about what he would say or ask him, he got out before his stop.

He had no connection with his new mates at the agricultural college. He visited his family now and then and had a return visit, once, from Eberhard. But there never was any real intimacy. He no longer appeared, out of precaution, in the Vartov parish. He tried out a less-crowded church, but did not consider himself, really, a Grundtvigian, and was not even clear about what that denomination signified. As for his faith, he was still a solitary seeker, and his mother's letter, which he had now read in various moods, only added to his sense of isolation. He could never overcome the discomfort of his first reading. Finally, he had to force himself not to think about it in order to avoid becoming again a prey to doubt.

Autumn had arrived. Woodbine berries bled all over the walls of the houses, and in the Frederiksberg Gardens, red and yellow leaves sailed down the dark, shadowy canal. He had quickly come to love this quiet place in the park, which he could reach from his house in just a hundred steps or so. He liked especially to go there in the early-morning hours when there would be few strollers. He could smell the fresh autumn nights off the large open lawns; the dew lay like silver webs on the grass, and the swans glided quietly by him in the canal's dark water with a bearing and grace of fairy-tale princesses.

Meanwhile, the days went by and he heard nothing from Colonel Bjerregrav. This began to disturb him; his small savings were used up and he had to pawn some clothes to pay the doctor. He wrote to the colonel to remind him and, the day after, got this answer: the colonel curtly announced that, after more careful consideration, he could not manage the errand Per had consigned to him.

Per sat with the letter in his hand and began to realize he had been taken for a fool. He laid it aside, but couldn't really be offended by the colonel. If he shouted in the forest, the same answer would come back to him. He blamed only himself for saving his pride by asking a stand-in to represent him. To be sure, it was not pleasant to go to a strange man to ask for money. That he must now beg was certainly an ugly turn in his story, for someone who had dreamt of being master and conqueror of his fellow men. But it served him right. God was no joker. He had not wanted to spare him the humbling condition of a beggar that could function as full penance for his past sins.

Councilor Erichsen's office was in Højbro Plads, on the first floor of one of the large corner buildings facing the canal. For some time, Per paced back and forth in front of the gate deliberating how he should begin and what he should say. Even on the stairs, he hesitated for a moment. One corner of a half-dark room was sectioned off by a bar behind which twenty or so clerks sat writing at double desks. A young man came up to him and asked what he wanted. When Per said he wanted to speak to the councilor, the surprised clerk stared at him. The councilor was not in the country, he said. He was abroad and wouldn't return for a few months. Was there something he could do for him?

Per had already turned to go out the door. In order not to have to say his name, he hurried out without explanation. Back again at the gate, he asked himself, What now? Before him lay the motley fruit and flower market bathed in the strong September sunlight. Large bonneted women from the isle of Amager spread out with their baskets and hawked their wares. Gardeners, their wagons in a long line, did a lively business while chatting, wrangling, and haggling. In the midst of all that harvested profusion, Per felt attacked by an anxiety, not over the degradation of the soul, but of the body, by life's real demons, hunger, cold, and dirt. He thought of the twenty kroner he was able to get by pawning some clothes. That could hold him for a week, maybe two. And then what?

He collected himself by force of will and went slowly home. He had to look for another way out and not become despondent. Whatever the imminent hardships, whatever the humiliations, he wanted to leave nothing undone. He felt no temptation to turn back and to yield to the power of the worldly Lord again. That the path of God was a path of testing was, to be sure, nothing new to him. He had already heard it sitting on a footstool at his mother's bed. If he had not been very surprised and frightened by the prospect of really suffering for his faith's sake, it might have been because up to now, in truth, he had thought of these terms as high-sounding phrases. He realized that Pastor Blomberg, especially in his sermons, could find so many heartfelt and striking expressions for happiness and rewards in a godly life, but lacked persuasive power when it came to sacrifice and suffering. Nevertheless, he reminded himself that it was time to learn how to take literally those words about "the path of thorns" and "wounded feet." And that did not scare him, because he felt that all this could lead him closer to God and make things clear that, now hidden away, made him anxious and unsure. But he still had to figure out a way to support himself, and he thought again of the master and his wife. But no! Better anyone else! Discretion was not the strong suit of those people, and, inevitably, the story would reach the ears of Inger and her parents. And what impression would it make if, after he had thanked them for their proven hospitality, he suddenly asked them for a loan? Besides, the result of the hint he had already risked with the master did not encourage him to repeat it. But what should he do? A written petition to Councilor Erichsen would surely be useless, and his recent attempt at one of the city's offices for technical affairs to sell his two patents had been unsuccessful.

He decided, then, to wait for a while and, in the meantime, to struggle through by pawning or selling his spare clothes and valuable objects he no longer needed. He counted on the possibility that the drainage project around Kærsholm would soon be agreed upon and he could simply ask the master for an advance. In her letter answering his thank-you note, the master's wife barely mentioned the project other than to say that she still had high hopes for it. At the same time, she repeated to him her invitation to spend Christmas at Kærsholm.

A few weeks passed. It was October, and he still had no prospects, but he didn't give up hope that things would brighten up for him soon. He simply couldn't believe that God would push him farther down in the dust.

In order to stretch his money as much as possible, he ate only what was essential. What mattered was to hold out at least until he passed his exam. Then he would be able to get one or another employment and, in any case, set up someplace as a private surveyor and wait for his opportunity. But without the exam, without money or connections, he had no choices other than to starve or survive simply as a workman.

The dark and sleety days of autumn went by in stress and strain. Every morning he stood by his window at the hour the mail from Jutland could be expected, looking out for the red coat. Any possible salvation had to come from Kærsholm. He was still exchanging letters with Fru Prangen, who took satisfaction in being a messenger between him and the Bøstrup parsonage. She wouldn't send him direct greetings from Inger, but let him clearly understand that he was not forgotten by his young friend and that they often spoke of him together. She was more and more reserved about the drainage project. Her husband had held a couple of meetings with landowners where he zealously supported it, but, unfortunately, they were not of one mind about it—she last wrote—so the outlook, at this time, was not bright.

As if to add insult to injury, there arrived with the Kærsholm mail, the same day, a registered letter from Rome that finally reached him after a long delay. It was from the young sculptor the baroness had commissioned to make a bust of Per. He wrote that the marble head was now finished and could be sent at any time. He had, he explained, informed the baroness some time ago and had politely asked her to send the agreed-upon fee. But to his astonishment, he had received a letter from the Swedish trustee and administrator informing him that the baroness could not recall such a commission, and, in addition, the request could not be sanctioned without the guardian's consent. For this reason, the sculptor asked Per, who knew the real story, to be his mediator and to help him recover this desperately needed payment.

This letter pained Per deeply, not so much because of the request, but because it awakened memories of a time that seemed to belong to his worst period of degradation. He blushed from shame when he thought of that bust with the impudent face of an emperor, and he wished he had been able to send the man some money just to have the right to ask him to crush his work to pieces and strew the useless shards over the road. For now, he was obliged to leave the courteous letter unanswered because an application to the master's wife or her husband about settling that debt would, perhaps, have a negative influence on the project upon which the whole of his welfare depended. They could well take badly his mixing into the baroness's affairs, all the more since the master's wife had never acknowledged to him her sister's insanity.

So several weeks went by, and at the end of November he had to face the catastrophe. Piece by piece his clothes were disappearing from his closet, and the greater part of his books. He even forced himself to sell, at a ridiculous price, the diamond studs he had received from Jakobe and that he had intended to send back to her when he could. And in a few days, his rent would be due and he had to pay what he owed the waiter in the public house where he ate. From sheer anxiety, he could no longer work, and his frugal nourishment had weakened him. For the first time in his life, the red coloring had totally disappeared from his cheeks. He stopped his visits to the family because he knew how bad he looked and he was wary of questions as to the cause.

In his dire need, he had ventured once more to try Councilor Erichsen, but with the same result as before. The councilor had become sick on his travels and would return only after Christmas. He would have to resort to the most extreme measures and turn to a moneylender—a usurer. One day, he read in the papers multiple advertisements in small print by which these "philanthropists" made themselves known. He decided, finally, on a man named Søndergaard. This name sounded reliable to him because a good-natured baker woman by that name had lived in his native village. Since he knew it was best to meet with these kinds of people in the evening when it was dark, he waited until six o'clock and went into the city. Herr Søndergaard, who called himself a real-estate agent, lived in one of the quiet, small streets around the law courts that people used as a shortcut when they were in a hurry but whose name was known by few. Per had to inquire and read all the corner street signs in order to find it. It was a narrow, empty lane with one light that happened to be in front of the house he was seeking. He stepped back and looked up at the second floor where Søndergaard was supposed to be living. All three windows were lit up, so the man was likely at home.

A little girl with red curls, about six or seven years old, opened the door just enough to peek out at him with a pair of large, blue, doll eyes. And when she could not understand what he was saying, she asked him, in a childlike way, whether he wanted to talk to her father. She raised herself on her toes to release the safety chain and showed him into a room, a typical Copenhagen, petit bourgeois living room with a rug under the table, pictures on the walls, albums and cheap knickknacks on a shelf.

Per was agreeably surprised; there was nothing unpleasant here. There by a desk at the window was a lamp with a shade of red silk paper. Among the portraits over the sofa was one of a pastor in vestments and a photograph of a country church. Then Herr Søndergaard himself came in from another room, a tall, massive form with a full, reddish-gray beard. At first, there was some uncertainty in his posture. He obviously found it a little difficult to judge Per, who was standing by the door in the half darkness, and Per himself had the feeling that, with his full, dark beard and long mackintosh buttoned up to the neck, he made a very odd impression in these surroundings. Herr Søndergaard bade him, finally, to take a seat and asked how he could be of service. They both sat down. Herr Søndergaard had just come in from his evening meal and was not quite finished chewing. The distinct odor of cheese bread hung on him. Per came straight to the point, named the sum he wanted to borrow, gave an account of his future prospects and the security he could provide. Since that consisted only of his two patents, he further offered to insure his life for the amount of the loan. Herr Søndergaard did not respond. He sat in his armchair at his desk, and now, when Per saw him fully illuminated by the lamp, he no longer made such a favorable impression. A pair of yellow eyes, displaying a most unpleasant, rigid, and impertinent stare, bulged out of a red-spotted face with large, spongy cheeks. He obviously had eaten well that evening. Every moment his round stomach jumped from the distinct belching he took not the slightest trouble to hide.

Meanwhile, Per thought his silence a good sign and began to ask about the conditions for the loan. But instead of answering, Herr Søndergaard asked him what guarantor he could provide.

"A guarantor? Is that required?"

Herr Søndergaard met Per's surprise with an incredulous smile.

"Well, didn't you think of that? I must have that security. If you have, as you say, good prospects, it couldn't be difficult for you to furnish a name or two. How much was it you wanted to borrow?"

"A thousand kroner."

"And for how long?"

"I think a year. In that time, I'm sure I can pay back both that amount and the interest."

"The interest is deducted in advance by installments," said Herr Søndergaard casually, as he took up a large book that lay on the desk. It was the Copenhagen Directory.

The little girl who had opened the door for Per had, in the meantime, come in with her doll under her arm. She leaned, for a moment, against her father, who, with pride, passed his fat hand over her red curls. When he had to let her go in order to turn the pages of the directory, she clambered onto his lap and observed Per with a spoiled child's saucy look of self-satisfied complacency. "I can't find your name in here," said Herr Søndergaard after some searching.

"I have been abroad for the last year," Per explained.

"Oh, so you have been abroad . . ." His yellow eyes slid up again with a suspicious and searching look over the book's edge. Then they were, again, lowered. "Here is a B. Sidenius, a retired rural dean. Is he part of your family?"

"No."

"And here is F. Sidenius, a bookkeeper. Is he?"

"No."

"E. Sidenius, bachelor of law, principal royal administrator."

Per hesitated with his answer. "Yes," he said.

"Is he, perhaps, a close relation?"

"He is my brother."

"Can't you designate him a guarantor? Then we could complete the agreement."

"No, I can't," answered Per decisively, even as he became confused.

"So, you can't." Søndergaard again looked over the book's edge. "You're not in a close relationship with that gentleman?"

"I can't, in any case, ask him for this kind of favor."

"No? Well, then, we can't carry through our business," said Herr Søndergaard in an altered tone, and shut the book. A pause ensued. Per stayed seated because he was anxious about leaving without the slightest hope. The dark street and the loneliness of his room opened in front of him like a yawning abyss. But to turn, in this situation, to Eberhard—no, no, that was impossible. That he couldn't do. Then he said he could settle for five hundred kroner, even less, and offered to pawn what remained of his clothes and books.

But Herr Søndergaard was now aloof. He dropped a tasteless remark about people who fancied they could get money by their nice face, promising prospects. I should think not! By those standards, anyone could run up from the street and get funded. What the devil! They all had promising prospects. No, a solid guarantor or pledges of real value—otherwise, there was no business to be done here.

Per got up and left. Entirely adrift, he didn't want to go home. What should he do now? A deadly battle raged in him. His pride wanted to revolt against God, but at the same time, he heard a strong and commanding voice in him saying: "You well know the justice of the judgment against you. Where there is sin, there must be penance. So atone! This is your trial. This is the eye of the needle you must go through if you want peace."

Without realizing how, he had come through the side street out to Kongens Nytorv, which, despite the fog and filth, was full of festive life. Vehicles shot across the huge square in all directions. Light streamed from the gallery of the theater. The hotel across the way was also brightly lit, and shop windows and street lanterns sprinkled gold over the wet pavement. In his agitated condition, and no longer used to this city bustle, he stood dazed for a moment. The clanking of carriages hit his ears like a lump of lead. The earth swayed under him. A shout—"Watch out!"— woke him up. A cab drove by so close to him that the wheels brushed his sleeve and splattered him with mud. By the lantern light he caught a passing glimpse of a couple in a cab in evening dress. The lady was in a light blue silk dress and turned a diamond-studded earlobe toward him. The gentleman was in uniform and had a chest full of medals. In a carriage coming from the opposite side, a young couple was kissing.

Per moved on slowly, farther and farther from his lodgings. Relentlessly he was led, as if by the hand of the Tempter himself, into Store Kongensgade and toward the residence of Jakobe's parents. Once again a voice inside him said: "Turn around! Hold up now! You are going toward your ruin." Nevertheless, Per went on. He turned a corner and was now at the small cross street where the Salomon palace was located. He stood in the shadows facing it from across the street and saw that there was a party inside. He could make out the lit chandeliers through the heavy silk drapes of the windows.

From dread of attracting attention, he went on a bit toward

Bredgade, but immediately turned back from there. And once again his soul was roused to complain against God: "I gave all this up for You! I'm standing here like a locked-out dog, freezing and splashed with mud ... and nevertheless You will show me no mercy!" Quickly he drew himself deeper into the shadow of the wall. He had seen the front gate open across the way. A little man with an umbrella came out. Who was it? He didn't have Ivan's rapid walk. Was it Eybert, Jakobe's old suitor? An absurd jealousy flickered up teasingly. Then he saw by the streetlight a profile with a crooked nose, a grayish beard, a pair of large, turned-in feet ... Aron Israel!

It shot through him like lightning: here was salvation! Aron Israel would help. Why hadn't he thought of him! Supreme goodness in person. It wouldn't matter to him that he would no longer be Philip Salomon's son-in-law. Even before Per's engagement to Jakobe, he had been very sympathetic and betrayed a respectful confidence in his future. He could speak freely to him.

He followed him into Store Kongensgade. But the voice within took over and said: "Go home! What can his goodness help? You know God's demands on you. Fulfill them. Don't try to get out of this. Day after day the command will sound louder in your ears and give you no peace until you follow it or harden yourself against it again. Don't put off the decision. Just because of your pride you are so sensitive about, don't bargain with a new temptation! Get to work! God is waiting!" He slowed his steps. On the corner of Kongens Nytorv, he stopped his pursuit with the look of a doomed man and watched the little man disappear past the light under the clock into the Grønnegade quarter. Then he walked back, slowly, the long way out to Frederiksberg. It was already past nine o'clock when he reached home. He didn't light the lamp. Nor did he want to go to bed. He sat in the dark at the table, his head in his hands, barely moving, for nearly half the night.

The next morning, he went to Eberhard, and his brother did nothing to make his difficult confession easier. He sat silently with his tight face and withheld from him any answer. But he didn't refuse to help Per. He wouldn't even consider security, but he wanted to think over the business more carefully and consult with the family, because, as he put it, it would feel most natural for them to act *in loco parentis* if the loan came from all of them in common. Per made no objection. He felt, suddenly, so strangely indifferent to it all. He noticed nothing of the anticipated peace and elevation of soul from his humiliation. On the contrary, it seemed to him that he had never before felt more depressingly empty, more deprived of any helpful power, than at that moment.

CHAPTER 24

WHEN IT WAS learned in the Bøstrup parsonage that Per had dissolved his engagement with the rich Copenhagen man's daughter, Pastor Blomberg's wife became seriously alarmed. And when she heard that Per was expected back at Kærsholm for Christmas, she talked frankly, one night in bed, to her husband about her concern and proposed that Inger be sent away during that time. But the pastor would not hear of it. Not that for him there was anything very attractive about the prospect of giving away his daughter to a man with Per's past; but it was important, he said, not to act in the name of Providence. The young man had, moreover, realized the error of his ways, and the great wealth he willingly sacrificed for the sake of his soul's salvation vouched for the sincerity of his conversion. "In matters of faith, we cannot use coercion, and love is a faith. But one day I will speak openly to Inger about the situation. She must know we will not put strings on her heart. That will strengthen her sense of responsibility."

From the outset, although she well knew her own worth, Inger had not attributed Per's break with the Copenhagen lady to herself. She believed this had resulted exclusively because of his acquaintance with her father. It was her friends, the two Clausen girls, who set her straight, and she had, since, lived in a thrilling giddiness at the thought of the many millions Per had given up for her sake. She was fairly uncertain for some time about her feelings for Per. When she thought of him, she saw especially before her his eyes, perhaps because her father had, the evening after his first visit to the parsonage, compared his gaze to an open seashore where sun-drenched seagulls circled a half-buried wreck in the sand—a "reminder of the destruction of dark winters and equinoctial gales." She had wondered about this expression, whose implications she didn't understand.

Now, when she understood it better, her imagination dwelled on these pale, melancholy merman eyes that dominated her remembrance of him. To give herself to someone who had been engaged seemed, to be sure, unthinkable. The situation was somewhat soothed by the fact that she did not know the lady concerned and had noticed how unhappy and pained he had been in that relationship.

She thought she really liked him, but whether she could actually grow fond of him, love him, she didn't know, because, up to now, she had only an unclear sense of what love was. Her two friends had willingly shared their knowledge about it, especially the hardy Gerda, who had always wanted to confide in her concerning both what she had personally experienced and what she ferreted out through others. But Inger had had no interest in listening until now.

She was perplexed when, one afternoon a couple of weeks before Christmas, while they were alone for a moment in the living room, her father began to talk about Per and his possible visit to the district. "As you well know, my child, Herr Sidenius is no longer engaged. And now I'll ask you frankly whether you, perhaps, are thinking about what people could be excused for deducing when they see him here in the parsonage. Just answer me that." Inger interpreted this question as camouflaging a proffered marriage proposal. She assumed that Per had written for permission to her parents, which so chagrined and embarrassed her that she couldn't answer.

To Pastor Blomberg, however, this silence and the glow in her cheeks were answer enough. That night in bed he spoke about it to his wife and repeated they must not put any pressure on the child; they must hope that God would give His blessing to her heart's choice and lead her to happiness. To the objection that Per was nobody and had hardly any prospects for a position by which he could support a family, the pastor answered confidently that also in relation to this, God would help. He was thinking especially of the current regulation project about which so much had been said, and that surely would yield something.

The outlook for this enterprise was really not very bright. In the course of the autumn, a couple of public meetings had been held at the instigation of the master, but it had been impossible to reach an agreement between the two or three hundred small and great landholders whose interests were involved and without whose unified consent nothing could be undertaken. Although basically convinced that the proposed arrangement could be advantageous for him, each of them showed himself unwilling to go along, from anxiety that a neighbor or a brother or brother-in-law would gain a more advantageous benefit. Nor did they want to let the master have the honor of carrying through such an important undertaking. Finally, the most prosperous farmers stayed away entirely from the meetings, and therefore the plan was considered irretrievably lost.

But then Pastor Blomberg suddenly mixed into the affair. With his happy ability to see in his small, personal interests far-reaching significance for community and church matters, he decided—as he said to his wife—to "grab the nasty stinging nettle." It seemed to him a terrible example of how the weeds of intolerance and mistrust could continue to shoot up in the soul of a purified and redeemed parish. First he tried privately to influence some of the citizens on whose consent a favorable outcome chiefly rested. But when he met resistance, he became angry and went on the offensive. At a large devotional service where the whole congregation was gathered, he brought up the matter in the middle of his talk and condemned, in words of forceful admonishment, the petty selfishness that would obstruct promotion of prosperity that promised to stimulate the development of a healthy, happy, and sincere Christian life.

His words caused great consternation as well as displeasure in several members, first, because they came in the middle of a devotional service and then because there were already rumors in the air about an upcoming engagement between Inger and the plan's young originator. Nevertheless, Blomberg would not be distracted. This was not the first time he had awakened a momentary indignation in his parish with a risky speech. He knew his power and let his people grumble. He had gained what he wanted: to blow new life into an undertaking that, in his eyes, concerned nothing less than the welfare of the whole district. Everywhere among the farmers and the cottiers, his speech was talked about and, with that, discussions concerning Per's project were taken up again.

The day before Christmas Eve, Per came to Kærsholm, where he found everything unchanged with the exception of the baroness's absence and the master's face color, which had become even more like a faded maple leaf than before. He noticed immediately the faint smell of peat smoke from the kitchen and took it for a welcoming greeting. It did not take the master's wife long, on the other hand, to recognize a change in *him*, and not only on the outside. She suspected that he had had one or another earnest experience, but despite all her efforts to win over his confidence by showing a motherly sympathy, she could not succeed in bringing to light his secret, could not make him talk about it, and, finally, she became a little offended.

On the first day of Christmas, Per went with her to High Mass in the Bøstrup church. The master did not feel well and had to stay home. When they entered, the hymns had just begun. With one hand in his robe pocket, Pastor Blomberg walked back and forth in the middle aisle and greeted friends and acquaintances, all while singing with his powerful voice. Now and then he stopped at the bottom of the steps of the choir, his face shining with evangelical joy, and looked out over the packed church.

Per's eyes had found Inger sitting in a row of seats opposite him, next to her mother. She was entirely in black, which gave her light blond complexion a particularly fine and soft appearance. She didn't look up even at the sound of the rustle of silk by which the master's wife announced her arrival, which made her mother turn around to greet her. But her cheeks had patently changed color. Per took that as a sign of victory and felt his heart beat strongly.

After the services, Per and the master's wife, together with some other churchgoers, were invited to the parsonage for coffee. With these invitations, always personally proffered, the pastor was sowing dragon seeds in the Blomberg community. Everyone always paid close attention to them and carefully assessed which parishioners were granted this distinction. At the parsonage, Per met four farmers and their wives with faces clearly written in different scripts but with a common sign: they belonged to the district's highest and most influential echelon. It didn't occur to him that Pastor Blomberg could have a particular intention in putting him together with these people, although the pastor was strangely eager to introduce him to everyone. The regulatory project was not mentioned by anyone. Moreover, the rendezvous did not last more than half an hour. The pastor still had a later service in the neighboring parish and made it understood that the company had to disband. The farmers left first, and, soon after, the master's wife and Per. Now Inger could breathe more easily.

The whole time her heart was in her throat for fear of being left alone with Per. She still entertained the fancy that he had written to her parents and secured, beforehand, their consent to the connection. But she wasn't sure about how much she liked him. Or, rather, she couldn't, in her inexperience, become certain whether what she felt for him was love. She did feel he was good and would be sweet to her, and she could not hide from herself that the expectation of seeing him again had made her restless and kept her awake the last nights. That very morning, just before church, she had suddenly had a stomachache. But was that love?

As long as Per was present, she had almost been convinced that she wasn't that fond of him. The change that had taken place in his appearance made him seem different to her, although she found it becoming. But now, when he was gone, the parsonage felt strangely empty, and the rest of the day slid by without granting her peace of mind. She moved from chair to chair, room to room, and began to consider it a misfortune that she had ever made his acquaintance. This restlessness, this uneasiness, so foreign to her nature, pained and humiliated her. Finally, she sat by the window in her own little room and stared blankly out into the garden, where the sun, going down behind the frosted trees, grew red.

She kept thinking of a fairy-tale figure, a mythical hero that Per reminded her of and whose picture had haunted her. With his reserved manner, his pale face, his large, dark beard, and those strange merman eyes, he resembled the "Flying Dutchman" in the opera she had seen a year ago in Copenhagen. Suddenly she laid her head down on her arm and thought that she loved him, even if it didn't make her happy.

She firmly expected that the next day would bring a resolution. Together with her parents, she was invited to dinner at Kærsholm, and, as far as she knew, no other guests would be there. But early in the morning, a dispatch came from the master's house canceling the invitation because the master, during the night, had become seriously ill with his old stomach pain.

In the afternoon, the master's wife herself came to the parsonage, accompanied by Per, to proffer her apologies. During the conversation, she alluded to the visit of the four farmers in the parsonage the day before and mentioned that, already for some time, there had been talk of convening a new meeting concerning the plan for regulating the current and that she was happy about that.

"Yes, the enterprise is already in the process of being arranged," she said, "and we ought to retain Herr Sidenius, here, for it."

Pastor Blomberg, who was pacing up and down in the room, his hands behind his back, stood still at these words, and, with an earnest expression, he said, "Yes, I have not given up hope that the spirit of cooperation shall win out in this affair." His wife said nothing. The master's wife, on the other hand, was more and more talkative and revealed that she had prepared in her head a whole plan for Per's future.

"You remember the little white house by the station. It is now unoccupied since the death of Pastor Petersen's widow, and I can't think of a more suitable place for Herr Sidenius to live. From the road, the house looks charming and could be prettily maintained with a beautiful garden and handsome utility rooms."

Inger got up. She was indignant and ashamed at these words, whose implication she well understood. Lately, the master's wife had gone down a great deal in Inger's estimation, not only because she understood the cunning lengths to which she had resorted to get Inger and Per married, but because she began to suspect that she hid, under her ardor, an outrageous pre-occupation with Per that she sometimes advertised to her in a most unsavory way.

After coffee, the company took a little walk through the garden and over the hill, but no intimate conversation came about between Inger and Per. Fru Blomberg kept her eye on them continually, and as soon as they got back the carriage drove up to the door. The master's wife had to go home to her sick husband, and Per was not asked to stay. At parting, the master's wife embraced Inger and wanted to kiss her on the mouth, but Inger turned away, sulking. Lately she had resisted the caresses of the master's wife that had once made her so grateful.

Several days went by during which the two lovers did not see each other. The master's wife was kept at home by her husband's sickness, and for this reason Per too had to resign himself to miss-ing the district's Christmas festivities. He regretted that only because it kept him away from Inger. He realized that, on account of her beauty and as Pastor Blomberg's daughter, she would be the center of attention among the young. But when he considered that there were no young gentlemen in the district other than the half-rustic farmers' sons and a few green students, he was no longer troubled.

That shelf in his room full of different kinds of books still hung there, and, wanting some light reading contrary to his custom, he paged through novels, plays, and stories that could fill up the time and soothe his impatience. Since the day he had to humiliate himself in front of his family, he felt an aversion to religious books. He could not reconcile the God he had learned to know during those autumn struggles with the picture of the kind, sociable, all-merciful comforter in the Blombergian edifying writings that so promisingly warmed him. He peeked into them a couple of times, but felt, while he read, the same kind of disappointment he had already experienced in church from Pastor Blomberg's Christmas sermon. His thoughts could no longer find peace in these pretty, but common, remarks about life, death, sin, and grace. He had passed the stage when his feelings could be satisfied and moved without consulting his understanding. His soul wanted to be nourished, his desire for truth answered. But here he was invited to substitute blossoms for bread. He had now decided to put his thoughts to rest. He was tired of fruitless searching and wanted, for a time, to bolt the gate to the impassable threshold of the Beyond and to concentrate his mind on the great throw of the dice that would determine his life and happiness here in the finite world.

Until now, he had not been able to think of proposing to Inger before he had passed his exam and had a post or a prospect of a fairly secure future. But something of his old daring had awakened in him as he awaited her arrival from hour to hour, and he was now almost determined to reach an understanding as soon as he could succeed in being alone with her.

The day before New Year's Eve, he finally had an occasion to again visit the parsonage. He had heard that a couple of requests had come from there inquiring about the master's condition, and when, just this morning, there had been signs of a good turn in the sickness, Per asked permission at breakfast to go to Bøstrup to bring the pastor's family the good tidings.

Immediately after, he set out. He had calculated that he had the earliest and best chance to meet Inger alone in the living room between one and two o'clock, when she was accustomed to practice the piano. To come as unobserved as possible, he refused to order a carriage. The weather was beautiful, the road in good shape, and, after being housebound for so long, he wanted the exercise. The winter sun cast long shadows over the fields, where, here and there, a few pregnant ewes were wandering and grazing on the scant grass. He was surprised at his confident and calm spirit. With a peculiar, almost religious thrill, he heard the sound of his regular, Sidenian steps on the frost-hardened earth. Something in that sound connected him to a world far away from which power, peace, and promise secretly streamed into his body and mind.

Nothing, of course, went as planned. The first person he saw when he came through the parsonage gate was Fru Blomberg, who stood in the middle of the yard feeding her chickens. With a restrained and measured dignity, she thanked him for the news he brought and asked him to come in. Inger was indeed sitting at the piano, but her mother did not leave the room, and the questions and answers circled almost exclusively around the master's illness. At last, the pastor came in, wearing his black, skimpy jacket, and immediately dominated the conversation.

Per was getting ready to leave without accomplishing his purpose when hoofbeats were heard in the yard. An old-fashioned carriage rolled up to the door. It turned out to be an elderly neighboring pastor and his wife, who had come to pay a Christmas visit. A tray with wine and cookies was brought in, followed by chocolate and coffee. Inger helped with the service.

After an hour, the visiting pastor and his wife left; in the few minutes that passed while Pastor Blomberg and his wife accompanied them to the carriage, Inger and Per got engaged. When Fru Blomberg came in again, she immediately saw that something had happened. Inger was standing at the garden window with her back to the room, and Per was by her side. "What's going on here?" she asked, almost brusquely. Per came up to her and said, with a slight bow, "I have just proposed to your daughter, and she has said yes."

The pastor in his short jacket came stomping in, and when he heard what had happened, his face became very serious. At first, he voiced the conventional, obligatory concerns, but he was easily won over, as he always was when it was a question of his feelings, and soon smiled, held out his arms to embrace Inger, and called Per his son, giving them his blessings with tears in his eyes.

How the proposal was actually managed, Per hardly knew. Afterward, he had to hear it from Inger, and she described it in a way that put him in a comic light. She said that when she was going to follow her parents accompanying the visiting pastor and his wife to their carriage, Per had suddenly seized her hand and held her back.

"You squeezed so hard I really almost screamed! You can't imagine how much that hurt." And this was posed as a serious complaint.

Gathering in the pastor's room, the family and Per determined that the engagement should be kept secret until Per passed his exam. It was Fru Blomberg who had insisted on this, and Per willingly yielded. Not even the master's wife was to know of it before anyone else. Inger expressly demanded that. But when Per came back to Kærsholm, it was out of the question. His expression betrayed him.

"You got engaged!" she blurted out as soon as she saw him.

Per again had occasion to experience the truth of the superstition: just as misfortune seldom comes alone, so, too, does good luck often have a twin. A few days later he had an unexpected visit. Two of the farmers he had met at the parsonage on Christmas Day came driving out to Kærsholm one morning and asked to speak with him. They were two tall and stout men in homespun coats with a natural kind of dignity in their bearing. Per asked them to sit down, and, though he was entirely unprepared for this and, as well, lacked experience in talking to farmers, they discussed Per's project for nearly two hours. The two men began with declaring emphatically that they had not been delegated by anyone. They had sought him out only because they had heard something about his wanting to undertake a re-regulation of the river to lower the water level in the meadowland. If that was correct, they said they would, perhaps, be willing, at his convenience, to take the business under closer consideration.

Their words were, on the whole, marked by a calculated circumspection and a bit of mistrust, strangely at odds with their strong and self-confident demeanor. Although they had shown, by the questions they directed to Per, that they had studied well both the technical and legal sides of the undertaking, they wanted to give the appearance of knowing only roughly about the proposal. And when one of them once let a word fall about the possibility of a new convocation, the other hastened to add that it was still doubtful whether anything would come of it. After that, the first farmer declared clearly that in his opinion, he did not think there was any stomach for the enterprise.

When they had gone, Per had the immediate impression that they had come to prepare him for a final rebuff. But the master's wife, to whom he afterward repeated the conversation and who knew better the farmers' way of doing business, congratulated him, and said, with a mischievous smile, that now he could be measured for his wedding shirt. The parsonage had the highest hopes as well, and soon it was reported that the two men had traveled to Copenhagen to discuss with the district's parliamentary representative the procurement of a state grant for the completion of the project.

By degrees, Per spent most of his day now in the parsonage, and Inger gradually overcame her shyness and became, at every visit, more open in her feelings toward him. She did not, to be sure, abandon her calm equilibrium and even pouted a little when he kissed her. But, in return, her tenderness toward him could be really touching. When he came in bad weather, she always took care to bring him a hot drink, which she forced him to swallow immediately while it was still almost boiling. And when he walked or rode home in the evening, at their goodbye, she would take her little silk shawl off her shoulders and tie it with her own hands around his neck so he wouldn't catch cold. Her love had not yet emerged from its motherly swaddling clothes, and Per without a murmur let her treat him like a child.

A happy change was also gradually taking place in his relationship to his mother-in-law. He had gone to a lot of trouble to overcome her resistance to him, for Inger's sake, and he really was succeeding. He had discovered that she liked to be entertained while she was sewing, chiefly, by being read to from one or another book lodged in her reading basket. Every afternoon, therefore, he would read chapters from one of the popular and pious novels that were cherished in the house. Although the books didn't amuse him, he gradually found those hours pleasant as he heard his own voice blend with the sounds of the diligent needles of mother and daughter and the comforting, soft crackle of the stove.

The day after Twelfth Night, he traveled back to Copenhagen. He dared not stay away longer from his studies, and besides, since the master's health had once again taken a bad turn, it was hardly the time to be a houseguest. The last day he spent in the parsonage he saw Inger really moved for the first time when he said goodbye. She had tears in her eyes and held on to his hand, as if she never wanted to let go. When he drove away, both parents-in-law and all the small children gathered with her on the stone steps to wave until the carriage was out of the gate. And afterward, Inger ran into the garden and climbed up on the fence to wave him a last farewell.

In spite of all this, he was a little disappointed. He had, until the last minute, hoped that Inger would ask her parents' permission to accompany him to the station. To be sure, the weather was cold and windy, but it surprised him, nevertheless, that it didn't even occur to her. Now, when he sat there in the carriage next to an empty seat, he couldn't help thinking of Jakobe. He remembered an expression she once had used in one of her letters about her longing for him. She had written that she would travel around the world three times to be together with him merely for a single minute. He could recall that he had, at that time, thought the words hysterical and hyperbolic. Now, when he himself was in love, he understood them.

After a good half-hour trip, he caught sight of the station in front of him and then went past the little house the master's wife had picked out for his and Inger's love nest. It lay a little way back from the road at the foot of a hill and was built in a cottage style with a pretty garden that even now, in its winter barrenness, gave the place a cozy and inviting look. He was seriously moved by the sight. Was it possible that the strange house would someday be his home, that this little warm nest was waiting there to shelter his happiness? Could he, who had offended against all life's guardian angels, be sitting one day behind the now-empty windows with Inger at his side, protected by the same gentle and good powers he had so arrogantly defied? Would his children's tears and laughter be heard here on the road from this bare and desolate garden? And there, on the hill behind the house, would his experimental windmill rise and, perhaps, one day, announce to the world a great triumph?

When he was in his compartment on the train jolting forward, he found himself together with a little, white-haired man he soon recognized as the pastor who had come, with his wife, to visit his parents-in-law the day he became engaged. The pastor, a cheerful and talkative man, recognized him as well, and they started a conversation. "You are the son of the late Pastor Sidenius, aren't you? I knew your father just a bit. He was a man who did not mix much with his fellow pastors, but preferred a dedicated solitary life. Your mother, on the other hand, I knew quite well in my younger days. We were from the same town—both from Vejle—and almost the same age. I can see that you resemble her a little. Already when I met you the other day at our dear Blombergs, it struck me that there was someone your face reminded me of. I did not, then, remember your mother's maiden name. Only afterward did it occur to me that it was the Thorsenian traits I had recognized. Now I see your grandfather alive before me. Well, you probably didn't know him. He was a marvelous man, cheerful and vivacious until the day he died, always interested in everything happening in the world around him. His hospitable home was a great blessing in the little town, and your mother was the center of the innocent amusements of the young folk. Oh, my! Those happy days! I remember once, during Christmas vacation, there was to be a masked ball at a gentleman farmer's house about five miles from the town and all of us young folk had been invited and were, naturally, tremendously happy. But it so happened that just that afternoon, a furious snowstorm came on that didn't let up, so no one dared to venture out, and there was a general despair. So as we were all sitting inconsolably inside, we heard sleigh bells and the crack of a whip in the street, and when we ran to the windows—who did we see but Kirstine Thorsen on the way to the ball. She would not think of staying home, and had, finally, declared that if no one would drive her, she would walk on foot in her white stockings. So, naturally, she gave us all courage, and the little daring adventure turned out to be really enjoyable. We all had a wonderful time."

"Excuse me," Per interrupted, a little embarrassed. "You must be mistaken. That couldn't have been my mother."

"But aren't you a son of the late Johannes Sidenius?"

"Yes."

"Well, so I'm not mistaken."

"My mother did have a sister."

"Ah, poor Signe, yes. No, indeed, she was weak, sickly, and died quite young. Your mother, on the other hand, was blooming with health, not tall in stature, but fine and graceful. I remember another time, in summer, when we young folk had arranged what we called a group forest outing and rode in three large carriages about ten miles from the town. The owner of the woods was a baron who, for one reason or another, lived on a war footing with the common people. Although the woods stretched over an area of many hundreds of acres and he himself lived far from it, there were placards up on all its entrances with strict rules of conduct. It was important not to leave the official road, not to yell or play for fear of scaring the wildlife, and, especially, it was strictly forbidden to eat in the woods. It was these precepts that had awakened much ill-will in the populace, and, in our light-headed mood, we decided to defy them. We camped, just like that, on a grassy clearing, got out the food baskets and coffee pot, and were quite content. Then we all, together, received, as it were, a punch in the mouth. Coming directly at us were two men, the baron himself and a forest gamekeeper. The baron had a reputation for being a big boor, and his appearance itself struck terror in us. He was a large, heavy, man with a purple face like a turkey. We didn't know what to do, and we were terribly frightened. But your mother stood up, quickly poured out a cup of coffee, and carried it across the grass to the baron. I can still see her clearly before me in a bright, light lilac dress and a large straw hat shaped like a basket with flowers on it, as was the fashion. She had a pretty figure and an airy step that was a pleasure to see. Then she curtsied to the baron and asked him roguishly to give us the great honor of being our guest on the green. That was more than he could resist. He was, at heart, a good man, and he ended by inviting us to be his guests in his manor house on the way back and to taste his champagne. None of us has since forgotten that day. Your mother never told you about it?"

"No."

The train stopped at the district town, where the talkative old man got off. Per was happy to be left alone. The pastor's stories had depressed him. As he rode on farther, he thought about how little he really knew about his mother's family and her youth. While it had always given his father a proud satisfaction to recall his adolescence and talk about the life of his father and grandfather in an impoverished parsonage, his mother was averse to speaking to her children about her home and her relatives. Per had never once seen her only brother, who was a doctor

somewhere in Funen. He did not come to the house, and his
name was seldom mentioned.

Per sat by the window, his cheek leaning on his hand, looking
despondently at the passing fields as it was already growing dark.
He began to understand the involuntary shudder that had gone
through his being that day when he read his mother's posthumous letter.

CHAPTER 25

IN THE NIGHT between the ninth and the tenth of January, there
was some distress in the small Silesian city of Hirschberg, near
Breslau, where Jakobe had been staying the last months awaiting
her labor in quiet loneliness. Early in the morning she had telegraphed a friend in Breslau, the only person to whom she had
confided her secret. Later in the day, a doctor was sent for. Jakobe
had endured twenty-four hours of such terrible pain that she,
who had always been intimate with suffering, could no longer
bear to think about it afterward. Her baby came out alive, but
died immediately after its birth. Jakobe hadn't even been allowed
to see it, because it had to be mutilated in order to save the
mother's life.

For four weeks she lay in bed. It was almost spring, and she
had regained enough strength to sit, well wrapped up, in her
landlady's little garden and to look out on the Schneekoppe and
the other white-capped mountains that rose up over the green,
spring landscape. However, all that beauty surrounding her gave
her no joy. She was in such despair over the loss of her child,
felt so empty, so unnecessary and remaindered in the world, so
helplessly weak, that she couldn't stop crying. In the last months
before the birth of the baby, she had lived so intimately and confidentially with it in her thoughts that she had bodily felt it was
the better half of her sense of self, and now there seemed nothing
left of her. She couldn't let herself think what a great burden she
had been spared: shame, humiliation, her parents' anxiety, and
her friends' sympathy. All that before had weighed and preyed on
her gradually became insignificant in comparison with the joy
she had expected, the hopes she had attached to the baby with
whom she was to start a new life.

Both her mother and her father, thinking her to be in Breslau, wrote her regularly from home about all that was happening in the circle of family and friends. She learned that Eybert had married a young girl of nineteen; her brother-in-law, Dyhring, now had a seat in Parliament, and Nanny had been at a royal ball and was introduced to one of the princes. But that was all so indifferent to her. She sat there in the little garden with a cushion behind her head and a footstool under her feet, looking for a long time at the children going by on the path.

They were mostly poor children, pale and undernourished wretches, the sort that swarmed in the factory towns, even in such a small and village-like one as this, where spring grass sprouted between the paving stones. Two times a day they walked by on the road, back and forth to a primary school in the neighborhood. Jakobe had especially noticed a little fellow of seven or eight with an unhealthy, bluish face and large scrofulous sores under his nose and on his cheeks. He always trailed the others, shuffling along with his tablet under his arm in a pair of slapping wooden slippers like an old man. When she became strong enough to move a little out of the garden, she stopped him one day and asked him a couple of friendly questions. The boy, confused and shy, stared up at her with a couple of large, blue, cheerless eyes and continued on his tired way without responding. When he had gone fifty steps or so, he peeked anxiously back, and when he saw that she was still standing there following him with her eyes, he drew in his head as if to protect himself against a danger.

"Poor fellow," she said out loud, and walked farther on. There was something about that little neglected boy and his precocious fear of people that made her motherly heart beat faster.

One day, some time later, she followed him at a distance to see where he lived, and she saw him disappear into a long, low workers' barracks with a door at every two or three windows. Through inquiry in the neighborhood, she learned who his parents were and in what condition the family lived. It was the usual tragedy of factory workers. Man and wife worked on the machines and left the children to the care of Providence. They were hungry at home, thrashed at school, and watched by the police in the streets. Under such circumstances they grew hardened and blunted, and became criminals or good-for-nothings.

Never before had Jakobe been so close to poverty, and these circumstances made a strong impression on her. She gathered information about the workers' wages, about their hours, living arrangements, the hygienic condition of the workplace, about support for the elderly, and so on, and with all she learned, indignation grew in her heart and mind. She was determined not to remain a passive onlooker of this oppression in the future. Every powerful impression evoked in her a desire to do something. She used this new feeling to help her, finally, to take action. With the assistance of her landlady, a good-natured widow of a warrant officer, and without lengthy consideration, she set up a kind of canteen out in the garden where the hungry children, on their way to and from school, could get something warm to eat and drink. The great sum of tenderness and self-sacrifice she had reserved for her own child was now being spent on that flock of homeless waifs, poured out on half a hundred scabby heads—and she was to go on from there. In the beginning, the children were frightened and held back, and the idea was inviting laughter in the town. But the smell of soup that wafted through the picket garden fence and the sight of the tables set at all times gradually conquered the children's shyness. Even the little, pale, blue-eyed child with the sores came in one fine day, sat down, and stuffed himself.

The experiment led further on Jakobe's part. As her body gradually got stronger, the stirring of new life exerted its old magic power over her and filled her heart. She wrote to her friend in Breslau:

> Have you ever really thought about what a despairing lot our time—our great, beautiful, progressive time—has prepared for children in poor circumstances, and how mercilessly little is done on the social side to help them to a humane, a merely natural existence? From an empty room that is called a home and where they seldom see the parents, the poor little ones are forced into schools that, for the most part, are nothing more than official penitentiaries. The state, which should be reliably and trustfully looking out for them as their unfailing protector and keeper, confronts them in its least attractive form: as an intolerant school-teacher, a brutal police officer, an offensive administration, a pastor who threatens them with dying, judgment, and the fires of hell. How, under these circumstances, could a kind of social spirit awaken in them, could, in the course of time,

a real feeling of civic brotherhood develop? It's useless to consider fortifying the dissipated life of the family. The parental home that used to be the foundation of society has become an institution that dooms development. But what shall we put in its place? I am obsessed with this question now, even dreaming about it at night. For the adults, some public relief is available: they have church, music, and lecture halls, pubs, theaters, and prayer meetings. But the children? Tell me, where should these poor helpless little ones turn? I see no solution other than that school should gradually step in to take the place of home. But, naturally, schooling must change, must gradually return to its origins; a school must become something that in the old days was a cloister, a sanctuary, a refuge, an ever-open retreat. But it must also be something else entirely. By its mere appearance, by beautifully decorated rooms, by its form of instruction, a school will function, someday, in a comfortable and happy way on the minds of the children. And the children will also be given the capital for a bright and fruitful sense of life that they can later draw upon, and that can make them more resolute in the battle for existence than the cloister-educated children of the past and a good deal in our time, who, at each disappointment, have immediately lost faith in life, lost confidence in happiness, and, when hurt, have looked for consolation in the lap of their old dry nurse, the church.

But I see a big question mark in your face. Why is she telling me all this, you ask? You may well wonder. But I have to tell it to you as it really is: here, in my solitude, a new world has, as it were, opened up for me, and I am still a little confused about it. Do you know, I am thinking seriously of trying to develop and carry out the thought I mentioned above. I am dealing with far-reaching plans to set up a school for poor children in Copenhagen on the model I have here sketched out. It will cost my future fortune, but how can I use it better than for this when I have no one now to leave it to? First I will busy myself studying what has already been tried in this direction. I would have to review the whole school question from the ground up. I remember hearing or reading that somewhere in America, a similar movement has arisen, so you ought not to be frightened if, one day, you hear that I am crossing the Atlantic. For the time being, I'm staying here with my foster children. I can't separate myself yet from the little grave in the churchyard. For that reason, you will not see me for a time . . .

In the spring, Per passed his exam with honor, but his happiness over that was diminished because, almost immediately, he had to walk from the exam table to a barracks and crawl into a soldier's uniform. This service was one of his derelictions from the past he had to atone for. Year after year he had sought a deferment of his military service in the hope that, by one means or another, with the help of Philip Salomon's influence, he could escape it altogether. He had been taken as an engineer recruit, and the whole summer he had to march out to the Copenhagen commons, and with a few hundred young men who were, in his eyes, only half-grown boys, dig trenches and braid gabion baskets for fortifications. What bothered him most was not the physical exertion, unaccustomed as he was to this, but the mental stupor that characterized the whole of barracks life. He had brought some books with him in the hope that he would find the occasion in his free time to read a bit. But, aside from his duties, he had bodily demands to satisfy. Meals and sleep were his masters. And then, he got so used to reacting only to commands that it began to seem unnatural to expect free time.

By the fall, he was liberated from that spiritual death. Once again, luck was on his side as he drew lots for the termination of service and got one of the very few numbers that exempted him from winter duty and from all future drafts. In the last days of September, he traveled, all refreshed in body and soul, to Jutland, where his engagement to Inger was solemnized. The master had died in the meantime, but rather than impeding negotiations for the water project, it forwarded them, and preparations had now gone far enough for Per, in his great joy, to immediately begin his work.

First of all he arranged his lodging in the little house on the outskirts of the station town that the master's wife had already designated for him. There were five small rooms in addition to the kitchen, and a couple of attic rooms. For the time being, he procured furniture only for two of the rooms and set himself up very thriftily. His lack of talent for creating comfort around

himself that had stamped all his residences both here and abroad
was again noticeable. He bought, among other things, a pair of
painted tables, an oilcloth sofa, and some wooden chairs at a
country merchant's auction. He was satisfied with his bits and
pieces, but it was not, as he himself thought, exclusively on
economic grounds, in order to pay back as quickly as possible
what he owed his family and Philip Salomon, but also because
he, like the Sidenius he was, had traces of a medieval cloistered
monk lodged deep inside himself that now seemed more and
more to be surfacing in his secret attraction to an ascetic and natural way of life. As a housekeeper, his mother-in-law got him an
old servant who had once worked at the parsonage and, one day
in October, when summer's last leaves were blowing in the wind,
he sat down for the first time at his own table.

The village itself, Rimalt by name, was one of the newly built
towns that were rapidly, and therefore with a stamp of arbitrari-
ness, going up around train stations in populated districts. There
was an inn, a secondary school for commercial training, a phar-
macy, some merchants and craftsmen, but no church or parsonage. Some distance behind the station, the tracks ran over the
river on an impressive bridge, and it was the train's hollow thunder passing over it that Per used to hear across the meadows at
Kærsholm. For ten miles around, people set their watches by it.
The province of his future work lay on both sides of that bridge.
It stretched along the river, four miles in one direction and two
in another, taking in the meadowland of Rimalt, Bøstrup, and
Borup.

Every morning he went out in his own small gig in order to
work with his map, mark out the borderland, and so forth, and
he gradually gained, in this way, personal relationships with most
of the district's farmers. But they did not win over his heart with
these transactions. Taken one by one, they seemed much less
impressive than when he saw them in a close crowd at the large
popular meeting in the woods. Besides, since he lacked the means
to judge them as individuals, they all appeared to act alike. Overall, he saw only their traditional attributes: money greed, obstinacy, and shameless suspicion—all those ignoble traits, bred in a
narrow and exclusive society. The impression he already had
gained as a soldier was strengthened. He had been in the
company of both provincial workmen and farmers, especially
West Jutlanders. It struck him what a fresh and active sympathy

the workmen manifested from the beginning, although most came out of Copenhagen's lower classes, while the farmers were altogether divested of fellow feeling and even seemed to have no clear understanding of its nature. They did not quarrel with anyone and were held together by mutual respect, but it never occurred to them to do anyone a service without being certain of a return, and they never asked for help without offering requital.

Per would come home depressed in the evenings when, as sometimes happened, he had wasted most of his workday because a couple of neighbors, who were, really, good friends, even fellow religious and political believers, could not agree on the property rights to a patch of trenched earth the width of a straw that could be carted off in two wheelbarrows. Despite the great revival work of the last generation here, the feeling of brotherhood clung only to the outside of clothes as a festive mood surrounding the crowd at edification meetings and at church, but was frittered away during the treadmill of daily life and, especially, in regard to the purse strings. Nor did he find any special cheer in the company of his compeers back in Rimalt. Every evening, after the mail delivery, the administrator of the commercial school, the pharmacist, the stationmaster, and a couple of merchants would gather in the reserved room of the public house as a kind of club, to which he had been invited. Here the company sat around a table under flickering lamps and read newspapers, smoked, and drank grog. Now and then a little conversation broke out. They talked about the contents of the paper, and nowhere were the daily events in the outer world treated more condescendingly than during those evening gatherings in this Jutland village public house. The school administrator was the club's guiding spirit. He was a crafty man of fifty or so with a sprinkling of general knowledge that he could use in discussions with a certain proficiency. He was a former graduate scholar and had, as well, once tried, unsuccessfully, to play a part in politics and now was ending up in this corner of the country as a director of a school for boys, with forty students. It was a personal satisfaction to him to reduce the significance of everything that had managed to attract the world's notice; the course of wars, North Pole expeditions, important developments in science and art, the labor movement, and the powerful advances of the working class all had awakened in him only patronization. Even the day's great technical progress, which the farmers followed with childlike wonder, failed to impress him.

"Well, look here," he said one evening when the newspapers had announced a newly invented telephone (a device whose mode of operation Per was best equipped to explain). "It's really puzzling why such a discovery was not made a long time ago. It's ridiculous that I can't sit here and quite calmly talk with a man in China—not only talk to him, but see him, feel him, smell him. And that goes for all provinces. We are seven days and nights from Europe to America. That's altogether shameful! We ought to be, at most, seven hours from there. We ought, in other words, to be able to go from Copenhagen to New York between breakfast and supper. When we have done that, I will take my hat off to science."

The pharmacist, as well, liked to hear himself talk, though he was wont to stop in the middle of his sentences because he didn't know what he wanted to say. The stationmaster, a pensioned officer, on the other hand, talked mostly when drinking, while the two merchants listened devoutly to the school administrator's expositions.

Per took no pleasure in these meetings and came to them only rarely. And it was too far to go to the Bøstrup parsonage every evening. His horse had to rest, and it was difficult for him, after a strenuous day, to walk six or so miles back and forth in all kinds of weather and road conditions. But it was lonely and sad in his house. To be sure, he had his books to keep him company, and he turned to them for solace during the endless evenings that now seemed almost longer than the days.

For the time being, he couldn't find the composure to work on his invention. For that, his thoughts were too busy, restlessly moving between the parsonage and his house. Only when he could secure his home and hear Inger bustling around, humming, would he have the peace of mind for an orderly schedule of work.

Already, toward Christmas, he began, therefore, to talk about the marriage. His parents-in-law, at first, would not hear of it because Inger was too young. Nor did they yet consider his future sufficiently solid. Inger herself thought about it only reluctantly, but after a protracted and, for Per, sometimes humiliating discussion, he got his way, and it was decided that the marriage would take place in May.

On top of the stress of loneliness and longing for a real home,

Per had a third, secret reason to move up the marriage date. He was not getting along with his father-in-law. His development had, gradually, taken him so far from the Blomberg perspective that he was almost hostile to it. The representation of a bourgeois God, who guides the world by common consent according to the most advantageous humane principles known, seemed to him almost comical. During the stormy moods that had oppressed his mind in the last year, he had imagined a universal will of a stronger sort with a goal of greater magnitude. The augmented insight into life, derived from his daily rambling through the district, had distanced him from the Blomberg faith in a fatherly God. The poverty of the cottiers, the devastation of sickness and ignorance, and, from a humane point of view, the whole despairing injustice of the distribution of life's advantages repelled any desire to renew a religious understanding. Instead, he wanted a deeper penetration into the mysterious logic of existence. And, as this did not long go unnoticed by his father-in-law, it occasioned various disagreements.

Pastor Blomberg, who was so liberal in allowing those around him to think of God and the world order in their own way, was, they soon found, very prickly about how they thought of *him*. He was so used to hearing his congregation echo his own voice that he took any contradiction as a sign of ill-will and a crooked heart. He, who seldom showed any particular respect for other opinions and was not afraid to childishly mock, from time to time, other religious convictions, assumed, as soon as *he* was attacked, the fatherly authority of the church; he did not in the least accommodate a born Sidenius. In regard to this, Per thought often of the words by which Jakobe had once described the self-deceiving zeal the church hid, from time immemorial, under the flag of piety to satisfy its egoistic craving for power. So he sought, in the long, lonely winter, entirely other influences and sources of nourishment for his soul to deepen his understanding of the mystifying side of life.

He had become, over the years, quite a book lover. His eye was automatically drawn to every printed volume that came within his horizon. What first caught his attention when he came into the rooms of the farmers were the small bookshelves that were usually there, and he seldom left without having examined their content. It was, moreover, almost always the same: the Bible, a couple of historical novels of Ingemann, Holberg's comedies, a volume of popular science, a couple of agricultural writings, some common, didactic, and sentimental so-called schoolteacher novels, or their counterpart: chaplain and folk school poetry, beside a row of genuinely edifying books, mainly, naturally, by Blomberg.

Per found, as well, fortuitously preserved, examples of old religious literature: small, thick books with strange titles. One was called *Salvation's Oil*, another, *The Little Golden Treasury*. A third, *Four Books About the Imitation of Christ*, and a fourth, *Jesus' Blood and Wounds as the Surest Refuge for All Troubled Sinners*. The families were somewhat embarrassed to be found in possession of this so-called pietistic literature from an ignorant age, and, since no one really read them anymore, it had not been difficult for Per to acquire some of these books for his own collection. He had procured them only for the sake of their oddity, but when, one evening, he started to flip through one of them as he was looking in special, favorite places worn by former readers, he made the discovery that the naive, rather primitive, inflated tone he was averse to in these old popular writers moved him in a strange way.

And he was led further. With his incessant and growing need to fathom himself, to understand his own nature even in its fleeting perceptions, he undertook a historical examination of the religious life from the time of the greater part of these writings. He was guided by this study back to the pietism under Christian VI and, from there, to the Moravian Separatists of the Enlightenment, to the strange Layman's Movement at the century's beginning, out of which the present great religious folk awakening had slowly developed. The picture of those peasants' sons and village craftsmen battling against that day's rationalist orthodoxy impressed him strongly. Those solitaries who, like apostles, wandered from village to village bore witness and were mocked by the crowd, persecuted by priests, and thrown into prison by the authorities, and those small congregations, with their evangelical spirit turned away from the world, reenacted the Christ story itself on our native ground.

A facsimile of these portraits of the past could be found here in his father-in-law's own parish. A clog maker, who stayed entirely to himself and wanted no contact with other people in the district, lived with his family in a neat little whitewashed house in the Bøstrup fields. Once or twice a year the man drove into town with a cartload of wooden articles and sold them to the tradesmen. But, generally, he remained in his own house, over whose entrance was a board with these words painted on it: "I and my house serve the Lord."

Per stumbled upon it when he had been traveling out in the district to assure himself of some able fascine binders for the summer work in the fields. In the main room, he found a young woman at a cradle. A couple of little children sat on the floor and played quietly. The door to the workplace at the side stood open, and there sat a man astride his bench, carving. At the sight of Per, he got up and came into the room, looking embarrassed. He was a middle-aged man, tall and a little stooped. His beardless and somewhat pale face with half-closed eyes was not pleasing to Per. Nor was the expression of his wife, who was observing him from the cradle with an almost hostile glance. The man asked him to sit down, but without any real hospitality. He refused Per's proposal to join the summer workers for the river regulation in a way that seemed to push the whole project far away. Still, Per kept sitting there for a while. There was, despite all, something about the domestic scene that attracted him. In the little room, there reigned a striking cleanliness and order. It was as if the house were ready to receive a royal guest. Here, patently, a kind of piety prevailed that not only generated an atmosphere of festive occasions but also was able to transform the inhabitants down to their very demeanor. For instance, just the way the man in the course of the conversation took one of the children on his lap to wipe its nose with his finger with such a unique and solemn gentleness seemed in no way ludicrous. In the parsonage, Per learned that the family belonged to a sect calling itself "the saints" that had, lately, spread to many places in the country. His father-in-law had called them straight-out "puritans" and said that he considered their presence a scandal for the Christian community.

Every time Per read about the "shoemaker's friend" Ole Henrik Svane, or about Kristen Madsen from Funen, or the other lay preachers from the age of the religious Revivalists, he saw before him the little, quiet, and expectant room in the Bøstrup fields. At the same time, he had arrived at a depressing recognition through his reading. When he compared the inner faith of those believers in Providence with his own, he felt that he neither was nor could become a really genuine Christian. It was, moreover, not so much the renunciation of the world that scared him off. He understood well the satisfaction of an introspective, unworldly life. It was the passion in their prayers, the kind of hopes they had, that dismayed him. He had in this last year prayed often, but for him prayer and devotion had served as a kind of guidance and purification for his soul, a flight from worldly pollution and desire. Still, he could understand those who trusted the power of prayer to really protect against misfortune and to provide help in the hour of danger and need.

But their deep, pious, Christian prayers were suffused with a kind of longing for pain and troubles. In their aversion to the world, in their anxiety over temptation, with their perception of the Christian life as a ceaseless pilgrimage, they invoked misfortune and persecution to come down on their heads: "Feed me, O Lord, with the bread of tears, and give me to drink a full measure of tears. I dedicate myself and all that is mine to Thee in chastity and humility. Thy punishment weighs me down, but Thy rod instructs me, for truly, it is grace to Thy servant to let me suffer torment out of love for Thee. I thank Thee that Thou hast not spared me as a sinner, but hast chastised me with hard blows."

When Per came upon such words, he involuntarily shuddered in the same way as when he read his mother's posthumous letter. Before such a burning belief that ravaged the basic impulses of mankind, his natural sensibility withdrew. "Truly, it is an affliction to live in the world," wrote Thomas à Kempis in his book about the imitation of Christ: "To be subjugated to eating and drinking, waking and sleeping, resting and working, and the other necessities of nature, that is truly a great misery and a torment for God-fearing men. Oh, if only there were nothing else to do but to praise the Lord God. Then you would be much happier than now, when each of your needs demands service to the body." What especially disturbed him in these readings was something that already, for years, had dawned on him during his random plunge into a translation of Plato's *Phaedo*. There he found a clearer and clearer understanding that Christianity was a lot older than Christ, in whom it only found its culmination, at least for the time being. And he couldn't take comfort in the thought that it would have been but a passing phenomenon if the powers and princes of the state had not seen some advantage in helping it onto the spirit's throne. It seemed to have taken root in a primal human need and to suck sustenance from an instinct that lay outside nature and that, wherever it was established, would finally conquer it.

"For the body causes us thousands of struggles, so arouses and confuses us that we cannot know the truth. And as long as we live, we will, it seems, come closest to that knowledge when we have had as little as possible to do with the body and only when it is absolutely necessary to deal with it, and do *not* let it take us over."

So spoke Socrates himself, and Buddha. There was a stray Buddhist saying that was burned into his brain and shone like phosphor every time his soul grew dark: "He who loves nothing here on earth and hates nothing, desires nothing—only he is without fear and fetters."

From all corners of the earth, the same answer! In all ages, the same demand: self-denial, obliteration of the self. Happiness lies in renunciation. But from the wings of the world the opposite advice sounds: happiness comes from a confident self-assertion, self-love, the power of the developing body and courage of the will. There was no bridge spanning the abyss between castrating the soul or the body. That was the choice. There was no getting around that for one who didn't have, like his father-in-law and so many others, the fortunate capacity for self-deception that could veil the horizon in a lyrical haze. It was necessary to take a standpoint, swear fidelity, without anxiety or hesitation, and with a willing determination and even enthusiasm, to the cross or champagne.

He always ended with the climax of faith as life's sustaining and justifying support. But he no longer had a comforting confidence in either heaven or earth. He could make no amicable settlement with the children of the world, and he no longer felt at home among Christians. Nor could he turn back to the Blomberg sense of naive innocence and, like a child, pluck flowers from the edge of the abyss without vertigo, insensitive to the compelling power of the demonic depths.

On a gray morning at the beginning of March, Per's gig stopped before his door and waited. Since Per himself had no stall space, he had to park his vehicle at the inn, and it was the inn's groom who now stood by the horse, cursing a bit, while he crossed his arms tightly to keep warm. He waited over a quarter of an hour.

Finally, Per, in his large greatcoat, stumbled out, still drunk with sleep, and silently mounted his gig, took the reins from the hand of the groom, and jolted off. He had, as usual, sat up half the night reading, and when he had gone to bed, his thoughts kept him awake, so he had not fallen asleep until the morning hours. But now, the fresh breeze quickly blew the dreamy fog from his eyes. The gig was not really suited for dozing. It was a superannuated rattletrap, so work-weary that the springs knocked together with the most trifling unevenness in the road. On the other hand, the horse was a reliable Norwegian fjord horse who had the habit, from sheer circumspection, of weaving from one edge of the road to the other as soon as there was the slightest slope. He had eyes as sharp as a leveling tool, noticed the least deviation from the horizontal plane. For the sake of his driving honor, Per thought, in the beginning, he had to scotch these bad habits with the help of the whip; but he had soon come to love his little, willful, and surefooted beast who, day by day, hauled him through the district in all kinds of weather, and he let the horse have his way.

As far as possible, he arranged things to be able to pass Bøstrup while riding off to work, to say good morning to Inger. He knew she went out into the garden to look for him, and, consequently, for this reason, these morning outings put him in a cheerful and expansive mood. The drive itself was, at that time of day, also very pleasant, especially on such a morning as this, with the fresh air, the clouds chasing over the earth, and screeching flocks of crows rocking on the wind.

He had to smile when he thought back on what had kept him awake at night and how he had not been able to find peace of mind before he had solved the riddles of life. Now, while his reflections were still drowsing and before the day's many small irritations had muddied his mind, he opened himself up again to the natural attractions of the world with confidence. Everything dark and doubtful in existence became, at this morning hour, so insignificant in comparison with the indisputable fact that he was sitting here, young and healthy, in his own gig, on the way to his fiancée, to consecrate the day with a kiss on her sweet mouth. He praised the God he scarcely believed in anymore and life, with its joys, sorrows, and troubles that seemed altogether worthy of his gratitude, wherever it would lead him. Why brood over it? Self-created miseries were the devil's work. It was really only pharisaic self-promotion not to let oneself accept life's struggles.

In two and a half months, his marriage would take place. On the twentieth of May, Inger's birthday, he would bring her home as a flower-bedecked bride, and his sad, lonely life would be over.

It was his intention, this day, to pay a long-overdue visit. In the meadowland that would be affected by the re-regulation, there were two properties that belonged to the parish in Borup, and he used this as a pretext to visit the pastor there. He had not spoken with Pastor Fjaltring since that chance meeting in the hay shed during the thunderstorm, a good year and a half ago.

He had driven by a couple of times when the odd man was taking his lonely walk along the road at twilight, and he had regularly greeted him, although it seemed that he wasn't recognized in return. Over the whole district he heard people talk about him and his unhappy family life. The least credible stories were those about his wife's degradation through drink.

The road dipped in a large curve down to Bøstrup, and suddenly Per's face lit up. There, in the parsonage garden, he saw Inger standing with a shawl around her head, peeking out at him.

"You sleepyhead!" she called out. "Where have you been?"

"Have you been waiting?"

"My whole body is frozen."

"You poor girl!" He drove up to her, so close to the fence that, under the shadow of a rosebush, their mouths could meet over the railing.

"Good morning, dear heart."

"Where are you going today?"

"Oh, I have so much to do. I have to go out right away."

"You're unbearable. You're always busy. Goodbye, then. Are you coming this evening?"

"Of course."

A fresh kiss, and then another, and "a little something extra," said Per. His dun horse started off, but the lovers were still holding hands until they were torn away from each other. "Goodbye, goodbye," they said again, and waved until the gig disappeared around the corner.

After having spent some time in the meadows with his surveying instrument, Per drove up to the Borup parsonage toward noon. Pastor Fjaltring was home and received him in his study, a large, half-darkened space, almost a kind of hall, with only two small windows. Although there was some furniture in it, it was so large it seemed empty. A reading desk with an open book stood at the wall between the windows, and a strange caveman came from the lectern to meet him as soon as he entered. The same eccentric mixture of shy self-consciousness, curiosity, and pride that had already been obvious to Per that day in the church was manifest in the pastor's manner. He stopped a few steps from Per and greeted him very politely, but in silence, and with his hands behind his back. It wasn't easy to tell whether he recognized him or not. When Per had introduced himself, the pastor gestured to a sofa and took a seat in an armchair some distance away. He asked him, in a businesslike manner, how he could be of service. Per put forth his question concerning the dredging of ditches in the meadowland attached to the parsonage. The pastor answered that, in fact, he did not have the right to make decisions about the grounds on his own unless it concerned insignificant matters. He requested only, in light of a possible future representation of the alteration, that Per draw up a model of the changes he desired to undertake, which Per readily promised.

The entire exchange took but a few minutes, and a long pause followed. The pastor sat bowed over his folded hands and, obviously, was waiting for Per to leave. Nevertheless, when Per really looked as if he were going, he seemed anxious not to appear impolite. He asked where Per lived and whether he liked the neighborhood. When he heard that Per had taken up quarters in a house by the station, he said that he thought the place would please him, and that gradually, a real little town had grown up around Rimalt. He mentioned the school director, the pharmacist, and a couple of other inhabitants. However, he didn't say a word about Per's future father-in-law or the family at the Bøstrup parsonage.

Since that meeting in stormy weather, Per had felt such great respect for the pastor that he was somewhat disappointed by this commonplace conversation. It hurt him, too, to be lumped in with the members of the grog club, all the more since the pastor himself, to judge from his tone, did not think highly of these people. He observed with some emphasis that his only social life in Rimalt was with his books.

The pastor raised his head a little. He still did not look at Per, but an attentive expression flickered across his little, sallow, beardless face.

"Well," he said, "the solitary life of thought can also have its satisfactions, to be sure, and its comforts. You might even say its blessings. And," he added, with a little smile, "the solitary life is, from time to time, very sociable. When you look inside yourself with sufficient thoroughness, you often have the strange sensation of having hosted visitors."

This remark hit home for Per, and he attempted to extend the comparison: "Unfortunately, such visitors are often very difficult and stir up anxiety and discomfort."

Once again, that surprised expression of interest flickered across the pastor's averted face. He didn't pursue the subject further, but added, as a conclusion, "We have recourse to the thoughts of others to drive away our own. Books are so pleasantly diverting, and the observations people allow themselves to express in them are usually not alarming."

Again there was a pause. The pastor obviously did not wish to say more. Per got up now, and the pastor made no effort to hold him back, but he was in no way impolite. At parting, he reached out his hand—a curiously hot and dry hand—and uttered a courteous apology because, fearing a draft, he couldn't accompany him to the door.

As brief and uneventful as this meeting had been, Per was absorbed by it. When he was eating dinner at the Bøstrup parsonage, he began to talk about it in a way that displeased his parents-in-law. "He is a poor and pitiable man," said his father-in-law. "I really am annoyed with him. He should never have become a pastor."

Already the next day, Per set about drawing a map of the project Pastor Fjaltring had asked for. He took a great deal of trouble with it, made a fair copy of it on a large sheet of thick paper, and added a painstakingly executed ground plan of the parsonage and the adjoining land.

A week later, when once again his path led him past Borup, he drove up to the parsonage to deliver the document. The pastor, who was so little used to anyone paying attention to his requests, became embarrassed by the sight of such a beautiful piece of work and thanked him warmly. When Per immediately made signs that he was leaving, the pastor became very disturbed and begged his pardon if he had seemed indisposed on the previous visit. To make Per stay, he pushed him back down on the sofa, and it didn't take long before a very sincere and open conversation got under way.

The starting point was the document Per had brought with him. Per informed the pastor that there was a significant amount of peat for fuel in the parsonage meadow. It lay fairly deep under the earth's surface and was a little difficult to get to. But it was, apparently, especially good just because of that. He was convinced, he said, that it would pay to procure a little mill pump that could keep an excavation dry and so yield heaps of mud peat. Pastor Fjaltring, who was standing in front of him on a small carpet runner in the middle of an otherwise bare floor, shook his head with a sickly, faint smile. He would have to leave the matter to his successor, he said. His health was not of such a nature that he could plan on the future.

"Besides," he added, "even if death grants me a truce, I know nothing about how long the church authorities and zealous administrative brothers will give me permission to preach to empty pews."

Per blushed and tried to make a polite objection, but the pastor did not let him speak. "I don't have any illusions. Our time has turned religion into marketplace wares, and you can't blame people for looking for the shops that sell the goods most cheaply."

Per felt obliged to defend his father-in-law's perspective. Without naming anyone, Pastor Fjaltring answered that a benign, half-patronizing, or, perhaps, merely curious relation to the great questions of life was, in his eyes, worse than no relation at all. Faith is a passion, and where that does not exist, it makes mere sport of God. To stir up a certain spiritual vigor artificially in the populace is so far from preparing the earthbound for a serious and sincere faith—or even for serious doubt—that, on the contrary, it destroys the seeds, which lie in the soul of every person, of a real relationship with God. He paced back and forth on the carpet and stopped suddenly at the other end of the room. It looked as if he were reminding himself not to let himself venture too far. But his desire to talk was aroused, and, as a swarm of thoughts were urged out of his loneliness, he could no longer hold back the words:

"The science of modern engineering cannot be absolved from bearing a good deal of responsibility for the superficiality and shallowness that is the curse of the contemporary world. The hurried progress of the machine age carries over to the religious life. When people from all spheres are habituated to satisfying their needs with the least possible personal effort, they demand also, in the realm of belief, that faith be acquired without too much strain or too much time. And the preachers of God's word—whether pastors or lay—generally do not have the will to resist that demand. To be sure, pitifully little is known about man's soul and the conditions needed for its vigorous development," he continued, with more and more passion. "But it seems generally recognized that happiness in the worldly sense has made mankind sterile. The soul's native element is grief. Happiness is an animal vestige in us. Therefore, you can see that people in prosperous times easily fall into all sorts of peacock and mimic manners, while in times of sorrow, if they looked inside themselves, down to the divine springs of individuality, they would take on an entirely transfigured bearing.

"To be sure, Christianity announced itself on earth as 'glad tidings.' But if that phrase were taken literally, mankind would be stuck in an insoluble contradiction. A faith that proclaims joy, peace of mind, and happiness has choked up the nourishing springs of the soul and extinguished spiritual life. Even the idea of a paradise beyond as a place of perfection can only with difficulty be reconciled with our present religious understanding. The words about abandoning hope, as Dante used them over the entrance of his Hell, could, with adequate justification and with frightening implications, be engraved over the gates of a so-called heaven when there is no longer any possibility for self-development. To the limited discrimination of mankind, it looks as if, for the time being, we are bound to stay among the unredeemed and provisionally damned to gain cleansed and purified souls and true salvation, understood as spiritual insight.

"But in all probability, we have not yet understood God's intentions in the Gospels. And in that case, we can realize why Christianity, after two thousand years, despite its great words and promises, still is not capable of accomplishing more for the sake of the moral progress of mankind. Certain theologians deny straight out Christ's divine birth, and, in reality, the affinity between him and the Old Testament God is not easy to understand. You could say, without exaggeration, that one is the other's complete opposite, even caricature. But if Christ is not God's son, who can guarantee for us that God did not let him be born, be tortured, suffer an ignominious death to serve as a discouraging example to us?" Pastor Fjaltring stopped his pacing abruptly, as if anxious over his own words. His forehead, during his long speech, had become red, and nervous spasms jerked steadily from his shoulders up into his face.

"Well, I hope you understand I am not saying these things to jest. I think that the figure of Christ and his mission finally will be made the object of critical examination, and that time is surely coming—so let it be thorough and without prejudices, because our salvation is at stake."

Per did not know how to respond to these wide-ranging thoughts, and Pastor Fjaltring apparently hadn't realized himself how far he had gone from his beginning point. Nor did he notice that the door behind him was opening and his wife had come in. Only when Per rose and bowed did he turn around and become silent.

Per conceded that common gossip had not exaggerated the description of the pastor's wife. She was shapelessly stout and had a large, copper-colored drinker's face with a pair of dead, staring eyes that seemed almost white against her complexion. Her slovenliness was all the more striking because she had obviously tried to dress up. Her hair had been hastily smoothed down with water, and she had on a fairly decent dress. But under her crookedly perched cap, the rest of her hair looked like pillow stuffing, and worn, unbrushed shoes were visible under her hem.

She smiled very invitingly when her husband introduced Per: "Herr Sidenius, you must give us the pleasure of sharing our meal. It's on the table."

Per did not know what to answer. Sympathy for the unfortunate pastor pressed on his heart. He would rather have said no, but fearful of hurting him with a refusal he accepted the invitation.

It surprised him that Pastor Fjaltring's manner in relation to his wife did not manifest any serious irritation. He was, to be sure, a bit embarrassed and fairly distracted through the whole meal, but in his behavior toward her he was considerate, attentive, even gallant. She apparently didn't even have the slightest realization she was a disgrace. It was she who led the conversation; in a fairly muddled way, she spoke of Copenhagen and her remembrance of North Zealand, where her father had been a pastor. Moreover, she had the habit of never listening to what others were saying so that, finally, she was the only one talking.

When both men returned to the study, Per understood immediately that the interrupted conversation could not be resumed.

The pastor did not ask him to stay on, but, at parting, accompanied him to the hall, where he thanked him again for the consideration he had shown him and stressed that it would give him pleasure to see him when he passed by again.

Per was happy for the invitation and paid frequent visits to the parsonage in the next days on the pretext of the excavation in the meadowland. Finally, he didn't need an excuse and always felt welcome. He never went, however, to the services in the Borup church, and it was not alone respect for his father-in-law that held him back. The impression he had of Pastor Fjaltring's preaching from the first time he had heard him speak did not tempt him to return. Pastor Fjaltring cut a strange Punch and Judy figure on the pulpit. He was not a spellbinder; still less, a prophetic speaker; but a truth seeker. It was necessary to see him in his cave, and even then he could now and then, during a spontaneous visit, flutter about anxiously and distractedly like a moth who suddenly meets the light. Either he felt self-conscious at the thought that his dress was not meant for the eyes of strangers or he was a victim of his imagined sickness and restlessly flitted from chair to chair or sat all drawn up with his hand supporting his swaddled head. With Per, this shyness, in general, passed quickly, and when he had overcome it he could talk for hours without getting tired.

In the Bøstrup parsonage, Per never mentioned his continuing connection with the heretical pastor. Nor did he speak of him to Inger. He knew that she would feel vexed like her father, and, for now, he couldn't make her understand his interest in this new acquaintance because she still trusted in her father's infallibility, in a childlike way. He would have to wait until they lived together. The few times there had been an incipient quarrel between him and his father-in-law about spiritual matters, she had become very angry at him afterward and let it be understood that it was considered youthful conceit on his part in such discussions to want to contest her father's opinion.

The secrecy that hovered over his visits to Pastor Fjaltring gave Per a mysterious aura. The pastor's extraordinary and wide-ranging knowledge contributed to that. Per became acquainted, for the first time, with something like a medieval theology. He was being led into a Byzantine think-temple of the scholastics consecrated by the pre-Reformation crowd of fantastic Gothic visionaries, men like Meister Eckhart, Johannes Tauler,

Ruysbroeck, and Gerard Groote, whose intellectual personalities had obviously tempted Pastor Fjaltring to thorough study. There seemed, in fact, to be no theoretical construction or direction of faith in the past or present that was foreign to him. He was even intimate with certain uncanny deviations of bizarre religious fantasy, like Satanic cults, Rosicrucians, and the Black Mass, and he could recite by heart long passages from the writings of those secret societies.

What interested Per most, during these visits, was Pastor Fjaltring's own character and the personal experience that marked everything he talked about. Just as he seemed so intimate with all modes of thought, he seemed himself to have undergone every human desire and pain. Even when he spoke of hell, in such a way and with such a sick look, he did it as if he had been there and were living through its series of torments again in his memory. Heaven could, in happy moments, play as well in his fine, vivid, and shifting expressions. A fleeting revelation could pass over his face, as if he had caught, from afar, the music of the spheres.

When Per, afterward, sat in the Bøstrup parsonage and listened to his red-cheeked father-in-law, he felt, even more than before, how poor was the worth of such a cheaply bought cheerfulness in comparison with the faith or the doubt that had cost blood and battles. He especially noticed the contrast in one of the so-called private conferences the pastor presided over a few times a year in the parsonage, where the district's liberal clergy gathered to discuss controversial church matters. Watching these men sitting there filling their pipes and jovially debating absolution, the dispensation of prayer, and hearing them jauntily competing with each other to lower the cost and accommodate the public's wish to have a cheaper religion, he understood the name "wholesalers" that Pastor Fjaltring had pinned on them.

The character of his father-in-law was becoming more and more exposed. When he again heard, by chance, of his strange relationship with Inger's old grandfather, to which the steward at Kærsholm had already alluded, his critical sense was awakened. The old man lived in wretched circumstances somewhere in Funen since the son had closed his house to him because his father, already an old man, had transgressed the sixth commandment and had a child by his servant girl.

Per suspected that his future father-in-law was, in fact, very happy to have that excuse to keep his troublesome, now almost blind father physically away from him. He was very cautious when it came to really rendering assistance to anyone.

Per repeatedly had occasion to hear how he dealt with the poor who sought his help with a promise to "keep them fast in his prayers." But, withal, that did not make Per doubt for a moment the sincerity of his father-in-law's religious faith. What determined his kind of faith seemed just the dubious part of the business it seemed. It didn't seem capable of ennobling or refining the mind, as in the truly "justified," where it entirely extinguished the natural man.

In his arguments, Pastor Fjaltring always came back to doubt as the presupposition of faith, the "ever warm and fertile womb. As the day is born out of the night and, again, night from day, and as all life on earth comes out of that exchange between darkness and light, so is the religious life conditioned by an inevitable relationship of contrasts, a conflict that keeps the soul restless. A faith that doesn't constantly renew itself through doubt is dead, a broomstick, a crutch with whose help we are, perhaps, able for a time to forget our lameness, but that could never be a life-enhancing power."

In one of his playful moments he said, "If it is correct that the way to hell is paved with good intentions, so the path to heaven necessarily must be paved with our worst. There is more truth in that," he continued, "than can be seen at first glance. For, as is well known, the body's march through life is continually interrupted by falls; so, too, our soul's development toward fulfillment is a constant fall through sin, from which we are raised by an instinctively active self-preserving power of divine origin."

As Per looked back at his own development, it seemed to him to confirm these words. And he looked again to the future with hope and confidence.

The parsonage at Bøstrup was already busy with preparations for the wedding. Sewing machines were humming the whole day, and, every Monday, Fru Blomberg went into town, where she had ordered the greater part of the trousseau.

From the moment Per entered the house, he was hit by words like "drill, sateen, insertions, ticking, horsehair, grenadine, and walnut wood." Inger's thoughts seemed more taken up with the cabinetmaker and upholsterer than with the imminent ceremony of consecrating love, and Per felt himself more and more superfluous in the parsonage.

He went back to his house to prepare it quietly to receive his bride. He now was gaining an adequate income. In addition to his chief work with the water regulation, he had taken on various small projects around the district from which he earned a considerable amount. He also had paid back, in full, his family, and had even begun to lay aside the first installment of what he owed Philip and Ivan Salomon.

He had the inside and outside of his fairly dilapidated house repaired. New wallpaper was put on and the old-fashioned cold, brick floor in the kitchen replaced with a wooden one. His ingenuity did not fail him in this work, but was reflected in various small practical arrangements, from improving the stove-chimney draw to the water runoff, and so on. He knew that nothing would please Inger more than a well-designed kitchen, a cool, airy dining room, a freshly whitewashed cellar, and an easily accessible and well-stocked furnace room. She had inherited her mother's sense of order and cleanliness and could be as enchanted at the sight of newly polished copper pots as others were over works of art. As it usually does, improvement in one area opened his eyes to the need for amelioration elsewhere. When the kitchen was finished, it seemed to Per that the living room, as well, must have a new floor. Without having noticed it, he gradually was infected by the fixing-up fever in the parsonage. For fear there wouldn't be enough time, both he and Inger were, in the end, close to wishing that the wedding would be delayed a couple of weeks.

While the new furniture was beginning to arrive from the city and getting settled into place, other problems declared themselves. A wardrobe turned out to be too big for the wall where it was supposed to go. On the other hand, a curtain rod was too short—and what made Inger, for the moment, quite unhappy, the new wallpaper in the living room did not look as pretty with the carpet and furniture upholstery as she had expected. Every time Per came to the parsonage, Inger assaulted him with worried questions about the length of the wall between windows or the dimension of the floor, and when he was leaving, she forgot, now and then, to return his kiss, as a kind of admonishment.

This kind of moving-day unrest lasted up to the wedding, and, even just a few days before the ceremony, it suddenly swelled into panic because of a problem. Virtually all the ordered furniture had finally come; the only things missing were the beds that had been expected week after week. Multiple inquiries with return requests were sent to the cabinetmaker in town, and he continually promised to send them. Inger and her mother finally were talking almost exclusively about these still-missing beds. Per felt a little embarrassed about it; he did not really understand the candor with which Inger, who was usually so tactful, expressed her anxiety not only to him, but also to others who came to the parsonage. The tension traveled out through the town, and everyone was talking about those beds, so it was a relief all around when, the day before the wedding, it became known that they had finally arrived and were in place.

On the wedding day, the summer sun was shining over a flag-decorated town, and everyone was on their feet when the wedding procession came up to the church. Inger sat in an open carriage beside her uncle, a handsome, older man with a pointed, cottony beard and a rose in his lapel. She looked very pretty and perhaps knew it herself, only too well. Her aunts, who had dressed her, friends who had placed her veil and myrtle wreath on her head, the house servants in the parsonage who had accompanied her to her carriage, had told her that no prettier bride had ever drawn up to the Bøstrup church. Among the guests were also two from Per's family, Eberhard and Signe. All the district's most distinguished citizens were there, the family of Councilor Clausen, the master's widow, the administrator of the college, several pastors, church and community officials, and a few select citizens from Rimalt—in all, over fifty people.

During the dinner in the parsonage, curious onlookers pressed into the garden to listen to the talk coming through the open windows. Afterward, tables were set for them under the trees. All the spectators were to be treated, and gradually, as the crowd streamed in, the marriage party took on the character of a folk festival.

Early the next morning, the out-of-town guests departed—first Eberhard and Signe, then Inger's uncle. The latter was a remarkable man, a bit of an adventurer, who had roamed around in the world and finally ended up as an expert director of a large and highly regarded shipyard in Fiume, where he still lived. After many years, he was taking the occasion of his niece's wedding to revisit his Fatherland and had been staying a week in Bøstrup.

But his eccentric manner and foreign habits had made it difficult for him to live happily with the inhabitants of the parsonage, especially with Pastor Blomberg, who called him, straight out, an old dandy. On the other hand, he was very comfortable with Per and had accompanied him a couple of times on his rounds to the excavation in the fields now under way.

Although he was not a trained technician, he had a very good understanding of how valuable the work was and had, afterward, expressed his amazement to his sister and his brother-in-law with words that cautiously suggested he thought their son-in-law was really too good to be digging ditches for farmers in the country.

During the whole morning following the wedding, Fru Blomberg had been very distracted and could hardly find any peace of mind when the guests had left. She accompanied her brother-in-law to the station and then looked in on the newlyweds. She found them at a late breakfast in an atmosphere that was anything but pleasant. Per was flustered and Inger pale, silent, and resentful. Fru Blomberg pretended that she didn't notice anything. She guessed what had happened and smiled a little to herself—it was, for her, as if she were reliving her own morning twenty-two years ago. She drank some coffee with the young couple and spoke of the party and the party guests. Afterward, she and Inger went into the kitchen and dining room to set a little order to the place. Per went into his own room and stayed there during the rest of his mother-in-law's visit. He sat there with his hand under his cheek and looked out over the fields. He well knew that no great unhappiness had taken place. He did not doubt that Inger's inhibitions would gradually disappear. But he still felt seriously disappointed and let down. What should have been the most solemn memory of his life had become an incident before which his thoughts would always turn away with shame and distaste.

He remembered another "wedding night"—with Jakobe— and he could not refrain from comparing them. But, suddenly, something uncanny stirred deep inside him. He felt as if a poison snake had bitten his heart. Was he himself to blame? Was it again necessary for him to do penance for his past?

CHAPTER 26

PER WAS NOT altogether happy in the early days of his marriage. His hopes of awakening Inger to a more independent spiritual life did not materialize. With her balanced nature, wholly suited to the practical world, and with her conviction that her father was Christianity's last great apostle, she could not even understand his desire to persuade her. And like her father, she considered his obsession with Pastor Fjaltring the result of a youthful need for rebellion and the wish to make himself interesting.

Undeniably, he was living a double life. The conflicting influences he was exposed to gradually rendered his feelings in relation to himself so confusing that he sometimes had the sense he was making a really disturbing impression on others. He noticed this himself and looked anxiously for solid ground. He found it where he had before, in that side of him turned to the natural world, and it was Inger who led him there. She was very pregnant at this time and, like so many mothers, was thinking of nothing but the imminent birth, and the preparations for it. She was no less composed, however, and that calmness and strength of soul with which, for all her youthfulness, she went about awaiting her hour, filled Per with wonder and gave him much to think about.

Then, the excitement of the delivery night, the fuss over Inger and the baby, Inger's week of recovery, his joy at being a father, and his newly awakened and sturdy sense of responsibility—all that planted him again on solid ground.

Still, he was unable to keep himself from the Borup parsonage. The large, darkened study with the carpet runner and desk between the two low windows had a peculiar magic power over him. But he stole off there with a bad conscience like a drunkard to the public house, and his visits became more rare until a terrible incident that was talked about for a long time in the district abruptly terminated them.

One day in the fall, a general alarm spread through the populace at the rumor that Pastor Fjaltring had disappeared. He had lost his wife six months before, but instead of feeling that as a deliverance, he became more and more anxious and secluded. Since he was missing, everyone immediately suspected a tragedy. Per moved to lead the search. He sent one group out to inspect the woods and others to the river and bogs. Finally, the pastor

was found in his own attic, where he had hanged himself in a
large, empty wardrobe.

Per had been, really, the only one Pastor Fjaltring was glad to
see in the last years, and with him he had expressed himself candidly. Just a few days before his disappearance, Per had spent several hours with him, and on that occasion he marveled at the
apparent calm and composure with which the pastor talked about
his loneliness. He joked about his bodily ailments and said we
should be grateful for our pains; they cleared the mind. And he
had obliged Per with a humorous story about how he had once
had such a breakdown from sinking so deep into thoughts over
the mystery of original sin that he had been on the verge of losing
his mind: "But a gracious draft granted me a terrible toothache,
a really good and blessed martyred molar—and devil if that didn't
chase away both original sin and other satanic nonsense, so that
I would gladly have traded my baptismal certificate for a good
bag of medicinal herbs."

Now that he was gone and, by his dismal death, had testified
to his defective life force and philosophy, Per had a sensation of
a lucky escape from danger, similar to what he had felt upon
receiving the news of Lieutenant Hansen Iversen's suicide.
Fjaltring, by his own feverish hand, had been led into a dark,
empty, and wild realm of the spirit world whose disappointing
mirages and deceptive hallucinations had lured him on into the
distant wilderness.

Nevertheless, Per would always remember the unhappy and
lonely man with gratitude and love. Even in his death he was a
teacher and a liberator. It vexed him to witness the gloating sympathy that manifested itself among the citizens who sat comfortably protected by their own lack of passion and had never felt a
titanic urge to struggle with the gods. Especially irritating was his
father-in-law, with his patronizing headshakes: "Well, it had to
end that way. It was almost predictable. What else should it lead
to when a man can no longer reach an understanding with himself? I have always been sincerely sorry for him, the poor man."
A sharp answer burned on Per's tongue, but, as so often before,
he suppressed it for Inger's sake and kept silent.

A year passed, another, then three, and all went by with the characteristic swiftness of time in the country, where the single day
creeps slowly away, but the years fly. In the little cottage idyll at

the foot of a green hill, three children were playing, a five-year-old boy and two small girls—genuine Sideniuses, with light, blue eyes and brown curls. The great river regulation project had long since been successfully completed, and Per had often talked about moving somewhere else; but Inger would not leave the district. She loved her new home as she had loved her old one and took pride in making it a model of comfort and order.

Per himself did not have the courage to break away from his accustomed life. The days slid by so peacefully here, the children were thriving, and Inger was so touchingly glad and grateful because she was permitted to live in the neighborhood of her parents and old friends. Outside his own home, he always felt like a stranger in the district. On the other hand, his own little world with his home and garden had grown so dear to his heart that it seldom took any lengthy persuasion to make him abandon the thought of moving elsewhere. In addition, he had sufficient work in the district with his surveying activity and lesser road and bridge jobs to give him a good living. Finally, he had become free from debt.

But his invention had not come along. He felt less and less desire to work on it, and his capabilities seemed to have disappeared as well. In any case, his formerly ingenious mind had become dry, and now he definitively shelved the project. Up on the hill behind the house where he had once thought his experimental mill would rise, there was now only a lookout bench, and there he often sat together with Inger, watching the sunset and chatting about the day's events, while the children played around them in the grass.

It was most often Inger who led the conversation. Once a big talker, Per had, with the years, become reserved. But sometimes, especially with the children, he could become almost cheerful. His moods changed so frequently and with such unpredictability that at times Inger became alarmed. Even in the best moments, when they sat talking intimately to each other, he would become silent and distracted, as if his thoughts had been caught by something he didn't want to discuss. This withdrawal could last hours or days, and then it was necessary to let him be on his own and not bother him with questions.

In the first year of their marriage, Inger had, like her parents, considered that lack of equanimity the fruit of his friendship with Pastor Fjaltring. Later, she thought it was the unfortunate "invention" that troubled him. When he had still been working on it, he had always been dissatisfied, could never be at peace, and steadily complained that the housecleaning and window washing were chasing him from his room just when he was in the best frame of mind. So it was partly her fault that he finally let the project go. Now she was more inclined to connect his unpredictability to his bodily ills that broke out periodically with the same symptoms and made him sensitive and peevish. He himself had no other explanation.

It was autumn again. In the garden, berries were ripening, and Inger was cooking and preserving them. One day, in the middle of September, she was sitting on a bench under the big walnut tree in the garden where she liked to pass an hour in the afternoon while the children, under the eye of the servant girl, were allowed to play in the field. Her rage for order allowed her a little time out in the day, but that hour was devoted to reflection on her housewifely projects and problems. She had snapped on a large apron and was holding an earthenware bowl full of dark, red cherries on her lap. At her side, she had an empty bowl in which she was putting cherry after cherry when she had pitted them with a needle. As with everything she undertook, there was something charming in the way she went about her task while the luscious red juice dripped from her white fingers. In the trees above her head, the first signs of fall appeared, and a dead, faded leaf peeped out here and there among the green. She herself was in the season of high summer, ripe, voluptuous, a little matronly even, for her young twenty-seven years. The physical weakness that had hampered her development in her adolescence had disappeared with marriage. She felt thoroughly sound and had, in all pride and happiness, been able to nurse her children by herself. In fact, she was happy in her marriage, though in a way different from what she had imagined. Despite the fickleness of his moods, Per was both an affectionate and responsible husband, but he was not the gallant knight she had dreamt of. Sometimes she wondered why she was as fond of him as she was. When she bore with his moods, it was because they called out her motherly instincts. During his continually recurring attacks of dark depression that had become more frequent and protracted through the years, she thought of him as a sick man who shouldn't be judged. And she well knew how much he himself was suffering.

One of his difficult periods was just coming on. The day

before, the family had celebrated little Hagbarth's birthday, and Per was still in his pleasantest mood late in the morning. He had gone out early to pluck some wild flowers to decorate the house, and when the children got up, he went with them to play hide-and-seek in the garden. The children were thrilled, and Inger, at the bedroom window, was amused to see him creep on all fours behind the bushes. The mail came, and they stopped playing. When she came into his room an hour later, she immediately saw that he was no longer the same. He sat by the window with a newspaper in his lap, and those deep shadows she knew so well showed up under his eyes. At the festively laid dinner table, to the surprise and disappointment of the children, he hardly said a word. At coffee, the grandparents came to say happy birthday; he had seized on the pretext of a piece of business to leave and didn't return until supper.

There was something in the abruptness and harshness with which these heavy moods descended upon him that had lately, in an eerie way, reminded her of the late master of the royal hunt. In him, as well, the mind's vulnerability was connected to his bodily weakness and even, perhaps, with the cancer that caused his death. She had promised herself that, when she had the opportunity, she would talk seriously to the doctor about it.

She was startled out of her thoughts by a happy shout from the hill. It was little Hagbarth and the oldest of his sisters, Ingeborg, who had crawled up to the top to look out for their father and now had spotted him and his horse on the road. Inger got up with her bowl to tell the servant girl to set out Per's meal. In order not to transgress the house's customs, Per had ruled that he shouldn't be waited for when he wasn't home at the usual mealtime. Inger had personally set aside his portion of sweet porridge, home-brewed beer, and mashed potatoes with smoked eel, but she didn't spoon it out. Per had been gone since the early morning with only a couple of sandwiches in his pocket, and she knew that after a daylong outing in the fresh air, he would return with the hunger of a wolf. It was again, like the master, whose depressions never seemed to affect his appetite.

Now Per was in the yard with the dun, surrounded by the children, hens, and servant girl, and, shortly after, the outdoor servant. The youngest child stretched out from the arms of the servant girl to get a kiss, and the two eldest children had already crawled up over the wheel into the gig and were playing with the whip. Inger stood at the open kitchen window and observed the scene with motherly rapture.

Per freed himself a bit roughly from the children's eager arms and got down from his gig while he gave the servant instructions about the horse. Though he too had filled out in the last years, he didn't have Inger's healthy color, and the big, rather untamed beard made him seem older than he was. At the dining room table, without thinking what he was eating and just as he was finishing the first mouthful, he asked, "Has anyone been here today?"

"No, I have been all alone," answered Inger, who had seated herself at the table with her knitting in order to have a conversation with Per.

"Did anything come in the mail?"

"No, only the newspaper."

"Anything interesting in it?"

"I don't really know. I haven't read it." A short pause followed.

"Didn't you read the paper yesterday either?" he asked, somewhat hesitantly.

"Yesterday? I don't think so. Was there something in it?"

"Well, no—just another account of the discussions at the engineers' convention in Aarhus."

"You should certainly have taken part in the meeting, Per, since it interests you."

"What would I do there? I don't know anyone, and, in addition, I'm not really an engineer."

"Don't surveyors go too?"

"I don't think so."

"But what they are discussing interests you, nevertheless."

"Well, yes, here and there."

"What's in the article you mentioned?"

"Only an account of a West Jutland canal and free port project with Hjerting Bay at the base. The papers call it the Steiner Project. But you'll remember, it is the same idea that I myself once had."

"Wasn't that what you wrote about in your book?"

"Yes, that was it."

"And now there's talk that the plan will be carried out?"

"I don't think so. The Copenhagen free port project is now an established thing. The other was competing with it."

"But isn't it wonderful that it is still talked about?"

"Oh, well, the local Jutland patriots must make themselves heard now and then. And it is advantageous for Herr Steiner that these discussions are going on. He is doing what he can to blow some life into them. It seems he was the object of impressive ovations at the meeting. At a previous dinner—champagne had probably flowed freely—he was called, in a toast, 'Denmark's Lesseps.' Do you have any more porridge?"

"No, I'm sorry. Would you like more to eat? There's plenty left of the second course."

"Well, that's fine."

"Don't get too full. Remember, we are going to the apothecary's this evening." Per made a grimace of annoyance.

"That's right. I had forgotten. Listen—shouldn't we soon begin to say no to the invitations? We never enjoy those kinds of parties."

"Well, they certainly aren't amusing. And I would really like to stay home, but we can't keep offending people—for Father's sake, at the very least. He wouldn't like that, and surely people think we already are more secluded than we should be." Per didn't answer that. He went on eating in silence.

Afterward, they were drinking coffee that had been brought to his room in the meantime. That room lay on the other side of the hall and was rather narrow and dark, with a gable window open to the fields and a hidden door that led into the bedroom. Per's original large, sunny workroom had been given over to the children as the family grew larger. And, really, he felt just as comfortable in this modest, still place that reminded him of his lodgings in Frederiksberg and Nyboder. He didn't always appreciate it when Inger sought to liven it up a little with some fresh flowers or a couple of potted plants. He didn't really like the scent, and nature's bright colors did not, in fact, complement the moods he felt most at home with. The one piece of art in the room was a large marble head that had been put up on the bookcase and just fit under the low ceiling. It was a sculpture of a young, handsome man with curly hair, a broad, strong forehead, and a full mouth that, like the classical busts, was a bit open to heighten the impression of life. His head was turned sharply to the side, which emphasized the telling play of muscles of a strong boxer's neck. A deep furrow on his forehead, cutting through his joined brows, suggested, as well, a strong will. The commanding glance and light smile hinted at extreme courage and youthful power.

This was the idealizing bust of the young Per that the baroness had commissioned during his stay in Rome. The master's wife, who had felt obliged to honor her sister's wishes, sent it on her behalf to Inger as a wedding present. But Inger found the bust detestable in every sense and wanted to put it in the attic. For a while it was allowed to occupy a corner of the dining room where it couldn't be seen until, one day, Per thought of taking it into his own room. In spite of Inger's insistence that it was not proper to have one's own portrait in one's room, he had not gotten rid of it.

While it was growing dark inside as well as out, they talked about the children and domestic matters from opposite ends of his room. Per was seated at the window with his coffee cup and had lit a cigar. It was always Inger who led the conversation as she tended to her knitting. Among other things, she talked about how little Hagbarth, all by himself, had found a way to make a doll carriage out of an old wooden shoe for his sister. He always had so many inventive ideas, that boy. And he had a pair of hands on him that could overcome any difficulty.

Per was attentive. "Yes, he is clever," he said, mostly as if to himself, and fell into his own thoughts. Inger twirled her yarn around her bobbin and went into the bedroom to get dressed for the party. As soon as she left, Per reached out to his worktable to take up a folded newspaper that lay hidden under some books and drafts, but when he heard her returning, he quickly drew back his hand and began looking at the red evening clouds.

The apothecary Møller was Rimalt's greatest taxpayer. He made it a point of honor to remind his guests that when they were invited to his party, he was showing that he well knew the obligation of a prosperous man to his less-fortunate fellow citizens. When the company had gathered, around seven o'clock, they were led to a table with three glasses at each place setting and fresh-baked rolls in napkins. The host had the satisfaction of hearing voices loudly confirm that his table was without doubt the best in the whole district.

That the dinner was not prepared by a master chef, and that the content of the wine bottles in no way lived up to their distinguished labels, took nothing away from everyone's enjoyment.

These were not people with fastidious palates. They judged the dishes by their number, were intoxicated at the sight of such superabundance, and mindlessly concentrated on the problem of gorging themselves as much as possible.

In this manner, the apothecary emphasized his calling as a splendid host while he liberally plied his guests with food and drink. His voice was constantly heard through the clink of forks: "Ladies and gentlemen! You really must do justice to the stuffed pigeon! Herr Stationmaster! I hope the Château Beychevelle pleases you. Ladies! The Sauterne is your wine. Enjoy it! Herr Sidenius! Has your glass offended you? You aren't drinking! May I have the honor? Gentlemen! The London Club 1879 that is being poured out should be drunk with reverence. I ask you to taste it and tell me your opinion."

The gentlemen emptied their glasses, contentedly smacked their lips, and expressed sincerely meant praise. "What I would call a good middle-course wine," exclaimed the veterinarian. "It tastes excellent on the tongue," the stationmaster said, with the look of a connoisseur. "Nectar!" proclaimed the new commercial school administrator, who rose at that moment to toast the host. That man was the six-foot-tall Balling with his lion mane whom Per had met at Philip Salomon's house. In the last years, he had had good luck on his side. After everything went wrong for him in the capital, he had sought consolation in the provinces, and quickly found there the appreciation he had sought for so long and with such ardor. Inger's friend, the outspoken and voluptuous Gerda with the warm eyes, the eldest daughter of the councilor and land agent Clausen, had immediately fallen in love with him. The wedding had been celebrated two weeks before.

Rimalt society had gained another addition. Five miles from the station, in the opposite direction from Bøstrup, Borup, and Kærsholm, lay an estate called Budderuplund. The owner, Councilor Brück, was an elderly man of an old landed Holstein family. He was very well off and had an only son who had spent some years abroad for his education but now had come home to take over the running of the large property. The son was a handsome, strong man of about thirty, but with a somewhat reticent manner, probably because he stuttered.

Per had immediately felt drawn to him, despite the fact that their circles and interests were very different. Herr Brück was an eager hunter and horse trainer and had his natural associations among the landowners. Per still hoped to be able to have a real friendship with him, and it therefore vexed him to notice that the feeling wasn't mutual. At the same time, he realized that a strong interest in Inger had attracted Herr Brück into this circle where he really didn't feel at home. The two had known each other from childhood, but Inger couldn't stand him and betrayed this, from time to time, in an almost rude manner. She couldn't give any clear reason for her aversion. To Per's repeated question about it, she always answered the same thing: namely, that even as a boy he had always been distasteful to her.

Per observed that Herr Brück, who was sitting diagonally across the table from her, had not been successful in starting up a conversation with her. Inger responded to his attempts with one or another indifferent platitude and looked away. After the meal, the party split up in the usual provincial way, the ladies to the living room and the gentlemen to an office room where they gathered to smoke and chat with looser reins. Here they felt comfortably emancipated from the constraints of the rest of the company, told indecent stories, drank liqueurs, brought up belches, and dozed off.

From where Per was sitting, he could see what was going on in the living room. The ladies were sitting at a coffee table under a suspended lamp with a dark red shade that cast a fiery glow over them as they crocheted or embroidered. Words were passing freely between them, and it was not difficult to guess what the talk was about. Only domestic affairs and the problem of servants could generate such a lively discussion. Even Inger, in spite of all her outer calm, was flushed with excitement.

Per, who had already been depressed, bit his lips at this sight. On many occasions, he could be proud of his wife; she was head and shoulders above her friends in the women's circle, not only for her beauty, but also because of her natural tact and taste. But he grew greatly out of sorts when he saw her sitting so comfortably in such company. Although she would insist to the contrary, in fact she felt fully at home with these kinds of people. Only when the group stepped over the bounds of respectability did she draw back.

She did not allow herself to become infected by the sometimes rather free tone used by the Rimalt ladies when they were sitting alone. The propriety in manner and thought that had marked her already as a girl closed her mature eyes and ears to everything that offended her womanly sensitivity. She had something of the Blomberg pharisaism. What she did not want to know, she did not hear. What was uncomfortable to believe, she did not believe. Thus, she could be friends with the wives of both the apothecary and the stationmaster in spite of the fact that it was an open secret that the first woman was the sweetheart of the second man and both were in love with the new administrator, Balling. And she could also borrow her father's saying about "the reprobate and ungodly life in the capital" despite the fact that the life around her was such a laughable caricature of *that* life that it couldn't conceal those most unpleasant things going on in both the seemingly idyllic farmhouses and in the pitiable huts of the cottiers.

The time dragged on to ten o'clock, when dessert was brought in. Pale and red-eyed from sleepiness, the good ladies around the coffee table made no effort to be on their best behavior. Several of them yawned unapologetically behind their housewifely hands. Even Inger's eyelids had become heavy. The hostess and the stationmaster's wife displayed an obvious nervous unrest; Director Balling had drawn back with his young wife to an empty private room where only a weak hanging lamp was burning. In vain they had been called back for dessert no less than four times, and when they finally came, Gerda appeared with flushed cheeks and disheveled hair.

Shortly after, the party broke up. The company went home in groups through the moonlit town, but they collected at each garden gate to say a more thorough farewell. Inger walked a bit behind the others with the doctor, a middle-aged, sound, and sensible man who had known her from her childhood. They were talking seriously about Per. "Did you notice, Doctor, how unusually silent my husband was this evening?"

"Well, now that you mention it. Is there something wrong with him?"

"I don't think so. But, well, I must tell you how it is. You know, my husband's spirits tend to sink. I really have been a bit anxious, lately, about him. Do you think he could have one or another hidden disease?"

The doctor pondered and said, "I'm glad you yourself are asking me. I was just thinking that I should surely talk to you about it." Inger became quite alarmed at the doctor's serious tone and stopped.

"Doctor!" she almost shouted, and grabbed his arm.

"Now, dear, don't be frightened. It's not so bad. Your husband is just a bit nervous. These attacks of weakness and side stitches that he complains about can be, perhaps, unpleasant. But there is certainly no reason to worry so much."

"Well, what is it, Doctor? You're mumbling so strangely into your beard."

"Yes, well, I think—it's difficult to say this—do you think your husband has too little to occupy him?"

"But he is out almost every day from morning till evening. You know that."

"Yes, but is it work that really interests him? In any case, I think that he needs a greater, more extensive kind of activity that doesn't leave him so much time to think about himself."

"I sometimes have thought that," said Inger after a little pause. "But there aren't any prospects here in the district."

"No, unfortunately, there aren't."

"We would have to move to a city—perhaps Copenhagen."

"You well might. And it would be a great loss for us who stay behind, but I don't want to be considered a bad counselor."

"I myself have been thinking of this, you know," said Inger. "But I am convinced that it is the best thing for my husband to live peacefully in the country. He himself thinks so, too. With the many concerns he has in relation to his health, he could hardly manage any more strenuous work."

"I'm not sure you are judging your husband correctly on that score. Despite all his minor infirmities, he has a naturally strong constitution that needs something more demanding to exercise it. Well, now that I've begun, let me suggest this. I know your uncle in Fiume has invited your husband, a couple of times, to come to work in his shipyard. Could you think of moving down to the much-celebrated Adriatic coast?"

"And be burned out by robbers?"

"Well, the place is a little unsafe. But the climate would suit your husband perfectly. The sun, the warm air he needs. I am convinced that a few years in the Italian climate would do wonders." Inger remained silent and instinctively drew back a little from him, without looking up. Shortly after, they stopped in front of the doctor's house, where the rest of the company had already been waiting to say goodnight to him.

Since Per and Inger had the farthest to go home, they had to take part in the whole series of farewell scenes. Inger had quietly put her arm under Per's, and when they were finally alone, they pressed together with the powerful longing that might have been dammed up in them from an evening spent among strangers. Inger yearningly laid her head on Per's shoulder, and in this way they went slowly home in the still, clear, moonlight, stopping, finally, in the middle of the road to exchange a kiss that promised more.

But when they got home, Inger, unfortunately, felt compelled to see to a domestic affair in the kitchen. She happened to remember some cucumbers that the kitchen maid was to pickle, and her sense of order would not leave her in peace before she had assured herself that her directions had been followed. Then she looked into the children's room to inquire of the servant girl how things had gone.

"Can you believe Ingeborg has a tummy ache again," she said when she came back to Per's room. Having, in the meantime, turned on his lamp, Per was sitting at his worktable with a book, pretending to be reading.

"Too bad," he simply said, and turned a page. She knew that tone, and she saw that he had just lit up a new cigar.

"Are you going to stay up?" she asked.

"Yes, I'm not sleepy."

She made no attempt to change his mind, because she knew how fruitless it was to try to influence his moods. Altogether calm, both too proud and too modest to betray her disappointment, she went up to him, brushed his hair off his forehead, and kissed him on the temple. "Goodnight, dear," she said. "Goodnight," he answered, without moving.

Shortly after she had gone, he pushed his book away and, supporting his head with his hand, he stared into the sputtering lamp. When he heard her going to bed, he took up the folded newspaper he had hidden under the books and drafts and spread it out in front of him on the table. It was the previous day's edition of one of Jutland's larger, provincial papers with an account of the engineers' meeting in Aarhus. His eye went immediately to a place in the second column:

The major discussion of the afternoon's meeting centered on the famous Steiner harbor project that our readers know about from the various reports in this paper. This topic attracted special interest because it was presented by the plan's designer himself, who both at his appearance behind the lectern and at the close of his instructive lecture was rewarded with enthusiastic applause.

The veins in Per's temples throbbed as he read this. It had, in the last years, been almost impossible to take up a provincial paper without coming upon Herr Steiner's name. He was on the way to becoming a kind of national Jutland hero. He was on the go everywhere, gave lectures, let himself be interviewed by journalists, and was setting in motion a systematic glorification of himself and his mission.

A dew-soaked branch scraped softly against the windowpane. In the living room on the other side of the hall, the clock started to strike twelve. He pressed his hand on his eyes and sat for a long time without moving. That Sidenian legacy—it was the curse of his life. Was it really any better or less ignominious to sit here, helpless and rotting, slowly dwindling from a castrated hunger for life than to shoot a bullet through the head from exhaustion and disgust like Lieutenant Hansen Iversen and Neergaard? His life was wasted, his strength dissipated. He was like a clock whose insides had been carefully removed, piece by piece.

Slowly, and with some apprehension, he looked at the marble bust glimmering on the top of the bookcase under the ceiling of the half-lit room. At one time he had wanted to annihilate it, but lately he viewed it often with an almost reverential expression. He had begun to fall in love with his own youth, and was no longer bothered by how naive he had been, how impudent and conceited a fellow, a fool in many respects, in others a good-for-nothing, and, in all, a soulless human being. Nevertheless, the music of life had sung in his blood then, and echoed in his dreams. Now his heart and mind were a silent wilderness. Only a single instrument, playing discordantly, remained from the large orchestra.

Those who were alone and abandoned, who were freezing in life's shadows, were to be pitied. Nevertheless, just the consciousness of being abused and cast off could become a great consolation in distress. He had always been able to warm himself at the fire of hope or anger. But he had never been as pitiable as he who, in the middle of sunshine, is chilled by the coldness of death and the grave, who sits at a high table in front of a royal dinner only to stay ravaged by hunger, who daily sees all his longing and dreams lived out around him while he is forced to flee the scene. But just this was to be his precise fate.

In return, he had the peace of home and hearth; three bushels of earth were his share of the world he wanted to conquer in the happy arrogance of his youth: Inger's love, the children's joy, the calm and comfort of home. This was compensation for what he had lost. In a certain sense, he had not even been injured. And Inger was too innocent to know or understand anything about his sense of privation. Was that so surprising? He himself did not understand his overwhelming sense of impotence. That he loved his little home, that it would be hard for Inger to live far from her childhood surroundings, that, in the course of the years, he had become a creature of habit, all this did not explain the witchcraft by which this patch of earth held him in spite of all his frequently oppressive loneliness. The fear that he couldn't take care of his family in another place was not what kept him back. In addition to the invitation of Inger's uncle, he had refused various other very tempting offers and even had a patron in an administrative officer who had found his river re-regulation project very interesting and, unsolicited, had, many times, offered to recommend him to his friends, the minister of the interior and the director of hydraulic engineering. Least of all was it the question of his health that troubled him. When he paid attention to it, it was mostly for the sake of Inger and the children. The fear of death that had, in his youth, scared the marrow out of his bones as soon as he felt ill had been entirely overcome. Now, instead, at burials, he looked enviously at the casket disappearing into the darkness of the earth, and there were times when no noise sounded more inviting than the dull, thudding tones of three shovels of earth falling on the casket cover—an echo from the realm of the dead, the comforting answer and assurance of Nothing.

Now and then, he had asked himself whether it wouldn't be best for Inger if he died. She was still so young and pretty. Probably, she would marry again, and then she could really come into full happiness. He often thought that there might be something in her aversion to the young landowner Brück that was hiding an instinctive, unconscious fear of his manly beauty and strength. There was so much in Inger that was still asleep and that *he* did not have the patience or, perhaps, even the ability to awaken.

* * *

A few days later, the couple was having coffee in Per's room, Inger sitting in the sofa corner with some sewing and Per at the window with a cigar. After a time in which neither spoke, Inger asked, "Should I leave?"

"No, why?"

"You look as if you want to be alone."

"Not at all. I'm happy you're sitting here with me."

"There's also something serious I'd like to talk over with you."

"What's that?

"Well, I've been thinking that it might be best for us to move from here before we are actually forced to. You yourself have said that our earnings are dwindling lately. And in the long run, it's impossible that there would be enough work for you here."

Per looked at her in surprise. "How is it you came upon that thought just now?"

"Oh, we have so often talked about it."

"Yes, we have. But why does it occur to you at this time?" His eyes rested suspiciously on her. She was bent over her sewing and didn't look up. What had happened? He started to remember how strangely quiet she had been lately, especially since the apothecary's party. Had she become wary of her fear of Herr Brück?

"When do you think we should move?"

"I don't know. But an administrative officer has promised to help you find a post."

"He was thinking mainly of one or another situation in the Copenhagen administration. He knows the minister of the interior. But you might not want to go to Copenhagen."

"In this matter, I would do whatever you think best. I was just reproaching myself that perhaps I have been holding you back too much. It was mostly for the children's sake. It seemed a pity to me that we might end up living up on the fourth floor where the children would feel as if they were in a cage. But now I think we can manage. We can stay in the summers with my parents and get all sound and browned. With God's help, we can make do with city air the rest of the year."

"And what about you, Inger?"

"Me?" She looked up with an open, innocent expression that released an oppressive weight from his heart. "Oh, don't worry about me. I'm strong now, and even if, in the beginning, we have to live in a bit of a circumscribed condition, because we'll surely have only a four-room apartment, we'll get used to it. I've been thinking we should give Laura notice. She isn't suited for city life and is too slow, as well. And then, it's better if, at least provisionally, we can manage with one girl. I myself can take the children out."

Per hardly heard her. He had laid aside his cigar. The blood throbbed in his veins, and he felt entirely flattened by the anxiety she had instilled in him.

"Only one thing worries me," said Inger in her calm way.

"What would that be?" asked Per. She waited a moment to speak.

"For a long time I've wanted to speak to you about this. But lately, you have been so inaccessible." To parry her, he said half jokingly, "Now you're being more like me. You seem to have been brooding so much lately. What is really on your mind?"

"I have wanted to ask you, Per, if you could make an effort to pay more attention to the children. I know, naturally, that you love them. But I can see, especially with Hagbarth, that they feel something is missing when you no longer busy yourself with them."

"What do you mean? Don't I engage myself with them?"

"Well, I know what you think. In certain moments, when you are in a good mood, you enjoy playing with them. But at other times, you reject them in a way they don't understand, and then they become unsure and intimidated. And now I'm afraid that you and the children will become estranged when we go to Copenhagen, where you will be even more away from home."

"But I don't really understand. I think, on the contrary, that I always—"

"Oh, perhaps you don't realize how much you are abstracted," interrupted Inger with a heavy sigh. "Naturally, you don't think about how clearly you signal the children that they are annoying to you. But for that feeling the children have a fine instinct, believe me. You ought, on your part, to pay a bit more attention to that. And since we are already talking about it, I'll tell you what Hagbarth said to me recently, the evening of his birthday, when you were gone for so long that he couldn't tell you goodnight. Sulking, with tears in his eyes, he said, 'I know Father doesn't really care about me.' I hope you don't resent my telling you this. And now, Per, if we go to Copenhagen or anywhere else in the world, I would like you to concern yourself more with Hagbarth, take him once in a while on a walk with you and chat about what you come upon. He is a very clever boy and so interested in everything that is happening around him. I well know how annoying all those childish questions can be, but you really have to be patient about them."

Per sat silent for a while. Then he stood up and walked back and forth over the floor, as he often did when something shook him up. Inger's words had frightened him.

Her thoughtful reproach had affected him more deeply than she could guess. She had stirred in him a remembrance of his own childhood he never talked of anymore.

Finally, he said, "In the morning, I'm going to Copenhagen, and this very evening I'm writing to the administrator to remind him of his promise. Are my clothes in order? Early in the morning, Laura should air out my dark suit, beat it soundly, as well as my dress coat, in case I have to see the minister. Are my boots presentable?"

Inger was altogether flustered. She was not used to such rash decisions. She asked him to take time to think through the question. There was no rush, and they ought, in any case, to first talk it over with her parents. But Per would hear nothing of it. He could conveniently get away now, he said, and besides, the question had been brought up often enough with her parents.

"Let's decide now. If we talk any longer about it, it will go the way it has before and we will never come to any solution. Oh, Inger, let's, for once, take hold of our fate. Do you know that I, myself, lately, have been turning over thoughts going in the same direction? Now I can tell you. You remember the engineer Steiner, the big humbug I talked to you about? It has really irritated me a lot that the cad has appropriated—right out stolen—my old ideas, and they have elevated him in the world. Think of it! He just got recognized in Aarhus, and now after overwhelming the provinces it is his intention to conquer Copenhagen. It was in the paper yesterday, and he has already been invited to a meeting in the next week or the one after. I could enjoy using the occasion to play a trick on the impudent boor and stand up at that meeting to calmly explain to the audience the history of the project. I have reason to believe that it would not be difficult for me to justify my claim to a Copenhagen public. It's well known there what a charlatan he is, and I think that among the engineers and the press there will be some, on that occasion, who still remember my booklet."

"Oh, why would you dig up that old story? You can't get any satisfaction from it."

"You don't think it's a good idea? Well—we shall see!" said Per, his hands behind his back, snapping his fingers.

"I think you should leave the past alone, Per. I don't know what you think can come out of this when you have waited so long to protest. But you won't do it, will you, dear?"

"What can come of it, you ask? Dear heart, I reserve my rights as the inventor, nothing more. I don't know what it might mean for our future."

"I am certain, Per, that you will only get yourself more aggravation. You yourself say that Herr Steiner is a coarse person who will spare no means to attack his attackers. And you aren't used to public performances, so—"

"I think the little woman already has stage fright for her husband," said Per cheerfully, and stopped in front of her with a smiling face. "Well, we'll see, we'll see. But where are the children? Where is Hagbarth?"

"He's out in the garden with the others."

"We'll have a nice game of hide-and-seek!"

"I think you should go on a little walk with Hagbarth, instead. He has been so idle. Why don't you take him out to Kristen Madsen's? They are running the new steam threshing machine these days. That will amuse him. He is so interested in that kind of thing."

"But there will be so many people looking at it."

"And just because of that, there's more for the boy to see. And if you can explain to him the way the machine works! He was so interested in it when it recently came by. But I couldn't give him any information about it."

"Yes, yes, I'll do that."

When he came back an hour later, he started to prepare immediately for the journey. But when he went to fetch the suitcase down from the attic, an invisible, ghostly hand held him back. It was an old, passing sensation. Another and greater anxiety drove him out into the world's turmoil. He felt as if he were standing at the last crossing on his life's track. If he didn't succeed now in running away from his depressed self, Rimalt would become his grave.

* * *

Per had been in Copenhagen only once since he had moved away more than six years ago from the city. A half year after his marriage, Inger and he had taken a pleasure trip there and stayed a couple of weeks; but already, then, he felt himself a stranger and ill at ease in the big capital. The noise in the streets, the clammy hotel beds, restaurant meals, tips, the large distances, the need to always be dressed up, wear gloves, and have one's hair done, which Inger certainly insisted on, made him, after a few days, long for home, for his small, quiet room and the unrestrained life of the country.

It wasn't much different this time. In the first days, he was a good deal preoccupied with the great expansion of the city in the last years. He went out immediately, the first mornings, to see the new harbor grounds, which were now being worked on. Later he viewed the newer parts of town and the whole or partly rebuilt quarters in the inner city of which he had read so much in the papers. But after his sightseeing ardor for all this was satisfied, he remained a helpless prey to the same provincial feeling of abandonment that had overcome him seventeen years ago when he had come here for the first time from his childhood home.

This was, as well, the city's most chaotic season, when summer and winter meet and call out a busier life both indoors and out. While the Tivoli shot off rockets in the evening over the city and brass orchestras blared in all the amusement gardens, the theaters were opened. Summer's German and Swedish guests still filled the cafés when the regulars gradually came back in from the country, extremely annoyed at seeing their sofa corners occupied by strangers.

Per felt alienated from all this liveliness, and his eyes and ears seemed to catch only noise and ghostly grins. While he looked at these busy throngs who swarmed into the streets, jumped in and out of streetcars, rolled through the city in open carriages, sat in restaurants as if in their own rooms, ate breakfast with a newspaper in their hands, or did business over a glass of beer and never seemed to reserve a quiet hour for reflection, it became clear to him that he had been mistaken to think that this kind of life would ever suit him. When he found himself in the middle of the crowd, a kind of missionary fever rose in him. He would suddenly be seized by an impulse to shout out to these people a warning: "Stop!"

Even after five days had passed he couldn't make himself seek out the interviews with the minister of the interior and the director of hydraulic construction. Every time he started to go, he was held back by an overwhelming perception that he was on the point of murdering the best part of himself.

"My dearest," he wrote to Inger, "I will tell you right off that I probably will come home without finishing my business here. The cause of that I can't explain well in a letter. I will merely say this: that every day that passes I feel more and more clearly that the situation here does not suit me a bit better than it did seven years ago. On the contrary; but dearest, let's not be despondent. There may be one place on earth I can call home, and I shall not tire of trying to find it. Nor do I consider my trip wasted. I have been decisively strengthened by that feeling deep in my nature that at one time, perhaps rashly, drove me from the capital. Because of it, I have found more coherence in my life and, in that alone, there is great satisfaction. It's not, as I sometimes have thought in weak moments, a blind chance that was my master. It is an inner power that I feel now has guided my life's ship, even when it seemed tossed by wind and waves. I have felt this before, and I now believe that when I merely allow that self-steering rudder to determine my constant course, I will land, at last, where I belong. You'll soon see me home again. Perhaps you are asking how the original intention of my trip has been relinquished so soon. And I have to confess that there is a certain feeling of shame that checks me. I left you with such great promises and come home so pitifully empty-handed. But I know you will be indulgent."

During his aimless rambling in the city, he happened, several times, to catch sight of old acquaintances from Philip Salomon's house. With a thumping heart his eyes followed, from the deck of a streetcar, his former friend and brother-in-law Ivan, who, as so often before, was scurrying busily off on his short legs with a briefcase under his arm. He caught sight, as well, of Aron Israel, Max Bernhardt, Hasselager, and Nathan, and it surprised him that they were all entirely unchanged. Then, too, while he was unrecognized, he came across many of his old fellow students from the Polytechnic Institute. They were now well-regarded men who had been placed in influential positions. He had carefully followed their progress in the newspapers. But now, when he saw them, he no longer envied them.

The one he was most eagerly and anxiously watching out for was Jakobe. He knew she was living in the city and had started up a charity school, a kind of asylum, written about in the papers. He had sought in vain in Jutland to learn more about that school and her goals. But in the provincial papers, there was not much more than that it was "a kind of provocative caprice of a rich Jew's daughter."

One afternoon, when he was sitting at a café window on the corner of Østergade and Kongens Nytorv, he saw Dyhring. He seemed remarkably unchanged, standing on the sidewalk talking to a young, pretty, elegantly dressed lady who looked like an actress and laughed continuously, a laugh teased out by his bold gaze. Every other well-dressed gentleman greeted him, and the ladies jabbed each other with their elbows. When he left the actress, he squeezed her hand warmly and got into an open carriage that had been waiting in the street. Hundreds of eyes followed him while he rolled over the sun-drenched marketplace, and his white silk hat could be seen constantly lifted as a greeting over his golden head.

Per remembered reading in a newspaper that Dyhring had recently returned from Paris, where, as a representative of the press, he had been specially invited to attend a dedication of one or another public institution, and, on that occasion, he had been presented to the president and had received a medal. He had become the public's self-appointed and indispensable ombudsman. Wherever there was something significant happening, he was there; or rather, only when *he* was there did the occasion have significance. All the doors stood open for him; all of life's both fine and coarse enjoyments came to him without charge. Men and women vied for his favor. Even the court, it was said, now and then used him in delicate diplomatic missions.

There was something of a world conqueror in that man for whom life was only a joke. Invincible in his divine, carefree nature, he made his days a series of happy parties, an uninterrupted procession of triumphs. And yet, Per did not envy even that modern Alexander. But where look for his real heart's desire? Where could he call home? In the previous day, he had, by chance, seen in a paper an official advertisement for a vacant post as a civil road inspector in one of the most outlying districts of the West Coast up near Aggertangen, and he had, since then, not been able to stop thinking about it. Once again, it came to mind.

It wasn't because he thought of applying for the post. Not only was the pay very bad, but Inger, who was, above all, in love with the peaceful, fertile, and cozy life, would never be able to thrive in that barren land of sand dunes where the North Sea storms and the salt-soaked, icy harbor fogs ceaselessly rushed in with oppressive harshness. The advertisement, nevertheless, continued to haunt him. The place had a special attraction for him personally, as he now realized, just *because* of its sterile and sad deserted nature, its full solitude. It seemed to him that he never had looked so deeply into himself as at that moment. It was as if he saw the ground of his own being uncovered and was staring at it. When, in spite of all the good fortune that had come his way, he wasn't happy, it was because he had not *wanted* to be happy in the general sense of the word. When he longed for home at Rimalt, it was not only Inger and the children, the peace of the hearth that drew him. The ghostly hand that had wanted to hold him back from this trip and that was the same that secretly seized him in all decisive moments through his whole life, to redirect his steps— that was his instinctive feeling that it was in solitude his soul felt at home, and in affliction and pain.

Feed me with the bread of tears and give me a full measure of tears to drink ... Now he understood the alluring and anxious power these strange words once had over him. The great happiness he had blindly sought was really great suffering, an incurable feeling of lack that Pastor Fjaltring so often had praised to him, calling it divine grace to the chosen. Per lifted his head and, as if awakening from a nightmare, looked around again on the sunlit square alive with its carriages and pedestrians. A little while afterward, he got up and went quietly out. He wandered aimlessly through the smaller streets and ended up in Ørstedspark. Here he had, in the past, taken regular early-morning strolls when other walkers were scarce. Now, at the city's dinner hour, it was again peaceful. Children and their nurses had gone home; the benches were empty. Long shadows spread out over the lawns and paths while the sun was still shining on the golden leaves and the verdigrised bronze statues.

He sat down on a bench by one of the central paths and, undisturbed, was drawing in the gravel with his walking stick when it occurred to him again that it would be a blessing for both Inger and the children if he died or, by some other means, slipped out of their lives. Perhaps especially for the children. He contemplated what Inger had previously said about Hagbarth. He himself had been noticing for a while something hidden in the boy's manner toward him. One day, when he had surprised him in an innocent chase after a bird out in the garden, the expression that came into the boy's eyes when he was discovered sent a deep shiver through him. It was as if he saw himself as a child standing before his father and, fearful and impudent, snatching at all possible abject excuses to cover up an offense. But Hagbarth's clean forehead must not be darkened by the mark of Cain; the father's curse that hovered over his life, making him a stranger and a wanderer over the face of the earth, must not be transmitted to his child. Oh, Inger! Now that he was fully conscious of his unconquerable inhibition in the face of life, how could he be responsible for letting her share his fate? Poor child! She still did not know her unhappiness. She still did not understand that she was bound to a changeling from the underworld blinded by light and killed by happiness. Should her eyes once be open to the love of another, she would close over the secret as over a deadly sin, wither and die without having, finally, even confessed it to herself.

He got up to go on farther when his glance fell on a statue that stood at the edge of the grass on the other side of the park. It was Silenus with the baby Dionysus in his arms. The old satyr was leaning against a tree with a naughty, wriggling boy, while his bearded face was shining from the peace, pride, and satisfaction of being a foster father.

Again Per sat down on the bench and remained staring at that happy statue until tears came to his eyes. He was thinking about how all might have been different for him if a face with a sunny smile like that had reflected delight over him as a child, if his life had not, from its earliest days on earth, been viewed with suspicion both at home and school. And most of all, if the two who had given him life had not consecrated him with a kiss from the mouth of a dead man. On the first day he saw the light, the grave's sign of the cross marked his forehead and breast.

CHAPTER 27

THE FOLLOWING DAY Per traveled home. He mentioned the vacant road inspector post to Inger so she could know he had looked even outside Copenhagen without finding anything that suited him—"since a position was impossible." So, while autumn glided over the country with all kinds of fickle weather, the days went by again in the old, monotonous groove. Per had some surveying work here and there, but had had no significant jobs for some time. Inger noticed a change in him. He had been touchingly happy to be home again. The first day he almost wouldn't let the children out of his hands and had brought every-one a gift. But there was something restless about him and, toward her, something reserved, almost shrinking, that was unlike him. He, who could sit by the hour at his window with a pipe or cigar and watch the procession of clouds in the sky, could not now find peace anywhere. She could hear him pacing back and forth in his room, as if travel fever were still in his bones. He complained of insomnia and every evening had his bed made on the couch in his room because he was disturbed by little Ingeborg, who had caught cold and coughed at night.

Inger kept her thoughts to herself. She was curious on many scores about his trip and its results. One of the reasons she was so reluctant to move to Copenhagen was that Per's former fiancée lived there. It was uncomfortable for her to think about it, that the two could meet again by chance. She imagined now that this had really happened and that Per himself had realized how disturbing that situation could be. She well understood why, in that case, he hadn't spoken more about the reason for his altered decision and why he must be feeling self-conscious in front of her.

But a way out had to be found. They could not go on living in Rimalt without falling into debt. She already had some unpaid bills that troubled her, but she had not wanted to talk about it yet to Per, who had, for the time being, enough worries, the poor man. Another reason for her anxiety was that she saw how con-cerned he was about their future, and it pained her that she couldn't help him with good advice.

One afternoon, a rider stopped in the yard and asked to speak to Per. Inger, who was busy down in the cellar and couldn't see the visitor from there, immediately recognized his voice. It was the young landowner Brück. Why was he here? she wondered, surprised and a little uneasy.

He was no less surprised not to find Per at home. When Inger came out instead and asked him in, he explained that her husband had made an appointment to see him here concerning some surveying work he had undertaken at Budderuplund. He had wished to compare his results with the old property map that Herr Brück had brought with him. Inger made many apologies and had to sit for a while and talk with him in the living room—a very unpleasant task, because, among other reasons, she had to iron some children's clothes and an iron was on the stove. She didn't know where Per was. He had been home for coffee and his gig was still in the gateway, so he couldn't be gone long. What bothered her in her intercourse with Herr Brück was, first and foremost, his stammer, which made all conversation with him difficult, all the more because he himself was so unhappy about his weakness. She had some pity for him, and might even have overcome her aversion to him if he did not also have eyes that were small and steel gray and, from childhood on, a masterful, almost brutal look that made her feel insecure. It was over half an hour before Per came. He made many, and it seemed to Inger, strangely awkward excuses. Then the two men went into Per's room.

Their examination lasted several hours, and Per invited Herr Brück to stay for supper. It was arranged that Per should go to Budderuplund when he could, to again assess the disputed boundary lines; he decided to do it already the next afternoon if the weather allowed good visibility, since he wanted to complete the work quickly.

"I might, if I remember, look in at the same time on your famous poultry breed. My wife has many times asked me about it. She takes a great deal of interest in that sort of thing."

It occurred to Herr Brück to ask Inger to come out to Budderuplund with her husband. "I think I can show you a breed of Cochins that you will envy."

Inger thanked him in the way thanks are given for an invitation you don't intend to accept, but when, the next day, from the bedroom window, she saw the gig taken out, she regretted her refusal. It was September's sunniest day, and she knew that the road to Budderuplund went through a couple of the district's most beautiful woods. She thought also that, perhaps, it would enliven Per if she accompanied him. And, finally, she had in mind the pleasure of seeing the old estate where, as a child, she had been a guest several times with her parents. If, in addition, she could barter a couple of her Plymouth Rocks for a couple of genuine Cochin hens, she would consider it a real coup. She opened the window and called out to Per, who was about to climb into the gig: "Can I come along?" She had the feeling that he didn't understand her right off, because he was staring at her with such a strange expression that she started to laugh. "Don't you understand, old man? I'd like to go with you!" He hardly nodded. The horse was again unharnessed and the gig exchanged for the pony chaise. The nicest harness was brought out, and in half an hour, they rode out of the yard.

The way went over the rails and climbed up from there gradually over the hill, giving a wide view of the river and fields. On the other side of the hill ridge, the ground sank down precipitously against a broad, wooded ravine whose multicolored sea of leaves shimmered in the sun. Soon the woods closed up around them, the road became soft and heavy, and Per let his horse go at a walking gait.

Per was silent the whole time. Inger, on the other hand, was lively and expressed her happiness at coming out by humming. She had been sitting so long at home, glum and moping. Here in the woods, she became exuberantly enchanted. How lovely it was: these gorgeous trees, these infinite colors! Just overhead, a single bird, which seemed to be following them, was twittering. She couldn't see the little creature, but she heard it constantly, now here, now there, while it teasingly repeated its "Look here, look there!" She breathed deeply and felt liberated from all that had oppressed and weighed on her mind. She wanted to sing, but remembering how depressed Per was, she contented herself with more humming.

Suddenly, she grabbed Per by the arm to make him stop. "Look," she whispered. She had seen something moving out of a thicket in front of them—a roe. With high, pointed ears and large, wide-open eyes, he stood there staring at them but ready to jump. Per kept still. The deer did not move from his spot, but stayed with his raised head and measured them somewhat defiantly with his glance. A couple of times he moved his ears and then stretched his neck out a little. Then suddenly, as if he were frightened of his own motion, he turned around and with a long leap ran back into the woods.

"Hello!" cried Inger spontaneously after him, but the sound of the rustling leaves and cracking twigs faded into the depths of the forest. The charms of nature were working on Per as well.

Some light came into his spirits. The touch of Inger's hand had spread through him like a shiver. The hope of life blazed up again, but it was a straw fire. A remark from Inger extinguished it precipitously: "It's a pity you aren't a hunter. That must be a fresh and delightful life. You should try it once. Wandering free and easy in the woods and fields would be good for your health, too, don't you think?"

"That certainly wouldn't work for me. You have to be brought up in that sort of thing. And in reality, I never was introduced into nature. That's why I feel a stranger in it."

"Who really owns the forest here?" asked Inger.

"It's part of Budderuplund."

"Think of it! The grounds extend all the way down to here."

"Yes, it's a large property. The councilor is a very rich man."

"That he is." Shortly after, they were out of the woods and a new view opened up in front of them over the wide meadowland to property on the other side. There was another forest and back of it, an even higher hill with a still wider outlook over fertile landscape. In the foreground on the hill's south slope was a large white building with two low towers and a stately park. That was Budderuplund. Inger looked at it for a while in silence. "The garden is so big," she said. "I didn't remember it."

"Yes, that would be a nice playground for Hagbarth," said Per with a strange sound like a little suppressed laugh. "It's getting difficult for him to find elbow room at home."

"What is that large building back there, the one with the high roof?"

"That's the granary, and behind that the stalls and dairy. Altogether modern in its arrangement and first class. To do the Germans justice, they do know how to put things in order."

"Do you think they will find it strange that I came along?"

Per held up the horse. He was willing to stop anytime. "We can turn around if you wish."

"No, I'm afraid they have already seen us. There's a gentleman up there coming along the avenue. Isn't it Thorvald Brück?"

"It looks like the young Herr Brück."

"Well, then, that's that. But remember, Per, that I'm terribly set on having those Chinese hens. You must promise me that we can go to the henhouse. The rest I can manage."

It was, in fact, Thorvald Brück who was coming up the old avenue of lime trees that led to the courtyard from the road. He had just caught sight of the little pony chaise and recognized the horse. When they drove through the gates, he was standing on the stone steps to greet them.

While a servant sprang forth to take the reins, Brück himself helped Inger out of the chaise and thanked her deferentially for coming. The councilor welcomed them in the garden room. He was a tall, stately gentleman with short clipped silver hair, a clean-shaven chin, thick brows, and an eagle nose. Despite his seventy-three years, he held himself as straight and courtly as his son. The old warrior's blood could be seen under his weatherbeaten skin. In his speech marked by a Holstein accent, he paid Inger compliments on her healthy appearance and asked about her parents. He treated Per, on the contrary, with some haughtiness. Wine and fruit were brought out, and a general conversation got under way.

At length, Per got up. "Yes, you go out to the boundary line," said the councilor. "My son has told me about your business. In the meantime, we'll take care of your wife."

"Fru Sidenius is interested in our breed of hens," Thorvald Brück inserted in a strong stutter. "I hope I may offer to accompany her. Perhaps it would give you pleasure on the way to refresh your old memories of Budderuplund."

Per went to the door, and Inger felt uneasy at being left alone with these strange gentlemen. She had a protest ready on her lips, but just then the councilor gave the servant an order to get the poultry roused.

Carrying his stock and measuring line, Per, with a few men, went along the ditch for an hour. He could scarcely concentrate on his work. The men looked at him often in some perplexity. He bitterly regretted now what he had been thinking. He had been mistaken. He had believed he was more finished with life than he really was. He couldn't and wouldn't give up yet.

In the meantime, Inger, together with the councilor and his son, went for a tour of the estate. They visited the stalls and the dairy, then the hen yard. Finally, the councilor led her into the kitchen and through the storerooms down to the historically famous cellar of the main building—the remains of a medieval castle on whose ground the new estate was erected.

When Per returned, all three were again in the garden room. The councilor, who seemed very taken with Inger, wanted them to stay for dinner. Inger looked questioningly at Per, who declined the invitation. In an almost offensive way, it seemed to Inger, he asked that the pony chaise be drawn up.

Thorvald Brück followed them on horseback part of the way. He rode a high, yellow, long-tailed mare that, obviously in honor of Inger, he allowed to caper under him so that her mouth was foaming. Inger tried to draw Per into a conversation, but without success. "Talk of hounds and horses bores me," he explained afterward. A little before the woods, the rider left them to turn into a side road that curved back to Budderuplund. He immediately went off in a short gallop, and when he was well on his way, Inger's eyes still followed him for some distance. "He looks so good on a horse," she said.

"He is from an old soldier-race. As far as I know, he could have been an officer himself if he had not had that tiresome stutter. It's really very painful to listen to him sometimes."

Inger was silent for a moment and looked straight ahead. "Yes, the poor man! But it didn't seem to me to be so bad today."

"Did you get the Chinese hens promised?" asked Per.

Inger blushed. She had forgotten to ask. "How annoying. I'm sure I could have gotten one or two pairs if I had only asked for them. The councilor was so excessively kind."

"Yes, that he was," said Per glumly. They arrived home as it was growing dark. Per complained of a headache and went into his room. He lit a pipe, sat by the window, but got up again right away, hung his pipe on a nail, and paced restlessly back and forth. He felt he was the most useless man on earth, an unfortunate half-man who loved life without daring to give himself to it and who despised it without being able to run away. There was a timorous knock on his door. It was Hagbarth, who was sent in to say goodnight. At the sight of the boy's uneasiness, tears filled Per's eyes. With a cry, he lifted him up to him and stood there for some time with his arms around him in the same position as the playful Silenus with the child Dionysus in Ørstedspark.

"You aren't afraid of Father, are you, little Hagbarth?"

"No-o-o," he hiccoughed.

"We two will get along fine together, don't you think?"

"Yes," Hagbarth said, and made himself heavy, to slide free. He felt, sometimes, more uncomfortable with the manifestation of his father's tender moods than with his sour ones.

One afternoon, a week later, Inger and Per drove to the Bøstrup parsonage, which they had not visited since Per's return from Copenhagen. Relations between Per and his father-in-law had, in the course of the years, developed into a hidden enmity that both sides held in check for Inger's sake. On this occasion, however, things fell apart. Pastor Blomberg was especially irritated by Per's general lack of attention to his words, and what fed his wife's hostility was the worsening economic condition in which her daughter had to live. That he now came home from Copenhagen without the slightest result did not soften her mood.

A couple of small clashes boded ill; they went into the living room after supper and into a heated confrontation. The agitated mental state in which Per lately found himself made him touchy and suspicious. When his father-in-law insensitively charged him with indifference toward procuring a more secure situation for himself and the family, Per was enraged and said he wanted no outside meddling in his affairs. His father-in-law reprimanded him for that outburst and especially for his tone, but that made Per lose control, jump up, bang on the table, and say in his father-in-law's face that he was no longer under *his* tutelage.

Such words had never before been heard in the Bøstrup parsonage. For about a minute, there was a deathly silence in the room. Then the pastor rose in all his diminutive majesty, pushed back his chair, and said, "I ask that you spare us this kind of scene in the future," wherewith he strode out of the room together with his wife, who, with a horrified expression, followed him into his study.

Per called for his carriage, and, shortly after, he and Inger rode away from the parsonage without saying goodbye. For a moment he had seen, as in a fog, Inger's ashen face on the other side of the table, and the sight had moved him to try to regain his composure. Since then, he hadn't dared to look at her, and during the whole drive, they didn't speak a word. But he noticed that, in spite of being well wrapped up, she was shivering so hard the seat of the carriage was shaking.

When they reached home, she became calmer. Not only did she allow him to help her off with her carriage coat, but she even asked him to hang it up for her on the coat hook. She went into the children's room to check up on them and then made her usual rounds of the house.

Per went into his own room and lit the lamp. When he put the chimney back on, he noticed he too was shaking. Sitting on his desk chair with a paper, he waited in anxious anticipation for what would happen. About ten minutes later, he heard Inger go into the bedroom, and, a few minutes after that, she come into his room, to his surprise, half undressed in her slip and dressing jacket. "You see, your bed is made up for you here," she said as she straightened his pillow. "That's how you want it?"

"Yes, thanks, that's fine," he answered from behind his paper.

"Ingeborg's cough is much better, by the way."

Per made no answer. Inger sat down in the rocking chair in the corner by the stove, and they were both silent for a while.

"Well, Per, now we must be serious about deciding to move."

"What do you mean?"

"You know very well. I realize now that what happened this evening was no accident, but has been gathering for a long time."

"I'm sorry for what happened, for your sake and for the children's. I should have controlled myself. But I can no longer think of going to Bøstrup and, perhaps, would not even be received there, and I hope that will not result in your being banned as well. It would be altogether unnatural for you, on account of this, to be estranged from your parents."

Inger sat bowed over with her head resting on one hand and looked at the floor.

"How you can wound without even knowing it! And you think that I can go to a place where you are excluded? And with the children?"

"It's your parents' home, Inger."

"Least of all there. But under these circumstances, staying here would be impossible for both of us. It will already be so difficult."

"Where do you think we should go?"

"You spoke recently of a post as a civil road inspector on the west coast. I think you should apply for that now, sooner today than tomorrow."

"Do you know what you are asking me to do? First of all the salary—I told you this—isn't even two thousand kroner, and there's no prospect for any incidental earnings in that neighborhood. As far as I know, it's one of Denmark's most barren districts, only dunes and heaths, and, in all directions, no inhabitants other than small farmers and fishermen."

"But we'll have each other," she said eagerly. "More, perhaps, even, than we do here ..."

"Dear Inger. You are so attached to your parents, your old

home, and the friends from your youth, and you so like to have it comfortable and lovely around you here. No, my dearest, it would be too great a sacrifice to ask of you. You would, with good reason, reproach me later if I took that post."

She held her face between her hands and sat motionless. "God grant I could know what you really want," she said, and burst into tears. In a sudden outburst, she sprang up and cried, "You torment me!" Without saying goodnight, she went into her room, slamming the door behind her.

Per stayed seated and stared at the closed door with a desolate look. He shuddered a few times and wanted to get up and go to her, but the ghostly hand held him back. "You must not do that! The hour of reckoning has come. Unhappiness is upon you. Her soul is about to awaken. And she is no underworld troll. She must be brought back to life and into the light." With him, it would go as it would.

The next evening, when the children had gone to bed and both servant girls were busy in the kitchen, after Inger had just lit the lamp in the living room and was sitting on the sofa mending the children's stockings, Per came in from his room. Though he had been home all day, they had exchanged only a few words since the previous evening. Inger had noticed how, in a strangely withdrawn manner, Per had circled around her and the children without wanting anything to do with them. After the dinner hour, when the children were resting, she had surprised him in the children's room, where he was standing over his sleeping son with an odd, bewildered face. Per paced the floor and, then, sat down across from her at the table. Neither of them was able to utter the first word.

Finally, Inger asked, "Have you thought over what we talked about last evening?"

"Yes, I have thought about nothing else. But before we take up the subject again, there is something we should be clear about. I mean, naturally, about what happened yesterday at your parents' house. You yourself said that the outburst wasn't just in response to the situation, and you are right about that. You realized that even if my words had been different, as would have been the case in a less agitated mood and moment, there was something more than a chance explosion in me."

"I have known that for a long time, Per."

"Yes, you said that yesterday, too. But, dearest Inger, if you have not been unaware of the deep difference of perspective that separates me from your father and his circle—and, in a certain sense, from you too—isn't it strange and even inexcusable that we haven't talked more about it to each other than we have? The fault is mine—I well know that. It's a kind of cowardice that has made me hide the full truth from you. But, in addition, *I* haven't understood the whole of it until now."

"You're wrong, Per. I well know your point of view. You have really never hidden it from me. Of course, I know you don't think in the same way we others do, and that has, naturally, often distressed me. But Father says that even he who sees only a noble and perfect man in Christ has the right to call himself a Christian and to harbor a hope for salvation if he is true in his relations with God and honest and upright in the whole of his life."

"But I don't believe in God!"

"You don't believe in God!" She let her mending fall to her lap and stared at him with the same white, stiff face she had had the evening before at the parsonage.

"Well, I haven't, to be sure, for a long time. Everywhere I looked for Him I only found myself. And for those who really know themselves well, God is superfluous. For him there is nothing either consoling or frightening in the representation of such a supernatural being that is thought of either as father or judge."

"How you talk! I think you will become, someday, a very unhappy man, Per."

"Perhaps. But do you know that there are those over whom unhappiness has a very tempting and alluring power in the same way bog hollows and dark forests have over solitary people?"

"Those must be the ones who are hardened in sin and who can only find happiness *in* sinning. That's what it says in the Bible."

"Does it? That's not the case for everyone. There are those who are drawn to unhappiness by their religious instinct that tells them that only through sorrow and privation—even, perhaps, total hopelessness—can they be emancipated as spiritual beings. There are also, you know, plants that thrive only in the cool shade and that still bear blossoms."

"I don't know those kinds of people."

"They're not so rare among us. Our history reveals that. It's in happy times we are most lacking in great men. On the other hand, our troubles can 'breed eagles out of sparrow eggs,' as Pastor Fjaltring once put it."

"Pastor Fjaltring! Is that who you are thinking of?"

"Yes."

"Well, I don't understand you at all! He hanged himself!"

"Yes, that he did, unfortunately. I have often missed him. And really, I never before now could explain to myself his sad ending. But lately, it seems to me, I have understood him better also in that regard. I see the reason for his despair in his relation with his wife. You, perhaps, remember I told you of his strange attitude toward that eccentric and totally ruined person. I now think that she originally might have had a nature entirely opposite to his, a rich, full-blooded one, made for sunshine and happiness, and that he had a guilty conscience because he had held her back in a shadow-life that was fruitful and emancipating for him but in which she was wasted. When she died, his conscientious scruples overwhelmed him. He blamed himself for murdering her soul and couldn't stand it. He outlived her only a short time."

"Why are you telling me all this?" asked Inger, looking at him suspiciously. "We were talking about something else entirely."

Per hesitated. "Because it seems to me, Inger, that that tragic marriage can serve as a lesson—and a warning—for us, too."

"For us?" Her mending dropped again into her lap. "For us? What do you mean?"

Per looked at the floor and didn't answer. His face suddenly became white, and Inger burst out with a short, spontaneous cry of anguish.

"Per! What has gotten into you! Have I done something you didn't like? Or the children? Tell me what is wrong!"

But Per couldn't say a word. Inger reached her hand across the table as a gesture of tenderness. "You are sick, dearest, and you don't know what you are saying. You are making everything in these last days so dreadfully heavy. And I, who just now have such a desire to be glad and to forget all our troubles. What is it now that is tormenting you? Is it our money affairs, dearest?"

"No."

"What is it, then?"

"It's something much, much worse, Inger."

"But say what it is!"

"I can't just like that!"

"Do you feel sick?"

"No."

Then a light illumined her face. "Will you honestly answer one question, then, Per?"

"Yes."

"When you were in Copenhagen, did you meet your former fiancée, Frøken Salomon?"

He looked up, surprised. "No."

She kept staring at him apprehensively. "You lie!" she said suddenly, and got up. Her mending was thrown on the table. "Now I understand everything!" With a heavy step she came forward: "You talked with your old love and are again enamored of her."

"But I'm telling you, you are mistaken!"

"Well, then, there's someone else! There's more in this than meets the eye. Now it is altogether clear. The whole of this conversation has been a disgusting masquerade. I should have been prepared. You want to divorce me and marry another. Isn't that the meaning? Say it right out!"

Per reflected a moment. It occurred to him that he might best help her by adopting her fantasy and confessing his guilt. Without an imperious reason, she would never think of a lawful separation; this might just serve his aim of bringing her to the point of hating and despising him. She would forget more easily. And since he had renounced so much, he could, at least, sacrifice his honor, too.

"Yes," he said, and bowed his head. Inger remained standing in the middle of the room. Her face was pale and her arms crossed on her breast. Her eyes were simply black pupils.

"And you have hidden this from me like a coward for nearly three weeks! And your insomnia, your headaches! I have to laugh when I think how concerned I was about you and how hard I tried to cheer you up. And you, meanwhile, were brooding and longing for another as you were figuring out how you could most easily leave us. Such a disgusting comedy! Such a mean and cowardly deceit!"

In the children's room, whose door was open, the youngest girl started to whimper, but Inger didn't hear it. She started pacing the floor again and was gradually talking more to herself than to Per. Only when the child began to scream did she go to her. Per got up, took his head between his hands, and groaned. Now he had done it. The sacrifice was made. And he promised himself to hold out to the end. Inger returned. After pacing again for a while, she stopped in front of him and asked, "Have you nothing to say to me? Tell me this isn't true!"

He shook his head: "No, Inger—what good would that do?" She remained standing, speechless. Then she turned away, sobbing, and went into the bedroom. "So cowardly, so mean!" he heard her say again as she slammed the door behind her.

Shortly after, he noticed agitation in the house. Doors were opened and shut, and he heard Inger give loud orders to the servant girls. The wooden shoes of the outside servant were clopping in the yard. The carriage house door was open and the carriage drawn up. She was already leaving this evening, he thought anxiously. Now the children were awakened. Ingeborg was crying, Hagbarth asked if there was a fire. Everywhere Inger's peremptory voice could be heard. One of the servant girls came running into the living room in a flurry in her stockings to look for something, but when she discovered Per, she turned around, terror-stricken. Then Inger, in full travel dress with her hat and coat, came in.

"If it's to be like this, Inger," he said, "let it be me who leaves. Or wait, at least, until morning." She didn't answer, and, standing in front of the escritoire, she took out her household money and some other small items.

"May I have permission to see the children?"

"Not this evening. You can see them at my parents' house from now on."

Half an hour later, the carriage rolled out of the yard. Per didn't move. When the last sound of the wheels grew dim on the road, he lifted his pale face from his hands and instinctively turned his eyes toward heaven: "Does that suffice?"

CHAPTER 28

ON THE WAY from Oddesund to Thisted you go by Ydby, with its many turbid ponds and puddles; then, if you go westward to the pretty little place called Vestervig, with the grave of Liden Kirsten, then further north, you get to a poor weathered country where even the sheep, at the height of summer, have trouble finding food. It is a terrain of swamp and dune, looking the same in winter and summer with only blue-green lyme grass, reddish horsetail, and heather to resist the salt sea wind. Impassable bog surfaces force the road to make wide bends, and, if there is, for a change, no wind, a thick snaky haze drives over the land as over a conflagration.

Here and there is a small farm or an isolated hut with a heather-thatched roof. But there are often several miles between the houses, and no real town. One place could pass as the start of a settlement. In a hollow where, on both sides of bog runoffs, a little meadow emerges, there are four houses, one of which is a school. In the second lives the steward of the meadowland and in the third, a shoemaker. The fourth is empty.

From this house, recently, the body of a middle-aged man was taken who, for a number of years, had kept those around him guessing. He was a stranger in the district and had never been anxious to talk about his past. Though a little curt, he was not really taciturn, and he had many friends here and, other than the pastor, no enemies. He was unmarried and lived alone with a housekeeper, an old horse, and some poultry. Though he was not a scholar, he had many books. Most of the time he spent by himself and with his thoughts when he traveled on the road on official business riding his rough-haired Norwegian fjord horse, who was almost blind from old age. The man was the civil road inspector, and the district's roads had never been in such good shape as on his watch.

In spite of his solitariness and frail health—which for many years necessitated a careful and strictly regulated life, especially the renunciation of the robust pleasures by which the other district inhabitants sought to compensate for nature's harshness—he seemed always calm and contented. That perplexed people and disturbed them, to boot, because he did not seek the consolation of religion, never went to church, let alone the Lord's Supper, and, therefore, was designated by the pastor as one of the unfortunate who were destined for eternal damnation.

His character had made the strongest impression on his neighbor across the way, the schoolteacher, a younger man with a lively mind. He liked to slip over to have a talk about serious matters. The schoolteacher was a man who endeavored, in all situations, to be honest and upright, even daring to hope for eternal salvation. Nevertheless, despite his conventional outlook, and though he lived the most comfortable of family lives with his wife and children, he had often experienced both sad and weary moments, and he couldn't hide from himself the sense that his godless neighbor, in all his solitude, seemed happier than he. When, once, he had had the courage to confess this to his friend, the road inspector had answered, in his calm, clipped way, that in that case he had not yet found his natural habitat where he could come to know the highest human happiness: to be oneself, fully, clearly, and consciously. When the schoolteacher asked him how it was possible to find that place, the road inspector answered that he himself could not give another advice, but it was necessary to hand oneself over fearlessly to the inborn instinct for survival in all creatures.

When, at another time, the teacher pressed him to tell him how this "highest happiness" feels, he answered, with some irony, not wanting to say much more: "Ask your pastor." Later, however, he elaborated that "what it comes to is that each individual has to bring himself, as far as possible, into an independent and unmediated connection with things instead of taking them from the mouths of others—as, for example, those who live by handed-down precepts and perspectives do. A genuinely immediate relation to life is the essential prerequisite for reaping a glad harvest from any experience, from the poorest and even most painful as from the best. Whoever does not know that happiness, how it feels when a hitherto-closed corner of the mental world or reality itself opens up, does not know what it means to live."

The schoolteacher Mikkelsen would often think about these words in the last years of the road inspector's life, when, in spite of his dreadful suffering from cancer, and without any outside comfort, he never lost courage. During great pain, he could be pitiable and moan so loudly that the inhabitants of the three houses around him had to stuff their ears with cotton. But when, afterward, he received a visitor, he would lie there with an expression on his face of one who had gone through a rich and deep experience. That no moment of life seemed to him wholly intolerable was confirmed by the discovery, after his death, of a loaded revolver hidden in the drawer of his bedside table.

During the last days, he lay quietly and wanted to see no one. To the end, he occupied himself with reflecting on the decline and decay of his body. When he noticed the death chill in his bones, he asked for a mirror, though he had almost lost his sight by then. "It will soon be over," he said to his housekeeper as he gave her back the glass. Shortly after, the death throes began. Toward evening, ugly weather came in from the Southwest. The wind whined like a sick dog through the crack at the top of the door, and rain slapped against the panes. A light burned at the bed's headboard. On the bare wall, the large silver watch of the patient's father was ticking. The old housekeeper had sent for the schoolteacher because she didn't dare to be alone with the dying man, but there was nothing he could do. The inspector lay snoring softly during the last hours. Shortly after midnight, his head fell to the side. A little sigh, and then he was dead.

A week later, in the most beautiful, placid October weather, under a blue sky, he was lowered into the sandy soil of the church-yard. About twenty people were in attendance. Only one verse of a hymn was sung, but no words were said, and the church bell was dumb in its tarred gallows. The dead man had ordered that. The priest, on the other hand, would not permit a fanfare Per had wanted blown over his grave.

Two members of his family were at the burial, Ministerial Undersecretary Eberhard Sidenius and Dean Thomas Sidenius, both out of uniform. After the interment, Per's will was opened. To the surprise and regret of the two brothers, he had explicitly denoted that his money should be given to Jakobe Salomon's nondenominational educational institution in Copenhagen, a bequest neither of them considered justifiable. Besides the furniture and some cash, they found a couple of savings bank books worth about ten thousand kroner. The strict regularity of habit, even asceticism the dead man's poor health had demanded and that suited his inclinations, had allowed him to put aside half of his salary as well as any extra earnings, among them compensation for a few of his small inventions. The brothers were astonished. "This is really a significant sum," the undersecretary exclaimed a couple of times, first with a great deal of respect, then uneasily.

"Yes, this is really not a trivial amount," uttered the dean in the same wavering tone. The brothers looked at each other. "I hope he came by it honestly. We certainly have no reason to doubt it."

When the undersecretary went back to Copenhagen, curiosity led him to bring the announcement of the legacy personally to Frøken Salomon at her school. One day, he went out to

Nørrebro, where Jakobe had built her much-disputed Children's Day School in the middle of the poor quarter. A caretaker led him across a large playground with trees and benches, and, when it became evident that the directress was busy with instruction at the moment, he expressed his wish to use the wait to see a little of the establishment.

An instructress came out and offered to show him around. At the end of the large building was a high-ceilinged, light, and cheerful dining room where half the children had just eaten while the others were being schooled. Off to the side were a couple of sewing rooms where the children—both boys and girls—learned to mend their clothes and stockings and patch their shoes. Above them was a row of bathing rooms. Every three days, explained his guide, each child took a bath. Light, air, water, and regular mealtimes were the means by which the school educated the children's moral sense, and that replaced religious instruction.

"So this is the way it is," interrupted the undersecretary, and cleared his throat. The children did not live at school. The theory was that their fresh bodies, well-kept clothes, and good manners would have an effect on their homes, as if they were little missionaries for belief in cleanliness, order, and discipline. But school was open from early morning, when the factories started up, and the children got their full board for a very little sum, which, in addition, was adjusted according to the parents' capacity to pay. The undersecretary thought, Yes, all this could be very good, but . . .

Just then, he received word that the directress was waiting for him in the office. Jakobe Salomon was now in her forties, but in spite of the fact that she had preserved her proud, upright carriage, she looked older. You could see that the project she had designed and executed with such energy and against a great deal of resistance and suspicion from various camps had cost her more than her fortune. The burden of struggle she had courted in her youth was given her in full measure. The face her admirers used to call an eagle face, her enemies and enviers a parrot puss, was now indisputably that of a bird of prey. With her already almost white hair, her sallow complexion, her large black eyes, her long neck, and her simple brown dress adorned only with a broad, white lace collar, she resembled a condor who, from a rocky peak, looked far out over the wide plains.

When the undersecretary came in, she went over to greet him

from her desk. "I suppose you are coming with the kind intention of announcing your brother's death. I already heard about it through others who had seen the death notice in the paper."

"If I didn't have another reason, I would not have bothered you with a visit, especially since my brother and his fate could hardly be expected to invite your sympathy."

"There you are mistaken. I owe your brother more than he himself ever understood. I kept track of him from a distance, as well as I could. We drifted farther apart from each other through the years, in more ways than one. About the last years, I know hardly anything. Now you may talk to me about them. Have a seat, Herr Undersecretary, and tell me of his sickness and death."

But the undersecretary didn't want to sit down. The simple, straight tone that this somewhat suspect woman used toward him tightened his mouth, so that his large, ungainly, underslung jaw was even more emphasized. "I would not, as I said, have bothered you if I didn't have a special purpose. I'll come right to the point. Your supposition that my late brother had distanced himself more and more from you, not only in the literal sense, but also in relation to perspective, to a way of thinking, it seems to me—and you will understand that I, for my part, say this with regret—is not really true. In any case, in his will, against whose legality serious objections could be raised, he designated you, or, rather, your institution, or whatever it is called, as the residuary legatee. Since my brother left children born of a legal marriage, the will is completely invalid. But I have been informed that there won't be objections raised from the heirs or their guardian, so that his last wish can be fulfilled. We're talking about capital of about ten thousand kroner, concerning whose origin I am not in a position to enlighten you. I considered it was my duty to inform you personally about it, and, as well, to learn from your own mouth whether you wish to accept this gift."

Jakobe Salomon stood by the side of a chair and supported herself with an elbow on its back. She was deeply affected. Memories from her youth streamed over her. She, whom few people had seen crying, could not, at this moment, hold back her tears. "Why should I not take it?" she said quietly. "Your brother and I were very different, and I often have thought that I really understood his nature poorly. But I am all the more grateful for the greeting he has sent me."

"In this connection, may I remind you of the conversation we had with each other, Frøken Salomon, sixteen or seventeen years ago? I used, on that occasion, about the same words concerning your relationship as I do now. I think you concede that it would have been best for all parties if you, then, had had more confidence in my powers of judgment."

She lifted her head and looked at him proudly. "There you are altogether mistaken, Herr Undersecretary! I do not wish anything undone. On the contrary, I feel it was a great piece of luck for me that I came to know Per. Through both the happiness and sorrow he gave me, my life first gained real substance. The work that you see around you here is, in fact, as much his as mine. And, therefore, I will always be deeply grateful to him."

"Well, hmmm—on this point, we will scarcely come to an understanding. I won't keep you longer. Goodbye."

One evening, a week after the burial, the schoolteacher Mikkelsen and the field steward Nielsen, who was also the parish constable, entered the dead man's closed-up house at the request of his departed brothers to draw up a list of the remaining household effects. The brothers had taken with them all the papers, letters, and other items that had been of value. But in the drawer of a table, by chance turned against the wall, they found a thick booklet filled with notes written in the road inspector's half-unreadable writing.

The schoolteacher could not help peeking into it. While the constable went into the other rooms with the lamp and made up his list, Mikkelsen sat in the bedroom and looked through the journal by the light of a candle stuck in the neck of a bottle. It was a kind of diary in which the road inspector wrote down his thoughts during the years he lived in the district—virtually a conversation with himself about everything that happened to him.

On one of the book's first pages, the schoolteacher made out, with difficulty, the following:

When we are young, we make immoderate demands on those powers that steer existence. We want them to reveal themselves to us. The mysterious veil under which we have to live offends us; we demand to be able to control and correct the great world-machinery. When we get a little older, in our impatience we cast our eye over mankind and its history to try to find, at last, a coherence in laws, in progressive development; in short, we seek a meaning to life, an aim for our struggles and suffering. But one day, we are stopped by a voice from the depths of our being, a ghostly voice that asks, "Who are you?" From then on, we hear no other question. From that moment, our own true self becomes the great Sphinx, whose riddle we try to solve. My true self? Was the man who rides out in the pouring rain this morning, depressed, bitter, and infinitely weary of life and its troubles my true self? Or is the one who, at dusk, sits by the stove and lets himself be lulled by the fire's crackling into happy memory-dreams of house and home, playing children, my true self? Or is the one who now sits here alone by the lamp, neither happy nor sad, neither young nor old, with a hushed and exalted sense of peace in his body that only night and solitude can grant, my true self, as it issued uncorrupted, unblemished from nature's hand? Or is my true self all these together? Is what we call the soul merely a passing mood, a residue of our night's sleep, or of our reading of the newspaper, something dependent on the barometer or market readings? Or do we have as many souls in us as there are cards in the game of Cuckoo. Every time you shuffle the deck a new face appears: a jester, a soldier, a night owl. I wonder, I wonder . . .

The schoolteacher Mikkelsen was surprised and could not recognize his friend in these despondent lines. When he looked in the journal for entries written in recent years, he came upon a letter that lay hidden between the pages. He looked at the address: "Civil Road Inspector P. Sidenius," and from the postmark he could see the letter was only a few months old.

After a short struggle with his conscience, he withdrew the letter from the envelope. It was in a woman's hand. At the top of the first page was the place name, "Budderuplund," and the letter read:

I have heard you are very sick, and therefore I am breaking the silence you imposed on me. I can't have peace of mind without telling you of my infinite gratitude to you for all you sacrificed for the sake of my happiness. I understand you well, now, understand that you only wanted what was best for me, and I can never thank you enough for that! I can greet you for our three children, who are doing well, like my two youngest. Hagbarth is now a student and will be an engineer. From what everyone says, he has an unusual talent, is a strong and spirited boy who will make his way well in the world. Ingeborg was confirmed last autumn. She and little Lise are still at home with me. They don't know you—you wanted it that way, and maybe that was right. Again, my deepest thanks for everything. God give you strength to bear what will come.

Inger

The schoolteacher hung his head and shoved the letter back into its envelope. What a strange man he was, he thought.

The last part of the diary consisted mostly of undated, short entries and several ended with the same sentence that was underlined here and there: "Nature is rich, and she is wise and merciful." In such places, Mikkelsen easily recognized again the thoughts and expression of his friend's conversations:

"Without the original human urge to develop, without the self-generated power that expresses itself as passion (whether it be directed toward the real world or the world of thoughts or dreams) and without that strong, even bold courage to will to be oneself in all our divine nakedness, no one reaches real freedom. Because of this, I am grateful that I have been living in such a time that calls out this instinct and strengthens this essential courage. Otherwise, I would have gone through my whole life half a man, a Sidenius."

In another place:

"The life and story of Christ teaches us, in reality, nothing more than this, already an older wisdom: 'There is only one thing that can conquer suffering: the Passion.'"

In yet another:

"Honor to my youth's expansive dreams! And I am still a world conqueror. Every man's soul is an independent universe, his death the extinction of the universe in miniature."

And in yet another, these words:

"Today the newspapers announced that Herr Steiner had been named a councilor. Why? For an entire life squandered in lies and headlong swindling—only for the privilege of a title: councilor. The world is a bad rewarder. Poor Herr Steiner. If only you knew how royally free and unresentful I feel in my obscurity, you would understand that it is you who are deceived. But you don't suspect that and are happy. You congratulate yourself and proudly receive champagne toasts. But nature is rich, wise, and merciful."

One entry was entitled "About God."

"This thought has been ascribed to Voltaire: If God did not exist, mankind would have invented Him. I find more truth in the reverse: If there really is a God, then we should seek to forget Him, to raise up men who will to do good for goodness' sake, not out of fear of punishment for their bad deeds. How can someone give alms to a poor man with a clean heart when he believes, and has an interest in believing, that there is a God who keeps score in heaven, who looks down and nods in approval?"

Lower down, there was a thought under this heading: "More About Faith."

"We are surrounded, in life, by so many things that become our property by chance. One day we discover that we need a dresser. We go to the cabinetmaker and buy one that happens to be there. We examine it indifferently. Perhaps it's not to our taste, but at the moment we have decided to buy it; when it becomes our property, a secret transformation takes place in the relationship between us and this chest of drawers. Carefully we brush our hand over the polished surface and, with love and solicitude, keep watch when the movers carry it up the stairs; if we are forced, later in life, to part with it, it feels as if a piece of ourselves is missing. That is the mystery of possessions. Is it also of faith?"

In his last year, he penned a note that bore the title "The Great Ghost":

On the island of Mors, a few years ago, this took place. A landowner had two sons who were still little. The youngest was a sulky boy with a defiant disposition whom the father wanted to humble. One day, when the youngster was in his tenth year, he had, again, done something wrong and needed a punishment. He sought refuge up in a high tree in the garden. Giddy from rage and (as has been claimed) from too lavish an enjoyment of his wine, for he had just returned from a hunters' lunch at a neighbor's—his father stood in front of the tree with his riding whip and

demanded that the boy come down. However loudly he
yelled and threatened, the boy stayed up in the tree and
even, in his anxiety, climbed higher, all the way to the very
top. Then a scream was heard. The branch he had put his
foot on broke off, and the youngster was hurtled to the
ground. He became a cripple for his whole life. The
father's sense of guilt drove him crazy, so that, until he died,
he had to remain in an asylum.

The sons, meanwhile, grew up. The eldest became a
strong and red-cheeked Junker, justifiably called a splendid
fellow. He married a pretty girl and put a crowd of happy
children into the world. Under his direction, his property
became a model estate. He did his duty as a good man. His
brother, on the other hand, lay pale and still on a stretcher
in the park, his bird friends fluttering around him and
eating out of his hand. He did not feel unhappy. Only the
stupid sympathy of people pained him and the thought of
the miserable lot of his father. I myself have seen him. He
was then about eighteen or nineteen years old, and
I couldn't forget the bright expression on his face. It was as
if streams of light surrounded his whole, helpless body. To
compensate for the health he was robbed of, he received
that sixth sense that bestowed upon his soul a deep joy. The
headstrong boy with the stubborn troll look in his eyes had
now become a poor cripple, neither a man nor a woman,
child nor adult. Nevertheless, because of that, he was a
human being whose eyes reflected the eternal in all its
transparency, depth, and peace. And I had to think of his
father, whose bad conscience had driven him into the
darkness because he did not have belief, the right belief,
the belief in nature, rich, wise, and merciful, who has lessons for all of us and who generously substitutes other limbs
for the ones we have lost, who

The schoolteacher interrupted his reading as the parish constable returned.

"Well, now we are finished, Mikkelsen. What do you have
there?"

"It's only the book we found in the drawer. What shall we do
with it? It's all handwritten stuff so we can't auction it off and it
is too good for burning. Do you think, Nielsen, that I can, in

good conscience, take it and keep it? Then I will have a kind of reminder of the road inspector. For, truth to say, many times I will be missing him and, in here, there is so much that is like what we sat and talked about, it is as if it were all revived."

"Take it, Mikkelsen. We have no responsibility for written material. And it has no monetary value."

The constable lit a lantern. The two men extinguished lamp and candle and left the empty house, locking it up carefully behind them.

The End

TRANSLATOR'S AFTERWORD

For lack of a translation, one of the greatest novels of European literature from the turn of the last century has remained unread by the English-speaking world, its author virtually unknown. Yet Henrik Pontoppidan's *Lykke Per* (*Lucky Per*) (1898–1904), rendered early into German, was praised by Thomas Mann, György Lukács, and Ernst Bloch as a cosmopolitan masterpiece of epochal sweep, as a profound social, psychological, and metaphysical anatomy of the modernist transition. It secured the novelist a Nobel Prize in 1917.

There is no question that Pontoppidan's scene is thoroughly Danish, but just as little doubt that the questions raised and dramatized by it are the central concerns of all major writers of early modernism: the problem of spiritual authority in the age of Darwin, of industrial and technological expansion and a rising proletariat; the problem of a psychologically and politically dangerous and deceitful moral language of idealism preserving a priestly and philistine power with its stultification of instinctual and political realities, relentlessly dissected by the irony of Ibsen, Nietzsche, Freud, and Marx; and the problem of the orphaned will, wracked by guilty desires and thwarted by a speculative world of bureaucratic materialism and planetary indifference.

As well, a shifting modernist dialectical play, favored by Nietzsche and by Kierkegaard, who viewed it as indirect communication, sustaining complexity without contaminating the passion braving paradox and contradiction, strongly appealed to Pontoppidan as his preferred literary strategy and stance. He had studied these masters by the time of the composition of *Lykke Per* and took them as temperamental and formal allies.

The powerfully influential and virtually stateless Danish critic Georg Brandes, a friend of Pontoppidan's, who is caricatured in this novel as Dr. Nathan, gave the name "radical aristocrat" to Nietzsche (a designation the philosopher enjoyed) and extended it to cover Ibsen and Kierkegaard for their common scorn and suspicion, in various shades and degrees, of all crowds and collectives, the promises of revolutions, the language of progress, for their antidemocratic investment in the individual as the only bearer of value, and for the touch of spirituality marking the passionate irony that judged their age worthy of anarchic subversion. Pontoppidan shares this disposition and a liberal social consciousness he acknowledged inheriting from his mother, evident even in his earliest short stories, which expose, with both grim and humorous irony, the poverty, superstition, stubbornness, and victimization of the peasant that could lead straight to the poorhouse. It surfaces most dramatically in the educational project designed by this novel's great heroine, Jakobe, for the children of factory workers, and in her outrage over the persecution of the tattered Russian Jews quarantined in a German train station on their way to America. We can see it too in Per's conversations with Pastor Blomberg and in his charge of parochialism against the potential banking brokers of his engineering project.

But Ibsen's confession that he was a pagan in the realm of politics, without much faith in the altruism of the socially powerful, could just as well have been voiced by Pontoppidan. His interest in the social and political problems of Denmark was always checked by the wide psychological and spiritual perspective he shared with the international radical aristocrats.

We can look, for example, at the presence in Pontoppidan's fiction of a central figure in Danish culture, N. F. S. Grundtvig, as a potential circumscription, since he is not well known outside of Scandinavia. Yet he, too, is typically subjected to Pontoppidan's cosmopolitan transmutation. As the originator of a Lutheran sect and an antiquarian scholar of Norse mythology, Grundtvig managed to join his own hymns to Danish history, to craft a curriculum for the folk high schools he designed to educate rural youth, and to promote a national identity, both patriotic and religious. For distancing commentary, he substituted the authenticity of the direct, living word of the Bible; for a classical and scientific curriculum, a national history and literature in the native tongue. His active and optimistic religious temperament advertised appreciation of the natural world and is embodied, in this novel, by the officious and breezy form of Pastor Blomberg. With the introduction of Pastor Fjaltring, however, whose Kierkegaardian temper and faith is dialectically nurtured by doubt, suffering, and guilt, and who has a crucial influence on Per, Pontoppidan pummels the Grundtvig denominational disposition.

He exposes it to the compelling and profound larger psychological analysis that promoted Kierkegaard to an existential father of modernism.

The often rehearsed account of Brandes's attack directed against what he saw as a sterile, static, and parochial aestheticism, of his insistence that literature should debate contemporary social questions, take a *developing* cognizance of naturalist emphases on heredity, milieu, and marriage, sometimes slights one of his most central indictments of special importance in this novel, against the Danish habit of seeking refuge from history in fantasy and fairy tales *(Drømmeri)*, rendering the country impotent in the face of a progressive European culture.

Ironically, Per, in love with Europe's advancing industrialization, calls the revolutionary Dr. Nathan, uninterested in technology, a mere aesthete. But Ivan, his sponsor, endorses Brandes's warning even as he dubs Per "Aladdin," and Pontoppidan's strongest structural design of stimulating realism by recourse to the fairy tale hounding the social plot by luck and chance both puts him in a central line of Danish writers—Adam Oehlenschläger (*Aladdin*, 1805), F. Paludan-Müller (*Adam Homo*, 1841–48), and Hans Christian Andersen (*Lykke Peer*, 1870)—and preserves his dialectical impulsion.

Pontoppidan's use of the fairy tale is anything but an indolent national escape, a satiric foil that shows up the hero's masquerade or, as in Andersen, an agency that generates an early entrance to social and artistic success so climactic the hero can happily die of it. The underlying fairy tale of this novel, *Hans im Glück* ("Hans in Luck"), leads the story, by its reverse structure, to a deeper realism than the one luck *seemed* to be serving. The peasant boy Hans is not happy until he has traded *down*, starting with some money he earned in service, to a horse, a cow, a pig, a goose, a grindstone, to the nothing that sets him free. This pattern, which prepares and parallels the backward spiritual journey, betrays an existential incommensurability between the modern soul's desire and will and what the world has to offer.

Pontoppidan subjects his aesthetic form to a dialectical debate that keeps it from being confined to a social or national cause, keeps ideas from dominating temperament, and even puts us in the position Kierkegaard promotes where spirit can snatch us. Taking up Brandes's contention that addiction to fairy tales is Denmark's "national weakness" and "a costly passion," Jakobe's suitor, Eybert, intent on undermining his competitor, Per, implies the latter's bold engineering project and inventions, which would put the forces of nature in the service of industry, are merely a magic tale: "Yes, a fairy tale. We have no lack of them in our land."

On the other hand, Aron Israel, a modest, generous, noble scholar and teacher, defends Per, the "fantasist" from a poor Jutland parsonage: "Is it such a bad thing for a young man to dream? I mean—haven't the greatest men really proved their worth for us out of their dreams? ... In fact, every actuality comes out of our fantasies." And he adds, anticipating the novel's ending: "Even if ... Herr Sidenius would not be able to realize his bold fantasy, which is undeniably possible ... it could have the greatest consequence for his personal development, and that, ideally, could be the most important consideration."

By banishing the fairy tale, we are reduced to a shallow realism; by letting it put realism through its paces, it leads us to a place beyond national and historical borders. But to get there, all national concerns in the novel are sifted through Brandes's international sieve. The secular exile Nietzsche called "a good European" admired the way the attackers of parochial self-protection like Kierkegaard and Nietzsche used psychology, symbol, and spirit to undermine the complacency of bourgeois and theological morality, the way Ibsen lets nature, in the blink of an eye, dissolve morality, the metaphysical shame the ethical.

The thrilling and perilous opening to what Ibsen called the "Great World" and to which Brandes gestured leads Per beyond Dr. Nathan's own European home in exile to the far country where Denmark's most obscure provincial corner becomes the capital of the universe of Being. Through Per's wide reading, discussions with Jakobe and Pastor Fjaltring, even his planetary monologues in the Alps and in the valleys where man and his buildings have been ravaged by nature, the radical aristocrats infiltrate his scene.

If these perspectives supersede the favored range of Dr. Nathan's arguments, they humble, as well, Per's competitive creative pride in the promise of technology. The dialectical tension between a deep, dwarfing, and timeless vision and the thrilling projection of a civilization wired by human ingenuity and ambition is a constant and rich drag on Per's will, a drag never dreamt of in Dr. Nathan's philosophy.

At the center of the subversive concerns of the fathers of modernism is the problem of the will in the modern world, a will more desirous than ever, but stranded in a leveling age so suspicious and envious of missions that partake, themselves, of the bad faith receiving them. This will prances forth in the tragicomic trajectory Schopenhauer sketched out as nature pays no attention to its plans while keeping the species going. Trolls and Christian ghosts of guilt haunt its unsanctioned efforts to be free, unconditioned, and an acknowledged power: luck's darling. But incommensurability between passion and possibility force disproportions that can be neither mediated nor managed. Ibsen calls this guilty gigantism a kind of megalomania characteristic of a mankind that has become an unnatural product, especially the Christian part, equally responsive to the priestly caste's call to duty and the instinct's urge to rebellion.

This misalignment is something Jakobe senses in Per's character when it shies away from what it ardently wants, a victim of the alliance between a new psychology and the reverse fairy tale. Ibsen's master builder of houses, rather than canals and ports, shares with Pontoppidan's engineer the urge and possibility of "wishing something, desiring something, willing something" so persistently that, at last, it has to be. Per's youthful spur is "I will," but his final retreat from the field spares him Solness's topple from the tower. As he leaves his last home, he is spared as well the fate of Mrs. Alving in *Ghosts*, who, haunted by dead philosophies and theologies, the general sickness of those who don't know how to listen to themselves, gains insight only to explode in a house that has *shut in* the disease of lies it would *shut out*, the abstractions and repressions that sustain the false idealisms seducing and shackling the instinctual life.

While Ibsen, like Brandes, chose exile to escape the sick houses of his native land, Pontoppidan's Per, after leaving his first unhappy home, restlessly evicts himself even from places of rich refuge that could give his plans and prospects a semblance of commensurability with the housed world. He cannot stay in Nyboder, where the Olufsens serve as foster parents, where their warm parties and neighborhood concerts, a first, innocent love, give him protection for his work; nor can he remain, finally, in the cosmopolitan Jewish Salomon circle as a future son-in-law with financial backing and a heroic fiancée who gives him passion, education, and an international perspective that forces

Christianity's persecutions and prejudices into a wider scene granting historical support for his rebellion against family and country. Nor can Per close off, for long, his incommensurability even with the standpoint of rebellion on his premature honeymoon with Jakobe in the Alps, nor with the domestic peace and order in the country at Kærsholm or in his provincial home with his wife Inger and his children. Those who will in such a world are subject to what György Lukács called a sense of "transcendental homelessness," for Nietzsche, a privileged place. Some, like Hardy's Jude the Obscure, unable to find anchorage in a sustaining medium, are worn down by their ceaseless migration. Some, like Ibsen's Nora, experience an anxious thrill as they slam the door of the Doll House and enter their creator's "Great World," unarmed. Brandes, anything but obscure and unarmed, unable to get a university post in Copenhagen, or, as a Jew, to speak in Russia, gained his missionary energy from exile, an ideal posture for a designated gadfly. Per has to back up into the farthest corner of Denmark's map, celibate and surrendering the ambition that made "transcendental homelessness" so feared and so desired. Here, in the most remote of spaces, he is at peace in the Great World , at last resigning himself to what Ibsen and Schopenhauer call life's most profound and humiliating mystery: the pathetic reliance of the human will on that which is will-less.

In his autobiography, Pontoppidan—like Per a son of a Jutland pastor—envies the Dickensian atmosphere of warmth in a poor workman's family that seems to allow the father to radiate, despite his class, commensurability with the world. It is a scene re-created in the novel, and, toward the story's end, Per feels the same sensation he did so often in Rome as he gazes, now, at a statue, in a Copenhagen park, of the satyr Silenus looking affectionately at his charge, the boy Dionysus. Even Jakobe, after her breakup with Per and the death of her baby, achieves a kind of truce with the world by her noble work with her educational home where factory workers' children will start a clean and well-fed life, no longer tortured by their national homes. But only when Per—who, unlike Jakobe, has a spiritual, not a social consciousness—moves into his final stage of a celibate natural theology does his will feel at home in a will-less universe.

Throughout the novel, we recognize the presence of the French realists as the young, provincial Per, like the more securely housed characters of Balzac, is busy getting the right clothes for the sophisticated capital, enough money, a name, relying on semi-magical means to push him up the social ladder before the final downfall. Balzac lives, as well, in the consortium of financiers and the nabobs of journalism. From Flaubert, Pontoppidan takes the notion of merging women in Per's sensuous imagination and a favorite provincial target, the pharmacist of Rimalt, a shadow of the hateful Homais.

But his passionate interest in bringing Per to an authentic and transparent sense of self, to an unconditioned consciousness, attracts him most compellingly to Ibsen, Kierkegaard, and Nietzsche. When Brandes, perhaps forgetting that Aladdin does not deserve his aleatory luck, wonders like other readers of the novel if Per may not be good enough to carry the kind of ideality Pontoppidan wants to get over the finish line, he may be best answered by the example of Ibsen rather than that of the French masters. The very signature of the Norwegian playwright is the use of severely flawed, psychologically celibate carriers to get us to the border of the Great World, leaving behind the better-adjusted, compromising couples, however painfully earned their marriages.

Pontoppidan shares a second major Ibsen pattern: the persistent presence of guilt for "soul murder" in the marriage of mixed natures, a guilt Pontoppidan, himself having left his first family, must have felt as much as Per. When the master builder confesses his regret that his needs crushed his wife's desires, we are in the presence of Per's depressed and anxious mother, whose gay childhood is recalled by a contemporary, of Pastor Fjaltring and his marital guilt, of Per himself when, in his final sacrifice for Inger, he lies and leaves her. Per fusses as well over the difference between his nature and Jakobe's before he abandons her in a less noble move.

It is hard to imagine that Pontoppidan did not see the parallels between the way Kierkegaard relentlessly worked his broken engagement and filial guilt through his literature, often representing his self-images as worse than he was, and the way he makes Per owe his selfish representation to his author's guilts. The forgiveness granted by Jakobe and Inger is testimony to this need.

While Kierkegaard crafted a design of successive stages of repetition to climb to the climactic one that transvaluates worldly loss into spiritual gain, and misunderstanding into a sign of God's love, Pontoppidan and his Per could become, finally, only

Knights of Resignation, just short of the last move to faith. But in the parable of the crippled youth discovered in Per's notebook at the end of the novel, we read of a rebellious boy who becomes paralyzed after falling from a tree where he is hiding from his father's wrath. The father goes mad from guilt, but the child grows into a beautifully spiritual young man who draws strength from his infirmity and far surpasses, in wisdom and grace, his prosperous Junker brother. He lies in for Per, who, in his celibate retreat, derives from his sickness a new kind of health, a sixth sense, a natural theology. As the youth, who had had, like Per, the stubborn troll-look in his eyes, now remembers his father in forgiveness and sweet sorrow, he lends meaning to the watch of Per's father, once rejected by the son and now hanging on his wall.

Per's strange, backward shipboard journey over water as an unsanctioned chaperone of his mother's casket, his review of her difficult life, ultimately prepares him to move past resentment at the lack of intimacy in his mother's posthumously received letter. The calm acceptance and transparency in the parallel lives of Per and the crippled youth come close to transforming misunderstanding into love, though, in contradistinction to Kierkegaard's dramatic transvaluation, this is a final reconciliation, not a first cause or conversion.

In *The Point of View of My Work as an Author*, Kierkegaard insists that the religious motive was present from the beginning of his aesthetic output. Similarly, in Per's life that finally expresses itself in writings, the ghost of the religious beginnings hovers over and besets his every aesthetic, willful, and magic move, even as he climactically shoots a roadside crucifix on his Alpine "honeymoon" with Jakobe, until it is appeased in a richly matured spirit. But it is in Per's intercourse with Pastor Fjaltring that Kierkegaard's haunting of the text comes through most strongly. He is considered too eccentric and solitary a figure to deserve a real congregation, in contrast to the bouncing Grundtvig preacher Pastor Blomberg. But like the Danish philosopher, Fjaltring keeps the wound of the negative open and gives Per, by his guilty example, sanction to leave his family to find his deepest self. And the pastor, like Kierkegaard, reminds him that the spiritual direction is always *back*, and that very cry is in Per's throat as he watches the mindless, pressing crowds hustling forward on his last trip to Copenhagen, the final stop on his own "progressive" journey. With the philosopher, he judges the rushing crowds he once envied as "untruth" and, perhaps, finds authority there to consider marriage and family a crowd.

In Kierkegaard's scorn for Grundtvig's version of Christianity, Per could have procured support for his own growing scorn of his father-in-law, who derides Fjaltring by condescension. And Per could have derived justification for his solitary retreat from Kierkegaard's insistent protest that Grundtvig did not understand that it is not in race, tradition, and nationalism that true Christianity abides, not in meetings, crowds, and congregations, but in the category of the individual.

In love with direct categories while canceling the dialectical play of the aesthetic and ascetic for the sake of spiritual security, Grundtvig is at home in the world. Per's philosophy of progress, always haunted by the backward movement of heredity and the inward pull of spirit, is subject to the torque of the fairy tale Kierkegaard regularly torments to get us past the comfort and potential philistinism of the ethical sphere. In chapter three, the first of Per's magic servers, Neergaard, worn out by life, writes his own timid postscript to the conventional fairy tale, foreshadowing a bolder, final regression. A young swineherd wins the princess and half the kingdom, but, in time, he is made miserable by his luck and looks back longingly to the chimney corner of home, the wooden clogs, his mother's soup, his father's dung fork. Even here, where the aesthetic is playing with a reversal far short of the deep spiritual purpose of Kierkegaard's torture of fairy tales, it can serve to start up the journey that climaxes in a bold, chosen return, liberating the first home from the job of merely propitiating failure and fate.

As a courageous conversion through *amor fati*, this move is practiced, as well, by Nietzsche, who is hosted in the novel most fully by Jakobe with her diatribes against Christianity as an agent of persecution under the guise of morality and humanistic promises that unmistakeably echo the philosopher's. In chapter ten, she gives a Nietzschean bite to her case against a Christian propaganda that, up until now, has covered up the reality of instinctual passions and fears by claims of brotherhood, justifying as well its persistent oppressions. It is a morality that refuses to recognize the higher soul it resents, and it feels quite comfortable in the consortium meetings of the power brokers that shackle Per's wide-ranging plans.

If Per's motives for rejecting the consortium's demands are anything but pure, his sense of being railroaded into crippling and curtailing his project so that it would be a mere shadow of itself gains our sympathy. It surprises neither Per nor the reader that the engineer Steiner, a poster boy for slave morality, sponsored by a consortium and living on plagiarism, is boosted into the place Per abandons and takes credit for imagining a great deal of Per's project. He is, to Per, a masquerade climaxing in a title. But Per could have taken comfort in Kierkegaard's reminder that inventions are nothing compared to self-knowledge.

In Steiner's world, Per realizes he had been "an unfortunate half-man who loved life without daring to give himself to it and who despised it without being able to run away," caught as he was in the slave dilemma of desire inhibited and perverted by the need for self-protection. The confession has the cast of autobiographical divulgence and describes the sickness that beds us down in the valley when Nietzsche would have us homeless on the heights, cleared of political lust and language and alive in transparent self-mastery that is not afraid to love its fate, to become and to overcome.

Jakobe reverts to the pagan world to retrieve an experience for Per. She writes to him of her viewing of the mummified remains of a master and slave from Pompeii. The slave's expression is confused and horrified, caught in an incipient scream. The master's, whose class is merely a spiritual metaphor, bears the noble look of a free soul in resignation, deriving from a life disciplined to self-mastery, not mastery over or submission to others. The distinction anticipates the stoicism of Per's death. Strangely enough, it is, however, the noble sacrifice of the fairy tale, the one Neergaard predicted would lead us home by reversing its direction, that brings Per to his climactic fulfillment. The dialectical relationship between the aesthetic and the ascetic in Per's life finally bears fruit. The phantom hand that draws Per back to his father's house of abstinence is just as tenacious as the generous, magic hands of Per's sponsors, Neergaard, Ivan, and the baroness. When the fairy tale is ready to turn around, to live on bread and water, it knows that its survival in the novel of social and psychological realism depends on its strange relation to the deeper spheres. It helps us to understand that Per's sexual attractions and distractions, his vulnerability to the planetary dwarfing of ambition in the Alps, his religious, domestic, and commercial blockages, are not causes but the plot's self-protective rationalizations, mere symptoms of a deeper desire that has been haunting Per from the beginning, the need to *be* himself, *by* himself. The fairy tale exposes itself to the fire of irony so hot Per can be free of ambition, magic, and God, and live his final years as a work of art whose chaste, open questioning form testifies to a grateful acceptance of the visible world and a willingness to yield to the mystery of its relation to the invisible world. The story gives up its disguises.

We remember that, on one of his childhood sledding expeditions, Per is asked by his beautiful partner whether he is the pastor's son. When Per lies and says no, he is asked, "Who are you, then?" Per answers, "Who am I? I can't say." This is no modesty, but a disguise of ambition both defiant and fearful. At the very end, when Per is, at last, equal to himself, he writes: "One day, we are stopped by a voice from the depths of our being, a ghostly voice that asks, 'Who are you?' From then on, we hear no other question. From that moment, our own true self becomes the great Sphinx, whose riddle we try to solve." In this authentic, questioning, celibate state, he sheds the epithets assumed and given him, in and out of the novel: Cain, Faust, the Prodigal Son, Christ, Aladdin, Caesar, Hans, Peer Gynt, and even that of his mad ancestor Sidenius of Vendsyssel. They have no more power to enhance or reduce by identification and irony. The cursed name "Sidenius," a symbol to him throughout the novel of the constricted life of clergy and philistines, has lost its power to shame, like the name "Pontoppidan," subject, as its bearer confesses, to childhood ridicule because of its odd difficulty. It refuses to hide behind a pseudonym as it moves into the Great World of literature.

ACKNOWLEDGMENTS

I would like to thank appreciators of the project: Professors Herbert Lindenberger, Paul Michael Lutzeler, Richard Watson, Milica Banjanin, Philip Boehm, and, as well, Jill Levin, Stephen Kidd, and Garth Hallberg. I owe much to those who helped me with translation problems and with editing: Professor Lynne Tatlock, Professor Frants Albert, Ruth Newton, and Inger Andersen.

For financial aid during the process of translation I would like to thank Kunststyrelsen Litteraturcentral of Denmark and Washington University in St. Louis. I am most grateful to have received the Leif and Inger Sjöberg Award for a portion of this novel from the Scandinavian Foundation in 2007. The afterword is a version derived from my essay "The World's Pontoppidan and his *Lykke Per*," published in the Spring 2006 issue of *Scandinavian Studies*.

Most of all, I endlessly thank my husband and tireless editor, Al Lebowitz.

Grateful acknowledgment is hereby made to copyright holders for permission to use the following copyrighted material: Henrik Pontoppidan, *Lykke Per*, Gyldendal.

Translated by permission of the publisher. All rights reserved.

Naomi Lebowitz
2010

5 The war referred to is the yearlong war of 1864, in which Denmark lost Schleswig-Holstein to Germany. The defeat left a lasting national sense of humiliation that surfaces here and there in this novel and often in Danish literature through the turn of the century. In his memoirs, Pontoppidan, like his Per, recalls the billeting of Austrian and Prussian troops in his childhood home.

6 Fru Sidenius: Throughout the novel I use the Danish forms of address for Mrs. (Fru), Miss (Frøken), and Mr. (Herr).

15 *Fædrelandet*: "The Homeland," a leading Copenhagen Conservative newspaper.

CHAPTER 2

28 The Dannebrog (Denmark) ribbon is a decoration given to veterans.

30 "Madam" is a form of address that indicates a class lower than "Fru" in Danish.

35 Hans Christian Ørsted (1777–1851) was a Danish physicist and chemist who studied in Germany, where he was attracted to philosophies of natural science. He was a pioneer in the study of electromagnetism.

38 The artists belonging to the Pot have generally been identified as caricatures of Pontoppidan's contemporaries: Fritjof, as Holger Drachmann (1846–1908), a poet who courted scandal as a free spirit and who was early associated with the naturalism of Georg Brandes's "Breakthrough" (see following note), though he also has been termed an impressionist; Enevoldsen, as J. P. Jacobsen (1847–85), celebrated author of the novel *Niels Lyhne*, in which the hero struggles to gain a philosophy of life that could accommodate his imaginative nature and atheist convictions. He has been labeled a naturalist, but, in fact, his reputation is primarily as an exquisite stylist; Berger, as Johannes Jørgensen (1866–1956), a neo-Catholic poet and critic who broke with Brandes after his

own alliance with the symbolists and his religious conversion in 1896. Hallager is the protagonist of Pontoppidan's
long novella *Nattevagt* ("Night Watch"), in which he is
allowed to exorcise Pontoppidan's own anarchic anger as
well as his distaste for schools of style.

41 Dr. Nathan is a caricature of Georg Brandes (1842–1927),
Pontoppidan's friend and the most influential force in the
Danish culture of the last third of the nineteenth century.
His "Inaugural Lecture" at the University of Copenhagen
in 1871 initiated the celebrated movement called the *Gen-
nembrud*, "Breakthrough," which affected virtually every
major Scandinavian writer. Brandes introduced the main
currents of European thought and literature into a more
provincial Danish scene by championing Nietzsche, Ibsen,
and Kierkegaard as fellow castigators and challenging
writers to release literature from its aesthetic quarantine by
debating, in the fiction itself, social and sociopsychological
problems and issues. Brandes complained about aspects of
Pontoppidan's portrait, but was generally a good sport
about it.

42 Gripomenus: An old comic tag for the police.

CHAPTER 3

57 Lucky Per: English cannot reproduce the double meaning
of *lykke* in Danish as both "lucky" and "happy."

CHAPTER 6

106 *Lyset*: "The Light."

109 Hans Lassen Martensen (1808–84) was a celebrated
Lutheran theologian, author of treatises on Christian ethics
and dogmatics, who, with Bishop Mynster, was a target of
Kierkegaard's attacks on professional Christianity.

109 Grundtvigian hats were broad-brimmed pilgrim hats named
for the vastly influential Danish theologian and scholar
N. F. S. Grundtvig (1783–1872), who initiated a highly
popular schismatic branch of Lutheranism marked by an
emphasis on the immediacy and living language of the Bible,

the natural and national world, and by a cheerful, open, collective worship and song exhibited in large, democratic meetings and congregations. He initiated, as well, the idea of the folk high school to further the education of rural youth through an emphasis on native Danish literature and history (instead of a classical curriculum) that could bind together patriotism and religion. Grundtvig was, as well, a famous composer of hymns and a noted scholar of Norse antiquities and folk legends, a translator from Latin, Old Norse, Old English, and old Danish material he tried to make compatible with Christianity. In this novel, Grundtvig's denomination is represented by Pastor Blomberg.

109 These plays are called *Ridderdramaer*, the Danish term for often patriotic and idealizing plays about medieval knights.

CHAPTER 7

128 *pensionsanstalt*: A boarding institution.

137 Herr Gott von Mannheim: "Dear God of Mannheim," one of many apostrophic expressions in German that punctuate the speech of Herr Delft.

138 Strøget: The central and, historically, most fashionable shopping street of Copenhagen, which now gives its name to an entire district.

142 troll nature: The figure of the troll, derived from Norse mythology, varies from region to region across Scandinavia. In Denmark, and in *Lucky Per* specifically, trolls are "hill trolls," slow-witted, sleepy, rural, isolated, and drawn to the gold they hoard in their lairs underground, yet perhaps no less powerful than the larger, fiercer trolls of Norway or the North Atlantic. Per's inertial "troll nature" can be inferred wherever sleep, greed, dreaminess, the rural or the subterranean are evoked, and in folkloric references ranging from Sleeping Beauty to the tale Neergard tells about the swineherd.

CHAPTER 8

153 *morsch*: German for "decayed," "rotten."

154 Skovbakken: "Forest Hill."

159 *Falken*: "The Falcon."

162 Bakken: Perhaps the world's oldest amusement park, Bakken is older than the Tivoli and rurally located in a beautiful setting in the forest near the Eremitage, a little hunting lodge on a big meadow with grazing deer.

165 *Dannevang*: Poetic name for Denmark.

CHAPTER 9

184 Strandveien: Denmark's most famous coastal road.

CHAPTER 10

201 *Industribladet*: "The Industrial Journal."

205 father-in-law: From the time of the engagement, Jakobe's family members are already called in-laws.

CHAPTER 11

207 *Kenn's nicht*: German for "Don't know it."

208 Per's German pronunciations and spelling difficulties are confessed and registered in the text. By *herrich* Per means *herrlich*, or "marvelous."

210 *Geheimecommercienrath*: *Geheimer Kommerzienrat*, "privy councilor of commerce."

210 *Gemahlinn*: *Gemahlin*, "wife."

212 *Tageblatt*: "The Daily News."

CHAPTER 13

244 *Industritidende*: "The Industrial News."

259 *Der Freischütz*: The famous opera by C. M. Weber replaced the tragic conclusion of the original story by J. A. Apel with a happy ending.

263 "Cottier" is, perhaps, the best translation of *husmand*, which has no real equivalent in English. The *husmand* was allowed

to build his hut on encumbered land usually in return for farm labor. He could use only some of the plot for his own domestic needs.

CHAPTER 14

270 *"Pfui! Hier riecht ja entsetzlich nach Knoblauch"*: German for "Whew! It smells terrible in here, like garlic."

275 The Copenhagen free port project, financed by a joint stock company, was actually realized in the 1890s.

278 the Prater: The Prater Garten, the oldest beer garden in Berlin, was in the late 1800s something of a cross between pub, café, theater, and garden—a popular place where women and men could appear socially together. Situated in the recently developed Prenzlauerberg district, it would have been something of a "country excursion" at the time of the novel's setting.

278 *Berlingske Tidende*: "The Berling Times," a major Copenhagen newspaper

282 *ganz und gar*: German for "altogether."

282 Laban: a complex allusion to Genesis 24–9. Upon hearing of Abraham's "flocks, and herds, and silver, and gold," Laban, brother of Rebekah and father of Leah and Rachel, contrives to join his family to the line of Abraham by marriage. The Colonel's implication may be that Per is somewhat conniving in his multiple approaches to joining the Salomon family, but it is notable that while his figure of speech posits Philip Salomon as Abraham, Laban is the one whose younger and older daughter are in play in the original story.

288 a provincial Jeppe: the equivalent of "a simple Jack," from the Danish diminutive for Jakob.

CHAPTER 15

292 *Borgerbladet*: "The Citizen's Journal."

302 Literary sources and structural evidence strongly suggest that mock naval battles were, indeed, held in the Colosseum during opening ceremonies in 80 AD and that these

"naumachiae" continued for a short time afterward, until the water proved too damaging to the foundations of the arena. In order to prepare for the naval battles, the lower gates leading to the arena floor would be sealed off, the heavy, wooden flooring removed, and the cells below flooded via an intricate pipe and drainage system. The arena could be flooded to a depth of five feet in approximately seven hours.

CHAPTER 16

306 "A certain man went down . . .": A witty transposition of a place name from the story of the Good Samaritan in Luke 10:30–37.
325 cothurn: the tall, thick-soled boots worn by stage actors in Greek tragedy to achieve an effect of height. Like "buskin," its English version, "cothurn" is now a synecdoche for the tragic manner more generally.

CHAPTER 17

341 "biblical lean cow": Genesis 41:1–4.
353 kleines Ding: German for "a little thing," meaning, here, a charm.
355 schlauer Fuchs: German for "a sly fox."

CHAPTER 19

406 Henrik Hertz (1798–1870) was a witty playwright and author of satirical letters and a versifier whose easy and accessible poems have affinities, at times, to folksongs. Frederik Paludan-Müller (1809–76) was the author of a Danish classic of great influence, Adam Homo, a narrative poem in the Byronic style that satirizes bourgeois Danish life and the crude insensitivity of political and social ambition. His irony fed Pontoppidan's, and his protagonist, the son of a Jutland clergyman, his portrait of the young Per.
415 "The foxes have holes": Matthew 8:20.

CHAPTER 22

476 Nanny is quoting well-known lines from a humorous verse romance of Christian Winther (1796–1876), *Flugten til Amerika* ("Flight to America"), in which the youthful hero is said to drown his sorrow in his sago soup and to find solace in the raisins at the bottom of the bowl.

CHAPTER 25

523 Bernhard Severin Ingemann (1789–1862), author widely know and read in Denmark for his hymns, poems, and historical novels, sometimes compared to those of Sir Walter Scott.

523 Ludvig Holberg (1684–1754), sometimes called the father of modern Scandinavian literature. A widely traveled critic, he became a professor of metaphysics in Copenhagen, but he is most famous for his satires and parodies, and, most of all, for his theatrical comedies.

535 These Catholic mystics are closely related. Meister Eckhart, a famous German theologian (*c.* 1260–1328), teaching chiefly in Dominican schools, influenced his many disciples, like Johannes Tauler (*c.* 1300–61), to become intellectual as well as practical preachers and not to separate holiness from learning, which Gerard Groote, a fourteenth-century Dutch reformer of Roman Catholicism and a follower, with Tauler, of John Ruysbroeck (1293–1381), did. The latter was a Dutch mystical Roman Catholic and great medieval preacher.

CHAPTER 26

547 Vicomte F. M. de Lesseps (1805–94) was a French engineer and diplomat who conceived the idea of the Suez Canal and supported its execution.

564 Silenus, the oldest of all satyrs, teacher and trainer of the child Dionysus.

CHAPTER 28

577   Among the many glories of Denmark's oldest cloister, the
Vestervig Church (1075–1125; rebuilt 1450–1500), is the
Romanesque gravestone, with two procession crosses
named Liden Kirsten's Grave. According to tradition, it
holds the remains of Liden Kirsten and Prince Buris, whose
seduction of Liden resulted in terrible family vengeance,
executed on both. They were finally buried together,
though the prince was set at Liden's feet, and haunted the
churchyard with the rattling of the chain he had borne in
prison.

ABOUT THE TRANSLATOR

NAOMI LEBOWITZ is the Hortense and Tobias Lewin Professor Emerita in the Humanities at Washington University in St. Louis. The author of books on Kierkegaard, Ibsen, James, and Svevo, she has also published work on Flaubert, Balzac, Dickens, and Nexø, among others. Her many honors include a Guggenheim Fellowship and the Lief and Inger Sjöberg Award from the American Scandinavian Foundation, for her translation of *Lucky Per.*

ABOUT THE INTRODUCER

GARTH RISK HALLBERG, a novelist and critic, is the author of *City on Fire* and *A Field Guide to the North American Family.*